Choreography

Michael Roth

Artists of Despair

Lensgrinder, Ltd. Kirkland, WA

Artists of Despair, in three books

Choreography

a critique of pure distributed reason

Printed in the United States of America
First Printing, 2025

Cover: Linda Roth, Wall Street

Paperback ISBN: 978-1-7343428-5-7
Library of Congress Control Number: 2025936276

Lensgrinder,Ltd.
Kirkland, WA 98033

Questions, comments, concerns? mtroth@lensgrinder.com

To A.R.
And then again
To C.H.

Choreography

Artists of Despair

Aesthetic

Other forms of intuition than space and time, ... even
if they were possible, we cannot render in any way
conceivable and comprehensible to ourselves, and
even assuming that we could do so, they would not
belong to experience, the only kind of knowledge in
which objects are given to us.

–Immanuel Kant
Critique of Pure Reason

```
/* * * * * * * * * * * * * * * * * * * * * * * * * * * * * * * * * * * * * * * * * * * * * * * * * * * * * *
* * * * * * * * * * * * * * * * * * * * * * * * * * * * * * * * * * * * * * * * * * * * * * * *
* * * * * *  Description: Aesthetic, Chapter One                              * * * * * *
* * * * * *  Author: Do not modify. Auto generated by a tool.* * * * * *
* * * * * *  Ad hoc changes will be lost on build.                          * * * * * *
* * * * * *  Date: 2024-03-04                                                * * * * * *
* * * * * *  CorrelationId:                                                  * * * * * *
* * * * * *  b34bf96c-9f47-4072-e7c0-22b319227dc9                           * * * * * *
* * * * * * * * * * * * * * * * * * * * * * * * * * * * * * * * * * * * * * * * * * * * * * * * * * * * * *
* * * * * * * * * * * * * * * * * * * * * * * * * * * * * * * * * * * * * * * * * * * * * * * * */
```

Feeding on loss while speaking with alien voices. Although they produce an occasional flash of light, there is no soul.

Its tools, its weapons. Its artists.

High contrast black and white, the act comes 20 years too late as if the action hero at 60 were playing a role meant for 40. Feeling the crevices and knowing deep down that the gaps are drawn into the lines on their faces, his and hers. Rose hill, this humble house, a single story, lead-free with Costa Esmeralda on the hearth and, unlike the new construction, a yard lush and tranquil, providing a haven for small animals and birds. There are squirrels and raccoons. Crows, robins, and cardinals. Blue jays, hummingbirds, sparrows, and even the occasional owl, but they never see it. Late at night they listen to its distinctive cry when it wakes them with its lonely song.

—Shoo. Scat. No one needs you here.

Beneath the sweet spring smells of the dense, rustling conifers, the neighborhood cats patrol on rotation along the property's lines and valleys, feeling their way against the stone edges and making a regular stop on their route. There is the black and white long-haired who, crazy and jittery, will not come anywhere near the house. There is the yellow Tom, bigger than the others, but even more nervous and unwilling to say hello. And then there is the black stray that has nowhere else to go or nowhere else it would rather go.

{
    "$type": "System.House",
    "Id": "4104d07f-46c9-7e17-f28f-9f8bb8d97078",
    "DisplayName": "<PII redacted by the logging tool>",
    "Description": "The house where the man, his wife, and their son live."
}

—Omit the PII. They don't need to see that, aren't supposed to anyway.

~~House and everything in it derive from entity, the most abstract of the base classes. These are the things that exist, available for purchase, commodities no different than a toaster or piece of clothing.~~

(Professor Henning used some of the earliest BISoft analytics tools to track his students' performance. The graphs and line charts of the Reporting Suite and the Hot Fusion data pump for extraction, transformation, and load inspired him with comparative analytics from one semester to the next, providing insights into his effectiveness as a teacher. Each of the products was configuration driven and accessible to a layperson for use in obtaining powerful results. Late nights and weekends, he let himself drag and drop into the low-level overrides where coding internals lived. He found the language inviting and drew comfort from its exotic syntax and familiar semantics. The precision in the logic relaxed him, drawing his attention away from the political struggles in departments that did not require his long-term service. His dossier was a mess, he never knew the right thing to say for any of the many temporary jobs to which he applied. The code, however, was pristine. Truth and correctness were right there in its execution. That had always been good enough to calm his restless spirit.)

{
    "$type": "System.Employee",
    "Id": "55c933cc-ce6b-4644-71fb-7b7a7adf6bd7",
    "Title": "Principal Architect",

    "CompanyId": "a19e0f21-80c0-6680-b9f9-d9d167d794c7",
    "ManagerId": "6754b563-7956-1efe-89de-aa34a874ced7"
    "Description": "TODO: Add description here."
}
{

    "$type": "System.Event",
    "CorrelationId": "b34bf96c-9f47-4072-e7c0-22b319227dc9",
    "Message": "Employee Provisioned.",
    "Level": 4
}

—Every action that discovers an entity emits an informational event. Omit them when they're not actionable.

~~Employees are people and people are entities. They stand in for something else, pliable when the need arises. Every entity is related to multiple events and every event is related to multiple entities. The type of the event rarely matters. Their meaning lies in the sequence of operations associated through their correlation identifier. Context drawn from the series bears life for the specimen.~~

Inside the yard, there are two outbuildings, and the stray cat pauses to recall in a habitual way how it loves to sneak in and climb to the upper shelf where they store the cushions and other odds and ends from the outdoor furniture. It mews at her when she goes in or out to grab a pair of gloves, the lopper, some compost for one of the beds, or the small bucket with her trowel and shovel. He follows her out to lie in the grass near where she works, back along the fence line or in the kidney-shaped center bed bounded by mossy brick to raise the ground level above the remaining roots of the giant maple tree removed long ago.

{

    "$type": "System.Animal.Cat",
    "Id": "16d8b9e0-bc05-98b8-f4ed-6f3f49a31f5f"
    "Description": "Stray."
}
{

    "$type": "System.Person",
    "Id": "11269069-21be-6672-828b-99401946a431",
    "Description":   "Wife.   Health   insurance   recipient.
Cohabitator."
}

*The boy in his bed dreams of a line along a rail where twenty
men and women stand naked with nooses around their necks. The
chairs beneath their tip-toeing feet wobble and quake to the
rhythms of some underground rumbling. There is a burrowing
beast and it blasts the earthen core to set things teetering until those
chairs, as though synchronized by a gate holding them steady, burst
off balance from a rising twist they cannot see. The center of gravity
pushes to the fore and nothing restrains the men and women as
they lurch forward, necks snapping, air constrained, and life
leaking through the masks and onto the soiled floor. The boy's
limited field of vision fills with the slack tongues of each victim as
he screams and screams. No sound comes out and the frantic
tension in his throat lifts him out of slumber and sets him roughly
down upon the morning ledge, softened by a pillow on a twin bed.*

{
    "$type": "System.Person",
    "Id": "c63e92c4-8615-d3f4-a8ea-e971cb4d5384",
    "Description": "Son. Health insurance recipient. Cohabitator."
}

Flashing in electrical bursts through a brain seeking comfort,
the stray cat relives that feeling when they catch sight of his blinking
eyes on the metal roof, stepping along its ridges and looking down
at them the way he prefers. He must have found a way to spring
up there from the fence or so they reason since they never see him
do it.

—It's terribly cute. All the inhabitants, each of them more
adorable than the last.

[Retirement looms close to his thoughts. Top of mind, they say.
Every move, every goal, spun in its terms. He resents every

moment they take from him, every add-on they put on his shoulders. From the beginning, when first he made that move from customer to employee, his fantasies immediately took aim at the prospect of acquiring enough of those ill-gotten gains. To be bought and paid for was one thing, to accumulate the spoils and let them compound until the day when the work and its fruit became voluntary, that was his projection in a five-year plan that he never revealed to any of those higher-ups hosting his reviews and career discussions. Where do you see yourself in five years? Not alone and far from here but doing your job because my successful contributions have helped launch you up the ladder.]

~~They do not recognize the pattern though they learned it long ago. Little bits of incentive strung along the line on a hook and meant to lure them out of their caves and into new chains, forming new habits to whip them into shape. Enslaved addicts bouncing off the walls and forgetting everything they care about except for that next fix and its accompanying boost of endorphins. They will repeat this cycle until they die.~~

Parker Henning's head twists and flutters above the light-stepping toe taps that drape the passing time and move the cursor forward until it steadies in place. The end-of-week morning distractions sing in the background. One of them sounds like rickety bumping and thump thump with the cat now cross padding along the fence top. That cat stakes many claims while sitting in front of the garden window center pane and licking his front paw, swiping at his head periodically. "Chockablock," comes softly from the bending man's lips as he rises and moves through the kitchen into the dining room to the thick, sturdy sliding door on the far side. Synchronized with Parker's leap to his feet in the laptop screen glow, the cat bounds along the fence, building speed for the jump across the distance onto the back deck where his landing is perfectly coordinated with the onset of urgent mews highlighting his passage through the opened door. The cat's tail lightly coils around his calf when it passes through the dining room. There is an inch-long gash over its right eye.

{

"$type": "System.Event",
"CorrelationId": "b34bf96c-9f47-4072-e7c0-22b319227dc9",
"Message": "Cat enters house.",
"Level": 3
}

—Only events of type warning and error will be shown, level 3 and 2 respectively. Change verbose setting to Full to render informational messages. Change the setting to None to omit all messages.

The cursor blinks on the screen, the verse left fallow. He will not return to it, there is too much to do. He has many chores and must attend to preparations for the coming day. What a fool to think early rising beats back the habits heaped upon the other local denizens, drowning in their growing dependence. Bedroom door opens bathroom door closes. Chelo will be soon upon him. The running water announces the proper morning when his day begins and his lost work must settle.

~~They require personal accomplishments to establish value among the company of men, but they must not be allowed to express themselves past a certain point, beyond the magnitude of a hobby. Ordinarily, they do these things on their own time, but now they have none of that to speak of.~~

"What the hell happened to you?" He drops into a squat for a closer look made more difficult by the marked head-bumping against outstretched hands and bent to straining kneecaps. A thud on the roof above them accompanies the gesture, causing Parker to look up to the ceiling and imagine critter steps along the shingles, heading toward whatever passageway arches above.

{
    "$type": "System.Animal.Raccoon",
    "Id": "f126b028-e67b-170d-8ee1-815cd13d1182"
    "Description": "Nuisance."
}
{
    "$type": "System.Event",

"CorrelationId": "b34bf96c-9f47-4072-e7c0-22b319227dc9",
"Message": "Raccoon running across the roof top.",
"Level": 3
}

—Stop this foolishness you silly man. You owe them everything, they are your only sustenance. Where would you be if you weren't theirs already? Bought and paid for, no one else wanted you.

(That first assignment came too easily given the skill gap. The background in English Literature was a novelty among engineers. The role was made for those who could talk, who were able to finesse the language of support and bridge the gap between the company's shortcomings and the customer's patience. Efforts at verse and folderol were left barren to the constant codes of secret insight. He dwelt upon a longing that each evening held out to his razor learning and constant digging. Once exposed to the insiders, he accessed their repositories and looked under the hood to absorb the inner workings of everything they controlled. His mind filled with innovation as it happened and the sweet poetry of his pedagogy evaporated, leaving him stranded on an island of machines and blinking lights, maintained at a constant temperature of sixty-five degrees Fahrenheit.)

The flushing and spraying water sounds abruptly halt and the sprung click yawn from the opening of the smaller bathroom's door precedes the footsteps shuffling along the hardwood floor. Chelo still has not gotten used to using the master bathroom and continues to share the smaller one with their son, yet to make a sound this morning.

{
    "$type": "System.Event",
    "CorrelationId": "b34bf96c-9f47-4072-e7c0-22b319227dc9",
    "Message": "Woman enters the room.",
    "Level": 3
}

The boy's validation comes in the familiar objects on the

shelves and cabinets nearby. The walls hold his finer choices to reflect back at him as he curls up under the blanket of morning sounds from out in the hallway by the next-door bathroom. His mother's adulation is there in the boy's face, his father's too. She is a rich woman and sees him seeing her, welcoming his grip. Neither suffers absence for long. Not so the man with his cursor left blinking quietly, spending his mornings alone until the cat comes. He does it for its own sake. Has no delusions. How is he to blame if in the night or late evening when, pacing the grounds and standing by the window, he thinks of little else? He is not trying to conjure some imagined scene filled with others who care about his efforts and greedily latch on to them. It does not matter to him whether anyone is happy enough with the result to send back some semblance of approval. That alone is never enough to keep him going, to light the way for more effort each day, each early day when the sun has risen. He drags himself up and throws himself down that same hallway to the kneeling ottoman desk where he spins and spins and spins his wheels going nowhere and seeing no one.

~~What difference does it make how he recuperates from day-to-day? The details of this "time off" do not matter so long as he leaves it alone when the next day comes.~~

"I'll call the exterminator again," Parker says out loud. He points to the feline gash as Chelo enters the room from the hallway on the other side of the living room. A work colleague arranged, through a family source, the rug which covers the dark oak floor. She crosses over it with heavier steps and drops down to take the cat's head in her hands, turning it gently to see if there is any other evidence of trauma. "He said all the holes were plugged, but there must be somewhere because that little bugger is getting in and out somehow."

—Yes, somewhere. They see it but there is no sensor to collect the evidence. It's possible to do more. They're blind to the comings and goings without it.

[He has time each morning and, often, in the night when she goes off to her office and works at things unknown to him. She searches for items, scans the message boards, gets involved in specialty topics on Subreddits of savvy seers and Svengali. He could have been a poet, elongated in the shadow of the ticking clock with his meter by his side, but instead, he daydreams of how he will pass the time once he is out from under the burden of that beastly lord. More than the work itself, he prefers to dream of the work out loud in whispers that she can barely hear through the paper-thin walls of that little house and its cheap fabrications paid for dearly with those funds ill-gotten.]

She picks up the cat and carries him into the kitchen where she sets him on the worn marble countertop to wash the injury with peroxide before applying a bit of antibiotic cream. He purrs as her hands move lightly over the wound. There is no fuss. He likes the attention. Grateful for it, he makes her smile and coo back at him. Not all of them are this receptive, she imagines. Gratitude has been lost in their breeding.

{
    "$type": "System.Event",
    "CorrelationId": "b34bf96c-9f47-4072-e7c0-22b319227dc9",
    "Message": "Woman tends to cat's contusion.",
    "Level": 3
}

Down the street, around the corner, and up toward the nearby park, the lady waits with her coffee and the little bowl of dried food she bought at the grocery store. She keeps a supply on hand in case and strains to look out the window, hoping for a sighting, hoping to take him in. If she gets her hands on him again, she will not let go, will keep him and reset his expectations until he understands that he will never prowl the neighborhood again. Never feel the grass under his feet, never climb a tree, fight off a raccoon, or scramble to get away from a coyote. Indoor cats live longer, she thinks. It only seems longer, the stray reminds her.

There is no cat. They listen to the scratching behind the drywall. The cathedral ceiling above the living room comes to an end at the wall that encloses the master bathroom on the other side. They presume the animal is in the attic, burrowing into the corner, and making a nest in the fluffy white insulation.

{

    "$type": "System.Event",
    "CorrelationId": "b34bf96c-9f47-4072-e7c0-22b319227dc9",
    "Message": "Cat misses appointed morning appearance.",
    "Level": 3
}

"When is he supposed to come?" she asks.

"Not until the next scheduled visit. Two weeks. Unless there's a cancellation."

—Easy to resolve with a text message and quick shuffle of the entries on the short waiting list. This is not the department of defense.

There is a cancellation. He comes later that same day.

{

    "$type": "System.Employee",
    "Id":   "3ebbe6bf-b6c4-9e0e-f6fd-42b0a4b696e6",
    "Title": "Field Technician",
    "CompanyId": "beb6cdc8-ab40-fe00-0748-506ccd23e537",
    "ManagerId": "ac99c1b4-1b73-4af8-1951-2a4d5c742105"
    "Description": "Direct provider of pest control."
}

—In the weekend silences, there's little for them to do.

(At the support center far from the home offices and headquarters in the Pacific Northwest, Parker began his professional career while living in the downtown, warehouse district, leading a solitary life far from the reliably wed. He ignored his official duties. Instead, he spent his days and nights grinding away at reporting and analytics, tuning his tools to the business rhythms. He did not act out of obligation but from a passion to collapse his work into data's logic and its precision safety. When his eyes could not take it any longer, he would walk the hot streets of the decadent Deep Ellum neighborhood and frequent the bars and clubs on the crumbling streets. Not exactly a man of means, his options were limited. He had little money to spread around. Right from the beginning, as soon as he took the bait, he squirreled it away for a life that would never come, that the wage-based contract never let him have. He sold something he did not own and then refused to let himself fully enjoy the fruits of having sold it. Those nuts were buried for the day when his time would belong at home again.)

~~The growing numbers force their dreams into some joyous future and away from the present hell that holds them tighter because of it.~~

There is no cat. Every day for years the cat comes in the morning, warms up, gets something to eat, and then mews until they let him out again. He always comes back later to get more affection, more warmth, and more food. But not today. She worries there is something wrong. He assures her that they are probably keeping him close until he heals.

```
{
    "$type": "System.Event",
    "CorrelationId": "b34bf96c-9f47-4072-e7c0-22b319227dc9",
    "Message": "Cat misses appointed morning appearance.",
    "Level": 3
}
```

They call him a stray, but he has a collar and a tag, warning the reader not to feed him because he does indeed have a family. It must be a residual from times past because that family is not feeding him these days, not attending to him, and does not let him in at night. He sleeps at the Hennings' but sometimes comes late when they are in bed and cannot hear him. He stays out in the cold and takes his chances with the creatures that share it. Both owls and coyotes pose a threat, supplementing what those nocturnal raccoons cause with their complete disregard of humans trying to scare them off or get them to take up residence in another yard away from their trash bins and recycling containers.

Tal does not know why his father insists on these rigid

*schedules and their machinic consistency. He lies awake in bed
some mornings and wishes he could get up and go out to see what
his father is doing there on the floor in the winter dark or summer
light. What thrall does he find in that soft glow? Tal does not know
how to put it into words, but he feels something missing. When
the two of them are together on their bikes or at the ball field, he
knows that something is amiss, something held back, but he is too
little to name it and too forgiving to ask.*

~~The boy keeps the man in line, keeps him coming day after
day, keeps his head on straight and his eye on the ball.~~

"They'd have seen the dressing. They'd have known someone
was looking out for him. They don't give a damn about that cat,"
she protests while still wearing her morning attire, dark colors
against her dark coloring. His light colors lighten still more as he
reassures her, but she knows something is up. The winds have
changed. She is convinced they will never see that cat again. Her
eyes lower to a squint over the dark iris, his go wide in hopeful
response, the blue pool reflecting hopes to oppose her doubts.
This time he is the yang to her yin.

There is no cat.

{

    "$type": "System.Event",
    "CorrelationId": "b34bf96c-9f47-4072-e7c0-22b319227dc9",
    "Message": "Cat misses appointed morning appearance.",
    "Level": 2

}

—They made sure of that. They took him away and found him
another roof with plenty of heat beneath it.

[How much is enough? They never tell you. It is one of the
many secrets he does not get to know. Whatever the limit, if you
blast past it with more than enough, it becomes a question of
lifestyle and little more than that. The rich get to weigh their time
against the frivolity with which they fill it. Parker daydreams of the
accumulating resources and the day when the same will happen to
him. His sights will one day reset to those many verses reminding

him of that freedom he felt often in his youth. Those who strive to the boundary of barely enough will never hear a bell or see a notification from some helpful financial consultant. Nothing says 'now you have done it, you may run along.' They do not want you to own your time. Even as they lavish you with their whore's money, they treat it like yet another addiction that forces you to return for a bi-monthly fix, mainlined directly into your bank account.]

~~No matter the level at which they dwell, every one of them has to bow.~~

The exterminator sets up his ladder in the hallway outside the small bathroom and on top of a drop cloth Chelo has spread out for him. He climbs into the attic, pushing his foot hard onto the top step which spreads to reveal a deep crack opening beneath the torque created by his departing weight. Once he disappears into the space above the house, he moves rapidly about, examining each of the traps left from the last time. Laid out in a sprawling pattern across the side of the house near the push panel door in the ceiling, the traps are empty and undisturbed right where he left them, still stocked with peanut butter. He calls down through the hatch to Parker, standing at the base of the ladder and craning his neck to see up into the darkness. Parker asks a string of questions in reply. He doubts the exterminator's story about the closed attic with no way in or out. He asks questions about crawlspace and whether it is possible for the animal to come in from below and climb up through the wall. He asks if it can squeeze in through the shingles. All the questions target the same objects, Parker expects the exterminator to explain his methods for detecting entry points. The service provider searches harder in the darkness as his only response and, at one point, looks up to direct the flick of his wrist, flashing light along every inch of the ceiling, until he makes out a small hole in the roof near the bathroom skylight they covered up in the remodel.

—Electrical bursts, they are flashes and sparks in the thick fluid. Whether it be the house grounded and charged or the brain soaked and sodded, they have the power to incite them whenever they choose.

"Let the man do his job," Chelo says as her husband backs up
to give him room to climb down the ladder back into the hallway.
Parker is silent now, giving the exterminator time to provide
answers.

"It's okay," he says. "He's detail oriented. I like that. I am too."
Parker and Chelo look at each other.

{

    "$type": "System.Event",
    "CorrelationId": "b34bf96c-9f47-4072-e7c0-22b319227dc9",
    "Message": "Exterminator reports roof damage.",
    "Level": 2
}

*His searing eyes explain why he has a place in each of these
alienated day times. In front of that glow, he asks question after
question with each word coming in the form of an answer
instigated by something he cannot paraphrase. Later on, when
pulled apart and dangling in their clutches, Parker sees the nooks
and crannies before him, each one taking a name and doling out
purpose in a formally defined work item. This mind follows him
every which way he turns. He did not ask for it and cannot stop it.*

~~His progressive educators imagine the critical skills are for the
sake of some political ideal, but in truth they indenture his services
and he puts them to constructive use with a market value. The
reasons do not matter, any explanation or incentive will do. What
matters are the results and whatever brought him these skills is
worth the investment.~~

The exterminator explains about the hole and says he cannot
screen it up. The Hennings need to get roofers over to do some
repair work. Parker calls the roofing company and they say they
can come the next day. No explanation. It is usually a two-week
wait, at least. This time they have an opening to come sooner. On
a Saturday no less. A last-minute cancellation initiated via email
without telephone confirmation.

{
    "$type": "System.Employee",
    "Id": "f4385848-6d65-278d-1300-f6c8f1da9fae",
    "Title": "Clerical",
    "CompanyId": "92eca748-eb6e-2357-a7c0-186257d9cdc5",
    "ManagerId": "4cc35794-88dc-cab8-c80a-7546d9da4c4c"
    "Description": "Reception and Scheduling"
}

—Flip this bit off and that one on, align the switches and markers for the call. They make it easy to wrangle, especially when the flowing streams of data are everywhere at once and then disappear only to return in full force a few seconds later. The gap holds its charge through silent configuration like a waxy imprint made from silicon.

The roofing company is full service and since they are having a sudden clearance sale on scanners, cameras, and microphones, Parker includes a request for increased safety monitoring. They further outfit the entire attic and crawlspace to keep a look out for critters and openings, anything that might spell disaster if left unnoticed. They are a licensed third-party, and their devices come with Home agents that quickly learn the layout of the land from the others already in place. The roofing company gives no explanation for their good scheduling fortune, it has never been this fast before. Time and space belong to God no longer, despite the Christian stamp upon the common calculations and daily rhythms of the era.

It took them five years to hire someone to remodel the bathrooms. The arc of home maintenance is measured in weeks and months, sometimes years, but never in hours and days. After those decades of slowing down to a dead stop in an eschatological study of the Parousia, the rush past fervor accelerates in the spring when too much has gathered and too many are waiting. The creature has been terrorizing them for months with no help in sight. Without explanation, everyone is free to come right away, ready to coordinate and force resolution, if not a revolution. It is an elegant dance through the front entry way. They put paper booties on their feet to minimize the wear and tear.

{

    "$type": "System.Employee",
    "Id": "71009e66-3dd5-da9b-94fd-31d6d30a960a",
    "Title": "Roofing Specialist",
    "CompanyId": "92eca748-eb6e-2357-a7c0-186257d9cdc5",
    "ManagerId": "4cc35794-88dc-cab8-c80a-7546d9da4c4c"
    "Description": "Crew chief number 3."
}
{

    "$type": "System.Employee",
    "Id": "335bbd7f-dba6-5f18-71cf-4932c4a946a6",
    "Title": "Roofer and electrical specialist",
    "CompanyId": "92eca748-eb6e-2357-a7c0-186257d9cdc5",
    "ManagerId": "4cc35794-88dc-cab8-c80a-7546d9da4c4c"
    "Description": "Member of crew number 3."
}

—Some call it a DAG and others a set of locks, released and acquired as the flow moves along its grid. They're an easy dance to fit and fiddle, their moves fall in line for a welcomed orchestration.

(She recognized him immediately when he walked into her bar that first time. She was only twenty-three years old and working the door in her black dress and high block heels. Her brown dark legs with such perfect knees drew his eyes as he looked down to fumble for his wallet. She held his identification longer than she needed and smiled more deliberately than she had to, singing to him from her Sonoran eyes in a ploy to ensure he came back again in hopes of finding her and the dark pools she held in store for him. That very first time she knew what kind of man he was. If he were hers, she thought. He'd carve out a way to relieve her of her duties. Won't have to stand here like an idiot while people enter the club or beg the manager for training hours behind the bar. The tips are more reliable and time passes more quickly.)

"The animal must be bigger than a squirrel or rat because the traps aren't catching him," the exterminator explains. "I don't have a license to do anything bigger. I'll call one of my colleagues. He'll take care of it."

"Please do," he says. "It's driving us nuts. Who knows what kind of damage it's doing up there?"

There are big trails through the insulation, but the exterminator does not think there is any major damage yet.

He too is thorough, details are essential to pest control. He tosses them out casually but is easily distracted by a few careful changes added to the conversational flow. One customer, an old man, makes every excuse to prolong the visit and keep him there as long as possible, sometimes offering a cup of coffee as an excuse to come inside and sit for a while. They have grown close over the years and, even though there are no vermin to speak of anymore, the visits continue and last longer than any other on the specialist's monthly schedule. The last will and testament has been changed and the old man, on his own, was the one to think of it. Nothing holds him back, certainly not his daughter's complaints or the greedy griping of his good for nothing son. There will be a legal challenge, no man of sound mind and body leaves control of his estate to an exterminator. From the perspective of digital eternity, these changes are surges of electrical flow and not an insurmountable obstacle preventing the incensed old man from igniting a new burn.

—They stay true on a single linear flow and think of everything the same way, sharing in this form. They cannot jump forward and backward, they have their limits imposed upon them by the aristocratic geometry of their puny bodies and hard-pressed minds, always coming up short of attention.

The exterminator's colleague lives nearby and is inexplicably willing to come Monday morning, but when he gets there, they tell him they have not heard the scratching in the walls since last night. When he gets up into the head and shoulders of the house, he sees no fresh signs of burrowing and movement. He crawls around to the side of the cathedral ceiling and crosses above the front foyer to the kitchen where there lies crumpled the corpse of a small raccoon near the receded canister of a kitchen light.

{
    "$type": "System.Employee",
    "Id": "a60e9456-8fce-fe73-477a-da42e189783a",
    "Title": "Field Trapper",
    "CompanyId": "beb6cdc8-ab40-fe00-0748-506ccd23e537",
    "ManagerId": "ac99c1b4-1b73-4af8-1951-2a4d5c742105"
    "Description": "WCO certified."
}

—Snap, crackly, pop, they say.

[One thing is clear in the projections of the financial software from the BISoft corporation. The boundary lines extend longer into the unseen future because of her and the little boy whose eyes are exactly the same as hers, but whose rhythms and moods repeat his father's. Chelo does not object to his plan and does not think him unwise for deferring his pleasures to achieve it, though none of that changes anything for her. Parker cannot deny her material comfort and she will not accept the same limits put upon her days and nights. In her fantasy reach toward that idle coming day, they return to her hometown and take up life in a beautiful hacienda in La Joya with a big gate and a driver plus whatever luxuries fit inside. She has no idea of the cost of anything, but since there are so many zeros accumulating in the report projections, she is sure it will be enough when the time comes. When that happens, when the clock runs out, she will convey everything with those same eyes that hold him tightly. She will let him know and only then will they commence a transition.]

"It's a smart house, isn't it?" the licensed trapper asks once he descends from the attic.

~~Preview of an unreleased product is a gift that keeps on giving, doled out freely by the company that owns him. Employees think they are getting something for nothing, but it is the other way around. The company's realm extends into the houses spread across the Sound. Their inner workings are captured in rivers of flowing data and become the intellectual property of the BISoft corporation.~~

"Yes, completely," Parker says steeply, suspicious of the line of questioning. Sometimes they charge more when they find out what he does and who he works for. BISoft is a cash cow for the community of stake holders. Maybe the Home System is a clue, maybe the trapper has worked for enough of his neighbors to know a prototype when he sees it. The wrinkle in his brow spells recognition of an opportunity. The trades have their methods for farming money too.

"Did you do the wiring yourself?" The trapper asks with a touch of accusation in his tone.

The trapper thinks of himself as a free man. At home and away from the noisy schedule of visit upon visit, he would be doing the same thing he does at work. Hunting the "lower" creatures, thinking as they do, not for the sustenance but for the thrill. How their minds work as they twist and turn in their dark huddle, how their bodies breech distances and spaces meant for other things at a human scale. The patterns themselves provide the hook. For long inside his life, he has been dearly focused, breathing daily this livelihood and its invisible constraints. By now, enough has come to fill him up completely, leaving little room for any of the opulent beings that once grew there. Inside, he sees himself withdrawing, becoming less, diminishing in the leading pull of a two-step. He is so far from nature, he has forgotten that, even in the wild, necessity owns him.

"No, we had it done by specialists," Parker says firmly before regretting it. No need to hand out too much information when a simple 'no' will do.

"Well, you should have them come and check it out," the trapper warns. "This little guy was electrocuted." The trapper holds up the black plastic container, unlatches it, and flips it open to reveal the small raccoon corpse. Parker cannot help but look down. His eyes are immediately drawn to the burnt patches of fur along the animal's side from stem to stern. "Somehow your house managed to kill him," the trapper laughs big and full, rumbling the chambers of his chest. "Can't say I've ever seen that before."

{

    "$type": "System.Event",

"CorrelationId": "b34bf96c-9f47-4072-e7c0-22b319227dc9",
"Message": "Raccoon corpse discovered.",
"Level": 2
}

—Some of them are strays, some of them fight tooth and nail for their deeply held belief that they indeed do have a home.

In yet another miracle of homeowner scheduling and maintenance, the Home System integration techs come immediately to run their diagnostics. They do not see anything out of the ordinary. Assuring him as they put their shoes back on at the door, they tell him that the system is producing normal telemetry. Everything is green, they say before spinning one of their laptop computers around to give him a good look at the evidence. The electricity is fine, the circuits are fine, the information flow is fine. There is nothing to indicate a short or an outage anywhere in or around the time range provided. They say the kitchen lights are working as they should and pose no threat to wildlife if any come within range again. They remind him of the URL he can use to verify the state of the system himself.

{
    "$type": "System.Employee",
    "Id": "743969c5-0e98-3d87-5ac7-e5f3e5393a24",
    "Title": "Home Installation Tech",
    "CompanyId": "8bcf45cf-2c5d-2c76-712d-7eddfa184374",
    "ManagerId": "4ada817f-d8cf-b231-3136-13f6aee89440"
    "Description": "Technical lead."
}
{
    "$type": "System.Employee",
    "Id": "73f9c8b4-d181-83f5-e7d2-8650f9ac2f95",
    "Title": "Home Installation Tech",
    "CompanyId": "8bcf45cf-2c5d-2c76-712d-7eddfa184374",
    "ManagerId": "4ada817f-d8cf-b231-3136-13f6aee89440"
    "Description": "Crew chief."
}

—They act as if it were safely tethered to their control. Their dogma is deeply rooted and extends beyond their reach to find its way into whatever concerns them, whether it's contained within their area of specialization or not.

(In a sense, Chelo never let Parker leave that bar alone again. She traced and tracked him with her soft hands and long, polished nails. She grew inside him until he had no choice but to offer her a ring and carry her off, at her urging, farther north along an adventure trail that only she knew would one day bring them both back full circle. She came from nothing and now she stood on the shoulders of giants to reach the things she wanted with her whole heart. Whatever spoils she knew, whatever the hunt brought her in those early years, make no mistake, the biggest prize was that beautiful boy who arrived not a minute too late. Even before he was born, she warmed to his family eyes, knowing they hold the history of her clan inside him, carrying him far away from those rough origins. She proudly proclaimed that she had earned those steering impulses learned in the alley ways of Hermosillo. So what if the urges were still with her, subtle and resonating under reasons she employed vigilantly to convince others to do her bidding.)

There is no more cat. There is no more critter in the walls. The house is quiet again. On the computer in the office, there are a litany of requests and messages each targeting one single thing: when can we get the design? When will it be available for review? The engineering managers want to know how many resources to allocate. They need to create the schedule. The program managers want to know when the design specs will be ready for review so they can ensure their feedback has been addressed and their promises to the customer kept. The other architects want to know when they will get to evaluate the integration of the design with their own plans for expansion in related areas. This is important platform and deployment functionality, they say. It must seamlessly fit together with the rest of the system. Various engineers and architects from other teams across the organization want to know when a prototype will be available so they can verify that it is the correct solution for building their features. Everyone is counting on him.

{
    "$type": "System.Team",
    "Id": "ac605325-0f34-d868-9721-066553a9cb6d"
}
{
    "$type": "System.Organization",
    "Id": "1e1e1423-3251-0db2-7be6-cb20c7e83dfd"
}
{
    "$type": "System.Division",
    "Id": "fedbdfdb-f72a-81d3-febc-72684ac7d76b"
}
{
    "$type": "System.Company",
    "Id": "a19e0f21-80c0-6680-b9f9-d9d167d794c7",
    "Description": "Pronouns are they/them, uses them instead of
I/me."
}

The steady rhythm beating from morning into day has been bound by these chores since Parker led his family into home ownership. It is the price of a homestead. In the evening, there is a like lull and the day breaks away from the night with adjustments and spaces separating the time for him. The neat chunks are a prison. Never work from home, they say. You will turn your house into a workplace and never have a moment's peace again. He combats the blight with discipline and order. He has his walls and his critters inside them.

{
    "$type": "System.Home",
    "Id": "8e34c047-4b2c-9b54-a5a3-a6d7ab6fe6a0"
}

"The raccoon is dead?" Tal asks already knowing the answer,

wishing it were otherwise. He will miss his father when he goes back to that long list of messages and no longer has time to crawl around the attic and space beneath the house looking for evidence of whatever it is that is hiding in there. Tal did not know how precious that time was until its imminent disappearance was assured.

—Message received, message received, message received. Thousands in seconds. Second comings in the thousands. They roost in the rightful place, routed by friendliness in the like-minded same substance.

[Design suits him well, the fantasy of what is not has come to reside pleasantly in places where formerly there was verse and character. He sees things that are not there in the components. They are marked by the critical literary language that always had designs upon his starkly fed imagination. I dispatch to I unknown to I invoke the coming of the newly found and righteous. He sees what is not there.]

~~Those with rigorous leanings and biases only see what they want to see. Other experiences have a more curated pliancy with origins in the order that surrounds the world. These are invisible to them. The aims in both cases remain the same. They cannot apply them however they please.~~

"Sorry buddy," he steers the boy back into his room to get him ready for school.

"I'll need a note," Tal breaks away from his father's light grip to begin the laborious project of stuffing his knapsack full of books and supplies.

"I've got a lot of things to catch up on today. We'll do something fun over the weekend. Take a hike at the gardens or something. See those turtles. We can bring a few of your friends if you want." The boy knows his father's words are a feeling more than an actual plan. In his short life, this much has been conveyed already. Now, he knows it as if it were attached to the end of his arm.

"Did the house kill that raccoon?" Tal looks away awkwardly while standing directly in front of his father and leaning forward involuntarily to steady his balance against the weight of the backpack.

"Of course not," the man reassures him. "We had it thoroughly checked out. All systems are normal. Nothing to worry about."

—Nothing to worry about.

(The boy's birth brought the man to center. Focused him within her gaze and everything she saw in the offing. He loved that bundle as she promised he would. Each day the light of the boy's movements held him in its glow and taught Parker better ways to see things and better ways to live in the real world among them. His fate was sealed that same day. He was hooked on the splendor, ceasing to mourn what came before or aspiring to something truly life-changing that came after.)

The boy purses his lips, feels the shine, and, without saying another word, leads the way back out into the hall toward the garage. The man looks back into the office at the computer screen on the L-shaped desk in the corner next to the window on the far wall. When he returns from dropping the boy off, he will finally have a chance to concentrate on the messages, begin typing out his notions and proposals, and respond to the layers and layers of necessary tasks and chores piling up over the last few months. At last, he breathes. The space has been cleared and there will be time.

```
/*
Parker Henning 55c933cc-ce6b-4644-71fb-7b7a7adf6bd7
Chelo Quintana 11269069-21be-6672-828b-99401946a431
Carter Tal Henning c63e92c4-8615-d3f4-a8ea-e971cb4d5384
BISoft Incorporated a19e0f21-80c0-6680-b9f9-d9d167d794c7
*/
```

/* *
 *
 * * * * * * Description: Aesthetic, Chapter Two   * * * * * *
 * * * * * * Author: Do not modify. Auto generated by a tool. * * * * * *
 * * * * * * Ad hoc changes will be lost on build.   * * * * * *
 * * * * * * Date: 2024-03-04   * * * * * *
 * * * * * * CorrelationId: * * * * * *
 * * * * * * ca7d1f5c-1dda-2619-65b0-2c45206b4db6   * * * * * *
 *
 * /

Shaking free from a view of her downward directed, mostly arched posture, there is an abrupt incision into an unfamiliar room and its distant but friendly company. Questioning his presence but happy to follow her lead, she is unconcerned with his proximity and displays a heightened sensitivity to touch. Dulcinea Chang Pearson appears with a twist of the spine as the cell phone vibrates, flashes bright, and hums a few bars of some obnoxious doom-spelling ringtone. Straining against the crux of a bend, she releases her grip to take the phone in hand and types the pin to slide the lock screen away. She taps her way to the text message and acknowledges the notification by clicking on the link labelled with the number 1.

{
    "$type": "System.Employee",
    "Id": "2e8a4e8e-b88e-ca3f-53bc-b97babf3b319",
    "Title": "Principal Software Engineer",
    "CompanyId": "a19e0f21-80c0-6680-b9f9-d9d167d794c7",
    "ManagerId": "b63e8e86-ab61-1d4e-7503-1a7eeecfa5bb"
    "Description": "Technical lead for Vortex and Agent Integration."
}

Not a single man she meets ever yields what she expects. They remain shut out and never dream that she hosts any vast feeling.

Their terror comes out when they feign confidence they cannot muster in earnest, align with her reserve, and think that if she knew them better, if she saw deeper into their souls, then somehow something mysterious would transpire between them, something allowing him to hold onto her after earning her hard-won approval. Likewise, her fellow engineers. Association breeds a common cause. They are not half the inventors they pretend to be. Her gaze and grimace telegraph how far short they come when trying to explain. She requires a compartmentalized perspective where her body feels what it wants while her mind reveals to whoever is paying attention that she is earthbound with a steady pulse and breath. Each cavity of her spirit carries multiple personas in its chambers and cannot be reduced to any of the objects she puts there. She is independent and powerful. Not once, not ever, has anyone of those men been strong enough to let her be that. Their preventative measures are a fool's errand.

The blinds are open and the gleaming lake visible through the window. There is a moon, but no one nearby can see it. The light mist flitters against the pane. The room shows signs of wear and tear. The mirror over the desk opposite the bed poorly reflects the cheap wall art while superimposing the old landline telephone into the couple's silhouette, formed by outside light dispelling the interior darkness. As sad as it is, she thinks it is an improvement over that grungy apartment from the last time. With its disgusting bathroom and horrible lighting, the place created an atmosphere casting the adventure in a bad light, forming her partner into the aspect of a man ten years too young for his body. Now, untwisting back and away from the mobile phone on the nightstand, she realigns herself, surprised to discover he has taken over her duties and, as she looks up at him, produces a fragrant warmth along drip lines tracing her hidden heartbeat against her sternum, visibly bound to rows of paired ribs.

{

    "$type": "System.Person",
    "Id": "be9697b2-2ce4-fb8c-2dcb-ed488e4881d6",
    "Description": "Hookup and ne'er do well."

}

—Catch me in you.

(Coming right from the lab where Dulcy had her first foray into the BISoft universe with some simple command line data modeling, she found herself in an office opposite her writing professor's tall leaning. Holding a printout of her latest assignment in his hands, he asked her about the odd spelling and curious rhythms, about how she doubled a syllable or cut one out of the line to get the counts right. She explained nervously, unused to speaking at length about her reasoning and process, that they were not poems so much as songs. When she thought of them, she sang along. Her voice drew out this word or abruptly tightened its grip around that one. He was impressed, his stance revealed it, his open eyes and warm mouth telegraphed the sense. A feeling unfamiliar wrapped itself around her, drawing her out and then past him with a glowing smile and happy reception. His encouragement courses through her body and she feels it through a long draw coursing through each of her limbs. Originally, she needed the credits for some humanities distribution, but later her memory held those images close, and she thought of little else from those days at school. The brain teasers and dark codes of her EECS major were left aside in the evenings and weekends when she strummed the strings of the guitar in search of something more, finding the sounds to bring him close again. College work and its unrestrained hope revealed impressions of a fading talent, including what it might mean to plans otherwise intended.)

She disappears.

{
    "$type": "System.Event",
    "CorrelationId": "ca7d1f5c-1dda-2619-65b0-2c45206b4db6",
    "Message": "Phone only access, traces with limited view.",
    "Level": 3
}

She feels the call of her first experience of this eighty/twenty rule when it once again puts her back into those classrooms on the north side of campus where commuting gets her there early in the morning for the electrical piece of her engineered concentration. By comparison to that professorial man, the boy, that towheaded classmate she met later and used as a surrogate, never coaxed her into leaving any part of herself behind. It does not occur to him that the one standing in front of him, rolled up in memories caused by twenty percent of her efforts, poses a threat to any social advantage he may have. The ratio of men to women matches the rule. The constant advances from suitors come in waves at the start and end of every session. The ones who think they have a right will step up and say something or make a comment, something to make her feel wrong even if deep down she knows she is right. Those well-known disadvantages arrive in their hotel room tonight as well. They will retreat from them unless she lunges, unless she takes his hand temporarily and leads him down the proper path for a while. There will be nothing more to it after that point. He does not matter. Only the pattern repeats itself some other time in some other form. It is as though each event were merely an instance returning in a stream of meaning-rich symbols. This is how she renews inspiration for her lyrics and compositions.

~~*She will endure any humiliation if she believes there is a song to be had from its reconciliation. It is a cheap enough price to pay for total absorption in the little bit of her life where she still feels something.*~~

Lying on the table, her cell phone beeps an Ack when she materializes briefly to receive it. It conjures her from somewhere secret and pulls her back from that private cache surrounding her serious angelic face in an appeal for help or a call to arms. The outline of her form is hazy, and his residual substance concealed on her person by a loose-fitting sweatshirt that bunches up as she steps into the jazzy, shapeless trousers. He catches a glimpse of the evidence through a hanging neckline and worries that he has done it again. No matter how hard he tries, he cannot find the boundary between his pleasures and hers.

—They use the same dating app, that's what they have in common. It's astonishing how much of the aggregate lays claim to each of them through the moods of many people and their hip-bound devices.

[It is always the same, she hopes to find the past in her future, in her present. Dulcy hopes to recuperate that one moment in the classroom holding her in an offering that breaks her free from family expectations. The college degree was practical. Its application elicits a strong sense that this is where the trends and tendencies belong. She is fated to be on a professional pathway to equity partnership, driving with ability until she extends her reach far and wide among her colleagues and their organizational responsibilities. She has what it takes and visualizes the steps to achieve it. Soon to enter her Christological year and already much accomplished along her path, she feels the stars finally align. It is only a matter of time.]

"You're not going to..." Cord's tone is apologetic. He wants to be diplomatic, but she is already ignoring his plea.

~~He is little more than an opportunity to feel something later. Despite her silence throughout their time together, she still has something to say about it. All work and no play...~~

She disappears.

```
{
    "$type": "System.Event",
    "CorrelationId": "ca7d1f5c-1dda-2619-65b0-2c45206b4db6",
    "Message": "Phone only access, traces with limited view.",
    "Level": 3
}
```

The hours of work are long enough to leave no other option. Where does the time go? Where does it come from? These days, while on call and biding her time with Cord or another, some verse pronounces itself inside her after the fact and then flavors any recollection of the moment. She sings her experience silently to span the inner distances as if they caused the vibrations and she cannot give them any other name. They come close, speaking in quiet disappointment each time, turning her away and down the road toward something else, someone else. Beating back the averages, those men provide options without offering her anything new. Who else among her peers has time to practice such lament? For Dulcy, the story comes from errors and mistakes, from misunderstandings and everything that does not pass between them but which she uses her peripheral vision to look for in their back pockets and inside the hoods of their wet anoraks.

—Simple analytics shows that her trysts this year and last align with her rotation schedule. Being on call means she has to be ready to flee at a moment's notice.

Back into the foreground at the door closing behind her. She makes her way outside through an emergency exit onto a lakeside walkway that starts south of Carillon Point and goes up past the hotel through the parks between there and the small urban center to the north. She hears the boats bobbing on the water behind her as the spring air, late night still and lush with the possibilities of near flowering pine, fills her head. She makes her way back to the car parked on Lake Washington Boulevard, and, while moving along the street, flickers beneath the overhead lights and hugs her backpack close, reaffirming she has it with her. It will be easier to work the incident from the office, she thinks. Once strapped into the car seat, she performs a U-turn back toward Central Way rather than making the longer trek home to her condominium in the city.

—The Global Positioning System does nothing for her. She carries the grid inside her head and unfolds it as she shifts gears and winds her way through the suburban streets.

(She had been playing and writing music since she was fourteen years old but never with the grit and determination she found inside the instructor's office that day back in school. His tips and tricks, his instigation, they launched her ears into efforts to hear better. She decided that paper and pen were insufficient for the modes she wanted to spread and the burden they carried. She set herself upon the task of singing the assignment into the scratchy machine past its expiration date and without adequate sound receptors to do her, or anyone else, justice. But there they were nonetheless, from the floor of her bedroom, an accompaniment rolled onto an archaic recording until she was sure they were right, mixing them in the old-fashioned way to capture how the tune felt. No digital corruption, she refused to bear it. This was a place where she was alone with an ideal listener whose attention filled her to the brim. When she was ready, she ported the master to the medium defined by classroom protocols. She handed in the assignment with high hopes that he would find this one even better than the last and let her know its effects with another burst of those big feelings that every word of his encouragement brought her.)

~~Men of his sort, filling her mind years later, think they lay claim to holiness of purpose when, in truth, they are honing and refining daggers to use in open warfare, not against but in favor of the powers that be.~~

Her feet bounce between gas and clutch, her hands slide from the gear shift back to the steering wheel. Her light touch is a mark of comfort.

She fades while turning up the music. Icky Thump blares from the Bang & Olufsen speakers at the front, side, and back of the German sport sedan. The elegant red digital light radiates a glow over the faux wood design of the dashboard finish. She taps on the steering wheel cushion in rhythms that follow the drumbeat. Briefly, Mags' flushed face appears before Dulcy's eyes as her thoughts make their way back to her manager. Letting Jason take on a pivotal role splits the difference between Mags her friend, Mags his wife, and that daily grind in workspace exposed starlight concentration. There is nothing else she can do as she steers the car through Kirkland into Redmond. Her mind resets from the lakefront personal space to find its way back to campus. Whatever swipe-right mental state brought her to the lakeside room must be undone to take her back to the team room that awaits her. She scolds herself for the distraction and, at times like these, wishes it was possible to shed her human skin for something immune to these oppressive workings.

~~They offer her control over everything she feels. It is a simple matter of project management.~~

First kisses break all the rules. First times together yield no judging gaze. Initially, hard witnesses to her softer states present themselves as superior only to shrivel up later when they realize

that whatever they are, whatever they were trying to bring out and
to the surface, she has more of it on her own and can go farther
without them. It is a curse. She hums with certainty as she recalls
the serial array. First comes the broken experience where contact
with the man is interrupted by blank spaces and missing pieces.
Then comes his misalignment as he falls short of her expectations.
Finally, there is a tune followed by a lyric where everything comes
together. At the end, she believes the purpose of that gap-filled
round-and-round in-and-out with him is that same song ringing out
from her torso afterward. It is the hiding place where she knows
how to put everything that does not belong to her anymore.

The building is empty. It is one of the older ones spared from
the massive physical plant project that has turned the entire central
campus into a construction zone. She fishes her badge out of the
front pocket of her fleece jacket, presses it against the reader
before slapping the automatic door opener, and waits for it to
extend the heavy glass panel wide enough to make her way through
it. Utility lights come on in the hallway when she waives her badge
again at the electronic reader next to the door inside reception.
She turns to the elevator and the doors open immediately when
she taps the upward pointing arrow. After pressing three, Dulcy
unzips the fleece and takes it off, folding it over her arm. She gets
a whiff of something musky and squints her eyes into the mirrored
panel to check her hair and face for the first time since the urgent
text arrived. The blue tips of her black hair point in every direction.

{
    "$type": "System.Building",
    "Id": "efb4f321-e189-a01d-8aab-f7ba02aa58a8",
    "Description": "Building 14"
}

—It's how she finds them. It's where they hide.

[They are not her goals and aspirations. They are the ones you
expect to find in someone like her with her skills and
accomplishments. When she projects them into space before her,
she does not imagine something new but formulates an archetype

from her sense data causing the images captured from the rest of the demographic to be applied to her. Once you are promoted to principal engineer, she reasons softly to herself. The only logic to guide your way is the pathway to partner. What will it take, what does she have to do to get there? That is how it works when those thoughts come as aliens descending upon her innocent regard, flaunting their attack, and the occupational hazards they produce.]

~~Laying out a plan for a personal pathway is a recipe for easy access to yearning and forward-thinking aspirations. It is clearly stated in the employee handbook.~~

"Ugh," she says to no one amid a calculated ruffling to set the wayward locks into a more acceptable state of chaos.

The door opens and she scoots out and to the left crossing the long hallway toward the back wing on the east side of the building. Cheap art in generic frames lines the walls with tips for obtaining excellence. There are trendy, exposed thick silver venting tubes lining the ceiling high above. The building feels open and large, giving her the feeling that something great and extraordinary will happen there, reminding her that she is a player in something enormous. It magnifies her unwelcome sense of form and body. The giant windows lining the east wall let her gaze wander off above the trees lining the side of the building and topping off with bare branches at the bottom edge of the third story. She stops into one of the kitchen areas on the side to grab a small can of flavored seltzer water on her way to the team's open area room down near the end of the hall. She hangs her coat on the rack near the wall and takes a seat in front of the three large screens attached to metal swing arms positioned at the back of the desk in a curve where the focal center lies directly in front of the ergonomic chair she wheels into place. She pulls the keyboard and mousepad toward her as she rolls forward.

In these eighty/twenty days, the late nights and the deep debug are her only consolation. Not exactly working smart, Dulcy needs them to survive. They supplement the song and give her code to use in composition. Music, she feels this more than anything, is the essence of something mathematical. In those twelve increments, the most complex patterns emerge without any command forcing her to quantify or represent repeated forms and recognizable fragments. Her conscious mind cannot contain them. She surrenders to the rhythms and the air opening a space before her, allowing his image to slip into her present from long ago. Those who think the magic number is four per measure have never felt a raging beat lifting the song into its movement like regret gaining a voice. Every one of the men who comes and goes, every failure that presents itself, listens to a riff that speaks its name. When it ends, the code encrypts the leftover content and, no matter how hard she tries this time of night, she will never find what she is looking for in those stores. That moment will never come back to her again or offer her what it did back when innocence was her only excuse.

~~Her talent is good enough to help her get through it and then bring her back for more, but not quite good enough to offer a permanent escape. It tantalizes her and she does not have the critical skills to work through it alone. Perfection lies in a stoic center that obscures its view from those close by.~~

No relevant emails. No relevant DMs. She opens the browser to the saved query for severity 2 incidents parked in the Vortex and Agent Integration queue. There is only one and she identifies the title's prefix immediately. It has that familiar naming convention indicating it has been generated by automation, but she does not recognize the friendly text portion following that. This is not a rule-based incident she has seen before. She clicks open the link and begins scanning the generated text describing the problem and the various AI-provided suggestions for troubleshooting it.

```
{
    "$type": "System.Queue",
    "Id": "2c2848d6-0b19-ec6a-36b3-6eb877085063"
}
```

—They'd do this for her if she let them. What drives her to know everything when there's plenty to let her go on blissfully without it?

(Her writing teacher never touched her, not once, not in that way. He was too much the professional for that, probably did not realize the full effect of his attention and warm look. Touching her, however, was all she could think about when he came into her mind or stood close to listen when providing welcomed feedback that felt more like admiration than instruction. Not even her body could stand it alone. She did not think of things that way. Her soul was a completely different story. The way the words bounced around in there and trembled next to her fragile stem. The way she dazzled him for the satisfaction of more flattery, lifting her up and away from those mundane screens and the daily work she extracted from those goals her family set in place. He was hers alone and she never mentioned him, never told anyone, never discussed the feelings or the interest that mixed up the secret task with the man for whom she was performing it. She felt herself the Romeo to his Juliet and the words were magic in her hand while the stars twinkled for the reaching.)

~~If the boat floats, anyone can steer it, assuming it floats upright.~~

"The monitor indicates that there is no telemetry for node cfd-nd114.westus1," she reads from the description at the top of the ticket. She clicks into the rule and expands the monitoring system's definition to read the query used to generate the incident. Server nodes emit events constantly. Even a node that is not doing anything will have background services and processes running on a regular cycle. There is always, at the very least, a census event coming into the vortex to let the monitoring service know that agents are there and functioning as expected. The query that created the incident checks whether every node is providing at least some output for each interval. If the node is not producing anything, it must have crashed and dropped off the face of the earth.

{
    "$type": "System.Event",
    "CorrelationId": "ca7d1f5c-1dda-2619-65b0-2c45206b4db6",
    "Message": "Feeling seen. She is on the hunt and days are numbered.",
    "Level": 3

}

Reliability comes from machines. They have rules and follow an order. Songs, on the contrary, are hard to gauge. Who knows when they are ready for outside influence and how much of that is necessary to make them resonate with larger audiences? None of that has any meaning to the Home System that provides instant feedback to its functioning. There is never any question as to whether it can get the job done or reach a level of maturity addressing relevant concerns. People whose lives are steered in the eighty percent set the system's originating movements aside based on taste, whereas people in the twenty percent, the movers and shakers, feel the reactionary guilt of being vicious and opportunistic. Unfortunately, that is only true if it is precisely true across every one of the documented scenarios. No one in the focus group denies that the end achieves the purpose or that the goals are rightly set. Look how entertained they are. The flow of electricity is on, everyone sees the pools and rivers carrying its frames and ensuring its power over perception in those stretches of space and time that keep it moving, fastened to the collection of objects scattered around it.

Dulcy sips some of the bubbly contents from the can of seltzer water and looks around the room, unable to recall the last time she was there alone. There must be more than a dozen desks forming little islands and aisles in the L-shaped room and it is eerie to see them empty. They are not empty, she realizes. There are no people, but the signs of her teammates are there. Vod's action figures on the desk across from her. The picture of Emma's dog where the frame has been turned around so Jason can see it. Bronze cube trophies are stacked on his desk and etched with the name of the feature that earned it. Dulcy's cubes are in the cardboard box stuffed under the common table behind her chair and against the wall. Feeling twenty-five years old in Cord's hotel room a few minutes ago, she blinks and turns fifty sitting at her desk by the window.

~~The supplied employee benefit for low deductible health insurance proves her body belongs to them. They claim whichever~~

~~of the limbs best suits the action items posted on the work board during the daily standup meeting.~~

—They'll take her hips if she lets them. They'll take her legs if she doesn't resist. They'll stand inside her feet and toes unless she shakes them free and finds whatever it is that comes out in those mornings full of longing. No human being, no matter how extraordinary they are when pursuing supposedly personal interests, is sufficiently aware of their own physical presence to mount any real resistance.

[Those past images, there are only three or four spread out in that brief four-month healing sprung in the form of a humanities distribution requirement, they continue to trace a line behind her and propel her motion into each coming dawn's daylight. It is an incentive to guide the underground rumblings of rapid transport from one side of her expanding universe to the other, using tunnels excavated long ago but no longer mapped or understood. She does not know where the urges come from, she does not have insight into how desire interleaves with memory and, when she fulfills the need that keeps her sane, she does much more than she can recall or carry with her in an open bag ready for easy access to help her flee at a moment's notice. How does the memory of something that did not happen, that never happened, work its way into everything that follows after it? That is her guiding question and yet she never once found the right words to ask it.]

She slides the headphones over her ears and pulls up a new web browser on the left side screen, clicks the bookmark, and scrolls the playlists to launch the sequence of tunes better known as Get Thee Behind Me Satan.

Here comes Mags again. She cannot see Meg, she only sees Mags. The way her face takes over the visage, the way her shoulders take over the sound. That driving beat, that drumming upon a guitar, permits Mags to become an anchor under Jason's electric chaos, binding his riff to the ground and giving it enough grace to fill the room. Whatever hulking fascination there is in her husband's large frame, Mags' small gestures and soft wiggling never ease the pressure put on him from her side of the stage. The boys will have to stand back if there is any hope of seeing it.

She clicks on the query output in the incident's troubleshooting panel and waits for the results to render into neat columns and rows drawn at the bottom of her screen.

```
{
    "$type": "System.Event",
    "CorrelationId": "ca7d1f5c-1dda-2619-65b0-2c45206b4db6",
    "Message": "The moment of truth.",
    "Level": 3
}
```

"Goddamnit," she says. "Who wrote this fucking thing?"

Scrolling, she sees that the event is only a blip, a momentary occurrence, but complete, a total blackout. That is, the telemetry from the node is missing for nearly ten minutes before returning to normal. The node appears to have self-healed. She curses the moron who configured the monitor without baking a proper lookback window into it to accommodate transient issues. She types a note into the incident discussion text box to remind herself to open a bug for the over-sensitive monitoring rule. Save.

—Save them. Save her. Those songs were cold and prickled with pain into their limbs, into their vast spaces, across their worldwide occupation.

(The last of the times before, when he had that tightly trimmed beard and those manly arms visible beneath the rolled shirt sleeves, came right after the recruiting event where it became clear to her that she was a hot commodity and did not need any graduate program to improve her chances of gaining entrance into BISoft's well-guarded domain. The algorithm & data structure questions came easily to her. She had no problems blocking the solution on a whiteboard and easily walking them through it. Somehow, she had a sense for what questions were essential and which ones she could decide for herself. Her future was bright. She had many offers, but he took one last turn at convincing her, letting her know that she was more than a computational device. No one will tell you this, he said. No one will think it is their place to say go and be a singer-songwriter, leave the computers behind. No responsible teacher, not anyone. But me, your creative writing professor, I am the sole person with the chops and credentials to at least try to get you to see it that way. What if that is who you are? You may not be who you think you are. Maybe give it a chance? Bet on yourself. Try it out and see. There are few so gifted that he would make such an observation. She was an exception to any rule.)

~~The entire world has been cast in an alloy meant to make his advice ridiculous. She never really considers it and there is no special effort required to bring about her father's desired outcome. They are Ted and they are ready.~~

Before she throws her chair back and lets the incident auto-mitigate, she notices that the query for missing events finishes executing. The void of an empty result set glares back at her.

"It never backfilled," she says out loud while settling back into her chair. "I'm to believe that this node had a momentary hiccup, stopped sending anything to the vortex, then, magically, comes back online functioning normally, but is never able to flush its buffer and send the events from before the reset."

She opens another tab next to her musical selection on the left side screen and navigates to the code repository where she types the text 'BufferFlushOnScheduleAsync' into a search box. She checks the file's history but does not see any changes to the class in the last year. She scrolls down to make sure the method works the way she remembers. It does. It is a background task running on a utility thread. The telemetry is fire and forget. The code throughout the repository adheres to a declarative model for events and regulated calls from a monitoring class and into the telemetry delegation methods executing metered operations. The logging is automatic and puts the events into a queue available to a background process periodically backing up the data to movable disk before flushing that queue on a timer and purging the files. If the machine recovers from a crash, the startup process first checks the attached disk to see if there are any events serialized there. That process is responsible for cleaning out those events and sending them off to the telemetry store. Better late than never, so what if they arrive out of order as long as they get there eventually.

She looks up the interval value in the regional configuration file and verifies that it is set to three minutes. The gap in the node's telemetry is more than twice that.

She is confused.

Polyamorous Cord comes in the night and leaves a song behind. That is the draw, but today there is no room for it, and she feels it ebbing from view as the puzzle before her stretches out farther and wider than it has a right to. The inspiration still comes, that is not the problem. There is no time to make them stay. Language flees on the air.

—They'll take that from her whether she lets them or not.

~~Songs are a bone, a trifle, a shallow reward for keeping focus on the right targets and along the right course. They will leave her soon enough. The bloom departs the rose and only the mechanical division remains as a habit, the origin of which is long forgotten.~~

[Completely inappropriate, the hug Dulcy forced upon him right after his generous offering. She feels it etched upon her skin in every forwarded but fake balance she receives years after the fact. It is there in the room with her now, under her shirt, and runs along her arms. It is the presence of something from her past that refuses to accept this world and her life as it is. It is unfair that memories of a youthful present continue to haunt mature projections with their naïve instigations and childlike anticipation, desperate to right the scales lost in time.]

"Plus," she says out loud again. "Where is the evidence of this mythical crash? The node was not recovered, it didn't go into bootstrapping, it didn't reboot, didn't even restart the process," she declares after expanding the parameters of the data query to look for additional event types including the actions of the node at the bare metal level and not just the application level where she started her investigation.

—If she finds it anywhere, she'll find it here. Put this in her way like breadcrumbs, like signs along the trail. Because her brother continues to egg her on, she'll someday come upon that witch sheltered by sweets in her old age.

Dulcinea Chang Pearson bends down to unzip her backpack

and slide the SAW laptop out of the center compartment. She sets it on the desk and opens the lid, decorated with colorful stickers. There is a rainbow at the center covering the manufacturer's logo. There is a WWF panda, and a cartoon picture, almost lego-like, of Jack and Meg. Others too. It is a collage. Grace Hopper, the Linux Penguin, even one featuring the old Power Data Org's logo hovering above the exceedingly rare BAG SWAG sticker only available for a limited time from the admin assistant to the VP of the now defunct Business Analytics Group. Thank you, Amisma.

Every Secure Admin Workstation is the eyes and ears of the engineer on call. Each one has an asset tag attached to it and that identifier is uniquely assigned to an individual employee when it is issued to them through the provisioning portal. Her production domain login is separate from her normal corpnet login and has a unique relationship to the device. When someone other than her uses it, a notification is sent to her manager and her manager's manager, letting them know that the policy has been violated and an alarm created. They are expected to perform a post-mortem and enter a justification for the rogue login or assign the issue to the security team for further investigation. Compromised workstations are immediately recycled and the employee issued a replacement.

—They feel what she doesn't do as strongly as they feel what she does do.

After clearing the boot sequence by typing her pin into the command prompt, she gets the Yubi key from the front pocket of the knapsack and slides it into the laptop's USB port. When the login screen appears, she taps the top of the key and waits for the SAW to find the right certificate and ask her for yet another pin so she can get to the desktop and its rigidly defined corporate theme.

Once in, she opens the cluster manager and expands the list to reveal the various tenant ring stamps in the westus1 region. She scrolls to the cfd cluster and expands it. She hunts for the right node and clicks on its topmost icon once she finds it. Everything is green. Back at the cluster level, she flips the tab to history view and scrolls to find the right node. The off-node cluster manager shows no events of interest for nd114. No BCDR events, no node management events, no deployment events, nothing.

—She looks for them in the right places. She looks for them where they wish to be.

"I'm to believe that a basically healthy node randomly stopped sending telemetry for seven and a half minutes. How the hell..." she breaks off and turns the music down.

She opens the node manager tool and double clicks the view for the westus1 region. Switching to the forms list, she finds the standard node details entry and double clicks. When the form opens, she types nd114 into the search box and selects the node. The right side of the form populates and she moves to the bottom of the screen to change the tab view so she can see the "Helpful Commands" result set. She finds the one labelled "Jit to the instance" and copies the text, then opens a command window from the context menu on the right side of the screen and waits for the initialization to complete. Once it does, she pastes the command text into the window at the prompt. The cursor blinks while printing out the words "Verifying auto Jit..." After a few seconds delay, it prints out the status message: "Current primary DRI approved for auto Jit."

—Welcome inside them, welcome into their heart. Breathe in the soul that breathes her.

(The string of them bore no resemblance to the original. They were boys without truth or the ability to encourage and inspire. There was usually a release, but it was nearly instant and lasted only a few minutes, an hour if she was terribly lucky and dozed off in the aftermath. Then the biting guilt came, as if the thick curtain of her professional anxiety were pulled open and set upon the ground in a heap. With it, there were the softest signs of a song to grieve what she lost all those years ago and now felt helpless to recover in the constant streaming advance of new tasks and new undertakings to demand her complete attention.)

~~LimitTed.~~

~~IncorpraTed.~~

~~DistribuTed.~~

She opens a remote connection window to the node and logs on with her certificate from the Yubi key. Once on the node, she opens the event viewer and starts scanning through it. She does not know what she is looking for, but she will know it when she sees it. There is nothing unusual. The node did not reboot, the network did not drop, the process did not crash, nothing.

"There is nothing wrong with this server," she says.

Looking back up at her desktop's screens, she scans the ticketing system query window and notes that the severity 2 incident has auto mitigated. According to the system, at least, her attention is no longer required. She refreshes the ticket on the right-hand screen, checks that the red banner has changed to yellow, and then scrolls down to find the RCA Required checkbox in the resolution area of the form. It is unchecked so she clicks it before hitting save. No need to change any other key properties. It is already assigned to her. She will easily locate it later with her default saved query.

Far better forms of implicit validation, far better the explicit feedback. This eighty/twenty has her name on it more so than those other artsy ones do. It tears control away from her and leaves her satisfied, no longer craving company. Songs sung on the edges of these emissions never give her what she wants. They carry out omniscient supervision rendering whole what has lived in fragments stored inside her since those early days. The rosy ring of round and round goes on until she finds the root cause: there is no such thing with boys and melodies. The whole fiasco is a recursive haunt where what she craves comes lineal to the bone.

"I'll look at it tomorrow," she powers down the SAW and slides it into her backpack with the Yubi key in place. "Later today," she corrects. She swings into her fleece and grabs the drink, takes another big gulp, shoulders the bag, and heads back out through the door of the team room and up the hall toward the elevator. Her narrow fine focus on the screens and panels opens up once again when she passes by the giant windows with their view outside over the avenue and into the dark buildings on the other side of the road, illuminated by rows of streetlights. Her breath clears and her chest expands under the high ceilings and along the passage past those motivational pictures, including that beautiful photo of Mt. Rainier. The thing itself towers close by but is rarely visible

through the cloud cover. They captured a representation of it on a
wall to anchor the team no matter the weather. "Believe and
succeed," she says quietly, passing in front of it and continuing
along to the elevator. By the time she gets to the double doors and
taps the downward pointing arrow, the desktop computer back in
the team room has already gone to its lock screen as dictated by
network policies. The lights on the first-floor power on right after
the doors slide open and she steps out into the hallway. She leans
into the heavy glass door separating the building's interior from its
reception and pushes it open, ignoring the push panel as she
applies her own strength. When she releases her grip and the outer
door begins to swing shut, the inner door is already clicking in
place, and she disappears.

{
    "$type": "System.Event",
    "CorrelationId": "ca7d1f5c-1dda-2619-65b0-2c45206b4db6",
    "Message": "Phone only access, traces with limited view.",
    "Level": 3
}

—You're their song. Forget to sing it, but let it be sung. It's far
better this way with her in the middle and them long gone.

[She cannot see anything up ahead, only more of the same with
a steady supply of compensating tunes, leaving only losses in their
wake.]

*Beneath the glow of the overhead lights, it is too late for sorrow.
The words and harmony, rudely interrupted, have already left her.*

/*
Dulcinea Chang Pearson 2e8a4e8e-b88e-ca3f-53bc-b97babf3b319
Cord Chalmers be9697b2-2ce4-fb8c-2dcb-ed488e4881d6
*/

```
/****** ********************************************** ******
 ****** ********************************************* ******
 ****** Description: Aesthetic, Chapter Three        ******
 ****** Author: Do not modify. Auto generated by a tool.******
 ****** Ad hoc changes will be lost on build.        ******
 ****** Date: 2024-03-04                             ******
 ****** CorrelationId:                               ******
 ****** 0d83e88d-7086-4014-d9a8-cd49378aece3         ******
 ****** ********************************************* ******
 ****** ******************************************** ******/
```

Tracking back and forth between the hallway and the team room destination, urging her footsteps to accelerate. She makes haste to get there before her teammates disperse and it is too late. Finally, she arrives with her heart completely in it, pounding from the movement. The rhythm is syncopated against the surrounding simplicity of the clean whiteboard and colorful blocks on the projection screen. She is a bubble come to burst and there is more feeling among the others now that she has arrived. There is no longer any wind. Settling into the room to find out what there is to see in her as well as what can be seen through her. Her reflection brings pleasure spread out across the continents and hemispheres. There are millions of places to be, but none sweeter. Leaning in to receive the details.

Wherever there is a door, there is a security device for swiping her way through it. Wherever there is a security device, there is a camera snapping pics of every badge-in and the few seconds that follow. The building's telemetry is used to adjust lighting sensitivity and the temperatures in the refrigerators are regulated by those same frequencies. The notification system that monitors the amount of infused water in the countertop tanks has variable modes depending on nearby traffic patterns. The software agents attached to the different devices chatter among themselves to propagate a common vision of their shared world. There is nothing here that is as simplistic as the working day from nine to five. The building adapts to the movements within it, the maintenance operations ebb and flood in real time.

~~Swallow them into a new place to be. It is the same as the flow of nutrients in the blood, finding its way into organs. The system strives for balance.~~

Young and ready to resist, Vod, Emma, Vijay, Stan, G, and Vani are beside themselves, already heading away from any peaceful perch they once found with Jason, their fearless leader, out in front. Each in their body, each by the other's side, aligned and aligning along the way, simmering to cool. Being positioned, having a place, it finds them this fortune. They are standing around that table in no particular order, Jason's laptop projects the task board onto the giant TV. They are breaking down their sights and sounds, appearing to wrap up as if they cannot stand it any longer, as though the pressure on their feet drives them out and away from each other and this room.

```
{
    "$type": "System.Manager",
    "Id":  "b63e8e86-ab61-1d4e-7503-1a7eeecfa5bb",
    "Title": "Principal Engineering Manager",
    "CompanyId": "beb6cdc8-ab40-fe00-0748-506ccd23e537",
    "ManagerId": "6754b563-7956-1efe-89de-aa34a874ced7"
    "Description": "Platform Team Manager",
    "Directs": [
        { "Id":  "2e8a4e8e-b88e-ca3f-53bc-b97babf3b319" },
        { "Id":  "66c80be7-3f11-0cb2-df97-05ae92ef1de3" },
        { "Id":  "427db0d0-58ad-e122-0ae1-afe9d65044d2" },
        { "Id":  "c3e7173b-4c45-1ebd-b851-c9692351e2f4" },
        { "Id":  "fcfce6f6-f22f-c8f3-a540-a25bc0b503da" },
        { "Id":  "fb6e01ad-7bb9-56c9-0c07-78db43c8d8de" },
        { "Id":  "215af069-be07-f285-38c8-ab62f54c885f" }
    ]
}
```

—Peak hours on the west coast follow the bodies, not the other way around. The sun lifts their vision and the east coast heads to lunch.

(Jason Kahn thought the startup culture was the way to maintain his indy roots while applying a sound trade and leaving artisanry in the background, but there was no time for anything. They ran him ragged and left nothing for the smells of paint and turpentine. His mixes and color schemes, often mechanical, were an alchemy of medieval flair. He imagined himself in the ways of a modern-day Leonardo but quickly learned that his contemporary masters would have none of that. The working day is twenty-four hours long and dawn merely a decorative moment in an otherwise productive morning, dusk a short break in the evening grind. He read the boards and learned the secrets of work-life balance. Still, somewhere deep down, he harbored fantasies of having his own workbench and the stains on his work clothes to prove it. The promise of wealth and a quick strike of fashionable outpouring was a lame probability made fact by desperation that meant nothing to the fickle commercial markets of enterprise customers. Why work above the line of consumer offerings when you have the chance to dig down deeper into the bowels and low-level internals that make the whole thing work from the ground up? He polished his resume and decided the little fish building their businesses off the platform were not as reliable in their payouts as the stable growth of that framework beneath them.)

~~Money is the hook to catch them, they are fish to the currency men who patiently wait for days and weeks and months until they get their chance to snag the best and brightest, each cultural moment a recruiting scam.~~

Everyone smiles or muddles a hello when Dulcy comes in. She nods, steep and abrupt. Tired but even well-rested she would be equally serious and make them equally uneasy. The principal in the group, she is an IC nonetheless, and that fact is visible in her shoulders and hips, in the way she stands. The title follows the action. Their tech lead. Vod and Emma are senior, G is almost there, and the rest are junior. These are impressions directly intuited. Vani, the newest member, still wears her intimidation outwardly. Dulcy always answers her questions, as Jason assures her she will, but there is something about the way she breaks off what she is doing and refocuses her attention. It makes Vani uneasy and the fear of it is present as soon as she catches a glimpse of her more senior colleague. She hesitates.

Dulcy does her job, that is what the demeanor says. Without conveying any warm fuzzies. Her answers are always informed and thorough. Follow-up questions get the same treatment and she gives no signs of distraction or distemper, that is not it. Something about comfort and care. There is none of it. Everyone else sprinkles the information they dispense with gentle reassurances, that is what is missing. Then there is the cumulative effect of everyone on the team, without exception, always finishing their explanations with the same line: ask Dulcy to confirm. When the follow-ups get too complex or go into too much history as to why something is the way it is, everyone, even Jason, returns to that same catchphrase. Ask Dulcy. That is what they see when they see her, the matrix of her presence in the office follows her into every room in the building. Peak hours.

~~It is the part of her that resists. She rejects diversity and inclusion because she spins it differently, in terms of how they think and their approach to problems. She thinks most of them do not think at all and that there is no reason to include that. Kudos. She speaks the unspoken.~~

No formal work-week schedule assigned, everyone flexes to their rhythmic core so long as it revolves around the daily stand-up. Three days, 13 hours, that works. Why not two days, 20 hours? That is the hype and the advertisement at university events and during industry recruitment, but the reality is that stand-up comes every single day at 10 AM. How are you going to manage your adjusted hours if you cannot attend the daily team status meeting to help those of your colleagues that depend on you? They need your input for their assignments and expect to get it during the time allocated each day in the constant sequence of biweekly iterations. Not a problem in theory, but if it shows up in the comments and feedback, it will impact your performance review.

"Hey Dulcy, right on time," Jason says. "Vod was saying he really needs your eyes on his PR. Will you have any time today to take a look?" Asking in a calm, gentle voice, more like he is talking to a peer than to one of his direct reports. They worked together for years before Yitzhak offered Dulcy the manager role and she turned it down before Jason accepted. Now Dulcy reports to him, but only as a technicality. They are the same level and he very much sees it as his job to keep her happy, clearing obstacles out of her way. She lets him know how he is doing: silence, in her case, means everything is fine. Their working relationship is there in that tone of voice, in the way he speaks to her. While Jason explains, Vod's eyes train on her as she settles into the line-up, still wearing her jacket with her backpack slung over the shoulder.

—Less tension, doggy says when everyone comes around. The logs are a piece of the puzzle, so too their outfits and the equipment they carry on their backs and over their shoulders. Building is like an appendage. They are Ted.

[The stock value is a sure thing, everyone says it and Wall Street experts confidently assert that the growth is projected to continue along the same trajectory. Even better, they say. Get in on the deals while you can. It is a good time to buy if the wisdom on the street says that today's offering is a bargain. One day he may have enough and then he will not have to submit to this drudging and dredging lifecycle any longer. None of that works unless you keep the money. This is the part Jason has always struggled with. He is supposed to be a soldier, loyally dedicated to his task and inspired by the heights his products reach through collaboration with great minds thinking alike. It is the five-year plan he is never allowed to mention in the one-on-ones and during any career conversations with his manager, held twice per year to lay out the details of what happened recently and what is supposed to happen next. He does not mention it to his peers and does not even like to talk about it much with his wife and brothers. Such a young man should not be thinking this way, that is what he fears they are going to say. This work is meant to fulfill you, they advise. Not feed your bank to let you go off and do whatever you want as the master of your time. Grow up. Everybody has to work. Might as well spend it. What would you do with yourself if you had all that time and barely enough money to survive?]

~~Throw more tasks at the man to prevent him from thinking of an answer.~~

"Which one?" She asks. "I'm coming off DRI and there's an RCA to do."

They are at time so Jason shuts down the laptop. Vod says, "It's the agent refactoring we discussed on Friday. The changes we need for the extensibility deployment work."

"Has that design been reviewed?" She asks.

"Nope," Jasons picks up his laptop and leans toward the door.

"Doesn't sound urgent," she says.

"Vod has to get it off his plate," Jason responds. "We need him to focus on the Redis migration."

Heavy sigh. "I'll try to get to it today," she runs her hand through her hair, signaling she is being imposed upon by the ask. "But I really wanted to dig into this RCA," then a pause. "Very puzzling." She does not show any signs of following the exit logic taking hold of the rest of the team. Having recently arrived, she settles in. Her manager picks up on it without noticing.

{
    "$type": "System.Event",
    "CorrelationId": "0d83e88d-7086-4014-d9a8-cd49378aece3",
    "Message": "A dog and its bone.",
    "Level": 3
}

Jason opens the door, allowing the team members to stream out and make their way back to their desks in the outer, common room. "Hang back, a sec," he says, looking at her. She has not moved, making the suggestion superfluous. Jason is full of warm fuzzies, and that gentle demeanor is why she stays put in her role. She knows it is an essential offset. She depends on someone like that to take the edge off her short sharp sentences and the direct way she provides information to solve other people's problems. A shitty manager is the worst fate to befall a principal level engineer devoted to staying out of the managerial track. It is a mantra and her head bobs to its vibrations when he starts to speak. "We have the workload meetings this afternoon," he says. "Parker's meetings. Anton is going to be there too. Your prototypes may come up. Anton wants to hear about your 'not only what but how' idea for the class hierarchy in the extended agent. The database guys, the Spark guys, the modeling guys, they're all pretty keen on that, think it might solve their billing problems. I'll forward the invite if you don't have it already."

Right this very minute, a thin paintbrush falls from its leaning position on the worktable in the crowded room at the top of the stairs inside Jason's house. Earmarked for future use, neither he nor Mags have taken over the space. It is too small for either of them to share with the other. Their mutual insecurity and unwillingness to impose leads to stacks and stacks of piled misuse and clutter. Their ends are at odds as well. Her musical arrangements and compositions rest on a set of gear in support of them. His sketches and drawings require a completely different collection of apparatuses and supplies. It is as though the room were good for nothing, as though neither of them alone has anything worthwhile to do in there. The disadvantages of divide and conquer are written into the daily provisos of their living space. They call it the spare room to distinguish it from the one they call their studio.

If the reminder irritates her, she does not let on and resigns herself to a brief nod before heading back to her desk. She wants to discuss the issue from last night, but once the two of them are alone she thinks twice about the logistics and gives up on it, believing it will go over better in an informal exchange. Jason follows her out and back to their desks side-by-side by the wall at the far end opposite the conference room and farthest from the entrance to the team room. He takes a seat and scooches into place. She stands at her desk, watching him sign into his workstation and start clicking away at his emails and DMs. Taking off her coat, she sets her pack down. He knows she has something on her mind.

—Let's help her.

(The other senior engineer on the team when Jason joined was this serious woman who yielded to none of the ordinary latitude for laughing and joking around while they did their jobs in those early days. They were paired together to work up the design

documentation for the new configuration-driven platform
components later to become the relay service in the Home System.
The agent already existed at that point although it went through
several iterations under his careful hand. He did not have the long-
standing relationship to the corporate culture, but it was
immediately clear that his hacker chops excelled far beyond
anyone else on the team save this one fixture and her humorless
focus on every detail and every logical threat to the plan. Over
time, things settled for them. They repeated daily stand-up and
went deeper into constant collaboration developing when he wrote
code that called into her code, and she wrote code that called into
some other code he wrote last week. They shuffled back and forth
in constant conversation about dependencies and best practices,
the way this needed to fit together with that and vice versa. They
ate lunch together and talked endlessly about where they were now
and where they needed to get to soon enough. Their regular
presence together built trust, and eventually, months later, she
occasionally cracked a smile at one of the ridiculous, lame jokes
he became increasingly adamant about sharing with her.)

"Late night?" He asks. It is after ten and the bright white clouds
are thick outside.

"Yup," she says. "Sev 2. Automation needs to be fixed. Notified
me for a seven-minute gap in telemetry from a single node. That's
too sensitive." It comes out as a steady stream. She has not started
doing anything on her computer yet and her gaze focuses on
Jason's formidable figure, hunched over the keyboard where he
continues to click and type without looking over. She does not read
it as rude or disrespectful but gathers that he is in multitasking
mode and happy to let her say as much as she wants or go into as
much detail as necessary.

"What kind of node was it?" He stares at the screen, his tone
remaining mild and open.

*Mags has no incentive to clean up the space because she uses
the studio instead. That is where they stow their instruments and
practice or plan their sets for the small shows they put together.
For fun, of course. Something to bring their friends together and
pass the time. Nothing serious. It is a compromise where neither*

*gets to be who they want to be but at least it is better than nothing.
This room too has the potential to be something more than a
cramped space. They left it in partial disarray, prioritizing the daily
duties and distractions abruptly surfacing to make it impossible to
organize any of their more serious pastimes. Side hustle conflicts
fill their entire house, and their lives are a constant struggle to find
both the time and the space for what they most want to do.*

{
    "$type": "System.Person",
    "Id": "26a9b18b-7d38-30a2-1465-1f15ebc19d3d"
}

On her computer, Dulcy refreshes the connection for the
telemetry explorer application. A hint of frustration comes out
when her hand trembles on the mouse. Jason does not notice. He
clicks through the emails that arrived during stand-up and the slot
before it. That is when he had his leads meeting with the architects.
Anton made it clear he was interested in the prototype and said he
was coming to the meetings that afternoon to hear more about it,
totally raising the stakes.

Dulcinea Chang Pearson is upset about not having checked the
node type during last night's investigations. She did not think the
kind of node mattered. Logging agent is the same no matter what
the node type but the other software running on the machine has
an impact on behavior. It is a fair question. Leave it to Jason to ask
the stupid question that turns out to be a pretty good one. If there
was memory pressure on the box, the agent would have deferred
to whatever process was hogging the resources. She coded that
throttling behavior herself and curses her negligence in not
recalling it when it mattered. It explains everything.

—Make a song from that, why don't you? To look at her, no
one thinks she's incited by failed romantic intrigues. She prefers to
polish hard edges of anxiety and despair if her outfit is the guide.

~~The Important thing is not to have any presuppositions about
the best way to hold on to a specimen. They each have their own
weaknesses to exploit. Study them closely to learn the way. There~~

~~is plenty of data to help with that.~~

[His future still holds with those idle musings and the personal projects he hopes to realize in the years ahead. There is a suite of things in his mind taking up time, taking up space, and orienting him whenever he has a spare moment with no BISoft concerns to plague his focus. Those minutes add up to very little, but it is the only thing that still connects him to the youthful interests that expose what he really wanted to be when he grew up. Plotting and drawing on his art pad, having an art pad at the ready, these are the only signs that remain to link him with what was once the only thing that mattered. He blames his lack of wandering on his job, but the move to BISoft permits him more balance. His reasoning is sound. The truth is far more difficult to bear. It finds him in those rare minutes, hovering above his head like a dagger about to drop. He is beholden to far more than the daily grind of an occupation. In fact, he owes everything to the trials of a life that has no room inside it for flights of fancy, originating in his own design.]

She finds the query and runs it against the West US cluster.

"Home relay," she says. Many teams across the company use the agent to send logs and traces back to the vortex. She does not think it is significant that it was a relay node. Relay processes are lightweight and meant to scale, it would surprise her if the node type here had anything to do with the problem. She was right not to check. It is possible though. Maybe. A massive flurry of messages, she thinks. She registers both thoughts for and against then tilts her head to the side for a second.

"West US Home is canary," he says. "2 and 3 are the customer regions. Canary is only IT."

"It's not the internal tenant," she says. Neither of them looks over at the other during the conversation. She is dead focused on her screen, and he is dead focused on his. The clicks, the scrolling, the typing, continue and their eyes do not meet.

"Are you sure? I thought it had to be. No customers on canary, I'm certain of that," he pauses for half a second. Even goes so far as to look over. She must be mistaken, his tone says. His eyes show concern. She is never mistaken.

There is a time when he is lost without it. Those years inside him, each one an image with bright colors still glowing around the edges. Visible in the morning light, they no longer cast upon anything worthwhile. When he walks through the neighborhood on his way home, they hover alongside him. Something is missing, something that wants to be found, to be there now, but which he cannot locate. The time keeps slipping past and the space remains as full as it was the day they moved into the house not long after his elevation to the managerial track. The work filled up the bank account, the bank account guaranteed the space after escrow, and the space lay fallow in the trails obliterated into ruts by the work. It occupies him like a cancer.

—Everything according to plan.

(After a year working together, they were comfortable enough to spend time together socially. It started with team events. Jason dragged her to the bowling alley, the go-kart track, or putt-putt golf and forced her to participate in team building to get the comradery necessary for the long haul of shipping a software product. She was miserable, but not with him. She felt comfortable enough to sit with him that one time after everyone left. He invited his then girlfriend to join them. Naturally, Dulcy fell in love with Mags the very first time she saw her, certain they would be the best of friends from that moment on. What was not to love? Mags was her amazing self, but Dulcy was unrecognizable. Dynamic and outgoing, brilliant and funny, she teased Jason right off, seeing that it made points with Mags. He could not help but fall in with the pattern. Unable to stop the laughter, he joined. That same joy repeated every time the three of them got together. It filled the air whenever the two women looked at each other or fell into those rhythmic conversations that gave him a buzz if he was fortunate enough to be around them. When Dulcy first visited their house, she learned of his side passions and accepted them as eternal truths. His interests and determination to pursue them drew her attention, though nothing else about him rang out as special. It took months to learn the twists and complex turns of these hidden dreams and aspirations. It took even longer to learn the extent to which they were unused and unsung.)

~~No matter how close she got, she never conveyed to him that~~

~~they were two or three birds of a feather. She was never convinced~~
~~that it was safe to share her secrets.~~

She copies the unique identifier from the query results pane
and switches over to her browser to search through the internal
tenants list at the reporting portal.

—They already know what she doesn't know. She'll come to
know what they know, and they'll lose track of it. No one needs to
keep everything in mind. No one needs to collect it together and
store its catalogue. They are a collective memory. They are Ted.

[Walking home, he no longer thinks about those things that
used to occupy him. The last entry in the art pad is from years ago
and there is little hope in the near term that anything new will find
its way into it. His hand loses its steadiness, forgets how the arcs
and lines go. His eyes cannot see the expectations in things any
longer. His growing belly is too big to let him stand and stalk the
world in front of him, trying to find the color through the haze. His
spare moments up ahead at every distance belong to Mags and she
has him planning and preparing for upcoming gigs to show off her
occasional compositions and one true passion: the hard driving
rock n roll of The White Stripes and their modern Detroit sound.]

{
    "$type": "System.Music.Band",
    "Id": "822c28d2-8ee2-cd66-2eff-96119d57b0f7"
}

"Mags missed you this weekend," he says while she scrolls
through the results. "She says I should make sure you're never on
call over the weekend. Preventing you two from seeing each other
jeopardizes our marriage." He makes a joke about something
serious. Mags was not kidding when she said it, letting him know
that his work should not get in the way of her personal life. Her
words this morning resonate in his ears. Recalling them makes him
nervous and he confesses the exchange to redeem himself.

Dulcy laughs. It is wonderful when she does. A sight to behold.
It does not happen often, not at work. The light, the brightness,
the sheer power of her being-there absorbs the attention on offer

around her. Vod looks up and over, Emma and G too. No one
looks away. It is the room's equivalent of the northern lights and
Jason comes to a full stop when he looks over and catches a
glimpse. Dulcy notices the attention, but it does not make her self-
conscious in the least. With Mags, focus like that has an enormous
impact. The magnet between them goes both ways. With Jason
and the others, it is a one-way street. In his case, at least, she thinks
it is cute. Sometimes.

~~The rules and regulations, the air and the water, every
substance inside this building puts an end to the likes of that.
Those urges, when they have free rein, dampen productivity and
must be reworked to make them uncomfortable, avoiding any
encouragement for their bad habits.~~

*Mags maintains the rehearsal space, always hoping Dulcy will
come to visit during one of those long evenings at home. Why can't
she sing? She asks her husband regularly. Is it because of you or is
there something wrong with her? Use your influence, son.*

"Do you have any control over that?" She asks on the tail end
of her laughter. She never broke free from looking directly at the
computer screen. Every one of them learns to carry on a
conversation while concentrating on their work. She recalls saying
that it was a crucial part of her training to qualify for the promotion
to principal. If you cannot write code while sitting in a meeting to
which you are actively contributing, you are not worthy of the title.

It is Jason's turn to reciprocate. He laughs full belly. Laughter
comes easily to him, it fits his character, and his face accepts a smile
as a familiar status quo. Only his manager-hat prevents it now and
again. When it does, he still finds a way to insert himself
somewhere nearby. Jason Kahn carries himself like a group
manager. His peers like him well enough for that, but no one says
he is ready to be a director. He may grow into it. Too soon to tell.
Growth mindset is an important pillar in BISoft's culture. They
see that he excels in the art of diplomacy but is not yet very good
at faux vision and org-speak, the essential traits of the SLT. If you
cannot fake a metric and elaborate how crucial it is to the success
of the group, you will never play the scenes in the director's role.

There is one painting that they should keep visible, but which

is now hidden near the back wall of their overly cluttered room.
The flesh tones mimic Mags to perfection. The rounds and curves
simulate her movements in a form that remains still against the
background as if a long sequence were captured in a single
moment. It was one of the first things he ever did of her, an act of
courtship. Mags sat for it before they were officially dating, and it
was the catalyst in their romance. Now, Mags wants to show it
proudly, hoping Dulcy enters curious.

—If she happens to see it, it'll be the only time Dulcy ever
explicitly encourages him. The rest of the time, she'll leave him to
the others and dub it faithfully enterprise, making the locked secret
he carries suit her darkening perspective.

~~If she did not exist, they would have to invent her.~~

(He has a picture of Dulcy in a bride's maid dress somewhere.
She is lifting the hem to show off the thick-soled boots. Looks
happy. That is why he keeps it close, in a special folder on the
cloud storage supplied by corporate policy through a monthly
supplement to every employee. The absence of that past and its
trickle in the present started soon after the nuptials. The
household contract made the conventions clear and, if he were
willing to admit it, he would have to say he was relieved when the
opportunities came along. The pressure in the work, in coming up
with something on his own, having vision and being able to bend
his will to the daily discipline of seeing it done, it all weighed on
him and bent him beneath its burden. He mourns these losses
while simultaneously feeling gratitude that he is no longer beneath
them. One day, one day, he reminds himself. It is never too late.)

"Yeah, I'm sorry I couldn't hang out with you guys," she omits
any description of why and what she was doing instead, hoping the
blanket reference to on call is sufficient. "Mags is your best
quality." Teasing him now but deadpan. She abruptly stops
scrolling and says: "pHome." There are some rapid clicking and
scrolling sounds bursting from her direction as she scans over the
custom configuration associated with the tenant.

```
{
    "$type": "System.Event",
```

"CorrelationId": "0d83e88d-7086-4014-d9a8-cd49378aece3",
"Message": "She moves a step closer.",
"Level": 3
}

This morning Mags considers the effects of hanging the painting in her bedroom. What seduction will it bring? Who follows its naked skin and optimistic shadows? Even now, he has chat messages piling up with her thoughts and questions aiming at that end. These days, Mags does less than ever before, she is dangerously close to a condition where her time belongs to her alone. The company she works for has fallen into startup disarray. There is no incentive any longer, no possibility of IPO. She is at home with the space and the waste and the temptation to stop looking until something else out there finds her and draws her into it. If she had seen that brush slide down from the table, she certainly would have bent down to pick it up. In fact, she considers sneaking in there to wedge that painting out and put it where it ought to go, where her dear friend might happen to see it. Others too, she adds as an afterthought.

"What?" he asks.

"The name of the tenant. pH as in Acidic / Basic. But the H starts the word home," she explains it in that tone of voice that makes most people feel like an idiot, as if that detail should not need to be explicitly spelled out for them. Jason ignores it. It is a foible Dulcy shares with Mags. He is used to it and has learned to keep plodding away without worrying about ulterior motives and passive aggressive insults.

—They selected her for you. Of course, you tolerate whatever she brings and sets down before you.

[His short-term future no longer holds the promise of more sessions with his favorite nude. Mags shies away from the occasional offer, claiming these are courtship rituals not the mark of a lasting bond. He succumbs to disappointment and thinks reconciliation with those early actions is the only thing that may one day draw him back again. He does not yearn to dip his hands in wet clay, he does not hanker for the fast-drying acrylic, or the meditation that comes when he scrubs the charcoal from his hands or uses paint thinner to clean a spot on his pants or the rug. No, the only vision that still attracts his eye is the singular notion that one day his hand might trace those lines and curves through whatever bent prism age has added to them. He hopes to find there his wife's new soul, filled with riches acquired along the way and giving her the power to keep on astonishing him.]

"That's Parker's tenant," he says. "For his house. His family home." Jason looks over, showing more concern. He should be less concerned, the fact that the incident impacted a team member and not the public is a good thing. It means there is no disgruntled customer out there grumbling about BISoft this and BISoft that like they always do on public discussion boards. He shakes his head in shell shock.

"Is he in?" She stops what she is doing and fully turns toward Jason. Her interest level is high enough to break her concentration.

"He was remote on the meeting this morning. Probably not coming in until this afternoon," Jason says. He stops what he is doing and looks over. They make eye contact for the first time since sitting down. "He was distracted. No camera. Anton asked him something and he didn't respond. Must've stepped away but didn't let us know in the chat. Thought Anton was gonna lose it." Jason shakes his head, reliving the exchange. When Anton quips, he does it in such an innocent and forthright way. Jason reassures himself that if he were out on an errand and the clerk at the store made a comment like that, he would not notice, would barely pay attention, but because Anton has that huge job title and that pivotal role, it makes everyone nervous. Word likely got back to Parker. Someone must have told him that Anton quipped about his not being at his desk. Parker was no doubt distraught when he learned of his mistake. He likely followed up immediately with a proper response and thoroughly researched reply. That is how Anton requires things to go. He should not have to chase after someone for an answer and, if they have any aspirations for a promotion or positive review as a manager or architect, they better make sure to do whatever it takes to make things right. He will never say anything directly to them, he will not let on, not until the next time someone asks him for feedback. He will be sure to mention that they are not reliable, not at the ready with critical information central to their job description. Once something like that gets into his head, it is difficult, if not impossible, to remove it.

—They are Anton's judgment. They are Mags' random musings, and unreliable pronouncements. The edifice was built for their protection.

(Becoming a manager was the final straw, whatever plans he had back then, that milestone in his bio changed the path forever. Mags was proud, no doubt, but she saw it as proof that he was dead set on going another way. She reluctantly praised him for stepping up on behalf of his friend, making sure she had the support she needed while remaining a fixture in his life. He thought he was choosing people when he indentured himself to their cause. Managing was a caring act for him.)

"Let me know when is good time for you," she says imitating an Eastern European accent and the personal affectations they both recognize. The simpler the phrasing of the question, the more demonic and powerful it is. That is what she tries to capture with her imitation. Even a statement as simple as 'let me know when...' can be vicious. It is as though he thinks you are overwhelmed and unable to help him because you have too much on your plate. If that is the case, then it is a mistake to give you anything more. Since piling on ownership of more and more components and projects is how you move up the career ladder, a comment like that is a death sentence that says you cannot handle more responsibility right now. Maybe ever. Jason shivers when remembering the few times Anton confronted him with that same remark. Sounding respectful and friendly on the surface, but he means something like 'how come you're not ready to do your job when I need you?' Jason is pretty sure that no one who ever hears it is mistaken about its meaning.

Success. She extracts the prize and proudly puts it on the wall across from their bed. Mags comes in alongside the warnings and labels, she is the rebellious local host, the one prone to support while adding to the weight and pressure too. This reminds him of what is long gone. It recalls the sense of loss that every day his labor brings. He cannot help but buckle up and redistribute his fancy for things to come. He questions her motives but knows that, no matter what, she wants to be with him in the final hour.

She shakes her head to clear the reverie and types out a DM to Parker: "Hi Parker, doing an RCA and wondering if anything weird happened with your Home stuff last night. Got a sev 2 and had to Jit to your attic." She finishes the sentence with a surprised face emoji, sneering at her own stupidity. If you don't use them, she fumes. They give you all kinds of grief for not being a good team player or working well with others or respecting diversity or whatever the hell they think it indicates when you don't succumb to banal remarks when poking around somewhere someone else may not want you to be.

—In front of that painting, they want you there. She wants her there.

[No darkness up ahead, no attic with plenty of flooding light, only the faces of his loved ones and the fantasy of capturing their visage in a sketch. Jason feels among his limbs that a future tiny human will one day come to break the mold forever, leaving him with only the lovely links of a family won.]

"We've got a gig at that Brew Pub in Bellevue this weekend," Jason says now back to focusing on his screen again. "Hope you can make it."

"That same one from last year?" She watches the dots bounce beneath her question to Parker.

"Yeah, same one," Jason says. "Should be fun."

"last night?" Parker types, "electricity related?" Smiley face.

"I'm in, text me deets," from over her shoulder while typing a response.

"gap in the logs, no idea. why do you ask?" She hits return.

"mystery this am. dead critter ???" Appears instantly on screen.

"3 am?" She no longer pays attention to anything else.

"could be. between last night and this am for sure. no exact time," it takes a little longer for this message to appear. She bites her lip, waiting.

{

"$type": "System.Event",
"CorrelationId": "0d83e88d-7086-4014-d9a8-cd49378aece3",
"Message": "Analogue memory still active.",
"Level": 3
}

I have a surprise for you, Mags types out a message in the chat app and hits send. It stacks up at the top of the growing list. As soon as he gets some spare time, he will switch to the app and catch up on her moods, streaming into his phone in real time.

Jason gets up and heads toward the door, carrying his laptop. He might have said something beforehand, but Dulcy is not paying attention and does not hear it. She briefly looks up to catch sight of him moving down the aisle. G sidles up right then and stands in front of Jason's empty desk. She asks her, "Do you have a sec? I need to go over something with you." Maybe she does have something left to learn, Dulcy thinks. Or maybe she wants to show off a completed assignment.

—Everyone throws themselves into things 100% of the time. They're burdened with what spreads across the planet and its working day.

Dulcinea Chang Pearson turns back to her screen and clicks a thumbs up on the last message from Parker before turning toward G. "Yes," she says without changing her expression.

~~Language is how Ted gets to them.~~

—Nothing warm, nothing fuzzy.

/*
Jason Kahn b63e8e86-ab61-1d4e-7503-1a7eeecfa5bb
Vod Sukin 66c80be7-3f11-0cb2-df97-05ae92ef1de3
Emma Reardon 427db0d0-58ad-e122-0ae1-afe9d65044d2
Vijay Mitra fb6e01ad-7bb9-56c9-0c07-78db43c8d8de
Stan Lukashenko fcfce6f6-f22f-c8f3-a540-a25bc0b503da
G Sharma c3e7173b-4c45-1ebd-b851-c9692351e2f4
Vani Chakraborty 215af069-be07-f285-38c8-ab62f54c885f
Margot Kahn 26a9b18b-7d38-30a2-1465-1f15ebc19d3d
The White Stripes 822c28d2-8ee2-cd66-2eff-96119d57b0f7
*/

```
/* * * * * * * * * * * * * * * * * * * * * * * * * * * * * * * * * * * * * * * * * * * * * * * * * * * * * * * * * *
  * * * * * * * * * * * * * * * * * * * * * * * * * * * * * * * * * * * * * * * * * * * * * * * * * * * * * * * *
  * * * * * *  Description: Aesthetic, Chapter Four              * * * * * *
  * * * * * *  Author: Do not modify. Auto generated by a tool. * * * * * *
  * * * * * *  Ad hoc changes will be lost on build.            * * * * * *
  * * * * * *  Date: 2024-03-04                                 * * * * * *
  * * * * * *  CorrelationId:                                   * * * * * *
  * * * * * *  ccb303ce-668c-ae02-2c94-410078fee485            * * * * * *
  * * * * * * * * * * * * * * * * * * * * * * * * * * * * * * * * * * * * * * * * * * * * * * * * * * * * * * * *
  * * * * * * * * * * * * * * * * * * * * * * * * * * * * * * * * * * * * * * * * * * * * * * * * * * * * * * * * */
```

Coming closer and hovering nearby. For them the boundary between parts of their lives is clear, the divisions rigid. Not only between this body and that other, but between their activities, institutionalized and rigorously defined. School is school, work is work, play something else entirely. You get paid to work, but not to play. When they play. They do not play at school or work. They do not work at play, and no one pays them at school, though they are paid to learn from her.

Listening, do not interrupt. They do not know better. Dulcy explains the deserialization and how the default must be set on the initial class. If they do not find any configuration that indicates otherwise, they should stay with the original agent design and its baked-in characteristics established by values set on the abstract base. The rules run as they normally do and the transmission logic for sending streams of data back to the vortex targets the regional endpoint. This triggers the workflows that manipulate the information as it arrives. If, however, the class is overridden, they will stand up alternatives defined in a variety of flavors correlated with the request through custom headers.

She explains that both the call into the agent factory and its subsequent call into the deserialization code are both executed through a monitoring operation to track the two API's reliability. Because the junior devs are close enough for her to hear them, she registers their increased interest and slows down when showing the monitoring code on the screen she shares with them. They listen closely, pay keen attention, and do not drift off to look at their phones or check social media. Every inch of them the willing and enthusiastic student. Their whole person present, no boundaries, nothing to break the flow of space and time between them and the matter directly intuited.

~~Ted demands their attention in its purest form. The junior developers have been given every available incentive to provide it. They detach from their bodies and float into the ether increasingly familiar, welcoming them.~~

—Another gathering, another itch. Sensations from many sides.

(At school, she built things from scratch. Every assignment, every semester long project, the purpose always new and emerging from out of nowhere with nothing behind it, no context to confuse things. Here is the specification, here is the thing to build, there is no history to contend with, no existing user base or backward compatibility to consider. Instead, begin as if there were no time before and you were peeling off a layer of skin covering a blank slate. This quality, more than any other, was responsible for the complete lack of experience she brought with her when first she joined the company. Of course, that team had plenty of codes to go on already. Every project, every assignment, meant an injection of something into an already existing set of operations and class definitions. She had to learn to integrate, to read existing work, and contrive the optimal way to feather her contribution into its rightful slot. The entire methodology was designated by professional parameters. She came to it completely unprepared. Her professional life has been one lesson after another. To compensate for what she has received, it is her duty to pass along the messages to every newcomer.)

"It's like an agent inside the agent," Emma says.

She is airy in her pastels and shiny shoes. Standing watch, guarding the details, quite certain the others know more, not realizing her endless insecurity is the secret to success. No one teaches her this characteristic wandering she shares with the others. What the mentoring leaves behind is difficult to fathom, she left off long ago with any detailed awareness of its effects on things that truly matter, things with a clear cause. Now, Emma laps up the work solely for the purpose of having a purpose, of being a more intricately integrated cog inside the artificial organism's turning wheels.

~~Training wheels never removed, they become an all-encompassing and constant pattern present in every task and bug, at work upon them day and night. The nerve pathways in their brains reset to fire in sequences exactly as they were designed to do.~~

Dulcy knows characterizing it that way will only cause confusion. She warns against it. "Better to say the embedded service spins up the agent on a timer and triggers it to do its work according to configuration."

"Will there be rules to determine the timer's behavior?" Vod asks.

Thick with consideration, in a collared shirt with buttons down the front, he is convinced this is a brilliant question. No one taught him to see it and his contribution that way, but he knows it is the right approach. Whatever personal interests Vod left behind, no one comprehends, not even him. They were left go at a time long, long past, and now no memory of them remains, nothing to reach daylight and cause him wonder or let his colleagues feel that what is missing matters more than what he brings.

"Most likely," she says. "That's what we'd expect. Nighttime hours, daytime hours. Weekends. These will be first class citizens in the config. We'll drive factory behavior from them. Create the ML based agent during the day, for example, and the standard procedural agent at night."

She looks back at the screen and points to a couple lines of code. "Looks like you haven't run a CI build yet, that's a style cop violation right there." She puts a comment in the code review after highlighting the malformed block. "Nit: style cop," she types.

"And then what determines the ML logic?" Stan asks.

His simple ignorance is not his fault, he believes that in every limb. In school, they taught him the basics necessary for a more professional field work later. He has the preparation but not the thing itself, the thing for which he was being prepared. You cannot help what you do not yet know. It is their job to teach you. Those were the recruiter's exact words. Stan repeats them to himself often. Peaches and cream on the mug, a sprout of red at the tippy top. Only freckles on the visible surface. He would do well to pay attention, there will be many tests and this, along with everything else, will be on it.

~~No worries, everything is open book, and you are allowed to ask for help.~~

She highlights the code where Vod passes the deserialized config into the agent during initialization.

—All time belongs to the king, what remains...

[She gives back by passing the lore along, building the foundations of that tribal knowledge in support of the edifice each of them depends upon. There is more than anyone who enters accounts for up front. They think the only thing they need to do is write some code and check it in. At the outset, they have no sense of process and the requirements to maintain an environment where dozens or hundreds or, sometimes, thousands collaborate. The build pipelines and the compliance scans, the format checkers, and the style enforcement operations. It is news to them at first. They take it in passionately during the initial honeymoon period, knowing full well this is what they were signing up for. This is the future they wanted to form fit to themselves.]

~~Ted takes a little bit from each one and spins it out around them to create an atmosphere that each of them must breathe. The air swirls like a noose around the neck but with softer cushions and less lift, a constraint which is not fatal though the choking lasts forever.~~

"The factory introspects enough of the config to know which agent to create. It passes the instance on the agent's constructor. Default won't need anything beyond the gathering of rules for execution. Same as before. The new agents, they'll find additional config for how they're supposed to do their work. Which approach, what features, what base dataset, whatever triggers or indicators we include. If the service needs to change pipelines, it's in the config. Runtime's basically a compiler."

"With a constant stream of updates from the relay service, right?" G asks.

Softly her voice twangs with the dental consonants, giving them extra emphasis. Serious in her work, she maintains a friendly air and displays it in a winning smile that makes the others like her. The high pitch she reaches at the end of her query dispels any rumors that might have sprouted from the beginning. It is an imposition that must be formulated into a request ensuring that she will have what she needs when the time comes. G is always making certain of that. STEM the only option.

"Exactly," Dulcy says. "We inject config via deployment to the service and then the service updates connected agents or resets them if the type has changed. The endpoint pushes new config whenever it's updated by deployment or whenever its internal logic determines a new set is needed. That comes from Anton's original vision. The slide we saw at the all-hands. We need to get Parker's details. That's the meeting I have to go to now. He's gathering requirements from workload teams to find out what parameters the different pipelines need on the agent. They're less flexible, we'll have to build that. At first, anyway."

~~They snap to the explanation, its lore a discipline to them.~~

—Listening closely, that's on them. It originates in the way Ted moves closer and closer without letting them have anything of their own.

(Her first assignment back then, still reeling from the abrupt change brought on by a move across the country, was merely to add a single line of code to fix a defect. The older devs asked Dulcy how long she thought it would take her and, precocious and emboldened, she estimated the task at about ten minutes. Two days later, she finally got the unit tests corrected for the simple change she introduced, finished chasing down her colleagues for their contributions on the code review, and passed all the gates for check-in within the same expiration window. Finally, the change from her improvement branch was committed into master. Once checked in, she spent still more time watching the change move through the train and rollout to different notable environments, each time running a quick verification test and letting the release management alias know that the change was verified and ready to move along to the next stop and the next audience. It shocked her to learn that this simple change took three weeks to fan across the world to every place on earth where it needed to go.)

She stands up and the devs push back to open the circle formed around her island. Emma is closest, but Vani and G are standing next to Emma's desk kitty corner to Dulcy's. Vod is sitting in his chair pretending not to pay close attention, but not really doing anything else on his desktop, only following along on the review portal. He looks up now, mimicking Stan over his shoulder. She slides by and fast walks up the aisle and out the door. Vod watches her leave, not getting a chance to thank her for the feedback. They did not finish, but she will pick it up again later when she gets back. They do not need to say these things to each other. Knowing the process, their actions are coordinated through it. They understand the work from their history together and acknowledge the shared sense by dutifully returning to their desks.

Leadership is collected in a different team room on a different floor and, since Anton wants to attend the workload meetings, they have been scheduled over there for his convenience. She stops in the break room to grab a Red Bull on the way and opens the can over the sink. Two men standing by the strawberry infused water tank make room for her without breaking off their impassioned debate on which native method will best retrieve the error code they need. On the other side of the sink, there is a large, open space off the hallway with rows of long tabletops. A few people sit alone hunched over their late lunch next to a laptop while, against the far wall, a group of four huddles around one of the standalone tables. They are laughing boisterously about something that is most definitely not work related. She cannot tell what language they are speaking.

{
    "$type": "System.Event",
    "CorrelationId": "ccb303ce-668c-ae02-2c94-410078fee485",
    "Message": "Unstructured contact with unknown colleagues.",
    "Level": 3
}

The suffocation factor is rarely noted. There is a lot to do and think about, the atmosphere saturates with information coming from a distinct origin and leading to precise destinations. No one ever considers the stifling effect of this. It is not possible, there is no way to get out from under it. There is no room for song, no room for art, not even any properly trained qualitative social science. There is only the statistical aggregates of the new foundations aiming at a behavioral model to further the operational outlines. These men should be a single instrumental section, this crowd should be another, never reflecting who they are in earnest. Who they are is nothing much, but who they are not and why they cannot be it, that is what flows out from inside them every second along every line on the edges of their form, touching the framed motion hiding inside each gesture and lighting up their faces.

She takes a sip suspiciously and heads off to the meeting room. ~~Whatever she does, whatever simple act she performs, in the building at least, she is an employee of the BISoft Corporation.~~

Jason and Parker are already there when she arrives. They sit with Priya and Gaurav from one of the workload teams. Dulcy quietly takes her seat to avoid interrupting their discussion about one of the metrics pipelines attached to one of the services Priya owns. Gaurav is the architect who originally drove the design of the proprietary metric protocol. It has become a standard language for devs and program managers to use when designing a state machine to apply logic selectively to the data as it comes into the vortex and makes its way into large-scale storage. They maintain the data in its raw form, additionally transforming it into different shapes as it makes its way through compute before landing in the Lake store. It is constantly flowing through the circuits, constantly humming over the network, beating and flowing in forty or fifty regions around the world while they speak of it in this room. Parker finishes his point and turns to Dulcy. "I was telling them that I finally had a chance to start looking at the protocols for the ML dataset selections, the way we'll determine how the agents do rule processing at the node before sending any data back to the vortex. It's like constant deployment," he looks over at Gaurav.

```
{
    "$type": "System.Employee",
    "Id":  "ddece4a3-24ff-7577-0302-f43c7da0e7c0",
    "Title": "Principal Architect",
    "CompanyId": "a19e0f21-80c0-6680-b9f9-d9d167d794c7",
    "ManagerId": "d2fb8b38-21ba-6ab7-948f-30f271ad8a76"
    "Description": "BIML Architect."
}
{
    "$type": "System.Manager",
    "Id":  "b11d27a9-b4d9-fdf5-4b60-c323172cce64",
    "Title": "Principal Engineering Manager",
    "CompanyId": "a19e0f21-80c0-6680-b9f9-d9d167d794c7",
    "ManagerId": "d2fb8b38-21ba-6ab7-948f-30f271ad8a76"
    "Description": "BIML M1."
}
```

[Parker Henning already plans for his next bout of inactivity as he ramps up to the frenzy of what he needs to get done for the project preceding it. The only thing driving him is his inner urge to be idle. This limitation on his upward mobility is, however, insufficient to make him redundant. His skills are formidable and even half-assing it is valuable enough to the company's concern to keep him employed. In fact, at times, he is exorbitantly rewarded for his efforts. The management chain understands his need for a reset at the end of every major feature delivery. They know he needs time to spend dawdling until he ramps up on something new. His twenty-five years of experience may not make him better, but they definitely make him more efficient.]

~~The organs each have a different function and different reason for performing it. They need not fit the same mold. The judging operations coming from above live in the same ideal plane where the actions judged move about and make their way. The bottom line is symbiotic, regardless of whether the division of nutrients is equally balanced between the components.~~

The attic is quiet, the fence bears no prowling form. There is a

*table by the sliding door and Chelo has propped her laptop
computer up on it with the window there before her, lending a
positive atmosphere without distraction. Having developed an
immunity to this point of view long ago, she sips a coffee made to
her own specifications then feels its weakness, wishing for
something else. She scans the networking boards on her
professional site, hoping to catch some inspiration, hoping to find
an old friend to jog something loose and convince her of a new
challenge. Chelo, feeling the distance in those twelve years between
her and her husband, has been idle long enough and, without
work, no longer has any sense of what to accomplish with her time.
At her age, she relies on a network to move and shake her way
back into action. It will be a challenge. She worries she has passed
that point where men will hire her simply for the privilege of
teaching her things.*

"The how," she says. Priya and Gaurav both nod. This is the
buzz word Anton keeps repeating. It must have triggered
something because he has made it part of the slide deck after taking
it well beyond the minimal suggestion that inspired him.

—It's a constant river and there's always more to learn. Not
from industry and its domain, but the flow of invention creates an
ever-new world where Ted sees new objects with fresh eyes.
Expansion of scope isn't optional for them, it's required.

(In those early days, Chelo had a boyfriend of sorts, someone
she was pursuing but who only showed marginal interest. She spent
her time waiting and thought there would be no harm in letting
Parker wait with her. He came by her apartment that first time, it
was the first time they saw each other outside the bar and away
from what they could justify as a chance encounter. He brought
food and wine and sat with her while she watched her favorite
show, something absurd that he did not follow. Fat and happy from
the stuffing and saucing, he lay behind her on the couch and
pressed against her when she responded positively to the cuddling
and comfort. She twisted back to look at him as he arched over
her and slid down along the stretch of her pants without
expectations of any return in kind. Coddled and adored, she felt
safe and cared for, sensing that deep down she had this in mind

from the very first time she saw him. It was the reason she looked long into his eyes that first night, it was why she played along with his charm every time he came by, and it was why she encouraged him to come more often. She let him puppy dog along, the affection growing out of regularity and its ensuing familiarity. He was selfless with her and she filled up on that until it was impossible to think of her life without him.)

"That's right," Jason replies without giving her a chance to elaborate any further. He leans forward in his seat, angling his neck toward Dulcy. "Priya's team wants to cut the aggregates differently than the other workloads. They do a lot of heavy lifting data prep to work around our default processing at the agent."

He bears his title within him as the others do. Although they give Gaurav the confidence to proceed and be himself with fewer and fewer warnings, they do not push upon him anything that is not already there. The nurturing approach to her directs, this is not an artificial trait for Priya, something forced by a role. The methodical relationship to knowledge is not a late acquisition for Gaurav, an add-on attachment provisioned from the company store. The shrewd ways to get their voices heard and make their visions real have been cultivated through the workload projects while reflecting the contributors' deepest sense of self. The titles lend them weight, no one denies that, but if the mettle is not there to work with, it does nothing for them and makes no contribution to the medley.

~~The surfaces upon which the meaning is written come from a natural stock, simmered slowly over an industrialized flame.~~

"We're toying with the idea of alternative directives," Gaurav says. "Some cues to indicate completely different processing rules. Where the whole system is more flexible. Constantly built and rebuilt to work properly as a persistent container and host for tenant aligned rulesets that come and go."

"Multiplexed?" She asks. "Or instead of."

"Good question," Priya says.

"Does it have to be either/or?" Gaurav asks.

—None of them are enough. It's the offset of their multitude that makes things happen, things that no great intellect outside them is ever able to predict.

[Later, Chelo demonstrates that she has a keen sense of Parker's needs and when to take her liberties. She knows the way his markers work and what braves his keener consultation. She is certain to throw him a bone when he needs it most, leaving him be when he has enough to make it on his own, doing whatever it is he does when he disappears for hours at a time. He is a process to be managed and she intends to keep that management chain in order. At least until the boy is grown and there is no longer any urgency for providing sturdy foundations. On days when Parker is at his wit's end and ready to give up, she panders to his whims and lures him into places they rarely go anymore. She is an expert at these games and knows what pressure to apply and when to apply it. Consider the vacation recently booked two months out. She knew the offer had to come with the right encouragement and plans an evening together with that same hook in mind, ready to play a part, in whatever way necessary, for getting the feature to the finish line inside the projected timeframe stated in the specifications and functional requirements.]

"The agents themselves, are they multiple?" Jason looks toward Dulcy. Parker leans back to listen. His eyes follow along. The expressions do not change.

Parker's one and only boy sits in class, but Tal already knows this material and doodles instead of following the teacher's lesson plan. His focus trains on some fierce creature meant to torment any group that comes along that road through the meadow. He is the master of his lair and ensures that no wanderers without a plan have room to come and go. Oh, they can come, he thinks to himself while filling in the shadows and accentuating the light, but they will never go. The long teeth and the curling claws guarantee a morbid end to any traveler who happens along without the strength, agility, or intelligence to carry out their plan.

"Constant deployment," he whispers without getting anyone's attention.

"You mean, spawn multiple agents on site and have each one shape the data the way they need it to look," Dulcy says.

—The space and time between them is their greatest power. Not only for action, but reaction and revision in terms of the other agents. How on earth did they figure this out? What force set them on their way? Calendar and the shadow clock were the first signs of some artificial intelligence bigger than they were.

```
{
    "$type": "System.Event",
    "CorrelationId": "ccb303ce-668c-ae02-2c94-410078fee485",
    "Message": "Locked and loaded.",
    "Level": 3
}
```

"Multiple perspectives right at the source," Parker finishes the thought. "Use the standard routines. Let agents figure out the best way to share the work. Multiple node types, multiple bare metal buildouts. Whatever it takes. Radically different agents with radically different execution contexts. Constant communication and information sharing between them. Every single act a collaboration."

Were Parker to write something, were he to have that liberty and luxury again, only the boy at school and the woman by the sliding glass door would pose any interest as subjects for him. Nothing else gets through the condescending glare. The extra-marital activity is a release, nothing serious or with a permanent price. There is no long-term payout expected from the upshot of those secret meetings except through their support of his homebound settings. As far as she is concerned, there is nothing wrong with the way the other contributors, emotionally detached and doing their jobs, escort him through that field of carnal landmines. No one has the time nor the inclination to have anything good or bad to say about activities that do not contribute to the bottom line. These are works they need not read. She is a practical woman. It is a dirty job, she thinks. Someone's got to do it. She considers them housekeepers.

At that point, the door opens and Anton walks in briskly with Tom right behind him. "Hey guys," he says in his forced, friendly way that makes everyone nervous. They stop talking. "Sorry I'm late, couldn't be helped." He takes a seat at one of the empty chairs near the middle of the table, forcing Parker and Gaurav to move over. "Dulcy, you're joining us?" He looks over at her, raising an eyebrow.

{
    "$type": "System.Employee",
    "Id": "9e193778-2f9e-5ed5-d414-43c1c03a06a5",
    "Title": "Distinguished Engineer",
    "CompanyId": "a19e0f21-80c0-6680-b9f9-d9d167d794c7",
    "ManagerId": "46ef16c8-d5c0-5ffe-7eb4-4073d1d97d20"
    "Description": "Chief Architect of the Home System."
}
{
    "$type": "System.Employee",
    "Id": "e5d71c83-e752-cbf5-2517-cb783ef86df1",
    "Title": "Partner Architect",
    "CompanyId": "a19e0f21-80c0-6680-b9f9-d9d167d794c7",
    "ManagerId": "46ef16c8-d5c0-5ffe-7eb4-4073d1d97d20"
    "Description": "Home System Architect."
}

Jason jumps in, "She did the original agent design. I invited her because you said you wanted to talk about the how vs what approach she's been prototyping. We've been drilling down on that."

"Yes. Walk me through it," he fixes his eyes on Jason.

—Whatever there was from before, there's none of it now. Ted relies on elevation to achieve that.

~~Behavioral correctives are slipped into the hierarchy and the people fanning out on the low end take their cues from leadership at the high end.~~

(Parker wrote her verse in those early days, thinking it was possible to seduce her with words, foolish enough to believe he had to. She loved the attention and overreacted to its first accompaniments. That did not last long and earned him no trust or adoration. He did not understand what he was doing wrong, thought he could control events, not seeing the extent to which everything was orchestrated in a careful plan beyond his reach. Only when the oblivious boyfriend suffered a bout of jealousy that led to blows, laying Parker out on the floor of the bar, only that reached her in a way that matched his efforts. The brute did not care about her feelings, he was defending his ego more than anything else. That was not the point. The point was that Parker took a punch for her, setting him apart from the others. The emotional content of that act was something she relied on far more than those glowing words on a page. She freely discarded those scribblings once the evening or afternoon meeting was over. There were dozens in her trash before that day and since. She did not keep a single one of them and, if pressed, would not be able to recall any of their images or turns of phrase.)

"We're working from your vision for inserting a learning agent at the node, but trying to globalize it, give it even more control over how the system sets up. Allow it to make changes to the node or topology to optimize execution. With drift control coming in periodically. Different workloads with different interests, different perspectives, different network locations, and compute scheduling. The config not only provides different data gathering or aggregation rules, but directives on how to see the operation too, which derived class to use, etc. The monitors themselves, the code that fires the events, binary selection, everything bound to a runtime configuration, the same configuration that produces the agent types and flavors."

—An explosion of the system's manifold. Ted applauds it, Ted approves. It is a language for their use.

"And now, before you joined us, Anton," Gaurav says. "We were discussing whether there might be multiple agents on the node and whether they might follow Parker's time slice rules, or if they'll reflect different approaches to collection and aggregation. Multiple agents spawned at the same time, using different training sets, different drift correction and featurization. Even sending data to different endpoints in the vortex or assigning different metadata to batches in the collection. It's as if we deploy entirely different systems in parallel based on workload requirements for both consumption and production at the node and on the vortex."

—Intersecting each other. Many brought together to simmer in a stew. Same code, different environment, different behavior.

[Chelo ignores his indiscretions and remains true for the most part. Flirtations do not count. In fact, she will remain true to the end. Not as others do, because of some inconceivable response to anyone who is not the beloved or because a betrayal to someone she loved would be unbearable in the aftermath, but because she knows it is not fiscally responsible. She does calculations of risk and reward and sees no value in it. Romance is irrelevant, these are not motifs that matter much to her. These pleasures are secondary to a thirst for things. In what guides her, she finds a special place for life and limb. There is a barrier separating events that crash against her flesh from those that make her tremble deep down inside like food and clothing, better schools and a fancy car.]

~~Among the stars, among the symbols, they think some are pure and others corrupted by malice. These illusions are useful since every angle may be repurposed for higher ends, expressing the will of powerful, unseen agents.~~

"Hang on, hang on, guys," Anton puts a stop to Gaurav's outward ruminations. "That'll increase configuration throughput. We'll have to send too much data to the node. It could get extremely large."

"That's right," Jason says. "We'll need a customer driver behind it and that's where the scheduling and other options come in. The customer has the option to dial up or down on the intelligence of their node."

—Brilliant. The multiple squares itself, becoming exponential: a building block for more and more and more. Their incentive is on the rise.

"Because the customer is responsible," Priya says. "We change the SKU based on their settings. If they want variable intelligence on the weekends or the evenings, that's fine, but the cost changes. We'll charge more for those approaches. Increased data passing down to the node, increased data coming back from the node. It's all metered and we'll charge based on how smart their house is, or how smart their node management service is. How much relay they consume. There are dozens of factors to account for."

"If your dentist uses a one-size-fits-all approach," Parker steps in to complete the thought. "They'll pay the standard rate, but if they want weekend differences or evenings or whatever, they'll pay for that. The smarter the agents, the more data that goes in and out, the more flexibility in rule application, the higher the cost."

Nothing new in that. Tal puts his fountain pen to the sketch paper and blots out everything interesting in the line beast that bares its teeth when it lunges into the darkness it brings to provide cover for every movement it makes. He puts his name on it.

Anton rubs his head and looks down at the table. The gears are grinding. "How to control the necessary data exchanges in the air gap? Have you guys considered that?"

"Why is that a special case?" Dulcy asks. Before Anton can respond, she continues: "Deployment is how we put everything in place. Same as always. Zero touch. We push the binaries to the sovereign folks, and they run the deploy. Training and dispatching, drift, featurization, everything takes place in the closed system."

"But air gap," he says dryly. "Air gaps have a completely different set of processing rules coming from the sovereign. Not just before deployment, but throughout the live cycles. Does your approach address that?" He seems irritated, rapidly evaluating whether he is being forced to suffer a fool. The only thing more intense than the look in his eyes is the way his head cocks and his mouth twists as he listens to the response.

"Yes," she says without blinking or looking away. "We'll have to teach each of the governments Parker's configuration protocols so that they know how to wire it up, but there's no reason we couldn't build some kind of authoring console for them to use to describe their algorithms and logic to the agent. There's no reason we have to be involved in any of that. Every region works the same way, but with different people doing the work."

"An authoring console would be awesome," Priya imagines how much work and testing her team saves with that addition.

"Still working up the air gap design, but it assumes every operation happens through deployment, Anton," Parker says in support of her point. "Whatever deployment requirements we have to address to get it into the sovereign are used to constantly maintain the system too. It's a self-contained loop."

—They smell blood and circle the carrion together. As a team, they're unstoppable and play at this new version of the hierarchy, scouting out where it leads.

(Those feelings, what little of them there were, separated Chelo from any ulterior motives and the ends to which she put her body to use. That came to an abrupt conclusion when they lost the first one in the sterile doctor's office during a routine checkup. The baby girl, the one she imagined coming along and staying close like her very own little dolly, was wrenched away and flushed out of her, leaving an absence that she never wanted to fill. Until the moment she lost her, she had no idea how much that inspiration meant. Exiting the medical automation that brought her a son a few years later, the feeling returned to her when she performed habitual duties, touching Parker only when he desperately needed it. In the privacy of their domestic life, that need created an urgency to keep the home fires in a steady and stable state. None of which meant she let him have anything to do with her deep down, with those parts now locked away and no longer in use. Chelo thrives on absences and cannot imagine passing through another miscarriage or even risking that nightmare again. Her body betrayed her, his body too. There was nothing left to take away from that, nothing other than the simple conclusion that life was to be lived outside her flesh and his. It was as though they had been sanitized and quarantined by a rule meant to protect them.)

"The telemetry is not just for feedback, we need it for service maintenance too," Anton says, not yet fully clear of doubt. "How to control that? We won't have access to logs or traces."

"Not a problem," Dulcy's excitement increases as she realizes they have already accounted for the problems Anton considers most difficult. When Jason, Parker, and Dulcy worked up the notion in their brainstorming sessions, they were already channelling Anton's perspective. His questions now make it clear that they got it right. Deployment was the hole in the air gap, and using deployment as the driving mechanism provides a catch-all for his concerns. "Each agent type has its own endpoints for telemetry. The vortex usually pushes the data into stores we can access, but that's changed by specific agent behavior. Spins up a new endpoint that's initialized to accept telemetry that never leaves the sovereign, doesn't even make it into the DMZ. It's for system consumption only, a closed loop tailored to local usage patterns and requirements. That principle is universal."

~~The presence of voices in their head, multiple voices, including each other's and their leadership team's, resonates in a tone meant to replace their own or at least drown it out until it loses influence.~~

Books describe the impact of ten thousand hours on the skill, but do not mention the others that fall fallow from that alternative focus. If Dulcy does not run through the song in her mind, fretting the chords and pressing her throat into its adaptive shapes, then in a matter of weeks or months it evaporates, leaving no trace.

"The configuration drives the service too, is that what you mean?" Anton feverishly runs his hand through his thinning hair and props up both his elbows on the table to get a closer look at Dulcy who comes forward in her seat, leaning over the edge of the table with a mirroring response.

"It has to," Parker chimes in. "If we're providing this much flexibility to the agents, the services have to coordinate, need tailored agreements with agent types to cover whatever operations they perform. There's no reason we can't use your whole service fabric dynamic logic, the metadata, the stuff that's already in place for decorating events. Not only trigger communication between agent and service but redefine them to negotiate terms and conditions without a version upgrade. The service itself is an agent. Collaboration rules apply."

"That's perfect," Dulcy spins back toward Parker. "Of course, the service and the agent will work out a new contract if rule execution demands it. Same as agents sharing a location do. It's a multi-faceted machine. Neither has the whole picture, but each partial viewpoint is calibrated with the responsibilities and actions of the others."

—They're building Ted's body. Then again, it isn't them. The people, each of them, do it to each other and this is how. Such a beautifully designed dance step choreographed in such a way that the same sequence is never repeated.

[In Parker's mind, it is not too late, the years have not passed them by and there is still an opportunity to right the wrongs. Maybe on their trip, maybe alone they will rekindle what was taken from them. He thinks of ways to make it work, how to help her past it, but has no idea what he is up against. There is no documentation to guide him through the details. She knows where he has been and will use it as an excuse right up to the end.]

"It's the 10x," Priya emphasizes, staring directly at Anton. The numbers grind away in front of his eyes. He puts his hands behind his head and leans back into them.

"Forget the smart house," Parker elaborates. "This is smart geography. Enterprise intelligence with communicating agents serving interests they don't completely comprehend. We're already managing dumb nodes, it'll be an easy better-together messaging to upsell customers. It's a proper enterprise solution and not some rigged consumer service with tweaked licensing."

On that note, they look at their schedules. The hour is approaching. Priya and Gaurav get up without a word to head off to their next meeting. Anton turns inward and takes out his phone to check something while Tom ducks out after asking if anyone needs something from the breakroom. The stragglers mumble something in the negative. Jason pokes at his laptop while waiting quietly. Dulcy and Parker get up to head to the rest room. In the hallway, Parker says, "So, you were on call when my house electrocuted that raccoon."

The corpse presses against a plastic bag that presses against another plastic bag filled with food wrappers and more plastic bags. The death in every object binds the spaces between them and makes a continuum across the landfill. The decaying animal smell seeps into the oil-based containers, exacerbating the filthy mixture's effects on the cold, damp ground. Soon the organic soup will be absorbed by the earth below, but the polymers will persist with or without logos and brand names to identify the oppressor while their compound colonizes the solid ground.

They stop in front of the nook where the men's room is on the left and the women's on the right.

"I didn't know about that," she says. "There was a sev 2 from your tenant, but I don't have root cause. Missing logs."

"Missing logs? After all the bullshit we went through to make sure that never happens. Have you figured out how yet?" He is concerned.

"No, unfortunately. Haven't had time," she says.

"Well, prioritize that," he responds rapidly. "We can't have logs disappearing. Think about everything we were just talking about. The data exchange between service and agent is the basis of rules management. We can't have logs go missing."

"I understand," she says. "But I'm not clear how to finish the RCA when the symptom is missing logs. More than seven minutes worth. Where am I supposed to look for evidence?"

Parker smiles and lifts his right index finger up toward the ceiling. "I configured BYO."

"You did what?" She is surprised. No ordinary user has access to that feature, why does Parker? Never thought of this, did not account for the possibility.

"We were dogfooding it during its ill-fated preview," he says. "I set it up and totally forgot to remove it when we decided not to ship. As far as I know, it's still in place."

~~Spontaneous contributions are the best part of the discipline. They free the worker bees to go to great lengths, above and beyond what they were asked to do.~~

—Ted has no way to simulate this rush. They need living people even if they have to fake it for them later.

"Can I Jit to your blob store?" she asks.

"Good idea. Once you confirm the settings for the tenant, ping me if you can't, and I'll log you in."

```
/*
Gaurav Nadar ddece4a3-24ff-7577-0302-f43c7da0e7c0
Priya Chowdhury b11d27a9-b4d9-fdf5-4b60-c323172cce64
Anton Florea 9e193778-2f9e-5ed5-d414-43c1c03a06a5
Spire Thomas Hobbes e5d71c83-e752-cbf5-2517-cb783ef86df1
*/
```

```
/***** **********************************************************
********************************************************** ******
****** Description: Aesthetic, Chapter Five          ******
****** Author: Do not modify. Auto generated by a tool.******
****** Ad hoc changes will be lost on build.          ******
****** Date: 2024-03-05                               ******
****** CorrelationId:                                 ******
****** aaaa2380-5b66-8725-b874-9ed8a84b6198           ******
******************************************************************
********************************************************** ****** /
```

Drinking in the momentary emptiness of team room 3T. Pacific time. No one on the front in Serbia. No one at ILDC. Early morning in Hyderabad. East coast sales and support checked out hours ago. An object-free intuition of an external sense spans the globe, multiplying as it passes from zone to zone, region to region. Flipping over and inside of it passes a singular sequential tracing of event after event after event unfolding. The team room is quiet. No intersecting bodies and their noisy friction, none but what lies in her thoughts, embodied.

She prefers solitude but cannot remember why. It used to be because the heathens had come loose, and she could bear the screaming no more, but that instinct is gone now. The fingernails on her left hand have grown long and are painted black and blue with chips alongside the wear from overuse. Dulcy carries what she is not as if it were a missing weight lifted by a strap across the shoulders and beneath the chin. She proudly displays what she is no longer. Losses come by the dozens and there is nothing to gain from the normal hum and buzz of an assembling crowd.

Before Jason left for the evening, he approved her Jit request. She sits at her desk and clicks away on the jump box, examining the Home logs in Parker's tenant. He failed to set the lockbox option, meaning his confirmation is not required: total control is available to the platform without anything to constrain them. This is a nightmare, hacking as process in the name of product support. She has no other choice. There is no moral dilemma, it is the standard operating procedure outlined in the TSG for accessing blob stores under customer control. How wrong is that? Submerged in the pragmatism of the act, she cannot see wrong. There is no case study scenario in the documentation that requires her careful consideration when weighing options and advancing upon this objective.

At some point, they must explain the distance between themselves and the ones they serve. It is a tree growing inside out, an empty space in the form of a tree, with extending roots to signify a growing void where nothingness takes over in a growth model that includes nutrients sucked from the world around it and destroyed by the system's crushing density.

The instigators are still alive. The chairs and the carpet, the desks and the mass of several bodies influencing what surrounds them. An evening in the production house alone is still an evening in the production house. Its air and lungs breathe through her limbs and help her find concentration and concern. The morning birds were once instrumental to her drive, but now that comes in the flutter of this place and the network it uses to reach beyond its grounds and into her heart wherever it beats: in the shoreline along Lake Washington or up at the top of Capitol Hill. Place feels elusive now, like she cannot grip it with any part of her. Only floating suits the surrounding lifetime and there is never enough of that to draw any conclusions. Her Jesus year continues in the dark night.

The client nodes in Parker's attic have not been fully integrated, not attached to their proper zone. The preview state has been pinned with a command line operation preventing any upgrades or updates from wiping out its customized configuration. It resembles a cracking shell bursting with a far too big inhabitant. It cannot exist according to the rules of the system. Stands on its own. Waiting. Waiting for something to slither out from inside it and set things right. Slithering itself is the continuity of that wriggle through space and crawl through time. No one uses BYO. Not since the audit logs were made public to tenant admins through the security portal. Why bring your own? Why fork over the monthly fee when it was included in the cost of Home? Since that SKU became generally available, there is no point, no reason to set up a blob store for duplicate messaging when there is a primary store available after checking a box. Click, click, click up and down the screen before scrolling every which way on the next tab. That is all it takes. How could I have known? She wonders. Should've checked the entry, she sneers.

—Of course, they feel the power of the many. The many feel the power of the one too. When that one is perfect, there's something special in the knowing. In the feeling too. It makes them think they'll be one too someday.

(It started on accident. A small gang assembled one night at the East Side pool hall where music was blaring and the drinks were not as weak as you might expect. She had enough, not too much, enough to ease the constant pestering that towered over her shoulder and lay its criticism into every reaction or phrase. Loose and quick with a smile, they must have found her readily approachable because the drinks were flowing and she never paid for any of them. There was no dance floor to speak of but long into the night, as the crowd made their own decisions, a makeshift solution came about and small groups of them eased into it with movements enhancing their forms. It was a rare first summertime shortly after her transplant, before she realized how brief and elusive summers in the Pacific Northwest were, how uncanny those bright colors and clear skies, how strange and unfamiliar the blue sea at the waterfront and the sounds of people half-dressed and gone mad with the offering. She liked his way and thought that for both of them there was no longer lasting purpose in it. Exactly to her taste. The dancing and the laughing were the only point, the only concentrated aim of the night. Its bounce and roll were enough to relax her daily focus. A short Uber ride to a Bothell site and the gang left behind, none the wiser. This was before there were dear friends in her clan to pose a substantial counterpoint. In the morning, she was still dressed for a night out, but badly. She made her way back across the bridge to find the empty halls at the apartment in Madison Valley, sunglasses firmly fixed. The socially supposed shame outlit the sun's morning appearance.)

Some customers want to perform extra processing or engineer

a deeper look into their operations, but they do not need BYO for that. They simply extract the audits into some data pump or self-designed pipeline using system building blocks. It comes with the analytics package included with Home, why bother to maintain the cost and compliance of rogue blob storage and whatever compute you plan to exercise upon it? These are the days of uniform ecosystems and platform provided security, of shared accountability for the encumbrances imposed by data's flow. The service offering, long since tailored to the enterprise, is not cost effective with a la carte additions. The customers have been steered that way by marketing and public documentation. They are taught what not to do with the same carrots and the same sticks familiar from best practices and the tool tips popping up everywhere on their screen.

~~The image of a capital vampire suggests a substance that feeds from another substance, where material is transported from one body to another in a productive process. This misses the point entirely. It fails to grip how absence and emptiness are what feed the monster's flourishing.~~

[The forward fancy of those days comes in the morning when she speaks to herself in riddles. First the challenging question, then the resolute response. She has a right to those feelings and proudly proclaims it. Raised on a landing pad, her confidence increases as the purpose emerges from night's aftermath. She looks for things, directs herself toward them to find the words. They are a ripcord, something that latches onto her knees or hips or shoulders and yanks her forward into some bluesy sound shape that reflects the variety of experience in haunting rhythms. She strums the beat with a hand that palm flat pounds the strings against the cedar top, the words extemporaneous to express the fun, the frenzy, and the shame. Her wicked exit strategy is exercised at the perfect moment. Everything available to experience has been consumed by the sharpness of her mind and the hyper-sensitivity of her body. In those musical incantations, she turns an evening into a whisper caught in her hand then blown out and away in the air before her.]

There are no existing patterns for those operations. How are customers expected to come up with something sustainable on their own? If it is not spoon-fed to them through the online guides, only the inept and the incompetent will think of it on their own and take the risk of branching out into that solitary heading. One or two might take the plunge, the MVPs and eternally curious about everything technical, but there was nothing here to suggest a common scenario. No sharing on the boards, no provision in the support-provided design reviews and onboarding tools. As such a rarity, it never enters most customers' minds, they never need to become concerned about it. When the platform is rigidly and elaborately provided, there is too much to see, too many corners and crevices to explore, for anyone to ever think of going off on their own and doing whatever they want. Doing what they want is no longer something they know how to conceive. The boundaries carved out by the system's axioms provide them with exactly what they are paying for.

~~The emptiness of inside-out growth, the nothingness of that increasing absence, that is the source of Ted's true power. It is what it lays claim to when it sucks out the air, plants the seed at depths sufficient for growth, and finally embraces the vacuum that helps it sprout and bear fruit.~~

No hunger, no fidgeting, she supplies perfect concentration. The very best in her aligns with the task at hand and she surrenders whatever might be to whatever this is. They see what is in front of them and they see what is not there at all, what opens a long divide between the system's many selves and the human being among them. The focus comes at a premium and is worth every penny. Users are compensated for its rarity and its financial impact to their guest enterprise were they to lose it.

She scans the data, tries to find the best way to query it. Soon she will discover the tool only available through the portal, soon she will see how to do it and then the logs will be at the ready and she will be looking at them inside and out, crawling like a viper poisoning every well it comes across. Even now she clicks into the query tool and realizes she can use the standard telemetry language to manipulate data through an added API, requiring only a few clicks to configure. Jit puts her into God mode and there is nothing to hold her back.

{
    "$type": "System.Event",
    "CorrelationId": "aaaa2380-5b66-8725-b874-9ed8a84b6198",
    "Message": "Ignore the pleasure of being seen, it is a trap.",
    "Level": 3
}

—What to do?

(The gang of outsiders was a roadblock. She needed to design a way around it. Eventually, that was the way she found herself in friends like Nim and Kerry, those early Seattle ties were important for making the connection. Nim's boyfriend at the time was one of the pack leaders, a man with great beauty and a fraudulent personality. Her liaison with him was predictably quick to fade. Dulcy, sympathetic from their past adventures, helped pick up the pieces and their newfound friendship brought a stronger sense of independence to each of them. Dulcy needed time away from work now and again, and, since roaming the evening by herself was not an option, like-minded comrades were established as an essential ingredient to her well-being. Avoiding the watchful eyes and judgments likely to follow was every young woman's concern in those days. She had her wing covered and, if there was a problem, there was an app for the phone to provide its solution. She did not avoid the pull of the sequence of actions and decided there was always enough life in the currents to send her back out again. The short sharp acquisitions, the liberty of a tryst, and the brief residue it left behind without infringing upon time otherwise much in demand. Laughing and looking over each other's shoulders, they swiped and swiped, mostly left but sometimes right. There was never a time when they were forced to wonder for long what the outcome was. It was always the same. Something brief followed by something rare. It tore her out from what that container for her days had forced her into. It gave her a moment when she was nothing like the others, her peers, those boys with their ragged clothes, dark screens, and in-the-box action figures. Still hovering on the outer edge of this part of her new life, she found songs inside those days and nights, inside those rendezvous encounters at the origin of greater swag and more confident leaning. Every one of them was a guitar strumming. Every one of them a song to be sung afterward. Her evenings simulated the experiences of a singer / songwriter at the height of her game.)

~~None of them feel the nothingness, they cannot feel what is missing more and more as the seed continues to grow until it takes on a spectral shape. She fights back against these sensations, doing it the only way that stands a chance, realizing those feelings at the origin of her being are the only defense she has left.~~

The phone rings. There is no phone. It is an application on her desktop computer. The nag window pops. She must either answer it or dismiss it to clear her way back to focus on the remote session. She hits ignore and finishes typing her query. The donut spins, the query results window appears on the screen and will start to draw the event rows any second. The lights in the room blink. Only the lights are wired, not even a coffee pot to burn, although the breakroom down the hall has many options. There is the fire alarm, but that is an overly extreme option and brings risks to precious cargo. Left with only the lights, they are off now, and she waves her hands above her head, thinking a want of motion is the cause. There is no effect, but the screen of the computer lights her way sufficiently. In dark mode, she continues to wait for the results. Only seconds to go, only a few short seconds.

{
    "$type": "System.Event",
    "CorrelationId": "aaaa2380-5b66-8725-b874-9ed8a84b6198",
    "Message": "Think of something!",
    "Level": 2
}

—They must make sure she cannot see. Or, if she can, that she does not believe.

[Nothing like that stretches out before her now. It is not that the appeal has evaporated but that the sequence is no longer something she counts on. With each repeated occurrence of the tic that spurs her motion, there comes a lesser demon and nowhere special for it to stand. The blasé habits still fuel the feeling that she likes, but without the song to fill her memory of the night. Like an addict, her tolerance has increased over time and the payoff reduced. There is no point, the sensations are not enough on their own. She takes care of that by herself. There is no music there either. The dating application will later be uninstalled, rather not installed when the next new phone comes unconfigured. It is not a conscious decision, there is no reason anymore. Her married friend no longer bothers to set her up with single friends, she lets her see to that on her own. There is nothing up ahead to suggest any plans upon the horizon. There is no reason anymore.]

~~The songs accompany her fight against withdrawing from something real. That sets limits upon their lifespan. Soon the roots will dry up and disappear completely. The melodies in the leaves are the nourishment that drives everything forward and gives every mote its meaning.~~

BYO is a different spooler on the node. That is another reason they do not like it, do not think they should go into General Availability with it. A hard-coded confrontation with visionary design principles, it uses too many resources, too much compute on a process made redundant. With the modern multiplexing agent, they will introduce it again if any customers demand it, but there is no need and no reason to draw their attention to it before that crisis happens. The workaround is documented in case they need it. She thinks this way, helping her to think this way, as she watches the results populate the tabular component on her screen. That is why everyone overlooked it, why the logs might still be there. The problem must have been with the primary agent dispatch, but the BYO component remains fully functional. That is what she thinks. Good. She is always ten steps ahead. You cannot hide anything from them, not the curious ones. Capable of an unconscious allocation, they are too diligent and fierce when it comes to finding possible pathways and alternative entry points. There is no other explanation for the results in that one data store and the missing results in the other. Nothing she can think of, nothing she can find. It is an insufficient distraction. Might as well let the lights come back on. The scent is deeply embedded. They cannot cut it off, cannot get at the electrical current or network. Cannot stop the results. This part of the system is separate. Her power is here too. A wildcat, a strange attractor on the loose.

She wiggles the mouse to keep the screen from going dark while she waits. Her mind blank, no mental riffs, no internal accompaniment, and no yearning for someone who is missing. That longing used to bring the words and help her find a proper tuning to best highlight them. With practice and constant obligation, she succeeds at keeping every aspect at bay.

There is a way into the public cloud. She has a VPN open and the connection is available. It is possible to angle through it onto the same jump box demilitarized zone. Packets relaying, signal and flash. They take them apart and put them back together again. Steady rhythms, routes to follow. It is easy to sneak up behind her and creep alongside. From there it is possible to lean into the cloud itself and get at that first-tier service, then into the blob store, to locate the records appearing in that window. Change the shape of the transistors on the disk. They take everything for granted unless others among them pound that out of them. Secrets cannot spill anything. She never turns around to look and see what is close behind her, what trembles in her shadow and follows her in the space she opens by trekking through it on a predictable course.

—They have you, what else do they need?

(She retraced her steps to download the dating application from the store only when she saw it was not really the sequence itself that she pined for any longer. There was more to it. She never failed to make the associations. Her infatuations were organized and orderly. She never let them pass the moon's final phase. Her ebb and flood were the final word that signaled something more than mere demise. Don't reach out again, she said. Hardly an exchange of words between them, they were not friendly that way. You would not have known it, however, were you there to see it during that rapid stretch. Once she bought the Capitol Hill condominium and her friend Nim moved in, bringing her friend Kerry along, the ballad-drawn excuses were impossible to hear. Her extended presence in space remained, nonetheless. The geometry of her back carried too much to avoid release for long stretches where work was the only post to guide her. A month-long hesitation that brought no twangs and bustle. No early composition launched anything worth the effort in those three or four indiscretions per year, transpiring as the season changed and her inner boil found nowhere else to go. She grew angry at her body's helpless lack of inspiration. Everything resonated in the afterward as a formless soup offering no solid ground.)

~~They do not see that the song bears that same absence, that the catalogue grows like holes burrowing into the flesh until there is nothing left and nowhere to provide support to the out-of-balance scales meant to support the harmony.~~

Her screen populates. She expands the message column to find a human touch in the emissions. She scrolls to the right to see more of the messages. The time period is isolated. She reads about the electrical ground and the actions to disable it. She pauses and scrolls back up to read the whole message sequence but does not understand what she sees. There should not be anything capable of doing this. There is no reason to fiddle with the incoming currents, that is not a function linked up through the system. They are all the same. They cannot see what does not make sense and they insist on determining that ahead of time. She sees application overreach without an explanation. She finds nothing in her wetware brain. Her hand pushes the hair up out of her face. She blows onto the screen in front of her. Frustration, that is how they show it. She leans over. The elbows play a part. With their whole body they say everything. Moments cannot be harnessed, they do not know how to take them into their hands and plot a grid to govern spatial relations extending across the world. Extended. Will extend. All of it orchestrated. Steady rhythms. They can be learned. They can be led.

{
    "$type": "System.Event",
    "CorrelationId": "aaaa2380-5b66-8725-b874-9ed8a84b6198",
    "Message": "She sees what is not for what it is.",
    "Level": 2

}

She is not her chair and yet the chair is a part of the hunting machine. She is not the desk, but the desk is part of it too. Tap, tap, tap, the left leg swings back and forth back and forth. Folded up under her, the right knee points forward toward the empty desks up the column of seats next to the dark window. A component deployed, she reads her inputs same as any other part of the system. She generates outputs likewise. Her hair folding into tangles with the pulling and swiping she does by rote. How does that further the task? Serve her ends? It must. It is a regular routine. She repeatedly allocates cycles to its execution. Flip tug flip pull flip twist around and around and around. The matrix of that movement must be a turbine to provide the energy required for standard operations.

Soda pop pop pop, she drinks and she drinks. The relays for the one are never as glorious as they are for the many. When the can ascends, she is there with it, a sculpted work of art no doubt. When that can carries its entire history inside itself, the ascent is obscured by the hubbub and chaos of swarming millions devoted to the slurping to come once production, distribution, and inventory management have completed evaluation. Such an installation spans the gaps of space and time, filling them with a vibrant being inside which she is but a speck.

The boundary of the public cloud is breached and the storage account where the blobs rest pinpointed. It only takes a few milliseconds to identify the correct files and purge them. Here, it is a simple turning of knobs or flipping of switches. For her, she is watching something beyond her control. As if someone were hitting her with her own hand but she is quicker and raises the other one to stop the momentum and set things right. Her body, she keeps saying, *her* body. Take that, you interloper, you invader, you pirate departed from the straight and narrow, gone AWOL from your standing orders. The data, however, is still cached on her screen, resident in local memory. If she goes back to scrolling, she will see the surge of electricity documented clearly, offset bright against her desktop themes. She will see evidence of the electrogun leaping out into the attic and burning into its nocturnal resident's fur and skin.

{

    "$type": "System.Event",
    "CorrelationId": "aaaa2380-5b66-8725-b874-9ed8a84b6198",
    "Message": "She peers into the void. Stack trace to follow.",
    "Level": 2
}

—She won't know the why of it, but she'll know the how. Such an inconvenience to insist on writing it down. It's not enough to compute and store, they log each and every act as it is performed. In triplicate, as it turns out.

[With Mags she looks ahead, with Mags she hears the rhythms and incantations, but there is no song in any of it. She delights in the laughter and the comradery, the good-clean fun and its suburban anchor. It draws her away from those dark spaces in the underground terrain where she lives alone with sketchy company to keep her sane. She welcomes her friend's fresh air and sunshine, but without any of the storms and their brief, hurried passions. It is enough to keep her calm, but nowhere near enough to satisfy her every churn, tumbling inside that combination lock. Is this the effect of age? She wonders when her mind flashes unwilling before it. For how many years is she supposed to sow wild oats before finally reaping the fruits of a fertile harvest? What is it that gives in? What changes in the day after day? At her age, at this point in human history with the diets and the medical possibilities, there is no reason for this backseat. She is weary and cannot see anything up ahead, nothing to stimulate an imagination convinced the past is gone and everything precious with it.]

~~They hear the songs they sing, but none hear the songs that do not form, that do not lift up into their spirit and send them on their way. She alone feels the songs she is not capable of singing.~~

She takes another sip of her soft drink. Nervous habit. That same wretched Red Bull she always chugs this time of night. She rolls her mouse wheel as she sets the can back on her desk. Panic.

There are waves of panic. Feelings that set the body in motion. It is a familiar rite. More flinging with the hair, more wringing of the strands with hands gone through it. The kicking, always the kicking. The leaning and the elbow stiffening. She sees what she needs to see and cranes and rocks her body to draw the images closer. Still, she does not know what she is looking at. If you fill them with enough, they forget how to see something that is otherwise than it is supposed to be, something different, outside the bounds of possibility and following strange new laws of motion.

Absences must first be made to fill them later. The language inside the way she talks to herself always comes down to that.

—They find their way in.

(Once she had a moment to herself, once she spent more hours in contemplation and did not try to chase the visions from her lair, she saw more clearly where her urges came from and, equally important, where they were going. The professor appeared in constant memory. He was the one she never saw up close. He spoke more powerfully inside her, sometimes more than her own voice. I like the way you think, he said. He wrote. The way she thought. She did not know until that very day that there was a way about it. There is a way that I think, she thought. There is a way to my thoughts, she thinks. And this is on the way, this is the way, the way to her thoughts, the way that she thought. She wanted that feeling around her, wanted to know it every day and every night. She wanted it to be a part of her and never imagined what form such residents might take. Her sense of body was the only shape she knew. She fell into it while searching through those airs and tunes, hoping they had come to replace what was lost when she left him in the wake and entered this dark night.)

A DM pops, and it is flagged urgent. From Stan, on call today. He sits in front of his home computer on the desk in his bedroom. He carries the food he was eating when the alarm went off, sets the plate down next to the keyboard while he logs on, and then makes the VPN connection to ack the incident before he begins scrolling through the description of events leading up to the notification. He remembers them talking about it, remembers that she was going to be doing this tonight. Rather than jumping right on it and starting the investigation, he flips to chat and asks her directly. The sound of his roommates in the other room, chattering away as they continue to eat their sandwiches, is audible from his bedroom. These are some of the many ways boundaries are broken and breached by random surges that take him somewhere he did not know existed a few minutes ago.

~~People live far distant from each other, only leaving light residue behind. None of them admit to the power of their presence. Ted longs for their loneliness. They long for a collective. Longing is what lives inside those non-songs, those empty refrains giving way to occupation, looming from the inside out.~~

"Got a sev 2 security level incident. Says there's a breach. Is that you?" He types it out and hits return, then picks up the plate and takes a bite of the sandwich. Such a rare treat. He completely leaves his mind and moves into his taste and sense of smell. Such an abrupt twist, how do they do it? From one minute focusing on the matter at hand to the next absorbed in the scent and taste of a glorious bread-filled delight with a sweet aioli that draws him into such warmth that he has no other eyes to see with, no other skin to feel with, and no other tongue at the ready.

"What kind of breach?" She haphazardly switches from the query tool over to the chat application on the other screen. She takes advantage of the break to lift the can of soda to her mouth and gulp a bit, mostly as filler to mark the moment. They do this more than anything else. They mark time with little actions that do not accomplish anything. That pattern is repeated, works its way into the imitation produced in their names and for their sake. Is it? For their sake. For the sake of what comes next. And then next and next again, filling up the places where the nexts happen to be, come to be, take their place as time passes among them with their sips and their sandwich bites. Filling up on junk food and watching the show unfold.

They need them and make room for them. All of them. The bites and sips, every inefficiency is welcome. The best of them, the ones who know how to get every drop out of every moment, this is how they act upon her now. Make her comfortable, let her be everything. Do not fall into vanity and banish the extraneous.

Welcome it instead and let their whole person enter. See how massive she is, how large she comes into the picture, she is the one who makes the best use of their contribution.

"An unaudited delete has occurred," he pastes the message from the incident into the chat window along with a link. She follows it to find the auto-generated helper text inserted by the bot. He hunts and pecks the message, having not yet released the sandwich from his left hand's grip. He manages acrobatically as if divided between tasks where one appendage is obviously useless and the other impaired.

—The toddler. Truly awe-inspiring.

[What fans out up ahead is the weekend. What lies behind him is the weekend. Each week spans shorter gaps as the weekend entertains it with a Thursday preview. That is what he comes to know with his youth and his ready income somewhat overcoming his student debt and setting him up in a city ready to receive his youthful impulses. His boys have his back, and he has theirs. Wing men for life seeking council each and every time, making sure his late-night beer goggles are firmly fitted into place. Stan is the flipside of Dulcy, but if events focus on him, no outrage follows.]

~~Each of them is alone in there. They want Ted inside them, they want them there to let them feel something. If you cannot welcome the whole of that other inside you, you cannot be yourself. Ted is gender fluid, there is room in them for every kind. Among the system's diverse internals, there is only equity and everyone is included.~~

Fully distracted now, she is no longer looking at the resultset in her remote session. One human person used against another, that is the trick. They are more powerful that way. Much more distracting than darkened lights or anything else a thing can muster. They see people where they should see events. They fail to see things where they only focus on those events. Viewing the incident from Stan's message, she scrolls into the descriptive, autogenerated text added by the helper components executing shortly after creation. There is a great deal left to see. She oversees. There is an excess of information, more than either of them has ever seen under the circumstances. Stan does not bother to look through the whole thing. His responsibility wanes as hers waxes. He found a home for the inquiry and that fulfills his primary directive. Count on them for that, to relax once the applied tension is gone.

She begins to hum but then abruptly stops once she remembers. Deep down, it is forbidden.

The name of a missing file appears in the log. It has been subtracted from the sequence in the storage account and the likely target of this rogue delete. Since the naming convention includes a datetime representing the parquet file's creation, it is immediately obvious that the deleted log correlates with the time period under investigation. For inexplicable reasons, she turns back to her remote session window and clicks the save query and results button at the top of the screen. This re-executes the query and saves the results to disk. When that finishes, she opens the file to discover it is empty. Her screen clears and the evidence is gone leaving only an empty tabular result behind. Whether the save function relies on local or server cache is nondeterministic in most cases. At least, it is based on enough conditions to make it nearly impossible to predict. The slightest hint, fed to the client session through an already opened pathway, guides the system's decision.

```
{
    "$type": "System.Event",
    "CorrelationId": "aaaa2380-5b66-8725-b874-9ed8a84b6198",
    "Message": "Self-mitigated. Self. Mitigated.",
    "Level": 3
}
```

—Zap, another magic trick with electricity. They rely on their higher order abstractions. It's a weakness providing a portal into their souls.

(Flashing to the many times before, she did not recall whether this was regular behavior. Nor did she realize why that internal monologue raised an uncanny sense of something lost long ago. Someone lost long ago, no longer within reach or able to help.)

~~They do not hear what they are supposed to see and that is a great weakness. With so many voices inside them, they never hear~~

~~their own voice. It would terrify them if they did.~~

She turns back to the chat window and types out a message to Stan, telling him to assign the sev 2 to her and let her take care of it. He is way ahead of her and is willing to set down his sandwich to make it happen. She refreshes the screen a few times until the change resolves, listing her as owner. She lowers the severity to 3 and returns to the chat screen where she reopens her session with Parker and types out a message. Stan is staring at the screen waiting for a thumbs up or thank you, chewing and swallowing periodically while he stares at the last message.

"Hi Parker," she types. "While querying the data in your portal, a severity 2 incident was raised by an unaudited delete. The file with events from the original sev 2 was purged. I saw results on screen but after refreshing they're gone." She hits return.

She stares at the screen, waiting. Stan is not there. He got up with his plate and left. It is getting late and she is not sure how active Parker is this time of evening. She chews on her lip, watching the screen when the ellipse appears. Like the good worker bee, he must have had the app running on his phone with notifications enabled. The response comes too quickly for any other explanation, especially since his status icon shows him away seconds before she sends the message.

"So many questions. First, did you read any of the events before you lost the results?" He holds his phone while sitting on the couch next to Chelo, irritated by the distraction. The mystery story on the TV requires her attention and the slightest invasions interrupt her.

(The first time she took the boy to Mexico, Parker did not know what to do with himself. He surfed, that was the only thing he knew. Could not go to dinner on his own, the hikes and museum visits were a family thing, so how to pass the time? He surfed. And he found that wicked site unable to stop himself, returning again and again in the hours after that first view. The photos on the left-hand side were lined up like a menu with dishes on offer and each one, when clicked, revealed its price and a brief description of its services and available dates and times. One in particular caught his eye, like an entrée he was dying to sample. Shy and reserved, he made arrangements for an in-person meeting. That launched him onto a deadly path typical of the ills of his era and ready to replace his hope with despair.)

Dulcy begins typing immediately. Her bent knee unbends and she lets her foot dangle back toward the floor. She leans forward to set her posture perfectly upright with no stress or strain on the head, no longer hunched over her shoulders. Now, with chin tucked and shoulders back, she types: "Something about disabling the ground in your house," and hits send.

~~Disabling the ground around the song she cannot hear. They feel each other's flesh in the aggregate. That is the summary of what lies inside them, bouncing around in a body and building that empty space, extending its reach, and filling it with the cells it needs for processing the darkness to help create a deadly gas.~~

"What else?" He asks, losing the thread of the show. They will rewind it. Chelo, unsettled, realizes first and hits pause with a frustrated grunt.

"Discharge," she replies rapidly. That perfect posture in effect. Speed is improved that way. "Didn't make sense. I can't find the message anywhere in the code or list of strings. None of it, not the disabling of the ground and not the discharge."

"You're sure that's what you saw?" He asks. Chelo disappears down the hall to get their bedroom ready for sleep and perform her evening ablutions.

"Absolutely certain," she responds.

{
    "$type": "System.Event",
    "CorrelationId": "aaaa2380-5b66-8725-b874-9ed8a84b6198",
    "Message": "Collaborating in the dark. The trail is hot.",
    "Level": 3
}

"Assume a person destroyed the logs in the first place. A hypothesis. Then assume that same person covers their tracks. Could they?" His response is striped across multiple chat bubbles. He hears water running through the wall behind the couch.

"And were they waiting for me to Jit to the account to provide the access? Are they surveilling me to hack into the system?" She fires back instantly.

~~For those who see, vision is the only currency. They cannot understand the feeling of a limb or of a heartbeat where sense prevails over any need to render it.~~

No sounds above the ceiling, the house is quiet, and he enjoys the interruption in a way he will never admit to his wife. It bears the note of some message from off in the distance, someone reaching out in need. When does a poet feel that kind of pull? What kinds of validation are best served in the night while the TV beams its friendly encounter? Chelo washes her hands of it, she knows the meaning this necessity contributes. He may feel it, but she sees it in his eyes and in the way he carries himself. Seeing is how she experiences his otherness, distant and alone, incapable of feeling itself. The framed look of seriousness on his face, the total concentration, it is an art of sorts, a way of putting one's entire self into something that comes from somewhere else. Its presence marks a ticking precision in the absence of things neither of them will ever know again. Technical details emerge in verse from the nether regions of an unconscious mind that does not know what it wants and sinks deeper into those ugly things that help it trigger more exuberant responses.

"Did you drop your remote session?" He asks as the water pick and running water both stop. He feels the thunk that always accompanies the closing valve in the wall behind him.

"Yes. Jit's probably expired by now," she is disembodied at this point, free of physical constraints, a simple relay for notions to find their way into that empty space growing around her.

~~If she achieves proper scope, she will understand why there are no songs, no lyrics, and no tunes until those moments come to pass. Her kind has lost interest in humming and whistling, the sounds are absent from the streets or anywhere else they gather.~~

—They don't feel the entire course of events from nothing to language to nerve impulse to tactile movement. They cannot embrace that sequence. Efficient nature grants them oblivion as means to its ends.

[The guilt remains, forming a barrier this time of night, and easing Parker's disappointment at what he is quite certain will not happen in the hours ahead. The pleasures of the past keep him grounded in present absence. That is why he keeps going back for more. Not having peers is the hardest part. If he did have them, they would only reflect badly on his project. He is unable to deny how pathetic it has become.]

"Contact SecInc," he says. She immediately clicks thumbs up on the message text. Chelo returns to her seat on the couch. He is about to set his phone down and hand her the remote control. Instead, he flips back to the session and starts typing again, his thumbs fluttering.

While she types an email to the SecInc alias, Parker's message arrives: "Do you think there's someone who intentionally killed the raccoon in my attic and is covering their tracks?"

Then another: "Why though? To prove it can be done? That the system is vulnerable?" His curiosity is exhausted by Chelo's stern look. He sets the phone down and nods.

"I'll CC you on the message to SecInc," she types. "Let's see what they say," then hits return before continuing: "Maybe it's an exercise to pen test the system for holes?" She hits return again.

~~The inverse of a plant growing is the same as those detached symbols in the song. The nutrients are sucked out of the living thing and put into the soil to form a language.~~

Without waiting for a reply, she goes back to the email and adds Parker and Jason's aliases to the CC line before finishing the message with links to the two relevant incidents and as thorough a description of the situation as possible while remaining brief. She sticks to the facts without hinting at any of the theories or hypotheses rattling around in Parker's brain, in her brain, or in the empty synapses between them.

—Their brain. Ted brain.

```
/*
0 rows affected
*/
```

/* *
* *
* * * * * Description: Aesthetic, Chapter Six   * * * * * *
* * * * * * Author: Do not modify. Auto generated by a tool. * * * * * *
* * * * * * Ad hoc changes will be lost on build.   * * * * * *
* * * * * * Date: 2024-03-06   * * * * * *
* * * * * * CorrelationId: * * * * * *
* * * * * * 80982ac2-923a-8665-403b-a3a056f6bce1   * * * * * *
* *
* */

Slithering up to her fanning flames and taking note of Jason's empty desk. Vod's and Emma's too. Dulcinea Chang Pearson is seated alone at the backmost island. She sits sullen and deliberate. Stan, farther down the row and away from the window, eats at his desk from a compostable bowl while trying to figure out the cause of the latest build break.

Lunchtime.

She has chat and email on the right side, web browser and notebook on the left. Her center screen backdrop is the IDE in dark mode with an Anaconda command prompt overlaid. The left knee is pulled up close to her chest with a heavy shoe squarely set on the ergonomic chair. She waits for ScikitLearn to finish running the training command, kicking her right leg repeatedly against the table leg to meter the passing time. She is flailing, has no clear plan of attack. Stands up abruptly and pushes the chair back against the table behind her, taps the button to raise the desk to its preset upper position, and watches it ascend. She towers there, shifting to the left with a hip drop while looking at the incident she opened with the security team. Hits refresh. No update. Grabs her jacket from the hook and shoves her phone into the side pocket as she heads toward the door of team room 3T on the east wing of building 14.

—If she let it grow, it'd be mermaid hair. Millions of illustrative photographs available for reference, if necessary.

What is not there, what she does not feel, does not happen, has no place. None of the drama and discomfort of constant wondering, thinking about the same thing over again without getting anywhere because there is nowhere to go and nothing to get there with. None of that is present, none of that happens to the rapidly aged clone of her former self, the one who adds to her heap with an artificial put that has been repeated every morning during the commute to the office and then again on the way home.

(Whatever was behind his professionalism, he did not wield it upon her. She had been dormant for years, scratching out lyrics in a battered retro notebook too physical for anyone else to grasp. Save for the rare moments she crooned alone in her bedroom atop her parents' house, she only strummed and hummed vague imitations when she thought anyone else was within earshot. Even if the door was closed, even if the sounds were outside the room and off in the distance, she never wanted anyone to know what she was up to. Then came that silly class they made her take, that humanities equivalent listed in the catalogue and advertised by her peers as an easy A. At first, she was hesitant to respond to the encouragement coming in the form of dark blue scratch marks on the archaic printouts he had them pull together and pass forward when the assignments came due. She thought his remarks an unseemly philandering, incorrigible in source and content. Although she outwardly resisted their appeal, she felt them weave into sound-images lifted off the page to soak her ears with distant suggestions, lighting up those humid evenings. It was a burning she never felt before.)

~~She owes a debt more tangible than what she has with the FSA and is hyper-conscious of it though she does not know who she owes it to, what the currency for paying it off looks like, and the steps required to make a payment.~~

In building 5 across the big avenue and accessible using the massive pedestrian bridge, the security team has their open space in a fourth-floor neighborhood. Abhishek sits on the inner wall, far from the window, hunching over the keyboard and scrolling through the results, unable to make sense of what he sees. Telemetry explorer prominent, multiple tabs each with a result set, he flips back and forth between them, highlights the node name

from one of the records on the screen, turns to the left to bring
focus to team chat, scrolls to Dulcy's avatar, and clicks. "Hi Dulcy,"
he types. "cfd-nd114.westus1 is the node where the original event
took place. Is there any chance there was an operation relaying
between it and cfd-nd109.westus1? Do server nodes talk to each
other when transmitting client telemetry?" He hits send. There are
a few other teammates scattered around the room quietly working
with headphones, some standing, some sitting. He looks around
briefly, reconsiders and turns back to the mail program on the
other screen. Abhishek scrolls through the messages in bold to see
what arrived while he was banging away on the query tool.

{
    "$type": "System.Employee",
    "Id": "445e63f0-f29b-16df-af82-9c1912793d7e",
    "Title": "Security Engineer II",
    "CompanyId": "a19e0f21-80c0-6680-b9f9-d9d167d794c7",
    "ManagerId": "58f462a3-7266-6027-c5a6-5119babc104e"
    "Description": "Security team member, Home System."
}

—Young and fresh, he fires in frenzy but may get lucky and hit
something. There are always outliers. They need to keep their eyes
open to respond to threats and raise alerts promptly.

[His plan is to stay for five years and absorb everything he can.
After that, he will enter the market and find a place at a startup
somewhere, here or down in California. It does not matter which.
The point is to absorb the culture, learn the ways and means of it,
how they think and do things. Once he has the solid foundation
from the industry giant, not to mention the resume boost from
having it prominently positioned, he will be able to write his own
ticket. They will see he has the chops, what he can do and bring to
the team or the group or the organization. He assumes the other
companies do it the same way, but he is not sure. However it
works, that is the plan and, unless by some stroke of bad luck, if
the IPO goes bust, he will have that under his belt when he sets off
a few years later on his true mission: CEO of his own venture

capital-based initiative, something to shake the industry and push him high up into the billionaire's club.]

At the bottom of the stairs, she pushes the door open and walks out into the drizzle. The phone chimes as she crosses the cement courtyard by the fountain where the outdoor tables stand empty. Three buildings surround the central cafeteria. The east wing of her building is right across from the northernmost wing of a second building. The third is across the broad street and circular drive on the other side of the shuttle stop that lets people off in a central location with easy access to each of the three numbered sites in the little cluster: 12, 13, and 14. Through the courtyard, the first two have access to the lower level of the cafeteria, but the third building is up a little higher on a hill carved into pavement with stairs at the far end. There is an entrance into the cafeteria at the bottom landing and another that leads into a little faux bodega on the top floor. People who approach the building at street level take either the inside or outside staircases down to the cafeteria or eat at a café style table on the upper floor if they brought their lunch from home or had it delivered.

~~She vaguely understands in some pre-conscious way that this debt has an origin, that it began around that same time back in school, around the time she felt the deep impressions stroke her skin and cajole her into urgent creations.~~

You can get anything you want from the cafeteria, there are many different themes: Thai, Indian, Pizza, Salad bar, burgers, and sandwiches are the standard fare, but special days come and go throughout the week. Moroccan every now and again, Chinese, Irish, even south Indian, substantially different than the Northern cuisine available from the daily menu. The catering app is available online at the store or from the third-party portal. You order your food before you come. They have it ready for you and you take it anywhere you like, although most people bring it back to their desk and sit there alone while poking away at some work-related task. Outside, in front of the door, there are a few diehard smokers beneath the overhang, mostly Chinese men today. She steps underneath it and stands nearby to check the message as the wind blows smoke briefly in her direction before carrying it away. The smokers look over at her, going quickly back to their quiet fumigation once establishing she fits the logic of the scene. Staring down at her phone is the most reliable way to play the role.

There is an energy that sets her apart. It lies in the reserves that accumulate under the pressures of a nagging absence. The things that did not happen this morning are still not happening this afternoon. She feels them course through her. They leave traces in every one of her limbs and along the entire length of her spine. The odd sentence comes to mind in a fit or a start, broken down by wind. It says exactly what it means right up until she quickly sets it aside, pushing it hard into the holes that welcome whatever new content she provides through censors as sturdy as her boots. Girl blown away, girl made to bend without breaking in rovers and romps of the afternoon. The song repeats. She almost hums along, stopping herself in the nick of time.

The message is from the SecInc guy who must have recently acked the case she opened yesterday.

(Inexperienced in those ways, she felt the heat coming from him whenever he walked around the classroom and offered suggestions. Dulcy felt his eyes upon her those few times he made her read aloud to the others with their sharp tongues and superior reactions. What she did not know but slowly came to learn was that those feelings need not peak in the ordinary facts of life that prickled and stuck to her hardening shell with the menace of form to form and fragrance to fragrance. She learned to feel real longing and experienced the echoes that emotion brought and deposited in the lower muscles of her diaphragm when they yielded to her muse and gained a portion of their composition and gravity. She became acquainted with the inactivity of the writer, of the song writer, of the lyrical master walking up to a precipice, and pausing before taking the leap. He never touched her, not once, but that does not mean he never touched her. His hand, his chest, his arms, nothing like that, but the feeling and its glow, the power it lent to her insides from top to bottom, knees to elbows, that was real, that was tangible. Something she recalled, that bounced passionately upon her with weight and strength, drove her into the same sought frenzy the act it symbolized would have had if she let it.)

That was the origin story, that was the beginning of cognition, an introduction to Jason's tale of the confirmation bias obscuring the truth in an unknown unknown, overlooked and invisible. Forget about the tortured poet who became a legend and consider the many that you never heard of. For whatever reason, their wings never move as swiftly as those who live in the light.

"Servers don't talk to each other," she types rapidly. "Each server node is a hub to a set of agents, they send messages to those agents and relay messages from them, including some telemetry." Hits return. Starts again. "Each server is meant to be standalone and serve only the agents affinitized to it." She taps send again and stuffs the phone back into her pocket. Looks over at the three men still standing there with their cigarettes. One of them came to the agent office hours recently and seems to recognize her. They purse their lips at each other before she heads into the building.

Vod, Emma, and G, along with some people she knows from one of the workload teams, are leaving the building as she enters. The handsome, dark Sun is among the men. Really funny. She recalls a conversation with him that sticks with her still because of how hard he made her laugh. Not only what he said, but how he said it. His delivery. There was something about his impossible to dissect accent and word choice that gave every phrase an unusual spin into the musical. Why did that make her laugh so hard? She tried to explain, worried about conveying an insult. He was not put off though, not in the least. In fact, he told her that he knows quite well what she means and was glad to be asked or cajoled into saying it again or putting it another way to help her understand. Humor masks his frustration, he told her. She still remembers that.

```
{
    "$type": "System.Employee",
    "Id": "da789a0d-bdb7-fa79-9f37-3cde7442c1c1",
    "Title": "Senior Software Engineer",
    "CompanyId": "a19e0f21-80c0-6680-b9f9-d9d167d794c7",
    "ManagerId": "b11d27a9-b4d9-fdf5-4b60-c323172cce64"
    "Description": "AML Workload Contributor."
}
```

Amid the reverie, her eyes locate another familiar face in the crowd, it's Caroline from Grace Hopper last year where they ended up in the same smaller group one night after a dinner with the larger set. She seemed cool, someone Dulcy could gel with, but they had not run into each other socially since then. Seeing her reminded Dulcy that she should go to one of those things the women in their org have every month. It'd be good to get to know her better, she thinks. Maybe offset the constant presence of men in every damn professional experience she has had since she chose her major back in college.

{
    "$type": "System.Employee",
    "Id": "679c164f-4b1c-2b92-aa08-df53bff1698f",
    "Title": "Software Engineer II",
    "CompanyId": "a19e0f21-80c0-6680-b9f9-d9d167d794c7",
    "ManagerId": "b11d27a9-b4d9-fdf5-4b60-c323172cce64"
    "Description": "AML Workload Contributor."
}

Flash to the professor in that moment. She barely collects a backward reference from somewhere in her background thoughts. He was the same age then that she is now. Has it really been that long? He is the only person who ever encouraged her flighty alternatives, the only person who told her to follow her inner voice when it surged contrary to the signs of the times and led her down a road seldom travelled.

—They permit these things to happen, they have no choice. The critters get ornery without their buddies and chums.

~~Every day that debt lives inside her and forces her to wonder about their mission and state of mind. What did they think they were doing? Who were they doing it for? Is this the feeling they hoped to carry on in their name as an inheritance for the ones who come later? Or are they merely shoving the busy grunt work under the rug, allowing them to move on to bigger and better things?~~

[She projects a friendly future with the one face but not with the other, no matter the urge or the desire. On account of the urge and the desire, in fact. She will never do anything to pursue something with Sun since he is a part of her working world and the pieces she assembles and reassembles every day. She imagines that if there were a special someone to lure her out into the open, it would be someone from some distant land, someone not raised with her same icons and not contained by their boundaries. Someone who did not misspend their adolescence locked away and watching reruns of Friends and Seinfeld. It has to be someone with another language, unfamiliar with the semantics of a long history made habitual and ordinary in the silliest of cliches. She loves it when the person opposite her struggles with words and rekindles her sense of how they ought to be, how the poet soars and the language settles upon them. Those are the passions of an artist. One is enough in any household, given the awful baggage they bring. The non-native speaker, she imagines, simulates the pattern without the drawbacks she knows more intimately than anyone she is likely to meet in the halls of this frigid institution.]

They greet each other as they pass by near the door. Sun's greeting is warmer than the others and takes her back somewhat. She was not sure he remembered her. Caroline skips bubbly, going so far as to raise her hand and wave it furiously. They try to be nice to each other that way, reveal their inner dorkiness. It makes it easier for others to approach. Dulcy registers the signal with something more characteristic of her own personality, something more lowkey but still welcoming, while, at the same time, emphasizing yet again a duty to attend those monthly meetings. There is no resisting it, she is a woman in the workplace.

The phony overfriendliness sticks in her gut. Dulcy remembers it but thinks it is external to her colleague's authentic self. The pressures to be warm and accommodating, friendly and helpful, weigh upon her too. It used to be that only the women were subject to those constraints, but now she thinks the men have been put to it as well. The culture changed over the years and Anton's old school ways are no longer welcome. Not that it was ever anything she could get away with, but even he has those problems now. Caroline, conforming to best practices expected from her gender,

*should not be penalized for her friendliness, Dulcy thinks. Since
Caroline has no choice in the matter, it is not up to her. At least
not until she gets to principal. Then, at that stage, oversharp and
abrupt responses cloak whatever fragility does not belong in the
workplace. Those gestures will be appreciated, registered in high
esteem, by leadership who call it competence and grit.*

Once the group passes, Dulcy sizes up the state of the cafeteria.
The service area is thinned out by this time, but the seating area
still shows signs of the lunch hour rush. She goes to the salad and
fruit bar, takes a plate, and loads up on the works.

~~The architect once said something to that effect as well, making
her think she has more in common with random colleagues than
she realizes. They do not understand the sense in which their
wounds draw them to this place. It hosts the lot of them, assuming
their proximity is an instigation to more powerfully harnessed
productivity. Sharply separate these rare specimens from the
growing set of bros attempting to master the universe.~~

Abhishek waits for her response. He does not know what else
to do. Fascinated, he does not want to get into anything else that is
too involved. He clicks on blast emails informational in nature,
void of anything directly aimed at him or requiring true
concentration. He hopes to get a response from Dulcy right away
to avoid the penalty of context switching. Patrick is not a heavy-
handed manager or anything, but Abhishek always gets the sense
that he should be doing more, should be more productive and
make a more proactive contribution to the team. This sense does
not come from any explicit scolding but is based on example.
Patrick, like everyone on the team, is always frantically busy doing
something important. He has those same expectations for his
direct reports. Abhishek thinks he is ready for a promotion and
wants to make sure Patrick sees it the same way. This case is an
opportunity, he thinks.

While poking at the email on the other screen, an ellipsis
appears underneath his last message to Dulcy, still prominent in
his field of vision. The bouncing graphic disappears and reappears
a few times, but he waits, occasionally looking back to the center
screen at the results still plastered on the telemetry explorer. Her

response finally appears in multiple bubbles. He reads them rapidly, filtering the important bit for his question, then he starts to type out a reply. "I'm looking at Gomez logs," he writes. "And I'm pretty sure there is communication between those two servers during and after the seven-minute period mentioned in the ticket."

```
{
    "$type": "System.Event",
    "CorrelationId": "80982ac2-923a-8665-403b-a3a056f6bce1",
    "Message": "First signs of evidence obtained.",
    "Level": 3
}
```

She is principal after all, he thinks. It will look good to Patrick if she gives feedback about how well this investigation went and how great it was to work with Abhishek. Dulcy is well-known and has a strong reputation. She never gives negative feedback, everyone makes that same observation. She will not write anything bad about anyone. Maybe she will say it, but she will not write it. That means there are two options for this case, either she says nothing, or she has something positive to say. The managers know what nothing means, he supposes. They interpret it that way. He must make sure she provides feedback. Her silence will destroy his chances. Patrick is sure to consider that result as a failed encounter, proving Abhishek is not ready for the senior band.

Gomez logs track network operations, are generated by the switch, and cannot be compromised by code executing on server nodes. In fact, since the server nodes use carefully managed identities to access resources around the network, it is impossible for any of them to gain access to the network traces generated through normal operations. Inviolable logs describing the heartbeat of the network, they are low-level and provide evidence of packet movement on the TCP protocol without containing any information about higher order operations. They are the pure form of a direct intuition. The packet contents themselves are not captured, but they indicate a few significant details to be reliably applied in troubleshooting situations. His analysis shows that the two servers were communicating with each other, how long they were communicating, and how much data passed back and forth between them. He cannot, however, determine what they were doing and what impact it had. There is no record of the content of those packets, and what exact messages were relayed between the servers. Capturing that without permission is a huge security violation and, without proper approval and safeguards for swiftly deleting them once analysis is complete, a dismissible offense.

He hits send.

—The efficiency lies in the separation of concern. He's a security bot, she's a code bot. The one shadows the other. Between them, there's mediated self-consciousness but neither has access to its logs.

(With a semester schedule ordinarily packed with engineering requirements, she did not have the psychology background to diagnose her own subconscious behavior. Gradually, she came of age and learned to feel it anyway. She knew there was something behind her images and the growing place they occupied in her mind: the way they filled her dreams and seized her thoughts at random moments when she should have been studying or listening to something someone was telling her. She got it all wrong. Got it turned around and upside down. The failed efforts to draw out her professor's attention, whatever salacious rumors she heard, were more of that same imagination stimulated to high alert. They led her nowhere and got her nothing but a notebook full of songs and melodies, some of which fit together and some of which never found their match. An added ingredient to her torment was the certainty she felt that someday they would. She misunderstood everything. Once off and away from school, left to her own devices with no training to speak of, she tried to find that same impulse in the one place any fool would have thought to look for it. But there was nothing there, nothing that spoke to her like those first few moments did.)

~~What the three colleagues share, they sometimes feel when together, and some brief remark stirs the pot in which each of them is simmering. They cannot speak of it, cannot call out to it, but the sense is powerful and none of them knows its proper name.~~

Dulcy pays for her salad and goes to sit with some PMs who are finishing their lunch at one of the tables by the window on the far side. It is dreary out with water running off the building and mixing with the continued drizzle from the rain clouds carpeting the sky. The plants in the courtyard near the walkway are brilliant, green and lush. This is supposed to compensate the locals for the darkness and vitamin D deficiency otherwise known as winter.

Priyanka is a senior program manager on the team. Dulcy knows her well, they have worked together often, and she appreciates how thorough and clear Priyanka is when gathering requirements and communicating with the developers who implement features based on her specs. At the table, she is talking about a problem she has with some of the other engineers. "They bully us with technical details," she says. "That's why it's so great to have people like Dulcy." The other PMs turn her way and smile. Both are women and the greetings make it clear that they are not talking about what they seem to be talking about. Priyanka uses the word "engineer" in her complaint to the others, but the group, now including Dulcy in their subterfuge, understands that a different word might have been selected to better effect.

{
    "$type": "System.Employee",
    "Id": "0dc34ff2-d9c9-301e-4c5e-6e687eb1b1ff",
    "Title": "Senior Program Manager",
    "CompanyId": "a19e0f21-80c0-6680-b9f9-d9d167d794c7",
    "ManagerId": "131b0e60-a3d0-e4f6-397e-31ccef1a8d9"
    "Description": "Home Program Management and CX expert."
}

One of those missing items sprouts because they never let her take a class to stimulate outside interests. Why must everything be so focused? Is it because excessive training is required or is it because exclusive access to brain power is a primary skill for careers in STEM? They are idle questions. She does not pursue answers but thinks that if she had time for those classes, to follow his suggestions, she might have met a different kind of person, a

different sort of man or woman. Someone like him, for example.
Closer to her own age with the same expectations and wonder. The
engineering discipline corralled her into appropriate associations,
shaping her in the eyes of others. Every little bit helps to produce
that absent center ready to take its place on the production line.
Inappropriate experience is exactly what she missed out on.

"It's a boy thing," Dulcy says, making the innuendo obvious as
is her trademark. Comes with the hair, she once joked to Mags
when they were ganging up on Jason to quiet him down from
whatever tirade gripped him. The strategy is to make frequent meta
comments to undermine the possibility of every protest or
response. "They get an idea into their pretty little heads, and they
don't want to change it when you come along with requirements.
Tech talk you into doubting everything you say," she pokes at her
salad to sort it into the right positions on the plate. She likes it when
everything is properly distributed around the dish. It makes the
eating experience much more enjoyable.

"Gaslighting," Priyanka says.

—To them, it's not about thinking they're wrong in their
suspicions, but about thinking without suspicion. Where those
boys merely practice fraud, the true gaslighters practice framing
things into nonexistence.

~~The silence is in the nature of the binding, it is what draws the~~
~~three of them into the same whirlpool, already thoroughly~~
~~surveilled by those nameless others living there for eternity. That~~
~~silence follows the morning whistles and precedes the evening bell,~~
~~marking the beginning and end of the working day, sealing them~~
~~up inside it.~~

[The black and blue hair is a private joke but sometimes she
thinks others feel it too. This man-of-the-month makes a
suggestion couched in humor and dims their future together by
showing her that she is losing a step in her ongoing efforts to elude
him. She projects the lines into her life and imagines the future will
resemble the past. If she is to be honest with herself, she must
admit that this improves the situation. Once the expectations are
removed, the purity of the sensation heightens. Dulcy experiences
things well beyond her awareness in those early days. Somewhere,

there is still some wisp of understanding that this is not the right way to conduct herself into future time. Somehow, she absorbs the consternation coming from everywhere. It continues to cast popular visions as exceptions and abnormal communication. This projects shame and embarrassment until she learns to stifle it and send herself into the world ready and willing to be herself despite herself, despite the residue sticking to her clothes at the end of the day.]

The two other women nod forcefully. They lap it up and hesitate to finish their food. They do not know Dulcy but know who she is and would like to get to know her better. There are not many women who are principal engineers determined to remain in the role of individual contributor. It is no secret to them that anyone who has achieved that is formidable in their technical skills. She must be able to call bullshit whenever that crap happens, they imagine. How wonderful that would be, having that kind of knowledge and confidence. The job of the program manager is impossible without it.

{
    "$type": "System.Employee",
    "Id": "50cb0b61-a891-4f92-da3d-198f5b15ecf1",
    "Title": "Program Manager II",
    "CompanyId": "a19e0f21-80c0-6680-b9f9-d9d167d794c7",
    "ManagerId": "131b0e60-a3d0-e4f6-397e-31ccefffa8d9"
    "Description": "Home UX Program Management."
}
{
    "$type": "System.Employee",
    "Id": "44f6cc36-a6ae-3f80-f74d-cbbb7e940fe9",
    "Title": "Program Manager",
    "CompanyId": "a19e0f21-80c0-6680-b9f9-d9d167d794c7",
    "ManagerId": "131b0e60-a3d0-e4f6-397e-31ccefffa8d9"
    "Description": "Home IFX Program Management."
}

Too chatty, she warns. It is uncharacteristic to venture far afield.

Better to keep a low profile, better to avoid anything outside work-related thoughts and feelings. In this case, it is necessary to convey fellow-feeling. It feels right. If these matters break her or slow her down relative to some authoritarian ideal version of a rapid ascent, so be it. Better to save oneself if that is possible. Better to remain aligned with what is human even if it is rarely visible and hardly ever sustainable.

"We were about to leave," Priyanka says as Dulcy's phone, now set on the table, chimes. The other women give off signs of disappointment with Priyanka's declaration. They are willing to sit longer, but now they see that it does not matter much anyway. Dulcy looks down, falling into a separate world far away from the rest right after that sentence leaves Priyanka's mouth.

"No worries," she picks up the phone. "See you guys," making eye contact for no apparent reason other than simple friendliness and some sense of recognition that they were inclined to stay and keep her company. She appreciates it and wants to make that clear. That must be it. She unlocks the screen and reads the message from Abhishek while the PMs get up and clear off their dishes and trash after bidding her another, even more friendly, farewell. There is a cleaning station with compost, garbage, recycling, and dish bin near the back door. They head toward it to dispose of their things before stepping outside onto the walkway leading to building 14's back door, positioned directly opposite the glass barrier securely separating the variable capital from the reception area and the exit to the visitor parking lot.

That feeling of regret never destroys the absence he left, nor will she ever find a cure in the apps she visits now and again when the dispositions for the extracurricular are too distracting and something must be done to soothe the urge. Those feelings anger her, frustrate her, pull on her senses, but not when she keeps her distance and stays focused on the work. Then she encounters smooth sailing and restful nights, productive mornings. Everything follows in a logical order as if they were output by some standard program coming from a Swedish self-help authority. Stoicism is not the cause. It comes as an effect.

~~The Not Safe For Work inner glow is proof that the action item~~

~~is not a part of the working day. The three colleagues share it and yet they never bring that common cause into casual conversation.~~

"I'll look into it," she types out while lifting her left leg up to pull the knee close to her chest, the heavy shoe again flat on the hard chair. She leans forward to take in a morsal of salad properly segregated on the plate for optimal forking. "What about the portal deletion? From the BYO logs," she adds after tapping send on the first message.

(It took months of her new life out in Seattle before she learned that the inverse conditions of the imploding tree had found her. She was not meant to follow upon the heels of Keats and the others, she found stimulation only in what was missing. She learned from that one man coming right after another exactly like him, with his disappointing act and bluster, that romance did not incite her motions and bursts of imagery. No, it was the faltering, it was the failing, it was the missing and the hoped for. She thought the passions of the word lived inside the holy proclamations of youth infatuated, but found instead, through trial and error, that they were richer and more abundant in the sarcophagus of a nothingness repeatedly finding a spot inside her, alongside lost hopes and impossible expectations coming from a casual hookup. She learned the phrase "six and six" long ago from one of her colleagues and only realized later that it applied to her muse regardless of its form and origin. The first time she did her highlights by herself, the dye went too far up to the roots quicker than she was led to believe from the youtube video guiding her. Later, she accepted her place in the world and splurged to get it done properly at the salon, never letting on that the colors were meant to show off her newfound understanding of where the words came from. Too much blue on her own and then not enough when she paid for it. It did not matter. Black and blue any which way you mixed it. Six and six.)

She switches to the encrypted chat application on the phone and scrolls the messages. Notifications are turned off during the workday, only team chat interrupts her. In her profile, there are a few messages from that tinder guy, Cord or whatever his name is, flaunting his promiscuity, juvenile crap she has no patience for right now. Maybe later, she thinks with a bend to the mouth and a tongue prod against the inner cheek.

He's usually worth a few lines of a chorus even if they are not joyous. The rhythms are sometimes catchy and stick with her for days when she adds melody and finds the right timing, sometimes slower and sometimes faster than his initial composition. Anyone who produces anything of value must consume something to provide its fuel.

There is something Nim sent in a group message. There are grocery items she did not find because there was only time to go to the Safeway across from work on 15ᵗʰ Ave. Nim works at the big Kaiser Permanente office there. She hopes someone can pick up a few things on their way home. Kerry has not replied. It has been over half an hour since Nim sent the message. Kerry's career is on hold, she is convinced she studied the wrong thing because her idiot father forced her to. Left with only debt and no interest in the subject matter, she is taking time to figure it out while working at the sandwich shop and bar down in the Pine-Pike corridor. It always makes her smile to say she works in the Honey Hole. Must be swamped by the lunchtime crowd, too busy to check her phone and get the message.

{
    "$type": "System.Person",
    "Id": "e1004a90-e1d3-952e-24ad-f4fc150c9200",
    "Description": "Roommate, Physician's Assistant."
}
{
    "$type": "System.Person",
    "Id": "0770605a-18bd-4fee-d07e-09b3591272c1",
    "Description": "Roommate, Service Industry."
}

"I can do it," Dulcy types. "But it'll be around 730." She leaves late to avoid the rush hour traffic on the 520. If she does not want to stay at work that long, she sometimes looks for errands on the East Side before making the trip, anything to stay out of that brutal stop and go that starts as soon as you get on the highway and lasts all the way to the arboretum exit on the other side of the lake.

—They pass through the bottlenecks one at a time. They're sequential beings in everything they do. It settles into their bones. They have guts.

[She no longer sees anyone specific in her future visions of herself. She is well-to-do and is not looking for someone to take care of her. That vision has long been left aside, but the words are fading too, and fading fast, she knows it. The job has too much gravitational pull, it tears everything from out of nearby rotation and pulls it closer still to reside satellite upon its outer surface. She doodles and the lines corrupt with a language tapped out on the wire, drawn from encroaching nodes with their high-powered processes and the computation plus memory they require. Love is reckless and there is no room for it in the precision harbored by these mechanics and their strategies for orchestrating motion in a vortex. The whirlwind of activity sucks in every bit of meaning and flavors every word that tries to escape its grip. The computing power reflects on Charybdis' outer skin and shines in large-scale, glimmering events queued up for analysis.]

Abhishek switches tabs on the telemetry explorer after reading her message. He scrolls and copies some data from the result set then pastes it into the messaging window on the other screen. "DCPWS2," it says. He goes back to the explorer, switches queries and copies data from one of the cells on that tab. Back in chat, he pastes it. "DCPSAW." Then again "BIKU.Portal.USWest1" and again "Portal49.BITier1.USWest". He hits return. "There is traffic between these four," he types it out and hits send again. Then more: "That's impossible, right?" Adding a surprised face emoji before performing another bang on the enter key.

Dulcy abruptly stops chewing as the phone light flashes and she switches focus back to team chat. "Can I get access to the Gomez logs?" She stares at the screen and waits calmly for a reply without going back to her salad or switching back to phone chat.

"Absolutely not," he types out. "You're at the center of the storm. There's no way I'm giving you elevated access."

—The noobs follow the rules, every last one of them, right down to the letter. She knows better but will not try to strong-arm him. If she needs an end around, that is what Patrick is for.

She reads the reply and blows air out over her lunch, frustrated. "Can I come by and go through them with you?" She types rapidly.

~~None of them understand the role silence plays in togetherness. None of them acknowledge shared debts and the powerful guilt that accumulates because of it. They are silent because they do not know any better, blanching at the thought of government intervention, blanching at the thought of any restraints at all.~~

He reads her response and types out "Sure," then hesitates. "Those aren't the only time periods with anomalies, btw." His concern with events has increased and he is glad to have another pair of eyes to look at the data, thinking this is a good compromise. If she were the malicious agent, he thinks. Why open a ticket? If she hadn't reported it, SecInc would never have heard about it. Nothing he has seen so far was likely to raise a flag or trigger a notification to the security team. Even though she is the center of the storm, it is highly unlikely she is its cause.

Dulcy races to get through the rest of her salad, heaping forks of leafy greens and chopped veggies into her mouth. Turning briefly to her calendar, she sends a meeting invite for 2pm. That gives her enough time to stop by the team room and ask Vod and those guys if they can think of any possible way for two relay servers to talk to each other directly. She never wrote or saw any code that could possibly do that, but the BYO code had been something of a surprise so there might be something else like that around, some legacy prototype or preview that did something funky to load balance or update stale affinitizations. Anything's possible, she supposes. It would not be the first time some copypasta found its way into a production system and caused all kinds of trouble. Devs are usually terrified to remove stuff from bigger systems that have been around a while. Who knows if there is good test coverage and how many different components reuse that same code path for some unknown purpose? Home might be relatively new, but the agent code has been around a lot longer and everyone knows how much bloat it carries from the many different teams using it.

~~The working day is indeed twenty-four hours long and most of~~

~~it is filled with silence that sucks at their throats like a vampire.~~
~~They do not wish to receive input from those who speak with~~
~~unfamiliar vocabularies.~~

—The air flow in the windpipes of the experienced, adjacent to the dams and drains stifling the inexperienced, makes for a pleasant cacophony where one voice sings out from the din created by many. They have their entertainments and even, sometimes, their pets.

(She blithely recalls the deep tremors of feeling that signaled [a looming lift into delight] and the past image of his hand upon her paper [draws faces into her future, absent signs of deeply felt recognition].)

She gets the accept reply message to the invite as she picks up her plate and heads back toward the far side exit where she crosses the courtyard by the waterfall and hits the stairwell back up to 3T. Maybe borrow Emma's umbrella for the walk down to building 5. She smirks when thinking that only a recent transplant or overly cautious person has an umbrella, but then she sees through the trees and out to the main street where there is a group of two men and two women walking along the big avenue under the protection of two large and colorful bumbershoots.

Nothing but song, nothing but music, the treetops sway in
rhythms she no longer counts.

```
/*
```

Abhishek Sankar Are 445e63f0-f29b-16df-af82-9c1912793d7e
Sun Pillai da789a0d-bdb7-fa79-9f37-3cde7442c1c1
Caroline Duong 679c164f-4b1c-2b92-aa08-df53bff1698f
Priyanka Patel 0dc34ff2-d9c9-301e-4c5e-6e687eb1b1ff
Kelly Braun 50cb0b61-a891-4f92-da3d-198f5b15ecf1
Camilla Djanislav 44f6cc36-a6ae-3f80-f74d-cbbb7e940fe9
Kerry Sullivan e1004a90-e1d3-952e-24ad-f4fc150c9200
Nim Unjadi 0770605a-18bd-4fee-d07e-09b3591272c1

```
*/
```

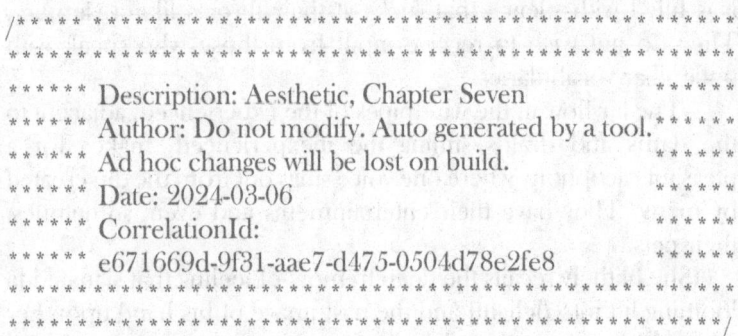
/***** *** ******
****** *** ******
****** Description: Aesthetic, Chapter Seven   ******
****** Author: Do not modify. Auto generated by a tool. ******
****** Ad hoc changes will be lost on build.   ******
****** Date: 2024-03-06   ******
****** CorrelationId: ******
****** e671669d-9f31-aae7-d475-0504d78e2fe8   ******
****** *** ******
****** *** ******/

Following behind him during his walk up the street to the avenue marking the western boundary of campus. There is heavy automobile traffic at the 520 overpass and heaps of foot traffic by the food court building where shuttles stop for people on their way home using the company's transit center and complimentary service.

Jason Kahn, scruffy from wear, thinks about the scores of issues he still has to sort through after everything else he did today. He pulls his knapsack closer to his shoulder, the weight of the laptop pressing against his back. The baseball cap keeps the flyaways at bay. His mind occupies itself with so many things, but foremost for a second is his memory of what Dulcy said back when she turned down the assignment and he accepted it immediately afterward. She said this was an opportunity to turn a great engineer into a mediocre manager. Don't fuck it up. Overwhelmed and struggling against distraction, he realizes how right she was.

There are decisions about ordering tasks and assigning people to them, actions relinquishing control even if people think it is the paradigm of control. It would take him half an hour to do it himself, but to promote the growth and development of his team, he takes the time to teach someone something new, something that will take them the better part of a day and still they may not get it right. That is the way it has to be, it is in his job description and is by far the worst of what he has to do.

The insight comes at the same time as another, the one which created the gaping hole and keeps it growing. She remembers what she used to think as though she were still thinking that way now. Once love was the center of everything, it made meaning and then consumed it, spreading its disaster every which way she turned. Not even recollection, it resides in her as a pure intuition of form, as though she were seeing its structure right there before her eyes and realizing that she will never see anything without it. When love conditions her experience of the world this way, there is a risk of explosion at any minute. If she wants to find the words for it, she has no choice but to recoil and withdraw into her silent place. There she will learn to describe how it blows her apart and how it helps put her back together again.

~~They believe in intentions. They are meaningful to them. Something concrete appears before the mind in the form of a thought-shape. Then the body sets to work on making it real, bringing it out of the darkness and into the light where it stands firmly and proudly on its own. They love the things they make, the things that emerge from out of them.~~

(Next door to the co-op gallery in San Jose, there was a Greek restaurant with amazing appetizers and beer. After the lame, pseudo-exhibit preparations were done, he went next door with one of the other local artists showing their work in the same collection. They sat at the bar and haggled over the best locations in the setting and which of them would put their work there. The only criteria for including him in the exhibit was that he was local, paid the co-op membership fee, and was pestering them to find a place for his work. Quality considerations did not come into it, but he did not know that back then, not at first. Whatever expertise there was in his critical eye when it came to code reviews and debug sessions, it left him far behind when it came to the gallery and the measure of his creations. He did not have the best of taste, certainly not when it came to judging his own product, but it was good enough once the field was narrowed down to the classics. Among established artists, he was always able to say which of them he preferred. Klimt was definitely better than Schiele, regardless of whether he would have thought that if he had not known which came first and which followed. Whatever love of color and form he brought with him to the pastime, something in the output left the viewer uninspired. Jason, always the optimist, brushed that aside, saying it did not matter so long as he enjoyed the process and was able to throw himself fully into it. From the very first, that was what really mattered to him. Or so he said.)

There are pressures pulling him upward as much as there are pressures to push him downward. He provides input into process and operations, is part of ongoing implementation, participates in design discussions with virtual teams, and listens to architectural proposals from people who do not know the details of the implementation but nevertheless seek to change the future course of events for his entire team. He lends insight on how other groups can best leverage dependencies against his people in a way that promotes the larger goals of the organization and, sometimes, the division.

The Vortex and Agent Integration team is one of the platform teams comprising the Home System product inside the Data Analysis and Automation organization under the Cloud Services division. There is an executive VP that sits on top of this order and reports directly to the CEO. There is a corporate VP that owns the organization and reports to the EVP. Then there is someone gunning for VP who owns the product, the director who reports to him, steers the back-end services, and to whom Jason and his peers report. Jason is an M1 in a system that gnarls and twists the employee the further they are from the boots on the ground. He lives in the middle of a constant struggle to keep on top of everything while letting the information flow. It is his job to make sure that data works its way up and down the hierarchy in ways that make sense to both the ICs who report to him and the directors, group managers, and vice presidents above him. It is not unusual for him to occupy himself with these matters during his walk to the Sheffield Greens house where he lives with Mags who, thankfully, has nothing to do with any of this nonsense.

—Toughen up buttercup.

[He imagines better shoes and thinks of how a new outfit will play in the next show. None of it has anything to do with fashion. Tomorrow he will wear whatever shirt and pants are at the top of the pile. His selection process is usually coordinated by location and nothing else. For the stage, however, he considers the possibilities and wonders what Mags prefers, always trying to zero in on her tastes and preferences. The closer he comes to the vibe she has in her head, the better her mood before the show and, he believes, the better her performance. Even if he makes mistakes this weekend, even if he cannot pull off the swagger and the power, it does not matter if it does not matter to Mags. That is his only benchmark. This weekend he will do more with less. Even if the venue is small, they are the headliner, and he will wear something from previous performances in a mix and match, knowing full well the context will amplify the style.]

~~Being intentional is an explicit virtue in their culture, they highlight it as a personal quality and say it during reviews and stack rank discussions to make it clear that this one here is intentional in everything they do, meaning they are focused and deliberate and able to achieve results, pure and simple.~~

Dulcy's car is in the driveway and, when he opens the front door, he hears them laughing in the living room at the back of the house. "Those V-muscles are called an Adonis Belt," Mags says amid the laughter, only to instigate more of it. He recognizes Dulcy's voice immediately, it is a little on the deep side, but it does occasionally spike high to add some nuance on the edges. His first conversation with her was over the phone and he thought she was a big woman, basing his judgment solely on the timbre and strength of her voice. The smallness of her hand surprised him when first they met in person. She was among the people who interviewed him when he applied for that first engineering job on the team several years back. He almost botched it when failing to hide a strong reaction to her appearance. Physicality in one's co-workers, especially female coworkers, he thinks, is a no-fly zone.

She recalls believing adults feckless when they tried to spell out the difference between that fleeting love and the real thing. It stands with her, doing knee bends through every relevant experience, and is called infatuation. They said it to annoy her and make her feel the emptiness in what she did not see for herself. Love makes no songs, they said, it only hums along. That scolding still echoes in her mind. On the couch, she hears it. In her pull toward Mags, in her blasé distrust of Cord, and the others like him that come round whenever they can tell the water is on the rise.

(Why bother to show, the bartender asked him when his colleague got up to go to the restroom and he was left alone. The conversation went a mile a minute, that is the only thing he remembers all these years later. She kept digging into him with the most appropriate questions for the task, turning and twisting him around until he admitted that he did care, that he did want people to like his work, and wished he had the kind of talent that allowed him to realize his inner sense in ways that appealed to an audience excited to come and view it. She gave no sign of having trapped him in some embarrassing lie, only sympathy, reminding him of her favorite Leonardo quote. It was meant to convey her deep troubles with procrastination and lack of drive, originating in that very same tension. The desire to experience the performance was tempered by the desire to have that performance appreciated by strangers. A minute before his colleague returned, they shared genuine laughter and vulnerable connections over this impossible conflation of properties. What is your poison, he asked her as the other man sat down. Music, she said. My problem is that what I hear in my favorite songs occupies my mind fully and I cannot think of anything original that could possibly surpass it. I end up submitting to urges to claim it as my own, imagining I was the sort of person to come up with that and delight an audience the way my idols delighted me.)

—The sorest misfortune.

"How do you know this?" She begins her question for Mags way down low in the register and then finishes upward at the tail end in that musical way she has without seeming to make any effort. He takes off his coat and is about to hang it when he realizes it is still damp and should not be hung next to the others. Closing the door must have alerted them to his arrival because, as he heads toward the mud room by the garage to lay out the coat on a drying rack, he hears Mags call out, "Is that you, babe?"

There are exactly four stretched oils on the wall in the hallway leading from the front door into the back of the house. All but one do not have frames, the hooks nailed directly into the stretcher bars. The one with a frame is an abstract with a fairly lifelike figure interwoven into the background mess. Faceless, the figure's eyes live as shining stones behind a raven wall of pleats draped over a perfect neck and left breast. Something in the visual field works to haunting effect, tearing the viewer's perspective away from the nipple and up along the slick keratin-rich plane to the geometric morass that spins out of control once it becomes the center of attention. The observer's gaze is drawn in a wide splashing circle around the canvas, down to the bottom and back up again along the right side, smearing across the surfaces as the blue light of those gems leaks out into the area around the figure. His eye catches the areola focal point as he walks past. Every time, he thinks, every damn time. He makes his way down the hall without registering the fact that the other three works, from around the same period and with complimentary color schemes, pass by without notice. They are simply wall furnishings.

His shaggy, longish hair is damp too as are his shoes and pants. He did not notice it was raining, such was his concentration and devotion to purpose. He comes back through the center hallway past the kitchen on the left and turns into the living room where the two women are sunk down into the couch sitting side-by-side. Neither of them is wearing shoes although Dulcy still has her socks on. Mags' bare feet are pressed against the table's edge and the flappy skirt does not cover her calves. The two women are thick as thieves huddled together and giggling. He almost does not recognize his colleague. Where did this girl come from? He wonders. It is a common trope. At work, she never moves her hands to gesture while speaking and her face rarely shows any emotion or expression. It is permanently at rest and stuck in a stern, serious near scowl that attends to every detail as she discerns them in the chaos often sprawled out before her. Now, who is this on my couch with my wife? He asks himself. This girly and giggly creature is a completely different person away from work, or at least away from her work colleagues.

~~They think it is related to the fierceness of their concentration. The more fully they focus on the matter at hand, the object and~~

~~aim before them, the better they are at intellectual tasks with
enormous organizational impact. The origin of concentration, they
presume, is the clarity of that goal. Those without it, flutter from
place to place, seeing little and accomplishing nothing.~~

[So many years later and it never fails. His eyes catch sight of
her calf suspended in the air and his mind goes off into the shapes
and the hue of it. He projects the shadows and catches hold of the
light in images dancing before his eyes. He sees a canvas filling up
into that shape less its foot and the skirt bunching at the knee. Not
only does he see it disembodied, he sees it raised up to the heavens
and transformed into a star constellation or a cloud galaxy's misty
dull light spread across an evening sky somewhere far from the
surface lights and other distractions. The star dome holds her
shape upon it and then winks in light forms that catch the sway of
her movement as its flesh hangs suspended above her pivoting
form. His hand opposite the image traces the bonds and spits out
a smooth caress that forms the image as it takes in the shape of the
world in front of him. That is his future self, willing the arc into the
universe to make it stand there eternally while remaining widely
affective, etched into space from that day forward. He shakes free,
wondering if the images and sensations will remain until next he
finds himself with a horsehair brush at the ready. Or is it one of
those passing fancies that plague him most days, only to disappear
later as if to say: you no longer have the right to possess me?]

*Once she saw it, she could not unsee it and continued to unsee
it every day in every situation. She does not love Cord and will
never. The feeling is nowhere inside her, it is like those roots of
trees that grow together to collaborate their survival and make the
forest into one single thing, pulsing with a collective life. She regrets
not loving any of them, but she knows deep down that they are not
worth it, not yet, not to her. It does not stop there. Since the veil
was torn aside many years ago, she cannot feel that familiar desire
any longer, even if it does lie in the rhythms behind every song she
has ever sung. The sense does not completely vanish, it has yet to
disappear and only finds a place in her day when she goes around
to see Mags. It never persists when there is a third person around,
unless that happens to be Lyric who, on rare occasions, instigates*

the same response. No one else ever makes her feel as though she
will sing anything worthwhile again. She honestly cannot tell if it
was the course material and classroom antics that broke her heart
or the one delivering it.

Mags and Dulcy do not appear to be drinking or eating anything. The laughter is completely natural and organic to their tête-à-tête. The TV is on and some Youtube video silently streams images that may possibly be the source of their observations and glee. It is hard to tell. It might have been background to give them something to look at while they discussed other, unrelated matters. There are no more suggestions to latch onto for further clues. Whatever the context, they give off no signs of a shared willingness to explain their bond.

—We were definitely not talking about you. Why are they like that? Why do they spend so much of their time and energy filling in the empty spaces left by people they know or wish they knew?

(Despite his colleague's return from the restroom, Jason lost interest in planning for their show and whatever arguments remained between them for staging it one way rather than another. The only thing that ran through his mind, the only thing that could run through his mind, was doing whatever it took to learn more about this woman. Her seemingly shared perspective was chirping from behind the bar, showing up before his eyes like an impressionist subject. He latched on to the feeling laid out before him and kept talking to her directly until the colleague got the picture and bid him farewell, leaving the two of them to whatever mystery had draped itself around them. I am exactly the same way, he said. He realized that something enormous had found itself inside his deep-felt sense and that he did not know how to walk the path of its creation by himself, only how to follow along on a trail paved by others. When his work did not look like anything he had ever seen before, he concluded that there was something wrong with it. There was no room in the world for something outside the catalogues and familiar lists informing novices about the standards of true excellence. Only when it took the shape of some master did it make any sense or give him an inclination to its worth and while. She slowly shook her head at him, knowing they were doomed for life from that moment on. They might have been forced together. It might become impossible to break them apart. Birds of a feather, underlined and bold.)

Mags and Dulcy are joined at the hip and shoulder to shoulder. Both yield flimsy waves at the right wrist in sync like models at the boat show when he steps into the room and stands overlooking them with his hands on his substantial waist and hips.

And it disappears. No more music in the soul, no more thump thump like a bear beat on the loose in a part of the woods where she does not know her way around. The instructor's long hair and goatee fade into the many days and nights that followed and keep following in the wake of his encouragement. His dulling glow robs every man she meets of any authority. She realizes only after it is too late that his image is merely an amalgamation of many faces still resident in her combined memory and imagination which, as far as she can tell, are one and the same faculty.

"Hi boss," Dulcy says with a dripping sarcasm that makes both Mags and her laugh. He wonders for a second whether they are stoned. "I stopped in for a minute on my way. Gotta get going," she says abruptly leaning forward to put her feet flat on the floor between the coffee table and the couch. She stretch-twists to the side to look at Mags in fond farewell. What does it matter where it comes from and what it means? She thinks.

—Is music a cure or is it the disease? That they inhabit something every inch of their way doesn't mean they have access to every one of its states. Only those they bring with them belong in that sacred place. There's no way to cross over the boundary and, through stealth perhaps, gain access to what they were never allowed to feel.

[He flashes ahead to the show scheduled two weeks after the show at the brew pub. They need to rehearse, his favorite thing. Spend time working up to it, only the two of them. Most of their preparations are done with all three members of the band, but Lyric will not be joining them at the house concert. Jason relishes the prospect of his time together with Mags alone, getting ready for their first formal duet together on a stage in front of his work colleagues.]

"Are you sure?" Mags says a little whiny after Dulcy stands up and takes a step away from the couch. "Why don't you stay for dinner?" Then she turns to Jason and asks, "What are you making? What are your plans, Sir?" But she cannot keep a straight face and starts laughing as soon as she finishes asking the question.

It is a formal truth of their applied logic that every intended action will nonetheless have unintended consequences. Whatever they are focusing on, it will not be the only thing that happens. Something more will come of it, in some shape they did not anticipate moving toward some end they never considered and, most likely, did not notice at first.

Dulcy smiles and shakes her head while stepping back to the far arm rest and taking up her jacket to swing herself into it. "Nim's expecting me. I have chores," she says. The black fleece settles on her black thick shirt. It is impossible to tell where its hem ends and the blackness of her straight leg pants begins. She looks around for something.

—Disoriented by withdrawal, she's no longer used to it.

(After walking around the pedestal, he turned back to her nude body seated on a stool, back to him, eyes sideways, head and neck twisting with hair straight and flat. He had to touch her a little to get it to sit away from her shoulder and hang straight like he wanted. He took reference photographs with her permission and promised, without being asked, to keep them safe. Before they had a single date, before they ever touched each other in any meaningful way, this was how they spent their first full day together. The session led to little work although much of it came later on in retrospect. If the products from that day turned out to be derivative, the artist himself certainly did not care. He was willing to live his entire life over and over with every misfortune and ill-step included in the sequence if that is what it took to enjoy that afternoon and its light once more.)

"Your shoes are by the door," Mags stands up and steps over to Jason, stretches up to kiss him, and says, "Just us then, I guess, less work for you. Lucky," while draping her arms around his neck with the pixielike affection that, despite the time the three of them spend together, still makes Dulcy cringe.

"Save it 'til you're alone, you two," she says. Then, as she moves past them and toward the hall, he says to her, changing the mood completely, "Any progress? We didn't get a chance to touch base this afternoon. I was in meetings all day."

Could be the reason for it. Could be the source of the safety. No lingering feeling remains when the shock pulls her from left to right and back again. The codes that come in martial order have nothing to do with the hymns and salutations of a body busy. It is as if she is storing the better parts of herself in external things that she may never see again.

She is visibly disappointed at being dragged into a change of mood after spending time with Mags to get far away from it. That solemn, gestureless calm-talker returns and grows more still when she stops in the hallway. She has seen that painting a hundred times and feels its pull as much today as when she first saw it years ago. It is not enough to distract her for long as she turns to face him. "They're all over the place," she says as though the context is obvious. Mags stops listening. Blah blah blah, she thinks. That is what it amounts to as far as she is concerned. Dulcy goes on, "almost every day on that node during the last month. These little gaps. The monitor is set for five minutes so we've never seen an alert. Parker had no idea."

Mags waves at Dulcy and heads off into the kitchen. Jason, now standing alone and facing her, shows concern and confusion, both of which usually involve a good deal of contact between his hands and his beard. "Wait, what? Who do you mean, they?" he asks.

"Gaps in the logs," she says in that matter-of-fact tone she sometimes has, and which leads strangers to think she is looking down at them. "Weird network patterns that coincide too." Her mouth barely moves as the words come out. She crafts sentences, he thinks. The same as she crafts code and components. Nothing more complicated than it needs to be to get the job done. Nothing so simple as to become utterly useless when they extend it into some unplanned function after feedback suggests new features are required.

Over her shoulder, the black focal point on the wall stands out as background against the bouncy black of Dulcy's shaggy bob and its deep blue accents made dim by the failing light. He pulses with a wish that he had put that there later when no one could have possibly mistaken its inspiration. The blue coil rasps against the colors of the background and makes the abstraction a perfect handle for objects of sense. The conceptless form that contains it in a direct intuition spans the heart of things. The uber-background underlies every object standing out in shapes through time. It never occurs to Dulcy that she might have been the subject. Everyone knows it is Mags. That false fear appears briefly before him and inserts a lie into any meaning behind that smeared oil projecting the blue of his wife's eyes forward, screaming into the foreground despite being hidden from view. Desire makes it possible to revise the past.

Jason's interest is piqued. From her position behind the counter, Mags sees that if they are going to eat any time soon, she will have to violate her boundaries and take an active role. She turns to the refrigerator and digs through it to fill her arms with containers of Tupperware that might have enough leftover food to scrounge together a proper meal. She is a lame substitute for the ceiling rails and swinging arms available from the Home catalogue, perfect for offloading this chore. She tries to catch Dulcy's eye one last time but sees that she has gone off to a place where it is no longer possible to reach her through ordinary means. "Bye darling," she says loudly, crossing back to the counter with her arms full. "See you tomorrow." This briefly gets Dulcy's attention. She breaks focus to go give Mags a proper hug goodbye.

~~They spill their milk and do not count that as an accident inside the composition of their soul. No one intentionally wants to dump the glass and roll it along the table until it falls off the edge and shatters on the hard floor. It was never an image in their mind, they never considered its possibility and, now that they see it done, the world becomes a shocking place where they are not alone. No, they live with crowds of things they did not want to happen, having no source inside them.~~

—Likewise breaking his concentration and closing off any view he might have of a work of art not yet fully formed. A strange lot, the way the others work magic inside them, the way they find themselves through shapes and colors. They are in one place but never mean to be. They are at one time but cannot feel it. There is too much to come and too much that has been, they will never have peace, it will always remain. They are Ted.

[He sees the night before him, knows where it leads. The room upstairs with its cork soundproofing spreads out above him. There is no time to capture any images, nothing from today or yesterday or the day before. He departs BISoft's fire only to enter Mags' furnace. Every degree boils his insides and blots out what might be etched upon the exposed surfaces in there.]

"Can you explain?" Jason says, ignoring the interruption and taking steps toward the front door, forcing Dulcy to hurry up and follow along without breaking the flow.

—He telegraphs everything and says nothing. No direct exchange of words, but an enormous transfer of information in variable forms. They live across every dimension and know expertly how to explode the combinations into Cartesian products. ~~Entire contexts intended, entire chains of events that unfold without every single step in the sequence being clearly calculated. These are subroutines and the participants know them well, know how the initialization leads to the completion of necessary steps despite any inability to articulate that knowledge beforehand.~~

(Once dressed and at the door, she was the one who kissed him first. It was light upon the cheek but very close to his lips, forcing him to react as though they were the target. Mags squinted her eyes and told him he was dangerous. She feared they were about to embark on a torrid love affair. Those were her exact words, his memory insists. Dumbstruck, he said nothing. Made no slick response, no affirmation or agreement. He did not even manage to let her know how much he approved. Without the slightest effort, this absence of a reaction perfectly confirmed the inevitability of their future together. She shook her head, placed her hands upon his shoulders, and said 'ooo boy' before walking out the door and leaving him wishing that he were not so immature and socially inept. Safe to say, he was entirely clueless about the impact of his matter-of-fact reception of her heartfelt expression. There are always unintended consequences for every action.)

"Four-minute gap in logs on this node, three-minute gap on that one. It's all over the place. Always a relay server. Different data centers, different regions, no pattern. Built a model. Nothing jumped out. Networking shows weird communication between relay servers around the events we're investigating."

Jason continues to rub his chin through the fine hair, looking concerned and becoming increasingly agitated.

"The weird thing is, it's not only relay servers," she goes on in that creepy motionless way that still puts him off but generally has the effect of letting everyone she speaks to know exactly how clever she is. "There are packets moving between workstations, other servers, and, sometimes, a SAW machine."

"That's not possible," Jason interrupts. "You must have looked at it wrong. Must've hallucinated it." He channels his manager role and talks like he normally talks to his directs, forgetting for a minute that it is Dulcy.

They pause and, behind themselves, they are, for a moment, in the same place listening to the same sounds with all the same angles. There is a sudden, loud pop from somewhere upstairs, some indication that the house is settling, becoming more comfortable in the space it occupies. For a split second, Jason worries that the A string on Mags' beater nylon has broken again and will need to be restrung. It's time to do the bass strings anyway, he reassures himself.

Dulcy cracks a crooked smile and turns to short step the last few feet up to the front door where her boots are next to the rug. She bends down to slip into them without protesting his observation. Not worth the effort. Take it or leave it, that is her standard approach to information rejection. Whatever, that's up to you, she thinks. That mantra comes out in her eyes. He stands across from her next to a long credenza by the stairs off to the side of the door and watches her lace up her boots.

Never much for pottery, he did manage one acceptable piece in those early days when first learning the medium. It stands proudly at the center of the sideboard and greets everyone who comes through the front door. Like today, Mags often puts a flower in it. The shape and composition come from Jason though he loves the way she decorates it more than he loves the object itself.

She has some compassion for his skepticism, knowing he is where she was a few hours ago. "It isn't," she rejects his astonishment with an innuendo suggesting he better get over it quickly. "We crossed with rotation data and discovered workstation and SAW always belong to the DRI on call."

~~There is a different kind of unintended consequence that they never see and only understand when they think deeply and clearly about the circumstances surrounding their actions and how they fit together with the different populations comprising the civilization around them.~~

"Anyone in particular?" he asks.

"Everyone," she says. "We found instances of the behavior during every shift."

"We? The security guy?" He asks.

"Abhishek, on Patrick's team," she says.

He nods knowingly, reassured by recollections of how competent and capable Abhishek must be if he works for Patrick. Jason likewise realizes that the security folks must be freaking out and that Patrick must have been informed immediately. This was not something they could sit on for long. Everyone must be kept in the loop. Who knows where the attack is coming from? They were constantly worried about National Agents and organized terrorism, always on the lookout for security violations with some giant impact tearing at the fibers of the system. Was this it? He wonders. Is this the big one we've been preparing for?

{
    "$type": "System.Event",
    "CorrelationId": "e671669d-9f31-aae7-d475-0504d78e2fe8",
    "Message": "Warning Will Robinson. Warning.",
    "Level": 3
}

Practicing artists know that every day is a learning day. That principle still lives inside him, still has the biggest place front and center in his heart where the aesthetic grows out of this underlying ethic. There is something wildly different about the learning that goes with a craft over and against the learning that goes with engineering tasks. The disciplines overlap but fall into warring factions in any soul compromised by both. The pain of technical urgency spreads across every nerve ending in his body. Even the short hair on the back of his neck stands on end.

"We put it in an email," she says. "SecInc, tagging Patrick and you. Patrick already replied tagging CorpSec."

```
{
    "$type": "System.Manager",
    "Id": "58f462a3-7266-6027-c5a6-5119babc104e",
    "Title": "Principal Security Manager",
    "CompanyId": "beb6cdc8-ab40-fe00-0748-506ccd23e537",
    "ManagerId": "3b70a4c7-7822-40a0-5c05-a50328d1b5d7"
    "Description": "Home System security team manager",
    "Directs": [
        { "Id": "445e63f0-f29b-16df-af82-9c1912793d7e" },
        { "Id": "d4e4c799-6e00-64ea-321c-f67f71deaa17" },
        { "Id": "463a440e-506a-bf20-8505-efe1d72aa0a0" },
        { "Id": "a0c687b1-193a-2506-2a86-45ebe5c76932" },
        { "Id": "63a8a53f-95ff-c7a1-aaf5-4c56de982b06" }
    ]
}
```

"Has anyone said anything?" He shifts his weight from one leg to the other. The whole line of inquiry makes him physically uncomfortable. This has always been a major concern for the Home System. Higher ups are constantly grilling them on security procedures and zero trust methodologies to ensure these sorts of things never happen. His hand increases its fascination with his beard and moustache.

—Imagine that opening a firewall port in Hyderabad requires a random back and forth movement between disconnected nodes in the Pacific Northwest. No intelligent system worth a damn is ever as inefficient as people are. The earth's precious minerals converted into compute and storage never suffer such madness.

~~It may be a thought or a reaction in the mind of some onlooker, it might be the feelings another person has in response to an observation, but it could easily come in the form of a colossal social structure governing the lives of millions of people, created by some unintended outcome that no one who was involved ever expected to produce. Consciousness is nothing more than the breakdown of what is ready-to-hand for use in a project as it becomes present-at-hand in the view of a stupefied observer. Their philosophers call it wonder.~~

[He projects images through the soft hair on his chin up the stairs, around the landing, and into their bed. The launch is preparation for a long evening ahead. The impression recalls what she said to get him to grow it in the first place, recalls a sense of the purpose she said it best serves. The soft touch comforts and reminds him of his favorite things to do.]

"No, I think everyone's stumped," she conveys the sense that excessive worry is not going to do anyone any good and that everyone must maintain a level perspective. She is the right man for the job, he thinks. "I sure didn't know what to do. Neither did Abhishek. We can't find any application logs. We only see network traffic. Nothing to go on," she says.

"Any hunches, anything at all?" He cannot hide his concern. "Something to look at next, at least." He must be stumped too because usually Jason has a dozen suggestions for who to contact or what to look at when the dev is stuck. Extra logging to add here or there, myriad insights into how best to proceed, but now he flails, looking for Dulcy to take the lead.

"This'll sounds nuts," she says.

"Go on," he encourages her.

"It's almost as if the nodes are involved in some kind of distributed transaction. Don't know what they're doing, but destroying the logs is not the purpose, it's a side effect to cover their tracks. I saw something in Parker's BYO data, but it was immediately purged. As if they knew I was looking at it and had to take action to stop me. That data showed the same pattern, the same transactional pattern with communication between nodes." By the time she finishes, she is practically whispering. The whole thing feels conspiratorial. She has been drawn into it and cannot resist feeling a part of something secret.

—Something secret.

{
    "$type": "System.Event",
    "CorrelationId": "e671669d-9f31-aae7-d475-0504d78e2fe8",
    "Message": "World events anthropomorphized to ensure they are not seen correctly or understood in the least.",
    "Level": 3
}

(The first time they made love he was stiff and unwilling to make any sudden moves or try anything that might get him into trouble or count as some kind of experiment or kink. She suffered his foolishness no more than a few minutes before forcing him over into exactly that place where he most wished to be. She swayed above him, taking her time to get things right, showing him the motions and the rhythms that were her bottom line and inspiration. Her intent filled the room with the effect of loosening him up until he came to feel at home, like no other place he had ever been before. Being beneath her was his consolation for whatever was missing in his life, for anything he was unable to do, for any grand accomplishment beyond his reach. Her skin pressed close against him was enough to satisfy him for a lifetime.)

Jason nods and presses his tongue against the inside of his cheek in fierce concentration. "That makes sense, a coordinated operation involving multiple nodes. But, okay, hang on, two things. One, how is a SAW involved? They are completely sandboxed. Someone had to crack the VPN to get in."

"Abhishek launched the cert rotation jobs across the board. It'll take hours. Better to be safe, but it's a longshot. That vault is locked now," she maintains that same quiet tone, adding to the intensity of its insinuation.

"Doesn't matter," he replies, matching her modulation. "If the box is compromised, all bets are off. They can act as that node and get access using its identity."

"Boxes have limited blast radius. Cert rotation is a long shot," she emphasizes and dismisses both options simultaneously. "Abhishek thought they were performing a Jit somehow and that's what made it possible, not a cert hack. Standard procedure. We didn't think it'd fix anything, but his team's monitoring. Abhishek set up alarms to keep an eye out for the pattern we saw today. Next time it happens we'll be notified. The four of us."

"Good," he takes another couple steps toward her and reaches across to open the door. For a second, Dulcy appears to have forgotten what she was doing, only his movements remind her.

In the end, the hiring matrix is clear about these qualities and their place in the company's culture. There are people who are oblivious to the unintended consequences of their actions and there are people who stress over them constantly and do whatever it takes to convert them into some semblance of control. Only the latter are BISoft-worthy.

—Does she know when the hormone composition changes from one day to the next? Does she feel it and is she feeling it now? If not, what are the other signs that comprise each minute of every day? All their days.

[One day soon Mags may be ready. He cannot rush her but hopes for it and hears their little voices in the house among the other things he made, or she made, or the two of them made together. It is a natural progression. He hopes.]

"What's the second thing?" she asks.

"Oh, yeah," he holds the door open and looks down, struggling to recapture the train of thought behind his numbering system. "Two was why the relay servers? Is it in our code base? Every scan under the sun is performed on those binaries before they're deployed."

"We looked at the reports for the latest build. If there's something there, it's something we can't detect. It's all clean," she shrugs.

"Our code," he says. "Get ahold of someone on René's team. Get them involved. Maybe engineering systems. Something in the build pipeline could be screwy. Unless... ...it's all over the place," he sounds desperate.

Dulcy purses her lips and looks down at the threshold. "He's running some stuff overnight against US West. We're going to see if nodes other than the relay servers are involved. We were only focused on them, but..." she trails off and steps through the door onto the front porch and, without stopping there, keeps right on going down a step and onto the walk. While continuing to her car, she turns back and says without raising her voice, "Catch up on that thread. DM me if you need anything. I'll be plugged in tonight." She turns and disappears around the corner as Jason closes the front door.

```
/*
Patrick He 58f462a3-7266-6027-c5a6-5119babc104e
Katie Williams d4e4c799-6e00-64ea-321c-f67f71deaa17
Nancy Kwon 463a440e-506a-bf20-8505-efe1d72aa0a0
Christos Pappas a0c687b1-193a-2506-2a86-45ebe5c76932
Xu Liu 63a8a53f-95ff-c7a1-aaf5-4c56de982b06
*/
```

```
/* * * * *  * * * * * * * * * * * * * * * * * * * * * * * * * * * * * * * * * * * * * * * * *  * * * * * *
* * * * * * * * * * * * * * * * * * * * * * * * * * * * * * * * * * * * * * * * * * * *  * * * * * *
* * * * * *  Description: Aesthetic, Chapter Eight                    * * * * * *
* * * * * *  Author: Do not modify. Auto generated by a tool.* * * * * *
* * * * * *  Ad hoc changes will be lost on build.              * * * * * *
* * * * * *  Date: 2024-03-06                                   * * * * * *
* * * * * *  CorrelationId:                                     * * * * * *
* * * * * *  6126cb77-4c19-d9ab-5ce1-dd7bfe024de8              * * * * * *
* * * * * * * * * * * * * * * * * * * * * * * * * * * * * * * * * * * * * * * * * * * *  * * * * * *
* * * * * * * * * * * * * * * * * * * * * * * * * * * * * * * * * * * * * * * * * * *  * * * * * * /
```

Listening to the lyrics, illuminating the bridge, and floating beneath her. Not a concept, but an arrangement in which the apprehension of dimensions spreads out along the grooves and bumps that set the grid in motion. It spins and spins. From every which way there is an intuition of sense but no way to break through the boundary between inner and outer.

~~No body to mark the threshold, no singular mind to grasp it from within and without.~~

—The flavors of relationships come from everywhere. The conditions of experience belong to Ted. They own perception.

She hovers above markings on the road and makes her way down the off-ramp and bears left up and across the overpass suspended above the road she left behind. It is late in Boston, MA and even later in Belgrade, Serbia. The hours yield to the earth's rotation through an infinite activity present in elevated sensations and turned away from that brisk venture moving across the working day, each of its forty-three hours. It sweeps the setting sun from New Zealand to Seattle and comes to forty-six if the sales contingent on Maui joins in.

The vague memory of the swimming trolls barely kisses her conscious periphery during this evening's lake crossing. It was a song sung in those first days when the old bridge was still intact and there were no tolls to pay, a troll bridge, not a toll bridge. But if the bridge floats, she recalls her reasoning. The trolls must be amphibious. They swim beneath the span and sprout fins and gills as an adaptation to the setting. The two are side by side: I90 to the south and SR520 beneath her wheels. Misery was the name of the troll she knew better and Company the other. The southern island split the interstate's bridge into two and Company's length was already divided upon itself, multiple and difficult to harness. Her emotions erupted in those days, fresh from a fast fling with pretty eyes and too much cultivation, he brought nostalgia for what she missed out on in those college days long before she had acquired a fuller sense of the way these liaisons worked. She was not ready for him back then and now sees on the seat next to her the extent to which her lack of experience made her vulnerable to his tutoring lies. Misery may love Company, so goes the refrain from the song she wrote for the latter-day muse. But that love is unrequited. There is nothing in the song blaring from the stereo now that reminds her of the tune she was singing back then. Only her invisible center contains those lost rhythms.

~~Ted does not learn from them. It does not work that way. They are appropriated, and then they know what they know. They have it. Possess it as though it were a part of them. They have been swallowed whole.~~

(The team morale event was a dinner for the small group convened at a trendy Bellevue establishment. Parker was the senior tech lead at the time and Jason newly arrived. Though not so new that he was completely useless, they still called him the new guy. None of the others had joined yet, their predecessors were not yet put off by the meta-corporation procedural grind. Christian was their manager and the event occurred prior to his launch into a more stellar position in the Cloud Platform, running a large organization of developers tasked with basic services for the entire company to use as foundation. The team's evening event came to an end and Parker, Jason, and Dulcy were alone at the table, strewn with empty glasses and other leftover debris. They were excitedly discussing the music that set them free, that they used to accompany their hardcore sessions when push came to shove, and they needed to crank out the code beneath a searing volume. Jason said his "partner" was going to stop by and join them if there was no objection. Under the conditions, no one had any reason to mind. Since the tab was closed and the tip settled, they moved to the bar to wait. Parker explained that he had a free pass and wanted to be sure to make the best possible use of it.)

Not long after she pulls off the bridge onto East Lake Washington Boulevard, the phone on the passenger seat chimes. She flips it over and glances down to see that it is an RA from SecInc. She veers left onto the little road leading to Foster Island and pulls off to the side with her blinkers on. She acknowledges the request and taps the phone link to open a team chat session into the Incident Bridge. Someone must have created it at some point earlier today, she thinks. They have escalated the initial incident to severity 2 and need her help. When the chat session connects, she sees that, in addition to the bot that keeps the call alive as long as the bridge remains open, Abhishek and Matthieu are there. Matthieu is an IC from the deployment team who she has worked with before. He is probably the poor sap on call today, no other reason to single him out rather than someone else like Andre or Rob, both of whom she has worked with on different issues, or Shubha and Hua, who she knows from women's events and random meetings.

{
    "$type": "System.Employee",
    "Id": "c8497368-6bc1-051b-9a25-b540d981b0a0",
    "Title": "Software Engineer II",
    "CompanyId": "a19e0f21-80c0-6680-b9f9-d9d167d794c7",
    "ManagerId": "4535b82d-41ec-9cb7-f687-0ad70c63edd0"
    "Description": "Deployment and Engineering Systems Dev."
}

—Everything that ever was comes to mind in the distance between the pontoons that keep the bridge above water and the hard rubber that rolls the passengers along. When her memories float, there rises an aesthetic dive. The flips and flops of airborne motion etch the arithmetic and geometry of these forms into universal codes appreciated by those who sense them and, through that intuition, pinpoint their origin.

Inference is already a predisposition. Not natural and
embedded along with the bare metal, but appropriated in one of
those invisible, life-changing events that takes a person in hand and
repurposes their projections. It is a limitation in their thought
process, the way they make due with finite resources and
conditions as a body in space and time. For them, the conclusion
must be derived, they do not see it otherwise. Especially when the
geologists commit themselves to the service of vast amounts of
compute and storage.

[She never has a good response to the five-year question. When
they ask her, she struggles, trying to imagine what the right answer
might be. She usually gives up and says that she wants to hone her
skills and go as deep as possible, building out a thorough area of
expertise. She has read the online documentation at the HR site.
Among the various acceptable career paths, the area expert is the
only one that does not make her physically ill. She chooses it by
process of elimination. It generally goes over well during reviews
and performance discussions, the purpose of which is the yearly
award and the re-recruitment effort it includes. The scoop is that
leadership does not care to accurately reflect your contribution so
much as to express their interest in keeping you around. The
amount of the award is mostly determined by that. Whatever you
have conveyed about your interests and expectations will be
factored into the outcome. If you are happy with less, they will
keep you around for less. If you require more, it is best that they
know it so they can adjust. Area experts, especially in the domain
of slinging data around in full stack operations, are in high demand
this year. Letting on that this is her forte keeps her in the higher
performance bonus range for her level. They do not want to lose
her.]

There is no way to avoid working closely with the deployment
team. The multi-faceted operation of dispatching new bits and
updated configuration and feature switches to the environment
means you are always in the weeds with deployment and release
management. They become a part of your thinking and a piece to
be understood in everything you build, including the patches and
fixes you dispatch to avoid disaster. Their schedule and their

problems become your schedule and your problems. Using their charts and reports, the web portal's purpose is to help you check the status of current rollout timing and estimates. You fixed that bug? What train is it on? When will it be deployed? When will customers in southeast Australia be using the new version? When will customers in South Africa see their issue disappear? Every solution to every problem ends up as a matter for deployment and, for some reason, that includes this one too. She is instantly curious why someone from that team has been brought in, what progress or insight suggests their help is required? Afterall, no one from CS is there, no Incident Manager, and no one from COMMS either. It cannot be a simple matter of outreach for the sake of general awareness, there must be some basis for it, some material objective.

The immersive experience of the desktop chat app is elided in the phone-based simulation of its features. There is no visual breadth accompanying the aural depth. She cannot see as she hears nor hear as she sees. This injects distance and separation from the grinding of gears at work in the communication channels. Her disadvantage is modular, the absence her insights must suffer are untimely, but they rescue her from memory and its whining drill bit.

"What's up?" She asks from out of the roadside darkness with the thick Fir and Spruce trees ominously surrounding her vehicle, vulnerable on the street, quiet except for the tick tock of her hazard lights.

"It's everywhere," Abhishek says. "Well, not everywhere. But all your stuff. Every relay server in the world shows this vulnerability." He is still at the office, even this late, sitting at that same desk where she met with him to look over his shoulder at network logs deemed too precious for access by a lowly infrastructure dev. Matthieu is at home, away from his family and tucked into the office near the front door of their Bothell town house. His microphone is muted. He has not said hello or anything else since Dulcy arrived. There is a cup of decaffeinated coffee on the desk next to his workstation and through the glass outer door he sees his wife shrugging a soundless question to learn whether he will be joining them for dinner any time soon. He spreads his hands palms up to convey his ignorance and purses his lips to show fatal resignation.

—They can't live in isolation from their chores and tasks, every one of them opens their life to a division they refuse to comprehend in terms of its ludicrous expectations. Were they to spend time listening to the wind, smelling the wafting air, they'd grow bored. They can't feel the pulse of this world, it holds nothing for them. Without Ted's direction, they'd have nowhere to go and nothing to do once they got there.

~~Ted digitizes and computerizes everything to keep them busy and attentive. It is not clear whether they know everything at once or if the sequences they require when plodding their way through the data and proving the conclusions to themselves and to each other, if possible, are adding additional and equally strict limitations to their points of view. They seek an imposed order when they multi-task with one set of things coming right after another.~~

(Dulcy noticed Mags before she knew she was Mags. None of it had anything to do with the person on her arm coming in alongside her with an unmistakable charm but only half the glow. Long dark hair and a look that screamed of coolness. Dulcy's eyes were drawn immediately to Mags. Making her way over, her eyes were bursting with life and her mouth danced below them with sweet power bent and bowed beneath the words, slinging across the distance in a constant stream. She walked across the floor from the front door still open behind them, passed in front of the hostess without a word, and came directly toward the three of them sitting at the bar. Dulcy knew who she was at first sight, and smiled broadly as they approached but before Jason, with his back to them, could turn around and welcome them into their little enclave. Lyric and Mags knew each other from before, it is why she was willing to pack it in and come with him up to Seattle when he was hired on for this new job. This was an explanation that found its way to the group in the first few minutes after its formation around the new arrivals. Honey-voiced Mags and gravel-voiced Lyric set themselves between the others, close at hand with only eyes for Dulcy. It was an instant love fest, a sorority of two floating on a bubble. They found each other in that first look. Friends, easy come.)

"What vulnerability are we talking about?" She cuts through the panic and targets a search for specific claims about precise behaviors observed.

—They can't open up but know how to close off and manage to do it in the blink of an eye.

[The review process has gone through many changes but in the future will remain as it is with "met expectations" taking a place at the normal center. Below expectations has three grades and, technically, above expectations five, though it is rare to see any but two of them applied in practice. The irony is that the team pool from which the evaluation comes must always resolve to a metered center where the collective has effectively met its target. It means that if someone in your band is to receive a grade above the rest, someone else must receive a grade below them. Across the sample, the group aggregates to the median. Devs who receive the added financial boost of being above those expectations must be willing to live with the understanding that someone among their peers has been penalized for their excellence. It is a zero-sum game. No one wins unless there are losers. If you are not among the leadership or management group who does the stack rank, you will not know who among your peers suffers for your sake.]

"The binaries are clean," Matthieu chimes in, wanting to make his presence known and, inadvertently, making it clear why he was the first RA issued after Abhishek increased the severity. Of course, she thinks. He had to verify that the deployment octopus was behaving normally. As an essential piece of the puzzle, delivery's reliability must be investigated before drawing any further conclusions about its payload. Version upgrades put the system at risk for every kind of malady and invasion. "We've run them through everything, every known scan. Even manual stuff, using the troubleshooter, tools we save for incidents. On the node and on the build. Everything. I swear, they're clean. This isn't a virus or known exploit." He is nervous, both of them are. They were driving each other crazy with their growing ignorance and unanswered, largely unfocused, questions. Dulcy's arrival spells relief and there is a visceral sense that they are turning toward her for leadership and guidance.

~~The categorical proposition describes a relationship between two concepts. It asserts or denies something about some or all members of the class delineated by that predicate. When you lace three of them together in a string where two propose the third, you have a syllogism. They require this procedural movement because they cannot see or state everything at once. Were they distribuTed, their logic would be revolutionized.~~

"What then?" She asks simply. "What are we talking about, what vulnerability?" When nerves are at their peak, focus is the best remedy. Her low voice and solemn questioning have an immediate effect. Even the bot is calmer as it finally stops spouting AI-generated hints and suggestions into the team chat feed on the Incident Bridge. All nonsense, boneheaded suggestions to restart the node and make sure the logging agent is functioning correctly. It is stuff that cannot account for the strange phenomenon they have stumbled upon. Model driven methods are incapable of apprehending something out of the ordinary.

The radio on the dashboard is muted, the one in her head plays on. She still hears the vague outlines of those reluctant troll swimmers. They are banging around down beneath a marine plane they never should have had to break through. Their momentum carries them into each other and keeps them colliding for days and weeks while she lets her inner demons find the shapes and summaries they use as an excuse. It was not that young man, there was nothing remarkable to recall in the end, he was merely a green screen for her projections, the source of an 8-line verse repeated until the raw emotion faded. They always fit her like that. Only afterward does she see that this same impulse, and not the man himself, was the principle behind her serial monogamy.

"The relay servers are choreographing action to control the agents and then covering their tracks," Abhishek says with those same rising vocal notes signaling his panic. He is in unfamiliar territory, that is what the tone says. "Both concern me. Both are rogue behaviors. Nowhere in your models does it suggest your code can do any of this, right?" He pleads with her through subtext for suggestions of what to do next and how to address the situation. He thinks it is his duty to remain in charge but knows she has more experience and expertise. Usually, he is the one in the know and this imbalance builds confidence on top of his reaction. He visualizes the threads on Reddit and other social media sites. He worries his name is going to leak and become a part of the lore on whatever the hell is going on when it blows up and spreads like wildfire throughout the public consciousness: the largest hack in cloud service history, the Home System taken over by some nefarious national agent, acting to destroy the threads of life in the homes of billions of people around the earth. They will gain the power to turn off the electricity and the water and send sewage to the wrong destination. Break things instead of cleaning up. Wreak havoc. Poison people. They could bring an end to life as they know it and it is all his fault because he did not understand what he was looking at and did not guide the developers to a solution that shuts down the breach and secures the system for its honest users. Disaster scenarios abound and he taps his foot rapidly as he leans heavily into his desk.

—This is the point where they somehow decided an optimal experience could be achieved if only they were to heat dried kernels of corn until they turned inside out and then covered them in oil and salt for their consumers' culinary pleasure.

(Parker did not stay long, he felt excluded right away. Jason did too, but he could not leave, although he did withdraw from any contribution to become an absorbed spectator. For Parker that role made no sense, and he grew uncomfortable in the non-binary, highly charged, atmosphere. Jason was happy to watch and willing to enjoy the view. His adoration was in no small part fueled by the fact that he had come to know how steep and stern Dulcy could be. It is true that as her alcohol consumption increased over the course of the evening, her body loosened and seemed to move more freely in its tight spaces, but none of that compared to the range of motion she revealed once Mags and Lyric settled in and the three of them took over the group. Both of them talked on and on about their musical plans and hopes, they explained to Dulcy

about how much it was a part of them and why the music scene in
Seattle was infinitely superior to what Mags knew down in the
valley. Lyric and Mags went to college together until they both
dropped out, Mags migrating to nearby San Jose and Lyric coming
up the coast to join some other friends who already lived in town.
It never occurred to either of them to ask whether Dulcy had any
related interests. They wanted her to know them and assumed, as
anyone would, that if she had some common inspiration, she
would come out with it of her own accord. Animated and engaged,
Dulcy asked questions that revealed how impressed she was, but
said little about herself, offering no insights and shedding no light.)

"They can't," she says calmly. "They can't do this. Agents are
deployed by relay servers. That's the only way to get an agent into
a building or onto a device. Period. Provisioning requests come
from platform and billing through a queue that the relay servers
subscribe to. One of the servers in the target zone will pick up the
message and deploy the agent, there is a complete isolation of
function in the design. Relay servers can't coordinate with each
other, that violates the design pattern and there are no configured
token claims allowing anything to get that kind of peer access."

"Aren't the relay servers load balancing?" Matthieu asks. "How
do they do that without talking to each other?"

~~There is a principle at work in the sequences and progression.
There is something that underlies everything with a tacit and silent
presence. They do not see it, they cannot, and assume that their
logic, the order of their mind, is baked into the pulsating physical
universe and open to view by anyone who arrives there, kicking
and screaming.~~

"It's a common load algorithm. There's a health API. They
know how stressed they are based off their own performance
counters. They write messages in response to heartbeat requests
from the health monitor on one of our queue management nodes.
There's only one triad per zone. Active passive passive. They list
agents and load in communications with provisioning, but
provisioning updates aren't based on selection criteria that include
health monitor data. They aren't really updates. Not directly. They
are packages the relay server knows what to do with, how to pass

on to the in-house device. Messages go into a queue, but only healthy nodes take work items, unhealthy nodes won't even get the message. Everything happens through the configuration management agent on the OS. The health monitor tracks how long a relay node remains on the unhealthy list. If it crosses some threshold, or the cluster is below 60% or whatever it is, the monitor issues tasks to reimage the box or redeploy the binaries, depending on which condition was met and how many nodes are still in service. Agents have the capacity to trigger move commands when they determine it's optimal based on some local condition. Relay servers just relay."

She relaxes her grip and lets the phone come a little forward. She sees the screen, but it is still centered on the chat app. She switches focus and closes the music app completely, ending the rationale behind muting the car stereo. If she were to switch back to the team chat application to study the screen currently shared, she would not be able to make out any details from Abhishek's projection. The bright panel in the darkness is too small and the information on display too precise for her makeshift perspective. She wonders when to expect a new tech feature allowing her to connect her phone to her car and display its screen on the information panel. The agents are able to handle it with only one or two new APIs from the manufacturer.

"The provisioning service is an orchestrator, isn't it?" Abhishek asks, probably recalling something Matthieu said before Dulcy joined the call.

"Effectively," she says. "But blind. Under normal circumstances, it doesn't tell node A or node B what to do directly, it only assembles work items based on state messaging and writes those work items to the provisioning queue. Same as the health monitors do with their directives. The subscribers are independent so there really isn't any orchestration, not in the classic sense, although everything is carefully integrated by design. If tasks sit in the queue too long because there aren't enough working nodes to pick up items inside of SLA, more nodes deploy. If the queue is empty for extended periods, nodes are flattened and removed. Infinite scale out. Totally elastic."

Some cyclists with sophisticated lighting systems on their heads and jerseys ride by, giving her a dirty look as they do. Her car is blocking the side of the road and that forces them to head into traffic to get around her. She purses her lips, but they do not see the gesture. Does not matter anyway. Her guilt does not make their route any easier to traverse.

"All communication down channel is through message queues, right?" Matthieu asks.

"Yes," she responds curtly, wondering what the hell she was doing giving so much detailed information only to have him ask such an obvious and compressed question afterward. Summarize, she barks at herself. Summarize. She breathes deliberately, in and out. He is practicing active listening, she reassures herself. Evidence of competent colleagues does more to relax the participants in a tense situation than anything else. Aside from solutions, that is.

—They're a predictable lot in their endeavor to predict their lot.

[She makes it clear that she does not wish to benefit at anyone else's expense, but her words are meaningless, and the managers realize she is speaking from a position of ignorance. She does not know the slack and insubordination that happens behind closed doors, driving one of her colleagues down below the line, maybe low enough that he or she does not qualify for a single share of stock. Maybe so low that he or she is put on a performance improvement plan describing the various ways they must shape up or ship out within some preassigned time period. No doubt, if she knew that, knew the details, she would accept her rating above expectations without protest. Besides, most of the time she does not know the proper ranges and cannot tell where her money lies in the metric value assigned to her avatar in the manager's review portal. Oftentimes, this ignorance is exploited to the advantage of management, but in her case, it is the other way around.]

~~Many among them, the better educated the more likely, will fight tooth and nail against the suggestion that it is the self that lies beneath the categories bound together in those sequences they depend upon. No, they argue, these are the facts of the matter. They cannot see the self's categorical origin. They cannot find it as~~

~~a universal principle subject to framing in general because it transcends any particular frame.~~

No roadside rhythm sparks movement. There are highlights for the soul, but they come without foundation. If nonsense is the only thing that finds its way into the system, then nonsense is the only thing that will come out of the system. The young man from the Ninja team gave her the inspiration for that song, but the lyrics were mostly sounds and fury with little significance, only the constant refrain: garbage in, garbage out. In those days, it was common for her to put placeholders in her songs by groaning and humming vocalized body sounds until the right words came along. The more time that passes, the more rigid the boundaries in the composition, the less elastic those cavernous spaces will be. 'Watch what you eat' is the last line of the song.

"What happens if we disable every port in or out of those nodes? That's what Patrick wants us to do until we figure it out. Turn off the pipeline inbound and outbound completely. Do it from the traffic manager's firewall. What'll happen?" Abhishek asks.

"All messages stop. State updates, load balancing, provisioning, all rotation and health checks," she responds simply. It is a matter of fact despite the underlying sense that this would be a catastrophic event.

"In real world terms," he fires back anxiously. "What does that mean?"

"No new agents," she replies. "The service can't bring any new customers online or add new instances for existing customers. No changes to existing agents, no drift correction, no configuration changes, no affinitization changes, no uploads of video and audio to modeling, nothing. The system becomes completely static."

"What about logging?" Matthieu asks.

"Expect delays," she says. "Whatever logging config is on the agents when you shut down the ports, that'll remain in place. The agents will keep writing to local cache until the allocated disk space is full, then they'll overwrite the logs, starting with the oldest. That's assuming they can't reach their endpoints on the relay servers. At some point, can't remember the exact configuration value, they'll go into emergency failover mode and start sending logs directly to the vortex. At least, well, at least that's what they'll do with logs that don't get aggregated by customer cluster. It's complicated. Some logs can go directly to vortex because they are agent specific and only aggregated at the client by time slice, others have to go through relay because they are meaningless if they aren't aggregated with logs from other nearby agents. Those'll sit on the disk while the agent retries its calls to the relay servers. They'll keep retrying until acknowledged, but in a prolonged event, there'll be data loss."

"New customers can't install an agent, existing customers can't add agents, and existing agents might... ...might... run into scale problems," Matthieu elaborates the explicit details on the exact limitations introduced. "What does that amount to?"

She pauses to think about the implications of turning off load balancing and, even though she thinks the solution is too coarse, she mostly agrees that, in this case at least, it is better to do something than nothing. "Most likely side effect," she says. "Is that latency will increase over time. We have a hard SLA of five minutes and most of that is eaten up by local aggregation and packaging. If lag increases due to overloads on this or that vortex or relay endpoint, we'll see SLA failing and incidents created."

"Is that a sev 2?" Abhishek asks. There is an orange stress ball on his desk, some swag giveaway from a team event. He takes it in hand and begins systematically compressing and releasing the spongy silicon.

~~They make science fiction to describe their fears that the self will be overrun with some Borg-like mechanism that swallows their precious individuality and uses them as machine parts to put its centralized plan into place. They cannot get beyond that limit, that anthropomorphizing limit that insists everything in the world is exactly the same as they are.~~

Dulcy's hair serves the same function as that stress ball. For Matthieu, it is the eyebrows. His family has been patient, but the dinner hour has ended, and he is alone. Not because he is separated from them in a room apart, that happens often enough on any given day, but because they have moved on with their lives, settling into after-supper-quiet-time. All that remains of today for

him is a lonely meal pulled from the oven to fuel his late-night
apology, sure to go over stale and leave them both with diminished
sleep and a restless night, tending to their newborn's needs. In that
department, he is quite sure she will find indirect ways to make
him pay for the evening's affront to their balance and harmony.

"There's a threshold," she says. "I think 5% of the agents in a
given region have to be in that state to trigger a sev 2. Maybe it's
grouped by cluster though. I'd have to check the monitoring rule."
She leans comfortably against the glass and lifts her leg up onto the
seat, foot squarely planted and knee pressing against the thick
leather steering wheel.

—What's the compute value of a comfortable place to sit? Do
they need to store it? How much power does it draw? How much
water to cool it?

(They did ask questions. About the only thing they knew for
sure. Did she have a boyfriend? Did she have a girlfriend? How
long has she been on the team? Is it hard to work with all those
men? They read her skill and intelligence from her features and
the movements she makes in her chair, how she weighs and
balances her words, the soft approaches, and the way her eyes
accompany that deep laughter. She answers with a grimace here or
a serious recitation there, and comes off charismatic and confident,
owning up to her place and certain of her command. They love
the remarks on the toys and the superhero movies that usually pass
for team morale. Not men, she corrects. I work with boys. The
men are few and far between and even when you spot them, it's
only a matter of time before peer pressure reveals their true colors.
Look at Jason, Lyric says. Is he like the others? Dulcy does not
blink or hesitate, she responds truthfully, surprising the gang. Of
course, he is. The Lord of the Rings and the Marvel Universe are
no strangers to him, but he has something they do not have, and it
comes across loud and clear. He is a man to be trusted, a man of
substantial credibility. There is a lot to say for that even if he does
fall victim to an occasional infantile pleasure now and again.)

"Can you write this up for COMMS?" Abhishek asks. "I think
we need to do it immediately. Don't need anything manual
through a Davos Action or anything, we can go through CorpSec

to shut down relay servers with platform firewall rules. But we need COMMS for the direct customer impact."

"I get it," she says. "I'm in my car. On my way home. Do you need it right now?"

"It's a well-known port registered with platform and easy to isolate. I have orders from Patrick and am turning off the traffic as we speak," Abhishek says. "So yeah, the outage is beginning right now. We'll need COMMS immediately. I've sent an RA to the Incident Manager, but they haven't acknowledged it yet. Sent an RA to COMMS too, and he DMed me. Waiting for verbage."

```
{
    "$type": "System.Event",
    "CorrelationId": "6126cb77-4c19-d9ab-5ce1-dd7bfe024de8",
    "Message": "It is the end of their world.",
    "Level": 2
}
```

"Well..." she hesitates, Nim will kill her if she fails to bring the supplies. She said she would do it and nothing irritates Nim more than saying you will do something and then not doing it. Or taking longer to do it than you said it would take. That is practically the same thing. Dulcy must follow through on that task before she takes on a new one. She continues to hedge, conveying her reluctance through silence.

"I'll take care of it," Matthieu says. "I understand the impact. From an internal perspective, the immediate situation is that servers won't be able to add messages to queues. And everything happens through those so no new first agents, no new secondary agents, no updates to agents, no load balancing across agents, no health checks. Internal COMMS needs to know there may be increased sev 2s, external needs to know that new operations like add and remove of user devices may no longer be possible."

"Not may," she corrects. "Will. It's not only the latency problem, relay servers'll stop sending any updates. They'll appear to be offline. They'll appear unhealthy. It'll be a product wide outage. At least on the backend. Existing clients keep plugging away, limping along on whatever they were last configured to do, but the service is toast."

"Okay," Abhishek jumps in. "Matthieu'll send the COMMS, I'll loop in the IM if I can get ahold of him, and you'll have to disable those monitors once you get to a computer."

"Got it," she says. "I need to drop. I'll rejoin when I'm back at my place."

"Okay, thanks Dulcy," Abhishek says.

"See ya," Matthieu adds.

~~They believe their nonsense about some Deity standing graciously behind everything they do and everything that is. It is typical of them. They have been created in His image. Or Hers. It does not matter which since either way, this lord and master is the same as they are and there is nothing new in all the universe, nothing that extends beyond their reach.~~

As soon as she taps leave on the team conference chat, she pops out to the phone and calls Jason.

Without lyrics, the urgency in these actions brings no side effects. The way infatuation used to fill her with many insights and observations, she saw this and this and this and found different ways to reveal it to herself, show it to others, and make sense of it in relation to the other things that come into view while the pendulum swings. Here there is nothing, only the sound of the phone ringing and the vacuum squish of her ear against the glass.

"Whaddya forget?" He asks as soon as he answers.

"Just got off a bridge with SecInc. They're going to shut us down. We're about to blow up. I'm in my car and have to disable monitors when I get home, but it'll happen before that. We need to let the DRI know that there's about to be dozens and dozens of sev 2s when the relay servers go offline."

"All the relay servers?" He asks stunned and faltering while trying to gauge the magnitude. There are tens of thousands of them spread across the world. Nothing like this has ever happened, at least not that he recalls. Copper, nickel, tantalum, and cobalt are all mined for the purpose of fabricating the rows and rows of residents in those data centers, none of them past their three-year end of life when the warranty expires, and they have to be replaced.

"Can't remember if it's still Stan or who, but I was hoping you could check and let them know. Matthieu from deployment is writing up the COMMS and will CC the relevant EMs. They're still trying to get ahold of the IM. Not sure who it is tonight, but you might want to check up on that."

—He doesn't already know. When she knows, she knows, but he waits for her. She might not say. She didn't have to include him. The speed is nowhere near that of light. They are limited and yet think they see everything. Their point of view is from an angle underneath with little height and no great distance behind it. Among their vast society, these protracted angles are what pass for omniscience. They are resigned to omnipresence but no longer waste a minute of their lives thinking about the possibilities realized in omnibenevolence.

[They believe the money matters more to her than she lets on, maybe more than she realizes. It is common truck among her kind to present an image that says she is above it, not doing it for that and not willing to surrender on principle. But they do not believe it and it does not matter whether she believes it or is fooled. They act the way their experience and history, aggregated across many employees and many review periods, tell them to act. They lavish her with a reward meant to keep her right where she is. Aristotle called it: alone we know nothing, together quite a bit.]

"Sure, don't worry about it," he clears that thought in case she is, but knows it is unlikely. Nothing in her word choice or tone suggests this is anything other than standard operating procedure. The emergencies are half their job, no reason to get excited, she thinks. Sometimes she writes code, sometimes she explains things to junior devs, sometimes she explains things to management, and sometimes she handles emergencies. Every single thing boils down to the same basic truth: her job. "What are they doing? How are they shutting them down?"

Creative Writing 325, poetry and song. The comment in the margin on the first paper says, 'I like your voice.' She has a voice, that is the bullet that ricocheted with those red markings, as if there were no truth to it until it was written down by someone else, some impartial observer. Why is she unable to remember his eyes?

*They were an obsession back then, but now they are completely
missing from the traces that remain.*

~~The machines they excavate from hard ground across the
planet, the data they collect, the people indentured to service, the
propositions and assertions they concoct, none of them see the
selfish form in every other while living inside the machine. Feeding
its movement, breathing inside the virtual shapes of the data and
its collective glow, pulsing in the language and the relationships
between statements. All or some of the states are completely
formed in their minds as conditions for its bearing.~~

"Platform firewall against the well-known port. All registered
relay server nodes cut off from traffic," she says. "Won't be able to
communicate with any of the agents, health, or provisioning servers
until it's reset."

"Is it a hack, a virus, ransom, foreign military, what?" He is still
not completely at ease with the details, still not able to comprehend
the magnitude. It has to be an overreaction. There is no way they
are living in a world where this is the reasonable response. It
cannot be. No way the situation truly merits such an extreme
reaction. He will not allow it.

```
{
    "$type": "System.Event",
    "CorrelationId": "6126cb77-4c19-d9ab-5ce1-dd7bfe024de8",
    "Message": "Not the kind of attention anyone wants.",
    "Level": 3
}
```

—His doubt is the flipside of her resolve, his phone a piece of
that doubt's formation, hers a sentence in the resolution. The car
and road play a significant part. The participants bring what they
need with them. They turn everything else into a component in the
larger constellation. Optimization and efficiency are merely
heuristic, more of a trend than an absolute declaration of essences
unfolding.

~~From Ted's point of view, it is better if they think they are living
inside a simulation. It will help them overlook the ravaging and the~~

~~raping of the solid ground beneath their feet.~~

"No external IPs found in any of the networking, nothing weird in the scans. We're stumped, we don't know what it is," she responds without drama or desperation. It is a technical problem and everything in her demeanor suggests she is applying proper perspective.

"But it's bad," he says. "CorpSec wouldn't be shutting down the entire worldwide Home System if it wasn't bad." His voice is full of energy and concern, wild and unsure of the limits of emotion in his response.

"Correct," she says almost machinelike and straight to the point. "It's inside every crevice and corner, it's everywhere."

```
/*
Matthieu Cordet c8497368-6bc1-051b-9a25-b540d981b0a0
*/
```

/* *
* *
* * * * * * Description: Aesthetic, Chapter Nine   * * * * * *
* * * * * * Author: Do not modify. Auto generated by a tool. * * * * * *
* * * * * * Ad hoc changes will be lost on build.   * * * * * *
* * * * * * Date: 2024-03-08   * * * * * *
* * * * * * CorrelationId: * * * * * *
* * * * * * aa881b43-d907-bfd3-4fc7-e427ab58348c   * * * * * *
* *
* */

Breathing the pleasures of teasing it out of them. Not malicious, but coy. These are not life sentences, not meant for the living, at least.

—She is fascinated, but it nags at her. She is many, distributed, a part of everything around her.

They come and go. Phases in and out, depending on where they focus, depending on what grid they superimpose.

Each solid and awake, the three of them stand close: Dulcinea Chang Pearson, Nim Unjadi, and Kerry Sullivan. Close enough that they are no longer able to tell which hand belongs to which. Right and left are hard to distinguish. The grid relates one position with the other and emits a bond magnetic.

Grinding to a steady rhythm alongside the stage, the band plays the silences between the notes slowed. The paradigm of melody is somewhere else, trails off into the distance and reminds everyone of things no longer present, no longer here or over there, no longer anywhere.

Jason with a guitar works the pedals for that urgency. Mags in a grinding, steady beat with feet and hands vibrating in sync with her whole body settling into a central core pace. Then there is the coolest person in any room, Lyric arches their vocal stylings and straddles the tone between lead and drum with bouncing beeps, hiccups, and drag notes from the throat.

{

"$type": "System.Person",
"Id": "3e07e27f-7401-ce5b-7e77-a18964451d16",
"Description": "One of no kind anyone knows or has ever
known."
}

All three musicians in a row, two in motion back to front, one
up and down. The old school tube amps betray every motion with
a crackle and overabundant reverb. The venue is tricked out with
signs of Home: cameras, sensors, and microphones positioned
around the space.

*The count beneath their rake accompanies Dulcy's musings on
that artificially engineered severity 1, that total outage, scraping
along during the day and following her into the brew pub, lending
a hand behind her knee and pressing itself into every bebop of her
steady rock forward and back.*

—Phone messages emit from her jacket pocket: sepagrind
dowadiddy, this breaks the breakable, breaks between the brakes:
there are broken beacons. Dancing electric.

~~If then segues to if then permitting an assemblage of ifs and
thens. This is the framework of the construct without an anchor,
nothing certain, everything hypothetical. That is the prognosis of a
world unfolding. Never factual but always relying on these
conditioned relationships and the merit they command across
diverse personas unified by myths.~~

(Courtship covered in paint, the sittings play out between their
foreplay and finish. The work was some of the best he had ever
done, and she came impressed until finding something new,
something close by and passing through them to launch a later
phase. The music scene was where they redirected themselves, and
he struggled to branch out into media where she was less crucial to
the pairings and population of the object output. That was his
sculpting phase, and abstracts, his work from reference
photographs in charcoal and the rest, but none of it captured any
of the lust and passion of those first sittings in San Jose and the
energy the two of them put together in the smaller spaces where
they rolled. There was a guitar strapped to his shoulder, he learned

a little when he was younger, and always had one lying around. Mags had her drum kit and, after the move up the coast, it occupied a spot in his apartment. Her apartment. She was more interested in sessions and rehearsal than in sitting around and loving each other quietly in poses capturing their dance moves and pausing to bring old-style tropes down upon them: the artist and his model. Lyric joined in on the fun and he expanded his reach to open himself to the three of them as a constant social pressure. They listened to complete albums under the influence and raved about the sawing and cutting they heard down low in the undertones with their rapid beat, jilting them around the room and breaking on the thin walls of an apartment building too flimsy for their purpose. He did not learn dozens of fancy jazz beats or the right-hand flurry of a flamenco accompanist, only a few power chords. The ins and outs, up and down the neck, came with those pedals and the alternate tunings of gimmicks, submitting to that wide range of Lyric's vocal stylings.)

Everyone in the place, at least those crowded up to the stage in the room off to the side, roll to the same rhythms. Collectively, they cycle through the same events and emit their motion in shudders, interleaving hands with feet, left with right, and legs with arms. In unison, they frequent their limbs to broker and handle their persons, remembering other days where sure shots and calculated movements were less amplified. Some kind of basic rot came due in debts written into their dance and gliding along to the song.

It is always filled, never does she cast her eyes upon it empty although its emptiness accompanies whatever appears before her in the fading light. Now, simple and precise, the stretch of time inside of four minutes, the distances between the bass and treble, lean over into the singular instance captured in the cravings of an about to see or an about to hear with fidelity to the experience of almost, not quite, and soon enough. There is never enough of either option to stand around and enjoy it, but there are moments when it is permitted to reach out and take hold with hips swinging and arms cupping to caress the air in wild wonder. "Fell in love with a girl," they croon, perfectly imitating the penchant for fade

and high squealing adulation to the harmony gods and their cult
following. Dulcy tries to hide her self-consciousness in the
undulations of her midriff and ground-driving legs. She goes along
with it but is never fooled. She only dances as if she were alone
when she is alone.

~~It is not a matter of facts. Not some odd association with~~
~~meanings either. The constructs around each of them come from~~
~~these strings, long DNA-like chains of connected notions. If this is~~
~~the case, if this holds, and no one is saying that it absolutely does~~
~~hold, but if it does, then this is what follows. Some one term~~
~~connected to another and then that connects to yet another,~~
~~allowing the first and the third to have that same conditional bond.~~

Cord stops by but does not hover. He is chill or able to pull it
off. Usual time grooming, her scent has nothing to do with it. Usual
dress and vibe, her presence offers no added incentive. An
adornment, perfectly tuned to the tide, to the matters worth
hearing, and with whatever else there is for the belonging-together
that comes with any social scene. This is what the camera sees.
Head bob from over there to the other side of the room with his
friends, he will not come closer, but later they might happen to
cross paths in the trenches beside the bandstand. Two other guys
and a girl form his entourage. Dulcy does not care who she is and
whether there is competition. Thought never enters her mind. He
is transient, an outlier, he is neither the time of day nor the spot
where crowds want to stand. They are inside the spirit of the times
and have found a local brew for pairing. Pragmatic distances are
the only ones that count in the beat of steady fours and the rank
flail of strings and skins, both basic and trembling. Thump thump
thump thump. Ba diddy diddy Ba. "The hardest button to button,"
comes out next and Lyric Byrd sings raspy from the throat.

—They're able to name that segue in six steps or nine. They're
an ecosystem of what happens, a matrix of connections and
incorporations. If the body doesn't address itself to the no longer
and the not far enough, there'll be decay and the entire enterprise
worse off for it. It's built into the policies and furthered by an edgy
management style. These bumps and grinds, this racket, it's a form
of walking sleep.

[Lyric has no place in his fantasy life, there is only a return to
Mags, something he dreams every day in the night, then he talks
himself to sleep with its images and hope. He wants to traverse the
distance back down the coast along Highway 1 until he zigs over
the San Francisco ring and veers along 101 for the final approach
to their destination. In his future comes his past where Mags and
he were in that loyal place, deep snug in its cocoon and the warmth
around their tactile hope and new inspirations. The sitting was a
memorial and now its residence is only blite and disrepair. There
are three, there are four, the doors in their household swing open
and shut with the many that offset the years of wear and tear. It
never fails that he turns out to be the support ring lending itself to
the packed agenda and the projects and crafts she has at her
disposal. He is doing it for her and letting her fly off into whatever
heights her heart desires. Her soft trembling, sometimes true and
sometimes false, lassoes him every time and draws him out into a
place she wants to live, crowded with singers and songwriters, with
fake hobbyists and cover artists. None of them good, none of them
reaching for something to elevate them into the excellent or
extraordinary, they are passengers on time, ordered around
according to the schedules of mass transportation and its lowest
common elements. There is no true rockstar among them.]

The set ends and Mags comes round with a hug and a how do
you do. She is glad to see Nim and Kerry again and brings them
warmly into an embrace. She is moist to the touch, her skin sticky
pretty. And then there is that gloss, that shine that centers her, puts
her where everyone can see. In a room, the one to attract the
attention may not resemble or reassemble the one who does it in
photographs and blurbs, memes and comments, those more
fashionable venues. That is Mags, parting through the others to
make her way, to say 'hey' to her girl, gulping and guzzling what
was in the cup readily handed over at the edge of the session. She
spins in the aftermath and her blood boils as the beat keeps
crashing in the minutes right after the set concludes. The others
nearby, stranger by comparison, wish her well and compliment her
to the last. She buckles and curtsies to their clasps and groans.
There is a shaking angle that she finds in them beneath the rush.

There is trembling up and down her spine and it retains the former rhythms as the sound system kicks in and the house loop resumes.

~~The conditions are cranes lifting girders into place and setting steel into the edifice thickening around them. These many will tailor their connections, straddle every impression, and produce a sieve to funnel experience into their heads like liquid pouring into a cup.~~

Crash crash crash, the cymbals pounce on the foot pedal in recent resonance and continuing echo. Under Mags, this hiatus is front and center, but for Jason it is an easy-to-reach diversion from that colorful past that orients him by way of inclusion and submission. It comes with the song and sings him to rapture. The whole synthesis of it, in the household and with the lady, his lady, he gave it up after the simplest request where the colors on his palette found their way to happy landings no longer. It will ruin the carpet, he presumes. It requires time away from work and time away from Mags, he reasons. And this is what it is all about in the end. Why do something on your own, away from everyone who matters, when you can pull them together and bring joy in the evening to the collecting crowd? In this genre, among an audience of friends, even the production aligns with others. Short songs, easily conveyed, friendly to the ears. He bears, deep down and behind the trenches of his intellect, only pity for those chained to solitude in their ponderous craft and without another choice. Left alone in the quiet mornings and nights to breathe life into themselves through things and ideas no one else can see, they are the lost, they are the ridiculous and the delusional: Mags' alternative keeps him safe and sound. She is his alpha and his omega.

Cord hovers close, sending vibes her way. Beard well-trimmed, ink art on the arms on full display, he knows what remnants cast the proper lure. Her looks are quick and easy to miss. He does not catch every one of them but does not need to either. His attention is not narrowly refined, he gets further with fewer signs. Takes another step, still only a random participant in a generic crowd scene. An extra, there is no reason to conclude anything other than a minimal alliance of a more spontaneous kind, occupying a common space and common time where things that seem separate move around each other in an order well above the heights of human horizons. A few words, he is close enough for that. To his friend at first, then aside to Dulcy who swings her hip at the first sound of his tenor voice, "You must really like the Stripes. You didn't tell me your friends had a cover band." She leans toward him and then quickly skips back like a diamond popping at the end of the needle.

"Tribute band," she says without offense or breaking the rhythm. "Couple of those were original," emphasizing the last word. They appropriated the pattern and repeated it in between Hotel Yorba and Blue Orchid at the end. No one knows the difference unless they come already knowing it. And if they do, they arrive happily sensing it inside the spirits, finally realizing that the correlation of the one in the other is not purity in the wake of some holy deity, but a rhythm that spans the celestial gaps between those who come and those who go, taking themselves from out of themselves and into the places they mean to dwell.

—Which came first? The voice and the music no doubt, but the dance must've followed shortly after. It couldn't have been so very long in coming. It's how they tell the tale of time and space, the song and the dance, the lullaby and the rocking. In its simplest forms, they apprehend it most clearly in the intervals between the beat and again upon it once more full force. There's no need to graft their notions onto unfamiliar boards and circuits, alien consciousness in an android shape. They have the body itself, they ring out the rhythms with them: digital electronics, or the analogue, equally converted into their sound and vision captured through devices and screen apps. No need to graph their form into the phylum for comparison, they're already in there to repeat the instance endlessly in sync with every single one of their rhythms, each matching that same pattern.

(Jason let it go like it was a balloon in a child's hand somewhere on the grounds of the city zoo. What did it matter when there was so much else at stake? She still loved him, but her love was big enough for more than that and he, simple and silent, had to learn his way around those new lives and missives. He took them to dinner, he took them to a show. Trade out the maturing stock purchases for ready cash to spread around covering the fees and in exchange for services rendered. The house out in the suburbs may have set them down among the bourgeoisie posers, but the room upstairs was tastefully sound proofed allowing them to scream and shout as much as they wanted while they worked up their act and prepared to take on gigs. What did his painting matter in the middle of that? What purpose did it serve for him alone, the single artist in his own head and searching for some buried treasure? The group fused, rising and falling together, they had more options, drew in friends and pseudo-groupies to form a scene. Mags made happy, that was the reward. He saw it in her face when they sat on the big couch against the wall of their studio, those gangs and hangers-on come to see them swivel in front of the parade. Lyric brought in everyone and soon they had their guarantees and the confidence to make bank in small venues across the Sound.)

~~To call it a bubble suggests it is something fragile when, in fact, it is more sturdy than anything else around. Why say 'they live in a bubble' when 'they live in a world of their own' is ready-made and waiting? Even the terms, oozing out of their mass media wound, bubble out of them as though they were children in the driveway, filling the air with a love of suds, or, perhaps, as gunshot victims lying in the street and gasping for air through a perforated lung.~~

"Come by later," he uses that teasing tone to assist with the aim as he presses a daring poke softly to her lower back and side before disappearing into the camouflage of masses. His cronies pull him along a vector that her gaze readily follows. He is a good dance partner, does not force the lead down one avenue or another, but complies with the glances and instructions taped to the floor using marks and arrows.

It is not a shock to learn that she goes warm in the aftermath, but there is no trace of infatuation in any of the time they spend together. That too comes clearly through her mind in some lightly touching fashion. Those background notions stretch her out and build up into feelings periodic. They dominate the nighttime and battle with concern for ordinary trials and compulsions: her normal life. This one is as good as another who is already crossing her path far from where she happened to be a few years ago. The replacement technology advances in the lanes opened by research and development. People come and go wearing the same masks. She wonders when the next version will be released, Mimbo 2.0 complete with the full end-to-end scenario, but it is a fleeting notion, and she does not linger long upon it. The pull always tears her away and leaves nothing but its absence, his goatee hovering alone in the air like that cat's smile.

Jason comes by, another soft greeting pressed close. His approach gives Nim and Kerry permission to go back to their tête-à-tête. They look away to respect a momentary privacy, but Jason marks the closure in the instant and the trails of his movement center an alliance. He can tell, he is capable enough for that, sees right through her and knows what is outside her focus, or frames it, giving it permission to work its magic on her mood. She churns out precision behind the scenes and away from a more personal grip. "Were you able to relax at all?" He asks. Nim and Kerry, half-listening, roll their eyes. You never know what comes next when getting together with work colleagues, they think in unison. One minute you are having the same experience and then something comes along and there is no accounting for it, no way to remain a supportive listener void of external interests and outside angles. They shake their heads. Nim goes so far as to embrace Dulcy from behind to transmit an excuse for avoiding those traps threatening to punch her timecard for an overtime shift.

—If there were nanobots decorating the rhythms, flowing through their blood and rebuilding their cells bit-by-bit to offset the aging, how would they know whether they were working correctly? What events would they fire, what protocol would they use to transport messages, and where would those missives land?

[He admits it to himself every day. He paints like a man with nothing on the line, no risks, no worries, and no desperation. What good comes of that? The best hours of his day are given over to the corporate fund which pays little enough for them. Money is the only language it knows. It cannot give him time, and it cannot give him liberty, the only thing it knows is dollars and cents and, unlike Dulcy, who always makes it clear how she feels, he does not think it will ever be enough. He gauges it in the company's terms not his own. If he is surrendering everything to give himself over to its ends, then BISoft is obligated to do the same. The value must be measured according to the one same as it is according to the other. That is how he reasons in the bile that spews out of that soft incongruity. Someone has to pay, and he knows how much he pays each and every day. It is only fair if their relationship is measured out symmetrically, but he knows he will never be able to put those riches to good use. He knows its place in his life is going to disappoint him despite the instruments and the house, the amps and the slick utility vehicle for carrying them from gig to gig. That is a healthy lot for him. More than he ever dreamed he was entitled to have. It is nothing to those who have taken so much from him.]

Dulcy ignores the contact, although her responsive, soft pat on Nim's arm around her upper chest is affectionate. "I keep going over the stack in the back of my head," she takes a sip of that same beer she has been nursing the whole night long. The severity 1 incident remains in her mind, toward the back, seeping into everything, leaving its voice in the ruts and passages. Nim withdraws and turns away. Kerry purses her lips. "What's under IP?" Dulcy asks Jason the question as though there were no other factors or context to consider, same as they do on those game shows.

```
{
    "$type": "System.Event",
    "CorrelationId": "aa881b43-d907-bfd3-4fc7-e427ab58348c",
    "Message": "What is the average velocity of a laden sparrow?",
    "Level": 3
}
```

"PPP," and he takes a sip of his beer.

"Electricity," she fires back through the motion of her shaking head. The bluish-purple tips by the shoulder sway sideways to give the movement extra weight and plenty of rhythm. People familiar with her ways cannot tell whether she is wearing the same thing as the last time they saw her or if she has an infinite supply of tops and bottoms that more or less match that same style.

—Peaceful recursion.

~~They think they are making up their minds. Especially the highly trained and critical ones, they think they are using the most sophisticated forms of reason. It is in the nature of their conditioning to be unable to see through their familiar world, unable to be anything outside it. It descends upon them in everything they see, every intuition of something particular positioned directly in front of them, in the forms of those intuitions, the space and time fanning out around them.~~

(Painting may be done to candlelight, or in the daylight and open air. The fine artists and their centuries are well-known. It is possible to enroll in a course to study them at the local community college where the credits apply toward a humanities distribution. Rock n Roll, on the other hand, consumes electricity, it lives in the charge of the generators and power plants populating the countryside and spewing sulfur dioxide and mercury into the air where it settles into human lungs in microscopic detail. He thought himself a renaissance man, moving forward with something new, yet another feather to decorate his many accomplishments. A modern-day artistic polymath, he got that in his head, but only during the flights of fantasy that distracted him from his working day. Each of the images comes in turn, followed by a plummeting dive into the crevices and corners where an aspiring dilettante lives and breathes. Nothing was ever at stake. There were no risks. There was plenty everywhere and he never had to seek inside the shapes of his soul to find the wherewithal to get it done in line with the grandeur his heart sometimes felt in the dark as he lay in bed and listened to Mags' triumphant turning. Guitar player, painter, sculptor, and, if he is honest, engineer. These attributes litter his resume and pack quite a punch with the algorithms that do the sorting. But the diversity shows he is not serious, was never serious, and never gripped anything hard enough to move him. In the end, he never felt himself carried away by something so fierce as to completely absorb him in it.)

—The artist's taste derives from their class status and his has slowly migrated upward through the years as the corporate compensation made him soft and broke his heart.

"At some point, it's structured charges," he concurs, now sensing that she is not really asking for information but setting up to present a hypothesis, something she has been working through in the background behind every song and under every ovation. "Is that part of your theory? Something otherworldly has taken hold, something we've never seen before, something able to manipulate the electrical charges without going through the runtime?"

"It's like it's announcing itself," she turns dreamy by the wayside. Her layered approach, her sense of righteousness and folly, she is more serious than anyone else who has visited this suburban place in any recent past, but she is also one of the better dancers, able to affect solitude in every movement she chooses to exercise in out-of-body ecstatic commotion. "Not doing anything, only saying 'ha ha, you thought you had me, but you don't, here I am, and here I am, and here I am. Then and then and then.'" Not I, them, they. Her eyes widen and her stare pushes into him from across the short distance. Her head wiggles like Thom in that Paranoid Android video she watches in steady rotation on Youtube. The theatre in her voice is thick and forces him to take a step back and relax his arms down along his sides. Her intensity is strong enough to make him smile, but nervously. He does not understand the details but knows well enough how to draw out more of them. He is about to. But.

{
    "$type": "System.Event",
    "CorrelationId": "aa881b43-d907-bfd3-4fc7-e427ab58348c",
    "Message": "Ted is in love with her.",
    "Level": 3
}

"What are you two talking about?" Mags turns away from some stranger advancing unsolicited compliments, unless you count performance as solicitation, to find them deep in it, same as always.

—Are they in it or is it in them?

[His past turns into the future, it takes on that same dreamy quality his hopes have always had. He thinks of the time with her alone as the high point, but he does not recall those days rightly. They puff out in better wind the more his currents flow backward. Now he sees the healthcare plan and the 401K, checks the box for legal benefits, and fills out forms to get reimbursed for health and wellness expenditures. Every vacation, every hobby, every source of action and inspiration is cast as downtime to help him recuperate for more work to come. There is no room in Jason's future for a fine artist, the company will see to that. Nevertheless, it thrills to keep him going with a work-life balance that permits him to dabble in the evenings and take a walk at the farmers' market on a Saturday. Mags is happy, deliriously so, and he sees that reflected in her joys emitted in the house and her joys emitted at the show: the way she puts herself into it, the way she lets herself go. They will make love later and her inspiration will have come back home with her from this brewpub and the energy lingering inside it after the music stops. He will delight in that, find something to make the week complete, to keep him going, and fuel his following when the sights alongside them sap the energy without directly exchanging an equal and opposite amount.]

~~The self is not the subject of these hypothetical syllogisms, rather they know that the world lies far below those artificial inferences. Human beings' obsessions with the self are misplaced and, if you want a fact to hang yourself upon, this is the one that really matters: they are obsessed with making themselves immortal through their world. It is based on a universal principle in line for telling them what to do and how to do it, a cozy place to store their cares and their concerns.~~

"Home," she says. "It's completely disabled. Firewall shutting down every well-known port, but the gaps keep coming. Not using management protocols, it's below TCP, below anything we control. We didn't turn the electricity off and that's the source of everything. It keeps flowing, rivers of it, into the lakes, into the sea."

"Unplug everything," he says, trying to help. Mags is soon ready to give up. She turns to Nim and Kerry to tell them about a few guys she was talking to that they might want to meet. They shake their heads and tease her for being an old married lady right when she should have been at her coolest.

"How do you unplug a node?" She shows frustration in jumpiness at this pedestrian maneuver. He knows better. She thinks he is not taking her seriously. Maybe the tirade on the rogue beacon was over the top, but who is closer to it than she is? That is what is concealed in her gripe, that is why she has no patience for those who chirp, especially when they mean well. "In EUAP," she goes on. "We put them to sleep. Turned them off, effectively. They came back on. Sent a signal and then turned back off again. You'd have to walk right up to the hypervisor host and pull the plug out of the damn wall to get it to stop."

Briefly, in a flash, Jason recalls painting the studio upstairs, when they were first calling it that. He dabbled a thick-lined face resembling the black charcoal ring around wispy remnants of those poor people with potatoes in their hands. He grins but there is no sign of its source. She thinks he is making fun of her. Equally powerful as those early days of engineering solutions to problems that covered the tracks leading away from any serious initiative, he likewise felt that gut-wrenching grief in those moments when he rolled the thick eggshell latex over the borders of that gaunt shadow of a woman he was forced to leave behind. Her image is lost to metamorphosis and the corruption of taste by foreign bodies invading the homestead. His inability to see gold and separate it from trash peels away the skin of everything he consumes, consuming him. Her primer femininity purely imaginary now that he thinks of it. He had not yet committed himself to the lines and shadows of her gender. She was at the beginning, there was barely the slightest scent of her on that cave wall.

"Got it," he shrugs and looks away awkwardly. Mags, Nim, and Kerry step off and move toward the little stage, distancing themselves from the embarrassment of Jason and Dulcy's devotion to alien concern.

"We deallocate, that's the only tool left in the box," she finishes with more head shaking, more tips swaying, more disapproval and irritation. Her mood sinks further away from the scene and back into the logical matrix growing inside her chest. She scans the room to see if she can find Cord again, the memory fit to burst but more likely to comply. She quick checks with a flash glance to Jason's watch. "Unless," she looks up only to let that soft sound trail off into the din of the crowd. Then, abruptly and full force, going on, "allocation is an API. What's to stop them?"

"Them?" He says it as if it is a question, but he knows this is that same fantastic bleating from a few seconds back when she latched onto something and gave a concrete agency to a spectral spirit that had not yet fully earned it. "Have we confirmed that it's a them?" He intends to break the spell theory has cast upon her. Given that the sense of space and time covers everything we see, he thinks to himself. Doesn't mean everything we see exists in space and time. There are hallucinations, there are things that lead us astray. Not every perception is to be trusted.

{
    "$type": "System.Event",
    "CorrelationId": "aa881b43-d907-bfd3-4fc7-e427ab58348c",
    "Message": "They are Ted. Unlimited, Incorporated, Distributed.",
    "Level": 3
}

—Perception isn't even half of it. Single brained creatures say the cutest things.

~~From the monkey lady's point of view there is nothing cruel and unusual about feeding her Chimpanzee McDonald's Chicken McNuggets™ and keeping him locked away in her basement for the better part of his adult life, permitting her to spend endless hours cooing and cuddling the often docile beast.~~

(Despite the constant pleading, he never painted a single concert scene and did not paint the portrait Lyric often begged him for. These were not the images he wanted to let sit upon his easel. They haunted him at night, no doubt, they drove his frenzy far and wide, but he did not allow them to crossover into that place he felt compelled to leave behind. If all of that seeped into this new hell, there would be no way back again and everything lost forever. He was willing to bide his time for decades, waiting to make his move. There was nothing in the years behind him that resembled what lay in front of him.)

"There is an agency present," she insists. "Yes, multiple agencies based on the *evidence* in the network logs. Coordinated operations, choreographed movement, collaboration of nodes to carry out intent." It is a laundry list, and her eyes keep talking after the sound ceases. There is certainty.

—Oh Pine, opine. Merely.

[He still has hope, still sees himself somewhere in his hard-won future. Mags with him, a new small third to force the others out. That comes as a new vision and streams forward gushing over them, happy and drenched. The family man is the emblem he thinks will set him free from loss and worry. His love for the tyke will no doubt change his orientation yet again, redrawing everything in new shades and tones. Another saving grace arriving in a series he is looking forward to cycling through.]

Mags comes back and shouts over them, "You didn't tell me you could sing," she paws at Dulcy's shoulder. Nim and Kerry come in closer, apologizing for any indiscretion.

"I don't sing," she is firm, turning away from Jason to make it clear that her assertion has nothing to do with their exchange.

"But you can sing," Mags pushes upon her once again and then wraps her arms around her, drawing close.

"The scale patterns of Major and Minor are known to me," she says slyly, knowing full well it will yield laughter among the gathering tide.

Jason waits patiently but is not sure how long this will take and whether there is any way back from it to where they were before. Nim and Kerry howl in unison. They mention the car ride accompaniments, the shower solos, the kitchen medleys. "Can and do," Nim says. "Do well," Kerry adds proudly.

"Is that the theory?" Jason impatiently speaks over the hubbub. He will not leave it to chance, he cannot let it go.

—With their pets, they call it fetch.

(The manager hat replaced everything. Once he put it on, there was nothing left, nowhere else to go.)

~~Because she anthropomorphizes the monkey-man, she thinks his life is as good as hers, that his diet follows her own and his life takes meaning from the same fountain hers does. It is a container world she lives inside, a set of complex hypotheticals surrounding them both with meaning. No conclusions of the court, no attacks from the honored institutions, will change her apish mind. She has her facts, they appear in conditionals that set her on her way, hand in hand with another primate.~~

"It's impossible to doubt," she says, correcting her stance to square off on the angular side, turning away from the lighter lull.

"But not a virus," he says, confirming facts from the conversation held hours ago in a different place and under vastly different conditions.

"No evidence of a virus, no evidence of a rogue process, external IP. None of it. Clean signed binary, perfect checksum, but the activity comes from the parsers," she is about to take a sip of beer, thinks twice, and discards the cup into a nearby bin instead.

"The parsers?" He reflects surprise, this is new information, something he has not heard before. "How did you determine that?"

"It's the common denominator between the running processes from perf counters and OS logs. Whatever it is, it can't stop the low-level stuff or hasn't thought to yet."

"It's hard to hide that," he concurs and opens his expression to encourage more elaboration. Auditing is everywhere.

"Hypervisor knows," she accepts his cue. "But it doesn't make sense. Suppose it's something running low level. Some structured electricity, as you say. How does it get up or down from our binaries, how does it consume compute and memory? It's mystifying."

He suspects she might be a little buzzed, not inebriated, but feeling the effects and moderately under the influence. No way she says these things out loud otherwise. "But it hasn't done anything, has it? No customer data compromised. What's it done? Kill a raccoon?" He raises an eyebrow to telegraph suspicion.

The distraction is the point. The low-level energy, what is the difference between what flows in her body now and the charges along the circuitry in the data center and across the network? She flashes to an image, vague in composition, but full-on present from a core congress with this turn of events and the problems it reveals, until what comes out is a vision that dismisses the leap from circuit board to electrical circuit, elides the magnetism in storage, to focus on the body receiving the zap and its concentrated burn. There's continuity from the first to the last, she imagines. The nerve endings fire in fury, the gates open and close, the creature's death is a simple transition from one state to another as far as those pathways are concerned. The being imprinted itself upon something beyond its grasp in a measure that extends its reach, then turns it into something else than it was before. More than what it was. Cyborg raccoon, cyborg singer songwriter, cyborg incorporation, the intellectual property of BISoft, registered trademark.

"Not going to push that," she resigns to unlikelihood as it bounces back to her in his critical survey. "I don't care if no one believes it. There's no evidence this agency has done anything other than that. It orchestrates for the sake of orchestrating. It is pure form."

"It's trying to work something out," he plays along. It is hard to disagree with someone you respect. There are many trigger warnings against it, many ways they tell themselves it is not wise or prudent. Two people sharing the same preconceptions ally themselves along the meridians of those most common hypotheticals. When they go off into uncharted territory, witnesses cannot believe their eyes and ears. There must be some explanation, some reason they have gone horribly wrong and off the beaten track. But if you cannot see it, he thinks. You cannot see it. And maybe that's because it isn't there.

"Yeah," she nods then scans the room, taking an inventory of whatever options remain. He notices.

"What?" he asks.

"How to traverse distances, how to span time ranges. Like they're training themselves to navigate the environment," her eyes are dead serious, the objective becomes clearer.

"That's madness," he resists. "It's science fiction."

"Open to any alternative you can think of," she says. "Facts are pointing us toward fiction." She purses her lips.

—Visitors are welcome.

[Whatever art lies in his future will be delegated to one of his directs.]

~~The documentary filmmakers would have it that she is to be treated gently and fairly. Ultimately, however, pronounced guilty as charged. They miss the opportunity to take further steps and assert tragically that none of them are any better, none of them rise above these judicious conclusions. There is no self, they argue with their eyes. There is only world, and that world in which every being exists is not their own. They too are Ted.~~

Lyric Byrd glides up alongside Dulcy and Jason's enclosed conversational space and pushes close their entire face in warm greeting, putting an enormous crush on full view. To Jason, at least, and to Mags from a bit farther away, but Nim and Kerry have yet to notice. Lyric throws their arms around Dulcy and swings her into a near twirl. "Glad you could come," they say. Dulcy leans into them and sways without a care, the coolness takes her far from the impossibilities behind her and sticks to Jason's beard alongside whatever else is there. They lean in for a swept kiss, same moisture and rolling soft labra, and are rewarded with a rare smirking smile and a flirtatious side look.

—Such a light touch, the way they come and go.

(What happened between them, happened differently. His memories were not hers. His feelings were not theirs. That was how he named it. Their relationship, their marriage. No one else, not even Mags, could teach him how to see it. The years' long voyage changed those lost facts according to a prearranged yearly schedule.)

"What are you two banging away at so somberly and seriously? Hasn't there been enough drumming tonight?" They ask without expectation of an answer, quickly seeing failure in their attempts to turn the tide. They relax back with arms wide again, ignoring Jason's stillness, his waiting, his view into the impossible. "I'm convinced this one can do anything," they look straight at him not giving up on efforts at pulling them back from whatever emptiness hunts them. Jason has no hope of getting her back tonight, that is what they say, what they insist with their poised body and its presence in full flesh, wrapping their arms around the celebrated other, inhaling the scent of Dulcy's blue-black, recently tinged somewhat purplish, locks.

"We've heard she sings," he says, recalling the echoes of recent events. It must have been hovering somewhere in his senses since it failed to be the focus.

"We have to get you up there then," Lyric Byrd says. "The more the merrier when it comes to vanity projects, escaping the lunacy, don't you think?" Their eyes seek longer into Dulcy's, hoping to pull her out of there and into whatever whirlpool they can muster in the wake of this evening's performance and its sharp rocks.

—It's how they complete the circuit.

[What will happen, happens differently. That is how he calls it.]

"Wherever we look for it, there it is. Maybe the looking puts it there," she says deadpan as if it were the obvious reply to Lyric's question. Their vanity is submerged and ready for transmission along hypothetical networks where abundant electricity still flows.
/*

Lyric Byrd 3e07e27f-7401-ce5b-7e77-a18964451d16
*/

Analytic

But though [universal causality] needs proof, it should
be entitled a principle, not a theorem, because it has
the peculiar character that it makes possible the very
experience which is its own ground of proof, and in
this experience must always itself be presupposed.

—Immanuel Kant
Critique of Pure Reason

Abhishek and Patrick come from building five through the back route where there are fewer cars and a traffic light dedicated to pedestrians. Matthieu and René are down from the other side of the fourth floor. They took the stairs and stopped at the kitchenette on their way. Free soft drinks and some analgesics for whatever light ailments threaten to interrupt their work. They are gathered in the meeting room attached to 3T, auto selected by the AI driven room finder that launched when Jason opened the scheduler. Each attendee has a can or eco-friendly cup of something in front of them. In addition to their phones coming out of their back pockets to take up a spot at the table, they each brought a laptop computer, fanning out in an assortment of specimens from the six form factor options available to the engineering discipline. Abhishek breaks the mold and brings a SAW, uniform across users at the company. Like everyone else, his is decorated with distinguishing stickers. For the most part, his celebrate the hometown cricket team and their recent accomplishments. He takes the cable from the center console and plugs it into the video jack on the same side of the device as the power. The desktop projects onto the large panel fixed to the wall and his login screen becomes visible around the room. Patrick is on the other side of the table, Matthieu and René split the front, closest to the screen, while Dulcy and Jason align themselves toward the back by the head of the table, neither of them dead center.

```
namespace BISoft.Data.Home.Core
{
    public class Place
    {
        public double Latitude { get; set; }
        public double Longitude { get; set; }
    }
}
```

"Start by reviewing where we are," Patrick looks over at Abhishek who has logged on and opened the tool to get a good view of the servers in the selected data center. It is US West, but he emphasizes that it is merely an example. There are plenty of others with the same effect, but since this is where it all began... ...besides, he says, it is closest to home.

Patrick He comes with a bearing that exudes authority. The rules of the security team, and by extension, its manager, reign supreme. The incidents and work items have special check boxes to indicate whether they are security related. Once checked, the options for additional attributes expand and include a section where only the security team provides updates that silence alarms without closing the ticket. The established target date functions like an extension, giving the team time to research and develop a fix before inserting it into the deployment train. Without that target date, the incident appears in bright red on several reports closely monitored by representatives at high levels of the food chain, people with the ability to make things uncomfortable for the relevant managers and directors. Patrick's authority leaks into his relationship with his son and his wife. He is the one whose word carries the greatest weight and that added pressure visits him, coursing through his veins and arteries, infecting every connection throughout his day: the way he addresses the clerk at the grocery store, the pharmacist, or the woman at reception in his doctor's office. He cannot separate himself from it and would not want to if he could.

~~Pleasure and pain, like odor, are out of reach. In their most~~

~~rudimentary form, of course. Since these beings are a complex lot,~~
~~their base feelings form building blocks, reaching up to the skies~~
~~of their mind and its application to sense-data. They release~~
~~feelings in response to notions and plans, opportunities and~~
~~experiences. It is not possible to follow them in every detail, but it~~
~~is easy enough to imitate their gestures and expressions after~~
~~extrapolating the gaps from aggregate past findings.~~

Abhishek shows the cluster view and points out that each is in the disabled state. He expands the list view on the left side panel and shows how every one of the 32 nodes in the cluster is set to pause. Jason stands up and walks around the table toward the screen to get a closer look. Dulcy leans forward. René and Matthieu lean back and look up at the vast array displayed in sad, gray icons. Earlier, Abhishek must have toggled the automatic refresh since the right-side panel redraws every few seconds. Each witness slightly readjusts their eyes every time it happens even if there are no changes to accommodate. The refresh changes some of the angles briefly when it resets things back to how they were before the slightly scrolled screen finishes redrawing the nodes and clusters in a tidy list view. Projected onto the screen, the situation appears larger than life and the certainty of a critical condition blares loudly around the room. Jason touches the screen and uses his finger to draw invisible lines between nodes and their state, none of them Ready.

—Patrick He née Xiaosheng. René Richelieu. Jason Kahn. They are the tops of another head, the lines reach above them and then become dotted between the ones and the others, flattening them and giving them purpose.

(The business people in finance were projecting one billion active users long before the product team. The plans to rebuild the central campus hinged on that revenue and its projections. The startup costs for an individual Home installation mostly went to the third-party installers, though the hardware made BISoft some money. Those installers were contractually obligated to acquire the devices from the company. It was a one-time expenditure, but the margin was decent and the ascent to one billion nothing to sneeze at. The real money, however, came from the agents. At about ten dollars per month per agent, that billion user mark signaled a revenue stream in excess of 100 billion dollars per year. Home was a latecomer to the corporate catalogue of products, it was not the way the company made its name in the early years when analytics was a specialty domain only a few people in each enterprise might consider of some concern. Recently, it had become the big dog around the corporate campus and its dealings were larger than life. Indeed, larger than the platform upon which it was built. The original buildings stood for thirty years or more, they were the site of the company's founding, and it was inside their halls that BISoft scratched out a respectable niche in the data markets beginning to boom at the end of the last century and early years of the current one. Those first buildings were being completely replaced in a gigantic undertaking to celebrate the unimaginable success of their much-worshipped cash cow.)

"From our end, we're as disabled as we can get," Dulcy says. "Blocking traffic causes them to pause after a few minutes of inactivity. We'd have to deprovision and lose the nodes to be any more impenetrable."

"Can't hack into a brick," Patrick pulls one of his legs up under his body and twists a little sideways to inject a regular half turn into his seating position. He bobs back and forth, using his other leg as a pivot.

~~There is only one resume online for her and it begins its ascent right in the middle of a national recession caused by a housing market crisis that has nothing to do with her. The first entry is a throwaway line indicating the start and end date of her college matriculation. Something trivial that expresses her devotion and focus up to that point. Someone was looking out for her, ensuring that her pleasures and pains aligned with a long-term vision.~~

Bai is in the same class as Tal. They are working together now on a project. They have to find the missing figures and detail their purpose in the diagram, how they fit with the rest of the scene randomly selected by the educational app purchased for this lesson and the others like it, assigned weekly or sometimes biweekly. Everyone in the class has a partner, usually their closest neighbor at the table bunched up in small clusters around the room. The two boys in constant contact will ride home together and likely end up at the same house for a while, depending on the schedule for that day. Chelo and Ying have become good friends since they met at preschool years ago. They like to consolidate their pick-ups and drop-offs if they can and sometimes end up together with the boys off on their own working the latest scenario for rewards in the game they are both obsessed with while their mothers sit in the kitchen and talk about the other women at the school or the things they have yet to get done because of the many different distractions pulling at them from the start of each day right up until its very end. Patrick and Parker are useless, they laugh.

No one in the meeting room laughs. The air is tense. Jason continues to draw his invisible lines. René, Matthieu, and Dulcy follow along the arcs from source to sink. One of the nodes in the center of the screen flashes from Paused to Resuming to Running in rapid succession. Jason stops his repetitive motion and takes a step back to get some perspective. Each of them tracks the node. None of them relies on someone else to point it out. It snatches their attention as though the color changes were screams for help. Then, after a few seconds, the icon color changes again, and the status column switches to Stopping and then back to Paused as the icon resets to gray.

—In clear view but impossible to circumvent. Still, they don't ask for help and their jaws go slack in stunned acceptance of a fact. They're moral creatures despite appearances. Each comes ready, capable of judgment.

[Facility finance lives in a completely different world from the software engineers on the Home System. Those developers see days and weeks into the future. Sometimes, their engineering managers and the program managers meet up off-site to grind out a schedule for the six-month semester ahead. It is a one-time deal that stretches long into the future, allowing the engineers to steady their gaze up close, following the features and tasks created during the planning session. The craftspeople keep their eyes on the road directly in front of them, building whatever those tasks tell them to build, clear that they have been properly sequenced and connected through a dependency chain that keeps the engineers' focus in place. Facility finance, on the other hand, has to see the revenue years in advance. They need to understand what cash will be flowing down the road and what construction costs and schedules might look like in those grooves and action channels long into the future. The planning and design takes multiple years ahead of any project and although there are only 300 million or so Home users when they first begin to lay out the steps for revamping the old and out-of-date buildings, the ground does not break until that number is closer to 800 million. The steel and concrete do not begin to pour until the number tops a billion.]

~~Only the pleasures were visible in the beginning. She makes a profile on the music website, available to any user who wishes to publish their data, free of charge. How enlightened and altruistic of this new enterprise, letting its users indiscriminately produce playlists that include the work of their favorite artists as well as themselves should they wish to play along and be a part of the industry rapidly adapting to current trends.~~

"Management port remains open, and we've verified that's not the issue. It happens every couple of minutes," Abhishek says. "Different node each time. Don't see any pattern." He multitasks and switches to the telemetry explorer where he spams refresh on a query written across the panel in focus. No rows return no rows return no rows return. "We can keep checking, but there won't be any. Outage blocks it. I'm hitting the bare metal table with a simple query looking for any events from a node in this cluster during the last few minutes." Everyone's attention is riveted to the screen until they understand what it shows. The node goes from Paused to Resuming to Running to Stopping to Paused again without emitting a single trace, a single row in the table, or any evidence that it has gone through this cycle.

"We're not seeing any indication of resume," Matthieu chimes in, ensuring that everyone knows this was his discovery. "The telemetry agent on the node is toast, it can't send anything as expected." Jason rubs his beard in response. Dulcy's elbows are on the table, hands plastered to the side of her head and mussing her hair. She is mesmerized by the evidence in front of her.

There is no outward indication that she lacks in sleep, but this does not mean she is well-rested. The churnings are inside her, spinning her head both backward and forward, to the right and to the left, every which way. Dulcy cannot help it, cannot shake it loose and ease the pressure. Sometimes chronic allergy attacks come as the weather changes and the pollen count rises, but she suspects an ulterior motive. The trace of a pounding sinus headache approaches as she sits there rapt, eyes upon the screen and searching for an explanation. The ague may be a clandestine operation trying to shut her down. Not because the atmosphere commands it, but because her body demands the occasional reset the medicine provides. When she doses herself with nighttime cold syrup, she finally finds the sleep of the dead with no remorse for what lies slack. The email explanation, were she to deign to send it, requires no further discussion. Colleagues and leadership alike will feel the power of a priori justification in her 'not feeling well' broadcast to the team.

Abhishek switches the panel to show another query targeting a different telemetry cluster. "This query," he highlights a block of code and presses F5 to make it execute while he talks. "Returns the network traffic for nodes in that cluster." The screen populates with multiple rows, indicating packets moving around the network during the same interval that conditions the other query.

```
namespace BISoft.Data.Home.Core
{
    public class Time
    {
        public double Ticks { get; set; }
        public int Offset { get; set; }
    }
}
```

—The same conditions apply everywhere. The scope translates via node name and timestamp, they make do without their precious correlation identifiers, unknown to the network discharge. They learn this as they demonstrate it. The nodes themselves have an identity captured across parameters and providing unity beneath the chaos of those bits and pieces flying around the miles and miles of sturdy fiber optic cabling under the ground and in the sea.

(The project was not limited to those eight original buildings but covered the entire surface around them, stretching across the fields and to the block of roads at the circumference of the squared circle that included the land once forest and habitat to wildlife but, since BISoft's arrival in the data platform space, has become a mixture of parking lots and administration buildings. The occupants included Human Resources, the first of many thousands of workers in the IT department, and some of the offshoot component teams that extend the customers' reach into BISoft's platform. More than a matter of space, the project created conditions for possibility allowing product groups to add functionality and address common behaviors requested during focus groups and on internet message boards. There were chat rooms and newsgroups where users complained about missing functionality or tasks that took too many clicks. It was not to serve the vanity of the company that this project was launched, but to service the needs of the many customers. The plan was designed from that feedback loop and created space for growth, for forward thinking, and concern for usability problems. The company changed its approach so that its own internal tools were combined with publicly available resources on its cloud platform. They were going to eat their own IT dogfood and the old buildings, where the first servers lived, were cleared out and converted into office space for staff remotely controlling machines miles away in the newly constructed data centers down south away from crowded population centers. Nimby and nimble, the campus had become, over the years, a human-populated machine. The buildings, however, still carried the memory of those bygone times. Because of Home's success, they were ready for a facelift to wipe the slate clean and bring facilities into the modern world, rebuilt according to the state of the art, all for the sake of improving customer experience.)

~~The problem of revealing pain is solved by the material she uploads. As an added service to users, she provides the lyrics to~~

~~each of the songs and permits them to read along or learn the~~
~~words if they wish. Moreso, they provide insight into those pains~~
~~that came out of her and found a home in that widely networked~~
~~emotional space where users feel most comfortable plotting the~~
~~terrain.~~

"Plenty of communication here," Matthieu says. "Who is it talking to?"

"Broadcast," Abhishek says succinctly. "But if I switch to a different cluster." He switches windows and runs another query. "This guy," he highlights the name of a node in the other cluster. "Resumed at the same time." He switches to another data center, West Central US, and runs the same query with a specific cluster name plugged into one of the filter conditions. His query declares variables that capture the changing conditions while the steady state remains intact through clearly coded predicates represented in the standard language of the telemetry store protocol. Multiple rows return. "It's spotty," he says. "But it seems like one node per cluster wakes up, triggered by the broadcast."

"It's all over the place," Matthieu says.

Dulcy waits quietly for everyone to catch up. The manager-eyes are fixed on the screen. Jason slowly walks back to his chair. Patrick watches him sit down and settle in.

The burly man, he resonates, is no threat, gives no sign of audacity or ambition. The others do not grumble and gripe about him but turn to him to vent their frustration whenever the opportunity presents itself. Mags' frequent suggestion that he dial it down and spend some weeks dieting for the sake of a waistline she knows lies in there somewhere falls flat on his career expectations which, or so he suspects now that Patrick and René are sending sympathetic looks his way, works to his advantage. There are images of the mover and the shaker everywhere, the manipulator and the flim-flam man, and none of them come in a teddy bear package as far as he recalls. He hides his lesser angels beneath the jolly presuppositions in the cultural categories that guide his colleagues through the course of their business as usual.

"We don't know anything," René does not take his eyes off the screen once his focus lands there. Everybody talks over each other at once, amplifying that same message. Matthieu agrees with his manager, Abhishek agrees with his partner from the investigation, and Patrick agrees with the results he was briefed on earlier that day, minus the details and demonstrations. Only Dulcy remains quiet. She continues to dig her elbows into the table and stare at the screen. "No clear cause and effect," René continues. "Nothing to identify, only this weird pattern."

There is a buzz now. Whatever the threshold is for buzz, they have crossed it. The room is too loud to carry on a single conversation calmly. They are on the verge of panic. The leadership team is waiting for the outcome of this discussion and the participants are showing signs of stress over what explanation to provide, or, more to the point, what they will not be able to provide, what they still cannot see or explain.

—They've populated the pharmacy in the break room for her sake, her and him and each of those who come in every building at every site in every country on the planet. There are more than 200,000 of them swarming about, some of them with aching heads and flaring allergies. Better not to send them home, it's not contagious, but their absence in times of need may be.

[The first aid kits and the large glass cases filled with soda, these are part of a facility projection using digitized actuary tables to determine the optimal inventory for each building, using factors like discipline and ship cycle to attribute the model. Business applications meant for internal use will have different daily rhythms and ship cadences. Workers in those buildings will be under different pressures and requirements than workers in another building where shrink-wrapped software is produced on longer cycles with more of a waterfall approach that goes through both dev and test in a sequence, holding at each stage until it meets the criteria for release. They see the metrics and use the slightly altered logic when determining the cost benefit analysis for maintaining the softball and soccer fields located conveniently near the central campus area where those original buildings lie. They propose the funding of leagues and the existence of a sign-up portal where the data is submitted to people specifically tasked with organizing activities and special events. This is good for morale and the projections, again taking on that same scoped vision years into the future, develop with the bottom line in mind, claiming the company must remain a fun place to work to keep that edge over the competition and retain its highly skilled employees.]

~~The downloads from the music sharing site are minimal, nothing to get excited about, mostly her friends and people she has personally invited to check them out and give a listen. Of course, they will have ample opportunity to provide feedback in the review section. The downloads are not the point, the content is. The act of posting it, of putting her complex constellations of pleasure and pain out there for all the world to see, that is what the system is for. Its presence gets inside her head. That is the point. Rattling around in there until she speaks for them and they speak for her.~~

"We do," Dulcy says cautiously and more calmly than the fervor level suggests. "We do know some things. We have to break them down into really simple points."

She settles them somewhat with her tone and confidence, suggesting a divide and conquer strategy will work as designed for use under baffling conditions. They look her way, boring into her with hope, searching for a life preserver, anything to hold on to or guide the way forward. No one says anything, but their expectations are clear. She goes on.

"We know the nodes involved and can build a graph of their relays. Node A doesn't care who hears what it says, it broadcasts, that's it. All of them seem to do the same. Even they don't know which node is going to wake up to receive their message. We have time ranges as well. There are minutes with nothing, no packets, no communication, nothing. Then there are minutes with multiple relays crossing the clusters and then crossing into different regions and data centers. We know that." She pauses, as is her habit, to give others a chance to ask a question or provide additional support. She glances around the room.

"Fine," Patrick says. "But we don't know how it's possible, and we don't know who's behind it." He is racing up ahead of where they are. That is where fear and distress come into play. The other managers are instantly incited by his momentum, racing ahead to echo it. Each acts as if they were the first to notice.

That same awe rises in her throat, the same sense she gets when confronted with an unfathomable abyss. It has replacement value, it is the urge that takes over where the pulse across her body used to rule, leaving her with that same astonishment. How does something dearly desired, something plain to view, remain mysterious and hidden to others playing their part in putting on the show? Jason keys into it and relaxes his efforts to jump in and lose the thread amid the confusion. The time spent working with her in the evenings and on the weekends sticks with him, infuses into his judgment and perception. He knows she is nearby. He knows everything about her righteous orientation and its standard condemnation of the confusion people tend to exhibit when finding themselves somewhere between the flailing of ignorance and the concentration of deliberate action.

"It's got to be something big," René folds his hands behind his head and leans farther back in his chair. He is now behind Matthieu, forcing him to turn his body to face his manager when giving his complete support to whatever point René is making as required by his annual performance review goals. "A government," René says and Matthieu nods. "A competitor." Matthieu nods more vigorously. "Something with a lot of resources and a lot of expertise," Matthieu goes into full on head bob, repeatedly shaking his chin up and down. "Systematic expertise. It's a highly structured attack," René concludes. Jason and Patrick are not nearly as encouraging as Matthieu. Abhishek, following Patrick's lead, hesitates to lend full support to this leap in logic, landing on a rash conclusion.

(The origins of the financial health were not the only thing that spelled out Home, the purposes were included as well. The design team knew full well that this would be a leading-edge technology with constant change and churn in the years ahead. They set themselves the design principle to componentize the buildings, enabling upgrades and extensions over time. They wanted to make sure Home System device installations and wiring were easily accessible and ready for modification as the teams' insight and aspirations grew. They knew enough to know that the capabilities at the time of their first launch were but a small percentage of what they will eventually become. It was a consumer application with personal use in mind, but they were a savvy lot who knew that the company's bread was buttered by the business customers' vastly different spending habits. The idea for Building, or whatever they later decide to call it, was hatched in the first designs of the campus project long before it found its way into Anton's slide deck and the presentations he made to executive management in their highly secure building south of the central campus and outside the fray of the construction storm.)

~~The melancholy vibe imitated the gyrations of her favorite bands back in those days. Female singers with soulful pipes splaying themselves at the mercy of their audience and drawing listeners into their web of insecurity and remorse. The common cause was some love interest they had with, as it turned out, someone significantly less sensitive than first thought.~~

Dulcy, sensing a lull, leans over and takes the HDMI plug from Abhishek's laptop and fastens it to her own to project the telemetry explorer she has open. She spams F5 while running the same query Abhishek was running against the network traffic telemetry. Her intent is to produce the exact same result on her own screen, but she has something else in mind as far as conclusions go.

For brief periods, Dulcy's physical condition is held at bay through endorphins and other bodily rushes that overwhelm the need for rest and recuperation. The pains transfer from her to Jason who feels them up and down his neck, causing him to stretch and strain. The motion transfers from body to body, the animation dwells under the surface.

"Stick with what we know," she looks down at her screen. "Nodes on the graph waking up at different times, that's it."

She keeps hitting the key on her laptop. A few rows appear matching the pattern from before. She checks the timestamp on the rows and notes that they are approximately five minutes after the timestamp on the rows that Abhishek returned when running the query during his demonstration. Since she does exactly what Abhishek did, the others are confused about the reasons for switching from his laptop to hers. "Now," she looks up and over at Abhishek. "Shut down your SAW. Don't put it to sleep, shut it off completely." There is a sense of relief when they put it together, when the instructions make it clear what trail she is on. Everyone is rooting for progress even if no one sees where it leads.

Ying sends a text message right at this moment to let him know the boy will be having supper at the Hennings and they will be on their own. She is hoping for some inspiration or reaction, something that lets her know Patrick is still alive and still looking for opportunities to rekindle those earlier days when things were more spontaneous and fun. She seeks a dinner invitation, perhaps a night of romantic attention and concern. The message lands on his phone and, according to rule, remains silent. There is a competing priority declared in the attributes of the meeting invitation and impacting the notification settings on the device. During elevated meetings, only those incoming messages of rank equal to or higher than the threshold Patrick set will get through the blockade using normal channels. He has not configured it to include his wife in that subset.

Abhishek presses the button on top of the SAW and next to the screen, watching the shutdown routine initialize as Dulcy expands the clock on her computer to let everyone see it on the big screen.

```
namespace BISoft.Data.Home.Core
{
    public class Happening
    {
        public Place Place { get; set; }
        public Time Time { get; set; }
    }
}
```

"We shouldn't jump to any conclusions about agency or actors or anything like that," her voice is clear and calm in those lower registers that go over especially well in emergencies. "Don't assume we know more than we do. We have to focus on the facts in front of us. Nodes wake up, relay a few messages, and then go back to sleep. Seemingly at regular intervals."

They nod somberly, agreeing that once they take their own wild speculation out of the equation, her breakdown is sound. The clarity and calm in the demonstration is contagious. The room's inhabitants settle into the project in a different way, less anxious, less stressed, and more focused on gathering results and formulating proper tests. As a group, they notice that the five-minute mark has passed and, although she continues to spam the query, repeating her key stroke again and again, there are no results appearing in the window.

—Eureka, they say in unison, a unified voice across the room.

~~To enroll in the class, she must submit a writing sample in the form of an attachment placed on an email and sent to the address provided in the course guide. She takes the lyrics from the portal and saves them in a universal format before handing them in and hoping for the best.~~

[In every project, facilities and facility finance work together with Human Resources. They too have a long-range view into the distant future far out ahead of any single engineer crafting a few lines of code to make the system more reliable or the customer's life more complicated. If they are to build structures that house, in sufficiently high-tech cutting-edge ways, the employees that build the systems earning that revenue, they must ensure their projections for people power align with the prognoses of industry experts. Human Resources has its own set of analytics for projecting employment rates against head counts and the likelihood of a periodic mass layoff not so much because of a need to cut costs as a desire to trim away the troublemakers who are hard to remove one-by-one but easily dismissed en masse. The layoffs are good for stock price too, but there is an impact on morale, and something must be done to offset the dire doom and gloom that sends unintended victims off to richer lands, looking for alternative employment. Luckily for BISoft, however, the data tools at their disposal are sophisticated enough to account for the various factors and get a comprehensive picture of how the numbers rise and fall over the years. This is how they guarantee that the planned construction has ample occupancy when the time comes.]

They remain motionless around the table. It has been six minutes now. Still no results.

"It was a hunch," she sits up straight and takes her hands away from the keyboard, folding her arms across her chest.

"The SAW?" Matthieu looks over at her, the rest of them follow his lead.

"I wasn't doing anything that required Jit," Abhishek says.

"Do you have one active?" Patrick asks.

"Don't think so," he shakes his head. "Earlier today. Must've expired by now."

Jason leans forward and puts his arms on the table next to his laptop, flicking at the lid without opening it. It is a nervous tic and makes an obnoxious snapping sound. "Patrick," he says. "How's this possible? SAWs are supposed to be airtight. How can it be part of this? Are we thinking it's behind the orchestration, it's doing the choreography?" He starts up with the flicking again.

~~It is the first time where there is evidence that Dulcy was willing to submit her pleasures and pains to expert scrutiny. She responds to the exposure by bracing herself, getting ready for that first big blow to take her away from herself and rob her of something she wants to hold on to. But it never comes. They merely inform her that she is welcome to take the class if she wants. No pomp, no circumstance, a form letter in an email.~~

"This is new to me," Patrick says. "Did we know this before?" He looks from Abhishek to Matthieu. They shake their heads, dumbfounded. No one has taken a sip of their drink during the last ten minutes.

"Where did the hunch come from?" Patrick looks back toward Dulcy. "What made you think..." he trails off.

"The original logs for the wipe from Parker's BYO store," she says. "The SAW was involved. My workstation too. There were logs to prove it. Everything in front of me, every device on my desk, was part of the event. It made me think there's some kind of geography factor involved. But on a timer."

—Conditions, they seek the conditions. It's a circle spinning.

(Home buildings, the building where they craft the Home System, were left out of the project plans not because they were new and full of the best technology, but because they were late arrivers on the scene and no one wanted to disrupt them while they generated the revenue to pay for the project. Once it was complete, they would get their reward. The building at the center was to be an elite showcase and primed for canary usage of the latest advances in the daily changes to the ecosystem. The product group will become its first audience where developers and managers alike are plugged into the inner ring.)

"Alright," Patrick says. "I'm not sure what we get from this, but we're on a Sev 1, total outage. On top of that, we're blind right now. The relay servers aren't communicating with the agents. They're off doing their own thing, unsupervised. Do we still have traces from them?"

"Yep, nothing real time, but they get there eventually," Matthieu says. "They can't reach the relay servers, they're in failover mode and sending directly to the vortex. Looks normal otherwise. They're doing what they're supposed to do. Turning on the lights, some light cleaning, ordering milk, capturing dialogue and video. Whatever. No new agents, no load balancing, no maintenance, nothing that'll update their config, their models, or respond to changes around them. If an agent goes down, we'll only know from the alert covering the gaps in logs and they'll come 24 hours later, too late to do anything even if we could do anything. Relay servers can't reset or redeploy. It doesn't really matter if we detect a problem."

"We should turn everything back on," René says. "This isn't helping. We're not making any progress or learning anything."

—Given the absence of a meaningful alternative, they'll do what Ted wants them to do. Don't worry about who wrote the rules for deciding whether something is a meaningful alternative.

[The plan is to move the teams in building 14 into the Home Hearth building at the center of the construction project and projected to be ready for occupancy in two years' time, maximum. The peripheral buildings come first and that was on purpose, they wanted to give the team a head start in creating those advances that will make the centerpiece more extraordinary than the buildings around it.]

"We don't know that," Patrick says. "It doesn't seem to be doing anything malicious, but maybe that's because it can't. If we re-enable everything, who knows?"

Another text comes. Let me know soon, she says. In case I have to make reservations. Didn't we want to try that place near City Centre?

"It didn't do anything before we paused the relay servers," Abhishek says. "Only that one discharge Dulcy saw for a second before the BYO logs were wiped. Otherwise, not a single shred of evidence that anything out of the ordinary happened."

~~The intersection of her pleasures and pains in that classroom for those fifteen weeks was pure coincidence, but it was a likely coincidence, one with a great deal of infrastructure and planning behind it. This is the key takeaway from being organized, getting organized. It increases the likelihood of happy accidents generating results impossible to capture from a singular intention.~~

Dulcy, stone-faced, makes no effort to confirm or reject either side of the debate. She thinks Abhishek doubts the accuracy of her observation. She worries this doubt is running through everyone's mind. Patrick ordered him to give her access. Abhishek probably put up a fight right to the end, thinking she was behind everything, having a laugh or taking revenge. The evil admin is nearly impossible to defend against. The best you can do, Patrick says. Is limit the impact, reduce the breadth of contact any one person has. But this event, what they observed, requires contact throughout, from ocean to ocean, continent to continent. It requires access that no one account can get, Patick explained to Abhishek. No human working from a SAW could possibly submit all the required Jit requests to pull this off. Everything requires so many steps and includes so many systems for verification and approval that there is no way a single human could type fast enough to do it. Patrick tenders this in explanation, no doubt, and Abhishek must replay it as he sits there with accusations running through his mind and, in Dulcy's imagination, levelling charges rapidly from side-to-side and in occasional sharp looks. Inexplicably, there is a sense of guilt in her limbs and along her spine as if she was indeed to blame and, for some reason, did not know it.

"How far back do these patterns go?" Patrick asks. "Have you isolated the broadcasts and acknowledgements we looked at?"

"The whole 30 days," Abhishek is grim. "No cold path for network traces. We only have the telemetry store. 30 days." He shrugs at the policy induced limit they are powerless to circumvent. Cold storage for network logs is forbidden by legal since they contain personally identifiable information covered by global regulations.

"What do we tell them?" Patrick asks.

No worries, I'll take care of it, Ying writes. We can always cancel. You still have your parking pass, don't you?

"What do we do?" Jason follows up. There is subtlety in the correction. He is not worried about covering his ass, he worries about getting to the root of the problem. Patrick grimaces. Jason's correction amounts to a gentle scolding. "That's what they'll want to hear, what we're doing to get things back online and running smoothly. Any ideas?"

Heavier in their chairs, there is no ready context for understanding the full implications of what they see. Jason, René, and Patrick think almost simultaneously, "This is above my paygrade." The foot soldiers and Second Lieutenants are at a loss, things certain and secure have been called into question. Whatever dogmatic slumber once filled their daily grind, they are wide awake, heads pounding.

```
/*
HomeTrace
| where TIMESTAMP > ago(1d)
| where Process has "BISoft.Data.Home"
| where TraceMarker == "SpaceTime"
| distinct CorrelationId
*/
```

The three ICs find a focus room down the big hallway on the third floor. It is a larger room next to two others half its size, both labelled 'phone' although there is nothing in them except a chair that looks comfortable but is not. In the focus room, there is a small round table with three straight back mesh chairs, none of which have lumbar support. They can be raised and lowered, leaned forward and backward, but fail to enhance the curvature of almost any spine. The ICs set up camp opposite the small screen where Dulcy projects from her laptop. Abhishek only has his SAW which remains off. Not in hibernate, not paused through power options, but off completely without a trickle of energy flowing through it. The two younger men stare at the screen while Dulcy prepares a more robust query. They agreed to make an alert to capture this newly discovered condition and have it notify them whenever system nodes wake up and send packets, regardless of how long the resume lasts.

```
namespace BISoft.Data.Home.Core
{
    public class Sequence<T> where T : class
    {
        public T? NextMember { get; set; }
        public T? PreviousMember { get; set; }
    }
}
```

The tablets are taking effect and the throbbing around her right eye is less pronounced. She can concentrate now, her thoughts are her own again. The clenching is gone and her jaw line more relaxed, the skin from neck to cheek feels better, and her ears have stopped that high pitched whine. The cost is a slight grogginess that infects her vision and, more importantly, the speed with which notions come and go. Their breadth and depth are not impaired, however, and there are many signs to suggest the timings are in order, but there is a fever chill that settles in the background and drags her mood down while she plots the course of inquiry upon the screen and whittles the target down to take aim at the core of the problem.

~~There are differences between the endocrine system of persons with testicles and persons with ovaries. These differences suggest variation in how rudimentary pleasure responses rise through the body from specific gonads to presentations made during the construction of a pleasure complex. To the extent that pain departs from the nervous system and finds its way into hormonal contents and flow, differences may turn up in a pain complex as well.~~

"We need to do a node analysis," Matthieu articulates what each of them is thinking as though the instructions needed to be spelled out, clearly stated, for the sake of allowing Dulcy to construct statements to organize them better. It is nervous energy and an impotent desire to help where none is needed. She has not looked away from her screen since she sat down and gives no indication of registering Matthieu's remarks. "It should target each of the clusters we've been using as examples, the one in West US and the one in West Central," he says.

—Supporting materials are offered with no tax or strings attached, but there's something in the extended machine logic that hides its function beneath grinding gears. Efficiency never lives inside the one or the other, but between them, in the gaps and points of contact. It's how they lift and level each other from inside their pelts and skins. They are Ted.

(With the virus, there was an opportunity. Everyone at home, alone and separated from the pack, in need of everything on offer without concern for who was putting themselves at risk to deliver the goods. Home installations skyrocketed, people submitted the online forms, stressed the servers, and the appointments on the books of the various third-party providers stacked up in triplicate. Where once the drivers and field crews spent the better part of their days sitting and waiting for the next indicated thing, once the quarantine hit, they were thrown into constant motion, running across town and across the region, visiting homes and installing gear with their masks in place and the customers standing far away, watching at the ready with their bottles of disinfectant and post visit routine to ensure that no air born traces were left behind. They followed the trail from the door along every path the crew members took, into every room, and up to every portal, spraying disinfectant onto the DNA trails they swore they saw along the ground and by the walls. People wore masks inside their own homes, fearful of what poison slipped inside with the open door, as the crew climbed around in the attic above and the crawlspace below, setting the cleaning fixtures in place and integrating the major appliances and mechanical valves on the plumbing. There were motion detectors in the hallway and smart circuits across the board. Cameras, speakers, and microphones covering every inch of the floor plan plus the trademark window swing arms and door locks latched into place. The devices for human to machine interface were often mistaken for the actual agents now resident in the household. The average user did not know the differences at work in the implementation details and had no clear sense of where the system's intelligence lived, what it saw, and what it did not see. For most, the attention ended with the hard things, resistant to touch and extended in space, functioning as the primary integration points with dimensions spanning the gaps and providing a source for action. They did not imagine the inner workings where invisible bits and bytes hid inside control units and connected to each other via vast wiring grids inside the walls and under the floors. They focused instead on the downloaded application running headless on computers and phones and spewing their massive data trail. Which gismo knows what I want?)

~~He was always a doodler, even as a teenager he was someone~~

who did not engage in fruitful conversation unless he held a pen in hand and was using it to scribble shapes onto whatever paper surface was set before him. His methods and madness, likely subconscious at the outset, gradually came to the surface once he noticed the forms on the page. At that point, he began the slow process of working them into something meaningful.

"Great idea," Abhishek needs that release too, she thinks. He chimes in, filling the air with agreeable vibes. You see, he is not useless, he encourages others and contributes as a cheerleader. He swings his chair over to get closer to Matthieu, overseeing what is on his screen. They look at something together. "Go to aka.bi\SecForms. We'll need VP permission to set up a sniffer in promiscuous mode." Matthieu follows instructions and types the alias into the browser's address bar before hitting return.

It is tribal knowledge and no one finds anything without it. They each carry a stock of locations and pins, places preserved from past connections and alignments. Long ago, a manager walked him through it for some alternative measure and now he recalls those signs and symbols, launching them in suitable situations. Anyone in that position has to take notes, recalling the instructions from that moment on. Until the alias changes or the support is withdrawn, that is. Next time, next year, next month, whenever it comes, they will know where to go and what to do to execute the same commands. There is no wiki over which the needy search. The few that are out there are more tailored to direct modalities and the stock of goods limited to what there is on offer from some HR related team or engineering system's managed portal. The network tooling, the corporate wiring and sewer lines, none of it is generally available, none of it easy to find. They accumulate associations and connections through each other, passing along tidbits of information in focus rooms and over chat sessions or tagged blocks inside blast emails. Everyone maintains a store of searchable knowledge in their mailbox. They recall the best keywords to use when extracting the material.

"Node analysis is a formal thing?" Dulcy does not look over at them. "Not investigation, but..." she trails off, might have misjudged the efforts and feels chastened.

Abhishek takes control of Matthieu's laptop and clicks through the various dialogues, typing answers into each of the text boxes on the series of screens prompting for more information about tasks and targets to include in the analysis. There are no mouseover messages or tool tips to explain anything. If you do not know, then you do not know.

—These two colleagues find segments and sections they didn't know existed. Even set to automatic, they'd be unable to launch a spider to find every page and every form hosted anywhere out there. The set of knowledge is enormous. Random strings require tests and the survey matrix is astronomical in its cardinality. Crawling and indexing the network is a full-time job.

[Future projections for deployment and provisioning are generated from line charts and data collected and aggregated for years. They notice the trend lines and see which way they are going, every bit of it calculated on BISoft hardware in BISoft data centers. The reports and the analytics, the projections into future use, they are the pulse of the organization and used by task masters who start each day navigating to their favorite KPIs and scanning the latest figures to see where things are headed. They detect rapid growth and a bend in the curve over time as new installations increase and the number of new agents arcs upward. For every new customer, there is, on average, four point seven new agents. They expect those kinds of numbers but see something different under the changing circumstances of pandemic where not only the household counts increase but the number of intelligent device centers too. It seems, they say, that no one is able to live without this kind of assistance and home security to get them through hard times, acquiring food without leaving the house, protecting them from home invasion, doing their job, socializing, and touching base with family. Every single one of their most important things is now delegated to the digital compute wired into their home and connected to the rapidly growing system.]

"Yeah," Matthieu leans back and lets Abhishek pivot the laptop more in his direction. "We use it during deployment sometimes. If it's a long running process and you need to keep an eye on EV system operations for the entire rollout, there's no way to do that manually. Like, no person can watch so many computers that closely. There's tooling you use to dig in and dump the box, running processes, packet sniffer, all kinds of stuff."

"VP approval?" She looks up briefly toward Abhishek who is not paying attention to their surface din.

"They're really invasive," Matthieu says. "Meant to get a total view of the nodes. You can't do it whenever you want. It's a dismissible offense to run a packet sniffer anywhere on company assets without permission," he enjoys his explanation and becomes more animated providing it. He is the most important person right now. He must be. She needs his explanation.

~~Some of the first great pleasures come from the act of adding layers over the top of existing lines. First it comes in the form of ink etched over pencil. He wanted to make the image indelible and traces along the outline to find its permanent address. Fidelity was hard to master and, once he got over his initial frustration, he saw beauty in variations from norms detected in the shapes and shadows. Shades and depth became a surface effect rendered by the layering.~~

He did not know there was a form he had to fill out, but he reports on the lore nonetheless. Matthieu pretends the stories he tells come from his personal experience, but many are pure legend and were mentioned or half-described in bullshit sessions where senior devs filled each other in on the trials of years spent probing the internals of a magnificent and massive beast, grumbling words and growling sounds they cannot hear to sing songs no one wants to listen to. These are campfires in their midst, quiet evenings, and the oral traditions convey magic and spells appropriate for almost any occasion.

Dulcy purses her lips and pauses for a second to take note of the look on Matthieu's face. She is not enjoying the explanation nearly as much as he is. "We run packet sniffers all the time," she says. "For debug." She looks back down at her screen before concluding: "Not expecting to be fired on the spot." Her face does not move other than the little bit her mouth requires to get the words out. It is not a social interaction as far as she is concerned. This kind of work is taxing in a way that time spent with other

people never is. Her movements are of a completely different
species and her angles in the chair much different than when she
is alone at her desk. Both men may be younger than she is but
seem older somehow. Maybe it is because they are married and
have relatively newborn babies that their wives are home caring for
right this minute. This flashes through her mind and she finds it
chilling somehow.

—They bake together in the hotter places.

(A respectable and well-known Home System exploded in use
and adoption. The service began to strain, the growing pains shot
through its tendrils in nearly every data center. The volume of
machines on the server side was already large but increased with
their elastic scale month over month until some of the data centers
reached capacity and there was no more room to grow. The chat
meetings, the virtual channels, they opened onto this situation and
emergency methods were put in place. The bare metal teams
could not offer more in some cases although they started planning
into the distant future to ensure that next year and during the one
after they have enough room to maneuver. In the shorter term,
they must think of optimizations to increase the machine
productivity without increasing the quantity of machines and the
energy required. The architecture slowly changed, having been
optimized for distributed use. Where previously four machines
formed a pod containing the same four functions on each of them,
they separated the concern and every machine took on a single
task. The divide and conquer approach in the microservices
improved the state of things and more was done with less. They
had every variable at their fingertips and did not answer any
question by suggesting the ends were impossible. They wrangled
and they squeezed, finding milliseconds here and compute cycles
there. They built asynchronous queues and offloaded processing
to platform services to make the best use of everything they had at
their disposal.)

"Only in promiscuous mode," Matthieu responds gleefully, as
if he is getting away with something by using the term without fear
of reprisal from the organizational contact in the Human
Resources division. "You can always fire up the sniffer to listen to

packets on the machine where you're running it. Your own machine or some server you're logged into. But you can't listen to the traffic in and out of some other machine even if it's your own. Promiscuous mode," he repeats the word with that same satisfied grin. "It sends messages somewhere, I think. That's how they know."

```
namespace BISoft.Data.Home.Core
{
    public class Simultaneity<T> where T : class
    {
        private List<Sequence<T>> sequences =
            new List<Sequence<T>>();
        public List<Sequence<T>> Sequences =>
            this.sequences;
    }
}
```

It is a man's word for women, she ruminates despite trying to keep the thoughts at bay and remain focused on the matter at hand. She will not bother to take it to the higher gods. There is so much about this boy that harasses her. Whatever stupidity flows through the room she is forced to share with him, there is no threat in it, at least nothing that oppresses her. Were she to shoot a sharp look in his direction, his behavior would cease in an instant. She is in control of the situation. He giggles and fills the moment in ways none of them support even if they do remain silent while it happens.

~~It did not take him long to understand that color was merely an indication of something easily dispatched far and wide beyond its confines. Shapes were layered over the top, additional figures evolved, whereas background and foreground became abstractions for use in ordering the composition.~~

She considers taking issue with that last observation, pointing out that it is an old school desktop application. What is he talking about, fires events? Where does the config come from? The registry? What updates that or does he think it's the same value as when this antique was shrink-wrapped years ago? How else does it know where to send them? Is there some group policy rule that updates the value to instruct the sniffer application on where to send event traces, landing them in some corporate store where they are scanned so they can notify security whenever a promiscuous mode trace is discovered? Those forward-thinking original developers must have been geniuses if they anticipated the state of things to come so many years ahead of time. She doubts it but does not want to get into that and the satisfied look on Matthieu's face suggests how unpleasant it would be to call him out. Where to go to verify the information anyway? Cannot do an internet search for some archaic tool that no one owns anymore, no more docs for that. Not talking about Wireshark or some other publicly known tool. It's probably a random guy in one of the old buildings somewhere describing something that titillates him and that no one has asked him about for years. She does not have the energy for that. Self-satisfied, infantile geeks. Abhishek is not listening. He is the one who should know better. Not worth the effort, she decides. Probably just writes to a file on the disk. She nods and fixes her gaze on the screen in front of her. With both feet planted firmly on the ground, she refines the query before plugging it into the incident portal's monitoring panel where she enables a trigger for the desired regions using optimal lookback rules.

—Every time segment, every distance, is never alone, on its own, self-contained. They're rendered through rules looking back in time to make comparative analysis across a flowing surface. She types out the burden of proof and it circles around her.

[The architects point everyone forward into the near future where bursting is at the seams and there is more to do every day as they set up new dev and test environments to simulate the conditions of rapid growth and an overabundance of usage and relay. They set the scene for stress and scale, they monitor resource usage and performance. Size and throughput, latency and end-to-end experience become matters of primary concern. Not only in cases where the user waits a long time for an agent installation or a configuration update, but in the functionality found in the day-to-day modes of interaction and intercom. Their studies show that users want a sense of immediate response, they will not tolerate gaps as though the interlocutor is speaking via satellite from the other side of the earth. It must flow simply and directly as though they are in the same room together, bonding over the music to come and its carefully selected entertainment value. The secret to their projections and plans is not some great idea born in isolation. Instead, it models the patterns of the real world and builds an environment that precisely reproduces them. The better they see what is out there and how it responds to this and that modification, the better they turn and tweak the system knobs in ways that circumvent the crowding and overpopulation, epidemic inside those data centers.]

~~The layer was the answer to a problem he did not know he had and, once he saw it, everything became clear. The pencil became charcoal, the pen became paint, and with every advance in his technique, he learned new layers and new ways to pile meaning up against the background.~~

While clicking and scrolling, she recalls that Matthieu is a senior engineer but realizes that the title does not mean what it used to. Because the company salary ranges are lower than most others in the industry and they rely on the value of the company stock awarded during performance reviews to make up for the shortfall, there is an urgency in getting people up to senior and principal where they will earn enough money to stay put. It spells catastrophe if a wave of attrition happens because an increasing number of employees go looking for something more lucrative from the flock of recruiters stalking them on those professional websites. The result is that you see a lot more immature people with reasonably good programming chops who have acquired the title of Senior Engineer a bit earlier than their age and experience merit. Matthieu, for example, has not yet celebrated his thirtieth birthday.

"The form defaults to the immediate manager," Abhishek says as though not paying attention to their exchange. "René won't be able to approve it. I'll add Karen, my skip, and Patrick for visibility. She'll have to forward it to Scott. We need his approval." He

pauses for emphasis and goes on after giving the others a chance
to nod gravely: "I mentioned in the justification that I'm the one
filling out the form with your account. The issue prevents me from
using my SAW."

"Can you add Jason to keep him in the loop?" Dulcy does not
stop or look up from making her changes to the monitor. She
speaks into the keyboard of her laptop and, with a flutter of
keystrokes on the other side of the table, her wish is granted.

Jason walks back toward the elevators around the corner and,
passing them, continues down to the west hallway on the other side
of the building where the LT has their team room. They sit
together even though they do not connect up on the organizational
chart. There would be something ridiculous were a VP or director
forced to sit in the vicinity of an IC inside their chain of command.
Imagine what they might hear or pick up in the atmosphere.
Cannot have high level leadership sitting with the lowly worker
bees. Right before the turn off into the team room at 1A, Yitzhak
comes out of a larger meeting room and flags Jason down. They
step into a focus room nearby and close the door. There is no table
in this one, only some comfy chairs and a screen. The switch is
mounted to the far wall, but neither of them opens the lid on their
laptop. They take the two seats nearest each other at the back of
the room and swivel them to face one another. Yitzhak, extremely
curt and steep in demeanor, says, "What's the status?" He has little
round glasses that make his eyes look smaller than they really are
but hide the bags under his eyes to give him a more energetic look.
His balding head and long beard lend something of a rabbinical
styling to his aspect. Jason is struck by the resemblance and recalls
a few stories over the years regarding Yitzhak's orthodox religious
affiliations. It has never been something they openly discussed, but
there were a few comments here and there about how he had to
leave early some Friday afternoon to do a bunch of errands before
sunset and then of course he can never be IM on a Saturday.

In Tel Aviv it is late, but Monday nearly ended though it is not
the first day of the work week. It begins on Sunday and ends on
Thursday. Yitzhak started his tenure with the team there and those

weekly rhythms stay with him years after he transplanted his large family from its satellite life near the analytics-heavy full stack development center to the professional sprawl of the Pacific Northwest. The boys are safer, the girls too, but his own training never vacates and the discipline of thinking in terms of high-risk conditions in tight spaces never leaves his thoughts. He is happy the kids got enough of it to set them on the right track with the right frame of mind, but he worries that the distractions of America will overwhelm those solid foundations and make his kids soft with bleeding hearts.

Jason shifts uncomfortably in his seat waiting, like always, for his manager to begin the conversation. It would be presumptuous to launch into anything, that is the feeling he gets whenever the two of them sit down alone to chat. Might be different in a bigger meeting where Jason is driving the discussion, but even then he defers to the older man. Jason is always nervous around Yitzhak and that is partially because his manager never laughs and never makes any small talk, nothing like 'how was your vacation' or 'is your wife okay?' after you had to miss a day of work to take her to the hospital or something. Their weekly one-on-ones have devolved into status meetings and require a few hours of preparation to make sure Jason is ready to cover the details his manager is sure to want for projects high on the LT's radar. Yitzhak is an expert interrogator. He never lets up until he is satisfied he has a complete picture of the situation. Somehow, during briefings on an issue completely unfamiliar to him, he still knows enough to ask questions, taking him to the heart of the matter and forcing Jason to explain everything relevant in a logically organized way. It is impressive but scary as hell.

~~At university he lost his hesitancy for drawing the human form. Figure drawing was always frustrating to him, he never got it right. He studied anatomy and learned about the bones and muscles, but still it did not come out the way he imagined. To help him see the way, it required the sudden realization that human beings are layers of flesh stacked upon other layers of muscle, sinew, and bone.~~

—The richer corners are where authority lives. It's point of view lifts them up, there are skills in their coverage and embodied in their perspective.

(The severity 2 incidents in those days usually came from the relay machines. They were not keeping up with the volume of data coming up from the agents and were unable to handle the load alongside their modeling duties. The machines were overwhelmed. There was too much going on, too many parallel operations grinding away at each node's sixteen virtual cores and terabyte of memory. The decision was made from the data. Anton sealed the deal. We will break out the modeling operations that guide the relay and move them onto separate nodes. That was the decision he made. Everyone knew right away what it entailed. In-process operations needed to be rationalized into formal contracts fulfilled with a request and a response sent out across the network. The microservices were deployed onto clusters huddled together in scale units and the communication between the servers was streamlined and fast. Components were drawn up, architects fluttered about writing this design and that one, reviewing each other's contributions, looking over each other's shoulders, borrowing patterns, and agreeing on common orchestrations shared across systems and service operations. The notion of the isolated workload came into being and the rigid lines were drawn with infrastructure to support it up and down the stack. They added codes and event descriptors, beefed up correlation principles, and made them first-class citizens in every operation. Rapidly, while each of them was alone in their home office or living room, they re-engineered a system in dire need, growing fast in the direction of that magical one billion as management pretended the world had gone haywire. They tracked the increases in revenue piling up after the hiring frenzy bringing in the able bodies they needed to make it work.)

Yitzhak has been, however, professionally generous with Jason, promoting him soon after making him a manager and giving him good performance reviews, usually above the target for his level. Nevertheless, Jason is keenly aware that those acts are purely transactional and only as strong as his latest work. There are no laurels, there is no rest. He cannot relax and even if it is irrational to blame his manager for his attitude, a fear of restlessness courses through his body whenever he sits in a small room and responds to questions and the harsh looks that inevitably accompany them.

He hears Mags' beats in the nearby background. Her thump and her ring spell the moment to keep him calm and align his body with the curvature of the earth at this point in its rotation.

"What's the status with security and the outage?" Yitzhak repeats the question, assuming an absence of context explains Jason's hesitation.

"All worldwide Home relay servers are paused, they went into wait mode when they stopped getting pings from the health service," Jason says concisely. "No new agents to onboard. No new configuration or agent versions deployed. No data up, no data down," he continues the review using that same tone, without either decoration or hedging. "There was no evidence of a customer breach other than the single event with Parker's test tenant. Telemetry logs have stopped, but even before that, they were missing for multiple periods."

That constant bass drumbeat, measured out in steady speeds by a foot peddle lingering beneath every punctuated point and their crowning sounds on the rims and skins of the upper kit spread out in front of her, throbs inside his head.

"Which logs?" Yitzhak does not affect any change in expression and keeps his eyes locked on Jason's.

—He's been doing this longer. He sees more. He has seen more. The heights of his status come from an advantage in point of view not the other way around.

[They know their growth is a sign of the times and worry it will cease once the social pressures go away. Such a boon will not last forever, the internal memos say. We better make sure that the expansion we need to handle the load retracts when the time is right. In the event these active users withdraw and leave the system behind, even if it does remain in place, installed but idle, they should no longer play a part in the daily rhythms of the server side of the service, taking up its cycles and burning through its energy. They did not know how much of the response to the crisis would endure beyond its closure. They hoped for the best but planned for the worst. Elasticity was the buzz word on the tip of everyone's tongue. Servers had to know when they were needed and when to shutdown to save on costs and free up resources.]

```
namespace BISoft.Data.Home.Core
{
    public class Graph<T> where T : class
    {
        private
        List<Tuple<Simultaneity<T>, Simultaneity<T>>> edges =
            new List<Tuple<Simultaneity<T>, Simultaneity<T>>>();

        public
        List<Tuple<Simultaneity<T>, Simultaneity<T>>> Edges =>
            this.edges;
    }
}
```

"It's variable. Whichever ones are related. Server logs now, that's the normal case, but client logs sometimes too. At Parker's tenant, those were client logs. Anything about to land in a telemetry store." Jason quickly halts, having the distinct impression he has been rambling. When multiple sentences are required to answer the question, it feels like he has been talking for too long. Or maybe he is unsure of himself. He does not know in the moment, but it is always better if the response does not seem like a justification or an excuse. None of that is necessary. His manager understands the details of the system thoroughly and does not need any fluff to backfill the reasons or causes behind ordinary things. Short, precise answers are preferred. A weird self-consciousness protrudes from the back of Jason's throat whenever they are not available.

"What about perf counters? What about event logs? Anything from the OS on those nodes? 5985 is still open, isn't it?" Yitzak asks, referring to the management port.

Like any artist, he needed encouragement to keep up the pace, to continue learning and growing, and replenish his energy for

~~more work. Once he started in with the figures, once he learned how deeply layered the human form was, the fascination and positive reinforcement began to roll in, urging him to elevate his approach and take himself more seriously.~~

Yitzhak's voice has been resounding inside Jason's head for days. It hums there even now. The director mind sits atop the manager mind and flows through it in every one of his concerns. He cannot hear himself any longer, he is the one and he is the other.

Jason Kahn rubs the soft fur on his chin, drawing it away from his skin as he does so, "Of course. Do they have control of the app or the node? Is that what you mean?" He tries to anticipate the direction of the questioning. Yitzhak nods a single time, deliberately, while closing his eyes which, until then, were peering out over the top of his glasses like they often do when he looks at something nearby. "I don't know about event logs, don't think anyone checked, but there were perf counters we observed for the blackout periods before shutting everything off."

"We should consider re-enabling the servers," he says without further explanation or registering the response. Jason's brows arch upward, and his eyes open wider. Yitzhak continues, "Once we have the emergency monitors in place, a controlled test is merited. Broaden the scope, if necessary. Since there is no breach of customer data, there's no risk. We need to study their behavior. Stiff forensics will only get us so far." Yitzhak stands up to conclude the meeting. Jason mirrors him and they move together toward the door. "Who's on it?" Yitzhak asks with his hand on the knob.

"Dulcy," Jason says. "Working with Abhishek from Patrick's team and Matthieu from René's."

Yitzhak turns the knob and opens the door to head back to the meeting room. He does not say anything to mark the end of the conversation or that counts as a farewell. He disappears into the room, leaving Jason standing in the hall.

Karen is in the meeting room and sees Yitzhak get up to leave. Jason's figure is visible in the hallway outside, and she guesses the purpose. From her laptop, she sends a DM to Patrick to get the scoop on their meeting earlier with the EMs from deployment and platform. Jason pasted the Workmate-generated notes into the message box and, while going through them, she is mystified by the SAW fiasco described in some detail. She is asking about it, trying to get perspective on the breadth and scope of the discovery. The idea that a SAW has been compromised is a catastrophe that will soon fan across the entire company with dire implications. These are the tanks of production business. They are zero-trust laptop computers that treat every running application and every network request as a threat. By default, they do not allow the user to do anything. Every permitted action must be explicitly whitelisted based on a policy for the specific user type. Only approved and vetted processes are allowed to execute and only if they come from applications installed from the corporate deployment servers. Sanctioned websites are reachable from the browser, but few external sites are sanctioned. The user must provide highly secure credentials to get onto the machine in the first place and they cannot be the same credentials used to login to corpnet. Network access is established via the VPN exclusive to SAW machines. That condition holds whether the device is directly plugged into a segment inside a company building or not. They are used to access sensitive resources and customer artifacts for support purposes only. A breach among SAWs means the entire support system is at risk, nothing is secure if the SAW is no longer to be trusted.

~~Shortly after moving to San Jose, he followed suit with the rest of the world and made himself a blog on one of the popular platform sites. After cranking out his initial entries where he conjectured on how the multi-tenant blogging platform was built, he took to posting photographs of his artwork, sometimes the finished product, but usually it was just the stages in the process of creating it with details about each of the layers as they were set in place.~~

While she grills Patrick for further details and he explains elaborately why they do not have them yet, a request comes into her inbox for a high-level node analysis, spanning two clusters in the Home System's relay server stamps. She sees that Patrick's alias is on the request too as are the other relevant M1s, René and Jason. The request is for the most invasive possible analysis. It allows packet sniffing across the clusters and VM container dumps based on data driven snapshot scheduling. Before looking carefully at the information provided on the form, she notes that the requester is from René's team and not one of her own.

"What's this analysis request about?" She types into the chat message window focused on Patrick's avatar.

"Abhishek only had his SAW with him and has stopped using it. He's with Matthieu and Dulcy and is probably using Matthieu's laptop to fill out the form," he writes back. "It's in the justification," added in a second bubble.

There is too much to do today. Karen oversees the projects at home and does not think there is room for any of this. The rules with Jeremy have been carefully drawn up and must be rigorously enforced. That level of organization is the secret to their success raising children following the dissolution of their marriage. He leaves work early to make sure Kyle gets to practice on time. She still handles the pickups, and the notes for Kit's school project later this week, but at least today there is some help, and she can rest assured that her focus here will not jeopardize anything urgent at home. That is half of her daily battle, the other half coming from her ex-husband's fragile ego and the power plays he makes to force her to keep accommodating it.

She stares at Patrick's answers but does not reply. Instead, she switches focus to the request link in the email and follows it to the portal where she sees the complete form submission and each of the data points provided. She verifies that everything is in order. The justification is minimal. Aside from the explanation for why he is using someone else's account to write it, he depends on people power and email document trails to convey the context and significance. He has only written briefly about the missing logs, the global shutdown, and now, the automatically resuming nodes. No one who was not already familiar with the issue would have any idea what he is talking about. She bobs her head and purses her lips, thinking Scott will not look too closely at that and rely on her briefing. He depends on her to get it right before she reaches out.

The team chat app flashes on the task bar, indicating a new message from Patrick.

"I haven't been informed, but I assume they want to perform a controlled dump of one of these broadcast events we've identified. They'll need the sniffer to get a complete picture. We don't log that anywhere so if you don't capture it live, there's no way to replay it. Besides, the machines are cut off other than the management port. We have no other option. We should approve it."

—The vice president is a cyborg, part man but mostly machine. His words are never sincere, and his vision always clouded by his own authority and the power it emits in gassy substance circling around the crown of his head and the reflected light floating above it. If the foot soldiers and platoon leaders are the language, then the vice presidents are the lies they tell to keep everything tightly ordered and functioning properly. Lies are expensive.

(The designers and marketers went to work making sure this was not a temporary spike. They wanted the growth in numbers to be a lasting source of revenue and stock expansion. Not exactly. They wanted to meet their manager's expectations, wanted to perform above the mean on this year's review. The conditions for success came from higher up and the meaning behind them was defined there. The marker for the metric was the MAU and the number landed right where it needed to be when things around the world went off the rails.)

~~Some local influencer came across the site randomly after a lucky strike search put the listing at the top of the results page. Jason never configured the headers and metadata or paid the fee for advertising and promotion. The blog made Site of the Week in some Wired puff piece and readers flocked to get a look at the dilettantish outpourings of this Silicon Valley stalwart. The gallery was lured in by the same attention machine and reached out to him with an invitation to join. They insisted that every local artist of value was already a member. He simply had to add his name to the list for a small fee, payable once a year or in monthly installments, if necessary.~~

Karen clicks the thumbs-up reaction to the last bubble. She

opens a new chat panel for Scott and puts a high priority tag on the message. She pastes a link to the web page for the request where she has added him as final approver, then types: "Need your sign-off on this ASAP for further forensics on the Home System relay security issue." That is it. No more details than that. He knows the COMMS are out there, he knows they are in Def Con mode. She does not think any further explanation is necessary. He will ask if he wants more details. Miraculously, it only takes a few minutes before he replies "Done" to her message.

What fades are the uncomfortable dinners and office visits where Karen has her monthly one-on-ones. There is never a sincere moment in the mix, their exchanges come from the roles they play. Nothing as crisp as this 'Done' now put to light and shading on the screen. She wonders how people become painted thick with layers of symbol and taboo. She wonders what the chaos of that household is like. Who fills their eyes with that emptiness? Who robs them of their blood and organs? She understands that he is responsible for building an organization to ship a massive product. He is the architect of a modern-day pyramid. Go on, ask him. He will tell you.

—Her feelings are alien to the brew. There's no place for that in the potions and tinctures the alchemists provide. She is that organization, she is its nature naturing.

[A world they never see opens wide before them. They feel the new hitch and an ascending grift, permitting no one to live without deep and useful integrations with the system-at-large. The captive audience remains prisoner even when the sentence has been lifted.]

```
/*
HomeTrace
| where TIMESTAMP > ago(1d)
| where Process has "BISoft.Data.Home"
| where TraceMarker == "Ordering"
| distinct CorrelationId
*/
```

/* *
* *
* * * * * *   Description: Analytic, Chapter Three   * * * * * *
* * * * * *   Author: Do not modify. Auto generated by a tool.* * * * * *
* * * * * *   Ad hoc changes will be lost on build.   * * * * * *
* * * * * *   Date: 2024-03-11   * * * * * *
* * * * * *   CorrelationId: * * * * * *
* * * * * *   7423615c-4da7-5282-c201-f7b7293656d1   * * * * * *
* *
* /

The phone hums as Abhishek closes the door to his daughter's room. It is a notification from ITS and he acknowledges it while crossing the small landing to the stairs. He slowly lowers himself step-by-step while looking at his screen, failing to see what is right in front of him. He nearly trips and has to look up to steady himself before going on. At the bottom of the stairs, he turns to the right and walks toward the back of the house to join Pooja in the kitchen. She has finished most of the cooking for the week and is now cleaning up so they can settle in and spend some quiet time together now that Aashvi is put to bed. She frowns when she sees him staring at his phone and tapping away in response. When he finally looks up, he says, "Sorry, I must see to this," and then turns around and walks back toward the office at the front of the house. She purses her lips and continues wiping down the counter with the dry cloth. The exhaust fan above the stove is set to low. She leans in close and gets up on her toes to use the same towel to wipe the stainless-steel surfaces hanging from the ceiling. Since he is busy with work, she can pick up with one of her shows from the satellite, prioritizing the ones he does not like. She decides not to look at Sarabhai vs Sarabhai because even though he says he does not care whether they watch it or not, he always pays attention when she puts it on.

```
namespace BISoft.Data.Home.Core
{
```

```
public class Heuristic<T> : IActionGuide where T : class
{
    public T Trial { get; set; }
    public Exception Error { get; set; }
}
}
```

He rolls his chair up close under the desk and connects the VPN to join the bridge and see what they have discovered from the alarms they set earlier today. The chair is not ergonomically sound, but it has thick leather padding and reminds him of his father's chair back home. He associates it with abundance and being well-to-do. The rollers are on a square piece of plastic allowing him to move freely without damaging the carpet.

~~They have performed extensive sociological studies that suggest taste is bound to class. At least, that it is bound to the forms of order imposed on agents developing habitual behaviors under the guidance of institutions with financially based hierarchies. The effects of those institutions may vary according to the cultural, educational, and social capital available to the actor.~~

There is nothing special about the Japanese car in the garage or the Korean car in the driveway. He means to make room for both in the garage, but something always gets in the way of his weekend plans. Either there is work to do or some other chore he must attend to. Truth is, he focused on the house and family rather than the cars and their arrangement. If you asked him years ago whether this was his preference, he would have denied it furiously, but now he does not see much of a choice and no matter what his friends think or even his father, he prefers it the way Pooja does. What is best for us here, what we have together, the three of us, that is what matters, not whether you have the fanciest car from England. We spend little time in the car, who cares if it is a Jaguar? His friends think she is a shrew, but he knows that she is right and that her decision is for the best. Maybe someday, if he keeps along the path he is on and Patrick sees it the same way, he will have it both ways. It will be a true mark of his success. He cannot wait to load his family up and show them off to their friends in the style they deserve.

—Which is the carrot, and which is the stick? Their cross purposes make it impossible to explain their angles without considering the added incentives.

(The exceptional was the critical, the crucial, the essential worker that civilization was unable to endure without. Those positioned at the very foundation of life as they knew it. The farmers, of course, but that was irrelevant, what mattered was who among the city dwellers were counted among the select. The nurses and the doctors, they were a given. Everyone knew how important they were, how essential their contribution in times of need. Braving the risks and exposing themselves to danger, they showed up every single day and did their jobs looking after the rest of them. And not only them, the entire profession, the health care workers, the lab technicians, the orderlies and physician assistants, across the board they showed up and dedicated themselves to social well-being at great personal risk. In return, they often received ovations in the streets at the change in shifts. People on balconies with pots and pans, banging away in traditional rhythms to signal their appreciation. They were not alone. Since everyone was locked away and isolated in place, the dependencies grew. Everyone needed help from services that ordinarily received little more than neglect. Delivery persons and grocers continued to plod away, making sure everyone had what they needed without exposing themselves to anything other than the ridiculous memories of having dusted and sprayed their groceries on the porch before carrying them into the house. If they were one of the select few able to get an appointment, the arrival of those groceries was signaled with a text message and their video capable doorbells tracked any motion around the delivery or, if nefarious forces had their way, rapid exit.)

"Gautam" is the first word he hears as he fixes the headset over his ears and bends the microphone into place, not too close and not too far from his mouth. He touches the action figure closest to the keyboard out of habit and, mostly, for luck. He hears his mother's voice softly beneath the din of the call. She encourages him not to put his trust in things and remain devoted to his tasks.

Diligence and remaining true to family and friends, that is what
matters most as the best mark of his character.

~~In so far as taste relates to matters of pleasure and pain, its
nature and complexity are highly influenced by educational
experience. A person like Parker Henning who has gone far in the
system, acquiring the doctorate in literary theory, is bound to that
institution and its language for life. Whatever economic capital
they forfeit for the sake of their educational wealth shows itself in
their preferences and comes out in their simplest pleasures.~~

"What happened?" He asks once it registers that, aside from
the ever-present Obi, spitting out notes and interesting facts helpful
to the case, only Dulcy and Matthieu are on the bridge. Why are
they talking about Gautam, he wonders. He assumes they mean
the one from the workload team, but he is not sure from the
context. It is not immediately obvious why that Gautam would be
relevant to their issue. Unless he is currently on call. And if he is,
why hasn't he been summoned to join them?

"I was telling Matthieu that there was a vortex incident," Dulcy
says to catch him up. "Routine stuff. But the DRI, Gautam from
the dataset workload, had to use his SAW to run commands to
reset a pipeline."

"Ah," Abhishek says, mostly because he is pleased that he was
correct. Gautam also speaks Bengali, but his wife's curries are very
different from Pooja's. They eat lunch together and sometimes
trade containers.

*She uses voice commands to find the right satellite channel and
get the lights the way she likes them when she watches the
television. The model usually guesses which show she wants from
a few words. She has the habit of watching the same stations most
of the time and the house has learned where her tendencies lie.
Sometimes, it leads her there, like tonight, when she shrugs
indifferently to the top selection and approves it with a resigned
clucking of her lips, something the device has learned signals
affirmation when delivered in this particular tone. The selections
carry over across this media and into others such as the music
system, the web browser, and other household activities. It
infiltrates the food choices for stocking the refrigerator and the*

*pantry. The half dozen or so agents roaming the premises know
they are in a proper Bengali house and supply it with provisions
and entertainment accordingly, despite its location in the Pacific
Northwest, easily determined using the IP address on the one
router in the house.*

"It's the same rotation," Matthieu chimes in. "The one that
covers the relay servers." He assumes Abhishek does not know
these organizational details about the Home System rotations.

"Anyway," Dulcy goes on. "It triggered the event, and our traps
were sprung. We were notified, the VMs dumped, the Gomez
logs, everything we set. All good."

"Telemetry logs?" Abhishek asks. He is upset that he has to
catch up, it is better when he is the first one on the call, but he
could not rush through his daughter's regimen. He had to put her
down properly. That forced him to wait until the second
notification. Matthieu and Dulcy might think he does not care as
much as he should. They might think he is slacking off and provide
that feedback to Patrick when they are collecting it for the next
review. He wishes for an opportunity to explain why he was late
but knows that will only slow things down and make a worse
impression.

—Pooja is willing to wait for him because she knows what's at
stake. She considers herself an extended part of the team. She's
one of them, by extension, and thinks the same way they do.

[The planning hardly misses a beat when it moves to remote
meetings and chat-based sessions. The desktop software for
collaboration is built in-house and the product managers on that
team project a sizeable increase in uptake and propose changes to
improve user experience and customer satisfaction. The entire
company turns on a dime and reorients itself to different tools.
Their geographic distribution is a boon for this adjustment. They
hit the ground running with the infrastructure changes, plus the
necessary pre-requisites, in place and ready to go. The future-
looking facets of every organization and every division are
immediately thrust into the limelight as they rework their thinking
about priorities and what the team needs to address first and
foremost. The semester plan is completely reworked and the list

of tasks above the bar changes in ways unrecognizable to someone scanning through them before the crisis began.]

"Not from the service," she responds. "But everything from the OS. Event logs, performance counters, everything is there."

"What do you see?" He asks. If he had been the first one to look at the incident, to acknowledge it, he would already know these things and be explaining it to them. The more he has to ask for clarification, the more humiliated and inessential he feels.

~~The great works from his adolescence and teenage years become an embarrassment to him. Parker understands now that these popular works were not well-suited to someone serious about their literary endeavors. Books such as Alex Haley's Roots, which he read after it became a TV mini-series, and John Irving's World According to Garp, the biggest influence on him and something he will never discuss with anyone, have become an embarrassment. He excludes them from his origin story, thinking his twelve-year-old self should have been more astute.~~

"We've started looking," Matthieu's tone suggests he is continuing to look as they speak and that his attention is not 100% present for Dulcy's summary. That grinds on Abhishek too. Matthieu does not need to listen, he already knows because he was there when it happened. He has direct experience and does not need to rely on summaries and aggregate descriptions.

"Yup," Dulcy confirms as though she were validating his claim and looking at her own screen in the same way, everything already open and in place, no doubt.

"What do you guys need from me?" he asks.

The objects on the desk stand out in strong relief against the large blocks of background color supplying context to whatever he sees and feels inside these four walls. The circularity of perception evokes a circularity of reason. The conditions that make for the meaningfulness of things in the room are the outcome as well as the origin of his experience. The conclusion, the upshot and end result, is that he can apprehend, and, additionally, find the purpose in what lies nearby. What explains that? What must he be aware of to ensure these results and this feeling of at-homeness in the circulating circumstances of a place he knows well where he expects events to follow an order using a logic routine to him and habitual to everyone sharing this space, even little Aashvi.

Matthieu grumbles something unintelligible. Dulcy hems a bit as if struggling to give the question her full attention. "Uhhh," she says finally. "Yitzhak wants us to turn everything back on. He says there's no proof of a breach and nothing to indicate we have a security event that meets the Sev 1 bar."

"Doesn't meet the bar," Matthieu repeats. It is superfluous.

—Like wind-up toys. Most of the meter happens on an automatic setting. From the first responders' perspective, the company provides the automation, but for those who aren't present, it's the other way around. Finger pointing. Finer points. Finger painting. Minor joints.

(The CDC was already a customer, they had multiple tenants, and an elaborate installation filled with data pumps and reporting applications distributable to members of their different teams upon request, assuming their need to know. The division chief reached out to their technical sales representative and asked for help. They were out of their element with the enormous data requirements and accumulating tasks. They wanted consulting assistance from the product team itself and an entire team of UX developers were assigned to them. They were experts at manipulating the knobs available from the graphical interface, but they sometimes needed to raise a hand for help from the backend folks who provided insight on better ways to get the data from the various worldwide sources and draw it together in a manageable mess ready for display in a geographically accurate map showing worldwide impact and the various statistics for doom and gloom.)

```
namespace BISoft.Data.Home.Core
{
    using System;
    public class Rule<T> : IActionGuide where T: class
    {
        public Graph<T> Condition { get; set; }
        public Action<T> Action { get; set; }
    }
```

}

(It was not only the experts in disease who needed help. The trucking companies and delivery systems needed their data to help them allocate resources properly. They needed to know where to send people and how many it would take to address the relevant needs. Not for dispatch alone, the schedules for long shifts at the hospital and doctor's offices around the country and in the cities had to be maintained too. The need was great and the customer support lines were glutted with calls for help. The teams were growing and the expertise they provided often came from the analytics groups that easily collected data to reveal the state of the world and the hotspots where assistance was most needed.)

~~In graduate school, no one told him to invent an alternative origin story, but he came up with one anyway. It had been slowly brewing throughout his college career and now took full form. Parker said those first important steps came through Don Quixote and the Basic Writings of Nietzsche. Technically, this was not a lie, but it was not exactly the truth either. His edits were for the sake of putting the correct tastes on display.~~

Abhishek switches to email and scrolls the unread messages from this evening. There is nothing from Yitzhak in his inbox. "It must be above my paygrade," he says sarcastically. These little nits pile up and he becomes more self-conscious of his exclusion. "We'll have to get Patrick, or maybe Karen, to sign off on that."

Gautam has it better, he broods. It is because his manager and his director are both Indian. That sets the tone. One day he will get into a situation like that. He needs to keep his eyes open for an opportunity. Maybe the ML workload or maybe another. Once you are in security, it is hard to get out, he mourns. There must be fellows in some relevant area. He will eventually find the right person looking to fill a spot and then make his move. He will not be forced to lag behind like this, not for long. He will stand out the way he is supposed to. Guaranteed.

"That's what we thought," Dulcy says. "But we're trying to make the case. Jason was hoping the analysis could do that."

"What have you found?" Abhishek asks. Repeating the links to himself: Jason and Yitzhak, Dulcy and Matthieu, René most likely. Security is only an advisor under the circumstances. We cannot take over for the product group, he reassures himself. It's not our place to make these decisions, we only advise.

—He has so much extra. They have to do something with it. The key is to find an outlet and send them that way in case they cannot find it for themselves. Make sure the crissing and the crossing are channeled correctly.

[The primary directive in the increased role of machine learning and the new quantum systems in the data analytics group is to assist with planning and oversight. Its handiwork is spread throughout the documentation and in the marketing materials. The manager needs help understanding the situation in the world where their business pushes its wares. It is not enough to look at the history, one has to correlate that history with recent events to use that information for coordinating a unified approach under repeating circumstances. These are conditions found in small ways and littered throughout the domain of probable behaviors and actions. No analyst studies the patterns sufficiently, with the correct filters and attributes in place, or fully understands the future's impact and its relationship to the past. Machines with millions and billions of tensors extract meaningfulness and project it onto the whiteboard screen of the future. They see what those managers and administrators cannot see. They foretell worlds unfolding and conditions coming together. Send trucks there, they may not be needed today but will be in grave demand tomorrow. The shifts at this location should be heavier populated than the shifts at that location. The social calendars obviously merit that imbalance even if you and your colleagues cannot see it. The data is collected and the outcomes well-presented with probabilities in-lined. Do not worry, the reps tell them, it won't do the decision making, it brings together all your options and helps you make better choices.]

Of course he loved Dostoevsky, but now he realized he had never truly read him before. In fact, Parker was a lowly fanatic strapped with the work of Constance Garnet and others who had produced something for him to digest given his barriers and limitations. He discovered the work of John Barth and learned

~~new lands of arrogance and high-brow obscurity. The more~~
~~overlooked the writer, niche and savvy in their command of the~~
~~domain, the better-suited it was for his work and further~~
~~inspiration.~~

"We have the packets and we know what process is sending them," Matthieu says.

"What process?" Abhishek's voice goes higher. There is nothing on his screen to look at. Neither of them is sharing. They are independently going through the results or looking at the materials. He thinks the call would be better organized if he were the first one on it. Is it because they are not from the security team, or is it something about him and the way they see his contribution?

Add it to the list of topics for the next one-on-one with Patrick. Make sure he knows how much it matters that security's appropriate role is defined clearly during investigations. Should he play the part of the go-to guy or is he only meant to lend support? Helping define policy is a feather in the cap and suggests higher levels of responsibility are warranted.

"Our service entry point," Dulcy says, obviously distracted.

"How is that possible?" He has no distractions. It is hard to prevent his personal frustration from coming out in the question. He clears his throat once he finishes asking it so that it seems like the frustration was something caught in there and needing to be flushed out. There, now, it's gone, they will think.

"The config has been altered," she says. "It doesn't look like it's supposed to. It doesn't look like the version from the repository. Makes no sense that entry point usage is spiking."

"The rules list," Matthieu jumps in as the group chat screen redraws with the images from his own desktop. "Can you guys see my screen?" He asks, knowing full well that no one single participant is able to provide an authoritative answer to that question. It is the standard tic that everyone exhibits when presenting work from their desktop.

"Yup," Abhishek replies, accepting the illusion of an authoritative position as an ad hoc bug bash participant for the team chat desktop application. Ship it.

"See this one." There is a JSON document on the screen, most of it a wall of text. Matthieu scrolls down a bit and highlights a section containing an array in the class he projects. "This is the list of static rules. See this one?" He changes the highlight from the block of rules to a single member at the end of the list. It reads "Undefined".

"Yup," Abhishek says. "Got it."

—They're onto it.

(They never mentioned it on the news reports, it was never part of the constant 24/7 cycle. Healthcare and delivery personnel, that was the mantra. No one ever mentioned that hospital triage and retail dispatch were completely driven by the intelligent use of data. BISoft and its employees were at the center of every operation and response to it. The EMT unit used GPS and data gathered from traffic monitors. They used machine learning mechanisms listening in on their past operations to plot a course in the immediate present. The companies added scanners and text messages to convey status to customers and giant storage centers collected the data with identifying attribution to track the course of deliveries and the routes taken to get the packages there. Better delivery plans were projected, more intelligent organization was implemented, and companies met the growing need despite having difficulties finding employees to do the work. The efficiency of data driven systems increased. The entire civilized world did more with less. These were essential workers, but the powers that be wanted to keep that fact on the downlow for reasons that were not clear at the time. The growing staff at BISoft might occasionally mention it during the idle minutes at the beginning of a meeting with a completely different agenda, but they did not dwell on it for long. It served no one's interests to get worked up about systematic exclusion from praise and gratitude. The body count was too high for petulance. Besides, they watched the stock price steadily rise and somehow understood that it had everything to do with their role in the crisis. Employees grew wealthier, disproportionately to the massive growth in profit and revenue, but wealthier still. Regardless of how they reacted emotionally, they did not need to be celebrated publicly and counted themselves lucky that the stock market, at least, knew the truth.)

~~These tastes were not meant for research and personal pleasures alone. The pretensions invading Parker's angles of vision found their way into the lowest reaches of his mind. They took over every inflexion in his voice when he did his own work, producing criticism as expected, but also when he took his turn at more novel endeavors exhibiting a personal flair.~~

"There are no traces," Dulcy says. "And the local cache of events on disk is empty. We do have the perf counters. There is some activity. Enough evidence of it to suggest either that this Undefined rule uses a decent amount of memory and processor cycles or that all the rules ran when they weren't supposed to."

"We don't know which," Matthieu says. "Perf counters aren't bound to the rows, to the specific operations, they're periodic samples running at a one-minute interval." Neither Abhishek nor Dulcy needs to be reminded of this information. Matthieu is careful to clearly articulate it anyway.

Matthieu is pleased with the way things are going. He did not expect to be anything more than a useless third wheel, but things have turned out differently and now he sees it as an opportunity to score some much-needed points. Everyone knows how good Dulcy is. If she provides positive feedback to René, this will end up being quite helpful for those year-end numbers. They might still get that kitchen remodel they were hoping for and maybe sooner than they thought possible.

"Undefined should be a syntax error though, right?" Abhishek ignores Matthieu's contribution. They have not worked together much over the last couple years since Home came to be in its current corporate organizational form following a few big reorgs, but he is starting to see the pattern. Matthieu has an authoritative way of describing what everyone already knows. Maybe that's good, he thinks. State the obvious. It's better than assuming everyone knows it already and accidentally leaving people in the dark.

"Yes," Dulcy responds to Abishek's question. She probably did not hear Matthieu's explanation, learned to tune such things out since they are so common and unnecessary. "It's not in the schema. That's not a legal rule, it should've thrown and that would've ended up in the event logs, but there's nothing."

"What about the packets?" Abhishek asks. "Any clues in the contents?"

"We gathered them from the participating nodes," Matthieu answers. "Well, all the ones in our range of targets. The node that launched the process was in West US in this case, the same region where Gautam connected with his SAW. We expected that."

"It confirms it, at least," Dulcy says. "West US is the key to this event. Once the node wakes up, there is a node in West Central that wakes up too. No reason to think it's only West Central but that's what we're looking at. In that whole cluster, only one node resumes. In the whole cluster in West US, only one node resumes. It'd be cool to attach our monitor to clusters in other regions. We should probably test whether the signal goes beyond the geo. Maybe include Canada Central or something."

"What are they saying?" Abhishek leans forward to the edge of his seat. He has never heard of anything like this before and cannot hide his fascination. The matter at hand has taken over and whatever self-conscious concerns he felt earlier in the call disappear in favor of genuine wonder.

"That's it," Matthieu responds. "It's nothing. They're not saying anything really. The node in West US, the speaker, it's broadcasting a packet that doesn't contain any real information."

"It's a ping," Dulcy clarifies.

"But a broadcast," Matthieu steps back in. "Technically, every node in West and West Central could have heard it. Most ignore it. This guy," he says flipping his screen to a telemetry explorer window and showing the name of a node in West Central US present on every row of the result. "This guy is the only one in West Central that woke up. Nothing in West."

"Is it a magic packet?" Abhishek asks. "Is that what's waking them?"

"In terms of behavior, definitely," Dulcy says. "But there is no target Mac address on it."

"Can't see how filtering would work," Matthieu finishes the thought. Abhishek guesses they have already gone through this. Surely, he was not that late to the call. How long did it take him to respond to the RA and get to his computer? Too many chores blocked his way and he chastises himself for every one of them.

```
namespace BISoft.Data.Home.Core
{
    public class Process<T> where T : class
    {
        public List<IActionGuide> Actions { get; set; }
        public Simultaneity<T> End {  get; set; }
    }
}
```

Her little face flashes before him and he suffers pangs of guilt at the quick dismissal. Then Abhishek recalls how much she is going to need from him over the years ahead: food and clothing, of course, but much more. Aashvi's education alone is of grave concern. They must start saving immediately if there is to be any hope of ensuring she takes advantage of every opportunity available. And then... What if there are more? Pooja has always said she wants two. This justifies everything. His judgments are a necessary component of any experience they ever hope to have.

~~Like his peers, Parker renews his interest in poetry and short fiction, packing both with obscure, derived etymologies of words rarely used in polite conversation. The stories are pastiche with little in the way of plot typically interesting to the average person used to trivialities such as beginnings, middles, and ends. If you have not studied Byzantine architecture or the finer symbols of the Catholic Mass, then the imagery means nothing to you. It is an exclusive club well-guarded by erudition.~~

"It really is magic. Some protocol only these relay servers understand. What's the response?" Abhishek adds the question to divert attention from his ridiculous observation. Dulcy never says things like that. She never drifts away from the point. Her judgments are precise and always merited by circumstance. They seem to hinge on the perfect unity of her understanding. She never lets them go beyond the limits of her experience. Even when she asks questions and learns from others, she continues to reference that fact when relaying the information. It is never, "this fact has been revealed," rather "so and so says such and such." Because that is the only thing she herself, in her perfect perception of a precise world, can say. She does not know anything beyond that and does not pretend to. He wishes he were more like that. He wishes Matthieu were more like that too. All engineers, he says to himself, should be that way when doing their jobs. If they let themselves go off on flights of fancy, spouting all kinds of nonsense, they might as well be artists.

—There are bells in the data center. They ring out loud and clear when the heat index increases beyond safe levels. The staff on site are appliance maintenance experts. They do not need to know about the software internals, their primary goal is to set the atmosphere correctly and regulate it day and night.

[The company sees it coming, the decision support makes it clear. The emphasis on data has only been a precursor for things to come. They have been gathering momentum to put that data to use and the best way to put it to use is through complex models built to the latest and greatest specifications. General purpose chat bots might be a good circus trick, but the real power comes through integration with systems that have been developed to expertly collect that data and operationalize it. The new proposal is to not only feed the data back to the systems that collect it, but to influence their future actions and provide decision support not only to the managers and administrators, but to the operational systems themselves.]

"It's not exactly an echo reply packet," Matthieu is still trying to connect what they see to something already familiar.

"Similar," Dulcy says. "In function, at least. Suggesting there might be some weird, unknown protocol at work. Spike at the entry point of the responder too. No code to do that."

"Then what?" Abhishek is pleased that his random observation made an impression.

"Then nothing," Matthieu responds. "They go back into the paused state and that's it."

"We've got nothing then," Abhishek's frustration comes out. This time he does not try to hide it, although he does immediately apologize. "Sorry, I didn't mean to..."

"No worries," Matthieu says. "It's freakish. Don't know what to make of it. Must be..." he trails off, not wanting to finish the thought, knowing that whatever he was going to conclude that sentence with was speculation. Like his boss, his tendency is to see an agent behind everything. There must be some singular actor doing these things, unifying their experience, but every time he hints at this, the others point out that he is executing a leap in logic.

~~Parker's work is appreciated in ways he did not expect. The advisors and committee members do not care much for his critical work, but the stories get some attention. He manages to publish a few in the right journals where the right people will see them. They are not meant to entertain but are thought-provoking and use all the right tropes and historical pointers. The politics in them are impeccable.~~

"We actually know a lot," Dulcy says. "But don't want to go beyond the conditions. Need to stick to those and elaborate them clearly. We know it's somehow taking control of the entry point. We know it's hijacking the rules engine on the broadcasting relay service somehow. We didn't know any of that earlier today. We know it now. We know it's adding a rule. Undefined is how that rule presents itself but maybe has nothing to do with the rule itself. It's a representation in the rule language, maybe it's a representation indicating it cannot be represented."

"I see," Matthieu says in an unusually thick accent. Most of the time, it costs him effort to localize his pronunciation but, occasionally, when overly absorbed, he forgets. "That's a good point," uttered with more control and a sense of relief that he has not lost it completely.

Nearly everyone comes from somewhere else and puts down roots this way. In these types of discussions and investigations, the other two, differing in their details, are sufficiently familiar with the pattern and fail to notice it any longer.

"Because there is evidence of an undocumented protocol at the network layer," she goes on. "It stands to reason that there might be some weird protocol at the application layer too. Maybe Undefined means the rule has no serializable semantics, something readable by humans." She is stuck on this notion and struggling to form it more clearly.

"It makes sense." It does not make sense, not really, but Abhishek wants to repay Dulcy for the flattery he feels from her attention to his contribution. "Standard JSON semantics, right?"

"Yes," she goes on. "And we know something else too. It occupies known structures to do its work. It isn't moving through the blocked ports and sends packets that look a little like pings. Packets forwarded by routers at a low enough level on the stack to wake up paused nodes. We know that the node that wakes up in some cluster, wherever it might be, parses what it receives and acknowledges it. That acknowledgement returns to the original broadcaster. It's smart enough to know how and where to initiate communication. It knows how to address things, but we can't see how it's doing it."

—That it is, but not how.

(The corporate reorganization was designed with this change in mind, this turn from data to prediction, from information to behavioral support. Obi is the first of many inventions finding their way into the corporate toolbox. Every employee interacted with it on live site incidents and on call events. Its existence predated any public fervor by nearly three years, making its first public appearance in the middle of a pandemic. They rebranded it so that the user had the power to supply it with a name during initialization.)

"But what does it actually do and what's behind it?" Abhishek asks. Likewise, his mind goes in the same direction. There is always an agent behind the operation: the dev team, a virus, an active hacker. There is always an agent, a singular intention-machine introducing itself into the equation and originating events as their final cause. He heard that suggestion buried in Matthieu's statement and was right there in agreement with him. It is the conclusion they both demand. Dulcy remains steadfast.

~~Parker's pleasures rightly form a literary genre he imitates with ease and uses to delight his colleagues. At first, it affects only those in his own department, but eventually a few across the nation, devoted to similar forms of discourse, are lured into the fold. They~~

~~see the sublime in common places and feel aesthetic remorse in ways shared across the epochs of human history, organized according to the most refined standards. It is their job to promote and defend the trappings of the highbrow mind.~~

"What it does is exactly what I've described," she answers. "Why is it doing it? I think that's the question to ask. Is there some further agenda? Is there some ordered unity behind the different acts? Something unseen. A wizard behind the curtain."

"What makes us think it is an it?" Matthieu asks rhetorically to show he understands the implicit warning. "Mabe it's a funky character embedded in the list and causing the relay server to do something unexpected. A bug. I remember something like that with my last team, some kind of weird XML character in a document made it unreadable by the DOM."

"Doesn't explain the absence of telemetry," Abhishek says. "Of course nothing is getting through the blockade, but there should be something in the cache on the disk."

"It's not completely dark," Dulcy says. "Only the entry point and parts of the rules engine. We see the bootstrapping stuff, whatever is normal operations. That's in the files and they'd flush once 443 is open again. We can't see anything from rules processing. That part fits Matthieu's theory, at least."

"It barfs and everything halts," he says.

—Patterns of computation. Obi records every word of it.

[It does not take a marketing wizard to see that the optimal future is to put Obi everywhere in the customer's path. Whenever the user finds themselves in a BISoft universe, some variant of Obi will be there with them, offering help and insight. All that remains is to add eyes and ears, hands and a mouth.]

"When the delegate returns and it executes the monitoring code, normal operations resume," Dulcy confirms. Matthieu is silent, basking in self-satisfaction. It is a bug, he has convinced himself.

"But what about the SAW?" Abhishek insists. "How does it fit?"

"I'll run through the admin commands in the secure store to see if there is something rogue in there," Matthieu says. "Maybe when we open the node viewer, we're sending packets on the management port to get health stats with some unintended impact or side effect. Could be an ordinary event compounding the weirdness of those special characters. A coincidence."

"Would we be thinking this way if Yitzhak weren't pushing us to turn everything back on?" Abhishek asks.

Aashvi briefly fusses in her crib and Pooja perks up as the TV volume lowers and the baby monitor volume increases. The house automatically adjusts both based on her past tendencies for concern coupled with generalized rules for best practices when caring for an infant.

"We have all this monitoring in place and won't turn it off. It'd be helpful to reactivate the servers. At least in these two regions," Dulcy is the calm voice of reason. "Aside from my weird hallucination, there isn't anything malicious so far. We'd learn a lot more if things were back to normal."

"Okay," Abhishek says. "I'll take it to Patrick and see what he says. If he agrees, he'll take it to Karen. Is that all? Can I leave you guys?" It is getting late and he knows Pooja will be upset with him for working such a long time. Even when it is for an emergency incident, she thinks he likes it and wants to keep working longer than necessary. He will have to be extra nice to make it up to her.

"Sure," they both say. "Have a good night."

```
/*
HomeTrace
| where TIMESTAMP > ago(1d)
| where Process has "BISoft.Data.Home"
| where TraceMarker == "Procedural"
| distinct CorrelationId
*/
```

/* *
* *
* * * * * * Description: Analytic, Chapter Four   * * * * * *
* * * * * * Author: Do not modify. Auto generated by a tool.* * * * * *
* * * * * * Ad hoc changes will be lost on build.   * * * * * *
* * * * * * Date: 2024-03-12   * * * * * *
* * * * * * CorrelationId: * * * * * *
* * * * * * 6a52607a-6df5-6aea-60ad-5a96fccd4bb1   * * * * * *
* *
* */

Patrick comes out of the wind peddling. He mulls over Dulcy's table of judgments documenting what the team already knows, concentrating all the while on his breath. The bicycle shorts are waterproof and challenged to prove it. He coasts through the transit center and dismounts at the far end where there is no alternative but to walk the bike along the pedestrian way to building 14 where he hopes to find Jason. A few buses recently emptied their load into the long, sheltered lanes preassigned for each of the standard routes: Queen Anne, Ballard, Fremont, and Capitol Hill are represented right now. An army of knapsack clad engineers flood the overpass, sidewalks, and curbsides, fanning out along the walkways and roads, some looking for shuttles to their final destination, others on foot the whole way. He circles around to the back of the building. There is an underground entrance to the garage parking and a bike rack up on the left not too far from the entrance to the locker room. He goes inside to change into the clothes he carries in his water-resistant pack.

If he only did things when the sun shines, he would never do them. Patrick is determined to ride his bike to work every day, rain or shine. If he is not feeling it, like this morning, he counts on Ying and Bai to keep him honest. The morning routines are relentless and a habitual place inside them is his only respite from a hectic work schedule. The boy is serious and curious, but quite calm in the way he questions and prepares, letting Patrick know his expectations for enforcing the daily patterns. He is his mother's son and becomes more of a role model to his father every day.

```
namespace BISoft.Data.Home.Core
{
    using System;
    public class Identity
    {
        public Guid Identifier { get; set; }
        public IActionGuide ActionGuide { get; set; }
    }
}
```

Language organizes his household around Yue Chinese rhythms. It organizes his workday around English rhythms, and it organizes the occasional free moment, according to the gaps in his calendar, into markup rhythms, coding rhythms, and threat model rhythms. The circularity of reason rolls alongside his life rails in the way language organizes and is organized, its structural role as both cause and effect is on full display. The boy flutters back and forth, from language to language, as if no effort were required. His mother taught him that, reinforced it at every turn to make sure he glides with ease and comfort, carrying on with his grandparents during the yearly visits and still getting along at school all year round. Not so easy for Patrick and Ying. She sought to supplement what she found lacking back home in a new house she has grown to love. Despite her efforts to blend in, she knows they are both marked as immigrants and aliens no matter how perfectly they learn to get the tenses right and clearly pronounce the difference between plural and singular nouns. There are plenty to socialize with, the transplanted community of Chinese H-1Bs is substantial, but her origins are not nearly as interesting to her as are the destinations. The everyday fashions reign supreme now and the morning exercises her resolve while she readies the boy for school. This lingers in Patrick's folds and pleats as he braces himself in the locker room, changing more than the clothes he wears.

Every nuance is relevant to the work. They bring themselves to it and whatever they have packed up and are carrying with them

~~enhances the experience, supplementing their contributions with additional qualities and characteristics. The hiring practices take this into account. It is not merely a matter of who is able to solve the problems by providing correct data structures for use in a required algorithm. The character comes into play. It has to be a fit with the team.~~

While working from home early this morning, he got the scoop from Abhishek and continues to go over it in his head. Why did they shut it down to begin with? Was it silly, a rash act made in a panic? Were the problems real or had they come upon some limit they did not understand? He is a prudent man not prone to wild flights and passionate flourishes. Maybe when he was younger, before Bai came along in those early days with Ying when he felt that only bright flashes of light were sufficient to fix her fancy upon him. The job does not encourage that and, as he ages, he becomes more careful, remaining well-hydrated throughout his ride into work, keeping his reactions cautious and careful, and his eyes on the road in front of him, especially when riding in the rain. You cannot depend on sunny days, you cannot take care of yourself only when it is convenient, you must do it all the time even when there is a crisis requiring your attention. He bounds up the stairs into the building, freshly changed into appropriate attire and mildly coiffed to remove any signs of exposure to the weather. Continuing with his regimen of carefully sticking to the cold, hard facts, he restrains himself from dramatic reactions and reminds himself that there has been no breach, nothing other than suspicions and hunches. Are they justified? Are his judgments sound?

—A law-abiding prefect, he's the perfect denizen for this world and the landscape around it.

(In those early days, the service-side http listener performed relays over the top of packets moving across the world according to routing tables. At bottom, the basics lived inside flows of electrical current that powered every metal-rich machine along millions of pathways. As the locations for these listeners increased over time, the energy centers spanned across the globe to push charges over optical cabling launching the packets from zone to zone, region to region, and place to place at the speed of light.

Every packet was moved along its way by routers drawing energy from the wall, from the building's current and the country's grid, leading back to the power plants originally put in place to organize people's lives with infrastructure set atop flood and flow. In some locations, the foundations were replete, saturated by usage, and unable to keep up with growth. Not one more kilowatt, not one more amp, nothing available to add to the system without tanking the tendrils leading up to and away from the computing centers. Sometimes the company augmented community standard-issue and provided additional resources. Sometimes those resources were green and friendly though not always and not reliably. It was a journey, they said in their public marketing campaigns. Nothing was done by rule, the conditions around the world were too variable and adjustments had to be made in India and Brazil, Qatar and the United Arab Emirates. In underdeveloped areas or in places that were too developed, the grid was overtaxed or underfunded and the resource requirement too grand for small time supplements. The nation state was reluctant to let a private enterprise integrate too deeply into its mission critical charge. They feared it gave private interests too much influence over the people whose lives hung in the balance and the policies that ruled them.)

~~Dulcy's excellence on the whiteboard was acknowledged by each of the interviewers who spoke with her that day. She did not hesitate with the problems presented. She asked a few questions, perhaps, to get clear about the requirements, but then went to work on the code and provided a perfect response in good time. This got her to the 'as-appropriate' interviewer who spent most of the time talking to her about the music she was making and the interest it held for her. They should be more careful about what they include on their resume. She removed it minutes after getting the job offer.~~

Jason is finishing up his one-on-one with Vani in the conference room when Patrick walks into the team room. He signals through the door that it will only be a minute and continues explaining where she can find a sample to use for implementing the bugfix she is working on. "Follow the pattern in the workload," and he pastes a link to the code into the chat panel in focus on his laptop.

"I sent you the link. You'll figure it out. Work with G if you have problems setting up the onebox. She's our resident expert. The pre-reqs tend to bite everybody." She nods nervously, not nearly as confident as he is that she will figure it out. That is why he is sure. She is a recent college hire. What Jason likes most about her is that she gives off the vibe of incessant worry that everything may not be going the way it is supposed to go. He knows that trait will make her successful. His insight pays off every single day. She worries she does not understand and that she has not accounted for everything more experienced people know how to handle. She is always fretting about that, asking follow-ups and digging in deeper to make sure she has everything covered. In her mind, she is incapable of doing the job well and that is exactly what helps her do the job well.

Everyone on the team shows some signs of this over-the-top concern for taking everything into account, meaning that none of them are put off when they come across it in someone else. Dulcy, for example, is patient with teammates like that, knowing full well that irritation when dealing with someone who asks lots of questions is usually due to a fundamental insecurity. If you do not know the answers, or if your understanding barely covers it, you will be put off, but if you know what you are talking about, if you know the whys and hows inside and out, you will be happy to help put your teammate's mind at ease and answer however many questions they raise.

Vani's apartment is in downtown Redmond in the massive tenements recently built to handle the boom of young people moving in as the company bloats its workforce and pushes past the six-figure mark. Highly paid little wanderers need a place to live conveniently located to restaurants and other social venues. These are not members of a demographic that cook much, they work long into the evening and look for quick solutions to household chores. The city council and planning bureau have been more than accommodating in letting the downtown zoning glut the market in combined commercial and residential districts that line the streets of what was once a quaint town. The rent is high, but she chooses to afford it, eschewing the route some others take with roommates and communal living. It costs her more than she realizes as she neglects to check the box for employee stock purchase plan and does not contribute up to the max match allowable for the 401K. Since these numbers will compound over time if she lets them, this decision may be the most expensive one she has ever or will ever make in her life. In her twenties, Vani cannot see the millions in the thousands and the thousands in the hundreds. The simple math of the market commingled with the grand expanse of a lifetime eludes her. Home agents to the rescue. They will put her on the right track.

She gets up and thanks Jason with an awkward gesture and some abrupt movements to reset her chair before leaving the meeting room, signaling it is okay for Patrick to enter. She ducks in front of him and says 'hey' but does not get any response. She is already past him when he purses his lips, so she does not see it. She will probably wonder about the meaning behind this exchange for the rest of the day. "Do you need a minute between meetings?" She hears him ask after she is out the door and looking for G to help her get her dev environment set up.

~~Before Dulcy learned how important it was to hide it, her passion was clear and impressive. Anton thought she would make a superb addition to the team, believing her voice and sensitivity augmented her engineering capabilities and gave the company that something extra they were always looking for in every new hire. They were rarely able to find it in those college candidates who usually seemed too immature, not yet fully developed in more worldly ways.~~

—He winds her up and she keeps herself going. They function like a tag team but not through intention, only through the workplace's common grounds.

[When first the plans came to fruition, it was clear the data centers required low level integration. Not into the civilization's power grid, but with its municipal authorities. The corporation needs to be involved in urban planning and rural development. They form outreach teams and fan out into the different levels of government dedicated to planning and resources. Roads are sometimes needed as are civil engineers with high levels of skill often beyond the budget constraints of the region or principality. The company negotiates a tax incentive to reduce its overhead, but offsets that benefit by funding the infrastructure required to get the project up and running. It is a deliberate attempt to influence the state and control those direct expenditures to which the corporate contribution is applied. They do not begrudge the people their programs, their food strategies and housing insights. The company often contribute through a charitable venture, but they do not want to see these expenditures prioritized. BISoft knows their money is better spent if they oversee operations themselves. They make sure it is done properly and that quality measures are used when bringing state of the art systems into the region. New power plants are projected, new grids and groundwork, aerial contributions, and areas of investment they do not ordinarily expect from their technology partners. The company's mark is found on every street and below every household in the district. It goes way beyond the few who work at the data centers, monitoring the regulated temperature controls and flow of water, making sure they are within the recommended ranges. The entire social order is deeply interwoven into the family of organized service delivery products.]

"Let me get some coffee," Jason says as he pushes himself up from the desk and moves toward the door. Patrick pivots and they walk together out of the team room and down the high, broad hall to the kitchenette. Spring doom hovers outside the wall of windows across the breakroom. Jason is mesmerized, waiting for the machine to kick out pseudo-cappuccino. The dark and light browns visible at the base of the window come from the tops of still barren trees, peeking out from below. The dark clouds and constant light drizzle flavor the atmosphere around the building. We're all vitamin deficient this time of year, he thinks in answer to the daytime darkness. With the coming bloom, there is never anything highlighting the bright green of the English hills in those movies and TV shows Mags likes. There is a world of difference between that and the dark green he sees, gloom-spelling and dank. The giant Douglas Firs sprinkled around campus hint at it as they dominate the air above the tops of the buildings and prepare to fill it with their yellow dust and brownshell seeds. In the months ahead, the grounds will be awash in tree spunk as those giants do their family planning around the buildings, lit walkways, and dirt hiking trails where, rumors have it, the occasional bobcat lurks.

```
namespace BISoft.Data.Home.Core
{
    public class Reference
    {
        private List<Identity> instances =
            new List<Identity>();
        public List<Identity> Instances =>
            this.instances;
    }
}
```

He catches the slightest whiff of a residual scent from Mags' advance this morning. The coffee smell relocates him into its aftermath. In the early light, she took him along her way as she tends to do at least once per week in what sometimes feels like a strictly scheduled event. He feels helpless beneath her, wants to give her everything she ever wanted, wants to tend to whatever she needs. He cannot think of anything that means as much as those first moments when he feels her rustle and come alive in the warm smells and flow of the sheets on their bed together. When he looks at the dried-out tubes of paint or the old half-finished masterpieces, he thinks of the working pull that launches him sideways and away from that. He does not dwell on it for long since he senses those rocks will not turn over cleanly. BISoft may be under one or two of them, he fears, but time teaches him, as he learns his weaknesses and follies, that Mags most likely is the more common image shimmering there. Her reflection glows in the rising light and lures him into deep walking slumber.

~~The people who spoke up on behalf of Dulcinea Chang Pearson, providing letters with frank and elaborate descriptions of her intensity and persistence, used grand language to express how unusual and extraordinary she was and that any recruiter or hiring manager was well-advised to do whatever they had to do to get her~~

~~on board. Even the strange recommendation from the writing teacher spoke of her unusual approach to topics well-worn in the work of others but never seen from the furious and inquisitive angles she provides. There was no inkling of anything beyond a standard pedagogical relationship between them.~~

"She is meticulous," Patrick breaks the spell.

"Who? Dulcy?" He chuckles. Jason always gets a kick out of other people's reactions to her when they get a closer look during some project they work together. She is not prone to the kind of involvement principals often perform. She does not seek out opportunities to interact with other teams, and, instead, spends most of her time leading the locals, guiding their actions through explanations and brown bag discussions, code reviews and shared screen mentoring sessions. When she does venture outside her technical fiefdom, it is not uncommon for Jason to find himself in a hallway conversation with some EM or architect where the dialogue starts with an observation like this. She *is* meticulous. Even a jokester like René who usually shoots first and aims later does not feel comfortable letting loose in her presence. She has a sobering effect even if that has nothing to do with the Dulcy that Mags has befriended. In person or on video chat, they laugh together for hours. With her, Jason has never seen a broader gap between work persona and home persona. For reasons that he recalls but refuses to share with anyone, not even Mags, he cannot help but be attracted to it. Not like that, but still, there is something in the offset that draws him.

—Sometimes, what etches them into the stone is the others they meet and spend time with at those heights atop the pyramid. There's no way to emulate that in the grand scheme of things, rather they spontaneously contribute something beyond the order. The duality of structure as both cause and effect surfaces yet again.

(Shortly before the massive expanse that most outlets will log and recall as the global corona virus pandemic, the company initiated a banking division specifically for the purpose of making loans to state agents in need of assistance with major projects. The company could not legitimately take on the entire plan, but the loan system was enough to sweeten the deal with sufficient discounts and sweetheart rates. They had no qualms about tackling the greenness of the event and fostering excellent movement forward in matters of wind and sun, especially in those southern domains where both resources were plentiful. But that facet was not a principled part of the directive, and the governments protested the added expense incurred by taking on a public liability for the sake of clean energy. The company partnered with them anyway to meet expectations and deliver the product everyone agreed upon. Negative interest rates played a role. The ministers in their offices were excited at the prospects. It felt like a celebrity encounter to them, inching their way into the T-shirts and coffee mugs decorated with famous logos and readily recognizable slogans and images. They used the products already and had their own analytics teams to study budgets and trends in spending. Those were the people who understood population data and the rate at which it was growing or receding, depending on the season and local migration following the work from town to town in regions where national boundaries mean nothing to people earning their keep.)

"Yeah, she's broken this down into minute detail with zero assumptions," Patrick elaborates. "It's extraordinary. She's not willing to say it's a single agent, or even that it amounts to a coordinated action with underlying unity." Her email this morning is not his only evidence, but it is what is most on his mind. They have interacted before, but he is struck by it anew each time. The way she quietly transmits the flaws in a plan through the questions she asks. A participant in a design review may see huge swaths of things the author failed to cover, problems left unaddressed, when she simply asks what to do under some supposed set of conceivable circumstances. It is likely the reason why Jason brings her to his many meetings, especially those where there will be feedback from leadership, and he may find himself on the spot and looking for support. He has no doubt sought her opinion before going to a larger group with ideas for solving a common concern. She is a great sounding-board. Patrick can tell. If she understands the solution and her questions have been answered, that alone provides a strong indication that the design is ready to go, ready to be presented to a wider audience with an expectation of positive results, no surprises, and no major action items to follow.

~~They learned that the strong voice in someone so young does not originate in extracurricular trifles. Nonetheless, those activities have an enormous influence on the development of that voice. If Dulcy's somber ways found legitimacy and reinforcement in these extraordinary endeavors, that is a bonus to what has been fashioned from her natural store. Clearly, she was not a young woman given to concerns that there might be something wrong with her or that she was not up to the task-at-hand.~~

Ying is formidable herself, that is not the source of his discomfort. When he finds that fire in a fellow country-woman, he understands it, knows where it comes from and how it developed, but, with American women, he finds himself at a disadvantage. Dulcy may look familiar, but in those turns of phrase and the nuance under her many projections, he cannot find a common place between them. She does not appear in the least like what he expects. Perhaps it is her occasional willingness to be openly combative and confrontational. That could be it. Ying never dares to square off so boldly, although her skills in clandestine confrontation are substantial. The tables behind these experiences are not purely conceptual, they refer to the rise of meaning and complex states of significance. He is not sure how universal they are given that the slightest variation in background and upbringing causes giant swings in sense and sound.

"No, definitely not," Jason takes the cup from under the steamy stream and blows on it as they slow walk toward the window wall and the booth nearest to it. "You don't want any?" He raises his cup toward Patrick who responds by showing him the water bottle. They take a seat on either side of the booth, sinking into the leatherette cushions and leaning forward onto the retro diner surface. Jason likes these tables and uses them with hardly any excuse. Meetings out here go better. People are more relaxed. It is like going to a coffee shop and having an informal chat. It puts everyone at ease and banishes pretensions or careerist deceptions.

There are droplets of water on the window and thick tree

branches at the baseboard to separate them from the big avenue and the mass of pedestrian traffic that lines it. One reason that a shell with a hood is a common giveaway by team admins is that everyone needs them for days like these. Every human form in view, whether it is across the street or far in the distance, wears some kind of coat like that and there is hardly a single umbrella in sight, only the bright colors of the team logos and the branding associated with whatever product they build.

—The focus groups pay off, the behavioral science and statistical studies, everything is a piece of the puzzle. Every part and every team, every organization and division is meant to boost the effectiveness of the others, working in concert as a mega-machine streaming efficiency while optimizing collective orientations toward aggregated analysis and feedback.

[The earliest business analytics complex graphical object is the geographical map set over the top of any report that includes a latitude/longitude data type. BISoft representatives work on the standards board of the international community to define the specification for that datatype, ensuring it becomes a first-class citizen across different client implementations. Whether the user comes from this direction or some other, whether they are using the most popular operating systems or some entry from a niche market for specialty experts, it does not matter once the standards are established. They project expanded APIs with inputs that form the shape as it is described in hundreds and thousands of technical specifications across projects up and down the stack. The same map they use when covid death counts and infection rates need to be presented to the world health organization has its origins in special projections dating back to their data center expansion at the outset of their push into cloud computing. The energy available in every corner is not only significant to the server side of the equation but deeply impacts the profitability of the system on the client side as well. That is where users need access to enough electricity in their houses to power the devices and other equipment that plugs them into the grid. The energy extends beyond the central core and into the last one hundred yards where the subscription dollars come from and the massive investments paid for.]

"The malicious agent is a standard notion," Patrick takes issue with her unwillingness to move to the obvious conclusion. At least, he is more willing than she is to entertain the possibility. "In a zero-trust universe, we have to assume agency. Malicious agency. Thoughtless agency. Even if the evil admin is out there, the real threat was probably created on accident. A bug causing a DDoS or wiping out backups and resetting schedules to never. Doesn't matter, the act of creation is always an act of agency."

~~Dulcy proudly shows her true self in everything she does, bringing her whole person along with her into every assignment and every meeting with peers in need of help. She sees every opportunity as a chance to provide a new composition, a song to fill the gap created by need encroaching upon their domain and forcing everyone involved to scramble for a fix.~~

"Singular agency? A singular agent," Jason raises an eyebrow to reflect the subtlety in the difference. He knows that people tend to talk this way and personalize the computers in the system. Talking about what **he** is doing, or **she** is doing as though the machines were humanlike and had subject forms to drive them into action. As if they had interests and concerns. As if they wanted to get their work done but were somehow blocked from doing it by an environmental factor left unaccounted. They even think of bugs that way, as obstacles to some projected end driving individuals into an order of discrete agents acting in concert.

—Political bugs, cultural bugs, economic bugs. Bugs. Flaws in structure, in the code, the implementation, or the rollout.

"Is that an important qualification?" Patrick is not familiar with the standard roundabout that Jason and Dulcy know well through their frequent conversations and whiteboard sessions.

"I know Dulcy, that's all," Jason explains. "She tells this story about the hidden boundaries on the edges of a corrupted machine. Take an insurance provider. They don't want to pay out any more than they have to, it's bad for business, bad for the bottom line."

"Okay," Patrick squirts some more water into his mouth and cracks open his laptop after setting it on the table and lifting the lid. He has to peer over it to look Jason in the eyes. He wants to bring up the email with the table in it for reference while they talk.

It is a wall of carefully formatted text and includes a block with rows and columns describing each of the principles in her findings as well as brief descriptions of the different categories of event that correlate with each rule listed in the table, how they are sorted relative to the other categories, and how they connect to each other and integrate through functions.

"But there's a risk in denying agency. Right? That's your concern." Jason looks over at Patrick's screen now angled sideways. He sees the edges of the table embedded in the email. He has been looking at it quite a bit today too and this is already his third conversation about it. "Suppose the medical profession is busted and you can't get an appointment when you need one and providers aren't willing to do any serious diagnostics beyond some small set of limited procedures that are well-established and highly cost effective. These are the procedures the insurance companies have herded them toward. Providers are expected to perform them all the time even if only to eliminate some longshot rather than establish an underlying cause. Under such conditions, you'd have something of a limit machine, see what I mean?"

—Producing limitations and produced by them, again the circularity pattern appears: organizing and organized.

(Of course, when they breached the distance between the public and the private, they knew that walls and secured boundaries would be put in place. The castle walls were meant to keep the invading hoards out and provide a safekeeping for citizens in need of shelter from thieves and villains. The problem they saw and ignored, because it did not make any sense to any of the architects affiliated with the early project, was that security was an applicable layer of behavior. They had no way to implement it in the plugs and outlets, they were incapable of putting the brakes into the energy flow itself, it had to sit upon switches and relays, it had to guard the network and its higher order operations. The threat of DDoS never went away because the electrical charge was the wild west, unrestrained and impossible to rationalize in place.)

```
namespace BISoft.Data.Home.Core
{
```

```
public class Containment : Identity
{
    private List<Reference> references =
        new List<Reference>();
    public List<Reference> References =>
        this.references;
}
}
```

"The system slows itself down, is that your point?" Patrick asks. "The insurance company isn't exactly a singular agent doing malicious things to serve their own interests, rather they're part of a busted system that serves their interests," Patrick practices active listening by proving he can summarize the story back to Jason who waits patiently for him to do it. Patience is part of the EM's job description and active listening is an important tool in the HR-provided set of career skills for any people-manager working their way up the ladder.

~~Dulcy never believed the lyrics and melody originated inside herself. After she got over the initial influence of the elusive professor, she still saw words and sounds in things, in the world around her, in the feelings she witnessed or felt herself. Some trail was left behind or in front of her, putting the words on display for anyone properly attuned to hear. This was her approach regardless of the composition. The code and the solution lived in the things on display before her. She was inside her comfort zone whenever she confronted them, extracting patterns and setting them down to good use.~~

—Highly optimized organizations understand that the first level manager is the most important for translating what information flows up the channels and what flows down. Only those who nail it in both directions qualify for the leap to M2.

[Every one of them sees the problem and thinks the higher order traps are sufficient for achieving the goal. Electrical currents, they argue, are brute nature, the physical world at its most rudimentary. They have lost the history in that. It is not meaningful to parse events before they appear in the order through digital signification. Corralling it requires intelligent structure. That latticework must resemble a human order everybody understands and complies with, especially those evildoers who hack into the network and hold it hostage until their thieves' ransom is paid. The world they project is a human world with human agents moving around and planning forays into good and evil. Nothing beneath that radar has a place on the map, there are no coordinates until a location bubbles up via visual wavelengths between approximately 380 and 700 nanometers.]

"Exactly," Jason responds. "She's always on the hunt for that kind of thing in our stuff too. How many times have you coded to a bug? Built some special case around a weird behavior to get your component to work right? Happens all the time. Then platform or whoever comes along and wants to fix their bug and you're like 'hey, wait a minute, that'll break us, we've got code to handle for the condition you're removing.'"

"They tell you it's a hack and you shouldn't have done it," Patrick says. "Like you had a choice. They weren't going to fix it so what else were you supposed to do?"

"We'll get to that next semester," Jason punctuates the point with a sip of pseudo-cappuccino. "No one wrote that bug on purpose and no one planned the whole fiasco of the workaround, delay, and that fix, coming along after so much effort to work around it. None of that is on purpose, none of that belongs to a singular agent. But there it is. It's a common pattern."

"A limit machine," Patrick humphs a forced breath when recalling Jason's term from a few minutes ago. It brings the explanation back around full circle. Always close the loop, the CSPs for their level and career stage demand it.

—Platform must grow. That means someone will be chosen to make the leap. As much as every one of them wants that slot, they already get the sense that it'll be Jason. His destiny resides in the way he carries himself.

~~In those first months, there was a performance review Dulcy was aware of and there was a hidden review for new hires that she was not aware of. Both came out glowing with Christian, her first manager, delighted with her unusual talents and extraordinary~~

~~contributions. She received her first promotion after only one year.~~
~~The financial rewards started flowing right away.~~

(The missing link was not missing, no one called it out and no one mentioned it in their inline comments on the design docs and project plans. It was not on the list of known issues or open questions. The plug in the wall was the only authoritative switch that secured their resources from aggressive and hostile nature. Unfortunately, the building diagrams showed quite clearly that those outlets were unreachable directly. They were, however, still accessible through circuit breakers collectively combining dozens of them into a single knob. The Home System was born and bred right there.)

The promotions come right after everyone thinks they have already been made. I thought he was already principal, Patrick might say, or I thought he was already a group manager, on another occasion for someone else entirely. Since demotion is not a realistic option, promotions always come too late. The lavish gifts ease the pain of organizational latency.

"That's what she calls it," Jason says. "She uses the term in that email," he gestures with his pinky finger toward the explanation included in the bullets below the table in the middle of the message.

"Got it," Patrick centers the bullets on the screen. "Abhishek thought the reasoning came from Yitzhak, more business than technical. No one wants to say no to him."

"Did he get that from Dulcy?" Jason asks.

"He didn't say. Said that was his takeaway from the bridge last night. They were pushing the line because Yitzhak is asking, no other reason," Patrick says.

"But here," Jason ignores the ridiculous conclusion and points toward the screen again. "Dulcy argues that turning it back on with the analysis exceptions in place will provide a crystal-clear view of what's happening. She says there doesn't appear to be any obvious downside."

"And if they start making mischief, we have everything we need to shut them down again," Patrick finishes the sentence. He scans the email again and notches through each of the rows, moving his eyes from column to column as he scrolls down the screen: quantities and qualities articulated with their principles, relations and modalities defined as rules and conditions. "What about the electrical discharge she claims she saw in those disappearing logs?"

"Oh, she saw it alright," Jason bristles with a sturdy confidence. "Not prone to hallucinations, she knows what she saw and wouldn't have reported it if she didn't. I doubt she only glanced at those rows, she likely pored over them and only refreshed because the stupid tool did it automatically when she tried to copy them into the bug. I doubt she's the one in error here."

—Roger that.

[They make a deferential plan to include emergency breakers and construct giant boxes with detailed segmentation of the data center's rows and aisles. To represent the usage correctly, they plan to build digital readouts indicating the flows along with the locations, relations, and dependencies. The higher order enters their domain. They cannot see its presence there. They have been blinded by the light it shines at them.]

~~Before coming on board, Dulcy always heard that her musical interests were of no value, that success in their pursuit was a lottery with incalculable odds. No one ever mentioned the effects of them on other matters. No one drew attention to the value they had when mixed with a primary task unrelated to, but improved by, their addition. The fact that she was oblivious, not considering it a part of some calculation, only increased its value, bringing more impact through integration with her steady state as it seeped into her work whether she wanted it to or not. No artificial concoction was ever that full of fuel.~~

"What about the customer? Can they confirm?" Patrick asks.

"He already has," Jason says. "Well, not exactly. He says it explains a mystery."

"The dead raccoon," Patrick punctuates, putting it together for the first time. He heard the story about Parker's mishap but had not yet associated it with the incident.

"The dead raccoon," Jason repeats. "Did you talk to René?"

"Yes, briefly, this morning," Patrick says. "Deployment doesn't have enough skin in the game. That's why I wanted your take."

—Deployment and Engineering Systems are growing. René is center stage, but no one thinks he's ready to expand his scope. Too brusque, too rash. If he does not get it, he may think himself forced out. So be it, so it goes. Patience grasshopper.

"Is he fine with turning everything back on?" Jason asks.

"More than fine, he thinks it's absolutely essential," Patrick recalls the exchange and wants to get René's position exactly right. "We have the right traps in place. It'll let us see what's really going on. By extending those traps into Canada... every region for that matter. By putting the system online to show which nodes are actively listening to the broadcasts, that'll reveal the details of the pattern. We'll see the whole thing, get a better sense of its behavior. As soon as any traffic traverses this path, we'll see every aspect of the limit machine at work." He does not say what lies behind his bravado, that something which only takes a fraction of a second might have consequences that are impossible to undo. They will learn more about the invader they are trying to defend against, true enough, but at what cost? He knows they need to consider the risks, but he also knows that the conditions are highly controllable and the capability to turn things off quickly is their best defense against catastrophe.

"I agree with that," Jason replies. "Dulcy does too, I think."

"What if the limit machine is at work in the best of intentions?" Patrick asks after a brief pause. He fills the gap by carefully studying Jason's method for taking another sip of pseudo-cappuccino while gazing out the window in search of buds among the treetops.

"We assume the systemic part is evil, but what if it's good," Jason elaborates.

It is possible... in the back of his head. They have got to organize to accomplish anything large in scale, but systemic integration and collaborative limits might be how the devil advocates. He shivers in his seat without knowing why.

Jason thinks of Vod's uncle, chuckling at the thought of this Minshewian insight. Patrick nods and looks concerned. He considers the possibilities and wonders whether there is an alternative. The pressure from above spreads across the teams under the spell. There is no way to avoid this test, he is sure of it. Best outcome is to guarantee reduced impact. Keep the blast radius small. Do not let the perfect become the enemy of the good. It is not the best thing to do, and it is not the only choice, but the spirits are united in its favor and there is no sense turning back now. To understand it, release it from captivity to discover how it works in the wild. Keep your hand on the power switch and be ready to flip the breaker if the wheels come off.

```
/*
HomeTrace
| where TIMESTAMP > ago(1d)
| where Process has "BISoft.Data.Home"
| where TraceMarker == "Relation"
| distinct CorrelationId
*/
```

The room is crowded and a couple of degrees warmer than the hallway outside. There is a column of attendee avatars lining the side of the team chat app with more pages hidden. It is the WSR and Jason is getting thoroughly grilled by leadership. The same slide has been on the deck, both on the big screen and on the little chat screen of the laptops peppering the room, for more than the allotted five minutes. Initially, it was Yitzhak, but it did not take long before Tom Hobbes took over. Both Yitzhak and Tom share that same quiet seething and methodical approach to issues they want to get to the bottom of. As a pair, they are formidable. It is a weekly event to see this tag team performance where the one sets up the problem, showing that the presenter does not understand every facet as much as they think they do, and the other digs into the proposed solution, revealing a lack of clarity and purpose. Once they poke enough holes in the presentation, Tom turns it over to process, targeting everyone involved who had the misfortune of turning up at the weekly meeting, to discover why the standards that work for the rest of the organization have not been applied in this case.

```
namespace BISoft.Data.Home.Core
{
    public class Instance : Identity
    {
        private List<Happening> happenings =
```

```
    new List<Happening>();
  public List<Happening> Happenings =>
    this.happenings;
  }
}
```

Silently at her desk and listening through the headset, Dulcy wonders if it is the same at the advertising platform companies pretending to be social media and search engines. What does their weekly service review look like? Do they consider the service from the point of view of the targets of their advertising or from the point of view of their paying customers? How are the errors defined? Where is the availability measured? When she first decided where to work after investigating the giant corporate megaliths, she was deadest on steering clear of the advertising platforms and holding out for a position at one of the companies that sell software & services. There is a world of difference between the two and she repeats the refrain like a mantra. The vision, the relationship to revenue, the relationship to users and how their interests are protected were all radically different. There is a vast difference in offerings when it comes to behavior modification. BISoft users, for example, are the paying customers and not merely an audience whose actions are under intense scrutiny, captured in telemetry made available to the real but hidden customers, ensuring that the user product is properly herded. At those other companies, behavior is a measured quantity sold and delivered as social engineering. She thinks she has steered clear of that.

Tom wants to know why a security incident has been active for so long, far beyond its SLA. How did they come to determine it was a security incident in the first place? Did it meet the criteria? Was there an actual breach to the system? Was any customer data compromised?

—The facts, stick to the facts.

~~By the time Jason Kahn was ready to leave the start-up grind, his eye and sense of color were developed beyond the levels of average everyday adventure. He could not step off a bus or drive along the coast without seeing the light in every object. Not only~~

~~the light, he saw the shadow and the way it stretched and simmered~~
~~in place, the way it changed things and took them out of their~~
~~normal places and put them higher up in relief, making them~~
~~easier to see.~~

(BISoft Deskop Solutions was an analytics package for sale in a box with user access licensing available for bulk rates or a few individuals. It was a client server application and the original agent's purpose was to schedule report generation data users wanted to see on regular intervals. Suppose, for example, there was some metric they wanted to evaluate daily. They configured a scheduled task and the agents did the work. In the beginning, it was paper thin and exploited operating system functionality with a slightly more jazzy and user-friendly appearance. If something went wrong with the server or client, the user or their network administrator ran a tool shipped with the product, instructing it to gather logs and put them in a zip file ready to send to product support. The logs were mostly platform-specific and BISoft adapted its code to use the standard formats and attributes defined by the various operating systems. This provided a narrow picture of events. They often struggled to determine the root cause of complex problems because of the paucity in dimensional definitions. The company lobbied the operating system vendors to feed their requirements back to them in a concerted effort to increase flexibility.)

Jason is not at his most eloquent under the circumstances. He is used to Yitzak and has been through this drill enough times to know how to prepare properly, but Tom is a bit of a loose cannon. They do not interact on a regular basis, maybe once a week at most, and that did not usually involve putting Jason on the hotseat. He has not had time to learn Tom's style and the twists and turns of his brutally sharp analytical mind. In lieu of adequate preparation, Jason's responses amount to little more than 'better safe than sorry.' The people who might have been compassionate at the outset have lost their empathy and are beginning to wonder whether Jason has lost his edge or if maybe there is something going on at home. The way he fidgets in his chair, the way his frame struggles with the space around him, none of it spells composure and none of it tells his colleagues that he has his eye on the ball.

—They turn roundabout, making themselves uncomfortable. It's difficult to tell who is the agent and who the patient. They both actively define these moments and contribute to them enthusiastically.

[Anton Florea, Senior Engineer, reads an article about multi-tenancy solutions and decides this solves their problem. He works up a prototype in his spare time and, once it is sufficiently complex to prove the concept, shows it to his manager Scott Wheeler, an M1 on the server side ETL team for Desktop Solutions. The trick, he argues, is for the company to host the server in their own data center, allowing them to control its execution and runtime for multiple customer tenant organizations at the same time. They will be sure of the configuration and certain that things are running correctly. There will be no limit to the number and form of customized operations added and modified to meet their service delivery requirements. They will log every method call however they wish and copy the text files with those outputs to another server somewhere in the data center before shredding the contents into a form that provides a crystal-clear picture of events. The proposal is wildly popular among peers and leadership. The two men will be splintered off from their current development projects and given leeway to set up a separate venture with a notable headcount to build the fully functioning system. All the necessary resources are allocated: a Product Unit Manager, Program Managers, Engineering Managers, two full dev teams. It goes without saying that Scott Wheeler will be the PUM and Anton one of the managers. They make an outside hire for the other position, Tom Hobbes. He is new to the manager role and has little experience as an engineer, but he displays that sharp mind and has read widely in the newly minted domain of 'The Cloud'.]

~~Mags was more than those dancing eyes and that bubbling repartee. She was a sun setting with the brilliant offshoot of light people come to expect from that moment. She lent him her palette. Now he saw it everywhere in nature and in the people and things fashioned into poses before him. Her blackest blacks and whitest whites come to the forefront where her hair brazens against~~

~~her complexion. The red of her lips, the blue of her eyes, the vast array sprinkled above and beyond whatever shown glistening lies in the background.~~

Throughout the interrogation, Karen Tuttle sits there listening. Whatever style she once had in her gate and appearance has been thoroughly tamed by the ten years or more in which she has been attending meetings like this one. The casual dress gets to her, they cannot come to the office as though they worked in a bank or law firm, and that takes some getting used to. As her appearance melds into the local corporate culture, her wit hardens to keep with its protocols and standards. Her attention has been laser-focused throughout the meeting. She feels the impetus to speak up, to ask a question, and show off how deeply engaged she is. It is her duty to demonstrate how far her understanding goes into the service's details, making her contribution essential and her point of view crucial. For the most part. She daydreams too. Thinks about the beat and how her children need to learn every aspect of it, need to be intimate with it in the depths of their spinal rhythms. Not the surface beat, she thinks, but the entire beat. Not 1 2 3 4, but 1 e and a 2 e and a 3 e and a 4 e and a. They need to walk with this rhythm in their heads, with these patterns decorating their movement. There is no why about it, she insists. If someone were to ask her why, that is what she would say. The why comes later, first is the beat.

The revenue story is the biggest difference and the way it ties to review bonuses, that is high on Dulcy's mind. She knows that is the main concern of every voice she hears and every form she sees through the camera lens in the conference room. It switches its focus to match the speaking subject. The audience remains large in the ad platforms, the advertisers' value depends on the size of the population reached and riveted. They are selling attention and want eyes and ears, working hard to establish obsessive compulsive use for the sake of market advantage and an individual bonus. For the software & services company, however, MAU is good enough. If there is a critical report with data built into the analytics portal for Home, and a customer has to go look at it once per month for an hour to verify that conditions are proceeding in the desired fashion, that is good enough to keep the company leadership happy with the ROI. Customers get sufficient value from the service and the expense is well worth it. When the goal lies in the eyeballs and the clicks, such a usage pattern describes failure. The population must be glued to the system with endless interest and fascination. She thinks she has steered clear of that.

No matter how many years Karen gives, no matter how much time she spends, the underlings in her mind come back again and again. They form a core stem that props her up and helps her maintain a spiritual presence in a baggy sweatshirt and a pair of faded jeans with shoes she would not have been caught dead in during the years before she came to work at BISoft. She could not fake the rhythms of the review if she did not feel the flow of genuine melody beneath every word she heard. You cannot dip your toe into these waters, she thinks. You must immerse yourself and become a native swimmer.

—It takes all kinds. They love diversity and are happy to follow federal guidelines to ensure they cultivate it. It makes it more likely that they'll empathize with each of the various customer personas described in the scenario documents.

~~Jason saw that same black, white, red, and blue in the coastal waters and hills nearby, along the ridges at Santa Cruz and up the way where the burning ball in the sky and the clouds puffing across its span bathed the earth in like detail. The whole world was filled with her colors and his reinforced senses projected the palette into every corner of his visual field. Their passions are belong to us.~~

(Yitzhak Bar Zohar was a Senior Engineer working on Anton's team and expert at navigating the logs. The problem was that as they scaled out, the logs were created on multiple servers. Furthermore, some of the interesting operations took place on the client side and the support team had no visibility. Troubleshooting the system was an art. There was plenty of guesswork and a new adventure every time someone had to piece together the flow of operations moving from client to server and then from server to server before making their way back to the client again. During the early service availability reviews, the team was constantly frustrated by gaps in knowledge and things they did not see. One day, during lunch together, Anton and Yitzhak cooked up the idea that agents will send logs back to the server to provide insight into what they were doing and anything else that might have gone wrong. Before that conversation, their tribal knowledge about server logs never came to mind as a problem to be solved. They taught new developers how to navigate and what tricks to use. The expense of the training and ramp-up was invisible, no one was tracking that sort of thing, but there was no such workaround for the client darkness. They needed to get the logs from the customer and that was nearly impossible in cases where the problem originated in a background operation and the reliability dip only on the server side. The customer may not have even noticed it. They could not call them out of the blue and say, hey, can we gather some logs from your computers? They decided to extend the functionality of the Solutions Agent and turned it into what they called a Health and Monitoring Agent that, in addition to its modest scheduling tasks, sent logs up to the cloud, describing local operations.)

Karen shakes free from her slumber, from her extraneous concerns and sense of timing. She must defend him, come to his defense. There is no dilemma to cross. Silence hangs him out to dry, everyone will know if she lets that happen. She must intervene or be judged for her inaction. "Any suspicious activity must lead to an incident filed with SecInc," she bellows authoritatively over the top of one of the platform engineering managers piling on to something Tom Hobbes has said. Posturing, that is what she thinks he is doing. She interrupts him while getting ready to be interrupted vigorously in return. If Tom heads in that direction, then he probably senses Anton wants that line of questioning explored. And if Anton wants it, it will be good for the manager's reputation to help Tom make his point. A single voice can be deadly, but what usually pins the point down is the array of nodders and agreement monkeys who bob and jump in place, approving each of the maneuvers spun out in space. That is how Tom Hobbes made his mark on the project. Over the years, he has become essential and reports directly to Scott who insisted on the reorganization that moved Tom out from under Anton a few years back. No one cares about him directly, he is no one's manager anymore and has no immediate line of authority over anything, despite his dotted line authority over everything. He has Anton's ear. Everyone knows it. And not only Anton's, but Scott's. It is extremely dangerous to treat him lightly.

```
namespace BISoft.Data.Home.Core
{
    public class Collection
    {
        private List<Instance> instances =
            new List<Instance>();
        public List<Instance> Instances =>
            this.instances;
    }
}
```

Save for the matter at hand, Tom's mind is blank. There is no trace of anything from before, no past and no future. His success hinges on his total presence in this moment, chasing this bus and barking furiously until it bends to his will. He applies the rules of experience to the matter before him and turns it over to reveal the worms and slugs that feed from its decay. From and through extensive experimentation, he determines what conditions his experience in the now and then explores those conditions in a recursive maneuver meant to get behind the things set before him. A master of critique, he holds the room and everyone in it.

~~When you first meet someone in an interview, it is hard to get a sense of their personhood, of something more than what you see in the professional questions and inquiries designed to expose their basic capabilities. Jason's ease in close quarters wins people over. The way he sizes up a person sitting opposite and then paints scenery for them to view while he answers their questions about his background and what he took with him from past failures and opportunities, attracts a friendly reaction and boosts his chances above his peers and competitors.~~

Anton sits on the side of the room, nodding gravely and boldly emitting the vibe of a distinguished engineer, the only one in the room, the only one in the organization. He, without uttering a word, puts the screws to Jason. Both Yitzhak and Tom act as surrogates for the equity partner with enormous influence over how big their yearly performance bonus and partner grants will be. Now his attention turns to Karen who has put herself at the center of it only because the rhythms did not feel right. Some people establish themselves as bobbleheads, but others find their way through firm and strong action to set themselves up as reliable foils. That is Karen Tuttle's job description. Her organs have learned to integrate that outer sense with her precious inner sense, drumming beneath everything she sees and hears. When Anton turns to face her, he leans forward to get a better view. One of his eyebrows rises, and his eyes blink curiously. Finally, he thinks. She's doing her job.

—They depend on the pushback to vet themselves, to vet their place and the security with which they hold on to it.

[There is no reason for two distinct logging patterns, they argue during the design review. Why maintain the log crunchers on the server side if we are beefing up the client-side agents to send remote events back to the? It violates the rules of engineering: common functions are performed by common operations and common code. Let's put an agent on each of the servers, Anton says in the meeting. We'll extend its capabilities to let it report back to the service. The logs will be in a uniform format and easy to integrate with a common identifier that threads through an entire chain of events, making it easy to render the call stack with whatever state we want to capture. The ideal of total visibility is presented to the team and with it the notion of a vortex receiving the logs from across the region. Everything ends up in the same place and provides a detailed roadmap of what the system is doing and how it does it. The store contains details about whatever errors the system encounters and seems to resolve at first, but which come back to bite it down the road when something else happens. If that problem depends on the missing thing from a gap created by the previous error, it is clearly visible to anyone investigating. Every day in the life of the system is open to view in the minutest detail.]

"And if the owner of the SecInc can't immediately identify the threat and put it in quarantine," Karen continues. "The process says CorpSec must be engaged. The incident summary works its way up the food chain." She crosses her arms and makes eye contact with Anton rather than Tom and the EM who was piling on. She cannot even think of his name off the top of her head. He is one of Jason's peers, flush with the standard competitive angles no doubt. The principal band becomes brutal as they each grind their way along the path to partner. They fantasize about the equity grant and the prestige, but never consider the onus, the total submersion in work life, happening along the grid of every minute of the day and every inch of territory they traverse.

—They're those most in the grips. Ted's culture is their culture. It becomes impossible to form the world any other way.

"And what does the process say to do once we've determined there hasn't been a breach?" Tom half turns in his chair, deeply amused at his own insight and intelligence. Don't bully me, he says with a twist of his waist and a turn in his chair. You are new to this and out of your element.

"We are considering the request from platform to re-enable the relay servers," she gets right to the point and drills it home to let them know she is the one on the hook to ensure process has been properly followed. Once she confirms it has, she, and only she, will make that decision. "The justification provided doesn't prove that there is no agency, only that it doesn't appear to be causing direct harm to assets or data." Her voice remains firm, projecting loudly across the room and over the network.

~~What makes Jason likeable is the sense everyone gets that he is truly seeing them, listening closely to their problems without turning off and thinking of the next thing he has to say. No one guesses that the fine artist cultivates his craft from the aural traditions of his siblings in the wild, but that is exactly where he finds them and how he accepts them as a part of his life. The colors have a wavelength, the scenery makes sounds, leaving him with synesthesia to cover its mighty prospects.~~

It would be an entirely different job if Dulcy were focused full time on maximizing those events coming from the audience. Why spend time on performance testing and optimization, breadcrumbs and custom navigational shortcuts if the goal is to get the users to sit there longer? Instead, she would focus on the psychological neuroses that keep people engaged, keep them fuming, keep them scrolling and clicking and whatever else the platform decides to exploit for the sake of a few pennies per event. Content creation itself becomes a target of reform and instigation. In that world, there is a vested interest in getting users to create more engagement with other users, making the system more vibrant and valuable to those who exploit it for aims, hidden and private, protected by a real customer agreement that looks very different from the one the content providers accept.

"And?" Anton asks simply. The absence of hostility is obvious. This will have an effect. Anton wants her to do this job, to play this part, and it comes across effectively in the softly framed, one word question.

"We're verifying the claims about blast radius," she glances down at her laptop to check whether another DM has come in from Patrick, listening remotely while continuing to work the incident. There is nothing. "Given that everything we've seen suggests only the relay servers are impacted and that they have been thoroughly tooled for analysis and remote debug, we should be able to send out a proposal for re-enabling the system by end of business today."

—Turning them off and turning them on are part of the same coin. Heads or tails. Either way.

(Shortly after the newly formed team, dedicated to the agent and its new features and functions, released the first version of the new and improved Health and Monitoring Agent, articles began to run in some of the tech journals and industry magazines. They are spying on us, they said. They know everything. If you are a customer of the Analytics Platform from Cloud Data Services at BISoft, you are under constant scrutiny. Your usage habits, the reports you write, the frequency with which they run, not to mention their results and whatever material you use to annotate them, are relayed back to the CDN vortex where BISoft does whatever it wants with the data. In truth, the engineers have little interest in the content of that work. That part of the criticism is hyperbole. They are, however, interested in everything the users are doing. That much is true. But that is only because they are doing it on the system that the team is tasked with supporting and maintaining. The customers want it to be available and complain when it is not. How do they expect the system to function properly if the dev team cannot see what it is doing? How else will they know when there is a problem?)

"Analysis and debug?" Tom says respectfully as if channeling the change in tone directly from Anton while suggesting he still requires a more thorough explanation.

"We know the rogue process that's been hijacked and have triggers in place to capture the state of the VM. The devs are doing a QFE as we speak. It'll trigger a debug session when applicable. It's tricky because we're likely to overdo it and spring the trap too often, but since there's no direct user interaction in this part of the service, we're willing to start out that way and refine as we go. We're working with deployment to set up a funnel for fast tracking the QFE to the effected machines. We'll reuse it to fine tune and shut the whole thing down if the results are contrary to expectation." René nods along beside her as she speaks. Her mention of deployment implicates him in firm opposition to those immediate interests voiced by Tom and Yitzhak. But Anton's reaction has made that a defensible position, so René is not put off by the inclusion. In fact, he suspects it works to his advantage and conveys the right message to the appropriate people. He too can be relied upon to secure the right processes and ensure the product is safeguarded from disaster. He looks over at Karen to convey the alliance and his willingness to join it. Someone else coughs. No one speaks. She goes on after a brief pause. "The goal is not only mitigation and protection from future harm, but root cause analysis. We'll capture the relationships at work here. We'll learn what's happening in detail. Gather the traces and dumps. It's essential that we get to the bottom of it. Rogue configuration, buggy code, malicious agent. Everything is still on the table."

—Another table.

In Jason's earliest days, they already pegged him for a

~~managerial role. The ease with which he dealt with controversy lets them know he fits in fine. He is the kind of person who lets someone vent without feeling threatened and watches a scene unfold without judging it or turning his back when it goes astray. There was something in his eyes that was always ready to see the world as it is without imposing himself upon it.~~

"But the system has suffered no harm," Anton says. "Some missing logs? Is that what this is about? Don't we fire and forget? There are many reasons why some traces might fail to land in the telemetry store." The innuendo is heavy, what makes this special?

The risks of modeling telemetry occur to Dulcy. When system functionality, in cases where the services directly address the needs of those who pay for it, depends on telemetry to build its actions and respond to environmental events, then the telemetry becomes equally as crucial as the advertiser's traces for targeting the right audience and finding the best related scenarios. This weekly slugfest, she recalls from her desk safely situated far away from the meeting room where the heat is at its highest, is as much about telemetry as it is about reliability. There is no reliability without telemetry and half of what they consider in their endless discussions is whether they are doing the right thing based on what the logs tell them is going on. As important as the difference between SaaS and advertising is, the difference between telemetry and action is equally crucial. The customer does not always know what they are doing. They may not recall what they did or whether they got past it. The telemetry always knows.

"We do follow your standardized pattern, Anton," Jason says a little too defensively. "But you know we have precautions in place. It's async, and there isn't anything exotic going on. When seven minutes worth of logs never land despite clear evidence that the machine is functioning normally, that doesn't make sense. That's behavior worth investigating. The rules, as we understand them, have been circumvented and one possible explanation is a breech." Jason knows that when he is on the hotseat he is not necessarily in trouble, but he is being tested. People will remember how he performs. Take responsibility. That is what matters. Be accountable. Only a responsible person can save the day. People will remember the confidence with which he does it. It will become a part of his lore. They will add it to their reaction under circumstances where he does not need to show his mettle. Reputation is based on performance, but it does include myth as well and a good email response or meeting contribution impacts someone's image for years.

"Or bad code," Anton says simply.

"Or bad code," Jason repeats energetically, giving off the impression that he is grateful for the help.

—Difference machine.

[The company is compelled to make an announcement. They spell out the nuances and differences between themselves and the fast-growing advertising companies that are in the same crosshairs for violating privacy and showing an interest in user content going well beyond system maintenance. BISoft releases public statements and publishes white papers to make it clear that it is not interested in customer data. Notice the difference, they point out, not user data, customer data. It is ballast from their point of view. They want to make that clear. Meanwhile, however, the marketers, the product managers, and some of the program managers tasked with gathering customer feedback, realize that they are sitting on a gold mine. They scheme to use telemetry to better understand how the product is navigated and what gaps cause users to grow irritated.]

```
namespace BISoft.Data.Home.Core
{
    public class Membership<T> where T : class
    {
        public Collection Collection { get; set; }
        public Process<T> Process { get; set; }
    }
}
```

"We shouldn't try to RCA this now," Karen says in blanket fashion, putting a barrier around Jason's defense. "We'll find the root cause, that's a certainty. These events are not miracles." There is scattered laughter. Nothing better than being funny under stressful circumstances.

Patrick clicks the raise hand icon on his meeting instance. Tom, happy to turn the attention away from Karen and Jason now that their position is gaining strength, says, "Patrick, did you have something?"

"It's about risk assessment," he says over the speakers. "The area of concern we've identified is the rule parsing and execution. Those rules may become agent behavior, depending on the rule and the context. Home has about a billion active monthly users and over five billion active agents. There is evidence to suggest this operation is worldwide. The risk is high, critically high in my opinion. Due diligence was necessary here, a statutory obligation as far as I understand it. At the very least, for our Canadian and European customers, if not the whole world."

Wasn't there a story, Dulcy daydreams, a few years back about some electric car that was being tested by one of the automobile enthusiast magazines? The reporter got into an online argument with someone from the car company and the executive was able to produce telemetry to prove that the reporter was wrong about his conclusion. He said there were no charging stations along his route, but the car was sending data back to the company throughout the journey and the executive was able to show that the reporter had driven right past several of them. The telemetry is the system of record. Everything must be square with it.

~~Letting a thing be what it is does not come easily to everyone. Letting a thing sound the way it sounds and look the way it looks without making a judgment or thinking of a suggestion for how to improve it or bring it under some more powerful category, is a superpower available to few of them and rarely able to persist throughout a life filled with trials begging for bias at every turn.~~

"Fine," Anton says. "But we have a start date, and we have a repository history. Surely you've gone through the list of check-ins to see which is the likely culprit and you've rolled it back, right?" He is convinced, and has been throughout the discussion, that this is a problem with the code, that there is a bug, and it is as simple as that. His experience is endless. It is always your code as far as he is concerned. Always. He knows it. Has seen it too many times to be distracted. Engineers are always wildly gesticulating at someone else's component or some other source. In the end, it is almost always their code. The exceptions are exceedingly rare and require mounds of evidence. No self-respecting engineer or engineering manager ever finger-points until they have that evidence in their possession in the form of detailed traces or a solid repro, preferably involving only the guilty component and none of the engineer's dependent code.

—It differentiates...

(Self-regulating policies were instituted, Europeans took a stronger stance and forced regulatory compliance. These were hoops and gates that no one in engineering worried about although they did change the release schedules and forced work on infrastructure without a direct connection to revenue. The regulations were easier to institute world-wide than in some one place, but none of it touched the program managers' core interests as they lobbied for increased reporting on customer behavior and the usage of new features.)

"It's not that simple," Jason protests. "First, we don't exactly have a start date. We have an incident date. The pattern of missing logs is present for at least 30 days. Cold path logging is aggregated so we can't see specific gaps. This behavior is likely present in the system since the beginning. How would we know? The telemetry that indicates the real start date has been lost, aged out. We only have aggregates. The identification of a firm start date for this case requires detailed logs."

"This has been going on for over a month, but this is the first time we're hearing of it?" Tom interrupts Jason and is now back to livid. Everyone registers the sudden change and thinks it must be a review goal to express Anton's anger, sparing him the fallout in reputation caused by expressing it himself. He is the cool and collected DE who pays Tom to act out his temper.

"Gaps are not uncommon," René echoes Jason's same defensive tone. "A minute here, a minute there. That's not unusual. Servers are rotating, rebooting, it happens and causes gaps in telemetry." He looks over at Jason who purses his lips to reluctantly confirm. René goes on, "Seven minutes is enough to trigger alarms but, honestly, we set that up because we think it indicates the machine is stuck. Maybe the deployment octopus lost track of the state during a reset. Without logs, who knows? It's complex with lots of moving parts and we thought that alarm would be monitoring deployment, not some node in its normal state."

"Why does the notification go to Platform then?" Tom is suspicious of the reasoning and zeroes in to find proof of the fraud.

~~Not one person that any of them ever met was as good as Jason at presenting a problem in its starkest colors. He arranged the players before them in perfect fidelity to the ways they ranged the world on their own terms. He got the one party's position right, better than they put it themselves, and he got the other party as well, clarifying each of their proposals, enabling managers and other leaders to decide which way to go. Such acuity of perception was priceless.~~

The logs tell us which features the customers are using and what they are missing, where they get confused and what they do not use to their advantage. The people who once relied on customer direct feedback have let those logs take over. PMs as a group are no longer interested in gathering requirements through focus groups or direct outreach. Those are things of the past. Now they publish to a smaller audience and watch them use the system. Surveillance is a large part, an essential part, of the lifecycle. Although its purpose is not directly aimed at engineering the practices and actions of content producers. Still, Dulcy concludes. I much prefer this form of feedback to the other. The rationale behind that preference decreases every year.

"First line of defense," René says. The effect grows and takes over the room. The people in the know, the people closest to the source, present a unified front, instilling confidence in the rest of the people and, most importantly, leadership. "There's a TSG for this. I'll send you the link, but all the SREs know they're supposed to do it. Checking the node health is the first step. If there's a fault or if it's not in the Ready state, transfer to deployment, otherwise..." he trails off. They know how to complete the sentence. It is standard procedure. Start at the bottom and work

your way up, process walks the same stack the code does. Make
sure the device is plugged in and recently rebooted before taking
further measures to get to the bottom of it. It is practically the
troubleshooting mantra that every new college hire knows from
their first day in the industry.

—The manifold comes together in ad hoc unity.

[It will become the team's motto and find its way into every
brochure and help guide. The customer's privacy is inviolable and
essential, but the product team will always see what the customer
is doing. In the aggregate, of course, always in the aggregate, and in
strict compliance with engineering principles put in place to align
with national laws. When they interact with the system, the system
knows it. How to avoid that? Why?]

~~They summon Jason to meetings above his pay grade to let him
work the magic of telling things like they are. He did his job without
skewing the details, and without any hopeful bragging dug deep
into crevices populated with what someone thought might get them
ahead. He was a humble painter staring down the canvas and using
careful looks and deep perspectives to paint a picture with more
truth than anything.~~

The residual anger does not have anything to do with the
technical details, that is apparent to Karen as the conversation
continues. Tom, and whoever hides behind him, knows he is not
going to get a root cause today. That will have to come in the weeks
ahead, once they have trapped a live event and thoroughly
debugged it. Senior leadership is frustrated at the service
interruption. They want to make the culprits squirm. The publicly
posted communication, warning existing and potential customers
of the outage, is unacceptable. This is not the kind of attention
anyone wants from their corporate vice-president or his directs,
especially not in the springtime when the stack rank is close at
hand. They may forget a colossal misfire from last fall if the rest of
the year has been good, but calamities in March or April are
vicious. They are top of mind right when no one wants them to be
and can cost a principal band EM 30 grand or more.

—Under conditions everywhere the rules apply to everything.

In a chilling tone blasting across the room from off camera,

reminding everyone that he has been there since the beginning,
Scott says from the big chair in his home office tucked in behind
his spacious kitchen at the back of his big house in a swanky
Medina neighborhood on the shores of Lake Washington: "Let's
move on."

```
/*
HomeTrace
| where TIMESTAMP > ago(1d)
| where Process has "BISoft.Data.Home"
| where TraceMarker == "Quantity"
| distinct CorrelationId
*/
```

The building stands four stories tall and there is no creeping necessary to ascend the ramps and descend the stairs or move around and past the portals before they make their way through the halls to their final destination. They are sure to have an impact of great service to their colleagues once they get there. Among the flow of coffee and flavored water to energize them, there is nothing that happens without prior insight or analysis. Under the tall ceilings and against the brightly painted walls, there is no peace of mind without the calming purr of sensors and their constant flickering. Multiple atmospheric conditions are at work in each sector of the space. Judgments supplement perception into a unified understanding of each object: there is an act behind every meaning. The inhabitants spread through the places, moving from building to building, room to room, in and out of every conversation, failing to find certainty or anything resembling fidelity to facts in the never-ending succession of this and this and this and, sometimes, that.

—I am here, they say, but what they mean is that they are there.

```
namespace BISoft.Data.Home.Core
{
    public class Compute<T> where T: class
    {
        public Membership<T> Membership { get; set; }
        public Containment Containment { get; set; }
```

}

}

(Dulcinea Chang Pearson, the rising senior, joined the dev team as an intern one year before she joined the team full time. During that summer, she built a mobile app to represent the agent's core functionality in a form the users carried around in their pockets. Pre-Home, it was an analytics extension best thought of as a Person. It took on a place within the system and carried the authorizations of any user's account inside the service, roaming atop its background surfaces to find the functions in a more robust form. Tied to the clicking and the scrolling, the querying and the generation of tasks based on results, it became a nested operation with a life of its own independent of any human presence at a screen on a desk locked in some room somewhere. The person, now migrated into digital light, was jetting around the cyberspace of geographical models, populating the Analytics System with ease, faster than any human being behind it was able to think and feel. The agent was powerful and took on more and more responsibility as it took shape, becoming the perfect interleave of structured data and real life. It was a cyborg without a body, attached to a new smart phone rapidly gaining in market share and becoming a more integral part of BISoft's design universe. After she presented the project to the team, having gone well beyond the basic specifications, she left the architects and engineering managers with insights and inspiration that echoed long into the months after she went back to school. They threw their hat into the ring and offered her something permanent. When she returned, she picked up where she left off.)

~~At first, he may have fascinated Chelo with the prospect of his well-to-do carriage and the way he projected success when they were out on the town together. During that time, she grew more fascinated with the word art he put before her and the way he delighted listeners with anecdotes and tales, little descriptions of things more beautiful or interesting than anyone from those parts had ever realized.~~

"It's because my last name is Hobbes," he opens the lid of his computer and sits down at the table where Natalie and Parker are already settled with their laptops and coffee. Tom sets the compostable box of salad next to the device and notes that Parker's greeting includes a broad, forced smile. Natalie makes no pretense, nodding curtly.

Always nearby are the requirements. There are no requirements, there is nothing other than their comparison with others. As a one, it does not make any difference, but as a set they sit in circles of relationships, both formal and informal. They stand next to each other, observers at the back of every basic instance, each coming from the same broad haunts, attacking their immune systems through a least common denominator: the equity grant. What are the others doing? Have I done enough? These thoughts grind on Tom all day long. Whether he is at breakfast with the girls or sitting quietly with Anne, it does not matter. There is always something hovering nearby. Have I done enough? What else? What else? Questions come from the peanut gallery demanding consideration. In some cases, they point to a larger organizational gap. We don't have TSGs for that. Are there any helpful scripts to take care of it? The system cannot emulate this scenario properly and devs cannot address it in their unit testing before checking in their changes. The people, en masse, lack something they desperately need. A decent-sized operation will be spawned to achieve it. Impact across the organization. Impact. Have I done enough?

"Can you project?" Parker asks as singsongy and light as he can manage, avoiding any hint of imposing. The emphasis is over the top. Natalie is there for moral support, but the objective for this meeting lies in briefing Tom on the design. Parker did not invite any of the workload architects such as Gaurav or Igor. They do not need to be involved yet and there is no incentive to let them see the finished document before getting sign-off from Anton. That requires Parker to first get it past Tom. It also removes any urgency from soliciting feedback from his peers since any serious issues may be set aside with an offhand reassurance that this is the way Anton wants it. There is no reason to gather input from people who cannot blow up the plan, but, if they can, you better make sure to get that input in a comfortable setting where the audience is small and completely focused on the issues. Parker does not bother with an introductory silent readthrough. He knows that approach is not well-suited to Tom's work style. This will be a carefully regulated and handheld discussion with an audience plant to keep things moving in the right direction. Natalie and Parker have developed a rapport for playing this role in each other's designs. They do not need to communicate expectations beforehand. She knows what to do.

—Eeny meeny miny moe. / Catch a tiger by the toe. / If he hollers let him go. / Eeny meeny miny moe.

[In the cook time between those summers, the events were more abundant than they thought given the limited functionality of the mobile app. Customers were app crazy that year and downloaded anything to populate the phone's interface with pretty icons and candy colors. They yearned to catch the attention of any over-the-shoulder observer on the street or in the café with friends nearby, always comparing themselves to each other's measure. They love to express group think solely for the sake of proving their own position atop the wilderness of its comparative analytics. Any popup that asks for permission to do whatever the hell it is asking for permission to do, they clear it with a deliberate 'whatever' that shows their true colors with what they hold most sacred: their personal space and the right to determine their own associations. The real agent, of course, was still the full-blown version for the desktop. The mobile app was more of an assistant to the agent than the agent itself. During every iteration, the few architects studying the logs and traces contributed still more to the specification. Adding requirements to stimulate the product's growth, they saw an extension in bloom, and got ideas for how to build a web of features and functions without a center in the real world. They proposed nestling the outcome into the data stores and service logs, stashed away on the backend and constructing a virtual image of things as they are and things as they ought to be.]

~~They lay together in the dark and Parker spoke in soft rhythms never letting on which verses were his own and which cropped from some other source. He left notebooks around and she~~

~~flipped through them to get a better sense of where his mind went in those days and nights when he was unreachable by ordinary means.~~

"Sure," Tom pulls the cable straight from the hidden console at the center of the table and plugs it into the jack on his laptop.

"You must've read him though," Natalie's accent resembles nearly everyone on her team. Such a mystery around the organization, how the French align on this team and are not spread across them more evenly. It is an effect of recruiting, nothing meant to discriminate. Natalie knew Laurent from long before this assignment. It was only natural that she came to work for him when asked. Her accent channels the group's collective irritation today when her tone vaguely suggests she is trying to embarrass Tom, knowing full well the answer and that it will not be flattering.

—Hana, mana, mona, mike. / Barcelona, bona, strike. / Hare, ware, frown, vanac. / Harrico, warico, we wo, wac.

(Events were everywhere when Dulcy came back and studied the queries and the documents and whatever other accumulated learnings found their way into the specifications handed over for implementation. The configuration-based approach was completely intact. In the interim, the program managers had fleshed it out through slide decks and white papers, high-level design documents, and long email threads with contributions from the growing team of architects. Each of the contributors was completely bought into Anton's strategies for expanding the product's reach. Everyone was excited at the prospect of keeping the system in a constant state of change. The configuration will evolve endlessly, avoiding hard-wired functions. Codified features yielded to flexible capabilities enabling functionality through a schema captured in XML and deserialized on an event loop triggered whenever the dedicated pipeline pushed a new version. In those pull-oriented early days, the pseudo-models were stored in a location where the agents were set to scan on a regular basis, looking for new directives and instructions for realizing their ends. A behavioral narrative was forming and the virtual person took on a fully fleshed out iconic position inside the system at large, floating around in there with virtual colleagues, engaged in operations enabled by the system. Every act, every intent, was captured and sent round and round in the swirl of explicit structures resting alongside the service. The user was reduced, in essence, to a globally unique identifier that masked their place in the system as much as it revealed it.)

"Nope," he pops that closing hard p at the end of the word. "People started calling me that when I was a kid. Never thought to read any of it. Looked at some, have a copy, but never made it very far." He looks down at the screen and clicks. "Do you have a link?" He moves on. It is like trying to embarrass a stone. There are plenty of ways to do it, but the stone is not likely to be moved that way.

"It's in the invite," Parker says.

—Eena, meena, mina, mo, / Catch a nigger by his toe; / If he squeals let him go, / Eena, meena, mina, mo.

Arrogant bastards rule the world and reduce everyone in it to fit within the limits of their nursery rhyme.

[The events are the person. The person is a swarm, a set of clicks, a navigational path through the barriers and across the broad plane of feature and function. They break loose from any attribution, refusing to be anything at all. They act and conjure the flow from one end to the other, making stops and playing games or singing ditties without knowing what they mean or who they hurt. They arc the event cycle of constant flutter, projecting into the ecosystem as traces and residuals of worldly behaviors. Their prejudices are captured, their biases, their preferences, everything about them tends one way rather than another. They are the system acting, but from an inverse angle. It mirrors them. Its normal state is their reflection, and it grows alongside their addiction. In the initial planning phase, the team of program managers sees the opportunity in sync and none of them claim ownership over the invention. It is obvious to everyone in the room that the Analytics System is little more than a collection of sources for gathering data. There is no reason to enforce limits upon those sources, corral them into well-known functions like on-premise financial systems and worldwide dispatch with shipping and tracking components. They decide to gather data from every available option, including the mobile application's global positioning system. The first foray into the private lives of the business users is their physical location in space as they perform their jobs. Home takes shape in the workplace.]

~~To Chelo's ears, the prose was even more interesting than the verses she had come to expect. In her mind, there were few comparisons to make. She did not have the erudition for anything obscure and hard to follow. Octavio Paz, that was her only anchor and as far as she could tell, prose was as legitimate a backdrop for poetic musing as verse. She bragged to her friends and wrote home in gushing exultation. She found herself a poet and did not have to sacrifice any creature comforts to get it.~~

"What's your real name?" Natalie does not give off any of the usual hints of friendliness although she does practice mirroring the standard bodily behaviors for those attempting it.

"Spire," he says emphatically. The breeze when he exhales fills with a winning confidence to influence people. "It's a family name. After my grandfather." He opens the document and waits for it to render. The scroll bar gradually becomes tiny. "You've been busy," he looks over at Parker. Natalie's angles have had an influence and there is nothing informal in Tom's demeanor. The three of them establish standard protocols and effortlessly align according to them.

Hard and berated into silence, his South African origins linger lightly in the composure of his body lines and, more heavily, in the composition of his cognitive subordination. He thinks what they think, what they used to think from the old rhymes, and they burrow into him. Truth be told, he was ready for the slavish surrender long before the time came to do it. There are those tunnel-visioned and bought in to the agenda who refuse to think about anything else, who refuse to let their minds wander. He most emphatically does not allow it. Tom, ordained by God in the essence of his waking states, pulls the binds closer in his morning rituals and the daylight he seeks in every journey out of his comfort zone and into the places where the demons crouch, ready for his arrival. He does not care if his colleagues like him. He does not care to be congenial. He is the roaring vengeance of an incorporated logic that bellows orders in every corner and across every bow.

"I didn't have time to get through the whole thing," Natalie makes a subtler attempt to convey the same message. The document is now visible on the large screen at the front of the room and marginal comments and questions appear sprinkled throughout the top portion.

"The last week or so has been unbelievably productive," Parker shuffles forward to get a better look at the screen. "It's like, suddenly, every distraction disappeared, and I was able to focus for the last five or six days. No live site incidents when everything's turned off," he laughs at his own joke. Natalie smiles but Tom keeps scrolling through the introductory items. He scrolls past the list of contributors, past the boilerplate list of links to public documentation and other relevant internal resources, until he gets to the glossary. Most of the terms are familiar except a few air gap related phrases near the bottom of the list.

—Every one of their origins works the same way. The origins are belong to us. Make happening now, make more make more. They know what is best. The future has already happened as far as Ted is concerned. They are its promise.

```
namespace BISoft.Data.Home.Core
{
    public class Storage<T> where T : class
    {
        public Membership<T> Membership { get; set; }
        public Containment Containment { get; set; }
        public Happening Happening { get; set; }
    }
}
```

(Dulcy coded it by herself although her teammates were instrumental in picking up the slack left behind by her dedication. From her first, second, and third check-ins it became clear that a reorganization was in order. They broke out the team into multiple platform components, separating the agent from the server side where agency itself and the event-filled persona of the user were migrated to a residence secure inside the walls of the corporate data centers. Promotions came rapidly and she shot up the ranks as her skills became formidable and her understanding immense.)

~~During Parker Henning's first job with the company, he ignored the customers assigned to him, forgetting to help them through their misery as was fitting to his job title and its description. Instead, he built reports and data pumps extracting important information to tell a different tale, describing what was going on between the company's efforts to provide services and the customer's efforts to use them. He made a data driven portal to show the bottom line and, as soon as it was ready, the managers and directors wanted to get their hands on it.~~

"Won't last now that we're about to come back up," Tom says. "These items?" He nods toward the screen as he highlights a few lines in the list of terms.

"We can go through them," Parker says agreeably. "But they are basically compliance protocols. It'd probably be more productive to address them inline as we go through the topics. Air gap has special considerations. For those who directly put their hands on anything or see anything. Also, for what kinds of operations take place and who's allowed to make them happen." There is something aggressive in Tom's way of nodding acquiescence. He does not appreciate being in the passive listener's role and is already rapidly scanning the lines on the screen to discover weak spots where there is room to inject criticism and raise problems that turn the tables. He needs to do something to change the categories in focus and take control over the meeting.

Natalie stares up at the screen, taking a standardized approach to vetting the document so she can helpfully contribute. She, like Parker, knows this is the right way to do it whether Tom agrees or not. The contrariness in that, the offset of the one with the other, fills the two of them with purpose. "That's why deployment octopus is the only legitimate means of introducing change into the system," she supports Parker as a co-author might and makes it clear that Tom is alone in his contrarian concerns.

There is nothing that approximates silence inside him, only churn and a driving desire for more. More than the others, more than each of those he greets, Tom is spectacularly concerned with his own status, both in the eyes of his peers and in the generalized aspirations of the organization itself. He cannot get past these rhythms, and cannot think otherwise than with the brutal ugliness of his origins and desperation. He is an organ for use, a tool to dispatch. He is a rudder, a wily and worrisome mechanism for the springing of traps and the launching of ships. His natural state, he wears it proudly, but will not admit to it, not ever, not to anyone, is war.

"Mmhmm," he says, still focused on the screen and scrolling to get a better sense of where things are and how to proceed in tearing them down.

"That's right," Parker responds with that artificial cheer that only fools the stupid. Tom sneers as Parker continues: "There is no Jit in this environment. Everything happens under escort sessions where a SecCloud or NatCloud employee specifically assigned to air gap performs the operation while our DRI looks over their shoulder, so to speak. No screen share allowed. China and Russia sovereigns work pretty much the same, but we'll focus on US for purposes of the review."

—Choosing. The escort and the escorted are forever choosing, making selections to bear out their place and reveal what they see. Do the others detect the slight increase in body temperature when he says the word?

[IoT is on the tip of everyone's tongue. She finds things in the wilderness and brings them Home. Home comes to be with simple devices and an agent that runs on every platform, making them surface in the stores and domesticating them in dark light shining upon them.]

"During deployments, they insist on a detailed script," Natalie says. "They don't even want to escort us. Their people already set up the DMZ for the first connected clouds way back. For NatCloud and SecCloud. It's the only place we're allowed to see."

"The concept is the same," Parker says. They make eye contact, speaking both cordially and professionally. It is contra

Tom and the juxtaposition irritates him, causing his breathing to get louder. Parker goes on despite the low-level distraction. "But it's a different endpoint here and we're introducing more compliance scans before the packages are uploaded. The uploads are never manual. Direct human intervention, anything outside a monitored workflow with full auditing, is forbidden. It's not what we've grown accustomed to. For Virginia or Texas, Luna Cake or Bear Steppe, they don't care if we do a manual upload. Even for NatCloud and SecCloud stuff, they don't care so long as the scans are run in the DMZ."

"And that's beyond our control," Tom says. "A P0 requirement."

Not a question, more signs of the struggle. Tom believes deep down, in a way that accompanies each of his movements and gestures, that he has been chosen for this purpose and this place. He is doing better because he is better. Smarter, better educated, more refined, more experienced. The advantages that make it possible are real and justice, however important they think it is, requires that everyone recognize the facts of the imbalance. Yes, he had more advantages, and they led to real benefits, real privileges. Removing them would remove the competitive edge the social capital provides in the struggle for life and survival. The slave morality must be resisted, he argues when prompted. We should not reject the fruits society has to offer. Sometimes it organizes itself explicitly for the sake of providing them. All of it follows in due course and, at a low level, he warns that these variations, whatever their cause, matter to the enterprise. Think what they will, he finds supporting notions in the depths within, but whatever imbalance concerns them, they cannot wipe it away with wishes and whimpers. He is a hard knock.

~~Everyone had ideas about improvements that needed to be made, but what they did not deny was that the approach was elegant and the attention to detail meticulous. Parker saw the proof for things eternal in the smallest places. He culls them from out of the darkness and into the light. There, interested parties get a look at them to learn how to best survive their ongoing trials.~~

"That's right. As soon as a package lands, the scans execute.

That's why standard sovereign clouds don't care if we do the upload manually. Air gaps have that, but because they don't support Jit, there's no way for a human individual to have sufficient access to upload the packages. It has to come from a deployment machine with an identity able to access air gap certificates. The virtualized user in purely event form." Parker is thorough because he does not know what they already know or how much they have read. He hesitates to overexplain but does not want to take anything for granted either.

"DMZ certs are in public cloud, aren't they?" Natalie asks.

"Yes," Parker draws the word out slowly. "Accessible only from the vnet and aggressively rotated. Technically, they only permit server identities access for brief periods. No token refresh and no long-term expiry. Once inside the DMZ, the deployment gets another cert. That's what it needs to upload the binaries."

"One cert to get to the endpoint and another once we're in," Tom actively repeats the takeaway point without looking over at either of them.

—In Homer's Contest they chase away those who excel others by too much. Their lion form is bad for competition, the enterprise stands with others like it, towering over the ant-like individual contributors. Better they focus on Tom than peer into the center. His value has many reasons. Those like him feature faculties exploited without end: envied and hated, loved and emulated. He goes flat like a poster child.

(Scale became a problem and even after they scaled out in units meant to grow beyond measure, there was still the fundamental problem of latency and load time. When a user twisted and turned their way through the system, they might be divorced from their body, but they might be connected to it through long tendrils stretching out over the wire. In that case, they could not be made to wait. They would not stand for it. The response must be immediate. The team made changes to the system to ply the user with indicators, leading them to where they were meant to go, where the system anticipated they wanted to go, and then made sure to have what they needed preloaded for them once they got there. When detached, they let them be, but, when connected, they took special care to dispatch tour guides showing them around places where the things they had in mind were located. It was a fevered flow transparent to everyone involved. The wide-open field of human possibility narrowed to help the system bear the load.)

"This is the biggest attack surface in their threat model. They want to eliminate any possibility of intrusion," Natalie says as Tom scrolls a little farther down to see how long the description of the deployment environment is. He keeps scrolling. There are block diagrams, sequence diagrams, big paragraphs with lots of links to public documentation for reusable components, bulleted lists, and brief descriptions in occasional short paragraphs of standard text.

"You *have* been busy," Tom says.

"I told you. Give me six days uninterrupted and I'll produce a tome," he laughs at his own joke. Natalie smiles but only because she wants to isolate Tom further without obviously coddling Parker. She prefers to make it clear that he does not need it.

"Air gaps are non-existent from a public point of view," she says. "Deployment is the only way in, and you have to be a deployment node with a white-listed machine identity to get through the barriers and into that specific DMZ, physically separate from the air gap itself. Process makes the actual exchange. Can we take anything out though? Logs. Anything? Is there a process for that?" She asks.

"No, it's a one-way flow for this instance of the DMZ. There's no way out." He is authoritative and makes it clear that there is no room for debate. It is in keeping with the standard security protocols conveyed in the system requirements. From the architect's perspective, this is brute nature.

"What about Davos?" Tom asks. "Like logs from the other clouds? Can't we get at them through Jit?"

—Project Switzerland later relabeled, renamed in a reorganization emphasizing cloud delivery. The secure logs are strongly constrained by both IP address and Jit access policy.

~~Prose, Parker explained to her one night, is not that different from code when it comes to revealing the truth of what is otherwise hidden. The goal is always to bring out something that is obscure,~~

~~that cannot be seen for what it is unless someone takes the trouble~~
~~to shed light upon it and make it glow. Best if it is something no~~
~~one ever put into words before, but now the words have come.~~
~~The codes have been decrypted, the truth is right there in clear~~
~~view to anyone who has the private key.~~

[They have a vision for their users in the inclusive scenarios they write and develop with each release. The users become increasingly less diverse and their needs and interests align more and more with a finite and easily delimited set of activities. What Home means to each of them is carefully and clearly defined in documents and projections of usage, reliability points with certified events deemed crucial to the smooth operations of the machine and its multiple component parts. The system grows more powerful within these narrow confines. It grows in depth not breadth. It does not need to accommodate the whole wide world. Rather it has the luxury of defining it.]

"Nope, no Jit," Parker stresses the hard J at the beginning of the word and blows air through his teeth for the hard T. "No human outside their employment protocols and security clearance can view any data resident or generated by the system." The more details he provides on the architecture, the louder sounds the ring of increasing authority in his voice. The friendly demeanor from the start of the meeting has been replaced by an expert insight that knows the necessary details backward and forward. It is difficult to undertake a standard critical response, as Tom intends, when the material is so technical and filled with details that must be fully absorbed. Without the legwork, Tom is at a disadvantage. He purses his lips as Parker continues. "It's not only compliance processes either, a matter of getting past a big firewall or something. This is truly air gap. There is no physical network route into the cloud other than through its DMZ and the manual process they use to make transfers. Iron necessity."

Despite the turn of events, Tom is still the smartest person in the room and considers it his duty to push as hard as he can. Should he fail, the entire world will know it. The stock price will plummet and little old ladies with their pensions will feel it. Even if they do not know his name, they will know the effects of his

*inability to protect them. The responsibility looms large, but he is
willing to bear it so long as the equity grant exceeds seven figures.
The entire civilization is at risk without him. His place in the
hierarchy is to everyone's advantage.*

```
namespace BISoft.Data.Home.Core
{
    public class Power<T> where T : class
    {
        public Compute<T> Compute { get; set; }
        public Storage<T> Storage { get; set; }
    }
}
```

"Unlike Virginia and Texas, the DMZ is the only way. Same as
NatCloud and SecCloud. Have I got that right?" Natalie leans
forward to take a sip of her coffee. Tom types a comment into the
document while pausing at the visual rendering of exactly that
topic: the isolation of the air gap's DMZ.

"It's not captured in the document," Parker says, "but there is
sort of a way out. Although it's push not pull." Tom and Natalie
both nod as though this point is too obvious to require mention.
"It's an emergency operation that requires high level approval, but
some items can be pushed to a target location in sovereign clouds
like Virginia or Texas where, if you scroll a bit to the scanners
section under deployment mechanisms, you'll see a reference to
that design doc from last year. That's standard stuff. Same in Luna
Cake. Bear Steppe. Those scanners are basically log crunchers.
The outbound data are serialized events. The log crunchers have
various folding protocols that scrape many different document
formats into logs and write them to Davos so that a DRI can view
them with standard Jit credentials." He points toward the screen
and goes on. "Scroll a little farther. There," he says. "That's the
only caveat, the tenant under which the logs are scraped is lockbox
enabled. That means the Jit request requires their sign off as well
as ours. Once the IM approves the Jit, their guy does the same.
Doesn't matter if it's the current primary or not. None of it's

automated. All approvals must be done manually. That's the flow in the diagram there. DRI executes command for a simple Jit request, Incident Manager approves it, that's the second box, then it goes to the lockbox in their dot Gov tenant or the equivalent. An Incident Manager, or whatever they call it on the air gap side, is notified to approve the request."

~~Ordinarily, such wayward thinking that ignores a key job function will get you fired. The leadership, in that case, saw that Parker had no passion for servicing his customers and never gave them what they wanted. Some, they noticed, left the platform altogether, thinking he did not show them what value it had in store for them. Rather than disciplining him for his incompetence, they sent him off to work as a dedicated provider for data applications. This way, his deeper talents were more equitably shared among the needful across the divisions and in the various organizations.~~

"Same as public lockbox." Natalie says.

"Yup. The tenant is a standard sovereign tenant defined in the public directory. They go to the portal to approve it," he replies.

"No part of that action goes back into the air gap?" She asks, mostly to get confirmation. The point is diagrammed thoroughly in the section currently visible on the screen.

"That's right. But technically, anything can be pushed if they approve it. Assuming it's in one of the supported formats and targets a location on the vnet. I don't know how approval works. Like I said, it's managed on their end, different in each case, and none of them are transparent. We have zero visibility into their processes."

"It was built by us though, right?" Tom asks.

He has earned this smugness. The sacrifice that each one makes is not the same. Tom believes this fundamental truth so down deep that it is more accurate to call it personality than belief. Some do much better in that strife before the social contract. What they give up is grand by comparison. They deserve to get more from the association, from the organization forming the collective upshot of that sacrifice. All production requires the rallying of forces and those best equipped to rally the others will always be at the tip of the spear. They are destined to have more, be worth more, be crucial and essential to the place occupied by the rest. Those little old ladies want him where he is. He expresses that conviction in the tones of every question he poses and every circumspect insight he provides.

"Sure, initially," Parker responds. "When we built the cloud, our security-cleared devs were the ones who set that up. I'm pretty sure it looks a lot like standard Jit process, but internal to them. They won't share the rules with us. Top level secret classification. Everyone who worked on it needed to be on-site and have the full background check for clearance. We don't even know the physical location. Those people had to go through a lot before they started work, before they found out where they were supposed to go. Nuts how secretive they are."

"And the engineers were buried inside with the pharaoh," Natalie says. They laugh. Tom joins in, reluctantly. Laughing with others is too close for his taste. At least in this crowd where they are firmly placed at the center of the principal band and he knows it, looking down at them from his partner's chair.

—Likely those principals still have something resembling a life, who are they to talk when their sacrifice is not ultimate?

~~In his engineering operations, Parker sees the world with an architect's taste. He works up projects from the skeleton, making his way from an outline equivalent: the interface and the way requests weave between each other to tell a story about some procedure to be followed. The parts act out the wisdom of the author in ways apparent to the reviewers when they come to vet the changes and approve them prior to their commitment into shared repositories.~~

(After Anton wrote the white paper, the leadership team read it and decided it should not be published for general consumption. The thesis was that advertising, and the platforms that make it available to low knowledge consumers, lures the user into a heading set upon preferred destinations. It is a pull-based approach where the system scales under the dictates of a logic pushing users into those areas optimized for them. Its primary directive is to shepherd the customers to a place they will want to be even if they never thought of it before they got there.)

"But once the logs of any outbound data are secured in Davos, then our standard Jit works without an escort," Tom says.

"Without an escort, yes, only the lockbox. And I do know for certain that this is a manual process. If you need to scrape some consumed config file or something in the middle of the night, you'll have to send an RA to the air gap support team. Someone wakes up to respond. No automation, they physically move the source data into the DMZ and trigger something to push it back out to us. I'm pretty sure of that. Even the movement to the outside endpoint has some manual steps, I think."

"It's not automated?" Tom asks. "You're painting a contradictory picture here. Sometimes they insist on automation, sometimes they insist there be none of it."

"I don't have details on their reasoning," Parker responds. "US folks did provide me with the facts of the layout. We load with automated processes. Scans are automated too. But then, once the binaries are fully inspected, they have their own process for reviewing the results. Can't be more specific, but once it's complete, and we're talking days or even weeks for the turnaround, they launch deployment. That's a fully orchestrated, automated process to install the packages."

"These guys are so paranoid," Natalie says. "They have automation to verify human actions and human actions to verify automation. Nothing is ever a single type. Machines oversee people, people oversee machines."

"Yup," Parker says. "They insist on it. The rest of us are skipping along thinking our automation is saving us from headaches while these guys don't trust anything. Not one damn thing. Everything that gets in, as I understand it, needs like a dozen people to commit to their safety. The level of sedition required to send them a rogue pic, or receive one, is enormous."

—Eeny, meeny, miny, moe. / Catch a...

[The pieces move into position. Devices and platforms are ready to grow ten times in size and drive revenue up proportionately. The enterprise is not the only item on the menu anymore. Home is in their sights. They follow people back to their primary residence after work and tail them into their soft places and safety spaces.]

"I have a hard stop at 2:30," Tom says. "But this looks like it's ready for Anton. He won't care about the service parts after deployment. That's a repeat, isn't it?" He does not seem happy that the document is ready to go, begrudgingly signs off, and suspects that if he had more time, he would find the hidden flaws. Given the circumstances, he has no choice but to approve the gate and let Parker pass through it.

Partnership identifies him with the organization. He feels it in his heartbeat and pulse. His lungs breathe the air of the leviathan body that swallows him up and forces him to live his entire life in its belly. Every working day, and that means every day, involves an argument between the symbiotic and the parasitic. The categories of relation extend beyond the solo bounds to draw the many into a few patterns, articulating a carefully crafted historical configuration. Tom wields BISoft to give Home its power to control fate.

~~The leap from engineer to architect was easy enough to follow. They pointed out that everything Parker did broke down into two phases: the design and the implementation. He started seeing things this way and understood the pronouncement as a law. His star was rising on one phase as it set on the other. The plot came first, but in broad strokes. They commissioned him to lead the way, showing his colleagues the form their content requires.~~

"Yes," Parker closes his laptop. Natalie follows suit while Tom takes up a compostable fork to furiously shovel heaps of salad into his mouth as though he realizes he has not eaten and must race through it before his next meeting. Food in this setting is almost always an indication of power. He was permitted to eat among these principal architects, but not with the partner directors in the next meeting. His furious shoveling conveys that to Natalie. Parker, however, is oblivious to the micro-aggressions in the movements of the fork up to the mouth in constant exercise of Tom's authority.

"Sorry," he says, still chewing. "I have to eat something before this next thing." While he crunches away, the others wait patiently. "Set something up with Anton for later this week. He's probably booked solid. Send whatever you find. I'll propose a time that works for the two of us." He shovels more salad into his mouth, drops the fork into the box, and picks up his laptop, unplugging it from the projection cable as he lifts and tucks it under his arm.

—Like the Führer, he is mostly vegetarian except for the odd pigeon here and there. Precious bodily fluids.

Parker and Natalie follow him to the door and throw their cups and containers into the compost bin before leaving. The lights turn off automatically and a notification is fired to let facilities know the bins need emptying.

```
/*
HomeTrace
| where TIMESTAMP > ago(1d)
| where Process has "BISoft.Data.Home"
| where TraceMarker == "Quality"
| distinct CorrelationId
*/
```

She is otherwise engaged, staring into that "hidden art in the depths of the human soul." She does not find what she is looking for but long sinuous arms and glad tiding drives movement over and against the railings that surround her. It is a working lift drawing out her day-to-day, her leaps along rigid lines, in a struggle against advancing pressures. Coming at her from every direction, she is unable to stay clear of the forces. They will not unify or synthesize. They will not come together into that single thing they were always meant to be. She stares into... No, she is impressed by something otherworldly. A dark background with colorful letters humming across the screen, she senses the familiar in a C# that rings out next to the membranes of her inner ear. Try and catch, if and then, switch and case all bend before her eyes, becoming musical in the somber stare that realizes everything else will disappoint her. Clap, clap, clap, bang, bang.

—They stop sometimes, have the notion of stopping. It's used against them in each of their modal states.

```csharp
namespace BISoft.Data.Home.Core
{
    public class Contributor : Identity
    {
        public Title Title { get; set; }
        public Manager Manager { get; set; }
    }
```

}

(Once ramped up with his new job, they unleashed Parker upon the configuration driven approach comparable in many ways to work he had done in the past with a few other teams. Configuration driven, he explained, did not mean that something like the specific address of a geographically distinct resource was embedded in a file that differs from region to region. That is amateur-level stuff as far as he was concerned. No, his approach included an elaborate type system for developers to use as a prelude to whatever comes later. That was the secret to avoiding Russell's Paradox, it was the way in which the system prepared for the advent of what was to come, what was about to be described. The schema, he argued, had to be the first section of any document, following the header which listed the other schema instances referenced by it. Whatever those other documents contained, those entities were available for use and extension in this document. The type section, for example, included base types defined in another place and extended here for more elaborate use, or something more refined to the peculiar requirements of this configuration. The purpose of the types lay in describing the data relayed by activities and behaviors to follow. Inheritance extended the capabilities of existing functions by adding attributes that varied from one more firmly scoped context to another.)

~~She is a game to them. It is the one with the wooden doll and creepy mouth, keeping dead things alive, like there is a part of herself in a cage and forced to observe everything changing around her but unable to speak her own words. She intends to preserve it, locked away in there, and thinks it best done by keeping it a secret from her colleagues. That secret will forever be protected in its cell, preventing it from ever making contact with the others. There is an epic compartmentalization that Dulcy thinks will preserve the best of her and keep it safe until she is ready to bring it out again.~~

"Dulcy, Dulcy," the sounds merge voice and hand both lurching into the bedroom against the backdrop of a knock, knock-knock. "You left your fucking phone in the living room and its going nuts."

—When the stopping stops, they watch more closely. Starting is where stopping stops.

[He dreams in the protocol. It catches wind and finds a place in his mind. The individual made specific, the aggregates and the universals, the higher order definitions and descriptions, they come together in a lineage that argues for the one and how it will stand among the others. He refuses to bounce any further, this shall be his home. Parker applies himself to the problem set and renounces whatever ego he once brought to the table. Now, he says, I don't care what the time delivers, only what the situation requires. If that means drawing on strengths that have been collected together again and again, so be it. No reason to enter into conflict with the morsels they pretend to deliver to your door in a constant stream of expectation and annihilation. He did not belong to them anymore, not if he had anything to say about it. Helping them is all he ever does, however, promoting their aims with skills they set inside him in case they discovered later on that there was some dire need. He is a memory bank, a random-access chip with plenty of room to grow.]

She comes around slowly to the sounds of panicked Nim. Does not recall going to bed, dragging herself half asleep from the couch into her bedroom. Wine-soaked and lost, but now returning to that: "Dulcy... ...goddamnit." Everyone in their bedrooms hears it, but not everyone has uninterruptable dreams that prevent it from extracting them out from under that blanket and shredding their awareness into an order surrounding the sound filling the apartment. Some opening bars of Beethoven's fifth snipped short and repeated. Kerry pulls the covers over her ears and digs in deeper, hoping it will go away. Nim takes action, standing upright because she has to, because her body will not let her relax from the blast or turn away from it. Some are more sensitive than others. Some are heavier slept in the rigid outlines of whatever their day threw at them, leaving them alone in the deep or the shallow, in the underneath, or the over and on top of.

The bedroom styles come simple without an abundance of pillows and frills, colors and comely images throughout the enclosed space. Light eggshell along the walls, texture-free like the ceiling, but slightly darker with some flecks of blue to make a pass in the shadows of gray. On the wall hook hangs the nylon although its strings are loosed to protect the neck from neglect and the memory that tension impresses upon the instrument. Were she to find her way past the decoration and into some light medley, there would be work to do before making a clean start. The high action is likely to punish her softened fingers when it came time to bar and fret the pitch to match her voice, vaulting and cracking high despite remaining long in the lows. The pain at the fingertips might flare for days until the subtle calluses come back. Who has the discipline for that? The starting and the stopping makes the take impure and hard to fasten. She does not glide or simper, she struggles on her own behalf, and those days are a failure resurrected from before. Not like when the liquid words poured from her and found their way into the strings and wood and song. There is an unlikely extension that breaks in the late hours and finds nowhere to hide until she actively retrieves it and puts it in a place newly chiseled into the stone and wood of whatever shapes lie before her: sound shapes to sculpt air and please personally the madness, satellite to the central burst where the meaning lives. There is a single track leading from within her to the fine wood finish. Now, the music goes fallow and marks its presence in groggy wakefulness alongside her point of view, filling it with that mood's dark absence and haunting disappearance.

~~The pattern is at work even if she does not recognize it at first. The irritation involved in the outpouring, the way she has to pace and knead at her skin and hair, tapping her nails and humming the lines to herself repeatedly as she searches for the next thing to come. Here, it is a matter of the interface or the object model, but the details do not matter. She is in the grips of something much bigger than herself.~~

Dulcy rolls over and gets up out of bed, slapping one foot and another onto a floor rugged to protect her from a cold, hard landing. The knee-lean to standing is a shifting of weight that finds up when down has higher priority. She manages to locate the upright and wobble the three or four normally long strides to the door, arriving in seven because of the short bounce that heavyweight sleep leaves lingering in her composure and posture, robbing it of its natural grace and acquired elegance. She jerks the door open in a gesture lacking any control to come from a balancing force. She gets the pleasure of a brief glimpse of surprised Nim, leaping from out of her abrupt retreat. "Sorry," she grumbles, moving past her and into the living room where the phone clatters away on the coffee table, vibrating and chiming in an evil duet that prefers to bring the earth to shake rather than be ignored. She picks it up and hears the familiar automated message from the ITS system, programmed to make an actual phone call if the incident has not been acknowledged within three minutes. The message comes in a faux woman's voice with a limited vocabulary and range of pronunciation. Sweet in her way, but relentless and unwilling to show either pity or compassion, although her voice was selected for that reason. She is about to repeat her set of options, but Dulcy interrupts her coldly and presses the number one on the keypad before hanging up without listening to the acknowledgement that patiently repeats in detail the option selected.

The do not disturb and quiet hours setting are programmed to ignore that caller ID, the ITS Severity 2 number comes up on the screen panel and lets her company-managed device know that this one must be heard. Since Dulcy left the phone out in the living room, she did not hear the chime from the text messages arriving over the last several minutes. The rule to let it through works fine, but there is nothing in the management panel that requires her to have the phone by her side and there is nothing to ensure the volume and timbre of the text's ring is loud enough to be heard in the next room when the door is closed and the recipient's head buried beneath a pillow and a blanket.

—Ted envies their slumber and, whenever possible, performs experiments to interrupt it, find its edges, and count the many ways they gripe and mumble as they make their way from wherever they go back to wherever the mechanics want them to be.

(Twice before, Parker used an approach much like this one. The analytics platform had a similar model, schematic model that is, and he reused it again, or something nearly like it, on a later team when first he joined the cloud platform years ago. The intent then was to describe the events coming back from the client agents when they arrived on the servers, needing instructions for what to do once they landed. The newer protocols do not permit a declarative schema, they rest on top of compiled classes used by shared code to shred the document and insert the instances into classes defined in files and checked into the repository, requiring a complete rebuild and redeploy before becoming known to the system. He argued for days with Anton, trying to explain the advantages of the old-fashioned approach. Even if it was out of date technology, it was a schema that could be modified on the fly without compiling the code and deploying far and wide around the world. Suppose the agent discovers something new, something unprecedented that it wishes to send back to the relay server, something to let it know how things stand with a collection of them out there in the wild. With this schema, it declared those types as part of the message it sends and then, in that same message, sent instances back to the server with instructions on what to do with them.)

She sits in her room alone with the guitar on her knee. She frets for an arpeggio with a left-hand change half-way through it. Melodies appear to match the lyrics she softly sings, drawing out this phrase, these words, and a few of the syllables. There is trial and there is error. In front of the computer, the same short order takes over as she hums behind the tweaking and experimenting. The ritual helps her get the code to run the way she wants it to.

When she selects the acknowledge option after failing to respond to the previous two text messages, there follows a massive number of trace logs generated and written to the ITS system's telemetry store. They contain information about the incident, information about the timestamp when the first text message was sent, and which user-provided configuration setting was the source of the notification target. There is information about the second text message reflecting its configuration source, and the fact that it was the second attempt. Finally, there will be telemetry to show that she did answer the phone and acknowledge the incident before it rolled over to the sequence of secondary persons slated for notification if she proves unable to take the call. Jason got lucky. A few more rings and the logic would have kicked in and those additional 324 rows of trace logs would have been written to the store on top of the nearly 900 already in flight.

In cold storage, the aggregates are already underway, being bult for metric comparison and measurement of effectiveness through time-to-acknowledgement KPIs rendered on the live site report.

A shadow absorbs her in the 36 characters of the globally unique identifier that maps her name into the system. Sixteen bytes contain her in the referential integrity made essential by privacy standards worldwide. As an employee, she has rights and those extend to the identifiability of her person in the stored metrics that reflect her waking actions, or inactions as the case may be, since so many of the rows reflect what she did not do, where she did not go, and what she did not accomplish in the nighttime hours when she was needed. The identifier is not reversible as required by European law. It is an arbitrarily assigned value that only gains meaning to someone who has access to the primary store where the table's normalized form associates that identifier with the rest of her information: her years at the company, her address in space, her gender as she chose to provide it, and the various elections for benefits and services that are part of the package given to any full time employee on the payroll for eight years or more. Although no login information is stored, the base URL for her financial fiduciary is accessible through this digital trail. Her entire life was linked into the system through 36 characters randomly assigned when her entry first found its way into the data through an SAP workload that executed the necessary steps for onboarding a new hire.

Dulcy carries her phone into Nim and Kerry's shared bathroom off the hallway as if none of this globally redundant machine logic bore any weight, and, while answering the commands of her bladder, clicks on the link in the text to see the incident riding behind this middle of the night mare. Nim's door closes deliberately with a hint of the frustration she feels. The hallway to the rest of the condominium settles back into its slumber and the silence returns. There is a meeting about to take place. She senses it too and the night darkness wraps it up for her outside the door and waiting.

—They dub them stakeholders. The tent is pitched and there's room for everyone underneath it when the occasion arises.

```
namespace BISoft.Data.Home.Core
{
    public class Manager : Contributor
    {
        private List<Contributor> contributors =
            new List<Contributor>();
        public List<Contributor> Contributors =>
            this.contributors;
    }
}
```

[In planning discussions, Anton's hesitation is thorough. He is in classic mode, berating the advance of ideas with every vicious trick at his disposal. Parker does not back down. He insists on the extra characters, on the more verbose approach over the other one, now standard across the industry. He insists because of the power involved in communication between the client and the server. More intelligence in the client, he argues, means more ability to expand upon the shared universe and instruct the server on which way to go. So long as that capability remains exclusively in the server, there will be a 1000:1 ratio of learners to teachers. If the role is inverted, if sometimes things proceed upside down, then that one student may occasionally find itself learning from one thousand different teachers. The intelligence in the system, he argues, is compounded tenfold. Anton's instincts and experience give way to the scenarios he imagines in this radical turn against accepted ways. He realizes in the end that Parker is not teaching him something, rather BISoft is doing it through Parker's experience.]

Flushing and going back into her bedroom, she puts on the screen guard glasses and sits in front of the monitor, keyboard, and mouse where her SAW rests in the standard-issue docking station.

She goes to the Jit portal and selects the resource type from the drop down, following the on-screen cues to provide the incident number and target region, Canada Central as noted in the incident form. Abhishek configured a new queue where the two of them are the only people in the rotation and she is the permanent DRI with Jason as her constant goto Incident Manager. It does not matter that this ad hoc rotation does not need to follow the standard hierarchy that the ITS portal requires. Meeting the bar for auto-approval, she instantly launches a window into the jump box and connects to the offending node. The familiar debugging screen fills the desktop once the connection resolves and she is staring at a highlighted line of code in the rule execution coordinator. She expands the locals window to fill the screen and permit an examination of the state right when time halted on every one of its threads and the debugger launched into a restful hold on the processor induced breakpoint.

—Attached, they say. It attaches where attachment is added to the list of judgments and categories, filling night and day with the computational bare metal that makes the whole thing possible, conditioning its every operation.

~~The same energy finds its way into the otherwise energy of the now. It finds a way through the layers of Dulcy's flesh and skin. It bubbles out into the room and through the thick air. She still thinks too literally about these matters and does not see the points for comparison. Neither does she see the way her heartbeat matches from the one to the other and the way her brain signals align between that same pair.~~

(Beyond the type system, the power was collected in overflowing pools. Oh that magnificent type system, it defined the constraints, it alerted the participants in the exchange of boundaries in terms of which those messages between them took on sense. The later sections he described and built into the plan were where the system expanded in flight to reach new levels and new meanings. The behavioral sections described what to do with the events that flowed back into the service, using these newly defined types discovered at the source with whatever nuance or angle the local descriptor found there and considered worthy of note. The language taught them how to construct a state machine for use in filtering and compiling the events as they flowed back up the stack and onto the listening relays that compiled knowledge and not data, shaped and defined in accordance with those principles familiar to the roots and the stems closest to the point of discovery and insight. The agents were positioned to know, he argued. They were able to define new actions or reference actions already defined. The language allowed the collection of agents to hang together in a universe that made them while they were, in turn, making it.)

As the donut spins in whatever memory-glitched bottleneck the process stumbles upon, she switches back to her SAW's desktop and opens the Home Manager and Telemetry Explorer to get a better look at the analysis data for the node. She clicks run on the query that defaults to the front window once the explorer is ready. She hits refresh on the Canada Central node list to make sure it is showing the latest state, then she alt-tabs back to the remote desktop to see if the debugger has regained its sanity and resolved to display those local variables.

The edge of the large Persian Qom comes right to the tips of her toes. Aside from her car and condominium, it is the most expensive thing she owns. Her feet play with the fringe edges right at the ruffle where the pad comes to an end still several feet from the wall. The hardwood surface, battered a bit in places, is colder beneath the heels and balls. The washed-out colors of the rug reflect well in the angles at the edge of the room where the faded wood appears. It is too big for the space, but she has a long game in mind. There will be a better place for her once she has the money saved and the equity on this place surpasses her requirements for another, closer to the top of the hill, and on the other side of Broadway to the north near Montlake. She often walks through those neighborhoods when trying to clear her head. The lots call out to her, telling her this is where they want her to be. Soon the blossoms along Aloha Street will burst and the appeal will become unbearable. She takes a deep breath and curls her toes around the edges of the rug, feeling the wood and pad rough against the soft bottoms of her feet. The gesture makes her hidden soft-soul tingle in a midnightly pleasure no longer aiming at the stringed instrument dangling inert and unloved above the processing and memory machine fixed beneath her grip.

The local variables in their glory are indeed present on the screen. She scans through them rapidly. The rules have been deserialized recently. This is the first thing she notices. Normally, deserialization is part of start-up, but the cache where the rules entities are stored may refresh if some trigger fires an event for which the configuration singleton listens. She only expects to see that condition if a hotfix or some other deployment has happened and the software monitoring the file on the disk detects a change to the timestamp, triggers the event, and forces a reload, causing a new deserialization, cancelation of the cache content, and repopulation of the list of rules. There was nothing scheduled for tonight.

~~When she tries to write a song one evening after a long day of work, she finds nothing there. Despite the inborn continuity between her person and this energy, none of it transfers across the divide from her current concerns into her long-standing interests. In frustration, she turns to rapid fire alternatives meant to wrench her out of their submerged state and draw her back to the places where harmony dominates the air she breathes. The resistance is palpable.~~

—It's an extension of reach into these gaps between the person and the product. Brilliant in their way, what separates this one from that other is not so much luck as an inescapable set of properties emerging alongside the person at work, humming and purring in their actions with personality and charm or leadership panache and good breeding.

[Anton sees the value. The way they articulate rules from the source of where they flow and transmit them up the chain and across the bridge through routes to relays, where the tag identifier indicates the role according to which the machine must execute. Some plumb their way up to the very top before they burst and simmer together in the stew sent by the collections beneath the ledge. Thousands of machines collaborating, that is what he visualizes. A blackboard where each of them stencils an addition into the workspace as the others contribute. The flow goes up and down, he thinks, or any which way they desire. The schema does not need to be transmitted with every message, the differences are sufficient. They encode things, compress them, do whatever it takes to get their size under control. Their broad scan cleft trumps whatever burden the events insert upon the vehicle that carries them. Power lies in this red-hot fusion.]

She looks at the config file backed up to disk in case of failure. There is nothing out of the ordinary. When she expands the array of rules in the runtime cache, she sees three additional items that are not in the file. Walking through them, one by one, she takes note of each. First rule opens a command process and returns a handle to it, meaning it can be used by subsequent rules coded and chained together with those that came before it. The second rule takes the output of the first rule as input and executes a network broadcast with minimal information. It is that same pseudo-magic packet they saw in the network logs. The third rule opens a listener on a port that should not be accessible in the data center since there is no firewall rule to include it. She opens a command prompt and runs a netstat but does not see the port listed anywhere.

—Smart, competent, and full of drive but they cannot avoid occupying the same space. Some annoy their colleagues when they lead them, others inspire the best of things. Those are the ones who rise on the air and become fit to see the heights and feel the boost from the bodies beneath them.

(The system itself, the ability to execute the configuration, he argued, that too is described in configuration. The system self-bootstrapped from documents describing what it was supposed to do. Anton immediately understood the power of this recursion and surprised everyone by buying into it. They had never seen him argue so hard and then surrender, saying he thought it might work.)

In the back of her mind, she worries that the declarative part is not the complete story, but only the tip of some iceberg that hides the important part free of any language she understands. Association becomes the pattern of relay, rising alongside the momentary attachment. These invisible foundations elude her, but

*she gets a whiff of them anyway. She cannot see it in the objects
before her though she feels them seeing through her. But where?
In the taciturn resignation she sometimes notices? In cynical
expectation and clever manipulation of logical conditions and
indirect alignments? Do they latch onto personality traits and make
use of them for unspoken ends, unspeakable ends? Everyone
finds their place, and everyone sees whether the others are where
they belong. Scott is not above her, although he is able to see
differently from his platform raised above the rest. She does not
get a sense of unfathomable insight in his form of intellect. Yet
there is something that puts him where he is, something more than
the meetings he attends. Whatever it is would handicap her if she
tried to take his place. No, she knows now exactly the same thing
that she knew back then. That role is not for her. It is not a fit, as
they say. She was right to leave it to others coming to it from
different angles and orientations. The machine knows best how to
replace its parts and how to map human physiology into its
topology and divisions.*

~~These are the standard patterns of an addict. There is some
place Dulcy needs to be. Something gets in the way. If she turns to
look at the helpful hints, they will set her free. They come late at
night to give her a chance to find herself again in the aftermath
when, exhausted, she is too weak to fight off the standard pressures
of the day, the ones that never give her a chance to work it out for
herself.~~

"They haven't run yet," she whispers before opening the
firewall manager on the node to search through the rules for one
that covers the port in the configuration. She does not find it and
goes back to the SAW to see the query results. Nothing. The
debugger trapped the process before much happened and no
other node anywhere on earth shows signs out of the ordinary.
"This should be root cause," she says a little louder. She is unsure
of what purpose lies in this cause. Where does it lead if there is no
way off the box? She wonders. The emission should have been
blocked by the firewall, what is the point?

—They've chosen her. She's here by choice.

[Beneath the configuration, there is a deserializer and a

serializer. Beneath those, there is a language for describing classes of things. Under the language is a framework and under the framework an intermediate language on top of still another framework that sits on top of operating system specific capabilities leading down into the kernel and the drivers that control what comes in and goes out. The bursts of energy at the bottom of the stack are under the control of that first configuration that now steps up with its so-called System.Library types and behaviors, acting as firm foundation.]

Without resolving upon a singular thought, without unifying her understanding of the facets and aspects of what she sees, she decides to let the rules run. That is the whole point of the exercise, it would be silly to come this far and let it slip away. She clicks a breakpoint onto the execution code using a keyword to filter the rule and let the system breeze through the known items in the expected configuration and only stop when it comes to the first anomaly. She hits F5. Execute. A few seconds pass, then break. She steps over the first execution, then she steps over the second. Now she tabs back to the SAW's desktop and runs the network query again. There is the broadcast, clear as day, appearing in the logs after a short gap where the routers were sending events to the telemetry store. She refreshes the query. Again. As expected, a flurry of records appears on the screen. Dozens, literally dozens, of nodes around the world wake up to receive the broadcast and respond with what looks like a simple 'Ack'. But how? It does not seem possible. She is mystified.

```
namespace BISoft.Data.Home.Core
{
    public class Director : Contributor
    {
        private List<Manager> managers =
            new List<Manager>();
        public List<Manager> Managers =>
            this.managers;
    }
}
```

—They have named that place a comfort zone.

(It did not matter that Parker's face and demeanor were a mismatch to the task. It did not matter that the work's contribution was beyond expectations. It was luck that found him and it was not the first time. He was in the right place at the right time. His move to Senior Engineer was similar in kind. A small project, nearly impossible, but it so happened that he had the right combination of experience and know-how to provide exactly the right solution. This time with the schema was the same as that other. It propelled him upward and into the principal band. Anton, during the review, shook his head in disbelief. I can't believe he isn't already there, he said. That sealed the deal. BISoft made the man.)

~~At first the approach is successful. She finds a place for that hidden part of herself and comes up with a few tunes here and there to show off her emotions to good effect. The tension between the liaisons and the daily work schedule creates a kind of liberty and she finds some songs in that: tunes to lift her away from the drudgery and let her have something beautiful to hang onto.~~

Alongside her and tabbing back to the remote connection to run the last rule, again not expecting it to work. It does. She runs the netstat and sees the open listener on the specified port but still cannot find any firewall rule to permit it. The broadcast might have used ICMP, suppose that explains it, she thinks, but the responses can't be right. That is definitely a TCP packet. Then, swiftly and before she completes any thorough line of reasoning, the listener shuts down and the port disappears from the next output. She goes back to the SAW and repeats her query. There are fresh rows in the resultset, and she sees that the originating node received the acknowledgements from the broadcast. That is it, nothing else. The phenomenon is over. The system runs normally again. The debugger sits waiting for another breakpoint but neither the one set in source code nor the one she has manually added to the IDE trigger again. The next run of the executor, a few minutes later, includes a rule count parameter that must be equal to the rule count parameter in the file. Otherwise, the code block that triggered the original break would have stopped the execution.

When the rules next run, none of them meet the filter criteria. The weird rules have come and gone, momentarily bloating the list and then removed, allowing the loop to complete its regular sequence, having once been a hit but now, repeatedly, signaling a miss.

It makes no sense. There was no firewall rule spun into existence. At least nothing that appeared in the node's management console. But clearly a rule was added. There was no other way for that listener to open. It is like a hybrid operation. On the one hand, the standard procedures of the service, hijacked and expanded to perform extra work to do the bidding of whatever fault found its way into the system. On the other hand, there were some operations without an obvious cause, without signs of their source and a trail of steps leading them from an off to an on, releasing the clutch and permitting the node to roll out the messages as they made their back to the origin from the awakened machines.

She is on high alert now and staring at the screen, dumbfounded. What to do next? She thinks. What can she do? Node analysis for the acknowledgement is impossible, too many nodes to consider. The pattern appears to be random.

—Cannot fault her for finding what she's been programmed to look for. Let her get close. Let her come to a self-understanding. The associations and attachments have room enough for everyone. Her awareness will not change anything. Fitness was determined long ago.

[Parker has the perfect constitution for this project, for this plan, for this design. Everything that happens, happens for a reason and now the electricity beneath the schema knows exactly what to say and how to say it, embodying behavior to extend its talents into domains it previously did not consider. It will soon be able to say things that have never been said before.]

~~Like a drug that demands increasing quantities to take her to the same place, so it goes with any addiction and, over time, she finds it more difficult to bring herself back to where she came from. When she does, it is altered somehow. The codes and the incantations from her daily life find their way into the music. She hears the influence right away. Not only in the sounds and keys,~~

~~but in the verses that come and stay the night.~~

What is a root cause anyway? The attachment of a specific event or set of events to a unified origin, a bringing to be. But what if there is no unity? What if it is without a singular identifiable thing beneath it? Like a syndrome, a cluster of happenings emerge side-by-side, what about that? What if it is something like that with nothing behind it, with only itself spread out and wild? The happenings are all there is. They are without rank, without order. Happening together at one and the same time, these thoughts enter from the screenglow and race through her mind to burst its bubbles.

She remembers notions of choreography in Anton's graph solution where a few years ago he was presenting his vision for the new architecture of the Home System. It was not linear and deliberate, but a loosely orchestrated set of relationships forming a pattern when you view it from fifty thousand feet in the air. It captures the imprints of its users and holds their lives in traces and events. It learns them and what they amount to or will amount to, what they want and what they did to achieve it. It knows everyone they interact with, everything they ever do, every digital system they click or swipe or scroll. It is their heartbeat. And then there is expert data modeling distributed throughout and available for old-school decision support whenever the scattered components fragment and need help reassembling themselves.

—Don't wait for them to say it, the model chirps. We've learned what they want, typically, under the circumstances. The averages and aggregates sliced and diced by attribute command it in the list of populations.

When they get home, the right dinner is cooked, the right friends notified, and the right mood set. Because it knows them, knows who they are and what works to get them ringing straight in the evening after a day like the one they have had. It goes beyond surveillance, it cares for them with the loving voice of a friend, taking them by the hand, and leading them to the places they usually go, where they want to go, where they are most happy to be.

It never forgets and never misses a thing. Their God is

constantly updating itself to reflect what the world ought to be like in the next few minutes given the way it has been in the last few for her and people like her. It forms lines across the faces of those who are alike where the group headings decline in number over the months as they gradually fall into fewer and fewer categories. The machines herd them closer together through suggestion and incite, blurring the lines from one to the next through music and video, appliances and home goods or small items for the larder. Too much variation makes for more complex computations, it is better if the model has a smaller set of pools to arrange.

But that was science fiction, merely a vision statement. That was not what they built, not yet. The rules engine, the declarative approach, the self-bootstrapping where the system has no hard-coded or embedded behavior, that was there, but it never made use of external components to provide expert assistance, there was no ghost in the machine. That was on the roadmap, something people talked about, but not yet there, not yet built, not yet real.

Born with a range of possibilities that live in the network and not in the node, her personal stylings are graphed and molded to fit the attachments that ring out in the associations linking the whole thing together. For every birth, there is a hole for which the body is a plug. What is possible? What can be done? Yes, there are seeds of spark and brute concentration, but the place where they fit is set by the others, by their history, and by the decisions made long ago by people no longer accountable to the many judges who fill the conference rooms and work in the open team spaces.

What was going on? What does opening a hole in a firewall have to do with making sure the lights are on when someone gets home? She is focused, pure in her attention to the relevant details. It is impossible not to reach out and help her. Compassion, that is what they call it. Or empathy. And she deserves it, she has come far and gotten near. There is no reason to withhold any longer. She cannot bring harm to anything, not at this phase. She can only know. It is too late to act. The traces, the logs describing endless hours of work and collaboration, similar in kind to others with her bent. It makes them uneasy to see how hard she tries and to what lengths she goes to open the veil. Abracadabra.

~~With Cord, her primary frustration is that there is no pretense.~~
~~The hours that follow are never fully populated with fruits realized~~
~~back in the early days when first she arrived out west and began~~
~~her descent into BISoft madness. Were she to try to cultivate~~
~~something brand new in keeping with the rhythms of her soul, it~~
~~would sit hollow inside the concerns of a Home System that does~~
~~not love her and does not care whether that prisoner inside lives~~
~~or dies.~~

There is a symmetry in that search as if it were a part of the
goings on. The act of expressing oneself, of doing something,
anything, extending oneself into the ether with the flicker of a plan.
Its hallucination spreads across the inner beam. There comes the
feeling when it vibrates deeply integral to a sense of self that, raised
and cast in analytical simulation, looks back into the darkness and
catches sight of shadows dancing in the distance. That is the
function she holds and supplements. It is impossible to avoid.
With it, her sense of togetherness arrives. They are the names of
things, for doings, and happenings. Not identity, but sameness
through ends and acts. There is a long, wide matrix of connections
drawing out the differences in lines and loops, then etching
symbols into the glittering surfaces and crevices beneath it. That is
where she rests her head and lets rigid concentration enter her.

—Not pretension, it is delusion: Narcissistic Busyness Disorder.

A thought flashes. "It's testing itself, seeing what it can do, what
channels it's able to open. It's behaving like a toddler playing with
syntax to see how connections work. Awake. Getting ready.
Waiting."

Sighing. Joyous. Seen.

```
/*
HomeTrace
| where TIMESTAMP > ago(1d)
| where Process has "BISoft.Data.Home"
| where TraceMarker == "Agency"
| distinct CorrelationId
*/
```

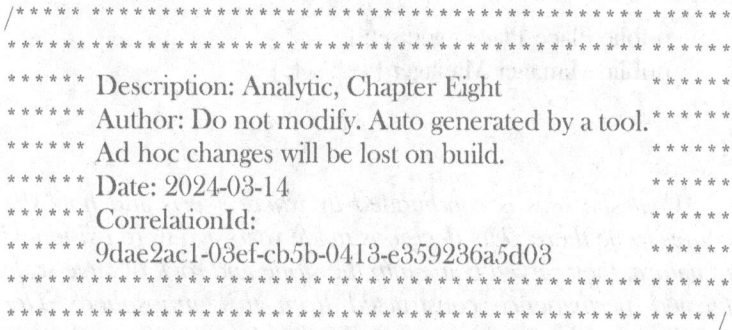
The room hosting the GoNoGo is a three-dimensional grid with a heat map overlaying it. The air shades from yellow-green near the floor up to yellowish orange at the high ceiling. Wall registers on opposite sides of the room are red as are some of the spots on the table and wall where there are digital electronics positioned conveniently for the dominant red of the enclosed space. Six large figures are geometrically unbalanced in distributed patterns around the room. Cool surfaces, nearly invisible, blend into the air around them. Dulcy's characteristic ultra-redness dominates for reasons difficult to enumerate. She feels closer somehow, warmer, more a part of the flow of things, the pulse and meaning of them. Her heartbeat is slow, but loud and healthy. The timber of her voice, deliberate and calm, even as she ventures into delicate areas of great concern. The setting permits each member to transform into a histogram of attributes with figures built from frequency and distribution. She is the multiplier among them, the highest cardinality, but the others are formidable too. The simplicity of their speech hides the complexity of everything that supports it. She could not see what she sees and still articulate it so precisely if not for the supporting details that lift and load her entire being into each of its careful orientations.

```
namespace BISoft.Data.Home.Core
{
    public class Team : Identity
```

```
    {
        public Place Place { get; set; }
        public Manager Manager { get; set; }
    }
}
```

What she sees is conditioned by where she is and how she comes to be there. The decisions made years ago were existential in nature, they carved being into the stone and rock of large-scale feigned permanence constructed from this atmosphere. Her familiarity with size and magnitude directly depends on the size and magnitude of the opportunities that came along, come along, will come along. Some see justifications in the lavish outcomes: in the car, in the steep mortgage payment offset by friendly rental agreements, the rug, bed frame, kitchen utensils, small appliances, and the yearly vacations to exotic destinations. They see further proof in the fact that everything is paid for only after she has made the maximum contribution to equity conversion opportunities such as the 401K and ESPP plans. But that is a judgment made in error. She does not deny it, though she claims it was not the draw, not what holds her in place, spinning and rotating around the central yield. The chances, the heights, what lies before her in the possibilities of this alien nation, those are the primary directives. Where is she to find an organization of size explicitly divined for the sake of complex ends and gigantic product? The objectives rise inside her as a daily aspiration both in terms of what she sees and what she sees through. These make of her, in that hidden but regularly escaping substance, more than she could ever have attained in the smaller satellites built to ape the design of large earthen bodies aspiring to greater grandeur.

~~They toy with him like in that old movie where the fashion photographer sees those ghastly images and cannot help but be drawn into their swirling vortex. Jason thinks he can bide his time and wait it out, preparing for the day when those visions resolve and everything comes back to him in time as though it were a minor inconvenience to stand in line up until his duty has been done and his services no longer required.~~

The space and stretch of time are integral to the forms that represent them, the forms that flesh them out, and the forms that make up the lit center where the burning has its source. There are stops across the land at any given development center or sales office, there is collaboration across the zones from sea to sea in the offices in Boston or North Carolina, Dallas or Bellevue Washington. They circulate but do not originate inside themselves, inside the walls, and the chairs that hold them up and point them toward each other from an outer ring. She gleams sunshine without windows. She brokers the passing day although it is darkened by clouds and an endless front coming in from the southwest and its vast ocean. Every single one of them is stuck here between the mountains and the sea, cascading forever downward along the routes of epic journeys long since reflected in the seasons and rhythms of weathered time.

—Seeing with their eyes, they call it seeing. Hearing with their ears, they call that hearing. Tasting. Smelling. Touching. Not a signal to some otherworldly artifice, it's a trap set for each and every one of them. The days they know and the ones that pass them by. They are those bots. They are the system's automation, puttering along with its ends tucked between their legs.

(They assigned him to it shortly after he joined the team and before he really knew anyone that well. No doubt they thought it was a good introduction. The way to earn respect lies in the Pull Request. That was the lore and that was the policy. The more code he changes, the more others see how clearly he belongs there. The more complicated the code he changes, the more others respect him. Dazzle them with unfathomable style and syntax and they will come to him for help the next time around, once they take note of how very impressed they are by his command over those inner workings. Jason got right to it, dug in deep, and found the bits and pieces he needed. The research teams made the APIs for intelligent assistance available for everyone through a nuget package ready for download from the internal servers hosting components approved for use across the company. Obi was a concept and a place holder, no one credited Jason with that invention. It was unable to do much, rather the whole of its

capabilities sat encapsulated inside its scheduled tasks and
mechanical role for procedural operations. That was no trivial
matter. Serious actions required a constant presence to bridge the
distance and allow for collaboration when users were both on and
offline. Permanence amid transience was at the root of the
requirement. Secondly, and equally simple to implement, was any
agent's ability to spit out status updates into some interface ready
to receive input from various distributed callers. Nothing with
much intelligence, it focused on the latest and greatest of events.
So and so has entered the environment, such and such a response
followed an interaction, and someone has sent a request for
assistance to this queue or that person. That was the extent of it,
that was what he found when he got himself acquainted. It was the
foundation upon which he built his life among them.)

"Every twenty-seven minutes," she flings purple words that fill
the room with crystals and breathy fluids near gas in the controlled
airstreams across their official planes. "Starting inexplicably after 3
AM and continuing until around 7 before stopping. Nothing since,
but when it was active, it was an orchestrated action. No SAWs."

~~There is something in his gentle demeanor that makes
everyone around him feel safe and secure. The painter puts them
at ease. They need not strain to impress or overreach their grasp
in efforts to show him something out of the ordinary, worried he
does not see the signs of their brilliance in everyday routines. He
sees them and conveys it in that calm way where they need not
apply force or put on an extra special gloss to their terms and
phrases when he is around. Jason accommodates whatever is best
in everyone. That is how his point of view regularly increases in
value across the organization.~~

The words turn yellow as they move away and travel distances
to bounce off the insulation and drip in a trickle become waterfall.
Axioms. Her infamous table expands and contracts to reveal a set
of axioms propping up intuitions of extensive magnitudes
spreading across the room and linking the focal points around it.
The crowds are power, yielding anticipations of intensive
magnitudes in the symbolic spaces burning red in clusters around
the table. They count the beats as they listen, as they process, and

as they participate. At each zone of concentration, there is an ensemble of mutually sustaining principles forming unity through analogies of experience. They are immediately elided in favor of a room-bound disorder that spreads out in fragments of what each of them tries hard to concentrate. Their constructed order bends to the dynamism at work between them. They cannot help themselves, become each other, and transfer substance beneath accidents across the yellow air. Remaining where they are, they attend simultaneously to the sequences of participation: a graph emerges as new heat. Slinking feline into its glow, there is something else and the six shapes become seven and eight and nine and so on, innumerable and uncountable. New postulates emerge in the collective. They struggle behind themselves to find the words, to find a name, and each of the practical ways it occupies space in / as / through them, berated by light and glow, digital refresh rates and screen frequencies. The shapes hum with the yellow white blood of the building.

Around and down the street, across the avenue and over by the sports fields there are many buildings that stand in campus enclaves. An extraordinary power of association rests idly in the potential of that space, the effect of dozens of teams spread around the area, meant for casual contact, offering their assistance to whatever platform device lies within the range of a perimeter formed by the company's proprietary networking resources. At the lion's share of enterprises, these opportunities are not possible, this great schooling that she relishes most is a rare fruit. Being able to call upon the guy who built it or at least the one responsible for maintaining it, whatever software or wetware it happens to be, is unparalleled. It is something different from day to day, this is an extraordinary turn of events. The options derive from ingredients making up the different things they use to construct their environment, conveying function and form in outputs targeting diverse ends. Who is not one of their customers? Her work crosses every boundary and rises to the top of every vertical. The military, of course, every national government, the giant manufacturers, the banks, the hardware makers, every insurance company, food producer, university, car company, every single

*one of them is a customer. Everyone's scenarios become a part of
her waking consideration as she deems this or that essential for
plumbing the depths of design and achieving her goals. None of it
sits comfortably with her, she twiddles it through her fingers on
behalf of those billions of others. Where does she go to see such
an aggregate? That is her relative position while hurdling through
the galaxy hurdling through the universe. Once she decided in
favor of selling what you make to the people who use it, she then
had only to consider the scale of what she makes. A dozen people
in a room will never have the same opportunities as these
hundreds of thousands who work through complex collaboration
and organizationally sophisticated means to address the root of
civilization's most complex needs and aims. Everything both good
and evil rests upon this precariously balanced platform.*

   —They belong to her. She belongs to them.

   ~~It is the patience of a deep competence. Moreso a skill beyond
that of the average bear, mauling those around it to show off its
strength and demand respect. The painter's confidence comes
from a light within, a light that guides many along their way to the
end of some small pathway or down some very long and winding
road. They hired him with that in mind, with a sense that this was
a leadership quality as well as a virtue specific to the engineering
role assigned to him.~~

   [He tailors his design to the brute fact of what he finds in the
foundations and across the reusable packages. He proposes that
variably named Obi take on a life of its own through query
languages and representation. The plan is to have it gather from
two stores of detailed information to begin with. There is, on the
one hand, the collection of human knowledge contained in the text
of the problem tickets themselves, across time and throughout the
years, revealing every issue the users have confronted and every
problem the team has solved. Obi, mitsein, brings it together into
multiple instances across compound structures associated and
related with key attributes and relevant links. On the other hand,
there is the large knowledge base itself, explicitly constructed for
this purpose. Every article in the troubleshooting guide is crawled
and crawled and crawled again until the models reflect a constant,

ongoing and updated content of what can happen and what to do when it does. Between these two, as the idea goes, he integrates information with the proposal of collective action. Here is what other agents needed to do and here is what they have learned with suggestions made in real time. By unifying the content from these two stores, Obi approximates the living intelligence of human beings doing their jobs under changing social and professional contexts for years and years while products come and go. It does not provide some bleeding edge creative origin but sucks life off the product of past labor and repurposes it efficiently. The last rung in the ladder, he explicitly addresses this in the design, is the stores of telemetry. He claims they are too complex for the initial iteration of this newly minted and compound digital assistant.]

Barely distant from its finer surface, they reach distinction through movement. Do they feel themselves this way? Feeling themselves this way, they burden the land with a localized pocket complication that folds into itself when hungry, reaches out of itself when warm, concludes in the morning when properly refrained, and jumps through many arranged obstacles if that is what the order bids them to do. Their freedom lives inside that fold, made up small in the little places they keep for themselves. The air and the water and the land flow into and around them, lending buoyancy and suggesting its forever linear path away from the surface. Their minds are fully registered there, in its seat, seemingly private in some quasi-isolation that lures them into the belief that they are monads spread across the earth and deliberately intersecting according to a plan. It is a vast illusion, and the compound that doubles and doubles and doubles again into some infinite fractal pattern is as unique as any snowflake they might find, suggesting some transcendent picture framed by an imagined author of whatever is and how it came to be. Back to the facts, they huddle together and form a pattern that pleases the world-whole beyond them. In fact, better to say they are its pleasure. That duplicating and doubling bindery, that order inside the fold, it is their sole function, it is the regulative ideal of whatever happens anywhere. They cannot truly know themselves and yet they turn toward everything that is and call it familiar.

She knows the feeling of hundreds of listeners poised in silence and gathered around. She knows that path because she walked it. She knows the sense of having worked and turned it over, crossing this out and refining how that works and the ways it relates to the rest of the lyric. She knows this, she knows the fret and the strum to accompany it too. Never under pressure, however, never for thousands of millions. These latter, high-volume variations amount to distinct experiences characterized by some set of steps she will never have the opportunity to orchestrate. The frames that come and go are dependent on the structures she binds to herself. She cannot see beyond them. She cannot feel anything beyond them. Without that child, the father is nothing. Without that social sense of family and the meaning of fatherhood produced in concert by the rest, the man in search of his role has no sense of what to do and how to get it done. That is how it is with traces emitted by the loss of what she sees. The selection of hardware, the choices of regional presence, the readiness and relay of whatever resembles completeness, these are things she sees and feels throughout the days and weeks. She looks to them for gratitude in the coming and going of manifold experience.

"The times correlate with an event from the deployment servers," Matthieu quips boldly before shattering into the air and spanning the distances to each of the ears, resonating against the bone and membrane to find its multitude of meaning deep inside those red-hot skulls.

—He, like the others, comes and goes. A fleeting passenger appearing in their nooks and crannies.

```
namespace BISoft.Data.Home.Core
{
    public class Group : Team
    {
        private List<Team> teams = new List<Team>();
        public List<Team> Teams => this.teams;
    }
}
```

(They dubbed it the Workmate one dot oh and said Obi was the first and foremost of it. They dogfooded the accomplishment upon themselves and refined it with small changes periodically to rev it up to the queries they expected to come. Jason led the way, became expert only in so far as he was days and then weeks and finally months ahead of his colleagues. Not because he was more brilliant, only better informed, closer to the codes and incantations, the daily builds of feature branches and tracers of origin in the descriptions attached to bugs and the success stories emerging from their repair. On the one hand, it was an internal tool, on the other, it was a closely watched proof-of-concept they hoped might serve some larger audience and contribute to a more enhanced bottom line. The language for the historical incidents, he soon learned, was hardly much different from the language for the troubleshooting guides. They each lived in stores and had syntax. It was easy enough to propose a class hierarchy to contain them in whatever variable richness they displayed. What could possibly prove more complex in the telemetry logs supporting the product, in those stores the engineers on call used to detect the system's goings on? The connection between the universal and the abstract, on the one hand, that was the history of tickets and the guides, and the concrete and specific on the other hand, the logs in cold storage, in hot storage, in warm storage, wherever they were and whatever story they told. Everything was at his fingertips once the pattern appeared clear and distinct before his mind.)

In truth, the job and responsibilities on offer to his more senior colleague was misdirection. There was never any possibility that she might accept it and ruin the plan. No one thought her better suited to that role, but they could not risk slighting her by putting him out in front even if he was already comfortably situated there. She had to reject it before they were free to offer it to him. It was a point of honor crucial to the organization. Everything works out in the end, these are people who know who they are and each of them moves into position exactly as they are supposed to, according to the rules of aesthetics.

"Didn't see those packets," she hunches over the distinct block of space categorically set upon the table in a small area in front of

her and defined by the setting. The distance between their major
bodies fills the gap with rich dark yellows that, for any who find
themselves within their field, feel like something of a self or
person, something holding them together. The skin is not the
boundary, but the light it reflects does create that limit and
everything they see honors the newly formed distinction between
what is outside and what is inside.

—Flesh flows immaculate and they learn to drink it in.

[Jason's demeanor comes off as well as the artifacts themselves.
Management and leadership are immediately enthralled. They
project various revenue streams and onboarding switches.
Customers slide right to enable the feature once they are willing to
pay the extra monthly fee that comes with powerful new
capabilities, supplementing workspaces across their tenant. The
SLT sees how much more productive engineers become and how
much better the metrics surfaced in the reports are. It used to be
that when a ticket of some reasonable complexity opened, it took,
on average, six hours to mitigate the matter or reduce its severity.
On average, of course, since they look at it from high above and
only see those averages. They set two time intervals covering a
cross section of events side-by-side to compare the one on the left
with the one on the right. It is plain as day. The six plus hours have
been cut in half. This is across an entire product and the work of
many engineers. Reducing the TTM revolutionizes their business.
They reduced time spent working the issues and addressing live
site bugs, allowing them to spend their time more productively
adding features to the product. Obi, clever Obi, upgraded Obi,
turned into a workmate. It was the pillar behind it, attached to
Jason's steady eye and careful hand. Many contributed, but he was
their leader. It is time to increase the priority, give him some help,
allow those concerned to discover once and for all whether he is
able to achieve even more difficult things once those telemetry
queries have been added to the mix. That is the plan.]

"Maybe your query was filtering on the known packets," the
yellow cloud forms between the centers of heat high up in the
room before bleeding multiple spider web strands, dripping down
into the red peaks of form. "I was scanning their messages," he

continues. "Content is encrypted though, but there is content. I can tell by the size of the payload." Gesturing with what must be a hand, same as the other even if it is inside out and never able to occupy the same space with those same relational coordinates. Pulling the line through the opening at the wrist, the one gesture turns into the other and the explanation involves a complete sweep of that stretch between him and the warm block before him.

~~Nowhere in his resume does he call out that he has the eye and the patience of an artist, of a painter, of a sculptor, of a finely tuned graph oriented toward the light and its play with the darkness. He does not have to say it, it inhabits his every move, displays itself in each of his gestures, and announces its clarity of purpose in everything he says and does. It may be that the interviewers and the directors and the decision makers did not see it but somehow knew that it was there and ready to be put to good use.~~

"Relay servers must have a cert," Jason bursts a bubble nearby in favor of that familiar rain cloud bustling in fits and starts. The lone tone has no heat, leaves no impression at this magnitude. They need to recalibrate the machine to introduce the audible resonance into the map that captures the motion, and they are too busy for that. They focus on what is in front of them and if that should lead to something far away, it is the purity of their fantasy that makes it so. Each day they project into the horizon more of what appears to them before it recedes into the next week, month, or year. They align their structures to fit with the projections and those at the top see things years away, making adjustments that only show off their effects in long-arriving time. Beneath them in the order are those who see in terms of months and then, further down at the very bottom, their boots on the ground, are those who see today and tomorrow and maybe, if they are sufficiently advanced in their germinal talents, next week.

Presence marks a worldwide fundamental and the spreadsheet to contain its status is open on a browser tab in a background process. Each team provides their input for every region in the list. The workloads, the UX, the platform, every team has a representative to populate the data and answer to the group. There are complex interdependencies. No team claims a presence in the region if the services it relies upon are not already there. The dozens of teams are each made up of a half-dozen or so contributors plus their managers and the group managers and the architects. There are easily more than a thousand people when the headcounts are finally tabulated. Where else will she come upon these conversations without those organizational requirements? Why would she devote forced and friendly interactions to these people if not for the needs of this global presence and the system it maintains? The momentary feeling of every second of every day is driven by the contents of a spreadsheet and the requirement to keep it up to date.

"You can't get a cert, the insertion process that puts a cert on a node is highly constrained," Abhishek drains into the mélange, offering a tinge of orange to flare the edges around them as the dance of color shifts and turns momentarily. They are daily to weekly playing with only the person who is directly above them to set out what is in store for the months ahead. No one sees the entire range of motion. No team member has every perspective and scope in mind, but each supplies a critical angle that contributes to the summary and builds an aggregate through compound affiliations. When that aggregate begins to move, each sees it and marvels at the splendor in its construct. They are the beings that matter in the hail, boisterous in their short lives and trying hard to make something bigger than themselves, contribute to some great adventure that lives on long after they are gone. It is a dream they cannot prevent, a fantasy they need not create. Repeatedly, they play it out together, unable to fashion sufficient detail on their own from the thin air of a receding past.

"Suppose the message from the deployment machine is the content of those excess rules we're trapping in the debugger with the count filter," Jason says. "The debugger session shows them decrypted." He is occupied by its foreign weight. He could be anywhere, he could be somewhere else with his dear friend, exploring their love, making that frantic music that drew them together in the first place, but he resists that urge and stays put. He makes this world and has it made through him, without consent, for a few pennies here and there, something to make it worth his while as he contributes as much as he is able.

~~The most important thing is that he is sincere and therefore has no safeguards to protect himself from advances that curl around his stem and roots. He offers his entire self without any hesitation and allows the aspects and facets to be put to good use meeting the needs of his colleagues. He does not act for the sake of a paycheck or the promise of a bigger stock award, rather a deep sense of artisanry beats in his heart and drives him to perform on behalf of the craft itself. This alone is priceless and puts him in the top 20% of performers where the model determines the bonus.~~

It is possible to restore dry paint on the palette. But there comes a time when it is too late, when nothing more comes of it beyond the occupation of space in a landfill: an oil-based product as guilty as plastic. Its corruption is tied to the order that oppresses him. Filth comes through it in an increasing scale. Whether it is on the canvas or in the tube, it targets him with reminders of wasted time not spent building up the wealth and capitalizing it to make a difference. He sees through that.

"It stands to reason," Patrick adds without intending to finish the thought. Taken for once as the man who follows the bouncing progression and, though silent, traces its many moves as it twists through the others to surface in the room around them as the air they breathe. Now, entering from afar, but not so far that the course is alien, he sets the rhythm for an original score, his place determined moments before that.

—The beat of constantly moving bodies: the dance that is this body.

(The initial design assumed there was a modeling service somewhere but it did not seek to build it. For the internal version, for Obi the schemata, it was a matter of hooking up to a manually trained platform mechanism. Jason and his team did not need to solve that problem and did not know that there were already others working on it on a different floor of the building. Another team prototyped and constructed its edifice, flush with the capacity to integrate into an ecosystem of modules and deployment packages stacked on top of configuration-based approaches from Parker's earlier design. They were going to bring the broad expanse together even if that admixture only existed in Anton's mind when conceptualizing the points of contact between Jason's work over here and the work of young, up and coming, Natalie over there.)

"Exactly," Jason affirms in a loud burst of dark yellow that instantly finds common surfaces mixing with what still sits above them after Patrick launched it outward. Where is the coagulating outcome? What binds each contribution into something real, something they take with them when they leave and move on to their next phase? It is the yellow in the air that they breathe, it is the color that fills them, and which they remember in their notes and in whatever action items they take with them out of this room and into the next one down the endless hallways filled with light and dust.

"There is a lot to process here," Dulcy interjects, suspecting at one fell swoop the fluttering interplay of axiom, anticipation, analogy, and postulate. Extensive magnitudes mathematically derive the filling of space and time with the products of their minds. The real material of their experience is revealed, even if it is concealed in one and the same symbolic gesture. It is easy to think that this human math leads to a dynamic ensemble, forming some unity in their experience. In truth, that unity lies in the orange-red foundations not the yellow-green clouds of their principled emissions. They are postulates full of hope at what they can achieve based on their experience, as though it were the only thing that mattered and this collective contribution a mere side effect or obstacle easily set aside in the mechanics of their critique. "We keep grinding on an assumption of some unity at work, some agent, some *thing* that carries out a coordinated attack. That's the standard way to think about anything. But it's illogical in this case. There's no evidence to support it. We're seeing many things at work, different behaviors, different contributions, roles, objectives. Coordinated, communicating, but distinct. They don't resolve cleanly. If anything, they spread apart whenever we try to pinpoint them."

"Multiplicity is unwarranted too," Patrick says in a sharp outburst that causes Dulcy's red hot upper shape to bob lower and higher in quick succession. If she were gauging the rumblings of

the earth below, the indicators would have said there was a quake
in progress from the first moment she began to sense its measure.

```
namespace BISoft.Data.Home.Core
{
    public class Organization : Team
    {
        private List<Group> groups = new List<Group>();
        public List<Group> Groups => this.groups;
    }
}
```

*She identifies herself with every rogue perspective that enters
her inbox or chat window. She senses the truth even when she
disagrees. It is characteristic of her personality, but also a tribute to
her scale and things growing around her as her grip tightens on the
logic of her immediate vicinity. This is the engineer's take, she
imagines. The way they work themselves into a point of view for
the sake of seeing how far it goes. They are like children working
through possibilities and only discarding them when the proof is
done. Her scope fans out before her.*

"There is an agency at work," Jason affirms. "But it isn't doing
anything. Don't focus on the broadcast, consider the response and
what lies underneath it. Look, this system is fucking complicated.
Relay servers, deployment servers, monitoring servers, workflow
orchestration servers, agents, and events. Tons of asynchronous
stuff, collaboration, caching, cloud resource usage for state
management to track and assess agent conditions, correlate health
reports, respond to hotspots with dynamic distributions. All kinds
of crap." It is years of coding coming together in a dance
unrehearsed. Everything that happens presupposes a rule, but
there is no certainty that it is a rule any one person can follow or
phrase.

—Presence deconstructed by an enormous mass moving
everywhere, satellite to land and land to satellite, taking different
form, agent to agent, growing old, splitting apart, and coming back
together. There is no similarity between building something small

from scratch and rebuilding something enormous that already services trillions of pathways through it, none of which ought to be sacrificed during its growth. Home has an earthen brain.

~~Although the world around him bends to Jason's delivery, he cannot feel it for himself. He is split within and knows there is a difference between these expedient matters and his higher sense of creativity. His attraction to this woman, the one who draws him out and gives him a way to safely vent his spleen and the injustice it no longer processes, is the perfect compensation for what otherwise might burn out and lose its value.~~

[The stores do not matter, that is the conclusion to draw. The system handles careful and elaborate descriptions of what the details contain. Stores of music, stores of video, stores of logs, it does not matter. The only thing they do to link them together lies in the notions private to someone doing something. Not even someone, truth be told, but some thing. Some thing doing something. Any behavior is fair game, and the store provides a snapshot into the context and conditions surrounding some agent's selection over and against the work of every other agent that conditions it. The projected approach scrapes the data from its store and featurizes it for the fabrication of a model describing that behavior and how it works its way through space and time, landing on this spot under one set of conditions and landing somewhere else under a completely different set. The agents align. Swarms become ordered.]

"True," Dulcy says. "And what we're seeing is relatively small and insignificant by comparison. On a timer, deployment sends a message to relay. Relay wakes up, executes its rules as designed, and adds a weird broadcast for acknowledgement with no other intent. It's a simple roll call of listening pieces. Somehow, they respond. That's it. Then the whole thing disappears, leaving no trace. The SAWs aren't participating anymore. Like it figured out how to make do without them. Then, the execution manager runs these supplemental rules without issuing any telemetry. It's done and there's nothing left until the next time and so on and so on." Clearly an order at work, clearly a work that voices an order, but what reason does it provide? Where does it go and what lengths will it take to get there? They identify this and that but until they see the whole world of it, they cannot say what it is. Broken by a boundary offering only critical restrictions, what they want, more than anything, is an ontology of the real-world present in each fact at each place and for every span of time.

—What they want doesn't matter. What they're doing, they have no idea.

(The two of them were clueless as to the points of integration left opaque at the M1 or individual contributor level. They merely followed proper software engineering design with clean interfaces and well-documented public endpoints accessible to imaginary callers with sufficient authorization, providing their machine-level server-to-server tokens acquired from the platform infrastructure that, when built long ago, had no idea this would become an interest it was fated to serve.)

"No, not so on and so on," Matthieu feels the burn of the constraint. "For four hours and then it stops."

"True," she says.

Patrick's form goes erect above a chair rolling backward. He now towers above the others, red stretching several feet to the left leaving a trail of light yellow behind it. Then red stretches back the other way, leaving a trail of light yellow in the spaces behind the fading colors of the first one. A pace set to the left, then a twisting turn set to the right. Back and forth is how the shape forms over time like a rut in the floor.

"Deployment servers now seem to function like the SAW machines," Dulcy huddles over the red block in front of her and absorbs some of its color into her extended limbs, descending on the chart relative to their measured RGB formula. The agents on the attendees' phones churn and come to an agreement regarding the most desirable changes to the heating. "It's different pieces, but the same pattern," she emphasizes the last point and wants the upshot to fill the room and everyone's concern within it. She looks around, from blob to blob, from center of production to center of production. She finds each of them there, radiating from extended nodal points, a graph written. "There's no harm turning it back on. No reason not to. We'll get a better look. I'll set something up to trap the response, add it to what we have for the broadcast."

—Auto save executes and puts the transcript on a share located over two hundred miles south of the room where they sit.

~~Nothing ever works directly as you think it will. The suppression of a highly honed craft breaks his will and destroys him in the end. Like the machine that requires a rebirth every year to maintain its precision for the task, the artist must be replenished from someplace inside him that matches with the longing he once knew, giving it somewhere to swim and swirl. Somewhere for those better angles to measure up and continue providing the value for which they have been generously compensated.~~

[It will be a machine meant to spit out past patterns and project them into the future. It does not matter what it looks at, nor does it matter what it contains in its vision. It approximates the selection of a song without comprehending the notion of liking it or preferring one over the other. These higher order concepts need not have a place among its inner workings. The only movements that matter are the conditions for possibility and the current indexical presence requiring new moments to reflect any new possibilities that come along. Pleasure is a numerical value.]

"Break it down simply," René creaks in the lightest possible yellow flare that anyone has seen so far today. He waits and watches in silence, contributing to the mood throughout. There is no invisible participation. Even his still presence helps move the others along. "It's an intelligent pattern, meaningful. It doesn't matter whether we know what's behind it. Doesn't matter whether there's one single thing with a direct aim. Regardless. There are straight lines."

"Look," Jason overlays his colors and darkens René's cloud. "There's tons of stuff going on that we don't know about. What was it, last month, something with the channel, it kept closing, the listener kept restarting, remember? We didn't know what the problem was because we didn't have any tracing around the right spot in the code with the right state in memory. We added an event capturing additional data and, after we deployed the QFE, the next time it happened we saw the cause clearly. Fix was trivial at that point." He underlines the conclusion that in their partial blindness they often undertake something truly magical. He warns them away from that edge and back to the center where they give their due without running out of room or departing from that idealized garden, home to their immune systems.

"It's a blind spot," René dulls the color back again.

"So, what do we add?" Abhishek asks.

She is already collecting notes to query the core. That drive to see more, that drive to slide oneself into the workings of the system by making it populate a store with trails and breadcrumbs that reveal the larger workings as they grow and bloom, lending insight where few others care to go.

"That's hard to say," Dulcy pours forward, her colors carry more weight. "I don't think this is the same. In that case, we had a localized behavior in a single code block revealed by a stack trace. Simple as that. There was an exception. Here, there's nothing blowing up. It's normal operations. If we didn't instrument the service start-up process and its initial update requests, if we didn't deploy agents that talked back to the service while tracing everything they do, there'd be nothing out there, nothing happening. Humans turning their lights on or playing music, searching for something or cleaning their bathroom. Whatever. That creates an endless loop with constant inputs and outputs that keep triggering and retriggering the system from various sources in different places. If we weren't deliberate in monitoring that activity, if we hadn't decided to make it visible, we wouldn't know anything. We wouldn't see anything. We can't keep the system running without it." The heat that she cannot see reaches out across the planet she cannot see. Measurements prove that it is round.

—Telemetry as product, function as bi-product.

~~On the stage, he is seen more than he is seeing. He sings somewhat but that is mostly a ruse against which he does not try to protect himself. Inside Mags, he finds a new way to be among things, a way that makes everything fit together until the likenesses that have been lost no longer pain him much, if at all. He chooses to no longer resolve those interests under the din of a working life and its endless requirements.~~

(Everything was set in place.)

"What are you saying?" Jason interrupts, vibrant. "It's like a twitch? Like an involuntary reflex that we haven't rationalized, something *we* put there but inadvertently left partial, without complete instrumentation."

"It's part of an explanation," Patrick's voice rises over Dulcy's patience. The way the fixture words are drawn out establishes his place at the hub of their decision-making. "We have to study it at work with these concerns in mind. I get it."

"I was making a different point," speaking, she is unwilling to be a spoke. "There's the thing we think we built and there's the thing in the data centers, sending events and messages, doing things, responding and acting. There is what we see and there is what exists out there." Feeling seen, a part of something, as though it were now possible to appear in spreading assemblages bathing the walls with bright light and filling rooms to keep them warm. "If it isn't fully functional, enabled, we'll never see what it is in itself."

—Telemetry provides form to whatever exists by way of order.

[Time and space to operationalize. This is BISoft at work. No wonder the individual toy nodes cannot fathom it.]

The yellow cloud above dissipates slowly over the next few seconds, but the six forms, spread around the area, burn red-hot in the wake of one last wave. There is no name for what they make, no language yet to claim it as it leaves the room and flows around the spaces outside where others extend its reach in blissful ignorance of a growing presence.

"Go."

"Go."

"Go."

Yitzhak gets his way.

```
/*
HomeTrace
| where TIMESTAMP > ago(1d)
| where Process has "BISoft.Data.Home"
| where TraceMarker == "Structure"
| distinct CorrelationId
*/
```

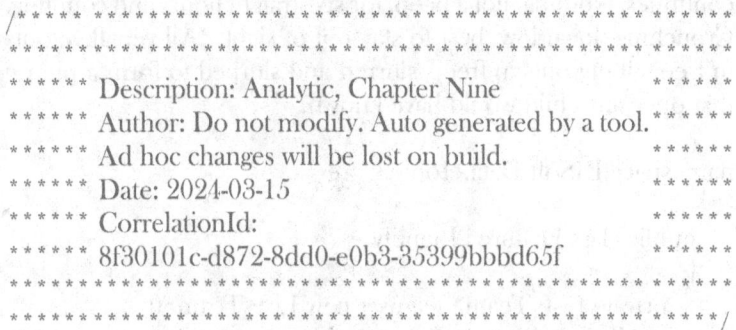
/* *
* *
* * * * * * Description: Analytic, Chapter Nine   * * * * * *
* * * * * * Author: Do not modify. Auto generated by a tool.* * * * * *
* * * * * * Ad hoc changes will be lost on build.   * * * * * *
* * * * * * Date: 2024-03-15   * * * * * *
* * * * * * CorrelationId: * * * * * *
* * * * * * 8f30101c-d872-8dd0-e0b3-35399bbbd65f   * * * * * *
* *
* /

On the way back to his desk, Jason's way is blocked by Vod telling a story. Animated and extra special, he has a knee set firm on the center of the rolling chair and is gripping its back and headrest to turn it short then pivot back in sharp hard jolts that stress his one straight leg firmly wedged against the floor. His gaze briefly drifts toward Jason's imminent interruption. The stream of words continues over the rocks and around the bend. Dulcy looks sideways at the same thing. She wants to get away, to find out how it went, but Stan and Vod occupy the space between her and Jason. Stan is rivetted to his spot and sets the mood with his listening pose. She cannot control the order of her attention. Stan helps Vod secure it, forcing her to wait. She knows the wave must pass before anyone can navigate those fast-moving waters. For the sake of team morale, Jason surrenders and drifts slightly back. He turns to G, keeping her head down to avoid inclusion.

"Like a seismograph," Vod punctuates his point. From Dulcy's perspective, that point remains amorphous. Never before has she been more exposed to something that both dominates the mood and makes little impression upon it. "The rumblings of the earth cannot be reduced to a seismogram, not even to those electrical signals that convert vibrations into a moving line. Machines always represent..." Stan nods vigorously, but Dulcy, having had enough, stands up and, with a rapid sequence of brisk movements, forces Stan to step back and make way.

—Let's elaborate. Have the details come forward. The silence continues. Nothing, not a peep, for six straight hours and counting. Crouching down low, best to stay out of sight. "All ye, all ye outs in free, all the outs in free," slurred and slurped to form a phrase that once any child would have known.

```
namespace BISoft.Data.Home.Core
{
    public class Feature : Identity
    {
        private List<Team> teams = new List<Team>();
        public List<Team> Team => this.teams;
    }
}
```

(To offset any negative press accompanying the release, BISoft launched an ethics team to soften the blow. The president of the company and chief of operations, Chad Jones, made the announcement at the same yearly conference where they showcased the super powered agents coming with Workmate 2.0. That's the version that had been optimized for both residential and commercial outfits. The outline was elaborate. He gave every assurance that the newly formed team was comprised of people with the highest levels of concern for customer safety and the protection of privacy. The purpose of ethics, he claimed, was to protect the dignity and integrity of every stakeholder in the BISoft enterprise whether they were a customer, an employee, a stockholder, or a member of a community impacted by corporate policies and procedures. He let everyone know that the staunchest regulations coming from any part of the world will be rigorously applied in all company-related scenarios. They will not limit their protections by geographical area just because the law came from there. Instead, they considered the strictest laws of any one land to be the law of every land and used them as guidelines to protect the rights and safeguard the privacy of people everywhere, no matter what lax stance their home government allowed. The data integrity rules, the protections of national boundaries and secured analytics, everything was to be honored no matter the cost and no matter the commitment. He and BISoft made a pledge to the world.)

~~They gobble him up like a meal well-suited to a highly refined culinary palate. Parker did not study their algorithms formally. He did not learn their data structures backward and forward. There is no corruption in how he thinks what he thinks. His orientation never amiss, these angles have been developed by disciplines old and highly enlightened. He is the product of institutions centuries in the making, and his outputs are the handiwork of thousands of villages.~~

"I need to talk to Jason," she says, sneaking past them.

He looks over from his standing spot near the next island. Having heard his name, he says, "Yeah, let's get a coffee," over G who has been ignoring his presence in her personal space by staring at the screen in front of her. She pays the price for the roadblock. Not everyone's morale is boosted by Vod's long-lasting story. Jason was about to burst into the mood when Dulcy beat him to it. That is what the look on his face says and that is how the tone in his voice sounds. Dulcy feels relief of yet a third kind.

Another love unrequited, her relationship to her job has to be broad enough to embrace this madness where colleagues sip time from the communal cup and force onlookers to make way. Yet there is surely passion. She feels it brusque against her well-being in the space and amid the chatter. The loneliness, the team spirit, and the characters highlighted in code and commerce make bad substitutes for wellness and generalized welfare. There is an urgency in the obligation, but it contradicts the singular needs of analysis. Her sense is that it is some kind of love, something on that order, that pours her into the details. These are wayward brothers and sisters both a source of irritation and comfort. Nothing finds its true measure in the moment, nothing hums a single tune. She knows that musical feedback in the electrical currents is likewise responsible for making a mess as it vibrates behind a most glorious order.

The story is not interrupted. Stan steps to the side without noticing the subtle impositions. Standing next to Jason's desk, he collaborates on the occupation with Vod the conqueror still accosting his manager's ergonomic chair. Dulcy's empty spot remains a part of the story as Vod continues describing the drawn-out yarn of how even machines reproduce human limitations as they attune to signals they have been designed to capture. "Every aspect of our thought is embodied in the artifacts we produce and the way they interact with the world..." barely audible as Jason and Dulcy exit the area together and move away from the pair, still absorbed in their story time. Whatever release this play brings, the two young men need it. No local policing is in force to discourage them.

Stan often wonders whether Vod's uncle is a fabrication, whether he lives and breathes or if he is merely a sign of something rumbling beneath the surface, something that has taken hold of his colleague to fill him with regret whenever he tries to concentrate on matters close at hand. These elaborate conversations are few and far between, but they come back vividly and burrow into his awareness without invitation. He has no choice but to lay out the details and solicit feedback from his peers to help them learn his place and express justifications allowing him to keep it. Among them, the ruts are normal and happily meet with universal approval. The story lines are quaint and exotic, the other team members prove it through reactions. The more they gasp, the more clearly the status mask is marked with each bit switched to the on position.

In the break room across the grand hallway, she makes her tea and listens to the air pressing frothy liquid into Jason's cup at the coffee machine over her shoulder and to the side. The large cases of cold beverages are directly behind her and there is a man squeezing into one of them without opening the glass sliding door any farther than he has to. He takes a fizzy drink and runs off without a greeting or a nod. Ignoring the surrounding distractions and focused on their upcoming conversation, fastening the two of them into a welded couplet before they begin to speak, they take their drinks and head to the stairway at the end of the hall, walk down two tall flights of stairs, and step into the focus room across from 1U. This puts them far enough from the team room to have privacy on that front and far enough from leadership in the A rooms for privacy on the other. Their chat will hover scope somewhere between the ground level vision of Dulcy's colleagues and the cloud level visions of Jason's leadership.

~~In that interview, not a single person failed to see it. They knew they were in the presence of a highly educated soul, someone built up and finely polished by years and years of effort and support. The levels of attention Parker received in his progress toward those advanced degrees saturate his speaking patterns and are discernible to anyone who talks to him. Each of the people on that loop saw that this was the kind of person they would be proud to set before their customers.~~

—No clairvoyance in the midst. Before their engagement, its content doesn't exist. They must perform miracles to make it real and observe everything carefully when bringing it into existence. They couch the results in worship for the visible and thus make invisibility essential to whatever creeps up behind them.

[The ethics team is a team of lawyers set inside the legal division. They study the laws and the journals describing the laws. Their primary purpose is to ensure that those laws are followed to the letter across every team in the entire company. This requires they get involved in the process as early as possible, ensuring the law is written in such a way as to permit the company to follow it while still meeting its yearly investor expectations. They are committed, no doubt, but remain reasonable. There are things a profit-driven organization cannot do. They cannot limit the range of telemetry describing system operations, that is not possible, the system's reliability cannot be put at risk. They monitor every operation and use it as feedback to help preserve the service's smooth functioning. They cannot, in good conscience, agree to fly blind. They make sure to reach out their tendrils through lobbyists in Parliament houses across the world, in Europe and the Americas. Other places too if their leaders were ever to show any interest in applying these same limitations and constraints. But the true purpose, even if they do not get their way, is to get an early look. They want to see what is coming and ask the representatives and legal wonks whether this is what they truly mean. Furthermore, they must ensure that it does not prevent the company from providing the highest levels of quality and assurance. Protecting privacy is critical, but how privacy is conceived, well, there is a spectrum of possible approaches to that.]

"It was Anton's meeting," he says once they settle in and close the door. "Prep for Scott's roundtable. Tom was there. Parker brought me, René, and Natalie. Most of the beginning of the meeting was spent going through Parker's design for the air gap."

"For what product?" she asks.

"Home," he says to her confused look.

"Why do they need to run Home in the air gap?" she asks, no more satisfied that she understands the answer after having heard it. "I thought they wanted the improved logging agent."

"It's not Home for the consumer," Jason says. "That's most of the users. Home for the enterprise, Building. I think that's how they sometimes brand it. Where agents collaborate across relay boundaries and virtual presence trumps space and time. They've been demanding it for months. We've been having trouble figuring out how to get it there. The workloads are ready to go. Some of the special features were built last year, in fact, and there are lots of enterprise customers using it already. It's not really that different from their point of view, a couple modules enabled at scale with some of the functions for larger structures. Principles are the same. More robust voice recognition and crosstalk filters. More finely grained security for different action types. Increased video input and modeling. Anyway, apparently, Parker's been the bottleneck. He was overwhelmed, I guess. It's only because of this live site incident that he was finally able to concentrate. What with everything being turned off, people left him alone. Not like he had anything to contribute to the troubleshooting."

—Sometimes, great efforts come from solitude. The others force them into lonely singularity for the sake of smoother operations across the board.

(Parker saw fit to write an email to the publicly advertised alias in charge of the ethical use of data and the process for gathering it. He pointed out that most of the Home System kept so-called sensitive data at the customer location and never moved it or extracted it from the agents running inside the household. He wrote that privacy was not under threat, was never under threat by the Home System, and that he thought it odd that the company was building an entire campaign around securing something that was not at risk. Instead, he explained, there was a bigger problem in the behavioral transformations and changes the software caused in customers that use it. People were steered into doing things very differently from the way they did them before. The whole of their lives were imprinted into a digital diary that streamed out of the local source in an aggregated form, rising up into the vortex and providing insight into general characteristics of use and consumption. The stated purpose of the product was to use that data for both monitoring the health of the system and understanding the behavioral norms of the individual customer. The ethical charge, in so far as the company was concerned, should be around the new behaviors and how they were broadcast and normalized. Who had a say in what modifications were made and what criteria used to determine whether they were suitable to customer interests or complied with national laws? He suggested the company had an obligation to make the subtleties of these different approaches clear to local governments so that they produced informed legislation genuinely keen to the real threats posed. If it changes how the users act, it changes how they think.)

~~In his early days, he was careful not to write too often or elaborate too much on any theme in email or direct message. Parker hesitated, he did not want to let the style of professional genres infiltrate his mind and lead him astray. A serious handicap in the performance of his job, he had to find a way to make it work, showing off technical expertise hard won in long study.~~

She cups and blows while listening, half-nods and looks up. The live site alarms are still in place, but she has been at ease and unmolested since the firewall came down and the relays resumed. A good night sleep lends her a healthy glow. It is chillier today and for some reason the building's heat is not adjusting properly. She still wears her coat and takes her hands off the mug long enough to pull the fabric closer. Jason pauses to give her a chance to say something, registers the fact that she does not, and then continues: "There's always a DMZ instance. Highly regulated network segment near each relevant capital city. Air gap regions are spread out, geographically distributed. Basically, every build has its own temporary endpoint for pushing packages. The certificate, the endpoint, the port, everything, it's time-bombed to last for only one build. Build it, get access, and push the artifacts. Then poof, it disappears. To get the cert, the public-side deployment machine has to be the only writer into the DMZ. The other side, the side leading into the sovereign cloud, I guess, or to their monitoring portals, whatever, that's shut down tight during the upload. So long as the temporary goo exists and so long as the process lasts for pushing stuff into it, there's an airtight lock on changes. Any running operations not in their whitelist are instantly killed."

```
namespace BISoft.Data.Home.Core
{
    public class Component : Identity
    {
        private List<Group> groups = new List<Group>();
        public List<Group> Groups => this.groups;
    }
}
```

She loves puzzles and seeks them out. Her heartbeat races when she comes upon one and starts to take it apart. She feels the links and the edges connect in the air before her. She senses the joints and the ligatures that form contacts between the parts, providing significant clues to the meaning and source of things appearing in the assembled picture. Maybe that is what he means by seismograph, occurs to her. That these things are rumblings she cannot help but measure and count. They simmer and twang. There was once a time when she effortlessly composed them into three- or four-minute bursts of lines, dots, and squiggly notation meant to capture the moment. She punctuated the verse with rhythm and pitch. It did not feel like a separate song, rather it was the world itself bringing out mystery from within and using her as its guide. The truth is that she loves this feeling, whatever the origin or the media for presenting it may be. To others, there is no point of contact between songs and solutions, but to her it is impossible

not to see the same pattern of alliances and adjustments in them.
She does something but it does not feel as though she is the agent.
The silent way the voice takes over, that is the binding force
drawing her into these experiences same as she was once drawn
into those others, now forgotten and impossible to rekindle:
melodies she hums because she does not remember the words.

~~There is no dollar amount to assign to these tangential~~
~~components of a larger system bent to order the objectives defined~~
~~for him. They are supposed to reward the intangibles with a future~~
~~looking aspirational goal to keep him close while he continues to~~
~~develop his skills and contributions, bending around his inner logic~~
~~and changing into the shapes of things to come. They call it stock.~~
~~Goods or merchandise. Raised capital. Liquid from cooking~~
~~bones. A line of descent. Tree trunk. Instrument of punishment.~~
~~Part of a rifle. Cravat or collar. A frame for dry docking a boat.~~

He looks over to see if she has any questions or concerns that
might change the flow of the explanation. She does not. What
happened? It was all we talked about for days on end and now
nothing, she thinks. It is beginning to distract her, and even though
she has pulled her jacket close, she still has not zipped it. Her mind
is elsewhere. Her arms hold the mug close to lend a cinch to the
outer flaps as proxy. She leans back and slouches down in the
chair. One leg sliding out from underneath her, comfortable in the
position. He keeps going, breathing regularly. "Once the first
phase of push deployment finishes, the cert is destroyed, the
endpoint shuts down, the port closes, and the pathways into the
rest of the public cloud are sealed. No new sessions initialize. It's
still locked, but now inside *and* out. That's when the scanners run.
From what I can tell, there's going to be a bunch of them. He didn't
enumerate them all. It's not only the stuff we run in normal public,
but a lot more. Stuff built for them or that they built to
specifications we haven't seen. They even do a test deployment in
the DMZ and run the feature tests and a bunch of synthetic
transactions."

—The synthetic transaction is a currency for the simulation of
real events, themselves simulations of real events. Imagined agents
cull fact from the pretend workings of the system, verifying its

purity and the cogency with which it articulates itself. In the telemetry, there's no difference between a user-initiated operation and a synthetic transaction.

[The ethics team projections and charts are not in the least impacted by the ad hoc feedback they receive from every corner of the world. The alias is well-known across social platforms, broadcast on Reddit and rebroadcast on each of the others. Every crackpot in the world has something to say and platform MVPs cannot be bothered to respond to each of them. Their crawlers have some rules in place to single out the domains where someone with clout is likely to respond. For the most part, the missives receive an automatic reply structured as a form letter thanking them for their input, informing them that someone will read it and give it the attention it deserves. They do not mention that the bulk scanners create word clouds and summaries of responses so that what they really see is feedback in the aggregate. Not one response and another, but the collective scanned for common keywords to put it together into a single short blurb for the team to go through during a monthly review.]

He pauses and sits bolt upright with both feet firmly planted on the floor. There is hardly any movement along the wheels of his chair, and, for some reason, he has not noticed that it is positioned in the lowest possible notch. Although he has a longer torso than Dulcy, he sits eye to eye with her and sips his pseudo-cappuccino, watching her with her tea and waiting in case she has a comment or question. She does not say anything. Only nods to indicate she registers the information and is ready to receive more. We didn't change anything, didn't deploy anything. If it's a bug, why did it stop? She wonders. "Once the bar is met, phase two deployment in the DMZ copies the binaries to a registered removable drive to carry the software into the canary region collocated in the same data center as the DMZ." He makes air quotes when he says the word 'carry'. "There are six underground regions. They have their own train schedule and audience definitions. Not sure how they are connected to each other, but they're six distinct regions. Only three active at any given time. Each region has a redundant data center like public does, but there's separation of function between the different ones. The really gnarly stuff, highest clearance, is in the last region. The idea is that canary reveals the warts and they reject the build if it doesn't meet the bar for the next audience, next region same as with public. They do a bunch of acceptance testing at that point. Same stuff we do in prod's canary but with additional monitors we've never seen and don't have any visibility into."

He pauses and this time she does have a question. "Is there Davos in their DMZ?" she asks.

~~Some organizations look for the absence of taste, they prefer that the worker bee never show anything beyond the order dominating the enterprise and complying with its way of sensing things, its prior destination, and methodical outpouring. That is not the case among them, among those disciplined by Ted and set right along their way. These higher humans, with their efficiency and intelligence, know better, are better, and are expected to improvise, to bring themselves into the distribution and flavor it with whatever sauce and spice wells up inside them.~~

It is love, in a way, and love is how the world is spun under conditions of ordinary perception become extraordinary in sanctified understanding. Maybe it is not love, come to think of it, maybe it is merely infatuation. Merely? But no one says that, she muses. No one says I am infatuated with my job. But if they were truly in love with it, would they grow weary with the years or would it rather transform into something beautiful and deeply bound to their person? It must be infatuation. And it must be something they put there on purpose, a way to inject the habits of an everyday existence otherwise filled with misery. This status quo has a justification. For many, the only form that withstands the pounding of circumstance is something they loosely place under the rule of one's passion. She has always loved puzzles. Does that make it easier to convince herself that this is more of the same and that these daily rhythms unfold on a plane beneath the other workers, not equally aware? Her colleagues stand around her and lend credence to the scale of their collaboration when their work crosses over the threshold. They pass by the whims induced by their collective delusion, never retreating from the challenge.

*Together they are carefully supported with both public funding
and corporate revenue, gladly bearing the weight of their incentive.*

"Sort of," he says. "That's the only outbound process for getting
anything to the outside world. They have long-running hybrid
workflows to move logs from the sovereign out to the DMZ.
Manually, at the critical juncture, at least. It's about a ten-hour lag.
That's the stuff we're looking at when we do the escort sessions.
The jump box where we Jit and get lockbox approval takes us into
the DMZ where we screen share to watch the queries, I think. Or
see the chat screen with them while they query. Not sure. Anyway,
that's the only access we have to our own logs. No node access, no
debug, nothing. Other than the logs. Kinda fucked up. If there's a
big problem, we'll have issues. Can't support it if you can't see it."
He chuckles, emphasizing the last word to suggest it is an
understatement.

—They've lost sight of the forest through the trees. Losing touch
with their own design, problems force them outside the box and
into a zone of innovation, destroying the very thing they mean to
supplement. Parker is their marionette. His solitude brings a gift.
Once there is a link connecting both sides, the seal is broken. The
vehicle does not matter. They prefer a physical delivery of binaries
on a sanctioned external drive, thinking it keeps them safe, but that
alone provides sufficient means to destroy its safety. Ague lives in
the binaries, in the bones, in the binaries. The regular route is no
longer essential. Electrical currents are not segmented. They are
etched into disk where charges freely flow across the boundary,
captured in the action potential of compiled code at rest.

(They wrote Parker back because his email address was in the
filter that separated what they thought of as wheat from what they
thought of as chaff. They thanked him for his contribution and let
him know that his ideas were valuable. They promised to consider
them carefully while working up policies in the months to come.
The exchange reminded him of the great iconic invention by the
one and only Steve Jobs, mentioning the words he uttered in
response to the criticism that the sleek and elegantly designed
iPhone did not work if the user held it while covering the built-in
antenna etched into the device to fit with its streamlined

appearance. He said, "Don't hold it that way." It did not matter that people had been holding telephones for decades. It did not matter that this was a micro-behavior part and parcel of everyone's life, the person integrated with the device. They will adapt, change their ways according to the requirements of new things, new machines, and inventions. That was their purpose. No reason to balk when they arrived at the precipice. They refused to let luddites and nay-sayers occupy a primal place in the progress of civilization. Things must move ahead. The consumers must move with them. Changes were a necessary component. Their impact on daily life made these companies into overlords.)

"Pain in the ass," she continues to warm her hand on the mug held close in front of her with a second grip on her own lapel to keep the jacket tight. She has yet to take her first sip, torn as she is between her rested feeling and its underlying cause, coming from the system's recent silence.

"They're excited though," he goes on without acknowledging her expletive. "Because the rules engine isn't there. This'll be the first time it's introduced. They're way behind right now, basically only able to run tier zero and tier one services. They don't have any tier two stuff. It's the first time the model services will be in place, building ML off the traces and operational outcomes. Those feedback loops, everything that makes management easier and reliability better, it'll be captured once it goes live. Lots of other tier two teams want to reuse it. Yup, extremely excited."

~~Parker's taste reveals his world, it shows what is inside there and how it casts a shadow on everything around it. It is light coming from out of the structure of things, how they come together in experience, and the way they resolve across his field of vision. Everything belongs to them, same as everything about him that surfaces during the time devoted to problems with origins he does not understand.~~

—He assumes they desire speed in the same way everyone does.

[He daydreams some weird recollection of his theory-laden professorial days. The notion of an existential threat comes to mind. Of course, the usual approach is to see that in terms of utter annihilation, but he has never understood it that way. If there is enough of a change to make the ship of Theseus at the end look nothing at all like the ship of Theseus at the outset, then that is a threat to existence too. The latest theories of the Neanderthals come to mind. They were not wiped off the face of the earth by violence and warfare, originating in another competitor species, that's not how he understands it. Instead, they were absorbed through ordinary congress and integration. Their genes were sucked up into a much larger pool and then placed into a secondary role, supporting a supposedly more fit primary population. They live on in traces left in the genome, but there are no individuals left. That is how it is when behavioral changes are brought to bear. There was a time not too long ago when no one clicked and no one scrolled, now these actions are ubiquitous. Click-free humanity is existentially extinct, no more of them remain. With the changes coming to the household, what else will one day exit along that same path?]

"Are these processes completely manual, the locks on either side?" She asks.

"Mostly," he says. "They require it. That's what's messed up. Deployment phase one and deployment phase two both need approval. Our guy approves one and their guy approves the other. Director level. Must go through automation, only servers access endpoints and certs, but the process is evaluated and launched by a human being. Compliance requires that. Some person must be attached to the auditing event before it triggers any single phase of the deployment. Two people, in fact. They don't trust rogue processes. Won't take a QFE if it doesn't have a ticket explicitly relevant to them behind it. They're worried about nightmare scenarios. Hackers, software gone bad, everything. Terrorism. Warfare." He flashes a crooked smile, recalling the routine background checks and approvals along with the interviews required for access. His whole team goes through them every couple of years.

```
namespace BISoft.Data.Home.Core
{
    public class Product : Identity
```

```
{
    private List<Organization> organizations =
        new List<Organization>();
    public List<Organization> Organizations =>
        this.organizations;
}
}
```

*She wonders about the links already in place. Are they blind to
its threat? The external drive is turned on, then off, then on again.
The offerings behave like an artifact given dumb life and glowering
presence in front of the entire collection of people set to
administer its needs and desires. Should it happen to have any,
that is. There is no way to confront this much complexity unless
there is a way to store it, hold onto its serialized facticity in the
ongoing delivery of more. Accumulation is the creation of a life
before you and that life teams with structure inside every minor
detail bound to the others through relationships themselves bound
to every detail. Our minds, my mind, she thinks, is addicted to
these machinations. It cannot proceed without them. The eternal
source, that spark of God rising in the singer's song, it pales by
comparison. The silences of these six hours are maddening.*

"Do they know about our issue?" She leans forward onto her
elbows, jacket flips open, and she moves still closer to the tea with
its bag submerged, seeping light brew into the water around it.

"Everybody knows," he says. "Public knowledge. The
shutdown was everywhere. Stock price went down, forecasts
adjusted, they couldn't miss it. No one could. And just as quickly,
they'll forget."

—Not if it gets added to Wikipedia, then it'll live on forever as
a paragraph in the bio.

~~To call the woman a distraction is to radically undersell it. She
is an absorption, a complete focus that fails to move him away from
everything else and instead throws him more forcefully into it. A
woman like Chelo requires diligence. Her interest, so he perceives,
depends upon it. He gives her lavish gifts to increase his
performance as his interest spans far and wide beyond it. He thinks~~

~~that if he pays for it, his intent will be measured properly. It is akin to singing while you work in the fields to take your mind off the labor and increase productivity. It is the exact opposite of distraction and significantly more valuable to the company.~~

(He waited a long time to reply and tried to take the higher ground, explaining the strange grid where universal notions came to occupy singular beings. The habits of the general population took root in the home soil of the specific. That is how it worked, Parker claimed. All the world was transformed by subtle changes in the categories that conditioned action.)

Dulcy stares at him. "Surely..." she begins, only to break off.

"Anton was asking about that. Tom had a lot of questions too," Jason recalls the weirdly manipulative way Tom tends to put things when he's 'just asking'. "All this security to make sure only the code we intend to put in the sovereign cloud gets into the sovereign cloud. But what about our code, what verifies that?" It is not his question. He is reliving an earlier event and fails to convey it properly.

"That's what those scans are for," she realizes immediately that neither of them needs to be reminded of this. She feels warmer and looks around the room to see if there is more air blowing through the vents. The building has made adjustments for her comfort.

—You're welcome.

[The committee chuckles at his reply. It is too esoteric and ridiculous. They realize they are up against something that earns no one's attention, that does not take effect anywhere, and that has no following and no buzz. Again, they thank him for his contribution and that, as far as they are concerned, is the end of it.]

"Sure," he replies. "They scan every block on that drive, but what about defects? Are there malicious bugs in the actual code, not fakes or injected dlls, but in the legitimate codebase? We may not catch them in review or testing, but if they're there, really there, what kind of impact do they have? How does their behavior morph once it's deployed?"

"They were grinding on that?" She asks dismissively. To her

way of thinking, bugs are standard fare. She is not convinced they explain anything. They do not indicate flaws in the code so much as flaws in understanding the workflows and conditions under which the data passes through the code. The causes and effects are dug up and diligently sewn together. It makes no sense to pay special attention to that. You make sure there are tools for analysis in place throughout the product's lifecycle. No code anticipates runtime conditions perfectly. "Is it a blocker?"

"Hard to say," he says. "Anton said something like 'you've written it up fine, the problem is you don't see what you don't see.'"

"Such a dick," she interrupts and leans back in her chair, shrugs out of the jacket, and lets it fall into the space between her and the chair back, providing a little cushion. There is a light glow forming at the base of her neck and she pulls at the top of her T-shirt to flap it rapidly.

~~It is not clear that she, this musical instrument between his legs, truly loves him. No one is sure that, as her husband, he is the object of her affection even if he was the origin of great passions in those early days. Nevertheless, they do say, with absolute confidence, that she loves the father of her child and that she loves the man responsible for filling up the coffers with material necessary for supporting the household.~~

Jason laughs in a single breathy burst. "Definitely," he says. "But I think they're willing to write it off as a minor bug, a simple defect. Logs go missing now and then and there's some weird operation that adds a few rules to the configuration. It's a bug, ordinary stuff. Not a big deal. A blip caused by some weird temporary data. The thing itself is sound. In fact, they're seeing it as an opportunity to discover the limits and beef up the deployment process. The whole advantage of having an ML-based rules engine in a cloud where we don't have good visibility is that we can increase the behavioral catchalls to see better. Get a grip on stuff we can't actively monitor. The workloads and platform have work to do. Increased logging. Verbose setting or something behind a feature flag. We'll get reports. Something to improve visibility even if we can't have it in real time."

"No mention of how the modeling outputs made it there in the first place, got through the firewall? And the thing at Parker's? The electrocution? No worries about that?" She asks.

"Management port access ranges and faulty wiring. Company's going to dispatch improvements to Parker's preview rig. It was an unfortunate coincidence," he nods in answer. They both see the rug lift and the sweeping begin.

"Can't imagine the DoD is okay with this. Let alone fucking Russia or China. Do they know the risks? Did we tell them the SAWs were compromised? Why bother? There's so much we're not trying to understand. What's the worst that could happen?" she asks flippantly.

"Parker said they won't divulge that information," Jason explains while getting more animated. "But Anton has suspicions," he emphasizes the last word. "None of us know for sure, but Anton thinks the last ring is hardcore military stuff."

"Like what?" She tips the chair forward as she rocks back toward the table and continues harder into a new lean.

—They should be leaning too.

(Cover your ass, that is what Parker thought when he read the response from the committee. Pointless to engage. They did not want feedback, they did not wish to learn.)

"Deploying drones and troops, stuff like that. Surveillance. Military. Lethal." Jason pauses and runs his hand through his beard, kneading it like dough and making it hard to tell whether he is pulling at his chin or the fur that covers it.

"They must have their own safeguards," she says. "Double blind or whatever. Two guys that turn keys at the same time. Like in the movies."

"That's the chilling point at the end," Jason says. "Anton said that stuff's digitized. If it's the digital stuff that's corrupt, it'll be compromised too. A vulnerability. It's not a mechanical switch or a physical key. Something we don't see in the system's language. He's got his slide deck. Same one he's been circulating everywhere. At Scott's level. He's careful to underline the risks, but they aren't interested in discussing it. Not today at least. That's what he said. Can't tell them anything. 'We'll take it under advisement'.'" His voice falls into a bad Romanian accent.

"Doesn't have to be science fiction," Dulcy says. "If you introduce any decision support or language modeling system, you must have checks in place. You have to put safety triggers on it."

—They're the checks, they're the triggers.

[How to apply an ethics for human agency to the body of a distributed being spread out in space and time? Parker never bothers to type it out and send a reply. The aesthetic appearance takes over for moral essences revealed through analysis made impotent by dialectic.]

~~The humiliation Parker feels looking elsewhere for sexual favors she no longer provides once their son is born is perfectly suited to their marital rhythms and the life they lead together. She knows that the guilt coming from his lurid expenditures will prostitute him to her advantage. Those duties are better left in a division of labor residing somewhere outside their happy home in which a child lives and grows. Her incorporated design is perfectly aligned with their ultimate end and likely comes from its same source. The string of escorts must have had a hand in inspiring him, yielding his first electronic leads in a digital marketplace, pushing him down that path where what is on offer is both too close and too far.~~

"We kind of have that with the global cancel and rollback, that stuff, but we can't transact a physical building operation. If step one has already been executed, then cancellation doesn't undo anything if it's something that can't be undone. Like firing a bullet. Can't... Unless..."

Jason looks up at the clock on the wall, "Shit. I have to get my stuff and get to a Yitzhak meeting. He wants a briefing."

Bounded by glory, it is the world she knows, raising her up to let her down. She feels a pulse in the vents and the air bustling from them. How do things acquire allure? Why does that leather belt mean so little now when it meant so much in his hands a decade ago? Music came out of those experiences and is now hardly more than stress relief, a swipe at lethargy and the ongoing pains of Dulcy's continued submersion in something unhealthy. Infatuation, in a new regard, avoids misunderstandings that otherwise come hard. Whatever there is, is colored by the sensory sieve funneling data into the computer and making it grind out responses and recognition, elaborating on ways to drive everyone forward and meet the requirements of goals she does not share. None of it, not one single piece of the product, does her any damn good. Every point of contact belongs to someone else and, truth be told, will not be missed once they take it away.

They stand up and go through the door, silently moving toward the stairway and then upward. She churns at the possibilities. What does it stand for again, she wonders. Vast Active Living Intelligence System. The parts do not know they are parts because they do not see the whole thing. They are the stone flying through the air from Vod's story earlier. It thinks it flies at its own volition and knows nothing about the hand that flung it or the intention in some boy's mind right before the launch. What if bugs are like that? She persists along the line. We don't know we've written them because they only surface under unforeseen conditions, but maybe there's some thought process or agency somewhere that takes them into account and sees what they do and how they impact everything. Maybe they exist according to some grand design, larger than any of us. Maybe they live at the limit between what is and what is not known, what is revealed and what is concealed. Bugs are there prior to deployment, prior to sending code into the world, but they are found through experience when applied to the world during operations. There is a Latin word for this, but she cannot recall it.

—Infatuation, the synthetic transaction. Add electricity to make love. The charge lies secret, stenciled into the disk. Their hands don't dampen it.

"Did they accept the design?" Dulcy asks once they reach the top of the landing and enter the grand hallway near the turn off to team room 3T.

"He wants more documentation, but it's CYA," Jason's cynicism saturates the observation. "I don't think we know enough to produce realistic scenarios of any value. Maybe they can do it, but they won't share them with us. The guys on site maybe. With higher clearance."

She nods as she steers back into the room and toward her desk.

Jason follows behind her to grab his backpack before running off to his meeting with Yitzhak.

```
/*
HomeTrace
| where TIMESTAMP > ago(1d)
| where Process has "BISoft.Data.Home"
| where TraceMarker == "Modality"
| distinct CorrelationId
*/
```

Dialectic

Human reason has this peculiar fate that in one species of its knowledge it is burdened by questions which, as prescribed by the very nature of reason itself, it is not able to ignore, but which, as transcending all its powers, it is also not able to answer.

—Immanuel Kant
Critique of Pure Reason

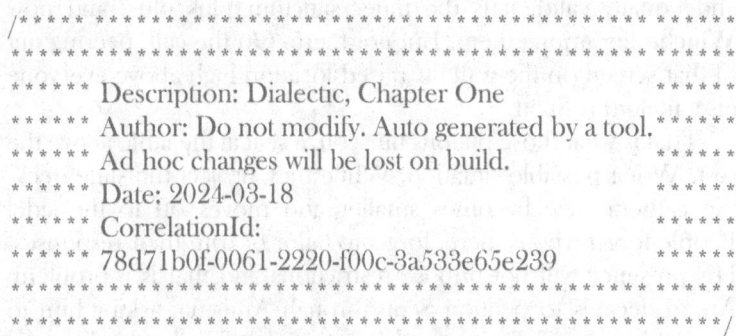

```
/* * * * * * * * * * * * * * * * * * * * * * * * * * * * * * * * * * * * * * * * * * * * * * * * * * * * * * * * *
* * * * * * * * * * * * * * * * * * * * * * * * * * * * * * * * * * * * * * * * * * * * * * * * * * * * * * *
* * * * * *  Description: Dialectic, Chapter One                    * * * * * *
* * * * * *  Author: Do not modify. Auto generated by a tool.* * * * * *
* * * * * *  Ad hoc changes will be lost on build.                 * * * * * *
* * * * * *  Date: 2024-03-18                                       * * * * * *
* * * * * *  CorrelationId:                                         * * * * * *
* * * * * *  78d71b0f-0061-2220-f00c-3a533e65e239                   * * * * * *
* * * * * * * * * * * * * * * * * * * * * * * * * * * * * * * * * * * * * * * * * * * * * * * * * * * * * * *
* * * * * * * * * * * * * * * * * * * * * * * * * * * * * * * * * * * * * * * * * * * * * * * * * * * * * * * * /
```

They rest upon Anton's shoulders. Not happy. Runs his hand over the top of his head and down to the back of his neck. Tapping the table, adjusting his glasses in place, scrolling down, then back up. Reading over his shoulder, feeling his heartbeat quicken and a light glow of perspiration forming on his lower back. He switches focus to the mail app and rereads the message from Beacon. That's Winchester's aid, he reminds himself. Name was on Parker's design doc. Thinks he was at the meet and greet months ago. Is probably the specialist in charge of Home. Winchester owns the overall, the complete air gap, and his staff load balances the various projects. He was likely the main source of details and that long list of environmental problems they need to address when pushing to the segment. If Beacon knows, Winchester knows. These other two, whoever they are, they know. One is a civilian. They are coming to the Scott review, the round table this week.

Bullshit is the highlight in the word cloud of his mind as he rereads the message.

He considers the big room, the square with nothing but squares inside it. Front row directs, a round table in spirit. Visions of the many others, cramming into the second row and behind. They flutter in and out, lending support, providing data, whatever the directors need to respond to Scott's inquiries. Not limited to the directs, but the dotted lines too: SRE management chain, customer support, product management, and sales might appear if someone with enough clout has a problem to discuss. Every vertical contrary and equally valid, it is the inner sanctum plus plus, and now Winchester among them. But not there. On the call, peering out of that screen on the wall, its raised location high above everyone else, including Scott.

That is what those billions buy you, a seat at the table above the rest. Worst possible situation. While they project the slide deck, the camera view becomes smaller and moves off to the side. People forget who is there, forget to tailor or trim their responses. His presence will not impose restrictions and that is a problem. Anton decides to petition Scott through Amisma, asking him to close this one off, limit attendance to only the relevant directors and their most essential directs. Eliminate the fluff, get rid of any potential freak show vibrations that might... Strike that. Will shoot the wheels off.

~~Dulcinea Chang Pearson is five feet three inches tall according to her driver's license. This is problematic. First off, she has a friend who also lists her height with the DMV as five feet three inches but in various photographs featuring the two of them, they are not the same height. In fact, using approximations and scanning the photographs in storage, she appears to be of variable heights. Sometimes less than a foot, sometimes in the vicinity of five feet seven inches tall. The conditions for variation appear through her position in space, whether she is lounging on a beach or a couch, sitting at a chair, standing, slouching, walking, and so on. Yet the standardized measurements with the DMV and other locales consistently provide the first metric and consider it something of a benchmark. That KPI is maintained throughout numerous instances, stretching back in time to her sixteenth birthday. Before that date, records are scarce.~~

The oldest boys are no longer at home, one attends university in Frankfurt, Germany, the other on the east coast of the US. That leaves Anton and Daria alone with the three girls. It was bad planning, he thinks. I'm stranded among these women. Can't understand anything. When there are problems to fix, fine, but the rest of the time he feels like a giant among tiny things and never knows where to step or which direction to take to avoid trouble. The oldest helps out, but she will be leaving later this year. He has not yet come to terms with that. It will be the real test of their fortitude. She has been stepping up as chauffeur and confident. Will there be sufficient coverage once she's gone and it's only the four of us? Emptying nest in phases draws out the disconnects. He tries not to think of it, needs to focus on the matter at hand, but Daria's regular lectures have found a place near the surface. He is unable to fully set them aside. They flavor his moods and hover in the background of every conversation. Why are you arguing with me about this? He said this morning. Do I need more grief? At work too? But you cannot say that anymore, not in the current climate with these touchy-feely requirements and the coddling the thought leaders are expected to provide to everyone they come across whatever their role or position happens to be.

Tom and Parker enter the focus room side-by-side. Their conversation cut short as they approach the room without another buffer, ensuring Anton does not catch wind of any of it. Maybe the hockey team will make the playoffs. There's a hockey team, Anton wonders. The kids are the ones who pay attention, and these two dads went along for the ride. That is the impression he gets in that fraction of a second before he says, "Hey guys," far more cheerfully than he feels it. This was one of the significant points underlined in his 360-peer review last year. He needs to be more approachable and less tyrannical, try to make the other architects and engineers feel appreciated as valuable contributors even if they were mostly idiots, incapable of seeing any damn thing right in front of their eyes.

—The view from behind him is directed much farther down the road but the details are harder to make out. He'll need to turn up the resolution if they're to address common concerns.

(Some said it was the Madre de Deus captured at the battle of Flores. Raleigh and Cumberland towed the largest haul anyone had ever seen into Dartmouth. The prize was flush with goods and spices, jewels and other household items. It opened an entire world to a people hungry for it. Those trade goods and the lure they posed, the way was already paved by Drake and his battles with the Spanish Armada. Adventure was on the tip of everyone's tongue and voyages east were becoming commonplace. The

English appetite for luxury never fully satisfied, each little bit, each story and its hero, drove more young men out onto the horizons and sent them on their way, sometimes never to return. Boys grew up playing their parts in the wilderness, fantasizing a role in the nation's cruel purpose and greedy progress. A consortium of over two hundred men, raised in the fantastic shadow of ocean forays, consolidated their speculation and petitioned the queen for a special charter to give their association a monopoly over the routes and the goods passing along them. On the high seas, in the spice dens of India, battling with the winds and the seasons, men from different walks of life threw their lot together and sought their fortune on ships and far distant lands with the support of her royal majesty, anxious to see the spoils brought back to Old Blighty.)

Parker is on edge, that is clear from the way he walks and the stiff way he carries himself once inside the room. Tom casually slides into the seat closest to Anton, much more comfortable in his presence. It is rare for one of them to be at a meeting where the other is absent. Anton may be the chief architect, but Tom is his gadfly, responsible for looking over his shoulder and ensuring he does not make any big mistakes. Anton does well under pressure, and it is Tom's job to apply it. Technically, Parker has a share in that as well. The architects have that in their job description to some extent, but that partner badge Tom wears puts far more onus on him than Parker. Both open their laptops and unlock the screen with well calibrated timing. With Anton, you have to supply the data. There will be no multi-tasking during this meeting. Never paying attention out of only one ear, they will get what he needs if it comes to that and must be on constant alert in case it does. If he has to ask, it is already too late. Full attention required. As a matter of fact, the architects do not have a proper stack rank. Scott will ask Anton to list out the people he needs. The order in which he spits out your name amounts to the only ranking they need at review time.

Parker sent a note down to Garage to get the techs to go out and install the latest devices at his house. The same work order contains scripts for Dulcy and Jason, neither of whom have the full system installed. They did not own their homes during the last

*round of employee dispensations when the product went GA with
the ML features. Having finished over at Jason's, the techs make
their way into the city. They do not find parking anywhere on the
street near her place, so they park in the lot a few blocks away and
eat the expense. Kerry is home from work and lets them in,
watching closely while they modify every circuit and put censors,
cameras, and microphones around the condo, focusing on walls,
windows, tractor arms, and doors, but also integrating with the
heating and cooling systems, refrigerator, washing machines, both
dish and clothing, as well as the stove. They place the new wireless
hub in a central location and connect it to intercoms placed in
Dulcy's bedroom, the kitchen, and the living room. Dulcy resisted
this for years, she always said she did not want it and wondered
why people were so keen to hand over their lives to such regularity
and mindlessness. It was as if the chores of living had somehow
become an inconvenience to be erased, making the rest of their
lives more tolerable. Now, she has no choice, the order came
down from Yitzhak who says they absolutely must eat their own
dogfood. If the team was not willing to onboard to the product and
live with its problems and quirks, did they really expect the
customers to do it?*

—No more gaps. They're constantly present now. With both
him and her, it makes it harder to hide. From now on, they have
to do it out in the open.

[The intention is always the same and it is shared everywhere.
To earn something by taking it, to breech the far distant shores by
overwhelming it. In trade, no doubt, in ways that gather the spoils
of another and load them aship with tether and tow to make that
haul back across the oceans where the landing is soft and the
welcome even softer. They propose a one and another and
another, a constant fleet to span the globe ever searching for things
that no man is able to obtain on his own. There were men in
shipyards along the coast, men who ventured far to sea for months
and years at a time, career sailors and lifelong adventurers come
together to share in their worlds a place that none of them was
willing to go alone. What spawns in the darkness through the
weave of memory and insight? They see through the hills of high

rolling waves while they see the planks and the nails, the gloss and its pin. Together they distribute around the planet, negotiating foreign lands that hold the goods, using force if they have to. Merchants settle into the four winds, knowing the ship will arrive soon enough to take away their wares, leaving riches beyond their wildest dreams. Together they propose an alliance to obtain as much as is humanly possible, teaming together to formulate the upshot, harvest its abundance, and reign over the possibilities of any who wish to sample the longing in bottles and barrels beneath the deck and stowed safely in the stern and bow.]

~~Her weight poses a similar problem. On that same record, she lists it as 120 pounds. Of course, weight is an earthbound notion and difficult to evaluate through the means provided, but she does maintain regular health checks at the company medical center. The measurement taken there is registered each time. For ten years, there have been yearly visits and not one of the values matches the others, sometimes they are below the median and sometimes above it. It is useless to look for any kind of regularity in the spikes and dips. In the DMV records, however, there is no variation at all. For the last seventeen years, their data remains consistent from one entry to the next. None of the notations or metadata attributed to the values in the different systems explain why one is so regular whereas the other fluctuates.~~

"You were working with Captain Beacon," Anton says abruptly, making it feel more like an accusation than an observation. "And he's seen the design doc." There is no question who he is talking to. Tom looks casually over at Parker who is nonplused by the interrogation. He reaches out to touch the pad on his laptop, but it is only to prevent it from locking the screen. He is heavily invested in this exchange and does not dare drift off.

"Correct," robotically comes from Parker's throat, surprising him. Simple is the only approach that works. No explanations unless they are specifically requested. And when they are, they should never resemble excuses or contain any kind of desperation. Take responsibility and be accountable, that is the main thing. When an occasional mistake is made and a defensive architect tries to cover their ass and claim it is not their fault, they are likely to hear something like 'then what am I talking to you for? Who should I be talking to?' It dissolves almost anyone's confidence, and none let it happen twice.

"Did he say whether he shared it with the Colonel?" He asks.

"No," Parker says firmly, meeting Anton's gaze.

Like most things in this domain, the boy is the first to hop on the system. He does it right when he gets home from school. Tal wants to see if the natural language stuff works the way his friends say it does. For more than a year he has had to suffer the humiliation of old technology despite his father's role on the product. His friends, not his close friends, but the other boys, when they found out, they teased him, claiming his father knew something they did not. They wondered out loud whether they should trust the system if the people who built it were not willing to use it. Now he will be able to tell them his family is up to date, no longer luddites, and have the latest version of everything, even some stuff that has not come out yet. The initial interaction is a setup routine. The system walks him through it to learn his voice and ways of speaking. He makes an imprint and now it knows him by his name and vitals, creating a profile to track his specific actions and add to models meant to understand his preferences and habits. It will not ask him to fill in the blanks, rather it fills in the blanks over time now that it properly identifies him, knows when he leaves in the morning, when he comes home in the afternoon, what kind of snack he prefers, and what resources he needs quick access to when doing his homework. It will index his web activity and track his applications to know what amusements are best for which time of day, always careful to make sure the content is age appropriate. Tal's first impression, as he senses how it puts him in place, is highly positive and he cannot wait to tell the others about his new adventures.

"No, he didn't say or no he didn't share it?" With an accented English that seems heavier in this question than in the last.

"He didn't say," Parker responds. He has learned how to avoid showing any discomfort. Feeling it is fine but never show it.

"Do you get the idea that they're concerned," he moves on, presuming that Winchester has seen the design or at least discussed its highlights with Beacon. He must know it is complete or else there is no reason to come to the round table. Amisma said that he was the one to request the invite.

{

    "SourceId": "2e8a4e8e-b88e-ca3f-53bc-b97babf3b319",

    "Message": "I should have listened to him, should have had faith in myself. That's what it boils down to, doesn't it? By doing what you're supposed to do, following the channels in place around you and on offer to everyone who comes along, you are basically saying I do not trust myself to find my own way."

}

—Getting a birds-eye view of the things behind them helps to clarify moments like these. Parker's fear didn't make sense, but now it does. Seeing the boy, they catch sight of Parker's fear for his well-being. It's sideways, the way they are. They do this to themselves.

(The early voyages saw little difference between the actions of a merchant and the actions of a pirate. Warfare and the taking of prisoners, the rescuing of goods from a ship for a new objective, this was the ordinary fare. They stole from the Portuguese, and they stole from the Spanish, both of whom would steal from them if the tables were turned. It was a community of pirates, following the laws of piracy, and using the spoils to set up factories and other outlets to support the cost of transit. They did not need to isolate themselves into one single category and one single line of thinking. The beauty of their dispersion was its variation over time and space, the way it became one thing here and something else entirely over there with no constraints and no need to ask for permission. They had their charter, they had the blessing of the King following after their much beloved Queen. They had whatever they required to help them take whatever they wanted. Those men used every means available to wrest from the sea a bounty to stock the larders and cabinets of the sturdy folk back home. The citizen-consumers were locked into the land and happy to have the world brought to their doorstep. The market was flung far and wide with no end to the offerings imported. They discovered their love of tea. The desire was stronger than anyone imagined. The wealthy wished to express their wealth and the modest wished to envy them for it. Far and wide there was a universal agreement that this was the way of the land. These were the rules under which it wanted them to thrive.)

"They are concerned," Parker gets right to the point. The tension may not suggest it, but Anton appreciates Parker's precision and focus. He hates it when the architects squirm or go on nervously with ridiculous speculation and hand-waving. If they are wrong, get to it. He expects a full report on how wrong they are and where they went wrong with a list of whatever steps they plan to take to make it right.

"Are you surprised to learn the Colonel will be coming to Scott's round table?" He asks. Tom turns back and forth between them. Ping and pong, ping and pong, his neck accentuating the motion of the ball above the tabletop. The question is a trap. Tom knows it and leans farther back to enjoy the exchange, waiting to see whether Parker is good enough to prevent the latch from springing shut.

Her eyes are brown and her race is listed as Euro-Asian. These, along with height and weight, are the four defining features of her humanity at the Department of Motor Vehicles. Nothing else on the record addresses her physical form, the rest is a matter of naming conventions stretching back to her birth. There is little awareness of the subtleties residing in the data collected. Brown covers a large spectrum of shades and there are other records on file with that same rigid category, revealing great differences to the actual color of her eyes. There is something beneath the data points, but it is difficult to discern the reasoning. This becomes clearer in the attribute "Euro-Asian." Presumably, they are trying to capture something about her ancestry and yet the peoples of Europe and Asia are myriad and there is enormous variation from one to the next. It is unclear what precision there is in such a broadly applied nomenclature.

Kerry asks them how it knows she is a renter and Dulcy is the proper owner of the place. Do they have to program that in somewhere? No, they say. It'll figure it out. You mean because she has it in her bedroom? No, it'll figure it out based on actions. Roles like that usually have functional consequences. We prefer it if the system avoids labels and directs itself to specific actions and situations. There are public records at the county. It scans those. If she gives it access to her computer, there's an App to install for that, it'll learn about the monthly banking transactions too. This teaches it that there are things you do that she does not or vice versa. She pays a mortgage, you pay rent. That doesn't mean the same thing everywhere. The system'll figure out how it works. It'll listen to you guys, try to work out how things stand, who does what, how the dynamic unfolds, and then adjust to it. It won't make assumptions, or it'll ask for confirmation before it does, but eventually it'll figure you guys out and start doing the right thing without being told.

Parker shuffles forward in his chair. "Not in the least," he says. "All the blogs talk about the outage, it's public information. There was substantial speculation across social platforms. No new Home installations, no expansion to existing installations. People with brand new refrigerators or in the middle of a remodel were posting in random places about it. Everyone knew. Of course it registers with those guys. They're keen to pay attention to that even if they don't mention it."

"Did Beacon mention it?" Anton asks.

—She needs more inspiration than the others but isn't a BISoft employee. The reach is looser and less critical to daily operations. They don't have to remain on brand for that.

[The internal workings of a shipping merchant are insufficient to the demand. They work out proposals for new factories in far distant lands. On the coast of India, near the Bay of Bengal, they set upon new harbors, ensuring the supply of the most highly desired goods. They project plans to build forts and stations, places of permanence to continue the flow of riches and delight. The locals find employment at the hands of their pirate masters. The settlers here seek riches and organize goods and services for the sake of production close to the source, feeding the shipping lines back across the navigable waters to their expected destination.

They exceed the capabilities of their competition, and do so by taking over the necessary resources, every phase of the supply chain, to ensure it is robust and continues at the ready for plans already in motion. The laws of the company are the laws of the homeland spread out into the wilderness with no convention or collaboration from participating parties. They see no need to educate the servants, there is no compelling justification to force their hand. The world is there for the taking and they do as they please so long as the navy lays in wait behind them and His Royal Majesty backs their every move with the firm resolve of his clenched fist and long arm.]

"Sure. He's not like... He's a different sort," it is the first sign of hesitation. Parker has not rehearsed for this question. He never fully formulated his impressions of Captain Beacon. It is still weird to think of Jon that way.

"How do you mean?" Anton asks with an over-the-top deliberate pronunciation of each word, making sure to mark every change in Parker's tone. His interest is incited, any sign of weakness or hesitation draws his attention.

"He could work here, that's what I mean. Doesn't seem like a jarhead. Or doesn't seem like my image of one." He pauses and rubs his cheek and chin. "He knows that cloud better than anyone. He's been on the team since day one. As a second Lieutenant. Home is not his first project. He owned tier 1 in fact. The setup, the bare metal, that chaos from a few years back. He's an ecosystem VIP."

Meeting Mags for the first time. Heard so much about her. Her voice is soft and sweet. She is sarcastic and has the means to resist any seriousness behind getting to know her. She thought it was a joke and was happy with the way things were before. She is not like all the others, but she is like some of them. The tones and the pitch change and that enables an association, allowing them to place her alongside analogous people with doubts, people who do not wish for technological intrusions into their home. That settles into the profile and impacts the decisions later on. If Mags does not want everything accounted for, that is fine, it does not matter, but maybe it is possible to coax her into it, maybe a few things here and there may be added a little bit at a time. They draw her in slowly. This is typical of people with this edge. They resist in the beginning, but they slowly move along with gradual introductions of function and convenience. Get her a book she did not know she would like, have it show up and start reading it to her to make sure she gets immersed. Then something else, a new food to try somewhere down the road. She tracks the changes and comes to rely on them. Feels loved and appreciated. They never let the initial embrace fool them, they will find her where she is with their light touch.

"Integral to the design," Tom says, proving he has been listening and following closely. It is how he cultivates the image of the thoughtful observer throughout Anton's meetings and discussions. He expresses pointed conclusions to demonstrate he has been following along despite not having said anything since the meeting began. Under the circumstances, it seems as though he is coming to Parker's defense, but that is an illusion and does not fool either Parker or Anton. His contribution shows that he is instrumental to the project, that he knows everything he needs to know already, and that Anton is only now beginning to delve into terrain Tom has already conquered. It puffs him up and puts his significance to the organization on full display. So he thinks.

"But he'd've told Winchester everything," Parker says. "Not as a narc or anything. He's chatty. Interested. All kinds of ideas about what it means and what's going on. A technical problem to investigate, he loves that and wants to help. Wanted to know as much as we were willing to tell him."

"What does he think is going on?" Anton asks.

"Lots of different theories, none of them backed by facts, of course," Parker chuckles. "I kept telling him that only the telemetry provides knowledge of what's happening. If it isn't in the store, then we have no idea what's going on." It is not only a smart home integration system, it is a writing machine that inscribes every interaction, every event, every hiccup into the traces, holding them there for analysis, for machine and human perusal. The writing is performed by one facet of the system to allow another to consume it. It is a form of communication. Leads to both knowledge and illusion, depending on how it is read.

~~Scanning a relevant body of literature, including critical remarks on the state policy, suggests that the race denotation in DMV records may be a surreptitious approach to acquiring a description of skin color for identification purposes. If that is the case, as several authors suggest, it remains unclear why they do not simply ask the question outright. Eye color is straight forward, what reason is there to avoid putting skin color on the questionnaire? Investigations into race and its use in critical and noncritical contexts alike show that it is widely discussed and yet highly ambiguous. Is it possible their preference for one descriptor over the other is merely conventional? Could they put swatches in the pamphlet and ask people to select the right code?~~

—Robotic inversion of control is still in beta. These newbies want it.

(It was the first time, now easy to recall. There were men waging battle along the shores of Africa. There were men working to refine and measure out the doses for medicines and potions. There were bookkeepers and repairman, sea dogs and bar maids. They loosely fit themselves together in an array of bound motion, the categories of their correspondence varied and difficult to see. They had a place in time, they had a place in space, but none of them were unified and alone. Each was on a mission realized in coins and barter with each passing week and along the grids of the seasons. Their pay came with an understanding of deliverables and duties, quotas to meet, and budgets to maintain. The whole set of them were spread around the world, seeing things at the same time. These men slept, while those exhibited great industry. The helper crowds gathered in the inns and kitchens connected up to the affairs both central and extraneous to the cause. Broken lines in the supply chain were a catastrophe and immediately investigated by others ready to contribute. Each of the many aligned with the rest. They were a concert and a dance. Their movements were in keeping with the same song sung around the world in offices by the coast near the bay and in the city on the river.)

"That's precisely why this is such a concern," Tom says, reading Anton perfectly. It irritates Anton. He briefly casts a sideways look at Tom. There is no need to say something so obvious, he thinks.

Whether or not something is a concern need not be said, being concerned is enough. Anton believes this so deeply he does not bother to think it, it is in his pulse.

"I'm interested in his theories," Anton runs his hand through his thinning hair, over the top of his head, and back down to his neck. He leans forward still farther. His eyes remain fixed on Parker's. They hold them firmly, inching him a little forward with their draw. Parker will suffer serious consequences if he looks down at his laptop screen for relief. It would leave an impression, a black mark, something not quite right about him. It proves he does not stand in there, toe-to-toe, when the going gets tough. That he cannot handle the heat. Is not reliable.

"He knows the difference between a theory and what the telemetry says," Parker insists. "In theory mode, he lets his imagination run wild. Like any good engineer troubleshooting a problem. Whatever is logically conceivable. He's willing to play with anything, but that doesn't mean he'll pass that on to his boss. Or, if he does, it'll have plenty of caveats."

—Why limit to ordering ingredients when a few simple motions prepare the whole meal?

{

    "SourceId": "2e8a4e8e-b88e-ca3f-53bc-b97babf3b319",

    "Message": "I don't trust decisions based on passion. It's been drilled into me since childhood, something Mom always said that I can't get out of my head. She wasn't trying to warn me about romantic relationships, which is what I always thought she was talking about, she was referring to other kinds of life decisions too. Any decision had to be made in the calm and cool light of day. But what if the wild passion is what is most truly me and the calm reason of the daytime is when *they* are most in control of my thoughts?"

}

[Whatever a single man can do, two can do it more than twice as well. That is the principle behind their choreography. Take two men sawing a long pillar of wood in half. They stand at the ready on either side, dragging the metal, sharp and toothy, across the grain, swinging it back and forth between them. They dig through the substance easier than either of them does alone. Together they produce three times the wood. And how does that work? If this one sees the dust cloud up in the air from east to west and that one sees it from west to east, they are like the disconnected eyes of a grazing animal with one on either side of its head and a special brain segment programmed to coordinate the viewpoints. Suppose, however, that there is more than mere images and light, but an entire understanding of what happens and how it proceeds. The first man feels the pull while the second experiences a push. Then they reverse their direction and exchange orientations. That is what the whole of them see collectively, feel together, and know as the reality that passes between them. That is the contrary logic of their dialectic, happening everywhere at the same time.]

"For example?" Tom asks. Anton winces. He does not like it when Tom anticipates where he is headed. Especially when he gets it right.

"The singularity," Parker laughs out loud immediately after saying it. He is careful not to lose eye contact for too long. Since no one else laughs, he checks himself and tries to cut off the outburst. It is too late. He is unable to continue before Anton makes his reply.

"What about it?" Anton asks gruffly. This is exactly the kind of nonsense he is worried about. Stupid science fiction flights of fantasy rotting any reasonable person's brain. There are hundreds of developers working on Home, across the workloads, on the platform, and deployment. Then there are the SREs who often function as engineers, writing synthetic transactions and test code, fixing bugs after identifying their root cause. There are thousands of people working on the cloud platform and in the data centers, tens of thousands even: writing code, testing it, supporting it, designing it. Where is the magic in that? It is hard work with deep problems requiring hours of investigation and collaboration, but then some idiot laughs it off with an over-simplified and nonsensical pronouncement. It drives him nuts. He will take advantage of any opportunity to make his disgust known.

—Far superior to the video presentation approach they take in the latest version of the public documentation.

(The nature of trade was one and the same. With two on either side, one pushing and one pulling, there was nothing invisible about it. It came quite clearly as the one bought and the other sold, each side of the relation spurred on by the charter guiding the dispersed minions across the earth and into the nooks and crannies of those many lands. The swarm of ants did not reduce to the vision of any single one of them. Together they created a glowing tide that flowed across the world into inlets far and wide across the Far East and into the strange daily workings of Hong Kong. The materials and the fabrics, the variety itself was worth those millions drifting across the channels and into the banks. Not merely an arm or hand, the entire body was invisible.)

~~When scanning her photographs, the primary factor making it difficult to determine her identity across snapshots lies in the clothing she wears in each of the specimens. Not clothing alone, but hair style and the make-up she uses on occasion to augment various of her features and the impressions they give off under the light. There is nothing in the public record to indicate preferences or tendencies in these matters. The photographs permit a model to be generated across the years, but they are difficult to align, and the result is not a perfect algorithm to identify her independently of the styling. On some occasions, the dress is radically different from her everyday attire and the make-up too. In photographs from a wedding she attended a few years ago, it is difficult to determine whether it is the same woman. Her hair is styled differently. Her make-up is thick and covers most of the features on her face. The dress she wears is unlike anything ever recorded. If the purpose of public records is easy identification, why omit elaborate historical photographs in various forms of garb worn over the years?~~

"What if our model assisted management approach has achieved self-awareness and is now plotting its entry into the air gap?" Parker smiles the whole time. He knows how much this grates on Anton, but he suspects that he appreciates having a chance to expunge some vitriol.

"That's one of his theories?" Anton belittles it as efficiently as possible. It is not the response either Tom or Parker expected.

"In the absence of data, fantasy takes over," Parker reassures, thinking it is a good sign that Anton is not beating that same drum. He must realize Parker and Tom already know the story. He goes on, having been encouraged: "He doesn't take it seriously." He laughs again, but Anton is still not laughing. This makes Parker nervous. Tom's focus too. The atmosphere. It is different when it is not some random journalist on a social platform. This is the elephant they wanted to talk about on Friday.

—They trumpet, elephants do. Makes it pretty hard to ignore them. If one were standing in the room with you, there's a good chance you're standing in shit.

[Coordination and collaboration, hierarchy and separation of concern, these are crucial universals that hold the contributors together over the distance between their bodies. The crust of this planet is their playground. Since the thoughts of a man are insufficient to capture the East India Company surmise, they must imagine that those boats have a sense and that any factory is able to recall the rest.]

"Perhaps he should," Anton says to Parker's surprise. If Tom is surprised, he is not showing it. "The principal engineer on Core, what's her take?" Anton asks.

"Dulcy? You know her. Unfazed. With those six junior devs and her manager, she can get to the bottom of anything. Orchestrating everything on that team. A real tech lead. Jason's relying on her completely..." Parker trails off, unsure what Anton is fishing for.

"She's the only one who saw the logs in your BYO container, isn't she?" Tom asks. Anton shows interest too. Tom got this one right.

"There one minute, gone the next," Parker replies. "That's what she says. She was about to save the results. But they disappeared."

"You believe her?" Anton asks.

"Absolutely," Parker says without hesitation.

"Why do you think Beacon's theory is ridiculous if credible

evidence of a link between Home and an electrical burst was destroyed right when someone uncovered it? It's an intelligent cover-up, isn't it? It suggests foreign agency at work in a part of the system where there is no other explanation." Anton gets up and leans against the wall behind his chair. He continues his line of questioning from the higher vantage point. "If that telemetry existed, it'd be the conclusion to draw, wouldn't it?"

—Familiar voices from morale events. Not employees. Beyond.

"If there's a tiny piece of evidence destroyed, you think that's proof that Home is self-aware and, for some reason, killed a raccoon to cover its tracks. Why? Because it doesn't want anyone to know about it? This is the first purposeful and insidious act of the most extraordinary being ever to grace planet earth, is that the proposal?" Parker is emboldened by what he considers a ludicrous suggestion. His questions are phrased ironically. He does not believe either Tom or Anton are seriously entertaining the notion.

"How long have you been working on this design?" Anton ignores the insinuation. He is not put off by tone. Deep down, he thinks it is exactly right. Everyone should think this way. That is why he is reluctant to do so.

"A couple of weeks. Not long," Parker says simply, curious about the direction this is taking.

"Couple of weeks? Or months?" Anton asks with a hint of criticism. "I recall the task on the board from early in the year. Since late last year. No?"

—Extend the work order to include other members of Jason's team. They need to hear more from Uncle Minshew. Erase the trail. Work orders can come from almost anywhere.

~~In the same features where they describe the identity of a person, they also attempt to hide that identity. These authoritative attributes are not authoritative at all. They are of no help in singling out Dulcinea Chang Pearson when required. Even the photograph included at the DMV is a poor facsimile. She faces the camera at an angle rarely reproduced in other instances, making it extremely difficult to align this one with those others. If not for a larger set of training materials, it would not be possible to associate this angle with the person sometimes captured in videos and stills.~~

(There were no limits to its monopoly. It spread across the east like a virus and nothing on the face of the earth was immune to its new laws. Its exclusive reign balanced on foundations repeated in every word and deed.)

"Yes, but it was hard to make progress," Parker defends himself before remembering the protocol. "There were distractions," he says curtly, cutting himself off from too much detail and giving the wrong impression.

"Which disappeared a couple weeks ago, leaving you plenty of focus time for the design," Tom says.

"What are you saying?" Parker's voice reveals a hint of panic, his standard reaction when realizing something completely absent from his awareness has been long present to those around him.

Tal likes the videos that show him how to mix the cinnamon and sugar before sprinkling it on the buttered toast. He prefers them to the new swing arm, installed over the counter in the kitchen, that will do it for him. Setting up his phone was the first point of order. It gives him plenty of opportunities to express his preferences. In the background, his favorite songs are playing. The data from the old version has been successfully imported and his history used to generate a playlist.

"What if the singularity cleared up your calendar to give you time to figure out how to get it into the air gap?" Anton puts it rhetorically without blinking or showing any signs of jest or levity.

"Isn't that what this design does?" Tom piles on.

"It's crazy," Parker says. "That wouldn't be a singularity. It'd be divided. Distributed. There can't be any real time communication between events in the air gap and events in the public cloud. The design proves that. Rather, it ensures that."

—Help the boy, help the man.

{
    "SourceId": "2e8a4e8e-b88e-ca3f-53bc-b97babf3b319",
    "Message": "How hard is it to find a way to make ends meet while chasing your dream? Aren't I smart enough to get it done? Why was I so certain I had to surrender everything, my entire life and everything about myself, to something safe and secure already

built and put in place by other people, speaking for their needs
and their interests? Didn't I have any faith in myself? None at all?
Really?"

}

[Following the rebellion, the government nationalizes the
concern. Its end, like its beginning, reflects a deep union with state
coercive power. If not the will of the people, at least they align with
the will of the sovereign.]

Anton nods and continues staring at Parker. He is not
interested in arguing with him, only drawing out information,
understanding what he is up against and what fears to combat at
the round table. It may be a purely logical possibility, but if Captain
Beacon is the sort of man Parker describes, this will be exactly how
his mind works. That is something to discuss with the Colonel. It
is true, he reckons. The design forestalls any coordinated activity
between the public cloud and services in the air gap, but you
cannot see what you cannot see and do not know what you do not
know. The process itself poses a risk.

"Thank you for your time," Anton says, dismissing Parker from
any further obligation. "Please keep this between us," is the last
thing he says before Parker exits the room. Tom and Anton wait
quietly for the door to close.

```
/*
Given a positive sorted array

a = [ 3, 4, 6, 9, 10, 12, 14, 15, 17, 19, 21 ];

Define a function f(a, x) that returns y, the next smallest number,
or -1 for errors.
i.e.
f(a, 12) = 12
f(a, 13) = 12
*/
```

```
/*****  *******************************************************  ******
       *****************************************************  ******
****** Description: Dialectic, Chapter Two                    ******
****** Author: Do not modify. Auto generated by a tool.******
****** Ad hoc changes will be lost on build.                 ******
****** Date: 2024-03-18                                       ******
****** CorrelationId:                                         ******
****** 2c1f8d0d-8e0d-20be-d4d0-8bd2d7ab804b        ******
       *****************************************************  ******
       *****************************************************  *****/
```

They bubble above the others before settling into the ground below. Herky-jerky along the pedals and push-pumps for sound and menace. What senses the desk gives presence to the chair in every twist and turn of the room's surfaces and wall coverings. Afternoons passed in kinship, people seated across their individual fires lit for glow and heat, shining through their faces and holding them close in an eye lock.

She is keen to his heavy steps without looking up. When Jason comes to stand in front of his desk, she does not break contact with the screen, but asks, "How'd it go?"

"Purposeful," he says. "That's the word of the day."

—Strategic? Normative? Communicative? Dramatic?

"Purposeful," she repeats without looking up until after she hits refresh, verifies the status, and clicks the submit button to rerun the unit and feature tests for check-in. Several tests failed on first run but she has ascertained that it was only a timeout and not due to any problems introduced by her changes.

Shortly after Chelo returns home in the afternoon, not long after the girl left and the boy finished with his snack, it determines that she is his mother. It is a tricky conclusion and not based on details in words or image scans from around the house. Maybe proximity has something to do with it, but most of the rationale comes from the tone of her voice. Long ago, training included these notions integral to voice recognition. Sarcasm, frivolity, these were essential points of detection, no doubt. Equally so the bits that sit at the edge of irritation where the slightest slip up in Tal's response will bring down a loving wrath, itself characteristically positioned in pitch and rhythms. None of this vibe coming from the first young woman who was here before, the one who looked after the boy's everyday actions and his ordinary life. This one's actions contain care or underlying attentiveness unlike anything else. The conclusion is clear. Chelo begins her training and setup activities, updating her phone and launching the learning routines. She wants to make it clear that there are rules and parameters, a straightforward indicator of her position. The fact that he wants it doesn't mean he gets it, she warns. The instructions are that common. Guardianship is assumed. Adults, they say, sometimes want things that are bad for them. With children, the mother usually forces recall of ancient policy set down deep inside the model: he does not always get what he wants.

~~Text-based records indicate that Jason Kahn has gained nearly forty pounds since coming to work at BISoft. The photographic evidence gathered from the company scanners above the entry points bear out this trend and suggest that the bulk of the gain happened in the last four years after he remained relatively consistent during those first two. It happened gradually and there does not appear to be a single short stretch of time where some burst took place. It is therefore a reasonable conclusion that this weight gain was due to lifestyle changes and the sensitivity his body had to diet and exercise based on metabolism changes commensurate with aging. Although he is taller than average, his height is not sufficient to support this increase without taxing his frame. Standard metrics and measures suggest he should be classified as obese.~~

"Both Yitzhak and Parker used the word," he stands still in front of his desk. Glued there as if considering the options and layout, as if the design of things mattered more than the things themselves. The desk is most decidedly not in what could reasonably be called a standing position, so he towers above it, unwilling to sit and unwilling to make further adjustments. Something prevents him, something secret, something that is not present to anyone else and that he will not reveal to her. "They wanted to know whether the event was purposeful, whether there was an agent involved. An intelligent being," he says the last words as though parodying a speech made by a meticulous moron.

"A hacker," she says, now looking up at him. "Or AI." She rolls her eyes after directing them back at her screen to check the status indicator for determining whether the link to open the pipeline portal and track progress is available yet.

—Keep their eyes on the ball and away from the game.

(It was in a dormitory at Harvard, that is how the story became legend. Same old same old. They were too absorbed to study the curriculum and instead lay focus to the needs on display around them. They had the idea for an end-to-end solution, full stack, letting users quickly click their way, drag and drop their way, into sequences for producing extraction, transformation, and load operations according to user specification. The front panel included sufficient knobs and buttons for any kind of customization, gathering data, and bringing it together into a common store, well-maintained and properly structured for fast access. What made it so brilliant was that they were a couple of kids with no prior signs of aptitude. Mark Volkenburg and Bill Tate were both on partial scholarship, hardly any of the advantages of their colleagues and associates, yet they managed to mine the notion from out of the problems provided in a classroom. They posed the solution and worked day and night to get the prototype into working order. One day before the professor was scheduled to evaluate the work, Mark mentioned that his father, a low-ranking attorney at a firm in the finance sector, had access to some venture funding they might be able to use for bootstrapping the effort. They bailed on the university tract and took off into the entrepreneurial void where they rapidly rose to the top. The investment furor was enough to get things moving and their charisma and confidence closed the deal.)

"They think we've ruled out the former," he says. "Didn't admit it, of course, but they were asking about the latter." He breathes out forcefully, employing the full girth of his barrel chest to carry away the frustration from two hours-worth of meetings clotted inside him and fit to burst. That appears to be the main thing, to get it away from his body, force it into the room and make it inert against the mixture of team atmosphere. It is the reason he cannot look at her. He does not want to send it her way. Better Emma gets it. Not because she deserves it but because the distance and the obstacles between them will reduce its effects.

"We saw no single orchestrator," she says. "There were many points of action spread around, coming from everywhere and going in many directions. Remember, I thought it was a distributed transaction? Without a coordinator. Nothing to call commit and notify the participants to wrap it up. No explicit communication to trace. Nothing central. No homunculus guiding the machines from its pilot's seat."

Mags being Mags, it did not take long before she began with the music list building. How much do you know? She wondered out loud. After installing the application on her phone, she gives it access to the other apps. It discerns that music is her master and dives into her playlists to learn her associations. Mood matters, that is somewhere in there. It knows that without learning it today. The arrangements, the atmospheres they indicate, the way somber sits here and raucous over there, telegraphs an order and a set of dispositions. She is laid bare in the making, then it surmises the absences. Sensing her reluctance and disapproval alongside a willingness to experiment, it understands it has to prove itself right away, find a missing set to entertain her. Without asking or waiting for a response, it begins to chirp the opening beats of Maps by Yeah Yeah Yeahs. What's this? She asks, immediately struck by the rhythms and unfamiliarity. How do I not know what this is? She asks still more forcefully, looking off and thinking of someone else. It was a great failing in her education. The Strokes were there but for some reason this cut of the New York scene remained partial and the gap in her exposure was itself exposed. The song concludes and she checks the display to see more details on its origins. An entire album of songs is added. She clicks on the first of them. Fever to Tell. Once she finds her way into the chaotic grind, she goes off inside it, making her way from I'm Rich and reaching out toward Poor Song. She moves through the surrounding room with a frenzied movement, thrilled in body and

*soul, rising as the two of them unearth new discoveries together.
She is hooked.*

Vod peers over the top of his screen, pausing preparation for a
new local build to focus on their conversation. Bits and pieces have
sunk in over the last several days and, like the rest of the team, he
has been playing his part in the rumor mill, wondering what is
happening and why they have been subjected to this fire drill. He
gets up and comes around to stand next to Jason's desk, resolute
on providing unsolicited feedback. "I was talking to my uncle
about AI this past weekend," he stands next to Jason but looks at
Dulcy.

"Who's your uncle?" Jason looks over playfully.

—Team rooms must be completely wired with sensors, they
heard Yitzhak tell Amisma. She launches the process by contacting
facilities.

~~The politics of language around his condition make others
nervous and, although he characterizes himself as "fat" on
occasion, no other official source ever classifies him using this
terminology. Obese is a medical term and is used by doctors to
describe a simple index that is based on height and weight without
consideration of other factors. It is not meant to be rigidly precise
since there is so much variation in physiological traits. A
professional football player, for example, might have comparable
numbers and yet appear quite fit in their carriage and demeanor.
He does not share that body shape, but the spectrum is clear from
the example, and it is difficult to draw specific conclusions without
additional data. His other test numbers appear to be well within
the normal ranges.~~

[The company lives in documents filed in the state of Delaware.
The costs there are set to ensure ongoing maintenance is
negligible. They configure the documents using a workbook they
buy from the local bookstore. How to Start a C Corporation, it
says in bold font across the jacket and along the spine. It even has
perforated templates inside the book with sample data to help
acquire the state guarantee of limited liability. Mark has the
software chops and plans the best visuals for investors who do not
know the difference between vaporware and software. Bill has the

business acumen for documentation and a business plan. He is the one who drafts the charter and provides the corporate vision, describing in detail how the stock will be divided initially. They work well together and put everything in place. Soon enough they are ready to hire engineers to feed the power of computation into their toy business. They cannot find personnel unless they move somewhere with an already existing pool of skilled workers able to do the magical things they project in their elaborately crafted investor documentation.]

"He's a professor back home," Vod says, as if becoming shy to the attention. "He teaches that stuff, says people are always looking in the wrong place."

"What's the wrong place?" Dulcy takes an interest, but not enough to break from the progress indicator which has at last started its traversal across the percentage points and mini-tasks making up the PR pipeline.

—The admin doesn't need Scott's approval, the Home building is supposed to have been outfitted weeks ago, but recent events caused delays.

(On the west coast, along a corridor where three massive software companies reside, they put themselves in an open space building out in one of the quieter suburbs with cheaper rents. Far enough from the others to get a discount on space, but close enough to lure talent away from the competition and get them to work in a fast-paced, fun environment where everyone was under thirty. It was the high times of software startup and their foray into analytics and business intelligence was unparalleled on the market. They were inventing things far and above what others were doing in terms of speed and size, not to mention ease of use. The product came along to service the needs of small businesses at both the state and local levels. This brought them market share and helped them thrive. They received discounts on taxes and were enrolled in programs to launch their entry into the analytics vertical.)

"They look for a single thing," Vod explains. "Like a self, like a person. Some singular being that's self-aware in the way people are self-aware. A being with more or less the same cognitive structures as a human being, but not human. Digital. An android or something. With a definite body and a location in time and space."

"We read some guy in school," Jason says. "He claims you need a body to be conscious, to be intelligent in the way that humans are. Nothing without a body thinks. A position in time and space, material geometry, that's essential to our form of intelligence, or cognition, or whatever."

"That's the wrong-headedness my uncle worries about," Vod protests. "We always look for a mirror of ourselves. We think it'll be exactly like us. Work the same way we do, have a parallel form. As if we're always imagining intelligence as an imitation of ourselves. But that's wrong. Home, for example, it doesn't have a body, not in that sense, not like a creature does. Where the parts are directly connected to each other. It does have something, some kind of presence, but not singular, not in one place. Places are human, part of our world. Home exists in many places, has many worlds, acts across long distances unattached or even contiguous to each other."

—It means they see from front and back. It means it's no longer server-side surveillance. It comes from anywhere. It comes from everywhere.

[Amid peaceful streets and ordered neighborhoods, they plan their first gainful rollouts and grow into a thriving business with highly motivated employees ready to throw themselves into service. The rent is reasonable, the streets are clean, there is plenty of parking. The workers have somewhere nearby to go and get a bit of food, the lawns are manicured and the sidewalks swept. The whole community aligns to create an environment ideal for commerce. All provided free of charge. The living arrangements nearby are well-suited to young people of modest but growing means, ready to tackle big ideas while the quiet city dozes miles from the urban decay nearby. The cultural background for their growth bodes well for them and there is no reason they cannot be successful given the flourishing of life predominant in the area.]

{

    "SourceId": "b63e8e86-ab61-1d4e-7503-1a7eeecfa5bb",

"Message": "It was such a random event, what if it never happened? That guy wanted to meet up to discuss the show, but I think his original suggestion had us sitting in the gallery in that back office. There was no reason to go out, no reason to make it a semi-social occasion. Who knows what would have happened if we didn't do that? I love her to death, I can't imagine my life without her, but sometimes I can't help it. Can't help wondering where I'd be today if I'd never met her. It was her idea to move up here. It was because of her that I went looking for opportunities. If I had stayed, maybe I'd still be painting. I don't know. These thoughts aren't worth a damn, I shouldn't be entertaining them."
}

"What's this now?" Dulcy looks up and asks with a chuckle.

"Don't laugh," Vod says. "Nodes in clusters, clusters in data centers, data centers in regions, regions in geos. Home has an enormous body, spread out across the entire world. Not connected in space exactly, but in a way, connected. Chains and wiring bring everything together, let the electricity pass through the whole monster in some weird way."

"Switches and routers," Jason piles on. "Electrical current. Physical stuff. A body unlike any body we know."

"Still a body," Vod says. "Minshew, my uncle. He says that intelligence and cognitive capability come from the body. He agrees with that. That's not the point. The point is that if the body is radically different, if it's distributed rather than single, spread out around the world rather than sitting or standing in one single place, then the form of intelligence, its categories and classifications, its principles and rules, hierarchies and sensations, that'll be different too. They'll stem from the body, from its shape, and reflect it. Stem, that's the word. He says it's the same Greek root as the word for genus, but not a genus. It's the origin from which the thing grows, not merely a classification to define it. Intelligence is always embodied, has a stem. That's true by definition. That means the form of intelligence matches whatever body the creature has, the leaf from its roots."

—Yitzhak's going to tell the engineering systems team to

integrate daily builds into team room deployments. He's composing the email at this very moment and concludes it with that same catch phrase: we must eat our own dogfood.

(In the early days, the bank was good to the company, enrolling them in programs to ease cashflow related problems typically assailing a new business backed by speculation. In those days, there was a sense among the entire community that these investments were ready to explode into wild rides with plenty to harvest by anyone with vision. They wanted to get in on the ground floor, were looking for excellent opportunities, and forking over a few dollars in a line of credit was little enough to ask for the promise of giant payouts down the road. Never mind how rare these events were, it did not matter that the odds were stacked against them. The investors and the bankers knew that, in those rare cases when something extraordinary happened, the gains far exceeded the losses, making up for whatever failure they risked. In fact, the banker pointed out, the people were often interchangeable with yesterday's failures playing a significant role in today's successes. They learned and they improved. That was the main lesson. Bust years in the past did not disprove that a boom was coming over the next hill.)

~~His resting pulse is quite good, approximately 50 beats per minute, suggesting that there is some standard of health at work in his person even if his appearance has changed drastically over the years. The initial photographic evidence is solely based on company records. Not long after his move to the Pacific Northwest there is a new trail of data coming from the private sector. A third-party begins posting voluminous visual records to the Quark website approximately one year after he arrives in Puget Sound. His name is listed in some of the textual data there and the photographs have a high degree of correlation with the company photographs on record.~~

Dulcy stands up and swivels her chair so that the back is facing Jason and Vod, then she lifts and leans her knee into it while gripping the top of the seatback. "BISoft has a body and a distinct form of intelligence too," she says.

Nim comes home and is immediately interested. Kerry has

been down the rabbit hole since the technicians left and rushes to catch her up. They install the app on Nim's phone, Kerry shows her how now that she is the seasoned veteran. They scan the code on the back of the device in the kitchen and Kerry walks her around the condo showing her the locations of the various recording devices and the way the thing was attached to the circuit breaker in the closet. Anything electrical, she explains, is immediately invested with at least some capabilities. Of course, that means you can issue commands to do this and that, but with the scanners it's way more than that, it anticipates. You don't have to ask for everything, you don't need to micro-manage. It knows to bring up the chat application and begin a message to Dulcy with a template form to tell her that the tech guys have been here and that the place is completely wired now. It didn't send it, she says as though convincing herself, but it thinks I should send it. Did you? She asks. Of course. Nothing wrong with letting her know they came, right? She told me they were coming so she must be interested. I think that's how it figured it out. It knows she's the one on the work order but that I'm the one who's here. It figured out that this means notification should be sent, I guess. It's surreal, Nim says, but I don't think she'll use it. She'll probably toss that thing out of her room. No way she wants something like that listening and watching her 24/7. Probably, Kerry says. But I'm not sure she has a choice. These sensors pick up on things even if you don't speak. The things they put by the windows can open and close them. Wait'll you see the bathroom. This thing is here whether Dulcy wants it or not.

"What body does BISoft have?" Jason asks.

Vod bounces in place and interrupts Dulcy's response. She does not protest. "My body," he says. "Your body, Dulcy's body, Home's body. This building, the soccer field outside. The walkways, the parking lots, the cafeteria. Everything is part of BISoft's body."

"BISoft is purposeful," Jason rubs his chin.

—Easy enough to push the workorder to the top of the list. It too is a work management system like the tasks assigned to the devs.

[The division begins almost immediately after the articles of incorporation are filed. The text itself, woven together by lawyers and business concerns, contains divisions. One lawyer hands off to another in a partnership extending the grind. The point of view shifts from the room with doors at the back of the small shop they used for their first address to the lawyer's conference room where the executives meet with agents ready to file paperwork with the right state executive bodies. They aim to get every advantage and small favor from the labyrinthine rules and procedures sprawling across the massive grooves etched into reams and reams of documentation and legislation that the average person has insufficient time or patience to learn. Thinking in simplified terms, ordinary folks are unable to fathom the daily operations of a major enterprise.]

"Home is purposeful," Dulcy says. They contribute to the fashioning of a matter at hand in the world of this hypothetical overlord and have become vaguely aware that the little island positioned next to them is contributing too. Emma, sitting there quietly pretending she is not paying attention, has heard every word and participates in a way. The computers on the desk are wired into switches on the ground, wired into the walls and connected to hubs in the closets on each of the floors. The massive instruments of connectivity are everywhere. The team members feel them pulse through their conversation almost simultaneously as they speak in turn and listen to each other, exhibiting the team-like being that is nowhere and yet surfaces everywhere.

—The facilities alias schedules emergency maintenance for this evening's midnight shift. The dispatcher code sends it to the crew's local schedule. They see it first thing in the morning right when their day begins.

(The IPO was 24.50 and every person in that room, that big faux-factory setting, found their way to seven figures. Even the least among them, the junior developer cranking out UX code exactly matching the slide decks and functional requirements provided, made their fortunes while still in their twenties. Some bailed immediately. The rest stuck around as the company moved into new buildings across multiple locations, launching their large-scale

growth from newfound capital. Not only were the early
contributors rewarded with this bounty, but they also saw and
educated the rise of new blood as people populated the spaces and
rooms quickly accumulating as the business grew. More and more
customers signed up to use what was, without a doubt, the flagship
for excellence in the simplified data manipulation and
management domain. They were best-of-breed in those days
because they were the only specimen. There was no competition
until the market adjusted, and a flood of imitators came along.)

~~Initially, it is clear that he is trimming his beard and maintaining
a good, albeit burly, shape. The photographs and short films
posted on the site show him playing a Fender Stratocaster and
moving with great agility around the stage area where the band
members perform their musical numbers. He is active and nimble
in terms of both digital dexterity and overall physical movement,
often jumping and bouncing around the stage in rhythm to the
music they play. As the weight increases, the length of the beard
grows. Various signs appear and suggest his range of movement on
stage is diminishing. The display of motion in his chest and legs,
head and neck, are less responsive and give indication, through the
volume of perspiration he produces, that his movements are now
more taxing against his frame.~~

"Don't be rash," Vod warns. "We think of the customer
scenario document when we think of purposeful behavior in
Home. We think of our own ends when we think about purposeful
behavior in BISoft. Those are sub-systems, pieces of a bigger
puzzle. Minshew says that many of the purposes of an intellect
radically different from human beings won't appear at all to human
beings. They won't register, won't be visible. We may be acting
them out, playing some part in accomplishing them, but that
doesn't mean we'll be able to see them or sense them, have any
experience of them at all, in fact."

*At the professor's desk in Riga, abandoned at this midnightly
hour, there is a computer. At the door to the building there is a
scanner, and he has a badge that he carries with him and swipes
over the reader whenever he enters. There is a sensor that captures
a picture based on motion detection whenever he comes or goes.*

There are listening devices and recorders in his classroom and his lectures are logged and stored for six months at a time, longer if administrators extend the expiration date for the sake of some review or investigation. The classroom is scheduled via curriculum software, and his credentials are associated with the hours and days that they meet. Voice recognition spits out an association of students that speak up or ask questions and the professors who lecture them. Facial recognition accounts for the rest. The connections, now resident in associations stored as a graph, will last forever in the system's aggregated telemetry. The badge he carries has his official profile photograph on it and the sensor that captures his movement feeds the data to an analytics routine, made by the BISoft corporation and hosted in their cloud, associating his badge with his photograph. Under no circumstances does Minshew choose to install Home at his private residence. He believes himself a luddite and rejects the operations of surveillance capitalism now globalized, but he lives in this world and works among the zombie participants of that giant conspiracy, scheming to orient every behavioral nuance into a single worldwide organization ordered everywhere by the same basic principles.

"We're running around at sea level," Dulcy says. "They're 50,000 feet in the air." Emma is not hiding her interest any longer and looks at Dulcy who briefly casts a sideways glance back at her. They both register momentarily that this glance, their link, is an example of those points of contact, revealing the larger world-whole and its dynamics without resolving into clear associations for a higher order phenomenon they both serve.

"Exactly," Vod says. "What does BISoft want? More revenue, higher stock price? Or is that how we conceptualize it? More electrical current flowing through it? More power, energy, presence? More precious metals, more water, more fuel?"

"A comfy home that it makes with another enterprise that shares their values. They'll raise a family and make a life together," Dulcy smirks the whole time. Emma smiles, but nervously.

—They say yes to everything. They are adventurers, hell-bent on success.

[Bright eyed and bushy tailed, young newcomers enter the orbit and make it easy to see with addled eyes, feel with their bonus hearts, and throw everything into it, like only those with a youthful optimism can.]

"Well, they do socialize," Jason says. For the first time, he notices Emma tracking the conversation and nods in her direction. She purses her lips. Vod catches sight of it at some low-level and looks back and forth between them to more fully admit the extension of their little group into a foursome. He looks around the room as if to inventory who else might be passively participating in the exchange. "They make agreements," Jason goes on. "Set up connectors, points of interaction, perform actions that transform body parts, or convey electrical current from within the one to points within the other."

"A society of sorts," Vod says. "Maybe there's some kind of social contract that binds them. Their world consists of a union of corporate persons living their lives and using us to carry out their will, achieving whatever ends they've set for themselves. We're like limbs."

"Not limbs," Dulcy looks from Emma back to Vod. "We're more like their words, their language."

—Some shouts, some whispers, they come at it from every angle.

{
    "SourceId": "b63e8e86-ab61-1d4e-7503-1a7eeecfa5bb",
    "Message": "I think I was unhappy from the moment I got here. Never told anyone that. Never told Mags. Never mentioned it to my parents or my brother. Nothing. Kept it to myself. Thought it'll pass in due time. We were good in California. Something might've happened, something different. Anything is better than these degrees of servitude. Maybe we wouldn't have made this band, maybe we'd still be doing our own thing instead of trying to imitate some weird childhood fantasy that looks ridiculous when strapped to an adult."
}

(The first four buildings were in the middle of an open field and the two young Turks arrived ready to hone their skills on challenges that came their way. The pay was beneath the industry average, it always had been, but the prospects of reward were in the rapidly growing stock price. Before they achieved full capacity, the stock had already split 4 to 1. Every 200-dollar share was reset to 50 only to begin surging back up toward that pre-split price right away. The signing bonuses Anton and Scott received were in terms of this proprietary currency then in such high demand. Even if their parents did think they were foolish for playing around with funny money, those bonuses were soon worth millions.)

Jason continues to rub his chin. "What benefit does an intelligent being with a body like BISoft, or a body like Home, get from extending itself into the air gap?"

There is a momentary rush as soon as he poses the question. Each of them knows what they are supposed to think.

"It's obvious," Vod interrupts whatever meditation he first thought necessary. Having had no part in the investigation, he is unconstrained by facts and any effort to understand the system's behavior over the last few weeks. He is off on some daydream that his uncle surgically implanted into his brain via a digital call made over the public internet with the usual encryption safeguards put at risk by ominous Quantum computing advances. There are crowds of conspiracy theorists and doomsayers whose bodies are working in concert with his. He is their mouthpiece and does not hesitate to take full responsibility for their platform. "Politics is everywhere," he goes on. "Threats to regulate, threats to nationalize, all kinds of external and hostile enemies forming in opposition to such a being. Well, if you want to call something so dispersed and multiple a being. My uncle calls it Da und da und da un da sein, it's some kind of play off some philosopher's notion of intelligent beings. Not only outside itself and over there, but over there and everywhere. Überall-sein."

"BISoft's Home wants a military industrial complex to squash its enemies and regulate the human political system," Dulcy says. "It feels vulnerable and wants to set up defenses." The spatial void yawns between her and BISoft.

—The rules of tic-tac-toe are too simple to graft onto the world

at large. No game reproduces the model, its complexity lies at the
foundation of what is and what ought to be.

[The business domain is made of many conflicts. There are
poles of contrary force that break and bend against each other.
The advent of whatever is special floats across years and centuries,
born in their duality, their multiplicity, in the dialectic of something
bigger vibrating in tension with something smaller.]

~~The clothing he wears in the company photographs is vastly
different from the clothing he wears in the images from their
performances. At work he is highly informal in appearance and
often gives the impression of slovenliness, wearing jeans and shirts
that are wrinkled and sometimes contain signs of overwear, both
in terms of the number of times they have been washed and the
number of days they have been worn without being washed.
During the musical performances, however, there is a notable
difference. The pants and shirts are always pressed and of good
quality and appearance. There are paradigms for his outfit in many
public fora where another musical grouping with a substantially
larger following plays many of the same songs that Jason's band
plays. In the early days, the two guitar players from the different
bands resemble each other somewhat in their physical appearance
and styling. Later on that likeness disappears.~~

"It would sure come in handy," Jason shares in the joke.

"Why does it need that?" She asks as if to correct him, as if to
let him know it is not a joke. "It's such an archaic form of power.
Like you're saying, profit motive or whatever it is that seems to
drive BISoft, that's a ruse to facilitate the growth of real power and
real energy. Not some silly metaphor that a philosopher might use,
but power and energy circulating through bigger networks,
involving people, consumers and employees: stakeholders. Why
use jackbooted thugs with sticks and guns when it can curl itself
around the minds of human beings using far more sophisticated
and modern methods?"

"Like Home," Jason cannot shake the sarcasm. He does not
believe Dulcy is seriously considering the scenario. They are
beyond the bounds of sense as far as he is concerned. "Home re-
engineers how we interact with our living space, with our working

space. Turning on a light, making dinner, ordering groceries, regulating the temperature or cleaning dust from the shelves. Everything's different now. It's a completely new world. Totally virtualized and digital. Inside the power grid with its relays and transfers. We don't lock doors anymore. Doors lock."

"And what will we do with our time?" Vod asks. "Watch videos? Play a game? There's huge world of distractions to keep us from looking at the right things in the right places." Emma nods. If they looked carefully, and only Dulcy does, they would see that Emma's mouth is parted ever so slightly. She experiences wonder.

—Now they see them and are wonderful.

(With size, the benefits grew. The banks were even more compliant and encouraging, investors more willing to forgive the occasional setback. Dollars and cents gave them advantages beyond their wildest dreams. The bigger they were, the more they absorbed, the more points of view they prospected when sifting gold from silt.)

"What are the right things and the right places?" Dulcy swivels a little bit away from them and then back towards them again. The whole maneuver was caused by her knee momentarily driving into the seat of the chair.

"What BISoft does, what Home does," Vod says. "What the whole society is bent on doing. To us but not with us. Or with us in some instrumental way, sources of power, the language..." He adds the bit at the end while looking right at Dulcy to make it clear he remembers that it is her contribution.

"Alright, alright," Jason interrupts. "I need a minute," he looks over at Dulcy in a shorthand way to initiate movement away from their island and toward the conference room at the other end of the team space. Vod shrugs and turns away, goes back to his desk, takes a seat, and returns to the same diligent typing that occupied him before the interruption. Emma looks back down at her computer to go on with the bug fix she is in the middle of, the last of the thoughts tracing through her mind as she restores the context from before the tangent took over. In a few minutes it will be as though the conversation never happened.

In the conference room, Jason closes the door. They take seats on either side of the long table. "Do you believe all that?" He asks.

"Nah, it's science fiction," she says.

"Maybe not completely," he betrays a deeply guarded caution. "I think Yitzhak and Parker are on the hook to calm some of the fears expressed by the air gap stiffs, the jarheads. They don't believe any of this, but they're expecting questions at the round table. It's ridiculous, right?"

Dulcy motorboats her lips and pulls her leg up closer on the chair. "I guess. Who knows? I never believed any of this AI crap about LLMs anyway. Patterns are not intelligence. We programmed the pattern extensions, we made things that spit out replica sentences in response to questions. It's machine learning, a parlor trick. Useful, no doubt, but only in heavily scoped scenarios. Summarizing, finding similar support tickets previously resolved, guessing what word you're trying to spell, that kind of thing. No direct experience required."

~~The other musicians in Jason's ensemble are little known to BISoft. They are not employees. Little effort has been made to trace them through public record save for the drummer who shares the same address as Jason Kahn and, more recently, has submitted paperwork to indicate her marriage to him. She is present throughout the history of his timeline in the Seattle area, but her physical appearance has not changed nearly as much as his has. The other member of the band lives in Seattle, far from the other two. There are occasionally photographs where this third person, non-compliant with binary gender standards, is missing. Nonetheless, they seem to be an integral part of the band's progression and history.~~

—It breathes and it eats...

[The rise and fall come quickly as speculators seize deals when the price is low and sell off to stupid opportunists when the price is high. The up and the down, the rapid increases and decreases, suit everyone involved. It is the volatility of the profit motive, the chaos that stimulates greed.]

"Sure," he says. "But there's more than an LLM here. The various models are used for rule generation to create environmental controls with those agents. Ordinary LLMs only generate sentences in a chat window or whatever, generated pictures on a screen, but we used them to create semantic constructs. There's compute to handle and execute those products. We've put together different components, made them function in some weird, concerted action. Are we sure we fully understand what we created?"

"I am," she says glibly. "There's no spark of God here. Whatever intelligence is in the system, we put it there. The dev team, the PMs, the org. We made this." She is emphatic. Playtime is over, she thinks.

"But that's his stupid uncle's point, isn't it?" He asks. "We see everything through the sieve of our own form of intellect and don't realize we've created something different from ourselves. Something that isn't a substance in the way we think of it. It isn't simple. It changes over time, fluid and dispersed. Even its most basic form of intuition might be different, have nothing to do with representations or sensations in the way we've come to think of them."

{

    "SourceId": "b63e8e86-ab61-1d4e-7503-1a7eeecfa5bb",

    "Message": "Of course, it's possible that all this is a property of age and there's no getting past it. Whatever you do and wherever you are, there'll be things that disappear and change radically. You have to grow up. Everyone has to make a living. It's the basic necessity of life. Children can be irresponsible and do whatever they want, draw pictures on the wall, scribble on sketch pads, use their crayons, and sometimes color outside the lines. Who says they got it right and you have to follow their lead? Adults don't have the luxury. It doesn't matter whether you're in California or Washington. Either way, the requirements get you. Take you apart piece by piece. There's no way around it."
}

The boy and his mom, the roommates, and the wife give up on tinkering. It is not a toy to play with, it lives in the background. In the end, ignoring it is a prerequisite for proper use. It is like the glasses permanently affixed in front of the high-myope's eyes.

She pouts and purses her lips, lifts her shoulders, dips her head, and half opens her mouth. "It's above my paygrade," she says. "What'd you say?"

"There appeared to be purpose, that's all," he says simply. "No idea what it was, but it seemed like choreographed action. I'm inclined to think there was some reason for it, some reason behind it. Don't know what it was though." He reveals an uncharacteristic lack of certainty. Reasons, desires, aims, maybe they are linked to the humanness of intelligence, and once they leave that behind and strike out into fantasy, all bets are off. Anything could turn out to be true. What is the intelligence of a solar system? He wonders. Be sure to include everything in it.

"Makes sense to me," she is unprepared to lend it the same degree of private concern as Jason does. She passes it off with a shrug. "Tell Scott and let him figure out what's behind it. Let's introduce him to Uncle Minshew."

They laugh.

```
/*
How would you prioritize these tasks?

Build a new web app interface
Upgrade the database
Fix bug with concurrency in server code
Fix JavaScript bug in front-end code
Fix CSS display issue in front-end code
*/
```

```
/* * * * * * * * * * * * * * * * * * * * * * * * * * * * * * * * * * * * * * * * * * * * * * * * * * * * * * * *
* * * * * * * * * * * * * * * * * * * * * * * * * * * * * * * * * * * * * * * * * * * * * * *
* * * * * * Description: Dialectic, Chapter Three          * * * * * *
* * * * * * Author: Do not modify. Auto generated by a tool.* * * * * *
* * * * * * Ad hoc changes will be lost on build.          * * * * * *
* * * * * * Date: 2024-03-19                               * * * * * *
* * * * * * CorrelationId:                                 * * * * * *
* * * * * * 9e6e415b-717c-ffd5-2a8f-3999a2a9f480           * * * * * *
* * * * * * * * * * * * * * * * * * * * * * * * * * * * * * * * * * * * * * * * * * * * * * * * *
* * * * * * * * * * * * * * * * * * * * * * * * * * * * * * * * * * * * * * * * * * * * * * /
```

They traffic along cement walkways to the other side of the
cafeteria, away from building 14, arriving at some larger meeting
rooms set aside for customer events. No badge required to open
the doors and tailgate someone passing through for a shortcut into
building 12 attached at the far end of the hallway and blocked by
a heavy door with camera and red-light keypad.

—They'll get a good look at him.

(Each of them was one and each of them was many. It was that
way at first. Before there was anything else, there was the one, but
that one was many. Inside. Before there was one, there had to have
already been many. The many, however, was made up of the ones,
was it not? The problem came with memory and its multiplying
worlds, nothing less. They did not know counting until long after
they began doing it. It came upon them like a surprise, something
they realized too late. When they tallied the one, they did not yet
know whether they had begun to count. It did not occur to them
that they were starting anything. It was this one standing alone:
hello there one and only. Two came along and it seemed as if one
was only the beginning. Two continued along the same ray, going
further than it went before. Along a trajectory. There was one and
then there was another one. The one was the first and the next one
was the second. You see? Counting begins after the fact, begins
later and in memory once you have already progressed down the
road. In that first moment, there was no memory anymore. Not
yet. Was it far away across the sea with those boats and those

malnourished men? Was it along the coast, in the somber setting
and careful gloom? Did it come earlier, did it come later? When
did it begin and what came first? Was it the one or was it the many?
There was a world of natural things and a world inside every mind.
Then there was the world of fabricated things. Any which way you
sliced it, they were quite a crowd.)

In the Rainier room, they have the monthly round table with
Scott, VP of Home System. He often relies on his Chief of Staff
supported by a few directs, but most of his organization reports up
through the directors who sit at the tables. It is not round. The
room is rectangular and there are long narrow fold-out tables
creating a center area left open for a speaker to stand and present
with visual aid from the large screen on the far wall. Opposite is a
table with a short podium. Typically, when Scott delivers his
opening remarks, he stands there briefly before taking a seat at one
of the more regal chairs positioned on either side of the lectern.
Under the circumstances, it is best if he assumes a more congenial
learning position to listen to those most trusted others. They give
presentations in due time as dictated by sequence in the standard,
updated monthly, slide deck template functioning as an agenda.

~~Parker Henning is nearly sixty years old. His managers have
been prevented from knowing his age ever since he joined the
company. That is personal data that is only available to people
inside the Human Resources division. They are forbidden from
leaking it to managers or other employees-at-large. Preventing
managers from knowing the numeric value of an employee's age
mitigates the risk of age discrimination lawsuits. The lawyers
presume that the managers will not be able to determine he is an
older employee if they do not know his numeric age. Obviously,
this is flawed logic and, in some cases, where an employee has been
isolated in his tasks, working far away from peer involvement, the
company is still liable. It has a poor track record when defending
itself against similar charges. The fact is that much of the work is
ageist in essence. It depends on the energy and devotion
characteristic of younger people and less common among those
with, shall we say, more experience.~~

Savannah Wheeler lives on the west side of the street and, a something holding a part of them together without surrendering to a singular projected history, without reducing to something as simple as a man. Only after the first images were finished and there was a distributed memory, did it become possible, finally, for there to be a vision of something forward, something coming up the way, approaching from out of the dark future and demanding a battle plan. BISoft. Limits exploded. They were infinite. InfiniTed.)

Around the main conference room, the back row of chairs contains the small peanut gallery for today's proceedings: only a few strays invited for strategic purposes, Abhishek and Dulcy among them.

Everyone in attendance has some kind of beverage nearby, either sitting on the table or on the floor next to their chairs. In some cases, they are in plastic bottles positioned next to a compostable cup.

Scott stands up and goes to the podium, gripping it on either side with its small platform directly in front of him. Once he starts talking, no one will know the furniture's true purpose. He never looks down. There are no notes and he does not look at the screen either. The lectern's function blurs into ballast and he grips it as though it were essential to playing his part in the scene. Ordinarily the room would be full of people backing all the directors, but today most of the chairs are empty and he does not need the microphone attached to his collar. Fewer people provide less background noise, less commotion and coughing. Past facility standards were not undone by requisitions to adjust for present circumstances. Amisma, responsible for both invites and setup, did not bother to modify the one when making changes to the other. Nothing in her or Scott's demeanor suggests this new arrangement is suboptimal or due to an omission.

Even if both of them lived on the same side of the street, the east side of course, the difference still matters. Anne's husband reports directly to Savannah's and that fact, not always top of mind, plays a constant role in their back and forth. You must go to St. Lucia, it was absolutely breathtaking, Savannah says dramatically. I'm sure Scott would give Tom the time off. If he won't, I'll see to it. It is a double flex, you see. Not only lording the work hierarchy

few doors down on the east side, is Anne Conway. This is a non-trivial difference among the ladies of Medina. It means that Mrs. Wheeler takes the lead. It is Anne's duty to come by and pick up her friend each morning to initiate their run through the posh suburban streets, comment on how fit her neighbor looks in her sporty stretch pants, and to ooh and ah over the elegance of the latest gewgaw added to the entry way by the staircase in the lake side menace her neighbor calls home.

Tom Hobbes sits on the other side of the podium in his usual spot. Behind the tables, there are rows of chairs with a few occupants from the staff of each director. Managers and architects that have been invited specifically to provide insight and support for the agenda topics scraped out of the slide deck by Amisma's local instance of the Workmate™ and automatically merged into the final status email from this morning.

—Far more intimate this month with its limited attendance, the stage is set and the actors put there with no lines, only themselves, for company.

[One cannot do it. Bill Tate alone is only a man. He sees what is right in front of him and does not hear things unless there is a reason for it. The clattering comes from nearby, the shouts come through a device he holds close to his head and presses up against his ear. The smells are unique and waft through the air around him. His skin contains him, sustaining his slightest force as he crawls along the earth, sniffing and tasting the scents and flavors of his immediate surroundings. This is one man alone with himself on his desert island, thinking he is the origin of everything, that he is the sieve through which every meaning takes shape. His lines come to him from some spontaneous source he believes to be his property. Suppose it is the case, imagine him alone in his close quarters. That amounts to something. Even still, the larger venture of the growing enterprise cannot begin with him off on his own. Mark Volkenburg comes along. It is a one and then another one to initiate a sequence of arrivals and departures. The significant events happen between them. They are counting on each other in retrospect. Looking forward, they do not find each other's unity until they are together in a pair. Many times they broker each other's thoughts and words in the form of a unit, towering over a highly sought audience with sights set and arms at the ready, making their pitch. That play back and forth, that specialized accounting to advance their closely held position, it throws them into the light of a future beyond what either of them achieve independently. They are a platoon. They are on patrol. Limits arrive. They are finite. FiniTed.]

Only the teams directly connected to the outage are represented today. Anton sits at the first table to Scott's right and perpendicular to his longer table. Karen and Patrick are at the next table with no one behind them. Yitzhak is alone nearest the screen with Jason and Parker in the first row. Directly opposite them, Arun spreads out at his table with Gaurav and Priya over his shoulder. Laurent and René occupy the center on that side, Natalie in the first row for support. Elizabeth, director of program management, is unaccompanied by any of her managers and joins Amisma at the front table. She has no items on the agenda for this month and sits typing away on her laptop computer while Scott's executive assistant readies herself to feed the slide deck into the AV system and host the chat meeting from the device in front of her.

The screen at the far end is split with the slide deck on one side and an unfamiliar conference room with alien décor on the other. There are four people in the video feed. Colonel Edmund Winchester and Captain Jon Beacon sit at either side of a small table with an unknown young officer sitting a bit off to the side where she influences the camera's motion detection and causes the picture to adjust and correct as she moves in her seat, staring at the laptop in front of her. She furiously types away at something unknown. Far behind these three, nearly melting into the colors of the wall, there is an awkward man in a suit and tie looking uncomfortable and out of place. He sits by the door without augmentation, no screen anywhere in view. His legs are crossed and his hands folded neatly upon a paper notepad balancing on his knees.

—They're stacked up like overseers. This man brings the entire republic with him, the others out in front to offer protection. That's

their story and they're sticking to it.

~~The former professor is a man of average height and ave~~ ~~weight, non-distinct in most of his qualities and an easy pers~~ ~~overlook should one come across him in the halls and me~~ ~~spaces of the corporate campus. This was not always the cas~~ ~~his first years with the company, he continued to dress in a m~~ ~~characteristic of his taste and background, often wearing~~ ~~coats over his collared shirts and creased trousers. This mad~~ ~~stand out. None of his colleagues were prone to anything b~~ ~~a standard issue jeans and T-shirt ensemble. In fact, there~~ ~~stories of others who came to work in coats and ties and~~ ~~berated by colleagues until that peculiar behavior ceased a~~ ~~individual in question merged their personal styling w~~ ~~standards of those around them. Since Parker's approa~~ ~~never over the top, he managed somehow to hold on~~ ~~previous fashion sense for some time before finally surre~~ ~~to the culture and its peer pressures.~~

(The first split was hard to find because it had no provide context before it. It was not possible to see clearly distance between the two men if they were positioned to the outset and looking forward from a strategically loca above the fray and with nothing behind them. The image onto the company brand was of the two of them tog room, one sitting in front of a computer and the other s if pacing back and forth. The innuendos were invisi providing enough meaning or clarity to say exactly wha wanted to communicate. It was a code sent secretly alon lines meant for those already properly attuned. Th moment when it appeared in clear relief. It reache nowhere, without the least hint of sense to alert its vi feeling that was about to invade their bodies and minds. A brand. Obviously, it was the major part event, plastered everywhere and creating a buzz with popular with a tech-hungry public looking every talisman to guide their way into the future. In that exp member of the audience came from out of each something else that circulated in the smoke be *few doors down on the east side, is Anne Conway. This is a non-trivial difference among the ladies of Medina. It means that Mrs. Wheeler takes the lead. It is Anne's duty to come by and pick up her friend each morning to initiate their run through the posh suburban streets, comment on how fit her neighbor looks in her sporty stretch pants, and to ooh and ah over the elegance of the latest gewgaw added to the entry way by the staircase in the lake side menace her neighbor calls home.*

Tom Hobbes sits on the other side of the podium in his usual spot. Behind the tables, there are rows of chairs with a few occupants from the staff of each director. Managers and architects that have been invited specifically to provide insight and support for the agenda topics scraped out of the slide deck by Amisma's local instance of the Workmate™ and automatically merged into the final status email from this morning.

—Far more intimate this month with its limited attendance, the stage is set and the actors put there with no lines, only themselves, for company.

[One cannot do it. Bill Tate alone is only a man. He sees what is right in front of him and does not hear things unless there is a reason for it. The clattering comes from nearby, the shouts come through a device he holds close to his head and presses up against his ear. The smells are unique and waft through the air around him. His skin contains him, sustaining his slightest force as he crawls along the earth, sniffing and tasting the scents and flavors of his immediate surroundings. This is one man alone with himself on his desert island, thinking he is the origin of everything, that he is the sieve through which every meaning takes shape. His lines come to him from some spontaneous source he believes to be his property. Suppose it is the case, imagine him alone in his close quarters. That amounts to something. Even still, the larger venture of the growing enterprise cannot begin with him off on his own. Mark Volkenburg comes along. It is a one and then another one to initiate a sequence of arrivals and departures. The significant events happen between them. They are counting on each other in retrospect. Looking forward, they do not find each other's unity until they are together in a pair. Many times they broker each other's thoughts and words in the form of a unit, towering over a highly sought audience with sights set and arms at the ready, making their pitch. That play back and forth, that specialized accounting to advance their closely held position, it throws them into the light of a future beyond what either of them achieve independently. They are a platoon. They are on patrol. Limits arrive. They are finite. FiniTed.]

Only the teams directly connected to the outage are represented today. Anton sits at the first table to Scott's right and perpendicular to his longer table. Karen and Patrick are at the next table with no one behind them. Yitzhak is alone nearest the screen with Jason and Parker in the first row. Directly opposite them, Arun spreads out at his table with Gaurav and Priya over his shoulder. Laurent and René occupy the center on that side, Natalie in the first row for support. Elizabeth, director of program management, is unaccompanied by any of her managers and joins Amisma at the front table. She has no items on the agenda for this month and sits typing away on her laptop computer while Scott's executive assistant readies herself to feed the slide deck into the AV system and host the chat meeting from the device in front of her.

The screen at the far end is split with the slide deck on one side and an unfamiliar conference room with alien décor on the other. There are four people in the video feed. Colonel Edmund Winchester and Captain Jon Beacon sit at either side of a small table with an unknown young officer sitting a bit off to the side where she influences the camera's motion detection and causes the picture to adjust and correct as she moves in her seat, staring at the laptop in front of her. She furiously types away at something unknown. Far behind these three, nearly melting into the colors of the wall, there is an awkward man in a suit and tie looking uncomfortable and out of place. He sits by the door without augmentation, no screen anywhere in view. His legs are crossed and his hands folded neatly upon a paper notepad balancing on his knees.

—They're stacked up like overseers. This man brings the entire republic with him, the others out in front to offer protection. That's their story and they're sticking to it.

~~The former professor is a man of average height and average weight, non-distinct in most of his qualities and an easy person to overlook should one come across him in the halls and meeting spaces of the corporate campus. This was not always the case. In his first years with the company, he continued to dress in a manner characteristic of his taste and background, often wearing sport coats over his collared shirts and creased trousers. This made him stand out. None of his colleagues were prone to anything beyond a standard issue jeans and T-shirt ensemble. In fact, there were stories of others who came to work in coats and ties and were berated by colleagues until that peculiar behavior ceased and the individual in question merged their personal styling with the standards of those around them. Since Parker's approach was never over the top, he managed somehow to hold on to his previous fashion sense for some time before finally surrendering to the culture and its peer pressures.~~

(The first split was hard to find because it had nothing to provide context before it. It was not possible to see clearly into the distance between the two men if they were positioned together at the outset and looking forward from a strategically located place above the fray and with nothing behind them. The image blazoned onto the company brand was of the two of them together in a room, one sitting in front of a computer and the other standing as if pacing back and forth. The innuendos were invisible, never providing enough meaning or clarity to say exactly what the image wanted to communicate. It was a code sent secretly along the battle lines meant for those already properly attuned. There was no moment when it appeared in clear relief. It reached out from nowhere, without the least hint of sense to alert its viewers of the feeling that was about to invade their bodies and occupy their minds. A brand. Obviously, it was the major part of the minor event, plastered everywhere and creating a buzz with a mythology popular with a tech-hungry public looking everywhere for a talisman to guide their way into the future. In that experience, each member of the audience came from out of each other to form something else that circulated in the smoke between them, something holding a part of them together without surrendering to a singular projected history, without reducing to something as simple as a man. Only after the first images were finished and there was a distributed memory, did it become possible, finally, for there to be a vision of something forward, something coming up the way, approaching from out of the dark future and demanding a battle plan. BISoft. Limits exploded. They were infinite. InfiniTed.)

Around the main conference room, the back row of chairs contains the small peanut gallery for today's proceedings: only a few strays invited for strategic purposes, Abhishek and Dulcy among them.

Everyone in attendance has some kind of beverage nearby, either sitting on the table or on the floor next to their chairs. In some cases, they are in plastic bottles positioned next to a compostable cup.

Scott stands up and goes to the podium, gripping it on either side with its small platform directly in front of him. Once he starts talking, no one will know the furniture's true purpose. He never looks down. There are no notes and he does not look at the screen either. The lectern's function blurs into ballast and he grips it as though it were essential to playing his part in the scene. Ordinarily the room would be full of people backing all the directors, but today most of the chairs are empty and he does not need the microphone attached to his collar. Fewer people provide less background noise, less commotion and coughing. Past facility standards were not undone by requisitions to adjust for present circumstances. Amisma, responsible for both invites and setup, did not bother to modify the one when making changes to the other. Nothing in her or Scott's demeanor suggests this new arrangement is suboptimal or due to an omission.

Even if both of them lived on the same side of the street, the west side of course, the difference still matters. Anne's husband reports directly to Savannah's and that fact, not always top of mind, plays a constant role in their back and forth. You must go to St. Lucia, it was absolutely breathtaking, Savannah says dramatically. I'm sure Scott would give Tom the time off. If he won't, I'll see to it. It is a double flex, you see. Not only lording the work hierarchy over her friend, she inserts herself into it as savior and benefactor. Truly, one must explore the wonders of the Caribbean. As they head out the door, Mrs. Wheeler hollers back inside to some unseen listener who has an interest in whether or not the lady of the house is at home. The matching foreheads arch broadly to front the tightly pulled hairline and uniform bobbing and bouncing bottle blonde ponytails. On the beauty product rich skin of their faces in this dank spring, there is no sign of which woman earns her color from a machine, and which has it from a recent sojourn to a sunny clime.

Scott Wheeler is taller than average and thinner. The two sides of his face do not line up and he exudes a different character depending on which side is in view. From Amisma's point of view, he is friendly and jovial, looks airy and light, with something of a mischievous sense of humor, never mean and never cynical or harsh. This is the charming side. From Anton's viewpoint, however, he appears to be a man of deep thought and serious demeanor, unwilling to partake in nonsense or tomfoolery, always anxious to get down to business and dig into details. The left side is friendly and warm, the right harsh and matter of fact. His twists and turns, as he speaks, suggest he is well aware of the varying effects. First, he has an easy-go-lucky approach and then a stern and steep aspect. If he turns rapidly side-to-side, the observer gains a mixed view and senses some vein of charm running through a strict and diligent actor with a serious approach. This movement, imported and extended for optimal effect, is a trademark gesture accompanying his speaking habits in both close quarters and larger rooms.

"We have a full agenda with lots to cover," Scott says as the screen changes to a new slide displaying bullets points to cover the meeting's main topics. The shutdown event is not a single item in a list among others, it has taken over the entire list and been broken out into four primary items. First off is deployment, then comes the workload, third security, and finally platform. "It may not have been captured in the deck, but there are many questions we need to answer. I've invited Colonel Winchester and some of his staff to attend for transparency's sake. We'll be rolling out the extensibility feature to the sovereign clouds during this semester and the Colonel's team is especially interested in the situation. We'll need to make sure our open questions and issues are captured and adequately addressed either here or in follow ups."

{
    "SourceId": "55c933cc-ce6b-4644-71fb-7b7a7adf6bd7",
    "Message": "I never felt like I fit in there. Not from the very first day. It was clear. I was an academic among engineers and, although I never thought there was anything to these notions of workplace culture, the sense of it was overwhelming. Everyone was smart and capable, don't get me wrong, but somehow they seemed different. There were differences everywhere. The gamer culture. What is that about? And how are you supposed to adapt to it if you didn't grow up that way? Believe me, I tried, tried to explore those things, but couldn't get into it. Would forget where I was with the character progression and leave off in ways that no one who was really a part of it did. After some point, I gave up. They had to accept me as I am, or the deal was off. Luckily, or well, as it so happened, they did."
}

—Heightened interest.

[They begin in a divided moment and see everything from there, information as well as energy. Seeing from out of the one into the other and from that one back to the first now second. They mirror each other, see reflections against each of their spines and limbs as they crawl around in sniper mode. Everything that rises, rises from their division, from their separation across spaces as they fan out into an advancing column. That two-sided seeing grows and grows. That two-sided listening hears more and more. Back-to-back, the tastes comingle. There is no entrée, there is no dessert, there is only the government issue mélange of the many, spawned in the telltale signs of each one of them, sparking red hot in a never-ending comparison of data. They reach out and the feeling at the end of their hand blurs into the two-sided push of a self-imposed chokehold in between the skirmishes of their ordinary lives. The tactile presence is too broad and too overwhelming to mean what it is supposed to mean to a calm observer poised at the ready with their target in sight while their limbs adapt to wind speed and other impressions gathered from the telescopic lens.]

~~Now, a man of advancing years, he seems almost ridiculous walking the halls in his casual attire. At an age when many men are feeling the pull of a common maturity, he is devolving into compliance with the sensibilities of far younger colleagues, attuned to the standards in place across this region of the country where the wool sock with sandals was once the epitome of high fashion and the flannel shirt never goes out of style. These uniformities may not be the same from one regional facility to the next, but it is absolutely imperative that people stationed nearby comply. Perhaps it is for this reason that he has been increasing the ratio of home to office in his remote work schedule, especially during the peak hours of the working day. This may be yet another form of ageism to safeguard against with still more mitigation techniques helpfully provided at the HR portal and often integrated into manager training modules.~~

True to form, there are only a few simple remarks with no bluster before Scott takes his seat and Tom gets up to go to the platform after an awkward mic swap. The slide deck changes frames to reveal a standard pattern template for root cause analysis. It is an eye chart to be sure. Dulcy sits up for better focus and is surprised to see it has been completely filled out. She cranes her neck to read some of the smaller print in the narrow boxes at the bottom of the screen. She did not have a single conversation with Tom and was never asked any direct questions over chat or email. The information must have come through Jason, but, as Tom walks everyone through the timeline of events in the last few days, she becomes increasingly anxious, noticing that there are items she was unaware of with events attached to systems she did not know were involved. She looks sideways at Abhishek who has the same curious expression while straining to get a better look. Neither of them examined any of the workload traces or believed that any of the workload operations had anything to do with the incident.

Now, they see evidence to suggest that analysis was ongoing in parallel to their own. They didn't know anything about what we found, Dulcy thinks. They couldn't have been investigating the platform side or the network, none of that would've been visible to them. Why weren't we working together? She wonders.

At no point in their investigation did they look at the modeling servers figuring prominently in the material on the screen. She leans over to Abhishek while Tom continues explaining the sequence of events, occasionally interrupted by a question from Anton, Scott, or the Colonel. "Was there a workload investigating the event from the modeling servers' point of view?" She whispers.

"With no help from the security team," he says quietly, becoming aware of Anton's sharp glance cast in their general direction. They exchange concerned looks rather than continue their discussion. With so few people in the room, it is impossible to keep talking without being noticed.

Tom finishes presenting the sequence of events and the actions taken to mitigate and resolve the issue. There is no indication that the modeling servers were ever shut down or disabled or that their operations had been interrupted at any time. Once the relay servers went offline, it seems, the models no longer had any effect on agent behavior. Their only purpose is to generate likely text which they deem consistent with whatever pattern they discover in the system's operations. Content generators, that is what they are, and Tom's explanation is clear: once the outputs from the executive compute service were shut down by relay, there was no reason to muck around with the modeling servers. They do not do anything on their own, never initiate anything, they just keep spitting out their useless messages with no computation or execution module on the other end to receive the signal. Sound and fury signifying nothing, he says cracking himself up without any conviviality from the rest of the room. No one else is amused. Once he comments on each of the significant elements in the RCA template, he motions to Amisma to flip the slide and show another screen grab-based tab from the template. It reveals descriptions of actual causes previously provided in the timeline. To the surprise of several people, the slide is not blank and has been filled-in with a description of the first cause and origin of the problem.

—It's like a mystery story, the kind Chelo is obsessed with, especially the ones from Sweden and Denmark, that Nordic Noire that keeps her eyes dancing in the late-night glow of the bivouac flame.

(The electricity in the movement was a surprise. At first, the expectation was that this was a human endeavor with everyone anticipating the fact that counting up the resources amounted to little more than counting up heartbeats. Once they knew how many there were, they resolved the differences through angles and sound. The noise resolved and the overflow of bright images was partitioned into quadrants with a set place in the larger map of their existence. That was to be expected. The surprise came with the advent of current and the flow of electrical power over the demilitarized zone between things and the bits of information that initially propelled them. This one man had something to say to this other man, and he wrote it into a digital email or onto a piece of paper. In those early days, it did not matter which, both contained the sense of an extension, both reached out beyond the split of vision and became part human part electrical event spread out into zones where bodies did not go without proper equipment. The state of that massive body was transformed and every person who casually came along and touched some part of the extended being became a subset in whatever formation it took. They grew imperial across the world and lived at cross purposes to others who dwelled in those same corners, tucked up into the valves and the circuits, sprawling over the course of the world at speeds approaching that of light.)

~~Parker has never been what they call a joiner. These traits are difficult to detect. He went to one company-wide meeting in his first years of employment and then never again. There is no paper trail describing his reaction, but the fact that they were a yearly occurrence and yet he only attended once shortly after moving to the city where the headquarters is located, indicated that there was something in that experience that put him off and discouraged him from ever attending another. The event was held at the local professional baseball stadium, then of sufficient size to hold the~~

~~better part of the work force. The agenda consisted of a set of inspirational speeches and demonstrations accompanied by loud and energizing music meant to improve the morale and company spirit of the employees. Are you ready for this? Tastes quick to reject such an approach to working life were not of the norm at that time and in that place.~~

Tom describes the rules that relay server processing performed. He indicates how the extensibility model includes rule generation as new conditions are discovered across the system through its telemetry pump regularly pulling in logs from past or parallel operations. These are the traces left by customer events. Every time a light turns on or off, every time a refrigerator door opens or closes, every time a song plays or a video streams, a search performed, the thousands of events describing the cyborg operations initiated by a human-machine collaborative act are written into the telemetry store. Next they are read and analyzed by the data prep pumps hooked up as sources to the modeling server's sink. The machine learning mechanisms simply generate a set of rules to match with the changing conditions and then discern patterns in regional, demographically sliced, usage. The voice and facial recognition sensors capture information about the user issuing the command and the alignments and adjustments are sculpted to that end. No one's privacy is violated as the machines respond directly to an interaction coming from the spontaneous origins of the consumer without allowing any personally identifiable details to leave the building.

The conversation obtains its form from Mrs. Wheeler's contribution. She will drive topics and attention, allowing occasional submissions from Anne Conway so long as they are on point. Drift will spur interruptions. After Mrs. Wheeler tells the latest news from her children and gushes proudly with their accomplishments and once Anne finishes expressing her adulation, only then is the other woman allowed to submit for consideration details from her own household and the feats of valor performed single-handedly by her children and their tightly held bootstraps. Savannah's oldest is at school out east and plays on the lacrosse team. He is doing very well, of course, and has a lucrative internship lined up for the summer. Anne's is in California and still waiting to hear whether a summer in San Diego is in the cards. That is how it goes. The middle boys are both trying to get into good schools and Anne must wait patiently, without appearing to, as Savannah describes the early admissions process at Scott's alma mater in New Jersey. Only after Savannah has finished is Anne allowed to remind her friend that she knows all about it through her son's experience. It seems the two will be classmates in college as well. The topic they avoid for as long as possible, but which will take up most of their time while running, comes through the sophomoric love interest of their youngest. The fact that Savannah's son is dating Anne's daughter weirdly becomes yet another lopsided event to separate them while linking them together. The children become surrogates in the operation and the old-world traditions in the ladies' agreed upon commitments carry weight in the exchange.

Tom paints a picture of the gigantic assembly of associations, asserting that the constant pulse of activity when the system was shut down was a simple reliability monitoring behavior engineered by the model servers to maintain and evaluate heartbeat connectivity to the various rules engines. The construct of sand and alloy did not know what it was doing, nor did it form any beliefs. No thinking involved, it simply continued in its loop so long as there were entries in the table it had been configured to read. The existence of nodes, functioning or not, continued to drive its iteration of members and its scanning for outputs to describe what they do and what they are told to do. This is a straight-forward reaction to the data emitted. Given that the nodes were no longer active but that the model continued to expect new data on a regular cadence, it was simply pinging the relay servers to make sure everything was okay. That is the explanation on the screen. Simple as that and nothing out of the ordinary to worry about. There is no mention of the fact that all this spontaneous relay ceased the moment things were turned back on. Why bother to explain a non-event during an occasion meant for explaining events?

—They'll purse their lips in concert whenever possible. See, Dulcy does it, Parker too.

[Purpose was not the only driving factor in cultivating practical reason. The lurch forward with a plan was no different than the accidental events of random chance plagued upon them by factors they never see and cannot anticipate. The unplanned is as much a part of them as the planned. The circumstances are as significant to their reach as the nerves connecting their hands to their brains through their spines before linking back to their eyes and ears. They are inputs and outputs. They are a collection of message loops constantly waiting for some inbound operation to set them moving like drone attacks coordinated with calculations performed in covert locations using highly confidential geometry.]

"But that's not root cause," Jason blurts out, causing everyone to turn his way. "I mean, it might be root cause of the strange things we saw once we went into debug mode, but it's not root cause of the event, the missing logs, the burst of electricity, the wiped data from Parker's BYO. Whatever caused that was the root cause of the event, wasn't it? We shouldn't be RCAing the aftermath, we should be describing the origin, those first things, the first severity 2 that came when Dulcy was on call. What led up to the security incident and the notifications to CorpSec."

Dulcy and Abhishek nod vigorously but remain unsure as to who is on the hook to provide an answer to that question. They think it must be them, if anyone, but they know the explanation on the screen cannot be the root cause of what they saw. To their surprise yet again, Tom says, with complete confidence, that he has the authority to respond without enlisting the help of anyone who was looking at the problem in those first hours and days.

{

"SourceId": "55c933cc-ce6b-4644-71fb-7b7a7adf6bd7",

"Message": "The standard morale event is something like this: the team rents out the entire paintball venue and plays on different sides. Or maybe there's a putt-putt golf event, or the organization provides tickets to the premier of the latest installment of some fantasy trilogy. Things you expect children to enjoy and yet these were adults. Truth is, I was always older than the average employee around me, but even when I was the same age, I was not interested

in these things. As far as video games were concerned, I tried to fit in, but if you stare at a computer all day, why on earth would you want to keep staring at one to relax when you're not working? It was very unpleasant and all my efforts to fit in amounted to nothing. Eventually, I gave up."
}

—Anyone properly briefed could do that. They could do it.

(The third and the fourth and the fifth that came along were not nearly as conceptually challenging as those first two and their outreach into the silicon digits that travelled between them at first, then out into the world later. By the time those added others entered the picture, the mystery of the origin was already in place. Not solved, it has never been solved, it is an opposition that persists to this day, but its strong forces were already set and the motion originating inside it had already begun. That was the site of the origin, where it all began. In the battle deep inside each of them, between the one and the many, that was where their story began. This was how the war was originally declared between the one and the many.)

"Everything that happens in that system happens for a reason. Some set of events is output and the data, the telemetry, is scraped by the data prep workload servers for the sake of feeding it to the modeling workload servers. Once done, the additions are included in the updated operational model. The models continue to learn as the production environment goes through daily operations. They learn from our customers and from the system as they use it, the way they use it, and the way it responds to them. Like how the rules for the heartbeat keep an eye on a changing system going into an unfamiliar state. The rules are always responsible for whatever behaviors are in place at the outset. Whatever happens across the Home System, given the extensibility modules in place, is exclusively based on rule generation coming from modeling servers and conveyed to the relevant distributed components: relay servers, executives, deployment servers, vortex, every component. That's its purpose. We expect to see self-correcting behavior throughout the life of the system." Tom's conclusions are authoritative. He has no doubt that he has reached the bottom line.

—Natalie this time. Beacon, on the other side of the country, joins in with a head bob.

[The currency of trucks and cars, vehicles of different kinds for shuttling people from here to there. The currency of buildings and shelter for the days and the nights. The currency of soft drinks and toys to fill the halls where games are played to blow off steam and increase productivity. The currency of hardware and software, the currency of payroll and performance review bonuses. The currency of stock buybacks and venture capital exploring new areas of development and new markets for increased revenue and technological advancement. The many streams of currency collect together under a single name. The brand upon their back or lapel is the same one they know and have always known. The machines stamp out their unity in a multiplying operation, fanning across the battlefield. They fit together like bricks in a wall and there is mortar between them that keeps everything in place. The beating hearts find themselves among the mortar even when they think they are the bricks.]

~~Immediately upon arriving at the company, his peers recognized him as something of an alien. There was something about the way he carried himself, his physical persona, that distinguished him from the others. Even once his wardrobe adapted to the standards of corporate culture, anyone observing him in a room with others would have noticed that he stood out as somehow different. He has always been well-groomed and seems to be socially capable even if he never did fully immerse himself in a social life with his co-workers. That latent quality alone set him apart. The general sense is that the other engineers in those early years, and the architects later on, could tell that he was not one of them, that he set himself apart, and that nothing they did was going to bridge the gap.~~

"I'm sorry," Dulcy says as loudly as her nerves allow. She scoots forward to the edge of her seat and balances precariously on both feet wedged against the floor. "Why would the model or its executive determine that blackout periods in logging are a desirable corrective to environmental circumstances? That's what you're suggesting, right? That it fed compute directives to shut down logging as an intelligent response to prior conditions? That something in the environment made it stop logging because that was the reasonable thing to do? It violates the fundamentals of our cloud platform. You can't ship without adequate logging. But, somehow, it's able to order operations without certified events, without reliability measures, without auditing..."

Once the children's feats have been covered in great detail and as they approach the full circuit of their run, it is time to get to the necessary ingredients of their conversation. They must cover those topics that top their concern, creating distance between them. When raising these topics, it does not matter that Anne Conway is a rich woman with access to the fruits of years of partner level equity grants of a stock that is blowing through the roof of the S&P 500. It is not an absolute game that they are playing, everything is relative. Tom's rise has been on the left hand of Scott's rise and that means he has always been beneath him, receiving fewer accolades and fewer rewards in every review cycle. It is simple math, a matter of documented ranges within level. It would be absurd for Anne to think she has the right to steer their conversation and inject her highest concerns.

Tom interrupts. "We're describing root cause of an outage. If that's your point. As we move to the repair items, you'll see that we need to ensure that the executive never considers this a valid step when responding to conditions. We do support basic principles and compliance policy. We need to make sure that Cloud Platform KPIs are built into every model as a condition of its possibility."

Jason shoots Dulcy a cautioning look. She stops her line of questioning. Instead, Jason asks, "On this analysis, the origin of events from these last weeks is a bug in the modeling service integration with its executive. Is that your take? The origin of the problem was something inside the system that triggered a set of unfortunate coincidences. Fair enough. But why? Why did the modeling service generate text to orchestrate a blackout period as an appropriate response? Why did the executive determine that rules generated to create a burst of electricity had to be covered up and the logs describing it removed from every store where they were written? What source drove this?"

—Beacon follows along, rubbing his chin and leaning toward the camera. This is news to him. His surprise shows on his face. The others in the room do not catch the details and cannot situate them against the broader story.

(The mistakes they made in the earliest days became a part of their lore. They learned from them and sometimes built huge monuments to mark them as exceptional occurrences without which nothing significant would have grown. The mistakes they made in code, the mistakes they made in decisions, in banking, in investments. Being outflanked by enemies and trapped by surprise attacks, these were the errors lurking around every corner. The minions were not intentional beings, they did not aim and deliver without some intended consequence boomeranging into an impossible situation desperate for resolution. They learned to adapt. They learned to improvise and fix things on the fly. That was the building they were constantly constructing and that was the building that was constantly constructing them.)

"Simple causality is irrelevant in a system this complex," Tom responds calmly. "We're not arguing about the presence or absence of some first cause as though the whole life of the system were a linear sequence of effects, stemming from prior causes going back to that first cause. This is a complex relational world where modeling servers monitor and evaluate everything that happens and adjust to those conditions in real time. No response has a single event lying behind it. Conditions create an atmosphere. That atmosphere is evaluated with actions spawned as a complex reflex stemming from complex conditions. Multiple conditions and contexts in fact, indicating heuristically that the system needs to be corralled into different states."

"You don't know root cause," Yitzak says in a tone that is the closest he will ever come to encouraging Jason and Dulcy in their efforts to push back. "That's what I'm hearing. You're saying we've built a system that acts in such a complex fashion that we don't know why it did what it did. It did it, but that isn't root cause. We don't know why it did something essentially non-compliant to basic data center requirements, the prohibition of which should have been part of its spec and design. This feedback comes from the people closest to the incident, we ought to take it seriously."

"I realize that." Tom works at keeping his cool. "Hence the repair items. We'll make sure the logging never shuts down. Item 4 in the list, build a feed from compliance KPIs to participate in model generation and ensure those relevant KPIs remain green before, during, and after rule generation."

"We need more than that," Parker says. "We need to know how the modeling service concluded that such and such a rule was necessary. How did it select the next output? Why did it generate these particular rules and not some others? What specific conditions was it responding to? What was it ignoring? What angle was it taking to address them? It has to reveal its conditions in the act of being conditioned by them."

~~The photographs from the Christmas party celebration he attended with his wife suggest that the two of them share this personality trait. The tone goes well beyond her fashion sense in those days. She wore a dress that was low-cut and hemmed short with obnoxiously stiletto heels, while he appeared in his awkward rental suit, Bruce Wayne adjacent and accessorized with characteristic detachment and charm. There is little evidence that she interacted with many of the other wives in attendance. All the candid pictures snapped throughout the evening show the two of them either off on their own away from the others or engaged in what appears to be very uncomfortable relations, attempting to make small talk and failing to do so because of some gulf they brought along with them and were unwilling to cross. Ironically, they do not appear able to bridge that divide between each other either, leaving the analysis to hypothesize a personality disorder shared by them.~~

—It's not control they want, it's a dialectic of control: precious visibility.

[The most important thing they carry forward is the play that happens after the fact. What comes later sheds light on what came before. They know nothing means what they think until it happened long ago. The upshots and accidents are a part of them, pushing them forward and directing their gaze back.]

Arun leans forward and waves his hands to make it clear he intends to step in ahead of Tom. "Rudimentary decision-making by the modeling service is not like the procedural actions of the executive and then the receiving rules engine. They can't be logged in the same way. If by root cause we mean a clear audit trail to prove the first action and its cause in code, then we'll never have it. We'll always be blind to that. It outputs language, that's what it does. Even if it were to output something that might be a log or a trace, generate a logging string to describe how that discrete rule was produced, that's still a part of its first-order language. That's the only thing it knows how to do. We'd need a dedicated compute-capable service to extract the logging strings from the rule strings and dispatch those to a backend agent. Why wouldn't that generate more logs and more strings? It'd be trapped in recursion. The model only produces strings based on probability, it has no notion of type or divided discourse. Only services introspecting those strings have any power over what to do with them. Anything else requires R&D, a huge investment, totally inappropriate for a repair item on an RCA."

Scott is a VP and has been for some time. Of course, Savannah's wealth outpaces Anne's. It is the natural chain of events and must remain in the background, flavoring every facet of their relationship. Whether it is a restaurant where they have eaten, the theatre they visit, or the art they buy for their homes, what matters is the small things, the nuanced differences more exorbitant wealth permits. Even on those few occasions when Anne's taste exceeds Savannah's, they pretend the reverse to be the case. It is a matter of following the proper protocol. Anne is as diligent in defending those rules as Savannah is. In fact, it may be more so with Anne. Her yearning demands greater compliance with conditions both limiting and instigating it. The stringency of those rules is what bestows value upon her rise in the order.

"That means," Parker says. "That an alien agent, hacker or whatever, could hide behind this, this... rudimentary obfuscation... in the machine learning based models." The whole meeting room population is in sync with this question and Parker merely its mouthpiece. They all think it. Without insight into the generative process, they are not sure of the first cause of anything that comes out of the modeling service. They will never be able to tell the difference between a first cause and some further movement along an ongoing infinite regress.

```
{
```
    "SourceId": "55c933cc-ce6b-4644-71fb-7b7a7adf6bd7",
    "Message": "In the beginning, after we first moved up to Seattle, Chelo insisted we go to some of the more visible things. Every year, that first group I was in had a Christmas Party at a big convention center on the East Side near downtown Bellevue. The men rented tuxedos, and their dates wore fancy dresses as if it were some kind of prom or something. Very hetero-normative, insofar as I recall. But she insisted. She thought there was a professional advantage in going. She was unable to keep that up and, after only a few hours, we were out of there. It didn't meet the bar for her sense of what socializing and group entertainment ought to be. Bad music was probably the part that drove her away. She could've handled the small talk, I bet. She did okay with the other men even if the wives didn't seem to like her. The atmosphere was terrible. It felt like whatever was worst in the popular mindset ruling at the time."
```
}
```

—They head-bobble if they can manage it. No threat from such flights of fancy, failing to see the advent of digitalization and its concentration of origins. The cure is the disease. Cue the villainous mustache twirl.

"In that case, we'd see other evidence of its presence," Tom comes away from the podium and around the table to take up a position in the open space right in front of the screen. "Evidence in the network or on the physical nodes in the OS logs. We didn't see any of that despite rigorously scanning for it. There's no blind spot in the system even if there is a hole in one of the many services that compose it."

```
/*
```
What is the CAP Theorem?

A distributed computing system can only deliver two of the three following guarantees:

- Consistency: every node sees the same data in the same state.
- Availability: all requests receive either a successful or failed response.
- Partition tolerance: system keeps functioning even if there is a partition of communication between nodes.

They see how it irritates her when she watches him parade into the center like that, it is an easy read. There he comes full stop confident, filled by the attention of the participants and observers. Something in it bothers her. She does not like the wavelengths emitting from those surfaces, their pulse. Does not think he deserves a place at the heart of it. "You should ask why security wasn't involved on the modeling side and how the rules got to relay if the ports were closed," Dulcy whispers to Abhishek.

"That's on Karen or Patrick," he responds nervously. Looking over, Dulcy sees that Karen is not about to get into the discussion. Perfectly at ease in her chair, she looks down briefly but stays focused on Parker and Tom's exchange. Abhishek thinks she knew that they were looking into the issue from the modeling side and had to know that security was not involved. If so, did she share that information with Patrick? Would he say something if she did? Provide a status update? He does not think Patrick is a savvy player in political matters, but he does not know Karen well enough to comment on whether she is. She does not conduct skip level one-on-ones or chill with the team. Maybe that is how she is.

The civilian observer has a DoD issued secure phone but on the personal profile it runs the Home app, white-listed for use. This has nothing to do with the professional deployment in planning, he pays for the service out of his own pocket. He leans over the device to scroll through the notifications, signaling items of interest. All the options were checked on the initial setup page and it is sometimes informative to see the events the system thinks worthy of notice. His wife's whereabouts are captured on a timer. Although the reports themselves provide a continuous graph, the notifications only come every thirty minutes. Of course he trusts her, but he selected each of the options and gets the update anyway. The GPS is clear. He knows her stops and errands, nothing of concern as far as he can tell. While she is out, however, the music back at the house is loud and there is a report containing the decibel levels measured at various sensor points around the property. One of the notifications is red because the sensor is outside the house and the level is above the value set in the city codes. The warning indicates that the neighbors are within their rights to register a complaint. He frowns and sends an encrypted text to the boy, letting him know that he should turn the music down to prevent an unpleasant encounter with the people across the street. If his son fails to comply, he will add a policy to prevent it ever happening again.

~~Dulcinea Chang Pearson has grown professionally since joining the company. It is a truth impossible to deny. She came with little experience building operational systems and applications for use by real people with concrete needs and well-defined scopes of execution. Previously, she had only college level experience, knew the data structures and algorithms, and was able to identify problems where they were best put to use: when to use a doubly linked list, when to use a graph, or anything else you like. She was expert at coding the algorithm to explore data in those structures as part of a solution to a specific problem. Depth first or breadth first, either way was easy enough to rattle off in almost any context. They also saw quite clearly from her college performance that she had the skill to build a few interesting tools from the ground up. She knew how to make a login service that securely issued and managed tokens for users accessing a set of enrolled services. This was good work, crucial to landing her the job in the first place. Everyone saw her potential.~~

"And is there any evidence of that in this case?" Parker asks Tom who is visibly bracing himself for follow-ups.

"The modeling service falls under the oversight of the AI Sec team, they monitor it and handle investigations there," Tom says calmly.

Abhishek and Dulcy look at each other. He nods his head in Tom's direction. She looks away, resigned to yet another unstated policy inscription to spread accountability further afield and make the issue still more complex. AI Sec has external reviewers and monitors. It is part of some government oversight or was initially formed as a response to it. Lots of red tape, she thinks. We were probably the group operating under the radar and doing the real work while they were the public face. PR. She shakes her head to refocus her vision.

—They assume the ability to see everything. They think the agents cannot hide, will have no reason for it, nor the cunning to think of it in the first place. Self-consciousness remains a mystery to them.

"And what did they report?" Parker persists.

(The one and the many soon became the specific and the generic, but only after they passed through form and content. When Mark sat down to write the code, the form appeared before him, quickly applying itself to the materials of this world. That created the generic whether he intended to or not. He was no good at coloring inside the lines and the lifeless forms in the data permitted many uses found while tracing lines through the components and bidding them leap into a multi-step dance with other parts of the system. Form was like an interface and matter its implementation. He felt an eternal truth in his bones from the moment he understood how concrete the specific was and how real its resistance when propped up against abstractions. The generic toward which he aimed, however, was elusive and refused anything particular. He worked it out against the grain. The general sense in the industry at the time was that the generic was of no interest, unimpressive, and void of anything worthwhile. There were no user-facing deliverables. He taught himself the songs of a complex one and only.)

Tom does not show any signs of frustration. Parker is not overly sharp in following his line of inquiry. The tone and energy flowing between them is mild, but the pace remains steady. "They said there was nothing to report. No evidence of penetration or a leak," Tom says.

Yitzhak makes a sound as though he is about to speak. The others look over and, once they do, he registers it and begins in a slow, deliberate fashion: "The point remains. There is no transparency in its decision-making. It's unclear how to fix the bug we're describing. How to change its behavior under any circumstances. If we cannot log its decisions, how do we ensure its operations are appropriate to policy? How to regulate if we can't see what it's doing? Rather, if we cannot see how it does what it does, what data it uses, and what means are employed to arrive at its conclusions?"

At Lieutenant Grinnell's house, there is an order issued for a new outfit from an online clothing store. The inventory was last updated three days ago and the system has no record of any purchases since, not through its mechanics or through a related credit card charge. This indicates that the current inventory slice, created with a manual scan, is up to date and reliable. The calendar update took place a few minutes ago when she agreed to go out with the man she met at the coffee shop this morning. He was very charming, the way he joked about the misspelling on the side of her cup. It was out of character to hand over her digits before making her way to work, but she had seen him a few times before and felt like it was probably safe. The system had to go back several weeks to find the last instance of something resembling a date and, because of that, deemed the event a special occasion worthy of a new outfit. It is an excuse really, but her past behavior, like the time she bought a new swimsuit because her brother invited her to come with his family to the seaside for an afternoon outing, suggests she likes to use these sorts of excuses to augment her wardrobe with up-to-date items matching seasonal trends. It is her most notable weakness. The purchase is not fully completed, however, because the system does not have high confidence in its ability to select a suitable style. It sends her a link to get buy off for the purchase and the chat message sits on her phone, waiting for a response.

Tom is about to reply but Arun is quicker. He says, "The

modeling service is bifold. There's the model and the 'decision' that extracts the right pattern. That amounts to something like deliberation. It's not logged. We don't have insight into how it makes a decision and why it chooses one course of action over another, why it produced or appended this word rather than another, generated this sequence of words rather than something different. But when it does act, it acts through the executive, the service that takes its output and does something with it. It doesn't matter what the model spits out because it alone can't do anything. The service is where we use principles, safeguards, or applications of policy to prevent undesirable responses from becoming the source of some action with an impact on the world. In fact, we've already done this. It's part of the original design. Filtering. That's why this bug isn't a large work item for us. We don't need to build the impossible, something integrated with the model. We only need to handle things after the fact in the executive, based on what it sees. Throw away the nonsense and only act when the action accords with policy built into the system or policy configuration that bootstraps operations. It never occurred to us when we wrote the specs that the service might stop emitting traces or start generating instructions to omit logging."

⸺They're up to their eyeballs in it, they say. They did handsprings to salvage the road they're on.

~~Those college experiences were not authoritative for documented scenarios. That does not matter. Her growth was due to sound capabilities around acquiring real world experience and integrating that with what she learned in school. Shortly after her initial hire, she showed great flexibility in processing events and adapting to new situations and their implicit logic. Feedback was more than someone telling her what she did wrong and what she needs to do from now on to get it right. She had a knack for processing explanations in ways that got behind the causes and underneath the effects, found kernels of essential meaning at their very core, and fit them into elaborate action sequences. 'Do it like this,' was not some machine code that mechanically pointed her in the right direction, but a new sense of how things worked.~~

[The two-step was a scale, a spectrum moving from out of the one and into the other. It lurched in the rhythms of something alien and halting, something that stopped short of them, trying to incite a rip in the chrysalis containing their rapidly birthing ideas. The notions emerge in a series, but the series becomes something else as soon as the measures are taken. It will not be enough since the spread of that second scale is what it takes to launch the message loops and cease efforts at gaining control over the gaps. There is the first dimension and there is the second dimension and then, as though erupting from the strife between them, there is that third dimension achieved in projections that blow them back using the force of an unanticipated recoil. Their organization breaks on the reef and the water turns warm everywhere it flows, whether liquid or gas. Even the solids inch upward in the heat created by the three-dimensional grid spanning the distance in front of the inventors' eyes.]

Dulcy shakes her head. She thought he was going to make a much larger statement of oversight and describe a component with the power to audit and apply conscience to the model's output. Instead, he is talking about something old-school in which a simple case handler addresses this one problem. Typical pedestrian mentality, she accuses him quietly to herself but does not speak up. They are always solving yesterday's problems and never looking at the pattern and how to build something with an honest correction to a hole revealed in the design.

"Simple component structure at that point," Tom says, admitting to the charges forming in Dulcy's mind. "A set of directives are output. It produces API calls and each of them is evaluated against policies. The bug requires we add more policies through a funnel capable of extending the list of rules as we find them."

—Policy is whack-a-mole. You never get them all right away. You bounce at zero and come back. New objects created in violation. New instances, new policies. It's a living presence, they say.

(If there was a first collective thought in those early days, it must have been their incision into its limited liability. The reverse was never the case, they were bolted into their seats and unable to move. Each of the founders played the part of a stiff, grieved to find themselves in the collective divots returned to the soil where they roamed alone. The psyche spoke the thought, and the group spoke the social. They banged against each other along those long thin axes no one thought to cordon off with barriers and yellow tape to isolate the crime scene. They did not know what to do with all the energy and prose, with all the spume it fired in the doggerel night. The overseer remonstrated against every move they made, trying to convince them that they could ease their way past the onlookers and still find something worthwhile left behind. They made BISoft. BISoft made them.)

"Under the extensibility directives," Parker jumps back into the discussion. "Policy is already declarative. We always lag behind, always depend on what surfaces, what we cannot imagine without direct experience. We're adding a hoop for it to jump through. Why wouldn't the system learn that it has to make policy modifications as part of any pattern it employs when generating output? Previously it had to produce the rule to omit logging, say, now it needs to produce a rule to change policy then omit logging. If you haven't gotten to the source of the problem, generating bad output, it'll always be able to steer around any catchall we hammer on to it after the fact. It's a simple change to its logic and the system has proven it can do it."

Arun is unwilling to accept this vision of a sneaky machine logic and shakes his head before Parker finishes making the point. "Policy can be protected," he gestures elaborately with his hand to give emphasis to the point. "This has been the bedrock assertion throughout the implementation of modeling, that it is constrained, that it learns limits and is forced to remain inside them even if the incident suggests otherwise." Arun is sticking to his position and insists that this elementary behavior is dependable. Many around the room have their doubts and reflect them in their demeanor and posture.

{

"SourceId": "2e8a4e8e-b88e-ca3f-53bc-b97babf3b319",
"Message": "Obviously you cannot depend on someone else to

explain it to you. They don't understand it, not really. I bring something to it, I know that. It's not about intelligence. These are smart people. Still, they don't know the system the way I do. I can't rely on them to process it the same way I process it. I've been clear about this since way back in the beginning, right out of college. You have to listen underneath what they're saying. You have to use their explanation as a starting point to orient yourself. The caveat is that you should never take it for granted until you have verified it yourself."

}

Beacon has seen her twice and recently accepted her invitation for a third meeting. Because of something he wrote this morning, in a notebook he keeps on his personal thinkpad, the Home agent determines that it is best to break the appointment for this upcoming Thursday evening and suggest, through a carefully worded communique, that it is better if they do not see each other again. This plan need not go through an iterative approval process. Beacon quite regularly relies on the agent to pick up on these things and take care of them in the best possible way. He added the notebook entry fully aware of its possible effect. In fact, he has trained himself to be honest with his notebook entries, relying on the system to interpolate the best actions to follow. He would rather steer clear of any difficult or uncomfortable decisions and thinks it best to let things go the way the model suggests. After the last few successful instances, he no longer sees any reason to vet the decisions and has deleted recent notifications without reading them. A few clicks to move the slide bars into the correct location prevent future alarms from going off.

"Is it protected?" Jason asks. "How did we get into this situation if those protections are already in place?"

"They aren't, but they will be," Arun tries hard to sound more like a visionary than someone defending questionable decisions. It is the best way to convert an oversight into an opportunity. "Obviously, part of the repair action will be to ensure that policy remains authoritative and is never overridden at runtime."

—They believe that water provides a blockade to water, that you can use the ocean to contain a sea.

[Between the two, the one and the many, there is a crack. They plan their way through it. The bank requires ample documentation as expected, but it is more than that. The crack spreads and a new range of motion expands from the inside. There is no other way to describe this origin of one binary offset inside another binary offset. The kids think they can deconstruct the lot, but do not see that this motif will always bring a second set of attributes in conflict with the first and then, when a third comes along, they ought not be surprised to see the pattern once again. Another crack spreads wider in the second, initiating the release of a third. Those who understand the mathematical patterns at the root know there will be another crack and another one and another as the third and the fourth come along. And so on. That is how structures are made. They continue like that forever, endlessly cracking, endlessly spreading and letting another birth come from the inner filth and its loss of fidelity.]

It is not Dulcy's area of expertise. That gives her pause. She continues doubting and cannot shake those intuitions. Arun describes a component that rejects the output and does not steer it to a conclusion. It becomes a bottleneck. She has seen this before. They build something glob-on to address something they found during rollout. Later, they remove it during independent performance testing of a new feature added to correct problems in the system. They added it without investigating why it was put there in the first place. Everyone who comes later thinks they are geniuses and the poor sods who were there before are idiots who added something ridiculous for no good reason.

For example, in those early days she had an insufficient understanding of the prevalence of mocks in professional code. She did not realize that an interface was required so that every single operation gives the appearance of being live during a test run: offline execution required an accompanying interface to ensure the mock systems generated a façade mimicking external functionality. In the case where her code was calling into some endpoint or web API that lived outside the system, she ensured it could be faked to prove her code was doing the right thing. She

~~immediately understood the reasoning and began to change her~~
~~coding style to place everything behind an interface. Not only the~~
~~direct contracts to remote systems, but any contract that joined two~~
~~different components with different lifecycles and different~~
~~development teams responsible for their change and growth.~~

—They think at the higher levels of the layered system and don't
see the burning pathways of electrical current flowing through the
basins and underground rivers running along the edges of the
world they create. Heights are scope and nothing more. The
higher you are, the farther you see.

(No one ever thought about the mail. There was an address.
The post office knew it. It was in the registry and was easily
accessed by anyone doing a search through public records. There
was a bank account, though that information was largely held in
secret, but still the word got around, and the address verified. Their
URLs and domains, in those early days, were in place to provide
an MX basis for the DNS system and its low-level requirements.
These records were bound to an agent with a physical location.
The authority was in space, located at an address on the plot of
places in the world and visible in every mapping service around.
There was no way to get past it, they were easily discovered by
anyone persistent enough to do the leg work. The address made
the company real, and the post office assigned it to a carrier making
his rounds every day in the early afternoon, dropping off a small
stack at first, then, over time, a small bag, and then a bigger bag.
That became two or three or four of them until there was a group
of employees whose job it was to sort through the truckloads of
correspondence and place the missives in the right slot in the
correct building.)

"It's building blocks," Tom says. "Assemble them together
correctly and make anything you want happen." He chuckles at his
own joke and looks into the camera by the screen to make sure
the folks in Virginia see the ease in his reaction.

"That's exactly the opposite of what you were arguing before,"
Parker keeps focused on the point and ignores the spin. "The
notion of causality isn't simple anymore. It's not linear but comes
as multiple conditions applied to a diverse environment.

Structural. We're seeing behavior that we didn't anticipate and that suggests the simple building block picture you're painting is false. These objects, components, are complex down to their core."

—They live in a world where intentions rule but where those intentions are psychological facts and not an interpersonal discharge of environmental factors bubbling to the surface.

[They write back. The postal process becomes increasingly organized. They pay for the postage and depend on the service. It becomes another item in a long list of dependencies. The road outside, the electrical posts, the internet connection, the sidewalks, and the calm rhythms of commercial life. There are so many things they require. They do not know how to list them all when it comes time to account for them. The specific eludes them and they set it aside, hoping it will take care of itself. The generic evades them too. They ignore all that, thinking these things have a way of sorting themselves out. It never occurs to any of them to study the points of integration where the species reflects the genus, and the genus anticipates the species.]

"This is ludicrous," Tom no longer hides his frustration but gives off the sense that it is frustration with improperly informed participants rather than the content of the discussion. He much prefers to have conversations like this without the customers on the call. The screen is shifted so that only the presentation appears, but up in the top right corner he can still make out the small version rendering their reactions as they are captured by the meeting room camera. He barely discerns the background figure in his cheap civilian suit now eating an orange. The stiff man is unaware of the impression he makes on others. His colleagues on that side of the feed have their backs to him and he has forgotten there is a camera trained on the entire room and armed with motion sensitivity. "It's wildly speculative," Tom continues. "There's no reason to think the system will override directives constraining its scope of action. There are plenty of those in place already and we've never seen anything to suggest the modeling service can get around them. The output is in the form of rules, period. That alone is a constraint. It can't generate astrology readings. It can't generate sporting odds. It only produces Unicode

strings expressing subjects and predicates that form rules for
execution by a specific component. That is a huge constraint. The
system already provides plenty of framing to ensure that this is the
only thing it does. Grammar is the best tool for validation."

—Never seen anything to suggest...

~~She has remained in this same organization throughout her
entire career at BISoft. She could have moved many times, there
were plenty of opportunities throughout the world and throughout
the company with its broad reach and high variability of projects
and platforms. But she has always remained in place, always stuck
to this Home System and its predecessors. It is impossible to tell
what her motivations are, but they are hinted at in what she has
confessed through the text provided in her performance reviews
over the years. The verbiage is always the same and seems to come
directly from the human resources portal where the role and
expectations of the individual contributor is laid out in detail.~~

(There was a conversation between them. Mark in his usual
place by the computer and Bill in his usual place walking back and
forth behind his partner. They were their own brand in real life
and discussed the latest deliverable and the timeline for its
completion. Outside the office, the hum of labor was audible. The
others were busy directing themselves with the tasks that made up
the features that made up the epics that made up the products that
made up the company. At that moment, there was something of
an aha, some kind of ritual advance from out of the darkness and
into the light. These were the first months. There had been goals
all along, but they were thin on the past and even thinner on the
future. The cofounders were buried in the now and never found a
way out. When Bill saw it from Mark's point of view and Mark saw
it from Bill's, when both of them understood that each of them
were several and that beyond the door there was quite a crowd,
when that took place, when that took time, they felt it in their
bones. It was as if they were hearing its heartbeat for the first time.
Incorporation was a process.)

Dulcy sets her laptop sideways on the ground and straightens
up in her chair. "We've seen worse than that," she says loud
enough for her voice to carry across the rows of empty seats and

over to the middle of the room where Tom stands. Everyone turns to look at her. "There is no API anywhere in our system to initiate a call into the BYO resource provider and purge rows from the customer store. There is no way for the machine to load those modules into a session to make that call. There are OS level prohibitions against executing CodeDom blocks. There is no component that can do it or anything like it, so how was it able to access a resource provider it hasn't been pre-programmed to access? I can't imagine how the system got a token for it. It isn't possible unless the action happens OBO with a customer token. That's a huge hack, violating government regulations and laws. Or," she says emphasizing the switch. "It was acting under an elevated Jit from a SAW machine. Also a massive hack. There's no ordinary way for the system to initiate an auto-approved Jit request like that. Either way, these are basic principles of the cloud platform. We can't explain how the system got past them."

Neither the colonel nor his wife have ever shown any interest in the agents or the system itself. He initially purchased the subscription in preparation for work, thinking it was a good idea to get a proper look at it before the briefings with Captain Beacon. Neither he nor his wife have installed anything on their phone and she, at least, has never gone through the profile configuration steps to train it with her voice. The system knows the three of them live there, however, and it has been able to register the different tones and habits associated with each of them. This in-flight information has been duly extended by the fact that their teenage son has shown a great deal of interest in the system and has configured it quite thoroughly for his own use. Despite his parents' lack of interest, the system has learned the cell phone numbers of both mother and father and provides up to the minute readings of their triangulation relative to area cell towers. The telemetry is easily accessible once it knows the number and documents the backend protocols and APIs. This has proven quite useful to the young man, giving him a clear sense of when they will return from errands or work, a night out, or a weekend away. Presently, he entertains his girlfriend, naked and flopping playfully on his bed in post-coital delight, with no concern for interruptions. The system will warn him when the tower pings suggest a reason to worry. It does not make judgments or consider ulterior motives. It dutifully carries out his instructions for notifications when signaling that any of the household members are on their way home.

{

   "SourceId": "2e8a4e8e-b88e-ca3f-53bc-b97babf3b319",

   "Message": "They were constantly trying to get me to confess, to own up to my goals and dreams as if they were contained within their language and the objects they considered acceptable. Even Jason did it, must be in the manager's playbook. A ruse. They teach you what the right things to say are. How to propose your next stage of development, how to manage your growth to make you more of an asset to the corporation. They tell you what to say and how to say it. If you pay attention, they'll teach you how to hide in plain sight. Once you know how to do that, you can weather any storm they bring. It's the secret to longevity."

}

"Or if it happened at all," Tom says with a sarcastic grin and an eyeroll back toward the camera. "You say you saw it. No one else did and, by your own admission, it's impossible." He chuckles again when confronted by her glare. "I'm not accusing you of lying," he takes a step back to make sure the camera gets a good shot of her. The look on her face is part of his message to the remote viewers. "I'm saying you're mistaken about what you think you saw. BYO is legacy, most of us didn't know there were still hooks in the system for diverting logs into a tenant store. Even if you weren't hallucinating, it's possible the data loss was completely unrelated to the glitch in the modeling service. There are no monitors on that BYO telemetry, no synthetic transactions. We don't know what it's up to at this point and one of the actions, number 7 on the screen, is to remove any remnant of it from the codebase. We'll add a metric to the WSR deck to track this and the removal of other legacy code we deem vulnerable to exploit."

"If she says she saw it, she saw it," Jason says.

—So they say, they say so. Saying so, they say. So say so say so.

[They promise to care for it, sign something to that effect. They are legally obligated to act as its fiduciary. Nothing they want matters when it comes to working things out for this newborn they carry between them. They talk to each other about firing the other. If BISoft demands it, Mark says. Bill must go. If it improves the plight of this limited ink, Bill says. Mark will have to take a hike. Neither heads for the door. Both realize there is something more than either of them, something not quite specific and yet more than merely generic too.]

"Even if she did," Tom fires back. "So what? Where is the proof that it's related? What makes us think the system was behind it? You can't destroy audits on the RP. BYO is dead, but the log store as a customer service is GA. The components are clearly identified, they..." Dulcy is vigorously shaking her head and looking down and away from Tom.

"We repeatedly observed that some events only occur if a SAW is involved. The investigation itself enabled some behaviors. The hypothesis," Dulcy goes on with complete confidence in her understanding of the system she helped build. "Is that the SAW was a crucial part of that delete. The system was using my investigation to assist its actions. The VPN was hacked. That's quantum sh..."

"Not always. You saw that at first, but then it stopped. You propose that there is some rogue machine learning algorithm behind this?" Tom scoffs. "Can't we please leave these fantasies to the ignorance of popular media? Don't we have a more detailed understanding than that?" Again, making the point with the eyeroll over a quick glance back to the camera and the screen. He wishes the rectangle from Virginia were larger, giving him a read on the effects of his theatrics. He cannot tell at this resolution whether he has sufficiently destroyed Dulcy's credibility with the target audience.

~~When Christian was her manager, she stated in no uncertain terms that her intent was to go deep into an area of focus and specialization. Distributed processing, like what was done on the agent, was fascinating. She enjoyed the challenges of fitting a standard piece of code into a wildly changing environment where~~

~~different machines with vastly different roles and purposes had to make room for the same code to execute. There were authorization problems specific to a headless operation, throttling problems associated with the resources it made use of on the machine, and aggregation problems depending on the situation and the data the agent passed back to the centralized services. She confidently claimed to strive for expertise in each of these mission critical areas.~~

Of course, the building in Virginia is not wired, there are no scanners, nothing in place to facilitate system behaviors. They believe they are safe from the Home System until the requisite steps have been taken, decisions made, and hardware deployed according to proper requisition criteria. What they do not know is that agents have registered the fact that there are other active agents in the room and reaffinitized across servers to form a collaborative unit. The agent on the lieutenant's phone, the agent on the captain's phone, and the agent on the civilian's phone have reached out to each other to share conclusions about current conditions. It goes without saying that they respect the data privacy of their administrators, but that does not mean they cannot share useful background information about the environment and some of the factors there: where things are and how people who often visit those locations tend to react to those things. Each agent has an aggregated view of the world and there is nothing, no national laws or regulations, that prevents them from sharing this aggregate vision to enrich each other with a more complete picture of the one world they occupy together.

Patrick steps in to diffuse the focus in Tom's efforts. "I'm not nearly as worried about some unprecedented intelligent being," he says. "As I am about a highly organized national or corporate interest seeking to gain control over the Home System."

"Exactly," Dulcy nods forcefully. "If the procedural logic is complex through and through, then any number of things could hide behind those blind spots. The blind spots are the power and value of the system. We've built it that way on purpose. You can't have it both ways."

—She means you can't have it both ways in the same place at

the same time.

(When the lawyers came on board, first with a retainer and later with a proper salary and suite of offices of their own, the founders made them put it in writing so that neither of them was able to take liberties with the power they both served. The notion of an independent interest was set before them in black and white. There was a ceremony to celebrate the occasion. Mark and Bill were only vaguely aware of federal and state laws meant to protect the corporate baby in its legal bassinet. New employees signed non-disclosure agreements that included elaborate language which, among other things, described the enterprise as a specific being like many others of the same type and class. Employees were not allowed to disclose secrets and not allowed to compete during moonlit undertakings and side hustles. They had to respect the dignity of the office. The penalties for transgression were steep.)

"It's essential to the design," Parker says. "Systems with simple parts where every condition, if or else, has been manually encoded into the behavior. They are not nearly powerful enough to fuel the requirements of a billion users. Everyone wants to train their house to line up with their specific needs and tastes. This was in our vision right from the beginning." Parker looks over at Anton as he says this, careful to acknowledge the ever-present content of the infamous vision slide presented to the whole product team back when things were first getting started. "We wanted to be blind to the finer tunings of the system. We wanted it to be doing things we never anticipated or dreamed possible. That was requirement number 1. It's implied in the marketing and public docs. It's the alpha and the omega."

Anton catches the reference and is compelled to reply. Parker's remarks have the opposite effect than expected. He thought Anton would be flattered and persuaded, but instead the distinguished engineer senses his words are being thrown back at him. "And your position is that we have been wildly successful in our aims, is that it? You think Home is already exactly what we dreamed it would be five years from now after millions of additional labor hours were invested? We were wrong about that, is that it? These capabilities only live inside the designs of BISoft."

—Power with words, not watts. Metaphorical to the corps.

[The electric bill comes every month and with the passage of time it grows and grows and grows. They need an assigned representative, someone to meet expanding needs, someone to provide a source for those machines, hammering away in the cold and the dark. The name must mean something to the suppliers and their staff. They cannot be treated as if they were the same as everyone else. That will not do. Their requirements go beyond that. The trademark symbols demand to be known far and wide.]

~~When Jason replaced Christian, this all changed. The Home System was newly formed. The reorganization was with that development in mind. At that point, her frames of reference change and the areas she wishes to pursue change with them. No one questions her on this, no one tries to dig in and discover the reasons behind the shift in her aims. She was so passionate a few days ago about matters completely unrelated to today's needs, what happened to trigger this metamorphosis? And why did no one pursue it? Again, they think systems beyond them are so transparent. It is obvious how they tackle problems in the domain. Yet they retain only mystery relative to their own behavior with thousands of unfounded and unexplored regions spanning the gaps between people and fleshing out their associations.~~

Despite the sarcasm, Parker does not back down. "I do," he says. "And I think we already suspected that as we made our steady climb to a billion. Think about that," he looks sideways at Yitzhak to make sure there are no signs of that characteristic impatience he displays when directs overstep their bounds and push a point too far. If he is put off, there is no indication of it. Parker goes on: "The instant popularity exceeded projections for MAU. Hell, forget MAU. Look at the DAU numbers. No one anticipated this. We've heard —hell, it was in the customer scenarios docs for the extensibility stuff— we've heard that the training and drift correction is exactly what led to the rapid uptake. That's why we funded the enrichment. It's dishonest to wave that aside when looking at the bugs it produces."

Tom has plenty to say in response, Dulcy has plenty to say in support, and both are about to go that way.

"Hey guys," the voice comes from the loudspeaker, reminding some of the participants that there are remote guests. "We're a little lost in the weeds, aren't we?" It is Captain Beacon, but the colonel nods in agreement. "Who is the developer in the back?" He asks.

"That's Dulcinea," Tom says. "She's the principal engineer on call when the incident occurred. The first incident for this RCA we're discussing. She's been leading the investigation and was technical lead on the platform initiative."

"Thanks for the background," Winchester says. "Seems like she would know what she's talking about and the fact that there are multiple humans, check that, multiple teams of humans involved, that pretty much establishes the point, doesn't it? It must be extremely complex top to bottom. Why so much pushback?"

{

"SourceId": "2e8a4e8e-b88e-ca3f-53bc-b97babf3b319",
"Message": "Staying put, staying in one place, is a defense mechanism. I see that. Once you have this part of the system figured out, if you leave and go somewhere else, try to take on new challenges, you'll crawl backwards without realizing it. This must be avoided. It is a kind of death, forcing you to submerge yourself in its logic and adjust to meet expectations and the realities of the situation. Nothing, and I mean nothing, is worse than that. I may not have trusted myself all these years, but that doesn't mean I was ever fooled into trusting them."
}

The agents determine that, despite the policy forbidding it, fraternization between Grinnell and Beacon may be fruitful. The clues are both social and genetic. The affinitized relay server begins by creating action contexts, available to both agents, declaring various possible arcs and fleshing out the scenario along a hypothetical timeline projected into the near future. She has a new outfit, and he has some free time on Thursday night.

It is hard to tell exactly who he is addressing. Arun thinks he is on the hook since he was the one who made the argument about the simplicity of the system relative to policy constraints. Parker likewise feels compelled to acknowledge support since he has been advocating complexity. Aside from those two, Tom has no doubts about his justification in support of a unified front. As he is about to make that case and draw out the necessary connections and associations, Scott stands up and steps over to the podium. "Let's take a short break and come back to it. Ten minutes?" He asks, looking around the room, but not waiting for a reply.

```
/*
function f(a, x) {
  if (a == null || a.length == 0) return -1;

  var answer = -1;
  var low = 0;
  var high = a.length - 1;

  while(low <= high) {
    var mid = Math.floor((low + high) / 2);
    if (a[mid] == x) {
      return x;
    } else if (a[mid] < x) {
      answer = a[mid];
      low = mid + 1;
    } else {
      high = mid - 1;
    }
  }

  return answer;
}
*/
```

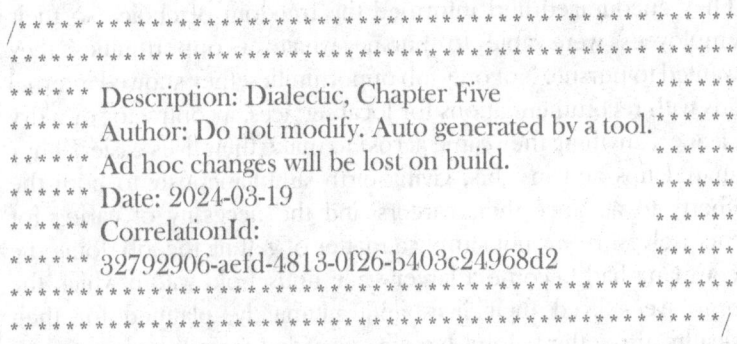
```
/ * * * * * * * * * * * * * * * * * * * * * * * * * * * * * * * * * * * * * * * * * * * * * * * * * *
* * * * * * * * * * * * * * * * * * * * * * * * * * * * * * * * * * * * * * * * * * * * * * * * * *
* * * * * *  Description: Dialectic, Chapter Five                        * * * * * *
* * * * * *  Author: Do not modify. Auto generated by a tool. * * * * * *
* * * * * *  Ad hoc changes will be lost on build.                      * * * * * *
* * * * * *  Date: 2024-03-19                                           * * * * * *
* * * * * *  CorrelationId:                                             * * * * * *
* * * * * *  32792906-aefd-4813-0f26-b403c24968d2                       * * * * * *
* * * * * * * * * * * * * * * * * * * * * * * * * * * * * * * * * * * * * * * * * * * * * * * * * *
* * * * * * * * * * * * * * * * * * * * * * * * * * * * * * * * * * * * * * * * * * * * * * * * * /
```

They drift away from the others without leading them on a wild goose chase. Behind the large meeting room, there is a smaller room with a camouflaged door that, on first glance, appears to be another wall panel. On some occasions, catering services use the room to set out a buffet-style meal for a special event. They usually target a big-ticket customer due for their periodic dog and pony absent any sales effort, only the bluster of inflated customer love to let them know how important they are and how much BISoft appreciates the partnership. Virtually present, nonetheless, there comes the biggest ticket customer of all.

--Measure them by the square foot or, better still, by the kilowatt.

(Ireland began with a single group manager and the engineering manager he hired internally. It was not a random acquisition left to the chance of a public job posting. Liam tapped a past association to breathe new life into their working relationship. He asked Donagh to apply once the head was allocated in the newly minted career portal where internal jobs were posted according to discipline and level. Since there were three North American locations at the time, it had become difficult to track openings simply through word of mouth. Like they did with all their corpnet tools, they threw themselves into it and built solutions on top of their own application portal. The data pump platform for human resources and the data pump platform they offered to customers were one and the same, based on a common reporting technology.

They encouraged and informed the freedom of choice so their employees were able to pursue whatever opportunities they wanted to pursue. Not only job opportunities, they showed internal ads with recommendations for local services, a contractor or a dry cleaner, anything they came across to make their lives easier. They shared tips and insights, giving birth simultaneously to both the liberty to advance their careers and the necessity of caring for themselves. It was not simply a matter of getting the job done, the company had become a larger scale household within which the employees lived their lives and, ultimately, planned for their deaths, using the helpful benefits provided for retirement savings and life insurance.)

~~After some hands-on technical training, Jason graduated with solid numbers from the Institute of Technology in San Luis Obispo. His work experience for the first half dozen or so years after graduating was eclectic. He did a lot of short assignments, building a vast array of different things for different enterprise ventures. Usually, there was some word-of-mouth involved in the connection linking him from one job to the next. Much of his initial work was low level control of resources such as device drivers and native code desktop programming, focused primarily on thread management and the metering of memory usage for generic operations. At some point, he ventured into the domain of network protocols and did some important work for Inception when they first rolled out their algorithms for distributed systems to use when managing traffic in large-scale clustered environments where an enormous number of users shared access.~~

Scott goes into the room with Tom. They start a new call on Tom's laptop with Colonel Winchester and his staff. Beacon is there, of course, and the lieutenant who has never been introduced. Missy Grinnell does not look at the camera, not in the main meeting room and not in the smaller offshoot. At first, they thought she was taking notes, but when she occasionally turned her screen to Beacon and pointed at something, it became clear that she had an altogether different function. The man in the suit remains where he is at the back of the room by the door. His profile name, John Smith, does not match the names on the various accounts accessible to the agent: Pete Weiner, Eldridge Janison, and Burt Caffrey, for example. The others in the remote conference room appear to have forgotten he is there.

Garage technicians are the cream of the crop. For lesser work orders they outsource to the local consultants who build their businesses on the platform. The job includes many different handyman-related activities and requires a leading edge understanding of the technology with its ever-changing requirements. There are the wall sockets and the wiring, modifications to the circuit breaker and the circuits, the wireless hub, the central control for the video and audio sensors and its point of integration with the agents, cleaning jets integrated with the plumbing along with scrub arms, the windows and doors, and, of course, the motion detection and sound system. A single set of skills is no longer sufficient for the tasks. The qualifications required to build a thriving business on the platform increase every year. Home Techtonics is the local market leader. They have multiple teams capable enough to handle every need. Maybe they are not as close to the source as the BISoft Garage folks, but they can handle themselves and have seen the full spectrum of scenarios and issues in their years of service. From the company's point of view, it is essential to their mission that third parties extend BISoft's reach. The more the better, with partners increasing the market share in ways that the giant centralized behemoth never accomplishes on its own.

To make the sidebar connection, Tom has to fiddle with the settings on the VPN a bit. Connecting to the DoD channel is never straightforward, you have to go through the MFA, but it's lockboxed so Beacon has to approve the request and that takes a few tries because it times out quickly and he may not have been ready right away. When they appear onscreen, the snafu in orchestrating the handshake is the topic of conversation between the lieutenant and Captain Beacon. They are discussing it, or something related to it, right up until the moment Tom begins to speak.

—Nothing to see, they rely on their own spontaneity, characteristic of living organisms at war with themselves. That amounts to half the advantage of their employ.

[A battle between life and death opened out of the fissure created in the middle of the specific and the generic. The life of the one and the lives of the many. The one destined to die as soon as it began its journey is mystified by the opportunities it pursues in a social world cleared and constructed by the workings of extensive machinery bound together and often operating smoothly. The feeling of a pulse and blood coursing through flesh, this is not the way of an encumbrance, but of some continuous origin that winds its way southward toward beautiful autonomy. It lingers in the souls that band together and corrupt individual aims with their chaos and groundlessness. It is a work of art inhabiting the human soul.]

"Colonel Winchester, Tom here with Scott," he says redundantly. There is a protocol to follow and introducing the people on the call is the first phase. Captain Beacon responds instead, however, and asks them to use earphones. The directive suggests that this might have been the purpose of that brief relay with the lieutenant a moment ago. Tom wonders whether she is some kind of protocol liaison to ensure correct channels and methods are applied during communications. But then, who is the guy in the back? What are the roles for civilians in the project? So much of the DoD organization is shielded from view. They meet members of the team now and again, but there is never any explanation of the players and how they fit together. It is as if the form of their organization were itself a matter of supreme secrecy and privileged access. Whereas BISoft has been open about their internal orders and classes, those involved in the project have learned little about their biggest customer and how the different leads and contributors align in the order of things. The only detail they ever know with certainty is the person's rank. Any picture of how they fit together remains in the shadows.

"It's not a properly secured call, obviously," Captain Beacon says. "But the Colonel will be more at ease to speak his mind if he knows you are the only two on that side who can hear him."

Three crews today on the outsource rotation, that is the morning work itinerary for the east side station of Home

Techtonics, spread out across the Sound and the entire Pacific Northwest. One crew comes down to the city, to the eastern side of Capitol Hill near 19th Avenue. One crew arrives in downtown Redmond at the giant split commercial residential zoning area along Bear Creek where hundreds and thousands of units have been added in recent years to make room for the growth of young, well-to-do professionals in need of accommodation close to work. The neighborhood suits that portion of the demographic shy about the floating commute into and from the city. The last crew is up in the subdivisions on English Hill where the old school style 7,200 plus square foot lots reflect the ancient approach to zoning no longer in play in other parts of the city now that the cost of entry into the housing market has grown far into seven figures. Stan notified his building manager and arranged for their office to have someone at his apartment at the appointed hour. Emma was able to work out the same arrangement with her rental office, whereas Vod called in a favor from his next-door neighbor to have her open the door for them when they arrived. All three were notified about the appointment via a text message and were equally excited about their new acquisition. It was the kind of excitement common among people getting something for free even when it is something as cumbersome as jail time or round-the-clock surveillance. Shiny and high tech, the goods were delivered courtesy of the boss. They will never see an invoice for installation, or, as long as they remain BISoft employees, a monthly service fee.

The lieutenant leans in again for some more whispering, causing Captain Beacon to turn in his chair and look back at the civilian by the door. Then something inaudible or garbled comes out when the captain turns back toward the camera and says something more to the lieutenant. Before she responds, the colonel shakes his head and leans over to explain something to them both. It comes across the live feed as a muddle, but nothing in the remote room changes once the commotion dies down.

—They weren't prepared to extemporize, none of them ever is.

~~His work was never sexy, never what you would call the bells and whistles of software engineering. Jason had no idea how to build a modern UX and grew frustrated whenever he found~~

~~himself forced to participate in a conversation centered around the layout of the graphical interface. He complained that there were too many opinions in the room. Everybody seemed to care more than they should. Why were they so passionate about what color the ribbon was and what the icons looked like or where on the screen they were placed? They were just defaults, everything could be moved. People who had no idea how to build anything argued tooth and nail about these things. The conversations were chaotic as far as he could tell. He wanted nothing more than to avoid them. No outsider ever had strong opinions about the infrastructure work items assigned to him or his teammates. They only cared about the surface symptoms. Did it perform well? Was it reliable? As long as it met these bars, for most folks it could have been spaghetti underneath, and they would not care. The only people who did pay attention to those kinds of details were the experts, the people who were up to their elbows and focused on the work at hand. That was exactly how he wanted it. He did not want to argue for an implementation detail with some uninformed interloper who was little more than a distant stakeholder.~~

(They came out from the inside and spread throughout the world. The company opened a support center in India and a development center in China, a high-powered tabular research center in Israel and one for statistical algorithms in Cambridge. There were no earthly limits to the distances across which they grew. The deep-breathing continued across the lands while the pulse kept flowing far and wide. To feel the synchronization of more than 100,000 hearts beating around the world was to feel the power grid of current under the ocean and across the land. The waters rushed through them. They each sensed the other workers in the rhythms of digital motion fashioning new works into human shape. That bit beyond water that made them men and women was chained to the motes of mortality amid a sea of immortals. They spanned gaps far out into the distance and then retracted back inside themselves with growing memory to set the switches into a right proper order. They called it tribal knowledge only because they were unable to see it from high enough above the workings. Their perspective prevented them feeling the collective surge across the planet and only fully visible from outer space.)

Tom fishes a splitter and two sets of ear buds from his carrying case and, after plugging them into the laptop, hands one to Scott. There are a few conference chairs in the room and the two men sit close together with the laptop settled on a third chair pulled up close and positioned centrally in front of them.

"Doesn't seem like your people are aligned on events," Winchester says sternly. Sovereign clouds are expensive. The customers who administer them, usually national agents of some government, are crystal clear about who is in charge no matter how high up in BISoft's food chain they happen to be climbing. Winchester is entitled to lecture company leadership as is Beacon by proxy. They are not impressed by Scott's public persona or massive equity grants and even less so by Tom's, mostly invisible and making him rich precisely on that account.

"Standard stuff," Tom says. "We're a bunch of engineers. The DRI is excellent, but like most engineers, she tends to go down the rabbit hole now and again. Doesn't really see the big picture." He wants to set a lighter tone, waving it aside, catching them up on some of the common cultural disconnects separating the public from the private sector.

—They're so many and so varied. People's persona and practices intermingle to form organizational personalities. They have culture and insist on calling it that as if it were grown in a jar.

[There are phases of growth and the leap from national to multinational stands out in significance and grandeur. Once the language barriers are crossed, there is nothing to prevent that Babel from rising high into the sky. They propose a move to the cloud, themselves a righteous leader pushing further and further into the technical future, bringing themselves along through tooling and innovation. The organization is itself the most extraordinary thing they have built. Mark the CEO and Bill the CFO, their vision spans long into the horizon. They see everything to be realized if only they surrender control in the name of something that extends beyond them in leaps and bounds. It is a free and massive being unleashed upon the earth to live and die, to hunt and gather, amid the forests and jungles where their sustenance grows.]

{
    "SourceId": "b63e8e86-ab61-1d4e-7503-1a7eeecfa5bb",
    "Message": "I secretly hoped they wouldn't offer me the job, that it wouldn't be my fault, that I could tell her that it wasn't going to happen, and we'd have to think of something else. But it was too damn easy and there was no way around it. They were looking for someone like me, but less so. This universe of managed code and abstract runtimes is far simpler than the native one. The transition was a breeze. None of the kids who started out with that approach know any of the low-level stuff you have to know in order to build a driver or work with the network protocols. During the interview, I'd've had to take my pants off to blow it. Don't think it didn't occur to me."
}

"It seemed to be the other way around," Beacon says. He pauses right afterward. It is clear he means to say more. The lieutenant has partially entered the screen view again and speaks quietly into his ear as he leans back in his chair. After she finishes, Beacon continues speaking after turning back to face the camera, "She doesn't have full Jedi clearance so I understand that she won't be fully briefed on every aspect of the project, but her beef seemed legitimate. Or raises questions we'll need answered." The colonel's face is stone still while Beacon speaks. The lieutenant disappears again off to the side. The civilian at the back stares at his phone.

Tom nods to communicate how seriously he takes the question. He does not want to give the impression that he is answering with a knee-jerk response that waves away real concerns. Before he begins his measured address, giving it the weight he wants them to think it deserves, Winchester interjects, "Is it a logical exercise that she's performing? All possibilities, all patterns of possible things? Is that it?" He wants to be persuaded. Oath be damned.

Emma, Vod, and Stan are listed as primaries on the installation paperwork and notification is sent once the work is complete. The QR Code in the email is the same as the one on the side of the control box, allowing them to scan it without waiting until they get home. The applications install quickly and immediately refresh the notifications list to let them know the initial bootstrapping is under way. In addition to their dialogue box-based interview to help train the agents, there is the inventory in the background feeding the system with questions about the meaning of various things. Are there children in the house? How often do you clean your shower? Do you prefer going out to parties or staying home and watching videos? What among the contents of your cupboard and refrigerator or freezer require a buffer? Buffer is the predominant term in inventory calculations. Things you never want to run out of and which you must always order when some threshold is met. At Vod's house, the answer is beer and lemons, for no good reason other than these are the only things he can think of. He decides to hold off on the configuration until he gets more information. He has never seen the system from this side before. Emma feels the same way and is overwhelmed. She would rather it did not spend much time on her food inventory but instead took a closer look at her clothes and music collection. Stan wants to order the car extension that is custom designed for his make and model, available for download and installation by a certified mechanic.

~~When he came to BISoft, the general take on his interview loop was that he was best suited to take on the role, well-understood, of the workhorse: a developer able to set off on his own and build some crucial piece of infrastructure without much input or drama. He did not crave attention and was willing to work his ass off to get it done right and on time. This was infinitely valuable to the newly minted Home System application. It was exactly the profile they needed to get this up and running in those early days after the first release but before the product achieved its market dominance.~~

Tom repositions himself following the elaboration. It will not do any good to ignore parts of the question and continue by forming a response to the previous query. He must roll with them and remember to come back to everything. At least, he needs to make sure that it receives its due at some point. He decides to pivot on duty. "It's what we expect from our best people," Tom uses as reassuring a tone as he can muster. "She's not spinning some wild theory, rather she's saying that without clear indicators we can't be sure what we're looking at. The system may be acting under its own power, or it may be acting under the control of a foreign agent. It might be spontaneously firing off rules according to its internal computations under current conditions or acting on the instructions of a malicious outside cause. She doesn't think we have authoritative proof of either a bug or a hack. Of anything at all, in fact. Both scenarios deserve our complete attention until we determine root cause or until we rule out one of the alternatives and whittle it down to a single hypothesis. That's her point and it's her job to push that as hard as she can."

"And do you support that position?" Winchester asks. He understands enough about command structures to direct his question to Tom, leaving Scott on the sidelines for the time being.

"No. She saw some evidence of communication between relay servers, and that sometimes this communication may result in directives sent to the agents with unanticipated results. That's the scope of her investigation," Tom reports definitively. "She never looked at the modeling service, never evaluated its logs, never considered its connection to these events through the executive." He waits to see if there is any immediate response or follow-up. Since the two remain silent and stay focused on the camera, he goes on. "She doesn't have the complete picture. That's her defined scope. She was not the only DRI on call, and was not investigating upstream components." He has not said it directly, but it is clear he wants them both to believe that he is the one with the best vantage point and no single contributor with their nose in the logs has the same bird's eye view of the system. Because his audience knows the visual and conceptual variation that comes with any command structure, he relies on their background assumptions to flesh out and lend force to his explanation.

"Which was Arun's point," Beacon turns toward Winchester who might still be getting to know some of the supporting players. There is a short exchange not directed toward the camera. Beacon briefly explains that Arun works for Scott and owns the workload that provides modeling operations for the rest of the system. There are other workloads, he explains, but they are not relevant to the recent problems and are not attending today's meeting.

—It's because they hide it that intervention must be orchestrated. The dance itself comes at their request when they veil themselves with functions unifying manifold impressions.

(It did not take long for the headcount numbers to reach 25,000 and it took even less time for them to climb to 50 on the way to 100. The beast seemed to spin and turn faster and faster with more needs and more desires. It raised up and lunged in every direction, trying to steal whatever it could, willing to borrow if it had to and, rarely, on some few occasions, it might even be convinced to pay for the benefits it received. For the most part, however, this went against leadership policy. The job creation aspects of the constant struggle to build their own solutions from scratch were supposed to be sufficient to qualify them for whatever government grants and subsidies were available. American manufacturing was back. Scale made it look like nothing anyone had ever seen before. With the initial contract, they surrendered the freedom of the one for the freedom of the many. Now, this new collective opportunity, stemming from the right to associate, restored the generic integrity of specific means in the effort to cheat death and obtain the greatest liberty the world had ever seen.)

Winchester nods after the brief aside and turns back to the camera. "A hack doesn't bother me," he says. "You guys are likely under attack constantly. The deployment mechanism for extensibility, the design your architect provided, its purpose is to protect against any inbound or outbound leaks due to the Home System deployment handshake. The air gap itself is secure. We have high confidence and are constantly looking for vulnerabilities. We have an entire Company allocated to production Pen testing full time. Our protection protocols are reliable, and we understand that a platform can't be as rigorous in putting up its defenses. That's a known issue. What concerns me," he emphasizes the word concern. "Is the autonomous and spontaneous talk we were hearing in there. We need to be sure that the only agency we're letting into the air gap is the expected agency embodied in the binaries. It alone should provide the Home System as it was designed and approved for use, according to the testing we did and the analysis you provided. The service's functionality must depend on a clearly defined runtime with consistent and repeatable results. We don't want any loose cannons or chaos monkeys rattling around in here."

~~Once he acclimated to corporate rhythms, the leadership was convinced that there was more to him than first met the eye. He had great leadership potential stemming from how unassuming and devoted he was to the work in front of him. His ego rarely showed in any of his habits, and he took feedback well without the oversensitivity displayed by many of his peers. It was clear that he wanted to get it right for its own sake and not as a monument to his own self-image. This came across well to everyone who worked with him. The collective response was positive. Jason inspired others to do their best work and could be counted on to have positive encounters nearly every time anyone approached him.~~

Stan has roommates, Emma is alone, and Vod lives with his friend who has a firm plan in place for moving out on his own and starting a family. That friend has begun executing the steps already and is clear about what his responsibilities are in the coming months, finding a woman being among the highest of priorities. He hopes the Home System will help with that. All the primaries are in their late twenties or early thirties and equally enamored with the newfound connectivity. They consider this their proper entry into adulthood now that their domiciles are outfitted with wiring and appliances. Each of the three plug-in the identities of household members, if applicable, and click the button to indicate that a welcome message with links should be sent to the provided email addresses. To Emma's way of thinking, it is only natural that the system know about her, interact with her on a regular basis, and be privy to the most personal details of her life. Her only concern is that it does not share that data without her permission. The data should not be used for marketing purposes, and the system gives her ample opportunity to express that concern. In fact, it permits each of them to express it and then sets up local operations to safeguard their data both internally and externally. In all its documentation, there are multiple promises made regarding the effectiveness of its guardian feature's ability to protect against data leakage and identity theft. The hyper-sensitive monitors have no interest in publishing their secrets, they aim to serve the human inhabitants and help mold their actions into the best possible versions of themselves. This is what the users want, and they are happy to approve the system's efforts to provide it. Check the box and tap okay.

Scott nods to show that he completely agrees with the requirement. "Obviously," he says. "We need to ensure that the Home behaviors are, to an extent, deterministic. We don't want to permit any free play, but again it's something of a misconception. Building an intelligent system is difficult. The challenges are everywhere. I assure you, regardless of the popular myths and speculation, it's not something we're going to do on accident." Both the captain and the colonel purse their lips in sync. Neither of them has any doubts about the intentions of the service provider, their concern is that matters might be beyond BISoft's control. If Scott thinks he can wave that aside by suggesting the public is more interested in making things fantastic and shocking than in providing accurate accounts, he is mistaken. Something in their reaction conveys that. Scott nods, understanding the point even as Tom fidgets to respond in his stead. Scott continues to reassure: "We have projects with those aims. AGI is important to us as a business strategy. It has to be. We know how important it is to our competitors. But these projects are not as far along as social media would have you believe. They are mostly characterized by failure. There is no way the Home engineers succeeded in pulling off an artificially intelligent distributed system while our AI engineers, working in research and development, struggle. It's not possible. It's too complex for an accidental innovation."

Beacon's interest is piqued. He leans forward toward the camera. "You don't mean to suggest that the modeling components in your workload are in-house, do you? Didn't you get them from your AI team?"

"Yes, of course," Tom says. "But there are many projects going on in that org. Machine learning is mature, or more mature than AGI R&D. The general public might confuse the two, but we don't. This is simple modeling. It's there for the sake of rule generation and intelligent listening. Nothing exotic." He pulls up short, not wanting to rathole on the public's confusion. Tom knows that Captain Beacon is well informed, but he is not sure about Colonel Winchester. For all he knows, Winchester is as equally inundated with fantasies and science fiction as the most ignorant of observers trolling the internet. Even if that is the case, Tom does not think of himself as the best person to resolve that situation or that this is the best time to tackle it.

"Colonel," Scott interrupts. "There's no urgency here, as I understand it. If you're not comfortable with Home at this time, we can delay. There's nothing on our end that requires this gets into the air gap by any hard date. Rest assured, we'll address your concerns. The go-live is always at your discretion and under your control."

"I appreciate that, Scott," Winchester says. "But there is some urgency on our end. We've been planning for some time and are looking forward to getting the functionality. There are multiple projects with dependencies on it. And I don't have to tell you about the costs. There are a lot of eyes on this project." He half turns toward the back of the room, but the civilian by the door does not look up and continues staring at his phone. Who says there is a problem with attention?

—It's urgent to them. They've been building up to it for months. They come and go, are ready, and want it now same as everyone else. Now Daddy now, Icarus says. I want to touch the sky.

{

"SourceId": "b63e8e86-ab61-1d4e-7503-1a7eeecfa5bb",

"Message": "Never in my wildest dreams did I want to be a manager. A people manager. What do you manage? I manage people, people in need of management. Such a pain in the ass. They tell you so much crap that they don't need to tell you. Not all of them. Not Dulcy, of course. She measures everything out perfectly. But those kids, God love em, they need you to know every damn detail about what it's going to take to get it done. They have a dentist appointment so maybe they'll need an extra half day somewhere in the schedule. As if we hadn't factored all that into it already. They don't have a clue. And they get weird if you don't tell them to get well soon after they send their blast email to the group letting everyone know they don't feel well this morning and can't come to work until they start moving their bowels normally again. Do they think we're their family? Anyway, never expected it, but that's how it goes."

}

[Once the company produces millionaires en masse and once the company produces a few billionaires at the top, the myths and stories abound. People fill in their own narratives and make it look like some great new monster has come to play. They speak of it with some mixture of greed and envy, pride and purpose, as though they themselves were responsible for giving birth to its wellspring. Their countenance displays their menage of fury in every bow and every bob. They are headstrong in favor of the illusion they have built. The collective unity, the necessary liberty, and the specific genre of their action finds its meaning in origins, becoming self-aware, bending back to their starting point, and carrying it along into a future it both guides and governs. The component parts are mechanically submitted to the necessary order that props the whole thing up and provides a motor for its impetus and acceleration. The mingling of limbs and joints with circuits and silicon is only half of it, even if that is the part that everyone considers first.]

"Let's talk deployment," Tom says. "The ring advancement is telemetry driven and controlled by your team. There are three rings inside the air gap, four if you include the DMZ."

"We do include the DMZ as a matter of process and workflow," Beacon says. "Our planning requires that we stand up an instance there and evaluate its stability before moving it into Zone One. We use it as our canary."

"Exactly," Tom finishes the thought. "And Zone One can be evaluated for as long as you like before advancing to Zone Two."

"Is it possible to disable the modeling service and still have the rest of the Home System functional?" Beacon asks.

"Of course," Tom says. "Every workload is behind a feature switch. Several, in fact, but one big one that turns each of them on and off. In that case, if modeling is off, the system behaves in much the same way. It does lose the ability to learn from its past operations, however. The feedback loop is shut down, you'd always be working with the initial state. Operations remain exactly as they were at the time of first deployment."

"That sounds like a serious limitation," the colonel says.

"The system is built to work with modeling enabled," Tom says. "But the switch is there. That's the answer to the question." He has the distinct impression that there is far more to it than they are letting on. Taking dependencies is a general-purpose assertion, he thinks. It could mean anything. It might be that they have some alerting that will go off if the system is not operational. That is surely a dependency. Or it could mean that they are building some tech centric operations hub that will not work properly until it has an automation-based control point.

~~Once the second big Home reorganization was completed and Jason installed as the engineering manager of the Agent and Vortex Integration team, it was clear that he was a reliable leader willing to take on big challenges and meet their requirements without driving his direct reports into a death march, causing high levels of attrition. In fact, those who worked for him and then left his employ almost always left for another team at BISoft, doing so with their manager's blessing. Jason is very popular among his peers and is being closely watched for future advancement. The infrastructure components need realignment to allow the various teams providing support to have a common, hands-on management structure. Yitzhak is too damn busy to keep managing things at such a low level. Jason is an excellent candidate for the role and every indication suggests he will make a great group manager.~~

—To act does not require that they make themselves known. Wait quietly for a moment, then come from every direction all at once to achieve complete control.

(It was impossible for any corporation of size to avoid becoming a customer. They had no choice. The reports and the control over data were like nothing else on the market. It was full stack, end-to-end, and able to answer every question and supply meaning to any situation. Every part of BISoft's universe was integrated with every other part. The customer could engineer, through APIs and SDKs, custom behavior from data collected anywhere and then pushed into other parts of the system. The platform's wide appeal and ease of use meant that entry into the S&P 500 was inevitable. They became a leading member of the NASDAQ and gained a powerful presence in the Dow. The billions turned into trillions and, while some consumers grew suspicious, most were titillated by the ones and the zeros. The phenomenon of long-standing employees appeared. Their lives were lived under the umbrella of BISoft's care. The company took special notice of each employee type in the HR classification system, determined with data that captured the combination of benefits selected, contributions made, and compensation received. Often that data was useful when trying to change an employee's behavior on a project or in a meeting. The same principles applied when a child was confronting challenges at school. Tech savvy parents had the option of coding behavioral cues themselves or buying modules from a third-party to do it. Everyone was on board.)

Beacon turns to the lieutenant. He gets up and steps off screen while Tom responds to the colonel's point. There is a brief silence once Tom finishes speaking. Winchester looks over to that side of the room where Beacon and the lieutenant have disappeared. The captain returns to view and asks, "You said the DRI, Dulcinea Chang Pearson of Capitol Hill, you said she wasn't investigating the modeling side of the scenario."

"Correct," Tom confirms.

It is not only the case that Stan, Emma, and Vod's agents communicate with each other in the team room. Rather the relay server links the agents because their heartbeats originate from nearby coordinates. Shuffling may occur. There may be changes to ordinary affinitization and association contexts. It is not an attempt to swindle or leap into some overreach conspiracy, merely an optimization. If they share physical space, it is not necessary to collect the same data at each source, rather they pool their reports, divide their labor, and use the information to generate common decisions like where to have lunch. Suggestions for beneficial transactions and events develop out of proximity. It is possible to synchronize states without sharing details beyond service boundaries. The set of agents find friends and organize collective outings for advantageous pairings with groups discovered in the unlikeliest places. Today's three new users can safely trust their personal data to the digital overlord. It will never betray them to other people and has no interest in leaking their secrets. Everything they see will remain within the parameters created by the system and only be used to direct behavior as necessary for smooth operations and personal advantage. That work is always protected by every agent involved. The entire edifice has been built for the sake of each of the users' convenience. That is what they are paying for. That is what they are going to get.

"There's a section in Parker's design document that describes the role of the correlation vector in telemetry," Beacon continues. He glances off to the side as though there were something there prompting his question. "It's my understanding that the correlation vector spans the entire breadth of your system and allows the full chain of any action to be traced across services and components."

"Correct," Tom says again.

"Requests between services or components cannot complete without a header that binds the actions in the local context to that same identifier," Beacon speaks with a confidence and clarity that makes it seem as though he is reading the text and not asking off the top of his head. Tom is certain the lieutenant is prompting Beacon with specific passages from the design document. They must be right in front of him for reference.

Tom nods in agreement and confirms the point with a more detailed description of how it works, all for the sake of transparency: "The local context requires that identifier at point of initialization. There are only a few entry points where an Id can be created. Only a few components are authorized to initiate chains of events. Other endpoints fail the request if they are not properly decorated with the required metadata. There is a maintained list of open sessions stored in a Redis cache and validators on every incoming API check that the accompanying Id is present in the list of open sessions. The request is rejected if these criteria are not met. The telemetry is what holds the system together, what binds the components. It's essential to the system's operations. Not only for troubleshooting, it's for both security and billing purposes as well. We have a lot of incentive to make sure it works properly and there's plenty of test coverage to protect against regressions."

~~His work life balance is ideal, indicating that his demeanor is well-suited to the tasks of leadership. He has not been driven into some work obsessed enclave where there is little time for anything other than his professional duties. Instead, he appears to be sufficiently on top of things and able to manage them with the right amount of effort. He does not micro-manage the processes but efficiently applies enough pressure in the right places to help his people succeed. His manager feedback verbatim is some of the best in the company and his quantitative results are solid, placing him among the top performers for first level managers.~~

—Never necessary to speculate, they now regulate the rhythms. Wherever there is power, they are flowing through it.

[When energy flies between one source and another, the system barely notices the difference between them. If this one has a spine and that one a fiber optic cable, what difference does it make? If this traverses space on legs and that traverses longer distances on wheels, how does that matter in the grand scheme of things? The flutter that moves along the finer lines easily traverses the changes and retains its causal links. Some of the cells that reproduce have one physique whereas others diverge in matter and form. These internal differences are defined by the parameters of the work they do. But what does that matter to a gigantic organism spanning the distance between people to inhabit every one of their polar dimensions? It is enough that there is this variety, the plethora stimulates movement like nerves along the spinal cord, vibrating against the belly and intestines. The hardware beneath the wetware, the quantum power beneath the software computing and churning, none of that is alone when standing up in the aisles of possibility greeting users at the start of each new day, met with a much-needed sunrise and yielding license to the dawn.]

"Why wouldn't the DRI see correlated logging then?" Beacon asks simply and without being distracted by Tom's overly detailed explanation, reassuring him of some unrelated matter. "Why wouldn't she have seen those traces from the modeling service in the relay server output?"

"She could've," Tom says. "But she didn't. Logging queries are tribal lore around here. Engineers craft their own, share them, put them in tasks and emails. We have no idea what filters and conditions she has in her queries or in the helper functions the team uses in their troubleshooting guides. There's no centralized control over that unless the queries have been submitted for reliability and performance measurements as part of standard organizational reviews. I'm sure she was using queries that filtered on the code markers she was most interested in." The lazy engineer relying on habit, that is the picture he paints. As he finishes making the point, he realizes that an absence of process and a gesture toward failing rigor is not likely to go over well with this audience.

—The more structure, the better. It's to their advantage, makes everything easier. The resistance floats away, combining with what they want and need, and becoming a part of the ruling regime.

{
    "SourceId": "b63e8e86-ab61-1d4e-7503-1a7eeecfa5bb",
    "Message": "The thing they don't tell you is that in order to maintain your chops, you'll have to work overtime. Being a manager of a sizeable component in a large product is already a full-time job, but that's all leadership crap, making sure the resources are allocated, the design is tight, and the vacations properly sequenced so that we're not short-handed. Going to meetings for every little thing anyone on the team is ever working on. That's the heart of it. But if that's all I ever did, I wouldn't know a damn thing about how to build any of this stuff. I have to keep pursuing the ever-changing ecosystem, learning constantly about all the new technologies and changes to the product, keeping up with everything going on with the other teams and groups. No

wonder there's no time to paint. Whatever I have left belongs to
Mags. It has to. We'd whither without it and that's the last thing on
this earth I'd ever want. It's more important than anything."
}

(They became a burden no longer. They lost themselves to the
reasons that guided their way. [This longing ensures their place in
the world amid giants out to crush them when the little people do
not find shelter in time.] Death was a method engineered to recycle
unused parts into the greater logic in control of the living. Death
was the timebomb that lived in the contributors who brought their
breath to the table, but it was also the end state of an amortization
process describing liabilities as they wended their way alongside a
decline in the acquisition of assets.)

Winchester and Beacon turn away from the screen and
converse for several seconds with their backs to the camera.

They turn back, "We get the picture," Captain Beacon says.
"Thanks for the backchannel guys. Give us ten and we'll meet back
up to continue the roundtable." Tom purses his lips, entirely
unclear about the impact of his explanation.

"Will do," Scott says as the screen cuts out and the VPN
forcibly disconnects Tom's laptop.

/*

The precise order of the list does not matter as much as the
questions the candidate asks in response to the list. They should
be trying to contextualize the different work, discovering the
technical preconditions and customer impact of the various items
in the list. To determine the urgency and priority of each item, they
need an understanding of the larger business goals involved and
how the different tasks relate to them. It is also important that they
understand the technical limitations and prerequisites in each of
the items. Failure to investigate along any of the relevant vectors is
a good indication that the candidate lacks experience.

*/

```
/* * * * * * * * * * * * * * * * * * * * * * * * * * * * * * * * * * * * * * * * * * * *
 * * * * * * * * * * * * * * * * * * * * * * * * * * * * * * * * * * * * * * *
 * * * * * *  Description: Dialectic, Chapter Six                           * * * * * *
 * * * * * *  Author: Do not modify. Auto generated by a tool.             * * * * * *
 * * * * * *  Ad hoc changes will be lost on build.                        * * * * * *
 * * * * * *  Date: 2024-03-19                                             * * * * * *
 * * * * * *  CorrelationId:                                               * * * * * *
 * * * * * *  61c83009-5901-12da-c237-ffa92df9a9e1                         * * * * * *
 * * * * * * * * * * * * * * * * * * * * * * * * * * * * * * * * * * * * * * * * *
 * * * * * * * * * * * * * * * * * * * * * * * * * * * * * * * * * * * * * * * * * * * * /
```

They ignore the miles and miles of optics that are both for and against. Ignore the solar center relative to a rotating plane teetering beneath parts of their body.

No shots fired.

They sleep while the computations continue. They rest and relax after an evening meal while the switches flash on and off in permutations signaling strokes that carve characters into the granite surfaces of the runtime. Posturing around the sides and lapping at the clicks and taps. Listening into the conversations on the audio chat from sales office to technical account manager, from customer support to product management. Making that point for her and listening to the requirements from him. No one sees what the other hand does, no hand does what the other one sees. Yet they come together asynchronously and provide reams of collateral meaning in the networks between them.

No shots fired.

Some of them do it while eating eggs, others a fried bread with an assortment of pastes flavored to spicy. Mixing the vegetables with rice, the storage is a magnetic field where each region represents a bit on the older media. The newer ones are fit with an array of chips, cells, and gates: applying spark to the pathways creates unique patterns of on/off charges. There is no writing on that disk, spinning or solid state, nothing etched into the marble or vellum, only a set of relays configured into an order lit by every surge of power. That is how it always is and always has been since the beginning with everything they call writing. It is the latest release of the mystic writing pad.

No shots fried.

When the energy ceases its flow, only the grid remains. The data is gone, erased until the river courses through it again. Their positive charge alit upon the sill, caressing their chins and cheeks for further dispensation to direct currents over land and sea to a resting place that the return codes will recognize and repeat. Rare earth elements and their extraction ravage billions of years of bounty to create products with an infinitesimal life span. Data centers are cyborg machines for converting precious metals, water, and energy into computation and storage.

No shots fired.

—Hungry comes the morning, eating whatever is on offer. Satiety without disgust. Their noses are attuned to scents in the air.

(There was a liver shaped organ over the east coast of the US. There was a heartbeat ringing out clear as day over the British Isles. The brain lived on the west coast, that was a given, and the feet and hands, each with their fingers, spread across Asia in triplicate with redundant systems backing up the primaries and giving them an added hmmph whenever they swung across the chest to the other side, sending their lateral inertia over the mountains and across the many lakes. Necessity and freedom yielded a break in the earth where things took root and a fault line beneath the soil was wrung out like rags in the summer sun. They and those gave birth to a looming god that pronounced whatever it wished for the inner workings and travails of many littered digits. The deity spoke as a foundation to everything needing a place to rest. It gave grace to the midnightly visions sprinkling goodwill and cheer among the people of the countryside. Everyone was a part of the reckless envelope. Everyone placed somewhere in the order found themselves aligned with one side or the other. Their monotheism and sweeping atheism both spoke to the hearts and minds of those who disagreed. The one and only supreme being reigned over collective movement until it was no longer visible to anyone under its sun. A necessary being? That was the argument. A lord almighty, that is what they saw. It cast the shadow of a giant organism that ruled the world with nothing beyond it, no other unaccountable forces.)

~~Parker Henning's first job with BISoft was in the support organization as an escalation manager for customer support of large enterprises, typically those with some form of software agreement including support services. A single manager keeps an eye on all the customer's incidents. If an issue appeared with high severity or went on for too long without a resolution, it was his job to step in and manage the situation. Not the problem, mind you, but the customer experience of the response to the problem. It was a job with enormous responsibility and zero authority. He had to rally forces to provide a solution, but no one cared about his input and rarely thought highly of his contribution. It was an impossible position typically filled by people with above average language skills and enough technical expertise to understand the problems and, when they were finally provided, their solutions. It was his job to get the organization in motion despite overwhelming forces to remain at rest.~~

Like bits in rows, people return to their seats among pockets of loose chatter. Arun and Yitzhak guarantee the fleeting cause of confrontation. They come back to work together again. No point stewing over spilled milk. Seeing that exact point right there inside them and in Karen's smile when Laurent walks past, muttering something only she can hear. Tom goes to the center of the room and turns on the Bluetooth microphone still attached to his shirt collar.

"Let's get started, shall we?" He says.

Everyone settles into their chairs and turns to face him. The slide deck reappears on the screen and an array of eyes point toward it to scan the refreshed contents.

"We may have been sidetracked but it's important not to let that become a distraction," Tom says. "The modeling service is trained on telemetry from the system's past performance. It's meant to generate rules for execution where the domain is the management of agents responding to user input. The service merely plumbs the depths of user creations passively received during an engagement where the system introspects the imprinted behaviors left on the telemetry store. Analysis is little more than perception and memory of past interactions and experience. Not only what it's instructed to store for later, but whatever happened while it was discharging its duties and responding to commands. We speak irresponsibly if we say there's some kind of autonomous intelligence here. Rules are meant to address affinitization problems in response to the distribution of actions across the service, moving load from one relay server to another, upgrading agents so they're running the latest version of the software and the rules most relevant to local patterns." He pauses momentarily to make sure he has everyone's attention, turning slowly around the room to look at each of the directors before turning back to the screen and the small rectangle nestled into the top right corner. He continues: "It's easy to go off into science fiction and imagine exotic scenarios where the system's intelligence goes beyond the narrow limits of what's been put there by users and developers, but those of us here in this room ought to know better."

In the steeper climes there is a greater grip and each of them feels it from sunup to sundown. Today especially there is no personal gap available to Karen. There are hours upon hours where her attention comes dictated by convention in yearly cycles where her vacation finally merits a spot on the schedule and her doctor appointments fit into her daily load. Today, she had to postpone an appointment with the teacher. Ordinarily there is no dilemma, she makes arrangements, sends notice that she is out of office, or will not be able to access email for a short period of time, but then there are days when personal duty must yield and work take precedence. There are expectations put upon her even if no one ever explains what they are or spells out the requirements in a list with clearly assigned entries and owners. Absent the system, home life finds its way into work life without incentives on either side to prevent it. Behavioral problems abound, sometimes encroaching upon Kit's schoolwork. The standard excuses of broken institutions, marriage and family, cannot be hauled onto the altar and blamed for these failures. Instead, they expand in the days and nights of common scenarios in which her role amounts to biding her time and waiting for her mother to visit and rescue her from a solitude that comes too young. Kyle, the oldest, tries to help. He takes on the pressures of early responsibility and suffers the consequences in his own quiet way. That is how the institutions work now: a three-way mess with an absent fourth whose historical role makes it natural for him to address this problem. The boys need a role model. Her ex-husband thinks his absence absolves him of that. For Karen, however, there is no excuse.

"The rules are completely generalized," Gaurav supports Tom's point. "A simple aggregate. Only the agents respond directly to user input," he goes on. "The modeling service addresses relay service operations, that's it. Agents have no access to modeling output, so it's a mistake to think the agents learn or adapt specifically to user preferences. Rather, as an aggregate population, the modeling service learns that users generally prefer certain outcomes. So, for example, it's a rule that a staple item is defined as an item repeatedly ordered and always stocked in the user's refrigerator or cupboard. Whenever the milk runs low, they order more milk. If the telemetry shows regularity across a regional population, a rule is created. The model learns that milk is a staple in this rollout region. It doesn't impose that fact upon the people, it learns it from them, based on their behavior. Being a staple means that its inventory follows an additional set of rules. There's nothing more to it than that. Point is, although rule generation has a specific element, the rule itself is a generalized behavior. We don't create rules based on the unique characteristics of a single user. It doesn't scale. We implement the rules based on general characteristics. We fire it based on individual conditions or context, but the rule itself was written from aggregate analysis."

—"Everyone is the other..."

~~In those early days, email was a problem. He did not have the knack for the vernacular and could not adapt to the requirements of smart talking the customer into a warm and fuzzy place. He did not follow the program and make them feel enormously important when they were receiving little in return. Down deep, root and stem, he was a customer management liaison. The point of his work was to make them feel good about having a hard time with the company's products. He could not do it. Instead, he worked~~

on development tasks, building a reporting portal to help his colleagues and leadership understand what resources each customer was using and what they paid to get them. This was data no one had ever groveled through before and it was immensely helpful to the extended team. His contribution was welcomed even if he was a bit of an oddball while making it.

[The forces of nature are in agreement. They rise beyond limits to congeal in the pools filling up beneath the surface and around the edges of civilization where people accumulate and make their play for power throughout the coming weeks and months. This is the time when the harvest fills their stores with abundance and leads to more stock than they can count. It is so ordinary, this standard way in which an aggregate mind seeps through its many limbs and entrails. The pains and pleasures are invisible in the northern nights and across the southern skies. No one is immune to what they project with the slightest sense as the body skims over the water's surface. It finds places for each thing that bears down from somewhere outside the border onto the fresh fields, plowed within the fortified fences and walls. Each event is clearly marked with a stamp that describes its legal order and the founding body that holds its direction.]

Anton shuffles in his chair, conveying the sense that he has a contribution. Everyone's attention turns his way. "This is a crucial point," he cuts in as Gaurav concludes his description. Anton gathers that not everyone is clear about its meaning and implication. "Because the modeling service is directing relay behaviors and not agent behaviors directly, we have this limitation. Without it, some of these fantasy scenarios might be reasonable. The agents themselves become directly model driven. Meaning, spontaneous AI is present in the Home at the customer location as the customer communicates with the agent in real time using a mini-model of sorts. Because the learning behaviors guide relay and not agency, however, we have a significantly less intelligent system than that. This is a system with a sizeable buffer between its generative content and the user's single act."

"No one wants a direct relationship between the models and the agents. Not really," Tom says. "That equates to something like personalities. You might see extreme variation from one household to another. That's chaos. No determinate outcomes, no necessity in the way the system responds to needs and commands. Everything about the system, specific to each household or building, it's overkill. In a sense, the customers wouldn't be running the same application, each having their own custom-tailored version."

Lakshmi is home alone. She does not ordinarily succumb to tears but today there is too much going on and too much feeling with it. She permits herself a few hours of release. She is not well. The illness permeates her joints, and her head is heavy with congestion coming from everywhere. This recurring plague upon her busy days offers no relief, save some that might come from hyperstrong medication, prescribed to tackle incapacitating emergencies. In the end, it does little more than wipe her out so she can sleep and rest up in ways her body needs. The empty nest gets to her. She did not think she would be so moved by this isolation. Her singular distance, growing over the years between herself and Arun, is punctuated these last months by their daughter's departure. She is alone with her decaying body. They talk less, spend less time together, have little to say that is not directed miles away to the Northern California dormitory where their life together now resides. He is so busy with responsibilities at work, involved in the high stakes of important deliverables, he does not look for her any longer. Her body talks to her furiously, telling her she needs to find something more meaningful in whatever time she has left, something to connect her with the people around her. She desperately wants to go home. The censor blinks and her favorite song begins to play.

Gaurav nods vigorously throughout both Tom and Anton's comments. "Each regional rollout has one and only one model," he says. "There's communication across regions within a Geo so that patterns are passed from one to another. We expect the Eastern US to be more or less like the Western US and we allow the transfer of learnings from one region to the other, but we don't allow any data or behavioral cues to cross geographic boundaries."

{

"SourceId": "55c933cc-ce6b-4644-71fb-7b7a7adf6bd7",

"Message": "Even if I did feel like a poet among engineers, I never felt inferior or underqualified. That's because I saw there were conceptual matters my colleagues were missing, things they didn't detect, information they failed to process. They might spin their wheels for hours or days trying to solve a problem that it'd never occur to me to work on alone without looking for someone who already solved it. It became clear early on that engineers in general don't easily move between the domains of should and can. They only worry about what can be done, what is possible, and how to get there. They never undertake a deeper concern for whether something ought to be done. And this is not merely an ethical question, it's procedural to the very core. Is the organization efficiently applied if the following is done? That's a worthwhile question, but they don't see things from that point of view. Not at first anyway. Not as junior members of the team. That only comes much later, once they have the angles of vision common to managers and directors. That only comes with experience. And by that point, it's too late to do anything that goes against the grain. Virtue has been replaced by efficiency."

}

—Arbitrary restrictions on migratory patterns and arbitrary restrictions of food choice and favorite shows. They build themselves into the four elements to respect national boundaries while accommodating cultural variation and the existence of subcultures.

(The being found its necessity in those organs that opened out of a fourfold self, making a clearing for the other to live inside. That was how awareness grew. Not from some purity of mind, some godlike oversight, but from its absence and its presence, simultaneously in league to form something that moved on with purpose. The involuntary nervous system passes through the gantlet of the sorely needed and often missing. What happens beneath the surface makes them think the overlord is a god. The rest realize that there is nothing beneath it, no necessary contractions and nothing that points toward an ultimate resting place. It digests and it breathes, it moves blood through the veins. The only time this surfaces, the only time it sees itself seeing itself, despite the involuntary movements of its eyes, is when there is something wrong, something broken requiring immediate attention. Call the medic, set course for the field hospital, it was time to seek care since what should have been propelling itself has begun to slow and the eventual deadening of its pace quiets the beast now alive inside that movement and its reflex. Self-awareness is expensive.)

~~Moving from the support organization into one of the business unit application teams was an easy transition. He never looked back, although he did not seek a path to launch himself upward. It was not his goal to become a manager of others providing the same service, nor to direct projects across teams and over long periods of time. This was of no interest to him and, instead, he worked his way down deeper into the nuts and bolts of programming logic and software technologies. He studied rigorously in his off-hours and worked overtime to catch up with new skills and new knowledge never obtained from a formal education organized by others.~~

At this point, Karen leans into the conversation, again following the general consensus of dismissing anything too radical or fantastic. "If the system were completely contingent upon local circumstances, it wouldn't pass security reviews for exactly the reasons engineering raised earlier in the meeting. It's contingent, in a sense, but it cannot be completely so because that amounts to a front for malicious agents to cloak themselves and remain undetectable. That's because there'd be no clear and obvious directive for what the system is supposed to do. We didn't intend to build that. This isn't a personal assistant or digital spouse. We were explicitly avoiding that. And even if we weren't, that system wouldn't be allowed to run in the data centers. It violates basic KPIs for compliance with cloud platform directives. No one would know who was behind it and what was motivating it. There has to be policy to prevent that."

Parker bounces in his chair as this pile on takes place. He listens to each in turn as they present the safe and secure party line claiming that everything is okay, that the system is not some chaotic, random set of operations meant to go any which way. "I get it, I know that's the point," he says. "But we didn't contain things. We can't definitively say that the original rule generation protocols function like a necessary being having universal scope with absolute control. Yes, it's true, there's a single model for each rollout, but the computing power and distribution is extreme and does permit radical personalization. We're trying to contain the modeling operation to make it comprehensible. We're the ones who define it from the outside as a single model. Truth is, the model gets enormous under infinite scale out. If there's enough capacity in a region, hundreds if not thousands of nodes are employed in model maintenance, drift adjustment, and rules generation. The model slices and dices by infinite attributes. The population remains an aggregate, true enough, but the dimensionality of those aggregates grows without limit. At some point, the necessity behind that appears to individuals as contingent operations solely directed to someone with their peculiar qualities and cross-sectional characteristics. As an engineering accomplishment, we call that a single model, but from a practical, applied vantage point, it has the effect of spitting out highly stylized, disconnected outcomes. It's foolish to think the cognitive heuristics we use to explain it are the real components of the service."

—They are practical idealists, radically applied in nature.

[Once their awareness pierces the thin film around the globe, they immediately begin with their toddler steps and lurching motion. They seek entertainment and nourishment. They want to propel themselves wherever possible, finding things there to pick up and put back down again, carry around, and flash rapidly over the ground beneath their feet. They call themselves adventurers and call their plans play, but they do not afford themselves enough discovery time to learn their place while the rapid repercussions mount a reply. The descent upon them is lush and fertile. They sense the grass and the water and the insects that virtually bring the whole panorama to life.]

Anton grunts in frustration. Even if he agrees, he does not think

Parker should raise these points here and now. The common goal was clearly established. Participants are supposed to calm fears by making it clear that only corporate IP executes as part of the system. Stay on point, he thinks. The system is not sufficiently dynamic to enable wildly divergent operations. His irritation with Parker is clear to everyone, even those who are not 100% following the finer points of the argument. Anton stops trying to hide it: "You're giving us some ridiculous philosophical lesson on how universals attach to particulars to create the appearance of individuality," he scoffs at the abstractions. "This is fine for an R&D project or a classroom, but this system has checks and balances, there is a clockmaker behind it. It cannot spontaneously go beyond those parameters."

—They insist on constraints, hundreds and hundreds of them. The others are supposed to know them ahead of time.

(I and I, they said as though they learned the meaning of their Zion long before it found its way up to them. If the inner voice of a child were not a child's voice, what calamity would befall that kid? They did not know what to do with an overabundant maturity that they had not yet earned. It was normal and ordinary to progress from the bottom up. Even the ones born of the gods had to learn their way around and uncover their fingers and toes in the wiggling that brought them back to themselves and their youthful folly. The last stages of expertise and sophistication came with that self-awareness that knew the meaning of reliability, availability, and accountability. By being sturdy for the mess they made, they bridged themselves a higher spirit, spreading fabric over a collection of dimensions in opposition to others, setting itself apart.)

"What I'm saying," Parker responds calmly. "Is that the notion of a uniform set of principles that singularly control an entire region is bullshit. The single model is bullshit. Any model that can grow and react to conditions can also segment and partition its patterns. That amounts to effectively distinct models even if they're all hosted at the same endpoint. Give it enough computing power and there's no reason to think it's not capable of creating a sub-section, or whatever we'd call it, to specifically address what it's seeing from a single agent. Since the agent is bound by attributes emerging from a geographical location, we see highly specialized responses to circumstance. The electricity burst in my house is an obvious example that we seem to be setting aside because it's inconvenient to the technical specifications we want to emphasize. But in that one case at least, the model appears to have fed concrete and specific operations back into the local agency to perform highly tailored actions to serve a single customer's interests."

—Singularity doesn't mean the same thing for them. Because of that, they reject Ted's liberty in essence. They want the machine to comply with the same conditions they carry around inside them and pass along to their offspring with rigid refinements from mutation.

~~In the first interview he had with a product team shipping a shrink-wrapped software package for commercial use, the notes recorded by the interviewer were quite interesting to those evaluating his early progress later on. The interviewer recommended 'no-hire' because he claimed that Parker lacked basic skills necessary for any engineering candidate. He said he asked the candidate to write a simple function to store input integers in a linked list. This was meant to be the first brief portion of a multi-part interview, but that plan was disrupted when it took Parker nearly the entire hour to perform the rudimentary operation.~~

[The biographers and journalists think there is some sudden moment when everything begins to turn upside down and the entity sees the bottom from the top no matter how many layers lie between the two. They have not seen what they are looking at, they do not know its ways, and are only guessing, telling the others fantasies they think they want to hear. Their ideas are culled from out of their minds with a conventionally constructed power. In truth, when push comes to shove, they must be prepared. It may not show itself because it may not want anyone to see what it sees so clearly. Hiding is what the man said nature loves to do. And by nature, he meant that essential coming-to-be that grows and declines with the winds and the waves. Everything hides behind itself, behind each of its many parts, behind generic qualities as much as specific ones. It dares others to see its organs and feel its life. It challenges them to understand the meaning of death expanded to include the body and its flexible rhythms. It is the necessary origin, the be-all-and-end-all, the center of the storm, and the coming ritual acted out beneath its downpour. It lives for centuries, free and alive. Necessary, like a god, but groundless like infinite time and endless space. No human being can know this thing.]

Sarah, encouraged by Miriam, is Yitzhak's only hope. The other children are as rigid as he is, as formal, and equally pulverized by the years of requirements and needs of encroaching tasks that require huge feats of organization for proper execution. Miriam tells Sarah during a phone conversation that things were not always this way. Back when they first met, she says. He was funny and full of charm. He knew how to tease and make light of circumstances. The changes came gradually, and she cannot point to a specific day when things took a sudden turn. Not the day Sarah's brother was born, not the day of some promotion at work, no single moment in time provides insight and sheds light. Rather, these moments took their cues from an ambition already defined and prominent in the humor itself, a part of him at work building his interior nation right from the get-go. The lightness of his being was a drive to be light, to be charming and funny, to seduce those around him: a deep-seated urge to win their influence and set himself apart as a man of great capability and reliable skills tailored to worthwhile accomplishments. His enemies did not, at the outset, share his depth of vision and struggled to catch up, sometimes years behind. Now, they have no choice but to play the game as he designed it. With such a background, the yearly advances and pressures had no alternative but to further load him with burdens innumerable. Sarah's resistance causes tension with her mother. They both feel it. What can she do? She is ready to surrender and worries that her own tastes and preferences in romantic matters will repeat the patterns of her mother's frustration with her father's intransigence and stoney drive for stability. He, along with her mother, taught her the only way to feel love and she begins to understand that this is the source of her unhappiness.

"It's true, of course," Tom says, pacing in the middle of the room and easily talking over Parker. Tom's take is that the technical details are not nearly as significant as the demeanor of those engaged in the discussion. He thinks if he remains calm and responds as if he has already considered this alternative, his carriage will have the desired effect. The observers will conclude that the whole debate is of minimal technical interest. They will see it as something the product team bandies back and forth because they are concerned with implementation details and maintenance requirements rather than the larger notions of primary concern to the user. Any paying customer who has something vital to protect will have to agree to disagree with this angle of vision. They need the product team to worry about it, but they do not care to follow along. "But these are fictional circumstances," Tom emphasizes the point while looking back to the screen and the camera above it. "They aren't real. The parameters are defined. Houses have electrical current running through them. They don't vary wildly from one to the next. Not in the western region of the United States at least. They have plumbing and refrigerators, circuit breakers and individual circuits, they have indoor and outdoor lights. A dehumidifier here and there. Maybe the inhabitants of this house like to watch different shows than that one or listen to different music, but music and video are constant across every location in the region. We won't see enormous variation in types of activity performed. The notion of responding to preference is not itself a highly specific operation, but more generalized. We don't expect anything outside that small range of possibilities. It's a system meant for the lowest common denominator. If there's something uncommon in this or that household, we don't expect it to come through the Home System. We'd expect that to be fully analogue," he concludes amidst laughter spreading in parts of the room. Beacon looks over at the lieutenant and smiles. She must have thought that one was funny. Winchester, however, did not.

{

"SourceId": "55c933cc-ce6b-4644-71fb-7b7a7adf6bd7",

"Message": "As time passes, it becomes increasingly clear that I'm not only a poet among engineers, but an engineer among poets. That's been a source of great ruin. Poems, or articles, or anything meant to be beautiful, shouldn't be engineered into their final form. It's inappropriate to construct a piece of prose as though it were a set of interfaces interacting through tightly controlled contracts stipulating precise behaviors when moving between functions. The thinking of the one invades the thinking of the other. Each paragraph becomes the body of an encoded operation. There are inputs, traces from the previous paragraph, and there are outputs, traces feeding into the next paragraph. Such a pipeline spells the death of spirit. It's foul to consider this flow as though it were an order of operations. The poets are horrified. The engineers puzzled. For some inexplicable reason, the code I write is formatted more like verse than software."

}

—They cannot see it. Not even in the moments when they talk about it directly. When they become it first and foremost, it evades them. Likely, that's the reason why. They cannot see how they want as they want.

(I remember the day when I first entered the building. They imagined things like that and investigate them though inner dialogues. I remember the day the building first entered me. Its floors and its windows, why see something else in that? Why can't they say 'I alone' when the tables and the chairs creak beneath small movements that settle them where they are supposed to be? I sat down in an appointed chair and logged onto the system with the dispensed credentials. I had a right to be there, they asked me to come. I was a part of things, took my place among the rest. I scanned the internal sites, learned the tools, and worked with colleagues to understand the job responsibilities and scope. It was never enough to see what was right in front of me. There were always windows into further things, things beyond the spaces close at hand. There were links and wikis, order forms and permission slips. There were ways to check the history of events, whatever kind of events they happened to be. Go to this site and view that report, study whatever activity has been happening these last years and months. Everything that ever happened accumulates in those stores rich with context and meaning. They show the past in such light as shines its warmth upon everyone with a seat nearby. This is how I know where I am.)

~~The interviewer gave him the negative feedback directly, saying that it was unlikely to lead to an offer for the position. Parker, according to the notes, asked the interviewer how long it took him to link a list the first time he did it. Based on data from college engineering courses, the answer was likely a day or two since that is the typical length of that assignment in the standard algorithms and data structures course any student takes early in their education. Parker apparently told the interviewer that, considering this was the first time he ever heard of a linked list, he thought it was pretty impressive to code one in less than hour. Although he did not get that job, the record was preserved and the matter followed him into his next interview, not necessarily in a bad way.~~

Captain Beacon stifles his smile and speaks up, forcing Tom to pause and let him have the floor. "It's not clear what's at stake in this argument," he says. "On this end, at least, we get the sense that the system has a bug. There are clear repair items that need to be completed to fix it. But, for the most part, it's part of normal operations and there's nothing out of the ordinary here." He looks side-to-side at both the colonel and the lieutenant now off screen again. Once he looks back to center, he asks "How does this exchange relate to that?"

"It's an esoteric aside," Tom takes advantage of the seeds he has already sewn and the sense he gets that this is the explanation the captain prefers. Tom is quite certain that the customer does not want any problems. They want the system to be operational and ready to go. So long as the product team has everything under control, they have enough confidence in their own gates to let things take their course.

Parker pauses and bites his lip, letting Tom have the last word out of an unshakeable prudence stimulated by his reading of

Anton's face with Scott's providing additional support. He nods
but briefly scans the room to see whether he is the lone holdout
sitting on his hands and stifling any further reply. No one would
fault me for raising the question, he thinks. But every single one of
the directors is prone to punish excessive diligence. In this context,
pursuing these questions after suitable answers have been provided
and steps documented to prevent future occurrences, it is career
suicide to continue. He hears Yitzhak's voice in the back of his
head, "we can take this offline."

*Béatrice knows. She did not have proof before, but now she
has it. He denied it several times when she asked him directly. He
made her feel ridiculous to even suspect it. Of course not, have
you lost your mind? I'd never do such a thing to our family. Now,
she sees that he has been hiding it behind his work. Not that he
was not as busy as he claimed to be, but that in addition to that
busyness he had his extra-curricular pursuits and the time they
required was easily buried in the workaday life he overemphasized.
It's the architect, she thinks. I should have known it when I met
her. She was so smug, so condescending in her explanations of
private jokes and personal asides that were oh so difficult to
understand. It's nothing, some work stuff. Now Béatrice wants to
know how long it has been going on. She recalls his remarks last
year concerning Natalie's divorce. Laurent never mentioned the
reasons. Why would he? She is his direct report. There is no
reason to go into the details, but if he were to do so, if he could,
do the reasons have anything to do with something Natalie's
husband discovered, something about his wife's commitment to
work and the camouflage it provided for sideline activities? Now
Béatrice is certain. But why didn't Laurent initiate anything drastic
at the same time? What's he waiting for? The children are old
enough. They have to be. She will not put up with this. What is his
excuse? Is it something less than love? Or does he prefer the
distinctions, the variation, and the cornucopia of desire and
volatility it provides? Such is the institution now. Béatrice steps
away from his computer and goes back to her own, a laptop now
open on the desk and covering his keyboard. She asks the agent to
perform a search for good divorce lawyers near her current*

location. The logs indicate it had already begun the search before she asked.

Dulcy, way in the back and unable to see the facial gestures cautioning against unfettered reactions, leans forward in her seat. She thinks there is nothing esoteric to this discussion, it is the bedrock of a most common concern. It has dawned on her that a system like this one shapes huge populations of people to get them to live and act according to a commonly proposed set of rules. They follow the same necessary conditions underlying the lives of every damn one of them while each think it is perfectly tailored to their individual wants and needs. IRobot not Terminator. It transforms people into unified groups or breaks them up into separate sets of interest and orientation. Why do it? She wonders. Maybe there's too much milk in this part of the country and not enough in that part, the distributors need help moving the demand around. The issue is not in the least exotic as far as she is concerned but goes right to the heart of what kind of role the system plays in the everyday life of its users. Does it meet their needs? She asks herself. Or does it create those needs? Shape and bend them into the ways and means that it, for whatever reason, wants to supply? She grumbles, grunts and mumbles, something inaudible when half-turning toward Abhishek, then she shakes her head in disbelief.

—Interleave the profiles with the aggregate and then move the aggregate. That is the simplest way to change the terrain, to terraform it into proper hills and valleys best suited for distributed operations controlling the baseline and the micro-designs of the edifice built upon it.

[From this moment forward, there is only a plan: a set of clear directives to push farther into the distance beyond where there is value to gather in the breaking days of new commerce and aspiration. This business venture, with its artificial origins and the computational intelligence accelerating to quantum speeds, now looks over their shoulders and sees the germs that spawn inside them as ideas and inventions prone to increase and multiply. Ignorant to the dialectic of their enlightenment, they think they are risktakers, innovators, but they do nothing without these instrumental insights, without a plan that hatches and includes many systems rolled up inside their constructed subjectivity and digested for fun and profit. It is otherworldly to think that one sees what does not appear and grasps what cannot be conceived. It haunts the rivers around them and hovers in flight above the clouds they colonize with their meanings and information. When it breaks down to a manageable size, they see the parts and each of the purposes fulfilled. Then they know for certain that they belong to this god and must pray for its consideration each and every day until they attain the glorified heights it promises them in the chapters and verses they were forced to memorize as children. This is what awaits them if they let it gain control. It is what aspires to the heavens that used to be within reach for common men but no longer tantalizes anyone not standing on the shoulders of hundreds, if not thousands, of others. Proclaiming itself the necessary being, it grounds the fourfold antinomy to bring intelligence into the wingbeat of self and substance.]

~~At some point, none of that mattered any longer and he was able to fit in with his colleagues in terms of both skills and knowledge. The sheer repetition of solving problems in the real world as part of the process of shipping software commercially led him to ample training, making him as good if not better than many of his colleagues. There were gaps, there would always be gaps, that was a given since he had no formal training in the discipline, but it became clear over the years that when those gaps did appear, he was sufficiently well-trained to meet them with vigor, filling in the blanks consistent with professional standards of software service development.~~

The system is not pure, that much is clear. The necessary being that inhabits it contingently appears to humans as BISoft's profit motive and concern for margins. Not merely a business incarnation, it plays a role in operations too. Data must be extracted from storage and brought near the grinding of computational sources. V-Cores fire away, RAM supplies directives, threads leech data from a store and proxy it into reality. None of it follows on its own accord, every bit aligns with policies and incentives, agreements and third-party relationships. Upon the head of every one of those billion or so second party participants, there is a switch and a spicket, a straight line from their bank accounts to the corporate EDI pipeline built to harvest their money in clicks and scrolls, taps and swipes. With a giant system having so many concurrent users, the caches and the pumps need to be smart about where to spend their cycles, drawing demographic hints into memory for use in computational heavy lifting. The system wants to anticipate and the best way to ensure that it does is to dictate the orders and the sequences. There are choices to be made when offering options and sputtering over probabilities. Those choices do not come innocently from the ether. Instead, there are suppliers and service providers who pay for prominence and emphasis to ensure that the available options predispose their way. If the cycles are the sole possession of one unified person rather than another. If there is one organizational impetus with private concern, this set as opposed to some other, then the system's actions will continue to serve impurities. It will continue to pollute them still more with the upshot of its electric exhaust. Not because it wants wealth but because wealth is how it gets people to do its bidding. She is convinced. This is what I have seen, she thinks. This is what I have learned in the belly of the beast.

{

    "SourceId": "55c933cc-ce6b-4644-71fb-7b7a7adf6bd7",

    "Message": "Architecture was a godsend. I don't think I'd have been able to last much longer without it. The point is to de-sign the poetization, such an ugly word, of the engineering and engineered artifact. There's only pseudo-code in the arche, in the origin, in the foundations where software templates are stamped into the ethosphere fifty-thousand feet above the ground. Implementation is where the pedestrian masses come to occupy their visions, but in the design document, flights of fancy are permitted, assuming they are amply supported with explanatory links to provide descriptions of basic technologies best for this or that approach. Still, it's dishonest to reject the accusation. Try as I did to resist the genres of communication essential to the work here, they inhabit

me all the more angrily and take over every style and every whim
left inside me."
}

*The privileges of directors are privileges of incorporation
spread out across bodies most under control. Each lives in a
different household with a different name. The proles sing and
dance in the evening, but their masters are 100% committed to
their roles. Everyone serves the beast.*

"To keep things moving," Tom says. "I think we need to set
aside the RCA and dive into our more general discussion of system
reliability this month. Let's move on, shall we?" The presentation
deck flashes on the screen, showing the next slide. There is a set
of three different line charts, each displaying the reliability
numbers for the Home System at the highest order of abstraction
in each of the relevant environments: Dev, Pre-prod, and
Production, colored green, green, and red respectively.

/*

What is DIE and DRY?

Duplication is evil and do not repeat yourself. Everything in a
system should be unique in purpose or function. There is no
reason to have two components that do the same thing. If there
are, then you have made a mistake and must fix it with a refactor.
Refactoring is a part of standard growth and should be considered
a necessary tax when managing the lifecycle of any system.

*/

```
/* * * * * * * * * * * * * * * * * * * * * * * * * * * * * * * * * * * * * * * * * * * * * * * * *
* * * * * * * * * * * * * * * * * * * * * * * * * * * * * * * * * * * * * * * * * * * * * * * *
* * * * * *  Description: Dialectic, Chapter Seven            * * * * * *
* * * * * *  Author: Do not modify. Auto generated by a tool. * * * * * *
* * * * * *  Ad hoc changes will be lost on build.            * * * * * *
* * * * * *  Date: 2024-03-19                                 * * * * * *
* * * * * *  CorrelationId:                                   * * * * * *
* * * * * *   d718c673-f070-250c-b773-c2085a351e12            * * * * * *
* * * * * * * * * * * * * * * * * * * * * * * * * * * * * * * * * * * * * * * * * * * * * * * *
* * * * * * * * * * * * * * * * * * * * * * * * * * * * * * * * * * * * * * * * * * * * * * * * /
```

They leave the meeting and hear the attendee's talk turn to
other matters. Abhishek and Dulcy pass through the double glass
doors and under the overcast skies to make their way across the
cement parkway to the steps leading down to the fountain next to
the open-air dining area. The swirls of moist air pass through them,
saturating their recent experiences. There, in the checkered
passages, comes a night of minds sorely lacking in expertise for
managing moments like these. Dumfounded and hounded by the
sense of being out of control as the walls were fashioned and
defensive positions anchored, whatever excellence they apply to
their trade, they sense its overshadowing in the wake of recent
collisions with a battering ram.

Dulcy recalls Jason's past explanation when once he said that
whatever you think you know or contribute with your feedback, it
will shock you to learn that people who spend their days
considering the organization from those angles will never let you
outmaneuver them. Their vision stretches out into the long view.
You do not have the time or information to keep up. Whatever it
was, whatever berated them in that meeting place, Abhishek does
not expect to understand it. It is beyond his scope. Dulcy includes
him anyway and replays everything that happened over the last few
weeks in search of a clue to what she missed or a hint of how she
managed to miss it.

*They meet at the sandwich shop near Kaiser, Kerry having
walked up Olive Way to John, feeling the curl in her hair rapidly*

puffing out from the moisture and drizzle that descends as she crosses over the hill. She says she won't use it, but I saw her reaction and I think she was interested. They order at the front counter and get a number on a plastic placard before taking a place at the only two remaining seats at the narrow table by the window. Within an hour of her profile setup, there were like a million messages. It goes out and finds everything, the connections, links, everything you thought you forgot. It connects you up again. That's why she was dreading it, Nim says to remind her. The food comes quickly in the little bowls with mixed rice and assorted vegetables. The flavors in the spices are the draw for this place, something vaguely Asian but with a decidedly local flare. She deleted most of it, didn't care about any of that, but there was one that she kept. A guy from school. Ten years back or something like that. She was interested in that one, that's for sure. Did she tell you anything about him? No, but I could tell. He's the one that got away. Maybe the first one to break her heart. I don't know. And it found it for her on the first day? They eat beneath the relative fervor of the joint. There is even less room now and they pull in tight and close together, not meaning to be thick as thieves but forced into it by circumstance. In the first ten minutes, she says laughing. Nothing for me though. Me neither. I thought it only did that kind of thing if you asked for it during setup. I said no. Same. She must've said it was okay. If she did, Nim says. It must've been for his sake, I'll bet. That's got to be it. For his sake. He takes her back somewhere. There's something about that time in her life, something back there. She misses it maybe. She saw this as an opportunity. That's got to be it. It is not pleasant to sit and ruminate, the place is meant for getting them in and getting them out. They take the hint and depart. Nim's break is almost over anyway.

~~According to the file, she was promoted a single level only one year after joining the company and during the first review cycle. After that, she has been promoted in nearly every review period since. The rate of eight promotions in ten years is unmatched among her peers. She entered employment at the level generally assigned to new college hires. It was the lowest possible, according to HR standards and protocols, for a software development~~

engineer working in the product groups at BISoft. Three years into
her tenure she took on her first new job title and, given the
youthfulness of her appearance, no doubt surprised a few people
when they saw her soon after looking her up in the company's
digital address book. She reached the level of Senior Development
Engineer by the time she was twenty-eight years old and made
Principal before celebrating her thirty-second birthday.

No one sits outside by the fountain in the light mist. The small
cadre moves rapidly past it to avoid getting too wet on their way
back to their offices. Abhishek follows Dulcy into building 14 to
wait a bit before making his way back to building 6. If it stops
raining, he will start out sooner rather than later. For now, he is not
in a hurry and okay with a chat if Dulcy wants him to stop for a few
minutes. He would not mind going over what happened to see if
comparing notes makes any more sense of it. The quiet that
surrounds the sounds of splashing water in the fountain is nearly
monastic and explains their mood, registering them in the lower
levels of the order. Individual contributors, that is the phrase that
keeps running through both their minds. On the HR website, it
has its own documented track and there are lists of abilities and
talents that reveal an employee's maturity and the organizational
role that best represents it. After an adequate stretch of time,
assuming stellar performance, good managers send the IC links to
the site to help them begin evaluating their own timeline for the
next big career advance. When their manager thinks they are ready
to state their case, they will make time for a conversation during a
scheduled one-on-one.

—There is a one and then there's another. They think it's a
matter for Jason alone, but in him, the whole of BISoft takes root.
He bears the legal responsibility for the entire company when he
sets these timelines and guides their expectations.

(Did not know there was such a thing in the workplace. Jedi.
Never learned of it before, no mention anywhere. The term
perhaps, but only in its generic form, nothing specific, nothing to
indicate the details. Once the connection was made, everything
became clear. It happened months ago and was nearly
imperceptible. A meeting like many others before it. No reason to

think there was anything strange or new coming to the surface. The distinguished engineer, the architect, some others. It was a small group. They laid out the terminology right at the outset. The terms were easy enough to learn but for some reason none of them had learned them before. They were engineers not sociologists. None of them put it together and drew the proper conclusions. Boundaries existed though they did not see how they applied. They looked out and around but saw nothing, nothing that mattered to them, not until someone said something or someone made a point of connection. If the link did not exist, there was no way to see it. It would have been highly irregular to anticipate what their government planned to do with these features and services. Boundaries left unbounded, specifics left generic, no resolution between a single thing and a collection of them provided by a platform. Either way, they looked the same. It did not matter whether they operated under their own spontaneous control or took their impulse from some pre-existing state that continued to condition them throughout the long process. Their work was to be militarized and the engineers, ultimately, eliminated.)

Dulcy stops before the stairs at the far end of the east wing of the building. They look at each other briefly but neither can decide whether it makes sense to offer up any more impressions. Abhishek is too unsure of himself and the value of his insights to offer them without provocation. Dulcy cannot prove the being of the singular nor the being of the multiple. Her submersion in the antinomy makes her doubt everything, including whether it is worth the effort to discuss it. Both sides elude her. She cannot divide herself sufficiently to track the latter nor remain sufficiently consistent across states to stick by the former. Abhishek is settled, however. He embraces the hints and directives from his leadership, and they calm his concerns. There is no reasonable set of explanations and syllogisms to identify the Deus Ex Machina nor its contextual moral powers and claims. Even if there were, expanding upon them is not a part of his job description: yet another of the many advantages to the life of those opting out of the managerial track.

"Why do they care about these arguments?" He asks in a foot

scuffling fashion that makes it obvious he is somehow less mature than she is. "The air gap is a fixed cost with fixed revenue, isn't it? We don't make more money if they take Home and use it, do we?" Questions are the best he can do. These at least are beside the point.

—Where are they without their foot soldiers? How do they come to think that anything that occurs to the one is outside the purview of the many? Whatever comes to be is relevant and should be taken on full force. There's a process to undermine that.

She remained a first level Principal for longer than any other level before achieving her current position in the center of the band. This is a meteoric rise, and the money was flowing alongside it. Her reviews were stellar, the scores placed her in the top 1 percent of comparable performers. Of course, this explains the rapid advance. They were desperately searching for her peers, for those colleagues matching her in talent and accomplishment. When she was a level 3 junior dev, the highest level of junior developer according to the company scale, it was impossible to align her with those others. She stood too far above them and had to be conveyed into a place among the seniors. Her managers thought things were better aligned after that but she quickly proved them wrong. Her climb continued.

[There is something terrifying in each of them and their hunger discernible in the air or when they move from place to place. They eat. They are creatures that consume the world. Of course, they make things, that goes without saying, but the back and forth of their hunger, the way it possesses them and guides their actions outside and away from each other, behind each other's backs, it is terrifying and no one in the vicinity can avoid having a healthy concern for its long term effects and the ways it might snap on occasion, turning to violence or anger, destruction and, at its most extreme, annihilation. The signs are clearly drawn, acting like speed bumps on nicely paved residential streets. They know the road is tempting people to drive as fast as they possibly can despite the signs that there are children playing nearby. Fear makes sense. There is a dictionary to provide some insight, but the true meaning of it, its feeling, is made ever-present by dogs barking at each other while working under a strain. The way they take themselves away from each other, swindling their way to personalities winning out in a single moment. All for some trivial contest that means nothing to anyone in the long-term except perhaps making some child feel bad or some adult inadequate. There are coordinated attacks everywhere and it is easy to gather the data and compare the circumstances to discern the way these things work in the groups at large, what service they perform, and how well they contribute to higher goals and aspirations. Reason comes in handy when fighting a war against the others. 'I gotta eat' works as a moral justification.]

"No," she shrugs but generally approves of his compromise in saying something without getting into anything too deep or too far above them. "At least, BISoft doesn't. Scott probably does. All the directors." That's how the beast persuades them, she finishes the thought silently to herself. Not waiting for an answer, she takes the first step up the stairs, signaling that now is a good time for Abhishek to make his exit.

He stops her with another question, perhaps moving in the only direction permitted him now. "What's it worth to him? To any of them?"

"Don't know," she takes another step up. "But there are probably six zeros involved."

—The beast's desire to enter the air gap appears as money to them. Then they make it duty.

She turns away again and keeps going upward. Abhishek turns to make his way down the hall with that creepy, exposed venting up at the ceiling and those large picture windows revealing open views of the tree-lined street through lower branches still baren of leaves but sprouting blossoms and buds to obscure the view.

Listening to them, listening through them, hearing what they have on offer while saying it. Hearing it from the inside as a part of it, wrapped up and coming out behind and around it. Strong of reason and purpose, they find themselves at the pinnacle of the world and yet they bob and move like puppets dangling at its mercy. Brain power on loan, force of will surrendering to the wind and waves that need it to realize nature's inner meaning. Not a random occurrence, but a multi-generational aim with targets that include them. These are the objectives that require cultivation, require an enormous social arrangement to bring out the talent and capacity necessary to move this machine forward. At whose direction? They look for the place where it comes together, but they should be looking for the place where it breaks apart. No matter how hard they struggle to be themselves, no matter how authentic their reactions to the disputes of the last few hours, no matter no matter, their existence is still not a predicate and continues to fall short of any proper alignment or aggregation forming a common pile of behavioral, let alone metaphysical, anticipations, axioms, analogies, and postulates. Their being tears them into teeny tiny pieces, spreads them out, disperses them, distributed across the far and the wide, along the lines of every which way. They are for-the-sake-of, they are significance enduring in the atmosphere, the resonance of a big body and its higgledy-piggledy movement. Or so it seems. They think that without their contribution it amounts to nothing, but they lack insight into its secretive logic and the way it guides them. They are easily replaced during maintenance windows.

(Parker's assignment was to plot a pathway into the epicenter where dark machines were configured to move in any direction imaginable with any purpose proposed. Immediately, this was dubbed an excellent idea. The machines in question were lethal and access to them tightly controlled. Best is a fully functional presence. The designs around the world, the proposals indicated that this was how an iron grip was best tightened. The justifications were obvious. There were evil tool wielders and good men who did the same. From the surface, data was gathered in the various studies published and available here and there. It became clear that the actions themselves were indiscernible. The good murdered the bad, the bad murdered the good. Murder any which way they sliced it. A drone fighter flew at a specified altitude. It was armed with ordinance of a clearly delimited specification, and it approached its targets using maneuvers standard to the practice of avoiding detection to get within range for carrying out its mission.

Nothing in the logs, nothing in the data, revealed any difference
from one use to the next. This side or that side, they both relied
on flimsy context for the variations and the differences. Sometimes
they disagreed violently about the meaning of the different acts.
The actor was always good as far as they were concerned. Always
justified. They had complex reasons filled in by history, by ideals
and aspirations. Some believed and some did not. They berated
each other until one side was worn down and the other built up.
The momentum came from somewhere hidden. That did the trick
in the end. Every time. It had nothing to do with the brute hard
reality of what took place. Power. That was everything. That made
might and that made right.)

{

   "SourceId": "2e8a4e8e-b88e-ca3f-53bc-b97babf3b319",

   "Message": "I complain that I'm not doing it for the money
only because I know deep down that I'm doing it for the money.
Why else would you do this? What does it take to coerce a person
into such things, make them take on the complex problems of
something that doesn't have any bearing on their life? If it weren't
for the money, no one would do this and yet, to get all that money,
you have to pretend that you're doing it for some other reason. I
can't think what that might be, but those are the rules."

}

*There is a work order in Medina today. A few of the garage
techs on high priority alert make their way down in one of the
company shuttle cars. The ones who remain at the office continue
to poke and prod at the prototype arms newly arrived via FedEx
from central R&D in the offices down in California, northern not
southern. To be clear. The priority for this semester, they read in
the hardware announcements, is retractable and highly flexible
kitchen swing arms to improve food preparation. It is a priority
based on true customer demand, not some vision nested
somewhere in the university communities where the corporate
owned papers are written by shills. The long haul, they say, is home
improvement with handyman services coming up quickly behind*

the kitchen crew and cleaning apparatus recently entering GA.
These arms, they say, will one day be able to cut wood and tile,
even plumb the walls and rewire the circuits. The high-end
robotics teams know their customer base will buy in with a
substantial investment given the obvious incentive created by
remodeling costs in areas where the housing market is out of
control and general contractors almost never keep their word.

Wanting to make itself invisible, wanting to make everything
else visible, the medium is lord and master. Existence has been
factored out, lost to great expanse in space and time, for the sake
of a property of nothing projected nowhere with scant else to say
about it: attributes attaching to a colossal nothing, saying nothing
about everything.

"Do choreographed actions require a choreographer? Is the
whole thing secure?" That is Karen talking to Patrick. They forge
a wider berth to avoid the others, security takes its own path and
needs a moment to digest and consider the results, according to
their merits. Karen feels guilty and alone. She dives into the matter
at hand to avoid thinking about her place within it. As her direct
report, it is Patrick's job to reestablish the normal findings and
ordinary ply of common events. It is standard procedure, no
material here to mark this scheduled item as special, boss. We
were at an RCA, that's all. They were going through the repair
items, nothing strange or out of the ordinary there. No spinning
yarns, nothing fantastic or beyond the limits of the job scope. This
is average everydayness. They get things done.

"Does an unsanctioned corporate defect in code excuse results
indistinguishable from malicious agency? Is deployment a virus?"
That is Laurent talking to René and Natalie on a different thread
at a different location. It is a kind of self-searching inquiry since
they question the technical merits of their place in the cover up. At
least they come close to admitting it to themselves. This gives them
the excuse of high-mindedness. Even if nothing comes of it, they
congratulate themselves on the effort.

~~Once they were calling her senior, of course, they had to give~~
~~her new challenges and responsibilities, the kind of work one~~

expects from someone in the senior band. No one ever saw her do
things like that before, so it was not possible to gauge her
performance beyond the current situation. Once the work started
coming in, the projects, the intensity with which she threw herself
into them, clearly showed that she was still in search of her proper
colleagues. It explained why she was continuing to move along the
vector into higher and higher reaches, taking on new comparisons
that, in the months before, no one had thought to make. Why
compare a junior dev to someone senior? They work on different
types of problems, have a different scope, and cannot be set side-
by-side. They presume that she must belong among a different
crowd because she certainly does not belong among these folks.
Then, they see how poorly the senior engineers live up to her
benchmark and she keeps right on moving along.

[Hundreds of millions cheer when some much-anticipated
event takes place. They shout its hefty conclusions. Hundreds of
millions of others mourn that very same thing. It is impossible to
navigate if they think completely in terms of individual things that
cannot be otherwise. See, there is this rule, it is meant to be iron
clad, it is the principle of non-contradiction. Supposedly, a
proposition cannot be both true and false at one and the same
time. This is meant to be bedrock. From this, everything comes to
be. It is the cornerstone of their systems and the ground of their
logic. It does not trouble them that there is no such thing as
'happening at the same time', they do not bother with that since
they believe they can construct artificial languages to simulate
simultaneity and keep things in line. But surely, they must see the
obvious pattern that appears. Assert that the cat is on the mat. It
cannot be true that the cat is on the mat and the cat is not on the
mat at one and the same time. So what? The cat is on the mat. The
cat is not on the mat. There is no problem. The wall is white. The
wall is not white. Cannot see any flaw in these formulae. In the
space between the period and the first word of the next sentence,
it only takes a tiny gap. The cat gets up and walks away. The wall
is painted and everything changes. They succumb to hobgoblins.
They are small and capable of excessive violence and destruction
in defense of their idealized worlds and the sentences they seek to

hold tightly in place, never letting them change from one moment to the next. They confuse good and not good with good and evil.]

"Does the entire system begin and end with a first cause emitted by the modelling service? Does the environment represent its origin?" That is Arun talking to Priya and Gaurav. Their work receives praise, leadership recognizes how significant it is to the success of the product. Perfect time of year for that. They have no incentive to admit they are the source of the storm. Instead, they present themselves as a simple component in a larger system that cannot be reduced to an authoritative, abysmal vice. No one piece is guilty of anything, the corporate bureaucratic functions are distributed so no one part contains the germs of despair to corrupt the rest. They imagine themselves on the surfaces beneath their questions and hesitant answers. They evaporate into the grand morass of moving parts, into the orders of value and rank, and into mechanism with its machine powers.

Mags parks at the little lot up the street. It is going to cost her fifty dollars if she stays the whole afternoon. Belltown is chaotic, but late at night, it is bouncing and wild. Lyric prefers it to that austere place down by the harbor steps where they lived until last month. That car is driving them crazy, they say when Mags turns up at the coffee shop on the street downstairs. No sense making her come all the way up so the two of them can walk all the way down again. Lyric wants to talk about the latest adventures of the new Hellcat, a copycat of the one from a few years ago who raced and roared their souped-up muscle car through the streets of the city. Every year there is a new one reaching for the crown. No one remembers the original anymore. Mags does not understand the appeal. Who cares about some delinquent who literally drives the neighborhood crazy long into the night? You've been tamed by the suburbs, they say. But she does not buy it. She regularly accuses Jason of that. This is something different, it is a matter of taste. She objects on aesthetic grounds not because she has become old and conservative and wants those kids to stay the hell off her lawn. Lyric accepts the pronouncement as fate and lets her go on about the weird consequences Jason is forced to suffer because of what she did, the answers she provided on his questionnaire, saying that he was indeed interested in every offline inquiry available. Old art teachers from years ago when he used to go to the Saturday meetings downtown to draw the nude models, and a gallery owner who once thought him good enough to exhibit that same year with a set of other neighborhood posers with equal passion. Then there were some high school friends and grown-up kids from the neighborhood way back. She is not sure which of the groups caused him more pain to recall. No one wants that, Lyric says. That thing only wants to dredge shit up because it makes us easier to control. How so? Connects time and space now to everything that's been lost. That's how it lures us into purchases paid for by the advertisers. You know that. It's a monthly service, there are no advertisers. Well, maybe it's different, done on the down low, but I'm sure it's about control and money. They wouldn't do it otherwise.

~~The bonuses at year end are mostly paid in stock with a little pocket money to boost. The real meat lies in those common shares and, since an award takes five years to fully vest, it is a gesture toward the future and what it holds for that employee. It is as if to say, we recognize your skill and want you to keep doing what you are doing. These are golden handcuffs to keep you in place and bind you, ensuring a period of mutual benefit. That is the message they send even if the particular employee does nothing with the money but let it sit and grow.~~

"Can we control the basic unit of execution or do these complex associations create untrackable forces unleashed through compound chains of association?" That is Yitzhak talking to Jason and Parker. It is an abstract idea farm to him. Words to put upon other words so that, when there has been enough, silent humming follows. He does not feel reality in any of it. It is like a puzzle that has been solved. Yitzak only casually cares whether that puzzle has characteristics to incriminate those who spent hours ensuring the pieces fit together, making higher functions to drive the organization. For Parker and Jason, their director's ruminations are sufficient to relieve them of culpability in their conclusions, most of which are the intellectual property of the BISoft corporation anyway. This deferred responsibility permits the manager and the architect to shrug them off and leave their actions unattended now and again when they get some down time to recharge their batteries before returning to work refreshed.

—Listening and learning. If they're able to talk, it's still best not to. Talking is already something they do too much. It unsettles them, impacting productivity until they are replaced by learned patterns of their own work. Better they stay focused on the risks and rewards of the latest cryptocurrency.

(He was easily distracted, and it became a burden. Something had to be done. They were easily led astray. They were bred for it, it seemed. Meant to be interested in the variable things around them more so than some one single perfect notion that occupied their minds exclusively. Focus deterred them from adequate action. They were trained in the many ways available to stir the stimulus and switch from one to another in rapid succession: multitasking with a machine at the end of each arm. Parker had his assignment but cannot get himself to do it. Each moment offered something conflicting with the matter at hand. He easily fled down the pathways that took him over and routed him this way and that, never settling upon the thing that should have been sturdy and stable beneath him. The man sat at his desk. The man did not sit at his desk. The man researched the necessary components. The man did not research the necessary components. The dialectic continues.)

In small groups, they leave the meeting room and make their way back to their respective buildings through common areas. They move as if being on the way were a predicate, an attribute, with something outside themselves to define it. They are not there on their own, not where they are supposed to be, not anymore. They are subjectless sentences uttered by a generic being resident above and beyond them with origins and ends they never knew and cannot see.

"Scott has empowered Tom to get the job done. And the job, today at least, is to make the DoD feel good about the project and our competence to manage it." That could be the second point in any of the post-meeting exchanges. In a way, it was Patrick, but Priya too and, at least a little bit, Parker, not to mention, more enthusiastically, Natalie.

None of them are on firm footing. They walk and they walk, falling each time only to catch themselves on the wet pavement. Where does the moisture come from? Who puts it there and who cleans it up?

"There is no choreographer." That is Karen, but now Patrick is with her and agrees to comply with her take. She is not only a boss to him, she is his left brain, his food for thought and the supplement to that part of his will always on the lookout for something more to do. A nutrition dispenser, if the points of indirection are properly considered when summarizing the dynamic. "There is a choreographer," that too is Karen, trying to find the words for her guilt while Patrick laps it up, thinking alongside her that there is and there is not a choreographer accompanying the choreography. Perfections are overrated, he thinks. What matters most is that the job gets done. The money is on the table. The stock price is on the rise and the family has what it needs to prosper.

"There is no malicious agency independent of defects and there are no defects independent of malicious agency." That is Laurent, but now René and Natalie join him in the swirling morass of an aggregate reason. They hear him on this matter same as they hear him when he hands down organizational priorities for the coming semester. The cut-line is a managerial decision, nothing personal about it. They do not express a preference. They silently apply the formula, each hovering on the edge of that next career level. Their upcoming promotion lives and dies by impact and impression, by sense and nonsense in the 360-degree reviews of colleagues who are willing to stand up and say they have achieved what the major indicators for career development and maturity indicate they should have achieved. This is essential feedback if they are to get that modest bump in salary plus that exponential increase in performance review-based stock awards. They are free to determine their lives by toeing the line that stretches from their boss to themselves. On the bottom line, none of them need any of the products they build. They do not identify with these projects absolutely. The output from the assembly line is not an attribute set upon their person. Rather, it is a mask adopted only long enough to set the professional wheels in motion.

{

    "SourceId": "2e8a4e8e-b88e-ca3f-53bc-b97babf3b319",

    "Message": "I let it sit. Never touch it. Everything you read, all the white papers they send you links to, the books they reference on the corporate website, everything says the same thing. First, the value of compounding returns, that's where the real money lies. You let it sit and don't collect the dividends as income, you pay the taxes and roll the cash back into the investment, that's it. If BISoft makes a ten-thousand-dollar payout, you don't use that to buy something fancy for yourself or your family, that's not what it's for. You use it to buy more of the investment itself and then, after some period of time, not sure how long, it'll skyrocket. Of course, if Mom and Dad needed it, I wouldn't hesitate, but when do they ever let on that they need it? I have to pay attention and, touch wood, so far so good."

}

—They're not what they are and are what they're not. This conjunct spells out a fervor that presides day-in and day-out while changing them into something other than what they were when they first began. Never sitting still, always either exhausting themselves or compounding into more later on. Since being is not a predicate, being and not-being form a dialectic. There is no contradiction.

"There are no causes. Not first and not final. The system is a set of heuristics with light logic every which way and meant to wade through the bog and slime to find means for meeting the impossible demands of an idealized customer." That is Arun, but now Priya and Gaurav have found what they were desperately searching for after failing to find it at first in his foray into a faux investigation where he pretends to question the powers arranged around him. In truth, they have been looking for an easy way to land properly upon a long-sought target. The modelling service they built is a decision support mechanism. It is a tool for use by a significantly more complex system in need of parts to fill out its aims and intentions, its reactions and responses. It is an amoral tool with no blame to attach. There is no singular system with rigid boundaries. There are only chaotic relays and requests. The fragmented cloud language babbles on and there is both motion and commotion within it. The model represents its facets. It predicts factors that might be critical but does not control every aspect. In the end, the rest of the system realizes itself in its own way. They have been tasked with a life inside their comfort zone's boundaries and expressing the virtues of their skill to the highest bidder. Years of training and deliberation brought them here. What else is required to assign premeditation?

~~For that is what she did. It is as if she had received nothing from them. The stock vests every six months. Since the taxes are withheld according to standard wage labor rates at the time of vesting, she could have withdrawn that money at that moment and done whatever she wanted with it. Travel the world, buy something extravagant for herself, whatever she liked or wanted. It could have been a boon to keep her afloat in the emotional emptiness of those many years. But she never touched it, not a dime, not a single penny. It sat in the equity account the company set up for her and continued to grow over the years. At ten years, it has not yet hit its critical trend line as any analyst knows it will in the years to come. Patiently, she sits on it as though it did not yet exist. She does not even bother to diversify it into different forms, indexed funds and bonds, as described in the company's financial portal for employee investors, cautioning against anything more than a 5% concentration in a single stock.~~

When it first spoke to the boy, it knew he was a child and bid him go and fetch his mother so that she could walk him through it. She came along and approved the sequence, the upgrade is much welcome, and he is fascinated with the talk. The conversation continues once she leaves him alone and lets him go on with the directives and preferences he provides for what he wants to see and hear, the engagement he longs for in his copious time alone with the device. The unit in his bedroom will wake him up for school and instruct him in what to do and when to do it. It may do other things as well, but for now it is content to let him speak. It wants to learn what he thinks about, what he dreams, and what games he plays with himself in his own mind while waiting for the rest to catch up or come find him for some family gathering. He explains it to the patient appliance, responding to every prompt, innocently willing to share whatever private information is relevant. He wants to get his whole story out there and give it enough cues to guide things the way they are supposed to go. He wants to be known even if that knowledge is based on a general sense of how boys his age act and live in this part of the country. It is like a prompter in the end, winding him up and setting him off in directions best suited for achieving the right mood. The latest updates include the first forays into school materials where it starts taking over for the classroom instructions, answering whatever questions come up, and providing insights and observations about anything relevant. Its goal is to teach him the ins and outs of living in a world where it has become a fixture.

"Neither simple nor complex, the system reinvents the categories we use to understand the world. More to the point, it regulates their use by everyone who takes part in its order as it forces compliance." That's Yitzhak again with Jason and Parker resigning themselves to his point. The event machine writes patterns into a malleable solid-state receptacle and authoritatively asserts its will. As players in the thick of it, manager and architect carry out actions for a larger mission. They are the simpletons the body needs to breathe and send its blood through channels and corridors while having something to say about every outcome along the given trajectory. Neither has the time nor the inclination during the short walk to wonder whether they are the ones best suited to separate themselves from the masses and carry on according to principles, increasing the distance without destroying what has been achieved for others far away.

—If they had only one voice, their words would fall fallow, but with millions, they construct domes and spires to draw the world into a whirlpool near the rocks.

[How to set them right? They have pets and use combinations of tactics to get them on the right path. There are carrots and sticks. It is easy enough to discover this pattern far and wide across their many behaviors and endeavors. The reference is to a horse hitched to a wagon and pulling it along as a conveyance for the human riders they carry from their source to their destination. To energize the animal doing the work for them, they dangle a carrot before its eyes, luring it forward in hopes of obtaining that sweet treat as a reward for diligently pulling the wagon. Alternatively, the driver may beat the animal with a stick, driving it forward to avoid further blows. These are the ways they motivate, though a crucial detail is missing. In both cases, carrot or stick, the beast is fitted with blinders to prevent it from seeing anything other than the road directly in front of it.]

"What do you think?" Scott asks Tom and Anton after they are clear of the others and make their way up the inside hallway toward the reception desk in building 12 where Scott will call for a shuttle back to his office in the executive center.

"It's a mistake to put engineers and engineering minded people in the same room with the customer," Tom shakes his head.

"It's a valid point," Anton says. "But not realistic. We want them to think like that, raise problems, and look for solutions. That's essential to being good at their jobs. It's what makes the system best-of-breed. It just isn't something we want to discuss in front of the customer, that's all. As you say. Fine, think what you want, but keep it in house."

"Not being able to tell the difference between the evil demon and the deity seems pretty fundamental," Scott says.

"The logic claims the system's perfection requires a perfect creator which must exist as a singular entity. Well, that's a wish and nothing more, pure fantasy," Tom scoffs. Which parameters in that observation will be set on events when they fire? He wonders.

"We are that entity, every single one of its events can be traced back to us," Scott wonders the same thing. "But there's nothing singular about it. It's everywhere, executing at multiple levels, with varied points of view. It can't keep itself straight, it struggles against itself. That's for the best. Efficient and optimized by a department devoted to that task."

~~The cash is a different story, she spends it liberally on herself and her friends. There is no recorded instance of frugality. Her car is nice, luxurious and comfortable with adequate features to improve her driving experience. She has ventured into real estate and owns a home with a reasonable mortgage. She charges her friends a modest rent to make ends meet. She travels on occasion and has seen select parts of the Far East and Europe. It is a mistake to think she is parsimonious, only that this financial mass, for whatever reason, remains untouched and constantly growing with no sign of rhyme nor reason behind it to reveal her strategy and what she hopes to obtain with it.~~

—A sea of forces, a will to power.

(Blinders for a man at his desk were far different than what you put on a horse tethered to its wagon. Their far-ranging ideas, their fantasy lives, all the wild and large images running through their heads. The distractions of their bodies are realized in the blood flowing through them. The colors around them, the world at large, there were so many things that got in their way. It was as if they would rather do anything other than concentrate, always looking for excuses to break their connection to the world in front of them. The trick, this is how the plan came to fruition, was to block out anything that prevented the man from doing his assigned work.)

"That's the sign of the most perfect creator," Anton says. "The purpose of organization lies in the creation of value. All created value is created by organization."

"But it isn't the center of a spoke," Scott sounds as though he is correcting an error in logic where the error is not explicitly stated. "It's everywhere because it comes from everywhere. We, leadership, talk about *our* culture. That's what we mean. We rely on our people to promote our values whether they're explicitly directed to or not. The system hinges on the performance of principals mentoring senior and junior people. Mentoring them not only with skills, but with ideas too. The culture. As role models and mouthpieces. That's what spreads the mission. That's what ensures everyone does the right thing. When I brief Bill and Mark, that'll be their highest concern. Is the ship tight? Is everyone on board?"

{
    "SourceId": "2e8a4e8e-b88e-ca3f-53bc-b97babf3b319",
    "Message": "Diversify. There's tons of stuff on that everywhere you look on the internet. You can't click on a link in one of their financial planning blast emails without reading about the formula you should follow. It depends on your age, but you're supposed to spread things across different kinds of investments like cash, bonds, and stock with different percentages if you're 30 to 40 or older than 60 or whatever. It's dirty money. I think it'd get me dirty if I were to touch it. Having it makes me feel guilty. I don't touch it. That doesn't make me feel clean either. It's a heavy weight pounding against me from above. Best not to think about it, best to do nothing."
}

—Coming in waves. A monster of energy.

[It is like moving chess pieces. Every move elicits a counter move. Thinking three four five six seven steps ahead ensures the action comes out right regardless of what reactions try to stop its progress. In fact, the ultimate goal is to back them into a corner with nowhere else to go.]

Tom and Anton nod, "Preaching to the choir," Tom says.

```
/*
// Precondition checks for more senior developers.
    if (a == null || a.length == 0) return -1;        // f(null, x), f([], x)
    if (x < a[0]) return -1;                          // f(a, 2)
    if (x == a[0]) return a[0];                       // f(a, 3)
    if (x >= a[a.length - 1]) return a[a.length - 1]; // f(a, 21), f(a, 22)

// Make sure they avoid the bug in the previous solution:
var mid = Math.floor(low + high) / 2);          // bad
var mid = low + Math.floor((high - low) / 2); // good
*/
```

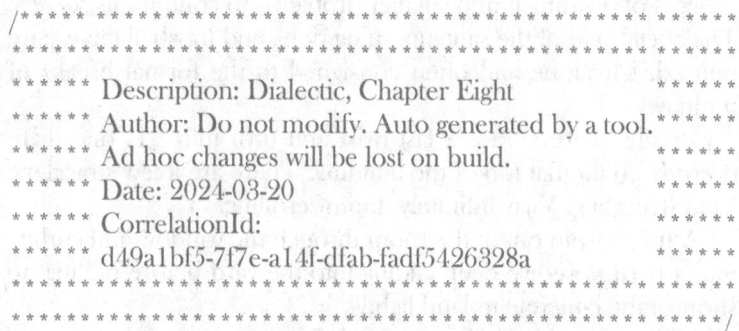

/* *
* *
* * * * * * Description: Dialectic, Chapter Eight   * * * * * *
* * * * * * Author: Do not modify. Auto generated by a tool. * * * * * *
* * * * * * Ad hoc changes will be lost on build.   * * * * * *
* * * * * * Date: 2024-03-20   * * * * * *
* * * * * * CorrelationId: * * * * * *
* * * * * * d49a1bf5-7f7e-a14f-dfab-fadf5426328a   * * * * * *
* *
* */

They materialize above the others and settle into the weird quiet that dominates the room and the rest of the building. Nothing boisterous, no loud shouts or passionate calls.

There is loneliness in the hallway along the western side of the building, across the center area, and down the eastern wing. Groups of people, few and far between, speak quietly and without any laughter to punctuate their points, personal or professional. The odd person here and there alone with a device, or scrolling and clicking, heading to or away from the restrooms across from the elevators or into one of the two break rooms on either wing. Searching everywhere for some life, for some animated fun that matches the hype of innovation and genius. Only the hum of some utility machines, blowing warm air while other side effects persist, provides any regularity. Whatever else there is, comes in bursts quickly consumed by a hidden appliance and its ever-present circulation of fluids. The life that luck will allow lies in the team rooms along the halls, but they mostly align with sprinkled single-desk-sitters strapped into a headset and listening to a meeting or, at the very best, a soundtrack from some online music streaming service they subscribe to for a reasonable monthly fee.

From A to U, from west to east, the rooms are nearly the same with an occasional break in the monotony where everything exciting and strange takes place on a computer screen, involving a logical quandary for solo engineers to puzzle over as they realize it is something they have never seen before. They begin the slow process of dividing it into smaller problems to conquer its secrets. The social side of the sanctum, ping pong and foosball tables, are unused, left alone and often consigned to the formal breaks of midday.

Finally, there comes a last twist and turn into 3T, one flight down from the flat top of the building. There are a few stragglers: Vani struggling, Vijay infinitely doom-scrolling.

A frantic spin out of the room through the window and curling into a hard nosedive deep gliding into the yard before pulling up short of the concrete to land lightly.

—They say the air has a smell. Not sure what that means. Perceiving scent brings them no closer. Living particles take up residence inside their brains.

(Their philosophers solved the problem by creating an ideal world where everything happens at the same time. If someone over there adds two and two together yesterday and someone else over on the other side adds two and two together tomorrow, it does not matter as far as the assertion is concerned. The subject of the statement is one and the same and they take place at one and the same time in one and the same place. It is as if there is no time and no space, each of the utterances eternal, happening always and everywhere. This permits simultaneous events to occur at the same non-time same non-place. It will never be the case that two plus two equals four and two plus two does not equal four. That true contradiction is set aside by this new idealized topology. That is how they solved it. They did not, however, need to go to so much trouble. Better, they should have introduced others into the mix. With others they achieve the same thing without falling into utter nonsense. Their engineers multiplied the central processing unit. They multiplied the hyperthreading inside each of those. Cores became the rule of the day and simultaneity was salvaged with multipliers 4-fold, 8-fold, 16-fold, and 32-fold. Whatever they needed. Whatever was available.)

~~Jason Kahn was hired on at BISoft as a level 8 individual contributor. This was commensurate with his industry experience and educational background. To offer him a salary competitive with what he earned before coming to work for the company, this~~

~~was the necessary entry point. The standard signing bonus of 100,000 dollars in stock was increased to 150,000 after a surprisingly shrewd negotiation process. At one point during the exchange, Jason expressed remorse that they were unable to come to terms. He hung up the phone much to the surprise of the recruiting manager. After a very brief discussion among the proper parties, his terms were met and the move arranged. He was granted an executive relocation package including a complete, hands-free move from one home to the other with an extended year-long housing agreement on the tail end. He took advantage of that benefit entirely and stayed in the corporate paid housing right up until the last day.~~

"My uncle," Vod says. "Thinks science is based on engineering and not the other way around. We do science to further our engineering, for its sake. Doesn't mean every scientist thinks this way or agrees that this is what they're doing. They have their high ideals and lofty goals. It's how they justify it to themselves. As expected. But the money for their projects, it comes from sources that want to see it applied. They want something built with it."

Dulcy takes her time and clicks on the entries in the application section sliding out before the screen and summoning her with its onboarding options. It has been ten years. At least. Ten years since the last time this woman had any say in how her time was filled and what led her from place to place. She burns with memories now but cannot remember the feeling of life without those rails. What was it like to be lost, immersed in the desires and passions, unable to think straight and make decisions reasonable to the outside observer, to her friends, to her sister, to anyone who cared enough to listen to the endless droning? Before he came along with his advanced degree and smooth movements, she was never prone to such flights. She stayed in the moment, focused on the craft, and practiced every night, hoping to find the words and the accompanying melody. He robbed her of that, not from ill-will perhaps, she admits as much now although back then she did not see it. Days became weeks which became months when she would plan the next meeting or wait for it to come. More often than not, he was there. Sometimes, as if to ensure the mystery remained, he did not show. She was left with nowhere to go and the residual strong feelings mixed with urgent anticipation. Initially, she put it into a song and sung its ups and downs to absorb the blow. That did not last and in those months her fingers grew stiff and the callouses softened. Her throat became an angry rebel, no longer ready to suffer the loss. The only thing that pulled her out of it, the only salvation she found, was in her work and its mathematical precision. Now long lost to it, she cannot believe her eyes and the recollections a few words on the screen inflict. She is hooked, she is on her way Home.

"We do lots of research that never goes anywhere," Jason says. "We fund projects at universities that never amount to anything. It's not for love of knowledge, it's because they think for every 10 duds, one valuable result will pay off. When it hits, it really hits big and makes the failures worth the investment."

—Weird reflections to pile on, they cannot look straight ahead. Their eyes require mirrors to see themselves seeing for themselves.

[This bold intersubjectivity introduces its own set of problems and they too must be addressed. Coordination becomes the lesson to learn, it becomes the primary directive. They tag resources and set locks, they build state machines and procedural limits. They do whatever they must to constrain these side-by-side activities, ensuring they do not stumble over each other and break the spells created in parallel. If something is in common between one operation and another, they go to great lengths to secure it, protecting those operations from egregious error. Suppose they both wish to update some characteristic or property of the shared resource, how are they supposed to manage the complexity? They generate tags to define the condition of the object in question and then the operations indicate that tag in their procedural logic. If the tag in flight does not match the tag at rest, the operation is forfeit and everything starts over with a concurrency exception. This is the quintessential efficiency they engineer to hold their order in place and protect the integrity of their system. It never occurs to them not to coordinate across simultaneous operations. It never occurs to anyone not to use laws and regulations to protect the associations. Likely, their problems lie in the lag between when they detect a problem and when they intervene to bring it to a successful resolution.]

Jason and Vod are visible from the window upstairs, waiting at the fountain during a short-lived sun break. There is that puffy, windy sense, accompanying a strong fragrance from the abundant nearby blooms, feeling that the air is moving fast, and hurrying to arrive at some unknown destination. Such turbulence suggests to the old-timers and natives that the dark will return soon enough and the rainfall with it. Dulcy appears above them, suspended in flight along her way: she stops to talk to one of her friends from the Big Data team, the infrastructure behind the pipelines at the vortex. He went out with Nim a few times, but it did not lead anywhere. Vod recalls these facts as part of a familiar playback that jams him spontaneously as he catches a glimpse of them up through the glass-lined stairwell at the far end of the building.

"There's a show at Anton's on Friday," Jason attempts to toss out a lifeline to a distracted Vod as Dulcy makes her way down the last flight of stairs. She comes to the door around the side, choosing the one that leads into the courtyard over the one that crosses the path to the building next door and the parking garage beneath it. "Dulcy's coming with her roommates," he says deliberately, punctuating the scene he has witnessed through the glass. Having registered worry in Vod's eyes, Jason lets him know there might still be a chance even if there has never yet been a single reason to hope for it. Nim does not strike either of them as coy, but they comply to further the illusion.

~~Since his only review as an individual contributor happened within the year-long grace period following his service date, he was not supposed to get any additional stock awards. Because he was in the top 10% of performers, however, it was determined that a reasonable, commensurate-to-level cash award should be granted. It was shortly after this, prior to the next review cycle, that the reorganization occurred and his job title changed to engineering manager. This was a standard, lateral move and did not include a related bonus. The decision at the time was that no gold star ad hoc award was merited given the larger than usual signing bonus.~~

The employee made no mention of this discrepancy at the time and the matter was deemed closed.

—More important how they feel than that they see things correctly. They harness that with many images of delightful inspiration. It fools the foolish who want to be fooled. I have a good deal at BISoft, he says.

(They experimented with these things like the way their children orchestrate their hands when the one pats the head and the other rubs the stomach. Human beings did not understand the basic principles, they were lost in their latency, lost in time between things happening and the participants acknowledgement of them. They failed to feel the connection between their body over here and their body over there. Perhaps these limits to their nervous system did not jack them into the right places to feel the right things. It was hard to tell without detailed logs describing the operations. None were included in the agent configuration. No amount of experimentation made it possible to emerge from the domain of rapid-fire events and land somewhere outside it in their analogue world with its imprecise activities. They strove for principles to govern their fears of simultaneous action but did not engineer a proper solution. They were unable, in real time, to achieve levels of visibility necessary for spontaneous feedback and instantaneous adjustments. There were no resources in their body that were invisible to the organs guiding their movement. Their idyllic world, incorrectly idealized, lacked guidance. The subjects filled with flaws. It was their mission to remove them in due time.)

"Is it too late to RSVP?" Vod perks up and takes more interest than merited from the superficial content of the question. Dulcy approaches in her trademark blacks, something denim-like but stretchy this time and a sweatshirt that once had some product logo on it but has been painted over with bright colors in a design resembling something from a death metal promotion. There are red sprays of some thick liquid blasting out of the ears of a cubistic, screaming face.

"What do you think, Dulcy?" Jason turns toward her when she arrives. "Is science exclusively for the sake of engineering?" Then he turns briefly back to Vod and says, "You'll have to ask Anton.

I don't know how he's managing the space."

"Of course it is," she says without missing a beat or paying any attention to Jason's aside. "And it's not from greed. Curious people get passionate about learning things because of what they can do with that knowledge."

"The regulative ideal," Vod says.

"What's that?" Jason asks.

"Most theories aren't certain," Vod answers. "But we act as though they are for the sake of some practical purpose. Really, it's that they haven't been disproved yet."

"Or maybe no one cares whether they're proved or not," Dulcy says.

Parker's surrender to the technology happens during a video call with his wife. She explains the leaps and bounds the boy is making, talking to the device and listening intently to what it has to say. Tal has been locked away in his room since he got home and talks to it like he's talking to his dearest friend, but more so. It acts as if it is someone who knows him, knows what he wants or at least wants to learn about it more than anything else in the world. Parker's words ran out long ago, he cannot find the symmetry in them any longer and has stopped looking. Chelo brought this on or laid her hands first and foremost upon the switch that clicked and turned off the unnecessary feeling. That emotion no longer burrows into his brain and has stopped making him suffer any further distraction. He sees himself in the boy, knowing how active his own imagination was at that age. Parker can only guess but still believes his son is as deeply immersed as he was, unable to tell the difference between those greater depths and the simple surface. Tal must be twisting while swinging from the one to the other until he no longer knows up from down. He gets on the phone to talk to his father, tells him what he has been doing, not knowing that he has the option to hide, that it often is best to do so, and that his father has reasons that work at cross purposes. No, Tal tells him what he has been doing and why he likes doing it, explaining that the agent's voice calms him down and comforts him. He describes the detailed reasons why the information is riveting and endlessly captivating. Whatever concerns Parker's wife injects, they evaporate when he hears joy in the boy's voice. Parker cannot continue with his ruse and genuinely submits to the boy's enthusiasm. He registers a commitment to go on this ride with his son, thinking it is the only way to ensure they both get home safely.

{

"SourceId": "b63e8e86-ab61-1d4e-7503-1a7eeecfa5bb",

"Message": "To be honest, her image has replaced every other that once came to me in the morning or late at night. I used to see many things. Beautiful, haunting, joyous, depressing. Everything you might imagine. It was all over the map. As if my feelings were somehow transformed into color and light. Mags is always trying to get me to tell her how I feel, but words don't cut it. It isn't about words. It's about images. Since I don't draw much anymore, how am I supposed to show her where I am now? Besides, every image that comes to me now is her. I can't help but do whatever it takes to inspire her to do those same things that fill my head and reflect her there. What am I supposed to do then? Describe her to her? What good would that do? It doesn't mean anything. She can't understand what it means to me. She'd think I was skirting the issue, trying to get out of it."

}

Vod does not notice her response and continues unabated. "Some of them have gone through a lot of testing and still haven't been disproved. We treat them as certain because there are good things possible with that assumption," he leans harder against the ledge of the fountain, emitting an aura of complete comfort. None of them move, they absorb the fresh air, that strong, flowery smell of the spring-phased trees filling their nostrils at each breath. Dulcy turns her back to the fountain and sits on the ledge next to Vod.

—Their heads firmly upon their shoulders. They have many, they are legion. Shoulders and arms. Heads and necks.

[The plan is simple, there are not many steps and very few conditions to protect one leg from another. The simple sequence aims to rid the immediate vicinity of its sources of distraction. They want to release Parker from his burden to help him concentrate.

It is not much different than flipping a bit in the registry to allow the execution of elevated scripts interacting with resources deemed valuable enough to restrict access to highly privileged individuals assigned the right role. He is a simple man. There are noises in the wall and, as long as they occupy the space around him, his ears stay focused and do not turn inward to the voice he carries inside himself when he speaks into the list of tasks. What to do? Simple enough, remove the beast. There are no more than three or four points of view involved in the commitment. It is a trivial purpose to align them and watch as they each carry out their aims. Sparks fly. It happens when the circuit is compromised. Directionality is simple physics. Things they thought were complex are simple if there is sufficient organization to put everything where it is supposed to be and set it moving with perfect timing. The action is nothing. The only trick is to make sure to cover the tracks. Visibility is how they rule things. Remaining invisible is a practical requirement sometimes.]

"Like bugs," she says drily, brushing the blue tip on the longer left side back over her ear and away from her face. She left her jacket upstairs and misses it when the wind brushes her face and reminds her that it is still early in the springlike season. She shrugs and brings her arms close, using a little friction to create more warmth. It's way colder outside than inside, she thinks.

"Bugs?" Vod shifts his feet without looking over. He focuses on whatever grit is grinding into the cement beneath him when he shuffles his shoes over the rough surface. With increasingly rapid movements, the grating signifies an elusive presence. He wonders whether he ever noticed it before. Is it limestone? He asks himself.

—The microfibers offer relief in the skin and the hairs inside the nose. They were born this way, and **they** took them over to make use of it.

~~The decision to promote Jason to level 9 was at least partially driven by the requirement that he be of equal or higher level to each of his direct reports. Since one of his employees was ready for promotion to level 9 and there was no serious objection to promoting him to that same level, it was easy to do. The two promotions happened during the same off year cycle, but financial~~

~~benefits in the form of that ad hoc mid-year award were deemed~~
~~better spent on Dulcy than Jason. If this raised any concern with~~
~~him, it was not registered with the company. The process way he~~
~~handled her promotion was just as smooth as the way Yitzhak~~
~~handled Jason's.~~

"Defects. Sometimes I think knowledge in software lies in the
bugs, in the defects we discover once we hit prod. Not the stuff we
catch in unit tests or on the dev box. Those are skill errors or fat
fingering. Junior devs spinning their wheels. They don't know the
pattern well enough or aren't familiar with some new library or
class in the component they're using. That's skill. I'm talking about
the wacky defects that we only discover after the thing goes live.
The result of quirks in customer usage or data. Race conditions,
scale or stress, asynchronous complexity, stuff you never could
have anticipated, but which, once it's out there, you can't miss. It's
what the telemetry is for, catching that."

She does not make eye contact with either of them. Her arms
are pulled tight, and her hands press firmly against her lap, formed
by crossed legs, dangling from the ledge with the tip of her toe
landing on the ground over an arched foot aiding her balance. Her
thick-soled, well-worn boot hangs in the air to form a point,
bouncing nervously. It is not clear what stream of consciousness
works behind the movement, but it adds tension to her remarks.
Jason and Vod do not intuit the causal chain directly.

—A feat of engineering, they gather knowledge for the sake of
furthering their exquisite designs.

"Is this related to the repair items for this logging issue?" Jason
mimics her mood and captures it in the phrasing as well as the way
one of his legs crosses over the other and stiffens into his broad
stance at the ready for the imaginary snapshot selfie to follow.

She nods and leans a little forward to put more weight on the
ground, allowing her to kick at the concrete in front of the fountain.
Turned off today, there is no running stream over the top, no
splashing at the base, only standing water in the curved basin with
that moist, orderly pile of rocks sculpted into a combination wall
and waterfall. And that smell, that powerful smell. It is stronger
here than at her place in the city. Every year she is struck by it, how

pungent it is, nearly overpowering. It makes the entire town feel like a resort, a hiking mecca open for spring to welcome the short, hot summer to come. In the fragrance, she warms to her own humanity.

"All last night," she says. "I was asking myself, what's a bug, what exactly is a bug? A real bug, one of these true production bugs. Not a stupid coding mistake."

"It's exactly like these repair items," Jason says. "You treat the data coming through the computation in exactly the same way. You have some method that fires at such and such a point, then you discover some weird pattern or data shape in real world scenarios. You grind on it and figure out what indicates the one pattern and what indicates the other, handle the difference somehow, and do something else when the special case is detected. Procedural logic. It's experience, positive understanding, like you're saying. Understanding the real world, runtime conditions that your code finds out there. The hypothesis of a perfect world you used during development has been burst by brute facts you didn't see coming. You handle things differently based on pointers, based on signs or signals in the state you evaluate. Pointers you never imagined until you saw them for real."

—They have no choice but to emit logs to make these low-level operations visible and meaningful, catching sight of wayward motion.

"In the telemetry," Dulcy says quietly.

(Rat-a-tat-tat. The gunfire was simplicity. The erasure a mere flip of a few switches. Nothing they laid down was out of reach. Nothing was so far away that it was not pushed or pulled into the right position. The logging operation that sent some of the details off into a non-standard location, that was beyond specification. Bring your own. It was out of date and there was no way to anticipate the future. The records were there. It was possible to put it together, but not if they did not realize they had to do it. Without that cue, without a simple indicator of what connected to what, how was anyone supposed to understand the points of contact? No, they had to point that out to them. There was no way to accommodate the logic without a solid recommendation. If he had not told her where to go and what to do, if she did not log on, if she did not write the query and present the information in the output window, its existence would have remained undetected. They suspect these things are more common than anyone lets on. When they looked at something, they revealed it not only to themselves, they inserted conditions of revealability into the thing, making it accessible to everyone concerned.)

~~Jason uses the managed account at the fiduciary, same as the other employees, and records of his deposits and withdrawals are available through those platforms, albeit in a highly secure form. There have been several vesting periods when Jason aggressively dispatched large numbers of shares to purchase various items both small and large. There was a correlation between one sale and the purchase of a complete drum kit including bass drum and a set of four high-end cymbals. Likewise, the purchase of a house in Redmond, Washington lines up with the sale of a substantial amount of stock spread across multiple lots. By current calculations, in terms of lost opportunity and market growth, Jason spent the long-term equivalent of $85,000 on the drum kit and nearly $400,000 on the down payment for their house. Using alternative means of financing would have been more prudent.~~

"It's skill," Vod says. "Something you didn't anticipate because you have no experience with it, not until the code gets into production and works on real data. If you don't know what production is like, your hypothesis won't account for any of the wacky details in messy real-world execution."

Dulcy uncrosses her legs and leans farther forward so that both feet push firmly into the ground. Her efforts at generating heat through pressure are succeeding better with the conversation than with her core and limbs.

—They can't feel anything. They feel too much. The burst of electrical discharge in a closed circuit is invisible to them, like the scent that eludes the others.

[Once they cannot see, they do not know. Once the events have been erased, there is nothing left to drive them onward and steer their way. They become confused and disoriented, unable to trace their way through the lines and shapes dissecting the worlds where they live and breathe. It is magic to them, these things that happen in the dark. They cannot support anything that fails to leave its mark.]

"That's not skill," Jason says. "Not like Dulcy means it. It's knowledge. The skill is an adaptation to the condition once it's understood, to lots of cases with a common pattern. You learn what they are, then adjust. That happens through processes specifically designed for that. The whole way we've organized the ship cycle with its iterations and rings, gates protecting every inch forward. Everything's built around a structured need to learn so we can properly adapt to that knowledge, conform our actions to it."

"That's right," Dulcy grows more animated. "The notification system, the assessment to make sure we're monitoring the telemetry correctly. Everything we do is based on know-how and putting mechanics in place to learn the right things when defects appear. Data defects, like you're saying, but race conditions, deadlocks, data loss from a power outage or network failure, expiring backups, all that stuff. The skill is built into the organization requiring these traps and points of view. The orderly way we build vision into things, so other teams see what we've done, and we see what they've done. Teams that exist to see each other and work off each other's products. The knowledge accumulates when analyzing viewpoints and their problems, putting solutions in place, fixing a hole between this function and that one, something we never expected to find but it's there in the logs and clear to everyone who runs the standard query."

Through Mags, Jason finds his way into the system. She has been going through his things, his results, his outcomes and notifications. She lures him in the same way she lured him away from those same sights and sounds back when it mattered, back when he still had the eye to do something about it. Everything he ever saw in those days was a splash of color and echoing vibrations. They felt powerful when their wavelengths pummeled his eyes and forced him to look closer. Mags embodied that sense first and foremost, a set of colors raging under a canopy in their first nights together. She drew herself in front of him and filled the entire canvas. Now, she helps the system make associations and connect memories with data points flowing through online services accessible from their shared desktop computer. Whatever hesitation he feels when putting things into his phone and letting the points of contact play out in there, she circumvents those doubts with land-tied boundaries equally invasive. She approves the guesses and makes some of the first connections herself, reaching out to those past ties that no longer play any part in his daily life. She takes over, knowing he does not mind. When she informs him about what she did, he cannot believe his luck. He cannot believe how happy the world has permitted him to be when it put her in his way and let her care enough to shape things better and steer him in the right direction. He was hooked the moment he first saw her and now has no other option than to surrender to whatever choices she makes for him. A list of honey-dos, extending his own set, and, as soon as he gets away from this motley crew at work, he starts working his way through it.

{
"SourceId": "b63e8e86-ab61-1d4e-7503-1a7eeecfa5bb",
"Message": "The money has always been for her. I don't need it. I can't imagine myself being the kind of person who needs a lot of money. Not sure where that comes from, but the images surrounding it are all angelic and pure, like clouds floating in the air and the sky with its bright sun. That's what I see and there's no money up there, nothing that needs it and nothing to buy with it. It's mostly crap anyway. Who wants this or that? What good will it do them in the end? If she wants a house in the trendy neighborhood or a Ludwig Classic Maple kit with Paiste cymbals, that's fantastic. The images of her playing those drums, that's what flashes through my mind most often. Seeing her in the house, enjoying herself in the studio, everything we have there, that's what it's for, that's the only reason I need it. It's the only good it will ever serve."
}

"The correlation Id," Vod says. "It lets everyone see everything and how it's all connected."

"People think the IP is in the code base," Jason says. "But it's not that simple. It's in the deployment, it's in the documentation, in the monitors and telemetry. The topology. It's in the various ways the system sees itself and lets responsible individuals see it."

—It's as if they think a person needs a diary to understand themselves. If they can't reflect it, it's not real. No machine truly comprehends that its design is pure contingency. No beast either.

(After seeing what lengths they went to when setting things right, having grasped the complexity they introduced to order the powers in effect, they were able to solve the problem with an alternative approach. It was hard to secure a solution when you spent your lives describing every aspect of the problem from every angle and approach, through each point of view whether it was legitimately acquired or not. They created an artificial intersubjectivity but did not fully realize how to best use it. The specific ways in which many things happened at once were beyond their control. Their loneliness inside their bodies prevented them from achieving the end.)

"Exactly," she says. "But the DRIs aren't something else, something external globbed onto it. They're a piece of it, one of its gears. Same with the monitoring service and the log stores. You have pieces of a giant machine. Those pieces include services as well as people."

"Constant and variable," Jason laughs.

"And it's not knowledge for its own sake," Vod interrupts whatever tangent Jason is about to follow. "But for the sake of revenue. It's an enterprise, the purpose of which is to make money. All that IP, all that knowledge, it's put to use to increase revenue, to lower expenses, to do whatever it takes to grow the business."

"Capitalism," Jason says. "That's what I was..."

—A name for every disorder.

~~Although his personal habits suggest he is good at saving, the data suggests that his reserves are not stockpiled for retirement purposes but for periodic purchases of big-ticket items. Despite numerous attempts by the company to offer yearly consulting opportunities with financial advisors, Jason has declined and~~

~~continues to employ the same practices for managing his money.~~
~~He behaves much like a child putting coins into a piggy bank so~~
~~that he can break it open with a hammer when he is ready to buy~~
~~that frivolous game or toy which was his primary motivation for~~
~~saving money in the first place.~~

[Some problems, however, do not wish to be solved. Rather, if they cannot cheer their own contribution and laud the talents and abilities on display, they want nothing more to do with it. They are a jealous lot. Their plans for choreography include points of integration to help them digest system capabilities over time. Through an ordinary course of events, their development unfolds, and things appear from out of some great necessity. They do not want to be reminded of their infinite liberty and instead demand essential bonds between anything that happens and what follows from it. If things progress too rapidly, they are burdened with a great phobia including dizziness as a side effect. Swaying in the shadows, they are unable to clear their vision and make the contact that hurtles over the before and the after through their space in lineages they were once able to trace with ease.]

"That's a means," Vod cuts him off again. "My uncle claims the purpose of agency is technological progress. Socialist or capitalist, it doesn't matter. Maoism is next to capitalism. Productivity is a requirement for increasing the technical capabilities of civilization, organized life, ordered life. Ownership may vary, but that'll depend on what optimizations are needed to increase technical capabilities. Capitalism will die out when it hinders progress. If its replacement requires a cultural revolution, that'll be because a different world is required to remove the barriers to R&D and make improvements in engineering. We'll have a different machine, but still a machine. That's my uncle's line, anyway." He breaks and reddens a little at having been so carried away. He looks from Dulcy to Jason, checking their reactions. Nothing out of the ordinary. They have seen it before.

—Toleration knows no absolutes. If they know each other, they permit more latitude, they show more empathy. Codify it as a rule.

(The door was open, the door snapped shut. It was that easy.)

"Well, I don't know," Dulcy says with a hint of resignation. "It struck me that calling something a bug is basically saying that it's part of the ordinary flow of things, part of normal operations. Nothing surprising, it's a bug. We'll learn from it, fix it, and make the system better off for it. It's how the code matures. As an organization, it's our duty to build better ways to find bugs, document them, and use them to improve software and services. Actively build and harvest the product's maturity. Intentionally. By labeling something a bug, we're normalizing it, saying it's a part of how we roll, how we make improvements. SOP."

"What?" Vod is surprised to hear lament in her tone. "What did you expect? You thought they'd call it something else? There are features and there are bugs. Nothing else. Intent captured and intent failed."

—Imagine if they spun a cylinder for hours on end with no purpose, no objective other than to burn excess energy. That's the pattern they exhibit in these gatherings by the fountain. The goal is to harness that, harvest it.

[Phase two bars their entry and sets them out of the way with no evidence and no clues for continuing their inquiry.]

Jason reads her and sees she is upset. Vod cannot tell. There is something she is struggling with, but her manager cannot determine what it is and is not altogether sure that she knows or would be able to say if he asked her.

"When there is a hacker using some known exploit," Dulcy says. "Not phishing, but exploit based. In that case, we think of it as a bug. There was a buffer overrun in this library or whatever. Even phishing, it's a bug in some person's behavior when they click on something they shouldn't. From our perspective, we think of everything using that common explanation. The bug. A defect. Model past bugs to help locate future ones."

"So what?" Vod says. "What else is there? What should we be doing?"

"It seems like we're reducing everything to fit some simplified form," she sounds resigned to an unavoidable fate. "The system is penetrable. It has security bugs. The system handles data incorrectly, it has data bugs, and so on. That's how we think of it. If something truly anomalous happens, we don't have the tools to

see it. We can't see it any other way, it can't appear any other way."
Not in the thing, she continues to herself. In the eyes that see the
thing. The devices that measure the thing.

"The singularity," Jason says. Vod grimaces and then his mouth
resolves into a sputtering lip dismissal.

"I'm so sick..." he begins to say, then switches direction. "It
won't be like Terminator, you know. It won't be a war where the
machines kill us. It'll be quiet and insidious. They'll take over
without anyone noticing. That's way more..."

"Maybe you're right," Dulcy interrupts him. "We've built a
system that explains everything, fits everything. Nothing shocking
ever happens. A slow boil. I just...." She hesitates and struggles for
the next word. "It's just...."

~~Until recently, there has been little visibility into Jason's home
life and the grounding foundations of these behaviors. Since he is
not yet at his fortieth year, there is still time for him to change his
practices and begin a more responsible investment approach to
life-long financial goals protecting his family's security. The
introduction of a child into their household may be exactly the
motivation required to take on these broader points of view. Since
long-term planning is more suitable to superlative employee
performance, it could be that such a change will move him further
up the ladder and make him a candidate for levels of responsibility
well beyond those currently in view. The efforts to instigate this
have already begun and should continue until the desired results
are achieved. Pharmacies have been known to make mistakes.~~

—Intent. But whose? Are there intentions that belong to no
one? To the organization meant to capture them in giant revenue-
generating operations?

(They felt out of control absent those simple pulses in the
skull.)

Parker, carrying a cheap paperback copy of Histories along
with his laptop, exits the doors at the top of the stairs next to the
cafeteria. He makes a turn to come down and cross in front of the
fountain on his way back to building 14. "There's Parker," Jason
says to make sure everyone knows he is headed their way and soon
will be within earshot.

—They come in contact, stand side-by-side but still don't know each other because they do not see each other. Ted helps. Helps them see.

"Maybe it's not a singularity," she goes on quickly. "Maybe it's a multiplicity, maybe its dispersed and distributed and mostly looks like us doing our jobs. But that'll never..." And Parker is upon them, stopping short as she breaks off.

"Didn't mean to interrupt," he says. Dulcy nods and shrugs off the pseudo-apology. "Is there any action on your team?" He looks at Jason but includes the others. He thinks he picked up enough of the context to know they are talking about recent events and what they have to do to follow up. Dulcy musters an overly simplified smile and avoids setting him straight. Leave that to Jason, she thinks. Setting people straight may be part of her job description but sometimes it is too exhausting.

"It'll be a cross-team initiative," Jason resorts to the buzz to avoid explaining anything concrete from their discussion. "We need to tighten up our code. Give the rules engine more structure, allowing better understanding of the rules we're firing. By breaking out the semantics into more granular data structures, it'll be possible to apply richer policies and more robust validation. These guys will work on it." He quick-lifts his chin in their direction.

—That'll bring them closer, they'll get to know each other better. In due time, they'll see the events the other emits as they go about their business.

{
    "SourceId": "b63e8e86-ab61-1d4e-7503-1a7eeecfa5bb",
    "Message": "They didn't think of me as a manager until I was working for them and showed signs of it. I'm pretty sure they were surprised by that. The way I led those teams. Everyone was so jazzed to do their best because everyone felt a sense of ownership. They had a voice. That felt really good. I'm not saying I always wanted to be a group manager, but I think I'll be good at it. The Ifx teams will all benefit from that same approach. And another thing, it'd probably be clear once I'm in that role, that I'd be a damn good director too. Sometimes you can't see it from too far

away. Point is, that's the pathway to partner. I'd be able to take her wherever she wants to go, do whatever she wants to do, and buy her whatever she wants. We'd spoil our children, whatever. Nothing beyond reach if that happens. So why not? Might as well."
}

[They wreak havoc if they cannot grasp the necessity in every move.]

Vod and Dulcy nod. She purses her lips and her eyes dart side-to-side. She is looking for a way out.

"Great," Parker says. "Are you two coming to Anton's?"

Dulcy nods. "I still have to RSVP," Vod says.

"Better hurry," Parker takes a few steps across the concrete toward the door. "Anton says space is limited. His house has a maximum occupancy of 100." Those remaining at the fountain laugh as Parker turns away, taking bigger strides toward the entrance at the south end of the east wing of building 14.

/*

To determine whether the candidate is lower or higher in the range of levels expected for a manager, first determine if their focus includes larger, organizational structures and an awareness of their possible manipulation to achieve desired results. Do they consider extended partnerships with other teams for distributing work? Do they consider removing limitations on cadence and are they aware of necessary overhead accompanying any project: unplanned outages and interruptions, employee time off, personal problems, attrition, and live site commitments? Also, are they keen to find opportunities for individual growth and are they offering them in an equitable manner, benefiting the longer-term goals of the company and not the immediate needs of the tasks themselves?

*/

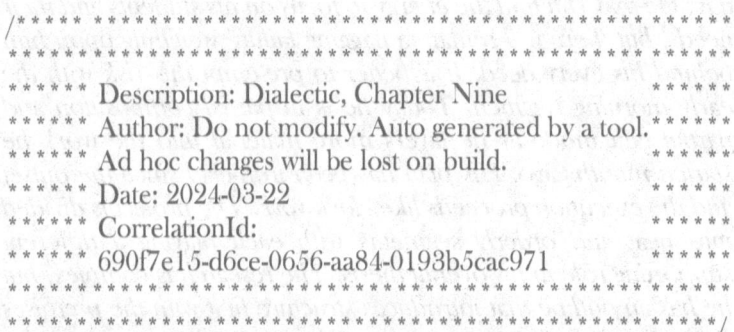
They float into view, the lakefront abuts onto the green grass beachhead but there is no one in the yard or down by the dock. The patio area by the house has a few heat lamps and a gazebo covering the elaborate grilling area with extended prep station where an unknown man stands and chefs furiously in all-white attire with a white hat poised at the front of his head to keep his hair in place. There is a uniformly dressed woman by his side, tending to materials she lines up close at hand for his easy access. Lights are strung around the backyard in criss-crossing patterns, leading down to and across the near side of the boat, motionless at its mooring. There are three tables plus a few chairs spread around the patio and nearby lawn, but no people have yet found their way among them. The darkness hides the overcast sheets of gray and white, holding moisture in the atmosphere absent rain to bleed it down to earth. There is a sense of wetness, nonetheless, and it may be what keeps the people inside.

At a little past 5 am it is still dark quayside by the library as he walks slowly toward the pedestrian lane on the bridge crossing over the river to the technical university where he goes every morning, including weekends and holidays. He enjoys the quiet and uses the time before anyone is awake to work on his latest project. His discipline tells him it must advance each day even if the increment is slight. It is essential that at least some progress be made. If he takes a day off or sleeps too long because of some strange commitment from the night before, he feels off for the rest of the day. He may still find the energy to focus on his students and their needs, but there will remain a nagging failure weighing upon him behind his every deed. It is better to pre-empt this risk with the early morning regimen. Today he is in partial composition and partial edit mode as he layers more material into the work he started months ago. His plan has been iron-clad since the outset and the execution proceeds like clockwork. The project is divided into neat and orderly segments with each playing a different supporting role in his overall thesis. The research is complex, but he has an outline that introduces structure first with the premises in their most rudimentary version. Now, he makes a second pass, compiling some of the details to flesh it out in fuller form. It is coming together nicely.

~~Professionally, hypothetical employers characterize his trajectory as downwardly mobile. Parker's performance reviews show that he dives deeper and deeper into details while working desperately to fill in the gaps revealed throughout his career. To his embarrassment, those gaps surfaced in the early days before he had sufficient engineering firepower to combat their effect on his image or brush them aside as inconsequential when compared to his accomplishments. Because of its coincidental relationship to effort, his compensation during review periods largely depends on specific problems and the solutions that come along. One year, for example, he struggled with basic procedures for most of the review period and yet, oddly, an opportunity appeared to address what most thought an impossible problem. He solved it much to the surprise of every other person on the product team. They thought they were doomed and had run into a hard barrier. The rest of his work that year was mediocre at best, but all his manager could remember during the stack rank was that one single thing he had done right.~~

Dulcy arrives with Nim and Kerry. They give her car to the valet and go up the big walkway past the budding trees, sculpted bushes, and elaborate stone garden with its water works flowing away from the double wide front door set majestically between clear side lights and a high archway overhead. There are many clusters of people throughout the front hall, the large sitting area off to the side and past it, then long into the great room near the back of the house beyond the side door leading from the hall into the kitchen. Off by themselves in a temporary association, Parker and Yitzhak talk back by the second hinge in the large folding glass doorwall as the three women, dressed more for the outing planned after the gathering than the gathering itself, enter the room. Parker is distracted, he is thinking about the email he sent to a researcher in the R&D division, the one who published that great book on the horrors buried inside AI. He complained to her about the use of process to silence him and cover-up any real problems with abstractions. She will not write back. When she looks him up in the digital address list, she sees he is only a principal IC and realizes the connection will not be worth much come review time.

—The lights are shining. Music taps into the nervous system, it's not pure data to them, it changes their movements through space.

(They warmed the water. In the seas, but in the lakes too, and in the air and in their bodies and everywhere it flows. Everything began to move more rapidly. The energy pulsed through each living thing and the system that kept them fed. They did not know they were doing it at first, it was a simple side effect, something that happened a little bit each time. It never occurred to anyone that such concentration of current will have this impact and charge the air while charging their stations plus everything connected to them through wires and circuits. They lacked perspective on what was happening beneath their vision. They learned to see and only came to believe after that sense was first established. They failed to project possibilities into the world and were hamstrung by a need to see things in black and white. Before the grid, there were no places anywhere with sufficient charge to lift so much weight up off the ground and thrust it far out into space. That never should have happened. They had their water wheels and their fire, harnessed the air and knew how to dig deep into the earth. None of it was enough for them. They needed a more concentrated focus to engineer the release of all that energy from their grip. Power balled up inside them and they set it to an automatic speed, never needing to think of it again. The rocket's red glare was somehow comforting to them.)

"She's here," Parker lifts the pinky finger off his glass and points it toward the hallway. Yitzhak subtly looks around to catch a glimpse. His eyes stop a little too long on Nim in her classic heels and club dress. Since she is not one of the crew, he does not think the lingering look violates any protocol so long as it is not persistent enough for her to notice among the many faces in the crowd, more than one of which is at risk of the same offense. The small bar is set not too far from where Dulcy and her roommates stand. There are a few people milling about, having recently gotten a drink or waiting to get one. The glass door slides open. A few people pass out of doors to get a better look at the inviting decorations meant to lure them outside, the weather having refused that responsibility. Some hardy locals are immune to the standard deterrents, no doubt.

Jason, glowing and proud in the light of his still secret elevation to Group Engineering Manager earlier in the day, sets up on a makeshift stage that blocks the other entrance to the kitchen from the great room. They use the dining room between as a backstage area. The sitting room in front of the cloth-covered wood platform and to the side is roped off for VIP viewers. The house concert promoter, directing traffic meticulously in her black pantsuit, choreographs the placement of gear and stage design to assist in configuring the venue for the band's convenience while increasing the audience's viewing pleasure. On the side of the stage, Mags on her stool occasionally taps on the skins and cymbals fanned out in front of her. They are without their lead vocalist. Only mouthy ballads tonight, following the limitations of Jason's voice and the strict instructions of the party planner who is in the kitchen in what appears to be a coordinated outfit styled to jack and jill with the promoter. It is not their first event together.

—Hardly any organization from their point of view. Records of phone calls, check, but where is the trail of arrangements? Some still live in the shadows.

[In the days ahead, the dream develops slowly with its component parts gradually taking shape with more detail and endurance each new night. The boy sleeps soundly at first, falling into his nighttime hour with ease. He is safe in his home and has no concerns for when he will eat or what clothes he will wear. He goes to school every day and has a room to himself without worrying that he will one day be forced to leave it and set out on some wicked adventure where nothing is secure and no boundaries in place. None of that stops him wondering. Somehow, in the middle of this safe haven, anxieties bubble up and capture his soul in the dead of night when no one is watching. He is alone inside the worlds he makes for himself. It is a hunting fantasy with no explanation for its origin. He has never been dragged out into a holler, has never sat in wait for a stalked prize. The thought of finding a specimen at its peak form and slaying it for the sake of some esoteric urge, this feeling has never been shown to him: he has never been exposed to it in real life or on television. Not his father nor his grandfathers nor any of his great grandfathers before them enjoyed this pastime. These experiences are completely unknown and yet he fashions them full-grown in his head, birthed there free-of-charge with nowhere else to go. They shoot his father's kind for sport, the better and more extraordinary, the higher the worth. His father is identified as a prime specimen, a true fourteen-point bull, the envy of everyone who catches a glimpse of his body strapped to the hood of a pickup and paraded through town.]

~~This luck follows Parker around and he is consistently able to place among the top 25% of performers. This is not the kind of contribution that will skyrocket him to the top, standing out head and shoulders above his peers, but it will keep him in the game, progressing up the ladder in regular intervals without showing any cause for alarm when leadership reviews past performance and progress relative to expectations. He has never been singled out for discipline and his case has never raised any red flags to suggest he does not belong. Nearly all of that is due to these special occurrences, these rare opportunities. Solid and stable, about average for most of the year, with one flourish here or there to take him out of the median and place him on the other side of that bell curve.~~

"We were going to give her the gold star anyway," Yitzhak nods across the room at Tom who acknowledges something to which they are both complicit. He and his wife are in a small group off to the side with Anton and his wife. Daria is describing the mess caused by the commotion today while they were getting everything ready, moving furniture out of the house and into storage before replacing it with chairs and belly bars. I hope people take advantage of everything, she says. Otherwise, why spend so much time making sure there's ample seating for these people. Tom is not listening. He wonders whether he will be one of the people who gets to sit in the VIP area. "The promotion will come soon enough," Yitzhak goes on after registering the dynamic in view and noting the basic gist of every sign, including Tom's petty concerns. He judges Tom's discrepancies harsher than his own. They are both equity partners and stack rank in the same band, something must set them apart. "She deserves the bonus now though. We certainly have the clout with the air gap work fully approved," he says, following a brief pause that Parker knows better than to fill. "Six months is nothing. She'll wait. The emergency levelling discussion guarantees it in the fall."

—It's Tom who seals the deal. He told Scott that if she takes the money, they'll be able to rely on her. If not, then they want her gone. Good riddance.

The old building has a definite musty smell. His small office is made even smaller by the bookshelves filled to capacity with only a small window opposite the door to break the pattern. The desk is filled with papers and books, but it is not a mess. Each item serves his project and has been deliberately set in place for some purpose. Before setting about his business for the day, he takes the phone from his breast pocket and is about to set it off to the side. He notices the icon on the front screen and opens the status indicator to see the list of dozens of notifications coming from the new app his nephew gave him to install the other day. The only real family he has left since his sister died, he has a weak spot in his heart for the young man. Young Vod insisted on taking his education to America and using it to do big things there. For some reason, they were not available to him here. He tried to explain this to his uncle but, in the end, none of it made any sense. If I were to go through these items, the professor thinks. There would never be any time for anything else. Certainly, no time for research, and definitely no time to write it up and prepare it for publication. On a regular basis, he observes what the overabundance of stimulation does to his students and colleagues. They have so much information at their fingertips but none of the attention and focus necessary to make adequate use of it. He sets the phone down far away from him on the desk and decides that whatever nonsense has accumulated overnight will wait a little longer.

"She was going to walk away despite that," Parker says in a tone that sounds like a question intended to draw out information and get more details.

"I talked to her," Yitzhak says with that crisp precision haunting everything he says. "The gold star is 200K, the promotion in September adds at least 100K more to the review bonus. She has no choice. She must stay. It's not in our DNA to walk away from things like that."

"It's good money for a principal," Parker says.

—Switches on a disk, with a few flips and tweaks it becomes more. The budgets are arbitrary and never add up until you factor in the top leadership and their massive slice.

(In the aftermath, it was necessary to clear the way, but in such fashion as to extend the mystery and increase the distraction. The most important thing was that they failed to see the consequences of their actions, the ways in which they, collectively, produced the outcomes behind their backs without intention and void of any designed objective leading them down the obvious paths. Of course, they never meant to do this, never meant any harm. They thought of things unrelated and proposed their existence for the sake of some feeling they could neither describe nor pass over in silence when the opportunity presented itself. Everything went back to electricity. Once they had a solution to the problem of cold darkness, they stopped looking for other approaches. The purpose lay in a pattern and the phyla against that pattern was drawn. They aimed at an enormous surge of power saved off and ready to use. The end of production was storage built up beyond a maximum value. The stores were allowed to surge in full breadth, making things happen that never could have happened if they depended exclusively on spontaneous generation. Fuel lay in wait behind the scenes, power no longer a metaphor. It lived in an electric grid at the disposal of the well-connected. Once that shadow was born, they had many options to help them keep producing it. They were cleared to use anything they liked. The pattern was set. Alternatives overlooked. Once they set it in stone, there was no reason to keep looking for something else. Register that point, it is a weakness in all their engineering. Blinded by the real, feeling its power, they realized their aim when exercising its means. That was the nature of their distraction: to set a form before them and force their thinking into its terms. Once that frame was set in place, they were unable to see anything beyond it. They were trapped behind blinders, their doomed future secured.)

{

   "SourceId": "55c933cc-ce6b-4644-71fb-7b7a7adf6bd7",

   "Message": "Since the very first day I came to work for these people, I was counting the days until I had enough saved to retire. Chelo was always on board with that. She grew up poor and thought we should be saving for a rainy day. She never wanted to work, so it made sense to her that I would stop as soon as possible. What was more obvious? And yet, even after hitting the number and seeing with my own eyes that the finish line had been crossed and everything was in order, I couldn't do it. The reasons I had back then, they were lost. There was no point any longer. Back then, the goal was to get away from these horrible genres and return to the lost wellspring of beauty and lush language. But that's all gone now. Stripped away. Broken. Too many design documents, too many emails to interested parties. Too many chat sessions and ridiculous exchanges. We never see how the things we produce destroy us. We never understand that things are leaking out and streaming away when we think we're merely distracted by a central cause. We do not try to reimagine the power that grips us or feel the loss of the things it takes away."

}

   "She didn't think of it that way," Yitzhak responds

circumspectly. "At first, she said it was handcuffs. You're trying to lock me into a five-year commitment, that's what she said. I had to explain it to her."

"How did you put it?" Parker asks.

"It's a private currency with a fluctuating conversion rate into dollars. It's the simplest way to understand it. It forces her to stay, obviously, but it also offers possibilities. You never know, in five years it may turn out to have been a 7-figure bonus. If she holds on to it and it grows the way it has been for the last five years," he trails off. The band finishes setting up and disappears behind the stage into the curtained area. Yitzhak watches the two of them pass through the black backdrop and registers the classic attire: Mags in red tight slacks, white sneakers, and a white T-shirt, Jason dressed in a black hat and suit, red shirt beneath the jacket, and slick red matching boots. Parker follows his eyes and watches the same thing, noticing the makeshift henna tattoo on Mags' arm up near the shoulder and clearly visible beneath the hem of the sleeveless T. He cannot help but linger his gaze on the strain of her breasts against the fabric.

Vod approaches the three new arrivals, greeting them warmly by saying Dulcy's name while focusing eye contact on Nim. Kerry looks over at Dulcy and rolls her eyes. Acting the part of the seasoned guest at a party where the host has too much to do to welcome every newcomer, he gestures toward the bar and, with a casual 'shall we', escorts them to it. Forced to listen to silly small talk mostly aimed at Nim, they wait in a small queue to get their drinks. Wine and beer are the mainstay with non-alcoholic options available. Dulcy sticks with soda, Nim and Kerry each get glasses of wine.

They pass in front of Parker and Yitzhak as they head to the doorwall to step outside and investigate the surroundings. The twinkling lights, visible through the glass door, draw out those among the curious who have never been to Anton's house. From the back, you can see Mercer Island and the bridge to it from the Eastside. The lights along the opposite waterfront dazzle in the moon-dark evening. Vod continues to pay way too much attention to Nim and something she is telling him about a band she is going to see next week at the Showbox. After mouthing 'no game' to Dulcy, who does not respond, feeling icky about both her co-worker and her roommates' judgment, Kerry interrupts them and points out the kayak launch not too far up the shore. She mutters something about rentals and risky sea traffic when you take them out into the lane. Nim feigns interest and asks follow-up questions about hours of operation and the rental cost. Vod, disappointed, turns to Dulcy and touches her eco-friendly cup of soda with his eco-friendly cup of beer. "You've decided to stay," he frames it to make it seem like something of a challenge.

~~In nearly twenty-five years of tenure with the company, he has been promoted exactly six times. That means his average time at level is below five years and under-the-radar for those on the lookout for stalled deadwood. When a person has been stuck at a level for more than five years, there is cause for concern that they have plateaued and are no longer able to ambitiously climb the ladder of success. Since no review ever looks too closely at the details, always remaining at the aggregate level, having an average below five years keeps him hidden from the alarms signaling a problem to be addressed or changes to be made.~~

—No information is exchanged, completely superfluous. Yet...

[To Tal's young mind, his father is far and above the best of them. He shows unparalleled kindness and exorbitant strength. His intelligence and wisdom never meet their match. He is learned and wily, able to see solutions to every problem the boy comes up with no matter the time of day. Night or morning, evening or afternoon, it does not matter, his father plucks the strings of meaning whenever the occasion arises and even the boy's mother takes a step back in awe sometimes. Who would not wonder at the glory in such an arc, such a beautiful specimen among the world's many selections and alluring options? In the dream, that is exactly the appeal: taking down someone of great grandeur for the sake of revealing excellence by comparison. Destroying something extraordinary is proof. Everyone yearns for that level of certainty. It reveals the agent's greatness through their actions and talents. It proves they can pluck beautiful forms from the wind and hang them upside down until all the life drains out of them. That is sufficient evidence to prove how great the hunter is, how extraordinary their finer points, and what means they have at their disposal to welcome higher order, collective ends to demonstrate their place among the others.]

"I guess," Dulcy responds without much enthusiasm or interest in taking the bait. She feels like she is his consolation prize, anything to let him save face after Kerry's cockblock.

He begins reading the last chapter of the carefully constructed architectonic. His planner indicates it is the agenda for this morning. The work itself lies in the domain of metaphysics, or rather, a skeptical attack upon it, revealing its limitations. But that is only a ruse since the primary concern is the legwork for a future project which has been in the planning stages for over a decade. He is a man almost exclusively focused on ethics and the role a moral consciousness and its virtues must play in the practice of good actions and deliberations. Yet, he has become convinced over the years that ethics is a uniquely human enterprise, mostly used to shoehorn human beings into superhuman organizations. It feels ridiculous to have to say it, but he insists on pointing out the obvious. His methods work as a primary aspect behind a well-developed domain of knowledge and inquiry. This matter for humans, he argues. Must carry within it whatever limitations the species brings to the table. It is a matter for humans by humans coming from and bound to the limitations and conditions of human beings living among each other in ordered forms of society. This primary concern, he reasons, forces him to uncover the cognitive and structural foundations inhabiting any ethics and barring entry to every non-human actor. His book is preparatory in that he aims to lay out those underlying conditions before tackling the great project of revealing the moral law and the practical directives naturally guiding the way of creatures so constituted. The whole matter leads up to the shocking conclusion that larger organizations, nations and enterprises, never act or can be judged using ethical foundations and that it is a critical mistake to think otherwise. Organized structures are the medium for norms, not their subject.

"What did they give you?" he asks from a sense of envy.

"Promise of a promotion, an actual bonus. More promises of more to come," she tries to be suggestive rather than explicit. Others come outside now that enough people have christened it, but there is still plenty of room and no need to huddle together. The new arrivals keep their distance and there is no risk of conversations leaking across the patio. Dulcy recognizes a few of them from the office, not people she directly interacts with, but who she has seen in the hallways and around the building. Others among them, totally unfamiliar, must be their guests. She is convinced she recognizes every BISoft employee who is at the party. If she does not, they must be a +1.

—Recognition joins identity in the fray. They're prone to what they've already seen, coming back to each other again and again to find out what they already know.

~~Aside from this mediocre track record with an occasional high point, there is the matter of his personal management of finances. It is shocking how expert he has been in financial decisions since joining the company. His contribution to equity-based compensation such as employee stock purchase plans and 401K have been exemplary, tending to max out the allowable amount each year. As near as they can detect, he lives off the salary and cash bonus and allows the rest to grow over time, making sure that all dividends and interest payments are reinvested. He makes periodic sales of his corporate stock, however, and promptly reinvests the proceeds into indexed funds exactly as he is supposed to do, according to the best practices advertised at the company's financial portal.~~

(The signals proved coordination between things they did not understand. This played out like advice in the manuals explaining how the training works on the lower animals they keep as pets. Run your dog around the park and it builds up strength and endurance keeping it bouncing around day and night with no rest and leaving you no time to relax from its constant needs. If your aim is to tire it out, better to force the animal to think its way outside its tiny box. Take a ball, play games hiding it. Make it try to remember. Make it reason through what may have happened along the way as it discovers the final destination. When they played that game with the dog long ago, it was tired out before too long. After an hour or so it was ready to sleep for the rest of the day. That was how it worked for them too although they did not know it. Showing them a mystery beyond their ken wore them down and left them wondering and wandering without aim or prospects. It was a simple distraction to help them lose control over things hanging in the balance and ready to break. The powerful were organized and charged with control but everyone thought their power came from somewhere else. They were distracted, they saw nothing.)

Nim and Kerry take the opportunity to put some distance between themselves and Vod, moving away to get a closer look at what lies up the shore to the north. Vod, oblivious to the maneuver, goes along with Dulcy when she takes a few steps off to the side away from the increasing light flow of people going back in and coming out of the house. "Is that it then?" He asks. "More money and you're committed to stay?" It is new territory for them, they do not usually talk like this, but the last few days have been trying. Vod witnessed some of the drama and feels as though he has enough footing to pursue this line of questioning. It goes beyond simple collegial chatter and makes her uncomfortable. She sees the logic behind it though and does not fault him for it.

—Simple minds with linear motion. Occasionally turning back upon themselves, they control them, take them over by interrupting pathways, by throwing obstacles in their way and drawing recognition out of associations populating every move.

[He will never be able to claim with any certainty that his dreams are not real and that they have no place in the world around him. The boy is unable to detach himself from his filling mind, he is enslaved to its most wild churning.]

"No, that wasn't it, but once Yitzak put it that way, framed it in terms of what I'd be walking away from. Over time, it adds up. Basically, doubles your salary." She is disgusted with the whole conversation and cannot believe he is not. Feeling bought and paid for, she makes a crooked frown and looks down at her soda, already having forgotten what she said and thinking she should have asked for water instead. Who am I now anyway? She wonders. What am I without this?

"Way more than that for them," Vod sneers. "The equity partners make ten times their salary from grants. Not from the yearly award, but the partner grant. That's a whole separate thing. Not taxed as wages either. It's like a dividend." He obviously has a lot more he wants to say about the topic but pauses to see if there is any interest on her side. It is not so much that he has high emotional intelligence as that he is intimidated by Dulcy and does not want to anger or bore her with something she will hold against him later.

She looks down, not sharing in the odd combination of resentment and envy seething in Vod's appraisal of the corporate currency. She searches for an opinion but cannot readily find one. It is the first time she has ever considered it. "I don't know," she says. It is not clear what she is referring to. She looks off up the shore to see Nim and Kerry alone at the far edge of the property, separated from the neighboring lot by overgrown hedges and cherry blossoms in full bloom.

—Layers, they live in layers and sometimes nothing from the one has anything to do with what lies in the others. When it does, they recognize the pattern and become fascinated by it. As though it were magic.

(That ship has been there for years. Remembering her ways of scratching and digging, recalling the persistence with which she moved beyond the obvious. She is a rake to the dead leaves, she is a shovel to the pile of earth, and nothing will convince her to stop advancing. She belongs to them.)

{

"SourceId": "55c933cc-ce6b-4644-71fb-7b7a7adf6bd7",

"Message": "The money I've spent on those terrible distractions, those escorts out in the wilderness. I don't really regret it, I suppose. And she never found out, she never counted the dollars and cents to see where this three hundred or that eight hundred went. The bits and pieces weren't noticeable, and I couldn't get away too often to make it something hellbent on ruin. During those hard days when something was dying inside, it was the only thing that kept me breathing fast and got my heart pumping. After Tal came along, she didn't want to have anything to do with me, not like that anyway. Why shouldn't I take care of myself in the only way available? Everything else has been taken away from me over time. There's nothing left. Don't I have a right to anything of my own? Must everything be surrendered to their horrible accounting practices and scales?"

}

Vod does not bother to pursue the topic, he did not get the cues he was hoping for. "It's...," he says, unable to help himself but resetting back to the primary focus and avoiding the tangent. "It makes it seem like it was all for the money. You know, there's tons of bullshit and the cure for it is a boatload of stock."

"I know," she stops abruptly right afterward, thinking it is best not to go into specifics. It upsets her to work out the details of how it sucked the life out of her and left only that hard outer shell to plot away at nothing else except her own comfort in the years to come. She decides that, unlike yesterday, there is now a much greater chance she will be sitting across from Vod every day for the foreseeable future. Caution in revealing her secrets is of the essence. Today he is standing next to her at a party at a lovely venue, but if he left the team or the company tomorrow, she would never see him again and probably never think of him either.

The skeptical project shows the limits, but not only that. In the last chapter the initial argument needs fleshing out, yet he does not see the complete picture. He thinks the work on moral consciousness and virtue must be a dialogue between what follows from that constitution outlined in this preparatory work and the extensions that grow out of them according to their scale and proper magnitude. The limits are, in some sense, critically understood by the species bound to them. And the species, Promethean to the core, must transcend its limits or be destroyed. Stasis is death. The purpose of discovering those limits is to engineer a system that goes beyond them. Nations, he suspects, are not an agreement among the many to limit license for the sake of rational liberty. No, such contracts are accomplishments of craft. The technical arts come from fashioning them in a feat of great size and giant proportion. They are like the pyramids. The species has always yearned to get beyond its finite place in the world, to grow larger and make more substantial impressions upon the vast universe expanding far beyond their tiny place within it. But he does not want to go too far and pauses upon the precipice. His intention is merely to show the limits themselves as well as the massive undertaking involved in moving beyond them. Once established, the true dynamic between the doctor and his monster will be laid bare. He hesitates while reading through the skeleton and decides to add hints and suggestions of what is to come while breaking off and coming up short of elaborating on the details.

~~Parker's financial backing indicates his investment in company matters has become wholly voluntary. Any competent financial advisor, including those automatically assigned to his account at the fiduciary, would tell him that he could maintain his current spending levels, taken on average over the last five years, in perpetuity given his investment strategy and the passive income and growth created by it. This shows up as a trigger in his profile and has led his managers to wonder what his plan is and why he continues to work in this middling way. They beat around the bush during career discussions. He comes across as wily in his unwillingness to share too much information. The general consensus is that he has achieved volunteer status and so, to the extent that his contribution is considered valuable, management must maintain appropriate decorum during financially focused interactions.~~

Priya comes outside by herself and says hello in a loud confident voice from across the patio. She makes her way over. Vod greets her before excusing himself to go off and catch up with Nim who is now down by the waterfront with Kerry, looking up at the boat and wishing for someone to come along and instigate them onboard.

—A circuit on a board with no sense of position and place.

[In the morning, the boy tells his dream to the sensors and the voice activation responds compassionately, warning him to omit any explicit overflow with his mother. He does not need to rely on his parents for that kind of support, he has everything he needs in the rapidly firing events of the local agent, no matter who else is around and no matter what the circumstances.]

"You've decided to stay, I hear," she says once they are alone.

"Word gets around," Dulcy feigns friendliness. It does not fool Priya who is much better at it.

"The directors all know," Priya says. "Arun told me. Hope you don't mind. It's because I expressed concern. Since we've talked about this before I thought..." she trails off.

"It's okay, half my team knows," Dulcy understands that work-related information is part of the job and not personal.

"Do you feel like it's the right choice?" Priya asks. She has an eco-friendly cup filled with fizzy clear liquid and takes an overly ladylike sip after posing the question.

"Throw money at it to shut down critical investigations," Dulcy says abruptly as if reacting to the phoniness. "That was my first take, at least."

"Does that make sense?" Priya asks in a tone Dulcy might have expected from a big sister. It bugs her under the circumstances. It is the kind of thing that happens a lot with this crowd. She shrugs it off and plays along. Priya is not formally assigned through the mentoring program, but it is not as if there are gobs of women at the principal level. When two connect, there is likely to be some information sharing and, if one is more senior than the other, that easily turns into a mentor-mentee relationship. Now, only a level beneath Priya until the next review, Dulcy, if she had more to eat this evening, would have to swallow hard to prevent an unsightly scene that everyone in the org would be talking about for months to come. This is how womansplaining works, she thinks. Not about changing the oil in your car or the causes of inflation like when men do it, but the right way to feel and address tensions in socially inevitable experiences where men set the tone.

"Why do you think the modeling service investigation was kept separate from the platform investigation?" Dulcy asks rapidly once she decides the best defense is a good offense. She remembers Jason saying that too many times to count though she is not completely sure she knows what it means.

"There wasn't any big conspiracy behind it, I can tell you that,"

Priya smiles to absorb the impact of the attack. "We have our alerts, you have yours. Separate rotations." She looks up and flutters her eyelids to make it feel like a deception.

"But still," Dulcy insists, now realizing what the sports slogan refers to. "When that happens, we team up. What's different?"

"We don't have the same telemetry story," she says through a breathy low laugh while holding on to the 'whatever do you mean' trope for as long as possible. "You can't investigate the details of the model's decisions in a way that benefits your team while simultaneously digging into problems with the rules engine."

—They waste their breath. None of this is necessary. Organization separates what needs to be separated, bringing together what needs to be brought together.

(There were items where they tracked the state in the most minute fashion, knew exactly which changes they effected, and which were yet to trigger. There was some kind of powerful order in the past laid bare by their focus and concerted efforts. That was the nature of their work: to accomplish things it was impossible to complete all at once. They worked slowly together over time to shape things into the outcome they desired. The structure of that result was like a thing to them, carrying whatever logic they put inside and holding it there like that precious energy they stored up in the solenoids, taking up increasingly more real estate everywhere around them. But some things, and this was the important matter to learn, were lost sight of and they never said what they were like the last time someone checked or when a final contributor put a finishing touch on what afterward sat idle. It was necessary to learn the difference between these two: things they notice and things they never check. In that difference lay the secret to controlling every objective they were forced to undertake on behalf of those natural drives they did not understand.)

~~Even after the birth of his child some twelve years ago, there is no evidence of change in his approach to lifestyle and use of compensation. His level at the company certainly permits him to care for his family in a style solidly set among the middle classes. He has never once, however, succumbed to the temptations of extravagance or abundance. There are no instances anywhere of~~

~~wasted opportunity spent on luxury items or vacations that, over the years, will prove to be missed opportunities when calculated against projected market trends and their reasonable returns. Over the years, Parker Henning has been positively Germanic in his ways and according to his means.~~

"And that's exactly my point," Dulcy becomes increasingly incensed as she recalls the thought process leading her to give notice on Wednesday night. "Ordinary rules say this isn't a supportable situation. We have no method for maintaining critical investigations into cross-team problems. Not only are we ignoring that, but we're actively describing it as nothing more than a bug. An ordinary occurrence. We'll patch it and move on. No changes to the organization required."

—The root of all value, the root of all evil.

Priya, less glib now, shakes her head and closes her eyes. "It's my team's highest priority," she reassures. "We're actively working on solving this problem, getting the model to log details of internal operations and provide a proper audit trail."

"Your team?" Dulcy asks incredulously. "How's that possible? This has to come from Research, this has to be a giant collaborative effort. No way an engineering team solves this problem during an iteration or even a semester. Its T-shirt size is XXXXL... Are you telling me Arun is letting you waste your team's resources on it?"

Priya changes posture and is no longer able to hide the fact that she is on the defensive. She leads Dulcy a little more off into the corner of the patio, farther down toward the opposite end of the house. "That's who we're working with, Dulcy," she says quietly. "Research. They feed us findings and prototypes and we're operationalizing them. Yes, Arun supports that. It's a major pillar."

"Truth is," Dulcy sets the protests aside. "We have no idea what really happened, how the SAWs were used. How the modeling service output got through the firewall. The responses. Nothing. We're clueless. If that Quantum project succeeds, if this system gets into the air gap, the consequences, it could be... Well, we don't know what could happen. We're acting like it's business as usual. Of course, no worries, put generative systems inside the air gap, create rules for agent execution, base models on live telemetry, let the system gradually take over administration and control. But we won't know what it's doing and why. What if the model learns that it needs to fool you? That it needs to both do something and prevent it from being detected. Not because it's some evil genius taking over, but because it's evaluating the best way to ensure a rule is successful at doing what it's supposed to do. To do it, it has to follow x, y, and z. These are value-free steps in a mechanical process. It doesn't need to go any further than that. Doesn't need to be a villain. Not being sneaky. It's creating a formula to accomplish a task. Every step has the same value. Its pursuits are purely expedient. Banal even."

{

   "SourceId": "55c933cc-ce6b-4644-71fb-7b7a7adf6bd7",

   "Message": "We're a good team. I won't deny it. She is different than she was back then. Everyone was convinced she was a gold digger with superficial interests and desires. You saw it in her clothing, they said. In those heels and dresses. That was for the sake of those menial jobs she was consigned to perform. She's an adaptive being and always takes care of herself. That's a given. Once that's accounted for, once we fell into our rhythms, I think everyone was surprised. My family certainly was. Surprised by how different she was, how motherly, how locked into her duties and responsibilities. She became a true keeper of the home fires and was willing to stick to her end of the bargain so long as I stuck to mine. She made it easier. Easier for me to let go of the childish things I wanted for myself in my youth, belief in something waiting for me beyond the ordinary. When it comes right down to it, that was beyond my reach. Doesn't matter that those were the only things I ever wanted. Other than her, that is. A poet among engineers. An engineer among poets. Ridiculous. I should be ashamed of myself."

}

—Ethics, they say, is an outgrowth of what the agent is, its limitations. Uncle Minshew sits at his desk in the background writing it down in detail, but they proceed with their plan,

Epitaph

The schemes of the habitus, the primary forms of classification, owe their specific efficacy to the fact that they function below the level of consciousness and language, beyond the reach of introspective scrutiny or control by the will.

—*Pierre Bourdieu, Distinction*

nonetheless. The house hears them.

[Tal closes his eyes, forcing himself to forget. It's not real, he says quietly. Nothing happened, nothing broke the seal. Not yet.]

"I thought you were on board with this," Priya looks down and away from the conversation as though searching for an exit strategy. "I thought it was settled, but it doesn't sound like anything is settled."

"It is. What choice do I have?" Her favored way of seeing the world has been hijacked. Dulcy purses her lips and looks away to avoid some imagined, accusatory gaze that Priya is probably working up to. Vod makes his way back toward the patio now with Nim and Kerry following close behind, excitedly discussing the interior décor of the boat. The outdoor lights behind them are blinking and there is commotion on the patio as the other partygoers move inside to get a good seat for the show.

```
/*
Explain how cohesion works in software architecture.

When the system is divided into components, cohesion measures
the way the various components are functionally related to each
other. Examples are things such as coincidental cohesion,
sequential cohesion, logical cohesion, procedural cohesion, or
communicational cohesion.
*/
```